THE SUMMONING

BRADY LONGMORE

BLUEBOAR
PUBLISHING

Cover design: Square 1 Creative Services

This is a work of fiction. Names, characters, places, and incidents are the product of the author's imagination or are used fictitiously.

Published by Blue Boar Publishing

P.O. Box 211
Iona, Idaho 83427

To Kimberly,

Your unwavering support was the fuel that kept me going and saw this work through to the end.

and to the countless unsung heroes: *warriors, law enforcement officers, and first responders, who bear the unseen scars inflicted by duty. May our nation never forget the debt that they are owed.*

Then certain of the vagabond Jews, exorcists, took upon them to call over them which had evil spirits the name of the Lord Jesus, saying, We adjure you by Jesus whom Paul preacheth. And the evil spirit answered and said, Jesus I know, and Paul I know; but who are ye? And the man in whom the evil spirit was leaped on them, and overcame them, and prevailed against them, so that they fled out of that house naked and wounded.

ACTS 19: 13-16

PROLOGUE

The terrified screams of the women and children echoed off the stone walls like the wailing of the damned; just hearing his own thoughts was becoming nearly impossible. The men were yelling and shouting as well, but the shrill pitch of the women pierced right into the center of his brain. He pushed his way through the tumult and chaos, shoving people aside. "Caleb!" he shouted above the din. "Has anyone seen my son?"

A great shattering sound induced a collective gasp from the crowd as all of the beautifully stained glass windows on both sides of the chapel imploded. For a moment, the colored shards of glass seemed to hang frozen in the air. The fragmented faces of The Twelve Apostles looked out from jagged, glittering edges before crashing onto the floor and scattering across the nearby pews in thousands of pieces.

A hot and strangely viscous wind gusted in from the broken windows and swirled through the chapel, ruffling bonnets and blowing away hats. A dark, moaning voice rode upon its billows. With the window glass gone, James could see that the church was surrounded by the rest of the townspeople; the people who had not sought shelter inside the church. Like a sieging army they stood motionless in the hot, afternoon sun, their faces blank and void of any expression.

Peter Ritchie, owner of the smithy just down the street, was suddenly in his face, his bright blue eyes nearly mad with terror. "You said we would be safe in here!" he screamed. "You call this safe, Reverend?"

"My son. Have you seen Caleb?" It was all he could think to say.

That's when Peter slugged him across the face. He fell to the ground putting a hand to the corner of his mouth, where he could taste the salty warmth of his own blood as it trickled.

Peter, his leather blacksmith's apron still tied around his waist, stood over him like an archangel on Judgment Day, pointing a finger at him. "This is all your fault, James! You brought this upon us! The only thing that Indian boy was guilty of was being in love with your daughter. But now he's dead, and the rest of us are damned."

A rage boiled over inside James's chest. "That heathen sullied my Elizabeth! What else was I supposed to do?" Tears rolled out of his eyes.

"Your own daughter tried to tell us the boy was innocent. She said she loved him. She begged for his life even as we were putting the noose around his neck! But that just enraged you all the more, didn't it, James?" Peter spat a stream of spittle onto James's prostrate leg. "You drove your daughter to witchcraft and she summoned the very devil here." Peter kicked him once in the side and stormed away into the terrified and gasping crowd.

The storekeeper was right, and the full knowledge of it crashed down on James like an avalanche of boulders.

Six months ago, Elizabeth had come to him and told him that she was with child. The fact that she, a reverend's daughter, had fornicated outside of the bonds of holy matrimony was bad enough, but when he had found out who the father was, it was more than any man could be expected to bear.

Billy WhiteFeather had tricked her; used one of those pagan dances or rituals to seduce his first born. It was the only explanation, and as far as he was concerned—whether she had been willing or not—it was tantamount to rape. It was a convenient little story that wrapped up the whole situation into a neat little package, taking his daughter and his family's good name off the hook of disgrace.

Billy had to die, but as far as James was concerned he deserved it, rape or no rape. So he had personally whipped up the mob himself, playing the role of a grieving and outraged father. Before he knew it, things had been set into motion. As unstoppable as the waves of the sea, mob justice was promptly meted out, and Billy WhiteFeather found himself swinging from a noose.

Elizabeth had gone mad with grief. The grief turned to rage and she vowed vengeance on the whole town. James figured that with time her anger would fade, but it only seemed to grow in proportion to her swelling, pregnant belly. The baby growing inside her was a curse, obviously. But there were practices out there, people who knew certain…methods that could cause a miscarriage.

He secretly made the arrangements. The procedure was painful—it took four men to hold her down—but it was a success, and his dear daughter was finally free from the curse and the sin of Billy WhiteFeather. So he had thought, until the day she went missing. A fortnight later, she was found deep in the woods, hanging from a large tree. Her dead body was nude, dozens of strange occult-like symbols standing out in etched, bloody crimson on her pallid, sagging skin. The wounds appeared to have been self-inflicted.

The disappearances had started shortly after that, then the murders. Now these ghastly abominations surrounding his church: former wives, husbands, sons, daughters, brothers, and sisters. All murdered, yet reanimated through some evil power.

He pulled himself up off the floor and saw that the ring of people outside had cinched, closing in toward the broken windows. Some of the men in the crowd produced revolvers. The women screamed and flinched as the guns began to fire sporadically, the acrid odor of spent gunpowder permeating the stifling air of the church. James could hear and see the slugs thudding into the bodies of those closest to the windows, but with little to no effect. They just kept coming.

The dead started climbing in through the windows on both sides, staggering and clumsy, some falling on the floor. Children huddled behind their mothers while their mothers trembled behind their men. The butchering began without mercy. James found himself standing behind his pulpit, helpless to do anything but bear witness to the awful scene playing out before his eyes.

A red-haired woman began moving toward him. The bloody tumult parted before her like the Red Sea. She was clothed in her white burial dress now stained with dirt and blood. The symbols that had been carved into her face nearly glowing as if from an internal light source. Her eyes burned with a grinning hatred. "Hello James," she said.

"Elizabeth, what have you done!" he choked out through his clenching throat. The fact that he was talking to his dead daughter barely registered in his frenzied mind. "All these people…your brother, they're all innocent, good folks —"

She came nearer, the stench of moldering decay preceding her. "I like them innocent," she said, a hungry flame leaping in her eyes. "We shall feast for quite some time, Elizabeth and I."

He saw it then; this…creature was not his daughter. Something dark, beyond comprehension, some devouring entity was in possession of Elizabeth's decomposing body now. A demon.

She nearly floated up onto the dais next to him. "We will feast on this town, gorging on the souls of all who dwell here, until nothing remains. Then we will devour the next town, and the next one after that.

Righteous indignation seethed through him until the fibers of his being hummed with it, like the tightened strings on a violin. "Let my daughter go, fiend of the pit!"

She laughed. "Let her go? Elizabeth is the reason I'm here. In her grief and rage she summoned me. Now, I am here to reap the pain and misery that you sowed, James." She reached a bone-white hand toward his face, the fingers stiff and hooked.

In desperation, he snatched his Bible from its resting place on the pulpit and held it in front of her. "Demon!" His voice had never sounded more firm, had never rang so righteous in his own ears. "I compel you, in the name of the—"

She sent the Bible flying with a swift backhand, the thin pages fluttering through the air like the wings of a wounded dove. She tilted her head in a show of mock sympathy. "You have no power, Reverend. I do not recognize you or your authority…murderer."

"I-I command you in-in the name—"

A bestial screech erupted from her, as if a portal to the very depths of hell had opened up deep in her bowels. She clutched him by the shoulders and threw him with preternatural strength, like a child throws her doll when she is angry. His body broke against the solid, granite blocks that made up the chapel wall.

Racking pain flooded every corner of his mind and he could feel the cold fingers of death groping and clawing at him. He writhed, coughing up blood, the screams of his dying parishioners and fellow townsfolk filling his ears. Suddenly, she was standing over him. He extended a pleading hand, his fingers trembling and clutching involuntarily at the air.

She sneered down at him, her eyes flat and lifeless like a faded garment that had seen too many days in the sun. She squatted down beside him, took his outstretched hand gently into her cold grasp, almost lovingly caressed it for a moment, and then pulverized it with one powerful squeeze.

The delicate bones snapping and grinding, the skin splitting wide open. It was a pain James would have never been able to imagine if it weren't actually happening to him. At first, he could only gasp in violent hitches like a man that had suddenly fallen through the ice of a frozen river or lake.

Then he screamed, and the cries of suffering and death that were filling his ears had now become his own. She let his hand drop like a wrung out rag, and still he howled. He howled right up until the moment she placed her hand across his bulging throat…and crushed his windpipe.

9

CHAPTER 1

Shuffling his way to algebra class, Daniel looked up to see Robbie Pritchard passing him in the hall. Daniel quickly lowered his head and averted his eyes. It was usually best not to draw the bully's attention to one's self—the kids who did often found themselves in a bad way. With a little luck Robbie wouldn't notice him today. *Please just let him keep walking*, he prayed.

All hopes of avoiding a confrontation were dashed into oblivion as Robbie's hand shot out like a snake and slapped the books out of Daniel's arms. The other kids nearby exploded in laughter as books and papers went skidding across the red and white tiled floor. Rage and shame shot through his veins as he clenched his fists and turned to face his tormentor in the center of the hall. Robbie was almost twice his size, exuding athletic prowess and ultimate confidence. He stood there, arms folded across his puffed out chest, eyes cold and threatening.

Robbie scoffed, "Dropped your books in my hall, Miller...pick 'em up."

The gathered kids barked like a pack of trained seals and, like so many times before, Daniel said nothing and submitted to the much larger kid by lowering his eyes. Any other reaction would have resulted in a massacre at the hands of the school football star.

"Well?" Robbie closed the distance to thrust his pug nose an inch from Daniel's face. "You gonna clean up this mess or what?"

Daniel felt his rage evaporating and turning to fear. He searched the crowd for a sympathetic or friendly face, only to meet cold, hard eyes full of contempt. In that moment time seemed to slow. A level of hate he had never known crept inside him, penetrating him to the core.

An invading, inky darkness washed over him, and that was when he first heard the woman's voice in his head. It was a beautifully soothing voice, but cold and hard around the edges. *"Pigs, all of them. They should be butchered like the animals they are."*

He knew he should have been frightened, but he wasn't. Not to say he wasn't disturbed and a bit taken back, but right then that voice was his only friend. It bobbed in front of him like a life preserver in a sea of hostility. He took a hold of it. He would have loved nothing more than to *butcher* them all, but he was smart enough to recognize the impossible fantasy for what it was.

Keeping his gaze on the floor, he turned to walk away only to receive a hard shove from Robbie that sent him sprawling to his hands and knees. Howls of laughter and taunting erupted from the other students. In defeat, he stayed down and avoided any act that would bring the wrath of the bully.

The crowd, realizing that their blood lust was to go unsatisfied, began to slowly disperse. Burning with shame, Daniel gathered his books from off the floor. With narrowed eyes, he watched Robbie swagger off for class, laughing with his cronies and lap dogs.

"Pigs," the voice whispered, and then she was gone.

He stared from his bedroom window into the dark mists of a moonless night. Even with the second story window open the air was stifling, the folds of his worn night shirt clinging to his damp, pale skin. Dark rings encircled his hazel eyes from too many sleepless nights. His breath came short and rapid, and though beads of sweat lined his forehead, he was shivering.

They were out there, beckoning, calling to him over and over, night after night. They were relentless. He could not see them. Others did not hear them. They were his alone to endure.

At first he was unable to decipher anything of meaning from the incessant, garbled whispers flooding his mind. The only thing he could make out from time to time was his first name being whispered repeatedly, *Daniel...Daniel.* It was *her*, from that day when Robbie had shoved him to the ground. The blackness and hate that overcame him that day lingered in him still.

During the day the voices were silent, but he could still feel their presence and influence. They pulled on him as if a cord had been cinched around his soul with someone on the other end gently tugging. The sensation grew in persistence every day. Sometimes, during his daily chores, he would cease his labor to look up and stare into the woods that bordered his parents' farm. He knew it was there she waited for him; he knew it was just a matter of time before he would go.

In the dead hours of night, they really came to torment him. fueling the blackness so that it enlarged inside his soul like a glowing ember igniting into flame, until it felt like it would consume him.

The Summoning

Tonight, the pull was strong. What did they want? His exhaustion and his need to find out were beginning to overpower his fear. He slid the window shut and the whisperings took on a tone of desperation as he turned away and fell back onto his bed. "Stop it!" he hissed, as he drew his blankets up to his chin. He tried to use his mind to send an angry emotion or thought back at them. The voices died down to a raspy murmur in the background of his thoughts and he was finally able to drift into a fitful, dreamless sleep.

He woke to the rooster crowing in the yard. The sun hadn't quite peeked over the low lying hills to the east. The voices were gone, the darkness diminished for the moment. He felt exhausted and remained in bed, though he was dimly aware of his parents beginning to stir in the final, gray hour before dawn.

After a short while, his mother came to rouse him from bed. Breakfast was ready and the chores had to be done before school. He sat up reluctantly, rubbing at bleary eyes.

She creased her brow with worry and placed the back of her hand on his forehead. "You look terrible," she said. "Are you feeling alright?"

"I'm okay, Mom," he replied, swinging his feet down to the hardwood floor.

"Well, you don't have a fever. Still…I wonder if maybe I should call Dr. Steinmetz and see if he isn't too busy to come by today." She sat at the foot of his bed and began to fidget with the hem of her apron while biting her lip.

"I'm just a little tired, that's all," he said, trying to offer assurance. "I've been having bad dreams lately."

She stood up and placed her hands firmly on his shoulders, easing him back down to his pillow. "You stay in bed and get a little rest then. I'm calling Dr. Steinmetz, I don't think school is a good idea today." She left the room, her slippers scuffling down the stairway. Daniel was reluctant, but the physical need for sleep won out and he slipped into a deep slumber, oblivious to the world around him.

He awoke to the sound of Dr. Steinmetz's cowboy boots echoing down the upstairs hallway. By the brightness of the sun and the rising temperature of the room, he guessed it was near midday. Had he really slept so long?

Somewhere out in the distance, he could make out the steady chugging of the tractor's diesel engine; Dad was busy in the fields. He propped himself against his headboard as his mother eased the bedroom door open and allowed the family doctor to enter ahead of her.

Dr. Harold Steinmetz was in his early fifties with dark, salt and pepper hair to match a bushy, graying mustache. A small, round pair of spectacles dangled from a silver chain around his neck. He was tall and possessed the healthy disposition and exuberance of a man half his age.

In one fluid motion he glided across the room and threw open the window. He offered a disarming smile as he dragged the chair from Daniel's writing desk over to the bedside. Taking a seat, he placed his black leather satchel on the night stand, unsnapped the clasp, and withdrew a stethoscope. "Well, good afternoon, young man," he said. "I hope you don't mind if I let in a little fresh air."

"Sure."

"So, you've been in bed all morning, how are you feeling right now?" Dr. Steinmetz asked, as he placed the earpieces of the stethoscope in his ears.

"Better than I was a few hours ago."

The doctor placed the stethoscope over Daniel's heart and listened. He moved the instrument around to different locations on his chest, listening some more. He had him sit forward, placed the diaphragm on his back, and asked him to take several deep breaths. He continued his precursory examination, checking pulse and blood pressure, all with a perfect poker face, keeping his conclusions to himself. Mother stood in the doorway, arms folded over her apron, her eyes tracking every movement the doctor made.

After having Daniel stand so he could check his muscles and joints, Dr. Steinmetz placed his instruments back into the satchel and rose from his chair. "What we have here is a perfectly healthy, fifteen-year-old boy," he declared.

Mother smiled, obviously relieved. "He's complained that he's not sleeping well at night," she reminded the doctor with a tinge of worry in her voice.

"You say you're not sleeping well?" the doctor asked.

Daniel replied, "Bad dreams." He wasn't sure how else to put it.

"I see." The man held out his finger and began moving it back and forth, then up and down. "Without moving your head, Daniel, try to follow the movement of my finger with your eyes."

Daniel performed the task easily.

Dr. Steinmetz addressed Daniel's mother, "There's nothing unusual about a nightmare here and there—especially in the overactive mind of a fifteen-year-old boy in the throes of puberty. What is unusual, is for nightmares to be so persistent that it affects one's day-to-day ability to function." He scratched the bottom of his chin with his forefinger in silent thought. "Do you experience any kind of headaches or dizziness, Daniel?"

Daniel shook his head.

"Is there anything going on in your life that might be causing you an abnormal amount of stress or worry?"

"No sir, not really." *unless you count hearing voices in your head as abnormal.*

"And these bad dreams are disturbing you the entire night, or most of it?" Daniel nodded slowly. "Once they start, they seem to last the rest of the night," he said, evading the whole truth. He was all too aware of how the whole truth would sound. He wasn't about to end up in one of those hospitals like Uncle Patrick had after returning from the war.

Uncle Pat had to be put in the hospital because he could hear Japs creeping around in his yard at night. Father had taken Daniel to the hospital in Clear Creek once to visit Uncle Pat. *Speaking of nightmares.* He could still remember the distinct, overpowering smell of sanitizer mingled with the stench of urine and body odor, the haunted moans of the deranged, and the hollow, vacuous stares of men who had lost their marbles. Seeing them had made him feel self conscious, almost guilty for his own sanity. His father had been back many times to visit since then, but Daniel had never accompanied him again.

"Son, would you mind sharing with me what these nightmares are about?" Dr. Steinmetz asked, sitting back down in the chair.

Daniel swallowed and suddenly realized he was parched. He knew he had to give up something here. To hold back would make the doctor suspicious, causing him to ask more questions. But he didn't dare mention the whispering voices that came to him. The sudden thought of the voices made him aware that even now, they were pulling on him. "I keep dreaming about the nut house," he finally mumbled.

Dr. Steinmetz nodded in understanding. "You've been to the county ward to visit your uncle?" he stated, more than asked.

Mother took a step toward the doctor. "I was against Will taking him to that place, but he insisted the boy see his uncle. Said a war hero deserved to see his nephew." Her voice choked slightly. "I tried to tell Will that he was too young to see the goings on in a place like that, but you know how stubborn the man can be."

"Mom, don't be mad at Dad," Daniel said, trying to sound calm and somehow grown up. "He just loves Uncle Patty, and it hurts him to see him in that place. He is a hero. He deserves a lot more than to be in that hospital."

Mother opened her mouth to say something, but was cut off by Dr. Steinmetz. "Well, that actually explains a lot Mrs. Miller. Young Daniel here experienced what was for him, a very traumatic thing. He was deeply disturbed by his visit to the mental hospital. and at the same time, he's burdened with guilt for feeling that way."

He reached and rapped with his knuckles playfully on the top of Daniel's head. "Dreams are actually the by-product of our own subconscious mind as it internalizes and struggles to process what goes on in our daily lives. A nightmare can often be the result of an internal conflict within us, such as Daniel's fear mixed with his guilt about his visit to the hospital. Sprinkle in a dash of traumatic terror and you can have some pretty vivid and horrifying dreams. Sometimes the dreams can be so vivid a person can't be sure if they were actually asleep or really awake. Not unlike what Patrick experiences."

Mother put her hand to her heart, her eyes growing wide.

Dr. Steinmetz was quick to add, "Just much more severe in Pat's case. I'm sure we have nothing to fear with young Daniel here, he's young and resilient. His mind just needs a little time to work things out and process. The good news is, with time, this sort of thing usually goes away by itself."

He produced a pen and a pad of paper from his shirt pocket. He scribbled for a moment and tore the top sheet away. "Here's a little something that might help him settle down at night so he can sleep." He stood and handed the prescription to Mother. "As I said, this should pass given a little time. In the meanwhile, just monitor his appetite and give him a little extra time to sleep in the morning if he seems to need it."

He turned to address Daniel still sitting on the bed. "It helps to talk about the dreams, son. Don't keep it all bottled up inside."

Daniel nodded in compliance. The doctor turned and strode out of the room, Mother conversing with him as she followed him down the hall to the staircase.

Daniel began dressing, wondering to himself why he didn't feel guilty about lying to the doctor and his mom. Something inside told him that the voices approved of the deception. A feeling of anger and self loathing flashed through him momentarily.

He was finishing the laces on his shoes when he heard Dr. Steinmetz's brand new 1947 Studebaker fire up. He stood and watched the black sedan cruise down the dirt lane that led from their house to the main road, leaving behind a cloud of dust in the warm afternoon air. The dust slowly dissipated as the car turned onto the black top and sped toward town. His gaze was pulled to the woods in the distance, and for an indiscernible amount of time, he stood transfixed on the old growth trees. Elms and cotton woods, their thick branches twisted like the limbs of a tortured man seized in the final moments of some unthinkable death.

As he was turning away a figure caught his eye. He paused. With both hands braced on the window ledge he leaned forward, squinting against the bright sun. At first he thought it might be his imagination, but a second look revealed a tall man standing on the edge of the trees looking back at him. He was skinny, almost gaunt, with impossibly thin, long legs like a spider's. His bones and joints jutted out at obtuse angles from beneath a black suit coat that was draped over his scarecrow frame.

The lanky man stood, both arms hanging loosely at his sides, simply staring back at Daniel. Sun-heated waves of rippling air rising from the ground made him appear to shimmer and dance in and out of reality.

On some level Daniel knew the man as the owner of one of the voices that visited him on a daily basis. Ice water ran through his veins as he stared back. He was too far away to make out any detailed facial features, but could feel the man's gaze as assuredly as if they were standing face to face.

There was a shimmer of warm air, the man danced in the ripples, faded in and out a couple of times, and was gone.

HAROLD STEINMETZ GLANCED BACK at the old farm house in his rear view mirror as he navigated his Studebaker down the Millers' dirt lane. Daniel Miller was there, standing in his second-story bedroom window, watching. He sensed a darkness about the young man that made him uneasy. He had been the consummate professional during his examination of Daniel. After all, a dark feeling about someone was not a medical diagnosis. But now, seeing him silhouetted and framed in his window—a picture of loneliness and fear—Harold had to admit, the kid gave him an eerie feeling.

A small wave of guilt swept over him as he steered his car gently onto Crowley Road and sped off on the ten miles back to town. He had known the family for years. In fact, he had delivered Danny into the world himself in that very house.

Will and Trina Miller had suffered through several miscarried pregnancies before they were finally able to have Daniel. He was their little miracle, and would be their only child. Harold had been there through all of it.

He hadn't been forthcoming with Mrs. Miller. In truth, he wondered if Daniel really might be heading down a similar road as his Uncle Patrick—insane and institutionalized. He brushed the guilty feeling aside. It was way too early to go and scare the family to death with talk of schizophrenia or psychosis. Besides, maybe it really was just bad dreams for the poor kid. Heaven knew, Daniel had not had it easy.

He had always been shy, quiet, somewhat a misfit with other kids. And although extremely intelligent, if the truth be told, the boy was a loner. Some of the kids in town had been pretty darn cruel to him over the years. *I'd probably be a little dark too*, he thought, as his car tires thumped loudly over the Fall Creek bridge. But the practicing Methodist inside him rallied against his logical reasoning. Deep down, he knew he had felt something different about Daniel Miller, something sinister and foreboding that his medical knowledge could not explain away.

He chased away the shiver running down his spine by reaching for the knob of his car radio and tuning into the local station. An Andrews Sisters song was playing, the one about the bugle boy of Company B. He pushed the Miller family into the back of his mind and began tapping his fingers on the wheel to the beat of the song, determined to enjoy the rest of his drive back to Clear Creek.

THE REST OF THE DAY WENT AS ANY OTHER late summer day on the Miller farm. Daniel missed school, but helped out with the chores. All the while, his mother vigilantly checked up on him to be sure he was eating and drinking enough and that he looked okay. Earlier, she had driven the old Ford into town and had returned with a few groceries and a small envelope containing some little white pills. On the outside was printed *Flossy's Drug Store* and some other handwriting that he didn't bother to read.

He was exhausted and hoped the little pills would work, but he had his doubts. Maybe tonight they would leave him be. But no matter what job or chore he was in the middle of, his mind was preoccupied with the voices—who were they? What did they want? Why him? Several times that day his blood turned to ice and the hairs on the back of his neck stood up. He made agitated glances around himself, expecting to meet the gaze of the tall man in the black suit, but nothing was ever there.

Dinner around the table that evening was a quiet affair. Father asked a few questions about the doctor's visit. Mother related that Daniel was having bad dreams associated with the hospital. It wasn't hard to miss the accusatory tone in her voice. Father stayed silent as he chewed his food, but shot a subtle glance of disapproval in Daniel's direction. It was obvious he expected his boy to be made of tougher stuff.

Before the voices and the darkness had come into his life, he would have felt a burning shame from his father's glance. But not tonight. He could feel the gathering darkness inside him acting like a shield, making him impervious to his father's disapproval.

After dinner, he asked to be excused to his room for the night, stating he was tired and eager to try to get on with a good night's sleep. Mother opened a kitchen cabinet, withdrew the small envelope from Flossy's, and dug out one of the white pills. He chased it down with a gulp of tap water, wished his parents a good night, and headed up the stairs.

"Don't forget your prayers!" Mother called after him as he shut his bedroom door. He snorted silently at her suggestion. Prayer had failed him long ago.

A thunderstorm echoed in the distance as he changed into his night shirt. The window was yawning open. Even though the cool breeze wafting in felt good he shut it and cranked the hasp to the locked position. He turned his back on the window and fell into bed. Pulling up his covers, he grasped the chain that hung from his bedside lamp, hesitated for just a second, and then gave a firm yank. The lamp clicked off, plunging his bedroom into darkness.

For a while he lay on his back staring up at the ceiling, waiting. He thought of the little pill he'd taken shortly before, imagined it dissolving in his stomach. He tried to imagine that he could feel it penetrating into his system, relaxing his tired muscles and easing his frazzled mind. The distant storm continued its rumbling march along the horizon. Occasionally, lightning flickered, illuminating his room in quick brilliant flashes, creating a strobe-like effect. He felt himself starting to drift.

He was dimly aware of ascending from a deep sleep. He tried to fight it. He didn't want to leave the comfort of that unconscious abyss, where thoughts, dreams and even self awareness are nonexistent. The first thing he noticed was the silence. The storm had moved on, the occasional flash of lightning in the distance the only evidence of its recent passing. His room was dead quiet. At the time, the only voice in his head was his own. No whispers. Was it all really a dream then? Did Dr. Steinmetz's little pills actually do the trick?

He opened his eyes. He was still lying flat on his back; he hadn't stirred a muscle since first laying down to go to sleep. He groped on his nightstand and found his wrist watch. There was enough moonlight coming through the window to see the hands pointing out the time: a quarter to three in the morning.

Groggy, he went to roll onto his side when a sudden realization dawned on him: he was not alone.

The fog of sleep fled instantly as his heart began to pound in his chest. He sensed something off to his right, in the corner. He didn't dare to look. To look at it would be to acknowledge it, so he lay paralyzed, barely daring to breath as he fought the urge to call out for his parents. A fifteen-year-old boy calling out for his parents in the night. He could just imagine his father's face.

After what felt like an eternity he finally mustered the courage to crane his neck and risk a glance out of the corner of his eye. A black, shadowy form of a man—barely perceivable—was standing motionless, observing him from the dark corner of the room.

As if it had suddenly realized it had been discovered, the form began to slowly flatten itself against the wall, gradually thinning and becoming two-dimensional. He felt the familiar, cold-blooded sensation he had felt when he was under the direct gaze of the tall man in the dark suit.

Eyes wide open, he fully turned his head toward it, the sound of his pumping blood coursing like a river in his ears. The form was mostly obscured as it blended with the natural shadows on the wall, but he could make out the shape of four skeletal fingers that snaked downward from a long, thin hand, tapering to points; the claw-like digits slightly trembled like dead tree branches quivering in a stiff breeze.

"What. Do. You. Want?" Daniel rasped through closed teeth. He tried to sound angry, but he could hear all too well, the quaver in his own voice.

A low, grating growl came from the wall, like the sound of a man who had been stabbed in the gut. The spindly form stretched and slithered across the wall, half-hidden and covered by the darkest shadows. It glided amongst them like a skilled hunter using his surroundings to camouflage his movements. Daniel watched as it seeped like a vaporous mist through the crack at the top of his bedroom door, and was gone.

As he sat up, his breath clogged in his throat like he had inhaled an oily rag. Standing at the foot of his bed was a gorgeous woman.

Her unearthly beauty was heart shattering, a specimen of absolute perfection. She was clothed in a white, satin robe, which left her right shoulder bare. The translucent material clung provocatively to the ample curve of her breasts and the tantalizing flare of her hips, leaving little to the imagination, but just enough.

Golden curls of long, vivacious hair played and bobbed about her long, graceful neck and marble-white shoulders.

Her full, red lips were slightly parted, a seductive smile touching the corners of her mouth. Her cheekbones and other facial features were soft and subdued, like the porcelain dolls his aunt collected. An intense pair of radiating blue eyes pierced him right to the soul. Her entire body glowed as if bathed in a halo of golden, autumn sunlight.

Effortlessly, she held his gaze as she stepped around the bed, her long, red fingernails tracing the contour of the wooden bed knob. Gliding toward him she was all beauty and grace, her hips rising and falling beneath the smooth folds of the robe. As she neared he started to shiver, and realized that his breath was coming out in small, white clouds. He could smell lilacs, but there was another scent lingering just below the surface, like the hidden undercurrent in a fast flowing stream.

She stopped just in front of him and looked down into his eyes, golden tresses of hair falling forward to brush against her milky cheeks. He was shivering so hard he could hear his teeth chatter, and he was on the verge of hyperventilating. Lilac blossoms again. Stronger. But what else? Something else.

She tilted her head slightly sideways, her liquid eyes large, cat-like, pleading. *"Help us, Daniel."* Her voice had an ethereal, echoing quality, but her mouth didn't move when she spoke. *"Help us."*

"How? Wh—who are you?" he stammered, through his chattering teeth. Her face didn't change expression. *"Come to us,"* she whispered.

Suddenly, a crackle of lightning flashed in the distance, strobing the room. As the lightning flickered so did the woman. For a few brief instants she intermittently transformed between ultimate beauty and decaying death.

Rotting, gray skin hung in fleshy tatters from yellow-white bone while pale maggots and worms oozed from hundreds of burrows. Her hair clung to bare patches of exposed skull in matted, frayed clumps. The lips and eyelids had decayed away so that her face was locked in a horrific, wide-eyed grin. It was then he recognized the underlying smell that had been eluding him: the fetid, foul stench of death.

The last flicker of lightning blinked out and the woman with it. He was alone again, trembling, his heart pounding like a hammer. He sat for a moment, unable to move and unable to make sense of what had just happened. Throwing back his bed covers he went to the window and shoved it open. A warm night breeze sent ripples across his shirt. A full moon bathed the distant storm clouds in a silvery, ambient glow as it glided silently along its eternal course.

His eyes were inescapably drawn from the moon to the tree line. There she stood, just inside the trees. She was as stunningly beautiful as before, like some dark goddess of the night. He felt his breath catch in his chest as he met her stare. He noticed that her robe and hair hung perfectly still and unmoving despite the breeze stirring the branches and grass around her.

After gaining his attention, she turned slowly and began walking deeper into the forest. The hard, rocky ground seemed to have no effect on her bare feet. As she faded out of sight, he found himself fighting the urge to run after her. And then what?

To pledge his devotion to her. To serve her.

Shocked by this sudden desire he quickly slid the window shut again and spun around, pushing his back against the panes. He turned to see his reflection in the small mirror that hung just above his dresser. He was startled by the ghoul looking back at him. A sliver of moonlight streaming in from the window cast deep, contrasting shadows across his pale, sunken cheeks. His eyes were pinpoints of reflected moonlight set into hollowed out pits. His dark brown hair was damp, matted and plastered to his forehead. He laughed a small, strange laugh, that didn't sound like himself. Then a whimper escaped his lips as he smacked his fist into his palm in frustration. His mind was going. He was running out of time.

He turned to fix a determined gaze on the black shroud of twisting, grotesque branches in the distance. He made up his mind that the next day he would follow the voices into those woods and bring this living nightmare to its conclusion. For better or for worse.

"You win," he muttered as he stumbled back to his bed and fell into a dreamless sleep. For the first time in days, the whispers went silent.

CHAPTER 2

It was a beautiful Saturday morning, and as far as Trina Miller was concerned, her son was a cured boy. He'd gotten himself out of bed at the usual time, and though he was quiet at breakfast, his appetite seemed normal. His face was still a little gaunt and his eyes were slightly sunken, but brighter and alert. According to Daniel the little white pill had really worked its magic, and he had slept soundly all through the night. She was so glad and encouraged him to eat another pancake, which he did without complaint. The metal screen door slammed shut as he headed off for his chores. She watched him march across the back yard toward the barn, his step quicker, his posture taller. Feeling relieved, she returned to the breakfast dishes soaking in the sink.

HIS MOTHER MAY HAVE FALLEN FOR THE RUSE, but on the inside Daniel felt darker than ever. He went about his chores as he would have any other day, but the pull from the woods was strong, and from time to time, the image of the gorgeous woman would flash through his brain. With his mind made up, he figured it would soon be all over, one way or another.

After a small lunch he informed Mother that he was going for a walk to clear his head.

"Don't be gone too long," she said.

He faked a smile as he left the kitchen, the screen door banging shut behind him. He noticed it didn't feel as hot as he strode with purpose across the backyard. There had been a slight breeze most of the day that had been increasing over the last while. It would most likely storm tonight.

He grasped the top rail of the wooden fence that separated the back yard from the pasture, climbed over, and jumped down to the other side. Landing on his feet, he looked up at the woods. They seemed close. He could hear the creak and groan of the branches as they swayed in the breeze. He started walking again, keeping his eyes forward, the trees looming closer with each step. He jumped an irrigation ditch, passed through a small apple orchard, and into the hayfield that bordered the woods.

It became a conscious effort to maintain his pace as he drew nearer. He could feel his courage and determination fading, so he drew on his anger. He had a lot to be angry about. He thought about the kids that teased him at school, how he never fit in no matter how hard he tried. The anger began turning inward on himself. He was a coward. He didn't have the guts to stand up to Robbie and the other kids like he should. If his dad could see him at school, he would be ashamed to call him his son. Well, that all changed today. It changed now. He concentrated on the anger and his pace quickened.

Before he knew it, he was at the edge of the hayfield. The woods were an ominous wall of contorted branches and thick, gnarled trunks a dozen yards away. He stopped, aware that his heart was beating too fast, even with his brisk journey across the farm taken into account. A gust of wind plowed through the upper branches, bringing the trees to life. As the limbs swayed in the invisible force, broad leaves twisted, rattled, and scraped against each other. They made a dry rasping sound, like the labored cough of an old man.

He was no stranger to these woods, he had been here many times over the years. When he was younger he built forts in the trees and explored the many creek beds and ravines. Sometimes he imagined he was a soldier defending the walls of the Alamo, or Captain Meriwether Lewis, leading the Corps of Discovery through the unknown wilds of America. As he got older, he had turned to hunting squirrels and rabbits. But, looking at the forest now, it seemed a strange and foreboding place where evil lurked.

He could feel the pull stronger than ever now and, for the first time, he didn't fight it or try to block it out. He tuned into it, allowing himself to be pulled straight ahead. He figured he had probably been guided this direction the entire walk, but just hadn't realized it. He exhaled loudly, put his head down and plunged past the first line of trees and into the woods.

After a minute of navigating through the undergrowth, circumventing trees and stepping over rotted, fallen logs he stopped to look back. Like a giant curtain the forest had closed him off from his old world. The safety and comfort of home seemed miles away now.

He felt his heart in the clutch of that unseen force compelling him on, and he continued forward, allowing it to lead him deeper and deeper still. The wind continued to pick up and the dry, scraping leaves overhead seemed to be gasping in anticipation. The rays of intermittent sunlight that had danced in changing patterns on the forest floor, were gone now. A squirrel chattered out a warning from a nearby branch as he passed underneath. It wasn't long before he reached the outer boundaries of his previous explorations and found himself in an entirely unfamiliar area of the forest.

He was following a dry creek bed paved with stones, smooth and rounded from eons of running water. They made hollow, clacking sounds as his steps disturbed them from their ancient resting places. The forest had grown quiet, the wind just a sigh; the only sound was the soft clatter of the river rocks under his feet.

There was a very old, primeval feel to his current surroundings. The trees here were bigger and older. He perceived that he was nearing the heart, the dark inner sanctum of some ancient, unholy temple. He moved more cautiously, his senses coming alive, probing into the dark woods. A part of him screamed for him to turn and run, but the pull was too strong now. Like a moth to the flame, he plodded onward, his feet and legs moving with a will all their own.

After a time, he rounded a bend in the creek and saw a small clearing just ahead, with a massive, blackened tree erupting from its center. As he drew closer he could see that it was easily the oldest tree he'd ever seen.

The trunk was thick and pockmarked with big, seeping lesions protruding from various places. Giant roots, bigger than a man's torso, sprawled out from the base, writhing into the soil on a centuries-old search for nourishment. The lower branches were bare and black, tapering out like large skeletal fingers clutching at the air. The tree had survived some kind of fire years ago, evidenced by the damage present. Only the very top branches sprouted leaves.

As he stepped into the clearing his head was immediately filled with the voices. The voices no longer came across as whispers, but the actual voices of men and women. He wasn't surprised to realize they were emanating from the tree itself. He stood staring at the dark, burnt bark, listening.

"Do not fear," a voice said. It was the woman's. "We have what you seek."

"I just want to be left alone," he said. The sound of his voice echoed irreverently in the silence. Suddenly, he felt a power seize him, forcing thoughts and images onto the stage of his mind. He saw images of himself: shy, weak, unsure, always the outsider looking in. He relived the taunting and teasing of his classmates, being picked last for a baseball game—or not picked at all—humiliated to tears in the hallways at school. But worst of all, he saw the subtle glances of disapproval in his father's eyes, looks that had escaped him before.

The honesty was brutal. It was like being forced to look into a mirror and see the plain truth for all that it was. He wasn't aware of the tears that had appeared in his eyes, until they ran hot and uncontrolled down his face. He dropped to his knees in utter self pity and loathing, his soul flayed wide open. The newly excavated truth of himself lay bare before him.

Through his tears he looked at the tree and he felt it beckoning him forward. He crawled forward on his hands and knees, his fingers digging into the dark, pungent soil of the forest floor. There was a sensation, like icy tendrils caressing his face, gently pulling him forward. The voices contained a tone of love and acceptance now, an acceptance he had long desired but had always been beyond his reach. His despair was being turned to hope, a sense of meaning, a sense of purpose.

He placed his hands on the rough bark of the tree and felt a tingling surge enter through his fingertips. The voices went silent, but he could sense their approval. He knew he was being asked to be a part of something. Something that he was destined to play an important role in.

A new voice—his own—rose up inside him crying with all its might for him to stop, but he willed it away. He locked it in a dark chamber and forced it deep down into the farthest reaches of his mind.

He began to feel a presence scratching away at his inner defenses and he consciously gave over a portion of control. He knew a bargain was being struck. The images in his mind began to change from what was, to what will be. He now saw himself confident, strong and feared. He liked the way it made him feel and he suddenly hungered for it, willing to do whatever it took to bring it to pass. He was ready to bury the old Daniel, out here in the woods, and trade him for a new Daniel, one that nobody would recognize.

He gave in and finally allowed the last of his defenses to collapse. He limbs became stiff as a powerful force surged from the tree, through his hands, coursing into his entire body. He watched his fingers digging into the bark; he could feel it writhing under his palms like a knot of snakes. The veins in his hands popped, but he felt no pain.

He couldn't breathe or move. His vision was fading as he began to lose consciousness. Just moments before he blacked out, he became keenly aware that he was no longer alone in his body. Like walking into a large room and immediately sensing someone else there, he knew that others had joined him. His little voice of warning cried in sheer panic as the dark tunnel closed and he knew no more.

Sometime later, as the sun arced on its slow descent to the horizon, Daniel Miller emerged from the woods bordering his parents' farm. He retraced his steps across the fields and entered the house, allowing the screen door to slam shut as usual. He reassured his worried mother in calm, measured words that he was fine. He ate dinner with a healthy appetite and even visited with his parents for a while before retiring to his room for the night.

Upon hearing Daniel's bedroom door shut, his parents exchanged smiles of relief with each other. It seemed their boy was going to be alright after all.

CHAPTER 3

Sheriff Chet Cooper wiped at his brow with a handkerchief. August was always hot, but by the end of the month things usually started to cool down a little. You sure wouldn't know it today. He stuffed the handkerchief back into his pocket and surveyed his desk with dismay; it was a cluttered mess. Stacks of papers and folders were strewn across the weathered, oak surface. A rattling old fan on the edge of the desk lifted and dropped the corners of the papers as it oscillated back and forth.

The office was quiet. Both of his deputies—his entire force—were out on assignments he'd given them. Rick Shelton was spending the afternoon monitoring traffic on Main Street, and Scotty Forks had been dispatched to investigate a fender bender over on Clark.

He gathered up some of the reports and tried to organize them by priority. It quickly became an exercise in futility, so he just stacked them off to the side of his desk next to his half-empty coffee mug. He hadn't anticipated this part of being sheriff when he had sought the job. Paperwork and filing were not exactly his strong suit. With just under a year into the job, he still felt wet behind the ears. Having to deal with the inner workings of the local politics and the unique quirks of the townspeople was a far cry from what he had come to know as a sergeant in the Marine Corps. Still, he felt he was in the right place.

After returning from the war he'd been given a hero's welcome by his hometown. Stepping off the train he had known, right then and there, that he never wanted to leave Clear Creek again. He had received decorations for his actions at Tarawa and Saipan, not to mention some Japanese shrapnel in his back and hip which had also earned him an honorable discharge from his beloved Corps.

The Clear Creek Register had run a front page story on him, and it wasn't long before he was enjoying celebrity status, despite his insistence that he was not a hero. The real heroes were the ones who had truly given everything, the ones who wouldn't be coming home.

He was offered a job as a sheriff's deputy on the small force and had readily accepted the position, figuring it to be a natural transition for him, considering his experience in the war.

A few years later, when the job for sheriff became available, he had the overwhelming support of the community. He had practically been forced into the job despite his youth—only twenty-nine years old—and relative inexperience. But, as the newspaper had pointed out, he was a war hero, and at six feet tall, with piercing blue eyes, a square jaw, and a head of wavy, dark-brown hair, he looked every bit the part.

Everybody seemed to be behind him when he first took the job, but it wasn't long before it seemed like he was inadvertently angering the entire town with every move. It was a tough transition, going from town hero to town heel.

Recently, he had phoned an old Marine acquaintance, Master Sergeant Bill Rumsey, and mentioned it to him.

"Hey, it's no different than when you were a sergeant," his old mentor had said. "You aren't doing a good job unless everyone is pissed off at you all the time. Don't worry," he consoled, "most people know a good man when they see him...even if they are pissed off at him." It was sound advice coming from a man almost twice his age, and he took it to heart.

Unable to stare at the jumble of papers a minute more, Chet rose from his cluttered desk, wincing as his war wounds protested the sudden movement. He tucked his khaki police shirt into his trousers, adjusted his duty belt, making sure his Colt M1911 was secure in its holster, and headed for the office door. *Just a quick drive around town in the cruiser, then I'll tackle the paperwork,* he promised himself.

As his hand grasped the doorknob the phone on his desk began to ring. He cursed under his breath and dashed for the phone. He was really going to have to try to find room in his meager budget for a part time secretary. He picked up the phone receiver. "Hello, this is Sheriff Cooper," he said.

Caroline Fishbeck, the switchboard operator, squawked into his ear, "Afternoon Chet, I've got Mrs. Henderson on the line. She seems pretty upset." Caroline was in the habit of screening his calls. It was totally out of the scope of her job, and border-lined on inappropriate, but it was pretty convenient most of the time, so he let it slide.

"Alright, thanks Caroline. Connect the line, please." There was a brief hiss of static as Caroline connected the lines.

An older female voice on the other end came through the receiver. "Hello, is this the sheriff?" Her voice was thick with worry.

"This is Sheriff Cooper. What can I do for you Mrs. Henderson?" He was doing his best not to sound irritated.

"Sheriff Cooper, my grandson's missing. He should have been home from school three hours ago, and still no sign of him." She was talking fast and it all came spilling out at once.

"Okay Mrs. Henderson," he interrupted, "I need you to slow down and answer a few questions for me." He walked back around his desk and rifled through a drawer for a pencil.

"I'm sorry Sheriff, it's just that this is not like him at all. He's always been very dependable, never goes off anywhere."

"Let's just calm down, I'm sure he'll turn up very soon. Now let's start with your grandson's name and age."

"His name's Levi and he'll be ten on October third. He's got medium-length, sandy-brown hair. He was wearing dark, denim pants and a blue, button-up shirt…"

Chet wrote as fast as he could while Mrs. Henderson rattled off about a dozen traits of the boy, from his glasses to his freckles, and the small hole in the left knee of his pants.

He cut her off again, "Okay Mary, I think I have what I need for now. I'm sure he just got distracted with something after school and has lost track of the time. Give me a little while and I'll take a drive around town, see if I can scare him up. I'll tell my deputies to keep their eyes peeled for him as well. I'll call you back in a while, okay?"

"Thank you, Sheriff," she replied. "My husband is driving around looking for him too."

"How is Rupert these days?" he asked.

"Just as mean and nasty as ever."

Chet laughed. "I don't know if he remembers me much, but he was my scoutmaster when I was a kid."

"Oh, he remembers alright. He's pretty proud of the fact, to tell the truth." A tone of feigned disgust crept into her voice. "He's always goin' on about how he taught you everything you know." A nervous laugh escaped her.

"Well, I'll keep an eye out for Levi and your husband while I'm on my patrol and I'll check back with you in a while."

"Okay, thank you."

"Bye now." Hanging up the telephone, he folded up the paper containing his hastily scribbled description of Levi Henderson, and tucked it into his shirt pocket. As he headed for the door he glanced at his watch. Almost five o'clock. The kid should know better.

Once in his patrol car, a new Chevrolet Stylemaster, he cranked the engine to life and rolled the window down. He raised Deputies Forks and Shelton on the radio and gave them Levi's description with instructions to keep a lookout for the boy. He put the Chevy in gear and pulled into the light traffic. The kid was probably down at Flossy's buying bubble gum and comic books. He reached speed and headed for the drug store on the other end of Main Street.

He scanned the sidewalks and shops as he drove, returning the occasional wave from pedestrians with a nod, but there was no sign of a ten year old kid anywhere. He struck out at Flossy's Drug Store as well. He asked Randy Ferguson, working behind the counter, if he had seen Levi. Randy knew who the boy was, but said he hadn't been in the store that day. The teenage couple sharing a fountain drink at the end of the bar said they didn't even know who Levi Henderson was.

Discouraged, Chet cruised over to Lincoln Elementary, a few blocks away. The grounds were deserted but there were still a couple of cars parked out front. After pulling into an open parking space he got out and headed up the cement steps to the front doors. They were locked, so he pounded a few smart slaps on the door's window with the flat of his hand.

A young, attractive woman appeared from an office door to the left. She pushed the crash bar on the door, allowing Chet into the school. She had a warm, genuine smile, and stood waiting for him to speak. Chet didn't fluster easily, but he found that words were hard to come by as he spoke. "Good afternoon, ma'am, I'm—"

She interjected, "I know who you are, Sheriff Cooper. I'm Kate Farnsworth, the new school secretary." She extended her right hand. Her handshake was firm, full of confidence. "How can I help you, Sheriff Cooper?" She had a southern accent, just like his drill instructor in boot camp, but the resemblance certainly ended there! Where his drill instructor's drawl had only served to accentuate his mean and nasty disposition, this woman's accent somehow made her seem more alluring…mysterious even.

Her large, almond-shaped eyes were sea-green, framed by naturally curly tresses of raven-black hair. Her full lips came together in a natural pout, but not exaggerated like the pictures of pin-up girls he'd seen taped to lockers and walls while in the service. She wore a light-blue blouse tucked into a cream colored skirt that reached just below her knees. Without the black heels, he guessed she probably stood about five foot seven—he had become fairly capable at estimating height and weight over the last year.

"Well, I'm actually looking for a boy, Levi Henderson. Do you know him?" he inquired.

Her pretty smile evaporated and a look of curious concern came over her face. It did not diminish her good looks in the least. "Why yes, Sheriff, he's a fourth grader here. Has he done something? He's a good kid, I can't imagine the police looking for him."

"No, it's nothing like that. His grandmother called me a little while ago and said he hadn't made it home from school yet. I promised her I'd look into it. I thought I'd stop by and see if anyone remembered if he'd been at school today."

She pursed her lips in thought. "I don't recall seeing him around today, but there's nothing odd about that." She thought for a second more. "His teacher is Mrs. Rucker. If you'd like, I have keys to all the classrooms. We could walk down to her room and check her attendance book for the day."

The alternative was to get back in his car and keep driving around. "It wouldn't hurt, uh Mrs—"

"It's Miss, and please, call me Kate," she said, as she darted into the office to retrieve her keys.

"Only if you promise to call me Chet," he called after her, immediately regretting it. It wasn't exactly the most professional reaction.

"Will do…*Chet*," she called from the office. After a jingle of keys and the sound of a desk drawer closing, Kate reappeared in the hallway. "This way, *Chet*," she teased, heading down the hall.

He felt himself blush slightly and inwardly kicked himself. With two large strides he caught up to walk by her side, her heels clicking smartly on the blue and white tile floor.

Lincoln Elementary hadn't changed an iota since he had attended as a boy. Even the same faint odor of pine-scented cleaner still permeated the air. As they walked past numbered doors and art projects hanging on the walls, he made an attempt at small talk. "I haven't seen you around before. How long have you been in Clear Creek?"

"Just a few weeks. This is my first job out of college, I got hired just in time for the school year."

"Where'd you go to school?"

"Oh, nowhere fancy. Just a little business school in Nashville."

"Is that where you're from?"

"No, I'm from a little town called Emmett, about two hundred miles east of

Nashville, at the foot of the Smoky Mountains."

"What brings you all the way here from Tennessee?"

She looked down at her feet for a moment when Chet asked the question.

Since becoming a cop he had learned to recognize many of the subtle changes people made with their body language when they were about to lie. Breaking eye contact was one of the most frequent and obvious things people did when trying to deceive.

"I guess I've always wanted to see further west," she said, reestablishing eye contact with him. "And how about you, Chet? Are you from around here?" she asked, quickly deflecting the subject back to him. She stopped in front of room nineteen, counting off keys on the key ring.

"Born and raised, like everybody else here," he replied, leaning a shoulder against the wall. She found the key she was looking for, inserted it into the lock, and opened the door to Mrs. Rucker's classroom. She headed for the large wooden desk at the front of the room while Chet looked around, childhood memories rushing back at him.

The room smelled like paste, construction paper, and pencil shavings. On the back wall of the room, hung a collage of hand drawn maps of the United States. Behind the teacher's desk a large blackboard still contained the day's math problems etched with white chalk. He shuddered from the memory of standing at the front of the room, trying to solve a math problem in front of the whole class. His eyes came to rest on Kate's striking figure as she leaned over the desk. She was flipping through the pages of the attendance book.

She flipped a page back and forth a couple of times. "That's odd," she said.

"What's that?" Chet stepped to her side to gain a view of the book. He couldn't help noticing the sweet fragrance of her hair and had to quickly remind himself of why he was here. Besides, she was probably just another one of the pretty faces that had led to nothing but trouble and heartbreak in his life since returning home. Best not to waste his time.

Kate ran her finger down the list of student names to Levi Henderson. Then she skimmed her finger to the the right, over a row of columns displaying the dates, each one marked with an X in red pencil for the day. The box for this day, however, had been left blank. Kate looked up at him, brushing a lock of hair behind her ear. "According to the attendance book, he never even made it to school today."

A familiar, hollow gnawing began in the pit of his gut. He had learned in his combat days to trust that feeling: something wasn't right. He rounded his lips and exhaled. "How's his previous attendance for the year?" he asked, leaning in for a closer look, no longer distracted by Kate's good looks and nice smelling hair.

"School hasn't been in for long, but so far, perfect for the year," she answered, straightening herself. "Until today." The concern on her face matched his.

"Do you know who his friends are, or if he belongs to any after school clubs of any kind?"

She sat down at the desk and pulled a paper and pencil from the side drawer. "I can make a list of the friends I'm aware of. I know there's some boys that play baseball after school, down at the park, but I'm thinking they would all be home by now."

"Yeah. Still, it wouldn't hurt to take a drive past the park just to see." He rubbed at the stubble starting to sprout on his face. "Do you have a telephone in your office, Miss...uh, I mean Kate?"

She nodded while copying a boy's name down from the attendance book.

"If you don't mind, I'm going to call his grandma and see if she can give me a list of names too."

"That's a good idea," she said, "I'm almost done here, then we can compare lists. I'll lock up the classroom and see you back in my office. From there I can supply phone numbers and addresses for everyone on the list."

"Sounds good," he agreed, heading for the door. He stopped and turned in the doorway. "Thanks Kate, for being so helpful. I'm sure you'd rather be on your way home right now."

"I just hope he turns up."

"He will," Chet said, trying his best to sound confident.

As he walked back down the hallway to Kate's office, he was dreading the call he was about to make. Informing Mrs. Henderson that Levi had been marked absent for the day would likely send her spiraling into a nosedive of frantic worry.

Kate's office was small, but neat. Late, golden sunlight filtered in through a four-paned window behind the desk. A row of metal filing cabinets lined one wall like soldiers standing at attention. Behind the big desk was a smaller table with a typewriter on it, a paper partially fed into the roller, and a wooden swivel chair pushed to the side. He must have interrupted her in the middle of typing.

The main desk was neat and clear of clutter. A large calendar was fixed to the surface of the desk with dates and appointments penciled onto it. One lone picture frame sat on a corner of the desk: it was a photograph of a smiling Kate in a graduation cap and gown, flanked by an older couple, whom Chet presumed to be her proud parents. The telephone sat diagonally in the opposite corner. The Marine in him approved of the overall tidiness of the office. Her desk definitely put his to shame.

He fingered the hammer on his Colt while Caroline connected him to the Hendersons' line. After four or five rings there was a click as the phone was lifted from the hook.

The unmistakable, rough voice of Rupert Henderson answered, "Hello?"

Chet was a bit relieved. Rupert was a tough old farmer and would be easier to deliver the news to than his wife. "Mr. Henderson, it's Sheriff Cooper," he stated. "I was checking in to see if Levi had turned up at home yet."

Rupert sounded dismayed. "No Chet, he hasn't. I take it you haven't been able to find him either."

"Well, I'm just getting started Mr. Henderson. Another reason I was calling was to see if you could maybe give me a list of his friends, kids he may have gone home with?"

"I already drove around to his friends' houses and checked. No sign of 'em anywhere, Chet."

Rupert was tough, but Chet could detect the worry in his voice when he spoke. "Still, Mr. Henderson, it might prove helpful if you could give me a list."

"If you say so," Rupert said, and started to ramble off a list of names.

Chet was bent over the desk writing, the phone cradled in his shoulder, when Kate appeared in the doorway. She raised her eyebrows questioningly. He just shook his head. Rupert finished his list and went silent. Chet continued his eye contact with Kate to ask his next question. "Mr. Henderson, did Levi get on the school bus this morning?"

"I would think so. I didn't drive him and it's too far to walk." There was a muffled sound and Rupert could be heard yelling, "Ma! Ma! Did Levi ride the bus to school this morning?"

Mrs. Henderson's muffled voice appeared in the background, and then Rupert was back on the phone. "My wife says she sent him to the end of the lane with his books and lunch pail, but didn't actually see him get on the bus. Why Sheriff, what's going on?"

"Mr. Henderson, I'm at the school right now with Miss…Miss,"

"Farnsworth," Kate whispered with a smile.

Chet continued, "With Miss Farnsworth, the school secretary, and we checked the attendance records; they show that Levi was absent from school today."

"Absent?" Rupert sounded incredulous. Chet heard Mrs. Henderson inquiring and her husband simply replied, "Sheriff says he never showed at school today."

Only silence followed.

Chet could perfectly envision the fearful looks the Hendersons were probably exchanging with each other. The silence was hard to bear. He was naturally a protective person. It was that protective instinct that had earned him a Silver Star and a Purple Heart at Tarawa, and consequently had driven him to this profession.

Many times as a marine in combat he had been forced to put on a mask of courage and confidence for his men, never allowing his own fear and doubts to peek out from behind the mask. It was a skill he had become quite adept at during the war, and once again, for the benefit of the Hendersons, he pulled out the mask and broke the silence. "Mr. Henderson, kids do this sort of thing all the time, I'm sure he'll turn up soon. I want you to know that I'm going to devote all of my resources to finding your grandson. I'm going to check out a few more places and check with some of these friends. I'll call you in a while, okay?"

"Alright. Is there anything we can do?"

"Chances are he'll come wandering in on his own. The best thing to do is to just stay put, so someone is there when he does."

"Okay, we can do that I suppose."

"Good. And don't worry, we'll find him."

Chet hung up the phone as Kate walked in and took his list from the top of the desk. She compared the notes and then walked around to sit in her chair. Taking the list that she made, she crossed off any of her names that matched with the ones Mr. Henderson had already looked into.

"I've got three names here that Mr. Henderson didn't visit," she said, as she opened a desk drawer and produced a clipboard with a stack of typed papers clamped to it. She answered his question before he could ask, "Addresses and phone numbers of all the students at Lincoln." She started flipping through the papers on the clipboard.

"You know, you wouldn't make a bad cop," Chet commented, with a grin.

She looked up from the clipboard, an amused expression on her face. "You should see me shoot a pistol."

"Now that, I'd like to see!" he replied, with a chuckle.

She arched an eyebrow before turning her attention back to the clipboard. The silence was a little awkward as she flipped through more papers. He folded his arms and leaned against the wall.

"Good news," she said after a minute. "Two of these students have home phone numbers. I can call them if you'd like."

"I would appreciate that. While you're calling those kids I'm going to go out to my car and check in with my deputies. I'll be right back."

He left as Kate picked up the phone to make the calls. He propped the school house door open with a pebble and jogged to his patrol car. He depressed the transmit button on his police radio. "Shelton, this is Cooper, come in."

There was a brief silence followed by a squelch break. "Shelton here, go ahead, Coop."

Deputy Rick Shelton was forty-nine years old and in really good shape for his age. A twenty-five-year veteran of the small force, he was instrumental in getting Chet up to speed on his new sheriff's job. Chet appreciated the fact that it probably wasn't easy taking orders from a man nineteen years his junior, but if it did bother him, Rick never let it show.

Chet spoke back into the radio mic, "Yeah, any sign of the Henderson boy yet?"

"Negative Coop, I haven't seen him."

"Rick, I'm making this a priority as of right now. I'm starting to get a bad feeling about this. I want you to make your way over to the park and check the baseball diamond and see if he's there. There might be some boys playing baseball. If he's not with them, ask questions and see if anybody knows anything, then get back to me."

"Ten-four, on my way."

Chet pressed his transmit button again, "Forks, did you copy all that?"

"Ten-four, I copy." Scotty Forks was a young rookie, twenty two years old, eager, and energetic. He was hired onto the force around the same time as Chet to replace the retired Bill Johnson. He had enlisted in The US Navy at age eighteen, but was still stateside when the war had ended. He'd always felt cheated by the fact he had never made it into a theater of action.

Scotty reminded Chet of all the bright-eyed, naive, eager beavers that he had trained and served with in The Marines—poor kids who had no idea what they had gotten themselves into. He did his best to convince Scotty that he had been lucky to miss combat, but to no avail.

"Forks, I need you to head over and man the office for a while till I get back. Keep an eye out for the Henderson kid on your way." He racked the mic.

"Copy that," Scotty answered, flatly.

Chet smiled. He could almost see the sour, disappointed look on the rookie's face. When he returned to Kate's office she was just hanging up the phone. "Any luck?" he asked.

She shook her head. "He's not there, and both boys confirmed that he wasn't at school today."

"I sent a deputy to check out the park, he should be reporting back pretty soon."

Kate stood up with the list in her hand, "I guess there's just this last boy on the list, Jimmy Parsons."

"Parsons, on Cherry Street?" Chet asked.

"Yep, two-forty-seven Cherry Street." She handed him the paper.

"Thanks again," he said. "You've been more help than you know."

"You are certainly welcome, but It was no trouble at all. I just hope you can find him. I'm starting to really worry."

"That makes two of us."

"So if he's not at the Parsons, then what?" she asked.

Chet wasn't so sure. "Well, Rick should be getting back to me soon from the ball diamond."

"And if he strikes out there? No pun intended."

Chet smiled nonetheless. "I suppose my next step would be to head out to his grandparents' place and see if there's any clues as to where he might be. Something happened between his grandma sending him down the lane to the bus stop, and him getting on the bus."

Kate folded her arms and nodded her head thoughtfully. "I was just thinking, maybe I should go with you to see Jimmy Parsons."

"Oh?"

"Chet, don't take this the wrong way, but to a shy boy like Jimmy you might be pretty intimidating to talk to…with your uniform and that gun. Jimmy knows me. A friendly, familiar face might be helpful."

Her logic sounded good, and he had to admit that despite his reservations about getting involved with yet another girl, there was something about her that he liked. Even though the thought of his own lack of professionalism chaffed, he agreed.

He waited while she retrieved her purse from a desk drawer. She closed and locked the door to her office, and they walked to his patrol car. He opened the passenger door for her and watched, making sure she was in and settled before closing it. As he walked around the front of the car he wondered how many people would notice the young beauty sitting beside him.

"Wow, taking a ride in a cop car, this is a first for me," she said, as he started the car and backed it out of its parking spot.

"If it makes you feel any better," he said, "It's a first for me too. This car has never had a woman in it."

"Really?" She feigned surprise. "What do you drive the girls around in when you're on dates?"

He grinned. She was obviously poking fun at the fact that he was considered one of the most eligible bachelors in town, according to the newspaper's recent article on public figures. "All the girls I date usually do the driving," he replied, dryly.

She smiled and shook her head. The truth was, he hadn't been out with a girl for a while now, not since the last breakup—entirely his fault. It was a sore spot with everyone he knew, especially his younger sister, who was always trying to set him up with girls. He was starting to believe that his job and a love life just weren't meant to mix. Or was that just an excuse? He wasn't sure. Maybe it was just too convenient to let his job run his life.

Kate crossed her legs and out of the corner of his eye, he couldn't help but take notice of the smooth, shapely contours. Maybe he really wasn't so busy after all. He deserved to be happy too, didn't he?

He caught the movement of her eye glancing in his direction and quickly forced his own eyes back onto the road. He hoped she hadn't just busted him staring at her legs, but he suspected she had. If he was alone, he would've slapped himself. Instead, all he could do was grit his teeth and hope she really didn't notice.

They were on Clark Street, heading into an older residential area of town known as the tree streets. These were a row of streets running parallel to each other, bisected down the middle by Clark Street. Each street was a little older and a little more rundown than the one before it. Not exactly what Chet would describe as dilapidated, but they were older homes, lived in by lower income families, mostly employees of Williams Steel, the small steel factory on the outside of town.

About halfway through the neighborhood, a green, tarnished sign appeared at an intersection indicating Cherry Street. Chet took a right.

"It's number two-forty-seven," Kate reminded him.

"Yeah, I know which one it is."

"That's impressive. Do you know all these homes?"

"A lot of them. I don't claim to know each one, but you never forget your first arrest."

"Oh, I see," Kate said, turning her head to stare out the window as they drove past uncut lawns and corroding cars parked in dirt driveways. "I suppose it's none of my business to ask…" She let the question hang.

Chet took his foot off the gas letting the Chevy coast. "It's all on the public record. The short of it is James Sr. had a bit too much to drink one night. He's a good guy that works hard and provides for his family, but once in a while he ties one on and I get a call. Usually, all it takes is for one of us to show up and he settles down. Except one time, he had to spend a night in my lockup." He pulled the car over to the right side of the road and parked on the shoulder. "And that's that."

He was about to climb out when his radio came to life, "Sheriff, this is Shelton, do you copy?"

Chet snatched up the mic. "What've ya got for me, Rick?"

There was a short burst of static as the radio squelched. "Sorry Coop, I got nothing at the park. No sign of him here, no boys play'n ball..." The radio went silent as Rick waited for further instructions.

Chet exhaled in slight disappointment. "Alright Rick, thanks for checking. Why don't you call it a night and head home to Alice, and I'll see you tomorrow."

"What about you, boss? You ain't gonna be up with this all night are ya?" Rick was never one to go home and leave all the work to everyone else.

"I've got a couple more things I want to check out. I'll just have to see where things go from there," Chet replied. "Scotty's got the graveyards for this week. You go home. If anything develops and we need your help, I promise I'll call."

"Alright, but do call me though, if anything comes up."

"Okay Rick. Have a good night and give Alice and the boys my best."

Chet climbed out of the car. Kate had let herself out by the time he walked around to her side. An old brick walkway led from the street to the Parsons' front door. Grass had grown through the cracks, obscuring the bricks and making the walkway lumpy and uneven. He could see that Kate was having difficulty navigating the walk in her high heels, and offered her his arm, which she accepted.

The Parsons' home was a classic two-story bungalow built in the mid-twenties that had seen better days. The brick that covered the lower half of the house was chipped and missing big chunks of mortar. The home needed new shingles, and the yellow paint covering the wood siding of the upper half of the house was faded and peeling. They reached the worn stair case that led up to the wooden porch, which was covered with a sagging roof supported by four square pillars.

Chet knocked with a firm rap on the front door. They could hear music playing inside, the evening radio programs would be starting soon. His experience in the war had taught him to take time out, once in a while, to let his senses probe his surroundings. He almost did it without thinking anymore. He soaked in the sounds, sights, and smells of Cherry Street while they waited for the door to be answered. The shouts of kids playing in the yards and street, the barking of dogs, a passing car, and the scent of a dozen different suppers being prepared presented a feeling of normalcy. No gut feeling raising its suspicious head.

The sound of the doorknob being turned brought him back to the task at hand as the weather-faded door swung inward. James Parsons, in his mid-thirties, stood lanky and lean in the doorway, the upper half of his work coveralls tied about his waist by the arms. A dingy, white t-shirt clung loosely to his chest, revealing a taught, sinewy build. A half-smoked cigarette dangled from his thin lips, the smoke curling up around his balding head. He was holding a dark brown beer bottle in front of his stomach.

James smiled politely. "What could I have possibly done, Sheriff?" he asked, holding up his bottle. "I haven't even hardly gotten started yet." He offered his hand.

Chet shook hands. "Only one more beer after that one now, James. Like we discussed, right?" Chet said, in an almost fatherly tone.

"Right you are, Sheriff Cooper."

Then, for the first time, James seemed to notice Kate standing next to Chet. There was an awkward moment as James blatantly eyed the beauty from head to toe. Kate blushed.

Chet cleared his throat. "Uh, James this is Miss Kate Farnsworth, the new school secretary out at the elementary school."

Kate extended her hand. "Good evening, Mr. Parsons."

James smiled and shook Kate's hand a little longer than proper etiquette called for.

"James," Chet butted in, "we need to talk to little Jimmy, is he around?"

James finally dropped Kate's hand and she took a small, subtle step backwards. "Yeah, he's here. Doing his studies at the kitchen table with his mom. He ain't in any kind of trouble is he?"

"No, he's not in trouble or anything. We just need to talk to him about one of his friends that hasn't come home from school yet. We're just looking for any information anyone might have."

James led them to the front room of the house. The smell of fried chicken was strong and Chet realized he was actually starting to feel hungry. James left them waiting there as he went to retrieve his son.

"Well, he's quite the charmer," Kate whispered as James vanished around a corner.

"Yeah, he's a real pillar of the community."

They both snickered and then fell silent, each glancing around at pictures hanging on the walls and other knick-knacks serving as decoration.

Jimmy appeared in the front room accompanied by both his parents. He looked like any typical ten-year-old kid, all knees, elbows, and teeth. His brown hair was cropped short, military style, and his large brown eyes stared down at the floor, just in front of his feet, that appeared too big for his body.

His mother, Eliza Parsons, stood right behind him, her apron spattered with grease from frying chicken. She was pretty plain looking, but any losses she had in the looks department, she well made up for with her warm and friendly personality. "Well, Sheriff Cooper, what a delight!" she exclaimed. "And Miss Farnsworth, also a pleasure."

Chet and Kate politely exchanged greetings with Mrs. Parsons for a minute and then Kate directly addressed Jimmy. "Hey there, kiddo! How are you?" She bent herself to Jimmy's height, her hands resting on her knees.

"Am I in trouble?" Jimmy mumbled, risking a glance up from the floor to Kate's eyes.

"Don't be silly," she answered. "A good boy like you, in trouble? Nah! Sheriff Cooper and I just have a couple questions for you is all. Are you okay with that?"

Jimmy seemed relieved and smiled. "Yes, ma'am, I suppose that's okay with me."

The boy was warming up to her quickly. She seemed to have a way with kids and Chet was glad to have her along. Kate looked up at him with a smile. He gestured with a nod of his head for her to continue.

"Jimmy, we were wondering, did you see Levi at all today?"

Jimmy shook his head, "No, ma'am, I figured he was sick or something."

"When was the last time you saw him?" Kate asked.

"Yesterday, after school got out. He got on the bus and I started walking home."

"Did Levi say anything about going somewhere, or that he was planning on missing school today?"

"No, we were supposed to shoot marbles against Richie and Mark today at lunch. He was planning on being there for that."

Kate straightened, biting her lip, and shot Chet a worried look. They weren't getting anywhere here. Chet noticed through the big picture window that the sun was starting to cast the long deep shadows of dusk as it sank closer to the horizon. Soon it would be dark, and somewhere out there was a little boy, lost… vanished. *People don't just vanish*, he reminded himself.

Kate pulled the list of friends she had made from her purse. "Jimmy, I'm going to read you a list of some of Levi's friends that we made. If you can think of any other friends that we missed let us know."

She read the names aloud from the list while Jimmy listened intently. When she finished she asked, "Is that all his friends that you know of Jimmy?"

Jimmy pursed his lips and stared up at the ceiling in thought. "All except the one new friend."

"Oh?" Kate furrowed her brow, "What new friend?"

"I don't know his name, Just that Levi said he'd found a new friend."

The gnawing in Chet's gut intensified. "Son, what did he tell you about his new friend?"

"Not much. He just talked about some kid he'd met, and that they played together sometimes after school."

"So it's another kid?" Chet reasoned, out loud. "From your school?"

"I think he's an older kid maybe, not from our school."

"What makes you say that?" Kate interjected.

"I don't know. Just cause I think if he went to our school, Levi woulda said who he was. And they probably woulda been play'n together at recess and stuff."

Chet took a small step toward the boy. "Jimmy, do you know of any secret places or hideouts of Levi's? Anywhere at all he might have gone?"

"He has an army fort in the woods that he built with his new friend. It's a secret though. I don't know where it is."

Chet didn't like the sound of any of it. He addressed Jimmy's parents, "Well, I think that's probably enough questions for now. I appreciate you helping us out." He made a move for the door.

Eliza stepped forward. "Can't you stay for some chicken? I'm sure there's plenty."

Chet smiled appreciatively. "Thanks Eliza, but I really need to tend to this right now. Maybe next time."

Kate followed Chet to the front door and they let themselves out. The Parsons wished them luck as they made their way down the brick path to Chet's car.

"You were very good in there with little Jimmy," Chet said as he opened Kate's door for her.

"Thanks," she replied, "but it's really nothing. You just have to remember back a few years to what it felt like to be a kid, and just get down on their level. You remember what it was like to be a kid, don't you, Sheriff?"

"I suppose, but I'm not kidding. You seem to have a good way with little kids. You should get into teaching."

"I don't know if that's for me. Maybe someday."

"Well, you'll make a really good mom someday anyway." He meant it as a compliment, but he figured he had struck a nerve of some kind by the way she quickly broke eye contact.

"So, now to the Hendersons?" she asked, changing the topic and sliding into the front seat.

"That's all I can think to do next. Maybe they know something about this new friend."

"Where do they live?" Kate inquired as he got into the car and shut the door.

He fired up the engine. "They live on a little farm about ten miles or so out of town." He put the car in gear and pulled out into the street. "Where would you like me to drop you off?"

"Oh, you don't have to take me home. I really want to help you find Levi, I'm more than happy to come along to the Hendersons with you."

She was being very kind, and a big part of him was screaming, *Alright, sure!* But, there was a professional line and he knew he was close to crossing it. "Thanks for the offer, Kate," he began, "but, I can't ask you to do anymore, you've done enough as it is, and I owe you one."

"Well, you are the sheriff, so it's up to you I suppose." She sounded curt, maybe a little offended.

"Look, it's not like I don't want you along," he explained, "it's just that—"

"It's fine," she cut him off. "I was just offering my help is all. I'm currently renting a room at a boarding house on Washington Street, just down from the school. I'd be grateful if you'd just drop me off there, Sheriff."

Sheriff? What happened to Chet? He wanted to say more, but wasn't sure what to say exactly. He exhaled loudly, feeling frustrated. An awkward silence hung between them as he made his way to Washington Street. Every once in a while a passing car honked, the driver waving with a smile. Chet would nod or wave back, all the time wondering if he had blown any kind of chance of a future friendship with Kate.

He cleared his throat. "I'm guessing you must be staying at Mable's then?" He tried his hardest to sound as benign as possible.

"Yes."

"That's a nice place. And you can't beat Mable, she's a great cook."

"I suppose so."

Alright, that does it! He pulled the car off to the side of the street and parked it against the curb.

Kate looked at him, confused. "Mable's is a couple blocks down."

He shifted in his seat so he could face her head on. "You interrupted me back there and I would like the chance to finish what I was going to say. I just wanted to explain—"

She cut in again, "There's nothing to explain, Sheriff. I get it. You have a job to do, and don't need me tagging along."

"It's not that... Okay, it's partly that, but it's not exactly like you're making it sound."

"Go on." She folded her arms, pursing her lips together.

He felt the palms of his hands begin to sweat. *What is the matter with me?* He'd barely met this girl and now he was trying to explain to her why she couldn't ride around with him all night in his police car like Nancy Drew?

"Okay, here's the thing: you are a very, um...very attractive woman, and believe me, I've enjoyed your company. Although, I wish we had been able to get to know each other under other circumstances." He detected a slight softening in her expression, the pursed lips relaxing.

He continued, "It's just that I've got this lost kid out there, who's seemingly vanished into thin air. I've got to go now to his grandparents and inform them that I've had absolutely no luck in finding him. I don't want the Hendersons, or anybody else, to get the wrong idea is all."

Kate began nodding her head slightly. Was he getting through to her?

She smiled and asked, "What's the wrong idea, Sheriff?"

"I just don't want people to think that while this kid is lost out there I'm out on a date, trying to impress a beautiful woman by having her ride around in my car with me."

She was silent and seemed to be pondering what he had said. After a moment she said, "I guess you better take me home then. We don't want people getting the wrong idea."

The last two blocks to Mable's boarding house was quiet, not a word passing between them. Chet was cursing at himself. Was there anything he could do to salvage this? For the first time since returning from the Pacific, he really felt interested in someone. There seemed to be a real connection with Kate from the get go. Or was he just letting her pretty face cloud his judgment? Whatever the cause, he hoped, given time, she might come to realize the position he was in.

Maybe he'd give it a couple of weeks and then make an excuse to stop by the school.

He rolled to a stop in front of Mable's and grasped the door handle to let himself out. Too late. Kate sprung out of her door on her own. He leaned across the seat to look her in the eye, half expecting her to slam the door in his face.

She bent down to see into the car, one hand resting on the open door. "What was that you said a little bit ago about you owing me one?" she asked.

"Yeah, you really were a big help today."

She brought her forefinger up to her red lips and tapped them as if in deep thought. "Dinner tomorrow night," she stated flatly. "That's my fee."

His heart leaped in his chest. "Um, okay," he managed to mutter.

"Alright, what time should I expect you?" Her expression was flat and serious, like she was conducting a business transaction.

"How about six?" he asked, a little too quickly.

"Perfect." A small dimple formed on her cheek as she gave in to a little smile, and then her face became serious again. "Chet, I'm really worried about Levi. If you need me for anything please let me know. Don't hesitate to call here and just ask for me."

"Thanks, Kate." He was back to being Sheriff Cooper again, cool and calm under pressure. "I'll keep you posted on any developments through the night."

"Okay. Well, good luck and I'll see you tomorrow night at six."

"See you tomorrow."

She shut the passenger door to the car. Chet watched, half mesmerized, as she walked down the cement path that led to Mable's front porch. Her long, black curls bounced as her well-defined calf muscles flexed with each step. As she neared the front door, someone from inside the boarding house flicked on the porch light, reminding him of the growing darkness…and the little boy lost out in it.

CHAPTER 4

As the final rays of the setting sun spilled through his open window, Daniel Miller sat on the edge of his bed studying the palms of his hands. Tiny dust particles slowly swirled in and out of the waning, golden shafts of light. The lone voice, locked away deep inside, cried out, *What have I done?* But was quickly silenced and buried even deeper, only to be replaced by the caressing reassurance of those who now dwelt within him.

He would never be the same after what he had done today—what *they* had done. He had defied God, and in so doing, his eyes were opened to another world, a world apart from the one he had always known. He had transcended from the old world of the pathetic and mindless to a new, enlightened world where chaos and absolute freedom reigned. The petty laws of mortal man didn't apply to him anymore. He walked on a plane between two worlds. He was a phantom, never completely existing in one world or the other. His face, now just a mask to conceal the truth of what he had become. He was a wolf in sheep's clothing, a deadly hunter preying undetected amidst the complacent, mindless flock.

He was a killer now, a murderer. He had crushed the life out of his victim, strangling him with his bare hands. The rush of power at that fatal moment had been intoxicating. He was amazed at his own physical strength as his victim's body went limp, the eyes glassing over, never to reflect the sparkle of life again.

He inhaled deeply and closed his eyes, savoring the memory. He replayed the murder over and over again in his mind, each time remembering new details of the kill. He smiled at his own cleverness as he recounted how he had deceived the boy.

His selection of Levi Henderson as his first victim had been the obvious choice. Levi lived on the neighboring farm alone with his grandparents. His father had been killed in the war and his mother, unable to deal with the loss, had run off, leaving the boy to be raised by his aging grandparents. Having faced such a deep loss, and so early in life, Levi was vulnerable, a vulnerability that Daniel had exploited masterfully.

At first, Daniel had merely observed Levi at a distance. From his bedroom window he could see the Henderson's home down the road, and the younger boy playing in the yard. He noticed that Levi mostly played by himself, the curse of being an only child growing up on a farm. Daniel could relate all too well, and he used that to his advantage.

Eventually, on a warm afternoon, he had approached Levi as the younger lad played army in the woods. Hiding behind the mask that concealed the lurking predator inside him, it had been easy to fool the lonely boy. He never suspected.

They played army together, building forts and defending them against The Nazis. They traded marbles and baseball cards. They explored the woods together, Daniel sharing hunting stories with the wide-eyed youth.

It didn't take long for Daniel to gain a clear understanding of Levi's emotional needs, and he effortlessly slipped into the role of the big brother Levi had never had. It had been too easy. He chuckled to himself, a guttural, hollow sounding laugh not completely his own.

Over a period of about two weeks, Daniel had carefully cultivated the friendship, continually gaining more and more of Levi's trust. He convinced Levi that he should keep their friendship a secret, that people wouldn't understand him hanging out with a boy so much older. During this time he was also working up his courage. It wasn't like he hadn't had the opportunity, but the time had never seemed quite right. Until today.

This morning, while Levi was waiting for the school bus to pick him up, Daniel had appeared out of nowhere. He made up a story about finding something amazing in the woods; it was a surprise, and he just had to come and see! Levi was reluctant at first, but it didn't take much to convince him to follow Daniel—the older boy he admired—into the woods.

Like a dumb animal to the slaughter, Levi allowed himself to be lead to the clearing. And the tree.

"Wow, what a neat old tree," the younger boy remarked, staring up at the contorted, black branches. These would be Levi's last words.

Once under the canopy of the tree, Daniel had sprung like a coiled snake, overwhelming the shocked Levi with his size and strength. To Daniel, the struggle seemed to last a lifetime, even though he knew it must have only been minutes. He remembered a strange sensation, like a part of him was floating above, within the branches of the tree, watching in horror, as the other part of him carried out the grizzly, forbidden act.

The Summoning

As Levi's life began to ebb under his powerful grip, Daniel felt like he was waking from a long, deep sleep. His senses were truly alive for the first time. He could hear every faint sound of the forest, from the slightest rustling of a leaf, to the sound of Levi's heart pounding out its final beats. The colors around him were vibrant and his eyes picked out every detail. He could literally smell the fear and confusion of his victim. He was like an all-knowing, all-sensing god. A god of wrath, an angel of death.

When the dark deed was accomplished, he actually threw up, right next to the lifeless body. He puked out everything he'd ever eaten, and still he lurched and heaved until he almost choked. This was his body purging out the old, weak Daniel, he mused.

When he had recovered, he dragged the corpse directly to the base of the great, old tree trunk and slumped it over one of the twisted roots. He gathered some debris from the forest floor and unceremoniously scattered it over the body, leaving it there to rot. He wasn't worried about anyone ever finding the body. Nobody would venture that far into the forest to look, and even if they did, there would be no proof of who had killed Levi.

Night had come, and black shadows gathered heavy and dark in the corners of his room. The symphony of chirping crickets outside his window was in stark contrast to his current state of mind. He was weary from the day and cursed his mortal body for the need to sleep. He changed into his night shirt and climbed into his bed, leaving the covers down, having no more need of their security.

The voices didn't need to speak to his mind anymore. He simply felt what they felt, knew what they knew. They were him, and he was them. Together they were gathering power. With this first kill he could already sense the increase in strength, but the task was not yet complete. There would be others, and he was the key.

As he lay on his back, hands behind his head, his mind traveled out of his room, across the farm, and deep into the woods, where the body of Levi Henderson lay cold, motionless, and alone. As sleep began to overtake him, a final thrill coursed through him at the thought of what he had done, and what he was yet to do. Who would be next? Not to worry, the voices would guide him, as they had with Levi. Contentedly, he rolled onto his side and slept like the dead.

CHAPTER 5

Deputy Rick Shelton snatched the phone off the hook on the second ring. Still in his uniform, he was helping his wife, Alice, clear the dinner dishes from the table while his three boys wrestled with each other in the living room. He spoke into the phone, "Shelton residence."

There was a brief pause and a click as the caller's line was connected to his. "Rick, it's Chet. I'm calling from the Hendersons."

Rick covered the phone with his hand and motioned for his rambunctious boys to settle down. "So you found him then?"

"I'm afraid not," Chet sighed into the phone. "I think it's time to take this to the next level and get a search organized. What do you think?" It wasn't unusual for the young sheriff to ask for some advice from his older, more experienced deputy.

"Yeah, I think you're probably right about that," he answered. "You want me to get the ball rolling?"

"I was hoping you'd offer. I'm going to be here for a while longer. I'll see you at the office in a bit."

"Alright, see you soon."

CHET HUNG UP THE PHONE and turned to face the Hendersons, seated together on the living room couch.

"I can't believe this is really happening," Mary said, as she wiped at tears running from the corners of her eyes.

Rupert placed an arm around her shoulders attempting to comfort his distraught wife. He turned to Chet, his weathered face pinched with worry. "So, now what happens?"

Chet walked over and sat next to Rupert on the couch. "We're going to organize a search for Levi. I just talked to Deputy Shelton and he's going to start making some calls. We should have a pretty good-sized group of volunteers within the hour. I'm sorry, but that's the best we can do right now."

He put his hand on Rupert's shoulder and gave it a squeeze. "I'm sure he's going to turn up." His attempt to reassure felt hollow and empty, like a promise broken before it was even made. He was no stranger to the feeling, and it dredged up a memory, buried deep down.

At The battle of Tarawa six thousand human beings were slaughtered in just the first seventy-six hours. Chet's platoon had been pushing into the jungle, rooting the Japanese from their fortifications, when a hidden machine gun emplacement opened fire on them. Everyone dove for cover, the burning rounds ripping through grass, trees and brush all around them. Chet ordered his men to return fire, hot and heavy, then sent a small squad, armed with grenades and a flamethrower, to flank the gun's blind side.

"Fire in the hole!" a Marine yelled, and chucked two pineapple grenades through a gun slit, where the automatic fire was coming from.

Chet didn't need to speak Japanese to get the gist of the sudden yelling and screaming coming from inside the bunker. Two muffled explosions rocked the nest followed by screams of agony. The Marine carrying the flamethrower on his back stepped up to the gun slit and shot a hellish stream of liquid fire into the small bunker. More cries of agony and terror echoed from inside, only to fall silent as the flames consumed the remaining survivors.

When it was over, like any good sergeant worth his stripes, Chet began moving among his men, making a head count and checking ammo. His heart sank when he saw a small group of his men standing and kneeling in a circle, eyes cast down. He hurried to the gathering, pushing men aside.

Private Conrad was lying on his back, coughing up bright, frothy blood. He was in severe shock, his skin pale and clammy as he shivered in the jungle heat. His best friend, Private Kovacs was hunched over him, pressing with desperate hands onto a gushing bullet wound in Conrad's abdomen. Chet immediately ordered a runner to locate and retrieve a corpsman, but deep down he knew it was a mission of futility. Private Aaron Conrad was going to die, and there was nothing he could do to change that.

"He's going to be okay isn't he, Sarge?" Kovacs asked, his voice quavering. "He's going to be okay!"

Chet didn't have it in him to level with the kid. He knelt beside the dying man and began to treat him the best he knew how. Conrad was incoherent, mumbling between coughing, and choking on blood.

"You're gonna be okay. You're gonna be okay," Kovacs kept repeating over and over.

"Make room!" the corpsman shouted, pushing through the gathered men.

Chet stood and ordered the platoon to stand back, then grabbed Kovacs and forced him away from the scene. The corpsman was starting his initial survey of the wound and digging into his kit when Chet ordered Corporal Smith to get the men ready to move.

"That includes you," Chet said to Kovacs. "Go join the men."

"What about Conrad?"

"He's going to be fine," Chet lied. "I've seen men survive a lot worse. Now get moving, private!"

Kovacs turned his back and ran to join the rest of the platoon preparing to move out. Chet took two steps toward the corpsman and the dying Conrad. The corpsman heard Chet's footsteps and looked up. He grimaced, shaking his head.

Chet slowly made his way to join up with his platoon, the weight of command heavy in his heart. Smith was barking orders for the men to check their weapons and get on their feet. Chet caught Kovacs staring at him from the jumble of men, his eyes imploring. Kovacs was on the verge of a breakdown. The news of his best friend's death might have been the tipping point for him. Chet needed every man at his best, so he forced a smile and gave Kovacs a big thumbs up. The grin and look of relief on the kid's face felt like a bayonet through the heart. At that moment, he would have gladly traded places with Conrad. Death would have felt nice. At least he would be able to sleep for a change.

A few days later Kovacs found out that Conrad was dead. At the time, Chet had justified his lie by telling himself he did it for the good of his men, and the mission. In The Corps you did what had to be done...period. But the look of accusation in Kovacs's eyes still haunted him no matter how he justified it.

Now, here he was giving false hopes and assurances to the Hendersons. What was his reason this time? There were no men to protect, no missions to accomplish. He forced the memory back down into its grave and buried it, along with the other memories that had earned a plot in his memory graveyard. Burying his memories, thoughts, and emotions had become like second nature to him since the war. Is that why he didn't have a girlfriend? Is that why he worked so many hours? *The most eligible bachelor in town? More like the most FUBARed bachelor in town.*

"I don't know where you're going to search," Rupert said, with a shake of his head. "We've looked everywhere."

"No we haven't," Chet answered. "We've looked everywhere we think he *might* be. Now that we've questioned all his friends and looked around his normal hangouts, we need to expand our efforts. We have to assume that something out of the ordinary has taken place, so we leave nothing out of the equation."

Rupert and Mary both nodded in understanding.

Chet continued. "We need to start asking, did he take a walk and get lost or hurt? Did he go chasing after a stray dog and end up lost in the woods?" He paused to let it sink in. "My hunch is, Levi never got on the bus, so I've decided we're going to start searching right here on your property and work our way out from there."

Rupert nodded and patted his wife on the knee. "That makes a lot of sense, Sheriff."

Chet stood up from the couch, tucking the back of his shirt in. "I've gotta get back to the office to get things rolling, but I'll be back soon with the search party." He turned for the door and stopped. "I almost forgot."

"What's that?" Rupert asked.

"Do you know Levi's friend, Jimmy Parsons?"

The old man's face was a blank as he turned to Mary. Mary wiped at more tears with a tissue, "Yes. Well, not really. He's in Levi's class and we know who he is, but I had no idea they was friends, I mean, he has mentioned him before, but—"

Chet cut in, "Well, I went by Jimmy's house today to see if he knew where Levi was and Jimmy said something about Levi having a new friend. Can you shed any light on this new friend? Jimmy said Levi won't tell him who it is."

Both the Hendersons' faces were blank as they looked at one another and then back to Chet.

"Does Levi play with imaginary friends or anything like that? I imagine he spends a lot of time playing by himself out here."

Mary said, "He has a pretty good imagination, but I don't think he actually has imaginary friends or anything like that." She stood up and crossed the room to an old writing desk, the kind with the rolling top. She slid it open and withdrew a piece of paper and handed it to Chet. It was an art drawing done in crayon.

"He drew that just the other day. You can see he does have quite the imagination."

Chet studied the picture. The elementary drawing depicted a battle scene. Two crude figures drawn in green, with American flags on their shoulders, and holding brown rifles, seemed to be defending a small fort against a horde of gray stick figures, with swastikas on their shoulders. Many of the gray stick figures were laying on the ground, their circular mouths open with an X drawn for each of their eyes. There was red crayon smeared on their rectangle torsos.

Chet felt some of his buried demons clawing at their graves in his memory graveyard. "Not bad," was all he said, handing the paper back to Mary.

"He wants to join the Army when he grows up," Rupert said. "I keep telling him, he should join the Marines."

"It'll put hair on his chest," Chet quipped, as he stepped across the room and opened the door. "Call my office if anything comes up. Otherwise, I'll be back in a little bit."

"Okay. Thanks, Chet," Mary said. Her spirits seemed to be somewhat lifted.

"Don't worry," he promised with all the confidence he could muster, "we're going to find him if we have to look all night." He shut the door behind him and made for his car. For a flash of a second, Kovacs's accusing eyes appeared in his mind, piercing his conscience.

CHET PULLED BEHIND THE OTHER TWO PATROL CARS parked in front of the sheriff's office on Main Street and checked his watch. It was going to be dark soon, not exactly ideal conditions for a search to be starting. When he entered the office, Rick was just hanging up the phone.

"Hey boss, how'd it go at the Hendersons?" The older man asked, standing and walking over to his desk.

"They're worried sick. Were you able to get a hold of everyone?"

"Most of 'em. I'm expecting about twenty five or so to show up."

Chet nodded. "Not bad."

Rick came back over to Chet's desk and set down a dinner plate covered with a white dishcloth. The aroma of warm food drifted to his nostrils.

"Whatcha got there?" Chet asked, his mouth suddenly beginning to water.

Rick uncovered the plate to reveal a mound of mashed potatoes covered in gravy, a chicken breast, and a pile of green beans. "Alice figured you probably hadn't had anything to eat for supper, so she sent it with me. It's still warm." He offered Chet a fork and knife wrapped in a napkin.

Chet gratefully accepted the utensils. "You have the best wife, deputy."

"I know."

Chet sat at his desk and began to wolf down the potatoes, while Rick poured a cup of coffee from the Coffeemaster percolating on a nearby table. He set a steaming mug in front of Chet and then poured one for himself.

"Where's Scotty?" Chet asked, between bites.

"In the back, scrounging up some spare flashlights and batteries."

"Good, they should come in handy."

Just then, the rookie appeared from the back room where they stored extra gear and equipment. He was cradling four flashlights in his hands.

"This was all I could find in storage." He settled the flashlights on his desk. "Combined with the ones in our cars, that gives us a total of seven." He started clicking the flashlights on and off, testing them out.

Chet stood abruptly from his desk as he forked one last bite of mashed potatoes into his mouth. "Rick, tell Alice it was absolutely delicious." He picked up his coffee mug and started for the door. "Alright men, let's go find this kid."

A small gathering of men had already formed in the Henderson's driveway when the three policemen pulled in, one after the other. The full darkness of night had now settled like a thick veil over the countryside. Some of the volunteers had the headlights of their cars turned on to offer light. All eyes turned to the sheriff as he exited his car and made his way into the center of the men. Rick and Scotty stood off to the side,

joining the others, Chet did a quick count in his head as he looked the group over and came up with twelve volunteers.

Alvin Skaggs, arms folded, leaning on the front fender of his Oldsmobile must have read Chet's mind. "We all just got here, Sheriff, there'll be more shortly, I expect."

"Let's hope so," Chet replied. "We've got a lot of ground to cover."

Porter Thomas had just finished lighting a cigarette and threw the smoking match into the dirt. "So, what's going on here, Sarge?" Porter was a former Marine and was in the habit of referring to Chet by his former military rank.

"It's sheriff now, mister."

There was a light rumble of laughter from the men. Chet went into a brief explanation of Levi's missing status and gave the group his description. He noted there were a few fathers in the group with sons who were Levi's age and didn't miss the empathy in their eyes as they hung on his words.

After giving the group the basic rundown of the situation he stepped aside and gave the time over to Rick. By this time, a few more volunteers had trickled in. Rick spread a county map out on the hood of a nearby car while the search party gathered around.

"Alright, listen up, men." Rick stabbed the map with his forefinger. "We are at the Henderson place, here." He slid his finger across the map. "To our west is the Miller farm, and over here, on the other side, is the Baxter place. All three farms border these woods, right here." He looked up from the map into the faces of the group to be sure everyone was with him. "Just between the three farms we have a lot of ground to cover. There's ditches, fields, and orchards, not to mention barns, sheds, and silos. There's a lot of potential trouble a little boy can get into around here, so don't take anything for granted."

"What about the woods?" Porter inquired, smoke from his cigarette streaming out of his nostrils.

"For now, we concentrate on the three farms. Once we've done a thorough search of those we'll deal with the woods." Rick began folding the map. "We'll split up into three groups, one for each farm." He looked at Chet. "Anything else, Sheriff?"

The young sheriff stepped back into the center of the gathered men. "I want everyone to pick a partner and stay together. No wandering off on your own. The last thing I want to do tonight, is organize another search party to rescue the search party."

Some of the men laughed. Chet allowed himself a moment to study their faces. How many times had he been here, standing in front of men and giving orders? At least tonight he wouldn't be ordering anyone to advance into machine gun fire.

"We'll meet back here in two hours," he continued. "That should give us enough time. Deputy Forks has a few extra flashlights if anyone needs one. If you find Levi, get back here as fast as you can and start honking a car horn. Any questions?" There were none. He clapped his hands together. "Alright then, let's find this kid."

There was an immediate bustle as Rick took over and began organizing the men into groups.

Chet put an arm around Scotty and pulled him away from the group. "Scotty, I want you to be in charge of the group that searches the Henderson farm, as well as manning the base here. Sound good?"

"You can count on me, Coop!" the eager rookie replied, his voice a little too high.

"I know I can," Chet said, walking to his car. "I'll be back in a little while."

"Where ya going?"

"Just gonna go have a little visit with the Baxters and Millers. Let 'em know what's going on here and see if they have any info for us." He opened his car door. "See you in a bit."

Scotty nodded, then turned to help Rick with organizing the search, as Chet pulled his car out of the Henderson's driveway.

Daniel was awakened from a deep sleep by the sound of someone knocking firmly on the front door of the house. He recognized the heavy fall of his father's footsteps echoing down the hallway that lead from the kitchen to the front door. He grabbed his watch: almost ten. Who would be knocking on their door at this hour?

He heard the door creak on its hinges as it was opened. "Mr. Miller?" inquired a young but commanding voice. "I'm Sheriff Cooper…"

Not possible! A hard ball of ice formed deep in his gut as beads of sweat seemed to instantly pop out on his forehead. He tried with all the force of his will to stay calm, to push the panic back down. He heard is father invite Sheriff Cooper in. He struggled to listen over the rapid pounding of his heart.

"I just wanted to inform you that there is a current search underway for Rupert and Mary Henderson's grandson, Levi. He's missing and we think he might be somewhere in the area. I hope you don't mind if we look around your place."

Daniel felt a small wave of relief pass through him. They were searching! Levi was just missing, no one had found a body. Of course! He'd been a fool to panic. He should have anticipated that there would be a search, perhaps questions. He had been too clever, the body would not be found. *She* would protect him from being discovered. He had been called to fulfill a destiny.

His heart began to slow a bit as he listened to the sheriff explain the details of the missing boy. His confidence grew as the sheriff asked questions. He smiled in the dark. The man had nothing to go on. To him it was as if Levi had just vanished into thin air.

Daniel rose from his bed and walked toward his bedroom door. The voices told him to stop, but he shut them out. He was much smarter than that pathetic, small town cop downstairs. He had nothing to be afraid of. He moved quiet and slow, like a cat on the prowl.

The idiots didn't even see him standing at the top of the stairs until he spoke. "Wha-what's going on?" he asked, pretending to be groggy, rubbing at one of his eyes.

His parents and the young sheriff all looked up, slightly startled. Sheriff Cooper took a step toward the staircase. "This must be young Daniel."

Daniel could feel them inside, frantic and scolding—*Danger! Danger!*—but he found he was able to suppress them. He had never been able to before. It was his newly found strength, it had to be! A small jolt of excitement shot through him.

"This is our son, Daniel," Mother answered.

"Sorry to have woken you up, Daniel," said the sheriff.

"That's okay," Daniel replied. "What's this all about?"

"Daniel, do you know Levi Henderson, from next door?" the sheriff asked.

He pretended to think for a few seconds. "Yeah, the little boy, the Henderson's grandson. I don't really know him though, I just know who he is."

"Well, he never came home from school today, so we've set up a search party for him. You wouldn't know where he might be, would you?"

Wouldn't you like to know, Sheriff? Daniel shrugged his shoulders. "Sorry, I'm afraid I can't help you with that one. Like I said, I didn't really know him much."

Instead of responding, the sheriff was just staring at him. It was a penetrating look, his brow furrowed over piercing, blue eyes.

What? What is it you think you know? Nothing! That's what. Daniel returned the man's stare without so much as a blink.

"No, I suppose not. You're a bit older than Levi," the sheriff finally uttered slowly, as if his mind had been somewhere else entirely, and had just come back around to the conversation.

Father spoke up. "Sheriff, me and my boy know every inch of this place. Give us a minute to get ready and we can help you search."

"That'd be really helpful, Mr. Henderson," Sheriff Cooper replied. "There should be a group of men showing up here in the next few minutes to help."

Father turned his attention to Daniel. "Son, go get dressed."

"Do you think that's a good idea, Will?" Mother asked. "We should probably be letting him sleep." She turned to the sheriff. "Daniel's been having a hard time sleeping at night. Dr. Steinmetz said he should get as much sleep as possible."

"If he's not feeling well I'm sure we can get by without him, ma'am," Sheriff Cooper said.

"No, I'm fine," Daniel interjected. "That poor kid could be out there, lost and scared. I wanna help find him." He sounded so concerned he just about had himself convinced.

Father smiled a rare, proud smile, and motioned with a nod of his head for Daniel to go get ready. It was ironic how just a few days ago, that approving smile from his dad would have put him on cloud nine. Tonight, it made him sick with disgust. Why should he care if his old man was proud of him? Who was Will Miller that Daniel should crave *his* approval?

"Yes sir," he said, and spun around to disappear down the hall and into his bedroom.

Chet chewed on his bottom lip as he navigated his car down the dirt lane that led to the Baxter home, the beams of his head lights casting odd shadows across the ruts and bumps, turning the driveway into an alien landscape. Something was nagging him about his visit with the Miller family, especially the boy. He had made it a point to try to get to know the teenagers in his town, but he didn't know Daniel. The kid had somehow flown under his radar. He couldn't place his finger exactly on it, but when he had looked into the boy's eyes, he had felt his demon memories stir slightly in their graves. He felt he had looked into eyes like those before, but the memory was eluding him for now.

There had been a strange feeling in the home. It was an eerie sensation he hadn't experienced before, and he wasn't exactly sure how to feel about it. It was like being watched from somewhere secret, accompanied by a cold, unwelcome feeling, as if the watcher in his secret hiding place wanted him gone. He realized the hair on his arms was standing up, as he pulled his car to a stop in front of the Baxter home.

He felt a little more at home at the Baxter residence, if still not a little unwelcome. He had been here more times than he wished to recall, thanks to their two boys, Kevin and Rusty, or more commonly known by his department as the Baxter boys. Even though it was late, and most kids were in bed by this time, it was no surprise to see both boys dressed and up—probably up to something they shouldn't—when their dad, Marley, invited Chet in.

Both boys greeted him with mischievous smiles that confirmed his suspicion they were up to no good of some sort or another. Mrs. Baxter set down her sewing and scowled at her sons. "Now what have you two gone and done?" she fired off at them.

Rusty, the older brother at fourteen, feigned a well-practiced look of shock and indignation, "We ain't done nuthin, Ma." He crossed his heart. "Honest!"

"Yeah, honest, Ma," Kevin chimed in, perfectly mimicking his older brother.

Marley took charge. "What have they done, Sheriff? They'll get a taste of the leather this time." His hands dropped to his belt buckle.

Chet seriously doubted the Baxter boys had ever had a *taste of the leather*. "It's okay folks, I'm not here about the boys."

Everyone looked surprised, including Kevin and Rusty, which Chet made a mental note of. But there were more serious things to worry about right now than cow tipping, or manure piled on the high school principal's front door step. Chet briefly explained the situation to the Baxters. The cocky smirks on the boys' faces quickly changed to sincere expressions of concern.

"Do you boys know Levi?" Chet asked, "Do you spend any time with him at all?"

"Uh, not really, Sheriff," answered Rusty. "We see him around once in a while in the woods and stuff, but don't really spend time with him. He's not really, um our type."

In other words, he's a good kid. "You say you see him in the woods, does he spend a lot of time there?"

"Yeah, I guess," said Kevin. "He plays army, builds forts and stuff. Pretty much just by himself."

"Kevin, you go to school with him, right?" Chet asked the younger brother.

"Sure. He's a grade down though."

"You both ride the bus?"

Kevin nodded his shaved head.

"Do you remember if Levi got on the bus this morning?"

"He didn't get on the bus. I remember cause we sat there for a minute."

"I figured as much." As an afterthought, Chet looked Rusty in the eye. "Rusty, how well do you know Daniel Miller across the way?"

Rusty shrugged. "He's quiet. Really smart, but weird. Stays totally to himself. Gets his ass kicked once in a while at school."

"Rusty!" snapped Mrs. Baxter. "Watch your mouth, for the love of Pete!"

Rusty allowed a glimmer of a grin to creep across his face.

Marley spoke up. "You want us to help out, Sheriff? We could help search our place, but I can't for the life of me think of where that boy could be."

"That would be a lot of help," Chet replied, as he put his hands on the backs of the boys' necks. "Plus, it will keep these two busy for a while."

It was a little after eleven o'clock when Chet drove back into the Henderson's driveway. As he neared the cluster of parked cars and pickups, flashlight beams darted in different directions off in the distance. As he pulled up behind Scotty's car and killed his engine he noticed some people gathered around the dropped tailgate of a Dodge pickup.

There was a gas lantern hissing on the tailgate, illuminating the group in its small orb of light, throwing contrasting shadows into the deepening darkness beyond. In its yellow glow, Chet could make out several thermoses and a large picnic style basket also resting on the tailgate. As he approached the gathering, he recognized Scotty and Porter, both leaning on the tailgate of the Dodge, sipping from steaming cups in their hands. The inviting scent of hot coffee filtered through the cooling, humid air.

Two women had their backs to him. They were talking quietly to each other as they made sandwiches out of the contents of the picnic basket. When Chet entered into the sphere of the lantern glow, Porter straightened and with a snarky smirk on his face called out, "A-ten-hut!"

"At ease," Chet played along, waving a dismissive hand in the direction of the former Marine. The women turned to look over their shoulders at him, but his focus was on Scotty for the moment. "What's the situation, deputy?"

Scotty, having served in the Navy, had instinctively straightened his body into a semblance of attention when Porter had called out the military command. "The search is well underway," he reported. "So far no sign of the Henderson boy though."

As if on cue, a distant voice drifted within earshot, calling out Levi's name.

The rookie continued. "I think we're about half way done searching the three farms at this point. I don't know what you want to do after that."

"We might have to call it a night after we've searched the farms, then come back and have a look in the woods at first light," Chet said. "After talking with the Baxter Boys, I have a feeling he might have gone off into the woods. According to them he spends a lot of time playing there."

"You want me and Scotty here to go check out the woods?" Porter asked, placing his cup on the tailgate. He produced a cigarette from a pack of Lucky Strikes he kept in his shirt pocket.

"No, not yet. It's not safe in the dark for starters, plus you've got to be careful when you start searching in woods and large areas. You have to plan it carefully so that nothing gets missed."

Porter nodded in understanding as he struck a match with his thumbnail and lit his cigarette. He extended the pack to Chet.

He shook his head. "No thanks, I gave 'em up."

Porter shrugged and offered one to Scotty, who accepted.

During the war just about everyone, including Chet, had taken up smoking cigarettes. Smoking was great for calming jittery nerves before and after combat, but most of the time it had just been something to do. Since being home, he had fallen out of the habit. Lighting up always seemed to stir too many memories. Even now, as the smell of the cig smoke drifted his way, the buried demons stirred and his suppressed memories tried to claw their way to the surface.

"A cup of coffee, Sheriff?" The voice was Mable Johnson's. She was standing at his side holding a steaming cup of the dark, swirling brew. "Hope you don't mind it black."

Mable was in her mid sixties, short and fairly plump. Her auburn hair, streaked with gray, was done up in a tight bun on top of her round head. She had the look of a woman who had swept a thousand floors, scrubbed a million pots, and probably rocked a billion babies to sleep.

"Black is just fine." He accepted the cup and began blowing ripples across the surface. "So, is your husband out there searching?"

Mable nodded. "Yes, I think Henry went on over to the Miller place with Clarence. When I heard what was going on I rounded up some help, and figured some coffee and sandwiches might be of some use to you tonight."

At the mention of sandwiches and help, Chet directed his attention to the other woman standing at the tailgate.

"Can I offer you a sandwich, Sheriff Cooper?"

Chet's heart skipped a beat as he recognized the voice and southern accent of Kate Farnsworth.

She turned to face him, her green eyes sparkling in the lantern light like jewels. She was wearing jeans and a light, flannel jacket. The high heels from that afternoon had been replaced with canvas tennis shoes, and her black, curly locks were tucked away under a baseball cap with a Cardinals logo embroidered on the front. A knowing smile touched the corners of her mouth.

"Sheriff," Mable said, "this is Kate Farnsworth, the new secretary down at the elementary school. She's new in town and staying at The Cozy Corner with Henry and I."

"Actually, the sheriff and I have met," Kate said, taking a step toward Chet and Mable.

"Hello Kate," was all he could think to say.

Kate rescued them both from an awkward silence. "Did I hear you say you suspect Levi might actually be missing in those woods?"

Mable shook her head. "How awful for that poor boy, lost and all alone in those woods at night."

Chet nodded and took a sip of his coffee. "Levi spends a lot of time playing in the woods by himself, It'd be the next logical place to search."

Kate's eyes were brimming with worry, as she stepped closer to Chet. "You really don't plan on waiting till morning to look, do you? What if he's hurt?"

"Those are really big woods ma'am," came Scotty's voice from behind. "Ain't no place for a bunch of us to go stumbling around in the dark. Wouldn't come to any good." Scotty stepped into the light, his shoulders pulled back, thumbs tucked into his duty belt, the cigarette he'd bummed off Porter dangling loosely from his mouth.

"It's also no place for a little boy to spend the night," Kate retorted, her voice growing louder with each word. "If you were the Hendersons and that was your boy, possibly lost in those woods, you wouldn't want people waiting until morning to look!" Her eyes blazed as she glanced at Chet, and then back to Scotty.

Scotty shrugged his shoulders and looked down at his feet, unable to bear up under the woman's glare. "Well...uh," he stammered, digging up dirt with the toe of his boot.

Chet let out a sigh and began to slightly nod his head. "She's right. We need to get looking in those woods...the sooner the better."

"We still have a while for everyone to finish searching the farms," Scotty argued. "By the time everyone gets back here and we get them organized—"

"What about the four of us?" Kate interrupted, motioning at the group with her hand. "It's not much, but at least it would be a start."

Chet rubbed at the stubble on his jaw, mulling it over in his mind.

By this time, Porter had shouldered his way to Chet's side. "You think letting a woman tag along on a night search in the woods is a very good idea, Sarge? There's no tell'n what could happen."

Kate took no time closing the distance between herself and Porter. "I'll have you know that I am perfectly capable of handling myself in the woods, or mountains. Probably better than you, for that matter!" The brim of her baseball cap was inches from Porter's nose and her finger was nearly stabbing him on the breast bone with every syllable.

Chet tried to hold back a chuckle watching Porter wither under the verbal assault.

She wasn't finished. "I've been horseback riding, hiking, hunting, and camping in the Smoky Mountains with my family, since I was three years old. I could have a rabbit shot, skinned, and cooking on a spit, before you could decide which of your pant legs goes on first!"

The look on Porter's face was priceless, as he shot a pleading look at Chet to rescue him. Mable was grinning from ear to ear, and shooting looks at Chet as if giving her approval to pursue the girl.

"Alright, alright," Chet stepped between the two. "I think Miss Farnsworth has made her point pretty clear." He turned to Kate. "Porter didn't mean any harm."

Kate took a step backwards and folded her arms. She smiled a bit sheepishly, "Okay." She leaned sideways so she could see around Chet to address Porter. "I'm sorry I lost it on you." Her eyes still held a slight smolder in them.

Porter took a big draw on his cigarette and tossed the butt to the ground. "That's okay," he said, "I probably had it com'n."

The foursome armed themselves with flashlights and piled into Chet's car. Scotty opened the passenger door for Kate, and she slid in next to Chet. Maybe Scotty had learned some manners somewhere in his upbringing, but Chet didn't miss the way his deputy was looking at the attractive newcomer. Could he blame the kid? Even in an old pair of jeans and a beat up baseball cap, she looked great.

Steering with one hand and sipping at his coffee with the other, he drove the car down a dirt access road that carved its way between fields and pastures, leading to the woods bordering the back of the Henderson property. Before long, the misshapen trunks and branches of the first trees were being lit up by his headlights. Just short of the trees the road emptied into a circular patch of dirt used as a turn about. He parked the car, killed the engine and lights, and the group climbed out.

Upon stepping out of the vehicle, he immediately felt swallowed up by the darkness and the profound silence. For a moment, nobody made a sound as they waited for their senses to adjust to their new surroundings. The moon was yet to peek above the horizon, but countless stars glimmered overhead, flickering in and out in the black heavens.

Scotty clicked on his flashlight and shined it directly into the forest. The beam of light struck a tree, illuminating the rough bark and making the leaves appear flat and colorless. The others followed suit, turning on their flashlights and shining the beams in different directions.

Chet broke the silence, "Alright, we'll form a line by spacing about twenty yards apart. I'll be on the left of the line and Deputy Forks will be on the right. Porter and Kate, you two fill in the gap. Move slow and methodical. Sweep the ground in front of you with your light using slow, broad strokes. Just follow my lead. If you see something, call out."

They quickly formed into a line and spaced themselves out until Chet was satisfied. Under his direction the line began walking into the forest, their flashlights sweeping back and forth in front of them. The heavy canopy of leaves and branches instantly blotted out the faint starlight, and they were enveloped in an oppressive darkness.

Kate put a cupped hand to the side of her mouth and called out Levi's name. The rest of the group began to call out for Levi in intervals. The line moved in increments, deeper into the woods, the sounds of twigs snapping under foot and brush scraping on pant legs echoed off the trees around them.

he estimated they had gone into the forest about a hundred yards or so, when he called the group to a halt.

"I think that's far enough for now. We'll double back to the tree line, shift to the left, and start again."

Everyone did an about face and began walking back the way they had come, stepping over fallen logs and through thorny bushes.

When they emerged from the trees Chet did a quick check to be sure everyone was okay to go for another sweep. He shifted his line down to the left of their previous position, making sure that the far right end of his line overlapped the last sweep. Once again, the line of searchers moved forward into the dark forest, calling out Levi's name as they scanned the forest floor with their lights.

About fifty yards in, during the second sweep, the beam from Chet's flashlight glided across a shape that stopped him dead in his tracks. The demon memories that lay slumbering under the surface of his consciousness, suddenly awoke in profound awareness as his entire body instinctively tensed. For a moment, he was no longer in a forest that bordered the town of Clear Creek. He was back in the festering jungles of the Pacific. His heart began to pound as he sensed the sights of a Japanese machine gun lining up on his chest.

He shook off the dread, forcing himself to come to grips with reality, driving his demons back into their graves with all the will power he could muster. Keeping his flashlight trained on the object ahead, he put two fingers to his mouth and whistled for the small column to stop.

"Chet?" Kate was slowly making her way toward him. "What is it?"

"I'm not sure," he answered, the words spilling out slowly, as he continued to stare into the near distance. "It's something that shouldn't be here, I can tell you that."

Kate trained her light next to Chet's. "I don't get it, it just looks like a pile of sticks and branches to me."

"Not to me."

She had made it to his side with Porter and Scotty not far behind, crashing noisily through the underbrush. The young woman looked up at Chet, her face frozen in a silent question.

"Find something?" Porter inquired as he approached.

Kate nodded at the apparent pile of sticks and brush. Porter and Scotty pointed their flashlights in the same direction.

"I don't see nuthin," Porter said.

Chet began walking forward. "That's the point."

"Huh?"

Chet kept his light forward as he walked, the others following close behind. "If this is what I think it is, then you shouldn't even know it's there until it kills you." He looked over his shoulder at Kate. "It's anything but a pile of sticks and branches."

Scotty piped up from the back, "Okay Coop...I mean, Sheriff. We all give up. What are you talking about here?"

Chet came to a halt in front of the mound. "It's a machine gun nest."

"A machine gun nest?" Kate asked, screwing her face into a look of confusion.

"Yep. And not just a machine gun nest, but a very well built and well placed one at that," Chet said.

Scotty was scratching his head. "Yeah, okay. But we know that Levi was big into playing army and building forts in the woods. This is probably just one of his forts."

Chet walked around the nest, examining it with his flashlight. "You'd be pretty hard pressed to convince me that a ten year old kid made this."

"I don't know," Kate said. "He probably had enough time on his hands to build something like this. Jimmy Parsons said that Levi had a secret army fort in the woods. What's all to it? You dig a hole, pile some brush and sticks around it."

Chet smiled and shook his head. "I'm not talking about how much work went into the construction, I'm talking about the know-how." He walked around behind the nest and found the access point, exactly where it should have been. Ducking his head low, he stepped down into the structure and held out his hand. "Come here, I'll show you what I mean."

Kate stepped up to the entrance and took his hand for balance.

"Watch your head," he cautioned.

She ducked to join him in the nest and relaxed her grip. He reluctantly let her hand fall away from his.

They were standing in a hole about five feet square and waist deep, that had been dug into the forest floor. The musty odor of damp, exposed earth filled their nostrils. Heavy logs had been laid parallel to the edges of the hole and piled up with dirt to hold them in place. The roof of the nest, which was too low for either of them to stand their full height, had been made by laying smaller sticks and branches across the tops of the heavy foundation logs, and then adding dirt and forest debris to the top to camouflage the structure. At the front of the nest there was a narrow, rectangular opening between the foundation log and the roof, about one foot tall.

"The gun port," Chet said, nodding at the slit.

Kate nodded and hunched her shoulders to ward off the colder air that seemed to be lingering in the hole. The smell of cigarette smoke drifted in. Porter was having another smoke. Scotty had come around the back of the nest and was squatting in the entrance hole, shining his light around, examining the inside. Chet gently placed his hand on Kate's back and guided her to the gun port. She stepped close and he secretly indulged in a quick whiff of her perfume.

He made a sweeping gesture to the outside with his hand. "Considering the terrain here," he explained, "this would be an optimal placement for a machine gun nest."

"What do you mean?" she asked, looking out of the gun port as if she could see beyond the darkness of the forest.

"For starters this was built on a little knoll, so right now we have the high ground. With a commanding view of the area, it would be impossible for anyone to approach us without us seeing them long before they saw us. Hypothetically, if this was war and this nest was manned, we'd be dead right now."

Kate turned to look at him, her almond eyes wide.

Chet smiled. "Hypothetically," he repeated.

A quick smile flashed across her ruby lips. "Of course." She laughed nervously. "I have a feeling there's more?"

"Well, whoever built this was keenly aware of the terrain of this whole area. This part of the forest comes to what is known as a bottle neck. There's a ravine to the left of this and to the right is a really marshy area. The ravine and the marsh work together to funnel anyone coming this direction, right into the field of fire of this gun placement." he shook his head and ran his hand along the bottom of the gun port. "This is the work of someone who knows what they're doing, not a ten year old boy—especially all by himself."

Scotty, who had been listening while squatting in the entrance asked, "What do you make of it then, Sheriff?"

"I'm not sure." Chet paused and shook his head. "This all gives me an uneasy feeling. I don't like it one bit."

There was an odd, unsettling feeling in the hole just then. Kate shivered.

"Come on," Chet said, grabbing her by the upper arm and turning her around. "Let's get out of here."

Scotty offered Kate his hand and helped her up out of the nest, Chet following right behind. The air felt cleaner and lighter once out of the hole, but somewhere in the dark recesses of his mind he could hear the agonizing screams and smell the unforgettable stench of Japanese soldiers being burned alive. He gave up trying to force the memories away. They were too close—swarming too near the surface now. His remedy for times like this was usually a cold beer or two, followed by a warm bed.

"Chet?" Kate's voice was soothing, forcing the demons away, back to their burial grounds.

He was sweating slightly, even in the cool dampness of the night. He looked around at the three faces turned to him, awaiting his next move.

"A couple of more sweeps, and we call it a night. We can resume first thing in the morning."

Nobody argued.

The moon was a shimmering, silver disk just above the eastern horizon when the foursome returned to base. A sizable crowd of volunteers were milling about Mable's Dodge, the gas lantern still burning on the tailgate. Most stood in small groups of three or four talking quietly—some smoking, others sipping coffee.

As Chet approached the glowing halo of lantern light he noticed Rick near the front bumper of the Dodge talking with Rupert and Mary Henderson. He bypassed the tailgate and the light of the lantern, making a straight line for the Hendersons.

Mary was a wreck. Her eyes and nose were rubbed raw from the constant wiping of a handkerchief as she continually broke into sobs. Rupert, a rock of the community, stood frozen with his arm around his shaking wife's shoulders. The lines in his face that had always reflected his wisdom and experience, now highlighted his worry and fear.

They looked up at him as Chet approached, their eyes mirroring their desperate hope—a hope that he knew he was about to shatter. For a second he felt Private Kovacs glaring at him. *See where selling false hope eventually leads you?*

"Oh, Sheriff!" Mary exclaimed, as she broke away from Rupert's hold and ran the last few strides, grasping Chet's hand in both of hers.

"Did you find him? Did you find our Levi?"

He Looked down into her bleary eyes but couldn't bring himself to say it. He didn't need to. His own eyes betrayed him. Mary knew. Her knees buckled. He caught her in his arms and slowly sank with her to the ground.

Sitting in the dirt she buried her face into his chest and a low, gut-wrenching moan escaped from a place deep within her. Chet was all too familiar with that dark place, and the kind of grief it gave birth to.

Professionalism be damned, he enveloped her quivering shoulders in his arms, whispering softly, "It'll be okay. It'll be okay. We'll find him, I promise."

CHAPTER 6

The walls of Kate's office closed in on her like a prison cell as she sat at her typing desk. She was transcribing a letter to the school board from Principal Grayson's hand scribbled notes. A lazy morning breeze sighed through her open window, bearing the slight aroma of fresh cut hay from some nearby field. She inhaled deeply and slipped out of her pinching heels. She allowed the sweet, pastoral fragrance to carry her back home to her family's stables, where her dad kept his prize Tennessee Walkers.

When she was a little girl it had been her job to get up early and water the horses before school. Her older brothers would have already seen to the mucking of the stalls and pitching in of fresh hay. She would always take her time with her chore, speaking softly to each horse while gently stroking their heavily muscled necks.

Often, a horse would nuzzle its soft warm nose into her armpit or the side of her neck so that she could scratch behind its velvety ears. Their hot, gusty breath on her neck would give her goosebumps and make her giggle.

Sometimes, when she arrived for her chores, her father would be working with a horse in the adjacent riding arena. At her approach he would often stop whatever he was doing and join her as she made her rounds. These were special times when he would impart to her his valuable horse knowledge—most people usually paid good money for that know-how.

As much as she liked hearing about the proper care of the horses, or tips on riding them, or how to selectively breed them in order to perpetuate their glossy, coal-black coats, what she really valued were the talks. Just father and daughter talking about whatever came to mind, each able to transcend their differences and come to a common plain of understanding with the other.

Not that he wasn't a good family man, but as senior partner in his law practice, Daddy was a busy man. What little time his law practice didn't eat up he devoted to breeding, trading, and of course, riding his horses. He certainly provided well for his family and included them as much as possible in his equine passion.

Many weekends were spent riding the nearby trails and the occasional multi-day pack trip into the Smoky Mountains. Daddy would ride out in front, larger than life, as he pointed out the different species of trees and animals, along with the names of all the peaks and valleys.

She missed home. She missed her parents, her brothers, and the horses. She missed everything. Maybe, after a little time, people back home would forget. Forget and move on with their lives. And someday, she could go back and everything would be as it was before. Maybe.

The absence of the rhythmic *tap tap tap* of her typewriter pulled her back from the stables and into the present. She sighed. She was having one of those mornings. She couldn't keep her mind on task. The open attendance log on her desk wasn't helping matters. Every Friday morning it was part of her job to walk around to all the classrooms, and collect the attendance rolls for the week. A little over an hour ago she had done just that. Bringing the rolls to her office, she copied down the attendance for the entire school to a master log, leaving it lying open on her desk.

From her typing table she could still make out Levi Henderson's name on the log. Eleven empty little squares next to his name glared like a desert island, encompassed by a sea of check marks. Missing for two whole weeks now, not a trace or a clue as to what had happened to him.

For the most part, the town had given up on Levi...except for Sheriff Cooper. She had to admit, the man was about as tenacious as a bloodhound on a coon's scent. He and his deputies still spent time every day poking around the three farms and the woods. Chet refused to officially call an end to the search.

A large scale search of the woods had turned up nothing. Kate had volunteered and walked the sweeping search patterns with dozens of other searchers for three days. The young lawman had organized the search well, including men on horseback, trackers with bloodhounds, and even a small airplane flying in low patterns just above the tree tops. It was all to no avail; it was as if Levi had vanished into thin air. Many guessed that he had run away and would be back eventually. She knew Chet didn't buy into that theory.

After the three days it was obvious that the sheriff was exhausted. She was positive he hadn't slept the entire time, or eaten anything for that matter. She had tried to use their prearranged dinner date as an excuse to pull him away from the search, if just to force some food into him, get him to take a couple of hours rest. It was useless. The man was driven to find Levi. To watch him was like watching one possessed. Possessed by what, she wasn't sure. Something was haunting Sheriff Cooper, but exactly what, she did not know.

Principal Grayson caught her staring vacantly at the attendance log and chewing on a pencil as his girth suddenly appeared in her open doorway. She jumped and let out a startled squeak. Embarrassed, she slapped the pencil onto her desktop calendar and looked up smiling.

"How's the letter coming, Kate?" he asked, a knowing smile splitting his round face. "I hope you're making heads and tails from my hopeless chicken scratchings."

Jonah Grayson was in his early sixties, rotund but large of frame so that he carried his corpulence very well. His thinning brown hair was neatly trimmed and combed back over his large ears, thick, gray bands streaking through it. A pair of black-framed glasses perched on his hawkish nose magnified a set of dark-brown eyes that swirled with wisdom, and if one looked hard enough, a great deal of tenderness and empathy.

Today, Mr. Grayson was dressed in his usual: a white button-up shirt, ironed and tucked neatly into thick khaki dress pants. A bright red neck tie flowed from a Double Windsor knot that curved over his belly. The tip of the tie dangled from the outcrop of his stomach, teetering back and forth in open space.

"I've seen much worse, believe me," Kate said. "Besides, chicken scratches are my specialty. You should see my father's handwriting."

Mr. Grayson snickered. "How are you getting along, Kate? Are you missing home yet?"

Kate liked the man. He reminded her of a caring, tender grandfather.

"I'm fine, Mr. Grayson, really. I do miss home a little but I'm fine." Her eyes darted down at the attendance log on her desk.

The principal caught the subtle movement. "I see." His face formed a grimace.

"Two weeks now," Kate sighed. "For some reason I just can't seem to take my mind off of it."

"Don't give up hope on him yet, Kate." He eased himself into the wooden, high-backed chair across from her, the chair squawking in protest. "It's possible he was just feeling a little adventurous and hopped on a train. Children do those kinds of things. He's probably out of money by now and on his way back."

She shook her head. "I wish I could believe that."

"Well, the cops have searched this town and its surroundings from top to bottom and haven't turned up anything. It only makes sense that he left. What's so hard to accept about that?"

71

"Because," came a man's voice, low and smooth, from just beyond the door. "It just doesn't add up that easy."

The tall, muscled frame of Chet Cooper appeared in the doorway and Kate felt her pulse quicken.

One of Jonah's knees popped loudly as he rose to his feet. "Don't shoot!" He thrust his hands into the air. "That was just my age getting the best of me."

"It's good to see you, Mr. Grayson." Chet greeted the principal with a smile and a handshake.

"Well," said Jonah, "it's a nice day to be out enforcing the law. How are things around town?"

Chet and Jonah began making small talk about some of the various goings on in town. While the men were distracted, Kate quickly smoothed her blouse and tapped under the desk with her feet in search of her shoes. She noticed her hazy reflection in the glass that topped her desk and checked her hair. Everything looked in place. She was just slipping into her heels when Chet's voice came into focus.

"Well, Jonah, to be honest, I was hoping I could have a minute with your secretary, if that's okay with you."

Jonah's eyes popped open as a smile spread across his fleshy face. Both men looked down at Kate. She tried her best to appear cool, but warm blood was flushing her cheeks.

"Why certainly!" Jonah beamed. "I believe Miss Farnsworth was just about to take a break anyway. Have a good day, Sheriff." He gave Kate a playful wink and pushed his expanse past the younger man and out the door.

Chet stepped to the center of her office. "Hey there, got a minute?"

Smiling, she motioned for him to have a seat.

He walked forward and took a seat in the high-backed chair. As he lowered himself his pistol got hung up on the arm. He chuckled nervously as he rose and untangled the weapon. "Stupid gun, always banging into everything," he said, looking at her with a slightly flustered look on his face.

She thought he looked cute. "Maybe you should attach a little rear view mirror to your belt," she teased. He was fun to tease, she couldn't help it.

He sat easy, leaning back, feet apart, his arms draped over the arms of the chair. The light brown sleeves of his uniform were rolled up past his elbows revealing tan forearms with thick, corded muscles running their length. He was definitely handsome: tall, broad in the shoulders and chest, olive skin, light-brown, wavy hair accented by blue-green eyes, and a strong jaw that ended in a proud square. He had a natural disposition of confidence—he could swagger while standing still. The best part, to Kate anyway, was he didn't know it. At the present moment, for instance, there was a boyish look of uncertain self-consciousness in his eyes.

"What can I do for you today, Sheriff Cooper?" she asked.

He began working his large hands together in front of his lap. "Well, first of all, I wanted to come here and personally thank you for all the help you've given through this whole Levi thing."

At the mention of Levi she dropped her eyes to the attendance log on her desk and the eleven blank squares. "It was...I mean, it *is* my pleasure to help anyway I can with Levi."

"And, I wanted to apologize."

"Apologize? What on earth for?"

A small dimple appeared on his cheek as a mischievous smile touched his lips. "Kate Farnsworth, I owe you dinner, and I apologize for being negligent in my duties."

A little tingle of excitement passed through her, but she kept her cool. "Why yes, you do owe me dinner, Chet Cooper." She placed her elbows on her desktop, interlaced her fingers, and rested her chin on the the backs. Tilting her head slightly to the side she asked, "So, what do you intend to do about this debt you are in?"

Chet leaned forward, his elbows resting on his knees, a hint of flirtatious mirth swimming in his aqua eyes. "Well, I was hoping that dinner tomorrow night might square up my account."

"It's a good start, but you've racked up a lot of interest. You can take me to dinner and I'll let you know how your balance is doing afterward. How's that sound?"

He laughed a hearty laugh. It was the first real laugh she'd heard from him. "Well, ma'am, you drive a hard bargain, but I don't see any other way out of it."

"My father is a shrewd horse trader and a very slick lawyer. I've let you off easy, mister."

They both shared an earnest laugh, and then just looked into each other's eyes for a brief moment.

He broke the silence. "Pick you up at Mable's around four then?"

"Don't be late."

"Be sure to wear long pants. We'll be outside a bit."

She arched an inquisitive eyebrow. "Just what are you planning, Sheriff Cooper?"

He smiled, there was that dimple again! "You'll just have to find out tomorrow, Miss Farnsworth."

The morning recess bell rang. Moments later the sound of dozens of canvas sneakers filled the hallway, as students clambered for the doors and to the playground outside. As kids filed past the open door, several looked in. There were greetings of, "Hey Sheriff!" and, "Good morning, Miss Farnsworth!"

An older girl looked in. "Alright Sheriff, way to go!" She ran off giggling hysterically with her friends.

Chet and Kate returned each greeting, both blushing like teenagers who'd been caught necking in a broom closet. The hallway eventually cleared and he rose to his feet. She saw him wince as he straightened.

"Are you okay?" she asked, coming instantly to her feet and moving around the desk.

He smiled and held up a hand. "I'm fine, really."

"No, you're not fine, you're hurt. What is it?"

"Well, let's just say the Japanese were kind enough to send me home with a little souvenir. There's probably going to be another thunder bumper tonight...it kinda lets me know in advance. It's nothing to worry about."

"You were wounded in the war? I didn't know. I'm sorry."

"Like I said, It's nothing to worry about." He straightened to his full height and stretched his back. "There, see? All better now."

He smiled, but instead of the joyous twinkle of a moment ago, his eyes now held a pained, faraway look. She felt a burning desire to help him, to ease him of whatever burden the man was bearing that seemed to weigh so heavily on his soul.

ROBBIE PRITCHARD STRODE THE MAIN HALLWAY of Jefferson Junior High, his chin thrust forward, powerful chest puffed out, stocky arms swinging easy at his sides. The biggest, strongest guy in the ninth grade. Not a bad position to be in, if he did say so himself. Having the president of the Clear Creek Bank of Commerce as his dad didn't hurt either. Nice clothes and a sharp car meant plenty of attention from the girls and green-eyed envy from his friends. In a very real sense of the word, he was king.

Coach Erickson had moved him up to the varsity team this year in football, and so far on the practice field he was more than holding his own. As a matter of fact, during yesterday's practice he'd knocked so many heads out there that

Coach had asked him to tone it down. "Save it for the enemy on game day," he'd said. The fact was, to Robbie, anyone in his way was the enemy.

According to his father, he was being brought up to be a leader, a go-getter. *When a real man is on a mission, everybody else better get in line, or get out of the way,* the man had taught him. When he shoved a kid in the hall, or gave them hell for being ugly or stupid, it was nothing personal. It was just the biggest dog ruling the pack, as he saw it. He smiled to himself, imagining a big dog with a spiked collar going around and pissing all over everything. That was him: the big dog of Jefferson Junior High.

He was so caught up in his reverie that he had totally tuned out the nattering voices of his loyal subjects, behind and to the sides of him. *Subjects.* He smiled again. It didn't matter what they were talking about anyway. All that mattered was they were there, fulfilling their duties. One of which was to laugh and embolden him whenever he chose to berate, belittle, or simply kick the crap out of one of the lesser minions scurrying in the halls.

One of his latest targets—or as he liked to think of them, *projects*—was Daniel Miller. For too many school years Robbie had been required to endure class after class, listening to the little smart ass answering the teachers' questions with his giant vocabulary and his annoying history knowledge. He was already irritated with the kid. Then, about a month ago, Daniel humiliated him by correcting him in front of the whole class. The kid should have kept his mouth shut. *So what if he knows so much about stupid history?* Well, it was time to take the kid down a few pegs. Time for the big dog to mark some new territory.

And there he was. Robbie spotted him just ahead in the hallway, walking slowly, head down, shoulders slumped. No books in his hands to slap away this time. Just gonna have to be more direct than usual.

"Hey Miller!" he bellowed.

The chit chat in his group of cronies stopped at the sound of his voice, but Daniel just continued to shuffle down the hall. He had to have heard him.

"I'm talking to you, Miller!" he sounded off, even louder.

Still no reaction from the little freak. Robbie quickened his pace, his temper beginning to spiral out of control. Nobody ignored the king! He came up behind Daniel, doubled and cocked his right fist back, and spun him around with his left.

"You turn around and look at me when I'm talk—"

He was startled, even a bit frightened to see that Miller was sneering, his thin colorless lips curled into a grimacing snarl. As unsettling as that was, what really cut him off was Daniel's eyes. They were flinty, black marbles, like that of a raven. He felt those black eyes boring into his, straight through his brain and into the back of his skull. It was a menacing glare that filled his heart with a darkness he'd never known before. And for the first time in his life, Robbie Pritchard was afraid.

The cronies shared a communal gasp and watched in silent awe. Robbie knew his kingdom was hanging in the balance, and it all hinged on his next move. He lowered his fist so that it hung low at his side. The sneer faded from Daniel's lips as he tilted his head to look at Robbie's left hand still gripping his shoulder. He turned his head back and locked eyes again with Robbie. Then, with fingers that felt like cold iron, the freak slowly reached up and pried Robbie's hand off his shoulder, never breaking eye contact.

Robbie's knees began to shake as a cold sweat broke out on his forehead. He was losing control of this situation and fast. His instincts took over, and he reacted in the only way Robbie Pritchard could; he slammed his balled up fist into Daniel's abdomen. Fully expecting to feel his fist plunge deep into Daniel's guts, he was surprised when his ham-sized fist met a rock hard wall of abdominal muscles that deflected the blow.

The force of the punch caused Daniel to stagger backwards, but he quickly recovered, maintaining contact with his dead, black eyes. The kid should have been on the floor puking up his lunch, but there he stood in silent defiance, practically daring Robbie to hit him again.

Caught off guard and shaken, Robbie was in no condition to take the confrontation any farther. It was time to salvage what he could out of the situation. "You're a damn freak Miller, you know that?"

Daniel just kept staring back with that malignant gaze. Robbie and his gang of followers moved past him, down the hall.

"A damn freak!" Robbie yelled again, as he shoved his way past Daniel, his voice a little higher than it should have been. As he made his way down the hall to his next class his subjects fulfilled their duties: slapping him on the back and praising him for a great punch, reiterating Daniel's status as a freak. But, even as he moved with seeming purpose and confidence down the hall, Robbie didn't dare look back. He could feel those soulless, raven eyes on him. Those eyes, that snarl. He tried to shake them out of his mind as he walked in a daze for his algebra class.

"POOR, LITTLE, FRIGHTENED BOY." Her voice came into his head, soft and sensual. *"He still thinks he's dealing with the old Daniel."* She chuckled softly, the sound of her laugh arousing him. The faint aroma of lilac blossoms lilting in the air. Her beauty was branded in his memory now. He rubbed the spot on his midsection where Robbie's fist had impacted with enough force to send him staggering backwards. He had felt absolutely no pain from the blow. He smiled, remembering the look of shock on Robbie's face when he hadn't collapsed in a heap on the floor.

"You see?" her alluring voice echoed in his brain. *"Your power grows already."*

"I want more," he projected the thought in his own head.

"And more you shall have. Much, much more."

"When?"

"Soon...very soon." Her voice faded into the background of his thoughts.

He watched Robbie turn the corner in the distance to disappear down another hallway, his faithful lackeys clamoring around him. Once again, Daniel stroked the spot on his stomach. The new Daniel pasted a smile on his face and headed for his next class: world history, his favorite.

CHAPTER 7

Chet pulled his Jeep up to the curb in front of The Cozy Corner boarding house and killed the engine. He checked his watch: five minutes to four. Right on time. He glanced at the neatly wrapped bouquet of flowers laying on the passenger seat. He'd argued earlier that afternoon with his little sister, Connie, that flowers would be too presumptuous. Connie insisted that there was absolutely no way you can go wrong by bringing a girl flowers.

Snatching up the bouquet he jumped out of his Jeep and headed for the front porch of the boarding house, butterflies wreaking havoc in his stomach. The Cozy Corner was a large, two-story, red, brick home with three big gables that spanned out opposite of each other in the shape of a T. Black shudders flanked the upstairs bedroom windows—he wondered which window was Kate's. The lawn was neatly trimmed and manicured with little, square hedges lining the walkway, leading to the large wrap-around porch.

He marched with purpose up the steps and knocked on the door. There were two tall windows on either side of the door. Their drapes were drawn, causing the windows to reflect his translucent image back at him. He heard footsteps approaching from inside and made a cursory inspection of himself in the glass. He was dressed casually in a red, button-up shirt tucked into denim pants, the shirtsleeves rolled up, and a well-worn pair of ankle-high, leather shoes on his feet. The ride in the open-air Jeep had tousled his hair a bit, but it always seemed to have that look anyway.

He was leaning close to the window, smoothing his hair when he heard the doorknob turning. He snapped to attention and, for some reason, hid the flowers behind his back. Mable Johnson opened the door wearing a flower print dress with a white apron tied around her ample waist, her red hair neatly done up in her customary bun. Her pale-blue eyes lit up as a broad smile stretched across her face.

"Sheriff!" she exclaimed, grabbing him by the hand and pulling him inside. "Miss Kate is expecting you, she's up in her room getting ready. I'll go tell her you're here." She winked at him before turning and prattling on up the stairs and disappearing around a corner.

Feeling foolish, Chet brought the flowers back out from behind his back and had a look around. He was standing in the main living room; it was filled with sofas, chairs, and a coffee table. Impressionistic, pastoral paintings were tastefully hanging on the walls. Elmer Johnson, Mable's brother-in-law and long-time customer, was seated in a green leather chair in a corner, smoking a pipe while reading the newspaper. They exchanged silent nods.

Seconds later, Mable came huffing back down the stairs. "She said she'll be down in a—" Mable saw the bouquet in Chet's hand. "Oh my goodness! Aren't those just gorgeous?"

"I hope she likes 'em. I'm afraid I'm not too versed on my flowers," Chet said.

"Oh, she'll love them! I'll fetch something to put them in." She disappeared again.

He got the feeling that her typical day was probably spent bouncing from one task to the next with infinite energy. He could hear the sound of cupboards opening and slamming shut in the kitchen, as if five people were in there ransacking the place. He allowed a small chuckle to escape him. He thought about his town, the people who lived in it. The ones like Mable: hard-working, caring, friendly, meeting life head on. Mable and those like her were the glue that held the community together.

He felt the glow of a small fire in his breast. He'd felt it before, many times overseas. It was the love he'd felt for the men under his command, combined with a fierce desire to protect them. The men of his platoon had been replaced by the common citizens of his home town. It was his job, his responsibility, to keep these people safe. There was great evil in the world; he had seen it first hand, fought against it, and knew it to be a real and powerful force.

He had witnessed his fellow man consumed by a darkness that the people of his home town couldn't comprehend. For him, there was a semblance of virginal innocence that rested upon Clear Creek. He had offered his life upon the altar— nearly losing it— to protect his country. And as far as he was concerned, his life was still forfeit for the sake of protecting his community. This little town.

Levi Henderson entered his thoughts. Today was the first day since his disappearance that Chet had failed to drive out to the Henderson place and poke around in the woods, looking for anything that would indicate where the boy had gone.

A small shadow of guilt began to creep into him, but was drowned away by the sound of Kate's perky voice from the top of the stairs, "Well, look at you. On time and bearing flowers even! You don't strike me as a flowers kind of guy."

He smiled. "Well, you know…with all that compound interest I've racked up and everything, I figure I could use all the help I can get."

She laughed, "That's for sure!" She pounced down the stairs with the energy and agility of a kid. She was wearing tan, form-fitting pants that ended mid-calf and a white blouse with short sleeves that revealed a pair of toned, athletic arms. The top two buttons were left undone, revealing a string of pearls resting gently above well-defined clavicles. A pair of black, leather flats on her feet made a hollow, thudding sound as she descended the stairs, one hand gliding on the banister. A red ribbon held her dark hair in a simple ponytail that bounced and swayed with each step.

The butterflies that had been fluttering around in his gut had now migrated north, and he felt his heart jump at the sight of her. She reached the bottom of the stairs, smiling with scarlet lips. "Am I dressed okay for the occasion?" she asked, spinning a quick three-sixty for him.

"You look fantastic," he managed to mutter, through a dry mouth.

"Well, that's nice to know, but I was asking if my clothes were appropriate for whatever secret excursion you have planned for us."

"Oh! Well, yeah. You're just fine." He felt sheepish shaking his head. How did she do that? How did she turn him into a blabbering idiot in one second of conversation? He extended the bouquet to her. "I wasn't sure what you liked…"

She stepped close, accepting the flowers with both hands and nuzzled her nose into the blossoms. "Mmmm, these are beautiful, Sheriff. They'll look nice on my desk in front of the window."

"Sheriff?" he asked, contemptuously. "Miss, do you see a badge, or a uniform right now?"

"Um, no, but I see you brought your Colt .45." She pointed to his right hip at the ever-present weapon.

"You know your sidearms, I'm impressed. All the same, it's Chet tonight, if you don't mind."

She gave him a mock salute. "Aye, aye, sir! I mean, Aye, aye, Chet!"

Mable burst out of the kitchen with a white, porcelain vase cradled in her hands. Her eyes twinkling with delight. "Aren't the two of you just a picture?" she exclaimed. "Now, I think this vase is just the thing for those flowers."

Kate handed the flowers over to Mable who placed them in the vase and carried them to a nearby lamp table, where she began arranging the bouquet.

"Would you like these up in your room, dear?" Mable asked, without looking up.

"Yes please. That would be just fine."

Chet clapped his hands once. "Well," he said, anxious to move things along, "we should probably get going."

"You two kids have a good time, and be careful," Mable said.

"We will," Chet promised, opening the door for Kate. "We'll be back later."

"Bye now." Mable closed the door behind them.

They drove eastward through town, the wind blowing their hair. She was curious and asked about his Jeep. He explained it was a 1945 Willys MB. He'd been so impressed with them during his military service that he just had to get one for himself when the opportunity arose. Besides, it was perfect for today's activity. She begged for more information, but he remained tight-lipped, informing her she'd find out soon enough.

It wasn't long before they were on a quiet road that wound and twisted into the hills, pine trees flanking each side. She said it reminded her of the Smoky Mountains at home, and shared some of her favorite childhood memories of horseback trips with her family.

He turned off the main road onto a rutted dirt track that climbed up at a steep angle. "Hang on!" he warned.

"To What?" she half laughed, half screamed as the Jeep bucked and lurched over a section of road that had washed out during a recent rain storm. They laughed as the same scene repeated itself a few more times.

The road grew narrower as they progressed, the trees encroaching closer and closer. At one point, Chet stopped the Jeep and folded the windshield down on top of the hood, so that they could pass under some low hanging boughs that forced them to duck their heads.

Eventually, they rounded a bend and the road emptied into a little clearing with a small, rustic, log cabin squatting in its center. The structure was a simple rectangle with a steep A-frame roof, lined with hand-split, wooden shingles. A door made of rough-hewn planks dominated the middle of the cabin with two small windows on each side, equidistant from the corners. A wide chimney made of large, rounded, river rocks sprouted from the left of the cabin.

He pulled the Jeep up alongside the chimney and shut the engine off. Instant silence.

"What is this place?" Kate asked, sliding down from her seat, her feet touching lightly on the ground.

Chet jumped out of the Jeep, his boots thudding. "It's the Cooper family hideout. I was just a little boy when we built it. Four generations of Coopers helped: my dad, grandfather, great grandfather, and myself, in the summer of twenty one. Of course, I probably wasn't much help at three years old." He walked to the back of the Jeep and hefted a large, brown paper bag from the back. He carried it around the corner, heading for the door, Kate walking beside him. "We come up here to hunt, fish, and to just get away sometimes."

Kate quick stepped ahead to open the door for him, and followed him in. They walked across polished planks that made up the tongue and groove wood floor, the boards creaking under their feet.

On one end of the cabin, yawned a big fireplace with split logs already laid in its mouth. A heavy mantle, constructed from a large, split log, was held up by two shorter split logs, all which were embedded into the river rock of the chimney. A round, hand-crafted table sat in front of the fireplace with four chairs pushed in around it and an oil lantern sitting in the middle.

The other end of the cabin hosted a couch constructed of pine logs with cushions thrown on it. Two wooden chairs of the same construction faced the couch at slight angles. Above the couch was a small sleeping loft with a little ladder leaning up against it for access. A double bed, draped by an old-fashioned, home-made quilt, prevailed over the majority of the loft's space.

"Oh my gosh, how cute!" Kate exclaimed, looking around.

Chet laughed, placing the paper bag on the table. "Well, I'm not sure if that was quite the look we were going for when we built it, but I'm glad you approve."

"I love it. I could really use some time in a place like this."

He surveyed the walls of the cabin as he spoke slowly, a thousand pleasant memories of good times gone by filling his brain. "Sometimes, I think I could just come up here, and never go back down."

She walked around the small interior getting a closer look, even climbing up into the loft while he emptied the paper bag. When she came back down to join him he had the first, fragile flames of a fire beginning to glow in the fireplace. Resting on one knee he fed the flames with increasingly larger pieces of wood from a cut stack until a good-sized fire was crackling. Orange and yellow tongues lapped up into the dark, gaping cavity of the chimney.

"Well, looks like someone earned their fire starting merit badge as a Boy Scout," Kate said, examining the contents on the table: carrots, potatoes, flour, baking powder, eggs, and a small package wrapped in white butcher's paper.

He rolled his eyes. "There's no fire starting merit badge in the Boy Scouts," he said, opening one of the cupboards mounted to the back wall of the cabin.

She watched as he produced two heavy dutch ovens from the cupboard. "Well, how do scouts learn to make a fire then, professor?"

"Learning to build a fire is part of the camping merit badge, if you must know." He pulled a kitchen knife from a drawer, stabbed it into a potato, and gestured with it at her. "How'd you like to make yourself useful other than debating me over merit badges?"

"Well…" She pretended to think about it. "I guess I could help, but it's going to reflect on your balance sheet."

He shook his head in defeat and pointed to a tin bucket sitting in the corner. "Behind the cabin, there's a little creek about fifty yards or so, back in the trees. How about getting us some water?"

"I can do that."

An hour later Kate was seated at the table, her hands in her lap while Chet spooned steaming beef stew onto a plate in front of her. She closed her eyes and inhaled the aroma. "It smells delicious."

"That's because it is." He used a small iron hook to lift the lid on the second oven. "Perfect." Using a pair of tongs to reach into the oven he produced a hot, fluffy biscuit, and placed it on her plate next to the stew; it was golden-brown. Reaching into the paper bag he pulled out two long-stemmed glasses, wrapped protectively in red linen napkins, and a bottle of red wine.

He poured the wine, served up a plate of stew and a biscuit for himself, and took a seat in the chair across from her.

She took a bite of stew, chewed for a moment, and swallowed. "Wow, apparently someone earned his stew making merit badge as well."

"That'd be Cooking, and yes, I did earn that merit badge too."

They ate in silence for a while, occasionally looking up from their plates and meeting eyes. It wasn't an awkward silence though, as it might have been with other girls. It was a comfortable silence and he realized he felt totally at ease with her, even though he barely knew her.

She took a small sip of wine and placed it next to her plate. "In all seriousness, Chet, that was really good."

He swallowed a mouthful of biscuit. "This is my specialty, actually. I'm afraid this is as good as it gets. Do you want more? As usual, I made enough to feed a battalion."

Kate shook her head. "It's delicious, but I'm stuffed. Why did you make so much anyway?"

"I just followed the recipe, it always makes this much."

She laughed. "Don't you know that you can reduce the recipe to make less?" The laughter continued.

He smiled, feeling sheepish. "I didn't dare mess it all up so I opted to go with the directions. Besides, I can always take the leftovers to work. Rick will make sure none of it goes to waste."

She took another sip of wine around smiling lips. "So what's your story, Chet? Mom and dad? Brothers, sisters?"

"There's not much to tell really. Born and raised here, my little sister, Connie, and me. We lost Dad to cancer when we were both still in high school. Mom died of a heart attack while I was away."

"I'm so sorry." She shook her head. "Now I feel stupid for asking."

"That's okay, we're alright now. Connie got married a few years ago to a foreman from the steel factory. They've got two little girls and couldn't be happier."

"I'd love to meet her, she sounds nice." Kate said, dabbing at her mouth with her napkin and scooting her chair away from the table.

"That can be arranged." He stood up and grabbed his wine glass. "Care to join me for dessert?"

She slowly rose from her chair, a puzzled look on her face. "Dessert? I don't recall you preparing anything for dessert."

Chet looked down at his watch. "Actually, it should be just about ready. Come on outside with me...and don't forget your glass."

She followed him outside, where he led her around the side of the cabin. They walked to the edge of the clearing, where a small trail disappeared into the pines. The trail was wide enough for them to walk side by side. With her hand buried in the crook of his arm they followed the trail as it meandered upward through thick pines. Off to their left they could hear the stream, where Kate had retrieved their cooking water, as it gurgled and splashed over rocks and logs on its course to the valley below.

After a few minutes they finally reached the top of a small hill, barren of trees and littered with scrub grass and wild flowers. At the very crown of the hill was a bench made of a big split log.

"Close your eyes," he said.

With her eyes closed he led her by the hand to the log bench and helped her sit down. He took a seat next to her.

"Dessert is served, mademoiselle," he said, trying to impersonate a French waiter, but failing miserably.

She giggled.

"Open your eyes."

"Oui Monsieur." She opened her eyes, her lashes fluttering like the wings of a butterfly. She gasped, a hand flying up to her open mouth. "Oh wow!" she exclaimed. "That is gorgeous!"

From their vantage point they could see the entire valley below them. The sun was low on the horizon, mostly concealed inside a low cloud bank. The clouds were erupting with every color of the spectrum: rich yellows, light pinks, and deep, saturating purples. Giant spears of light burst through parts of the cloud bank like gigantic spotlights, highlighting fragments of verdant farm land and lush countryside below.

The town of Clear Creek sprawled in the distance, surrounded by fields and forests. The windows in the buildings caught the last rays of the dying sun and glittered like hundreds of tiny fires.

Kate tore her eyes away from the surreal scene to look at Chet. She smiled a wide smile, her white teeth contrasting with her red lipstick. "It's the best dessert I've ever had." The sun glinted in her emerald eyes.

"I thought you'd like it," he replied, with a smile of his own. Then, as if seized by some unseen force beyond his control, he suddenly snaked his right arm across her back, and draped it around her shoulders. *What are you doing?* a voice inside screamed at him, but it all just felt so right, so he left his arm there. Her face was a blank as he looked into her eyes. Did she approve? Too afraid to find out, he tried to play it cool and turned his gaze back to the sunset. "Yep, that sure is one heck of a sunset."

She turned back toward the picturesque vista as well, drew her feet up under her legs, and leaned her head into his chest. She sipped from her glass. "Like I said, best dessert I've ever had."

His stomach and heart were having a somersault competition as he inhaled the sweet fragrance of her hair. One of her dark curls brushed his hand lightly. He began to twirl it around his index finger as they sat silently together, sipping their wine and watching the sun regress behind a low mountain range. The demons buried in his memory graveyard had never felt so dead, so far away.

The sun was all but gone when Kate stirred, tilting her chin up so she could look into his eyes. "This spot is perfect. This is where we should have our first kiss." She patting his chest with her open palm.

He just about fell off the bench. "What? You mean right now?"

"No silly, not now! I never kiss on the first date. What kind of girl do you think I am anyway?" She pulled away in feigned resentment.

Chet busted out laughing. "You're a firecracker, is what you are!"

"That's right, and I have a short fuse to boot."

He laughed again, shaking his head. "You aren't like any other girl I've ever met, Kate Farnsworth."

"Well, I should certainly hope not!"

They sat in contented silence a while longer, until he felt her shiver slightly.

"Alright," he said, "we better get heading home. That Jeep can be a cold ride at night."

Reluctantly, they rose from the bench. Kate grasped him by the arm and they carefully made their way down the path, back toward the cabin.

Cleanup was easy enough; Chet simply loaded the dirty ovens, plates, and left-overs into a big burlap bag, which he stowed on the backseat of the Jeep. After helping Kate into her seat, he reached behind her and pulled out an army-issue wool blanket. Unfolding it, he placed it across her lap. "There, that should keep you fairly warm for the trip back," he said, tucking the blanket around her feet.

"My hero," she cooed softly.

"Someone's had a little too much wine," he muttered to himself, getting behind the wheel.

Coming down off the mountain was like slowly waking up from a pleasant dream, only to wish one could immediately fall back to sleep and resume the nocturnal bliss. He drove in silence, content for the moment to be with his own thoughts. Something had happened up there, on that hill between them. A connection had been made for sure, but what it all meant, and where it would all lead, remained out of his immediate grasp. One thing was for sure: the couple coming down from the mountain was not the same couple who had gone up a few hours ago.

The half moon was riding high in a hazy night sky when they got into town. Chet was reminded that it was Saturday night by the abundance of older cars, packed full of laughing teens, dragging up and down Main. Most of the kids recognized Chet's Jeep. Hoots and whistles greeted them from rolled down windows as cars passed them.

"Cat's outta the bag now, Sheriff," Kate joked.

A passing car of kids honked.

"Yeah, I suppose it is."

Kate laughed out loud, then cupped her hands to her mouth and yelled at the top of her lungs, "Extra! Extra! Read all about it! Sheriff Cooper takes girl to dinner!"

His cheeks grew warm as blood rushed to the surface. "You are out of control." Ten minutes later he was walking Kate up the cement walkway to the big, wrap-around porch of The Cozy Corner, the porch light burning bright. Crickets chirped loudly in the cool evening air as the couple stepped up the stairs to stand in front of the door. They faced each other in silence for a moment. He thought it was strange that he could feel so sad and excited at the same time.

She broke the silence, "That was one of the funnest dates I've had in a long time, Chet. Thank you."

"I had a good time too," he said. "It was nice to just get away from everything for a while, wasn't it?"

"Oh definitely."

Awkward silence.

"We'll have to do it again sometime," he said.

"I'd like that."

"Cause, I imagine I still have payments to make on my account." He smiled.

"Actually, after tonight, I think you overpaid a little." She wasn't smiling anymore. Her eyes burned like a liquid flame and it felt like he could fall right into them.

"Overpaid, huh?"

"Yep. And here's your change." She raised up on her toes, placed the flats of her palms on either side of his chest, and kissed him on the lips.

The kiss was chaste, lasting no more than one full second. She pulled away and Chet opened his eyes. He saw the curtain in the window behind her move and he caught a brief glimpse of a red bun disappearing behind the curtain. He grinned.

"What?" she asked, using her thumb to wipe off the lipstick that was smeared on his mouth.

"I think Mable's spying on us through the window."

Kate laughed. "Well, let's not disappoint poor Mable!" With that, she kissed him again. "There," she said.

"I thought you didn't kiss on the first date."

"Oh that lil' ole' thang?" she asked, allowing her southern drawl to really come through. She mocked innocence, batting her long lashes. "That wasn't a kiss, that was a peck." She put her hand on the door knob and began to turn it.

"Oh? Well, thanks for clearing that up," he said, "cause, I could have sworn I just got kissed."

She opened the front door a crack and slipped one foot inside. "Trust me, Chet Cooper, when I give you a *kiss*, you'll know it." She smiled, her eyes swimming with mischief. "See you later?"

"If I have anything to do with it, you will."

"Good night, Chet"

"Night."

Kate offered one last smile, then stepped inside and closed the door.

As he walked back down the walkway to his Jeep, he was pretty sure his feet weren't even touching the ground. *You've really done it now, buddy.*

Behind the wheel, he caught the fragrance of her perfume lingering on his shirt. He sighed as he cranked the engine over, the jeep coming to life. He flipped a u-turn and steered back up Washington Street, making his way to the office. It was his night for the graveyard shift.

CHAPTER 8

The closet door was slightly ajar. Daniel watched through the crack as Robbie Pritchard finally staggered into his bedroom, reeking of liquor. As Daniel had predicted, the jock had spent a good portion of his Saturday night drinking. Good. His task just got a lot easier.

In complete silence he stepped back, allowing the clothes on the hangers to absorb him, and listened to Robbie cursing as he struggled to get undressed. Eventually, the bedroom light clicked off. He heard the sound of rustling sheets and blankets, followed by the creaking of mattress springs. What, no prayers? Not even an *if I die before I wake?* Daniel smiled and waited in the closet patiently. Silently.

EVEN THOUGH HE WAS ASLEEP, he could hear someone whispering his name.

"Robbie…Robbie, wake up." It echoed like it was far away, but it was loud at the same time. He was swimming, fighting up out of the depths of some alcoholic delirium to reach the surface where the voice was coming from. With considerable effort he finally forced his eyes open. From the way the room was rocking back and forth, he figured he was still pretty drunk. Oh yeah, the voice. He looked around, but couldn't see anyone.

He figured it must have just been a dream. That's when Daniel Miller stepped out of the shadows. He was dressed all in black, his skin pale, his eyes, obsidian, a look of malice in them that chilled Robbie to the core.

Through thin, sneering lips Daniel whispered, "Hello, Robbie."

"What the?" With inebriated fingers Robbie fumbled for his Louisville Slugger that was always propped next to his bed. It wasn't there. That's when Daniel held it up for him to see. *Oh, shit…*

The Summoning

The crack of the baseball bat impacting his skull seemed impossibly loud. There was a sharp pain, a flash of light, and he knew no more.

NOW THAT REALLY FELT GOOD, Daniel admitted to himself, staring down at the unconscious football star. A bloody goose egg was already beginning to form on Robbie's forehead. It took all of his will power not to bash his brains out right then and there, but he knew better than that, he was smarter than that. He cast an admiring gaze over the baseball bat before placing it back in its spot. He placed two fingers along the side of Robbie's neck, on the carotid; the pulse was strong, albeit a little fast.

Next, he placed his ear by the slack mouth, listening and feeling for breathing. So far, so good. He pulled back the covers. No pajamas. Robbie slept in his underwear? For some reason, he thought that was funny. The kid was all bone and muscle lying there. This next part was not going to be easy, but he was certain he would be given the strength to accomplish the task.

It took him a minute, some grunting, but he was able to get Robbie off the bed and onto the floor. Once he had him on the floor, he quickly made the bed, just like it had looked previously. Then, rummaging through Robbie's jeans, laying rumpled on the floor, he found his tormentor's car keys and put them in his own pocket. He paused to check the pulse and breathing again. Still good.

He muscled the limp body into a wooden chair that sat next to the bed, the head lolling to the side. A small trickle of blood had run down the side of Robbie's face and pooled in his ear. Daniel hooked his arms under Robbie's armpits and hugged him close, chest to chest. Then with all his strength he stood, pulling Robbie up with him. He quickly bent forward, allowing Robbie's bulk to collapse onto his shoulder. Finally, with unnatural strength, not of his own, he straightened, carrying Robbie over his shoulder like a big sack of potatoes.

He stood for a moment, testing his strength and balance. He grinned, even snickered as loudly as he dared. His muscles felt like straps of iron. He had the strength to do this and more! He quietly carried his human cargo down the upstairs hallway, right past the master bedroom and down the stairs. He got his load out of the door and made his way to the driveway, where Robbie's car was still parked, crooked and skewed.

By this time he was grunting from the exertion, glistening rivulets of sweat streaming down his face. With one hand he popped one of the back doors open and literally threw his burden onto the backseat. He observed his victim for a moment while catching his breath. Through his dripping sweat he grinned.

He got in the car and shifted the transmission into neutral. He got out and pushed the car into the quiet residential street, the tires making little popping sounds on the gravel. He pushed the car several houses down before climbing behind the wheel. Starting the engine, he drove away, Robbie Pritchard, the king of Jefferson Junior High, bleeding and unconscious on the backseat behind him.

CONSCIOUSNESS BEGAN RETURNING in little broken fragments of self awareness to Robbie. The most prominent, a knowledge that his head was throbbing with pain. Next, his stomach was churning and he was probably going to throw up. Then, he became aware that he was sitting upright. A familiar smell: his car. As his mind shattered through each new stratum of subconsciousness, the pain in his head grew worse, making him reluctant to continue. It was like falling. He could no more stop himself from waking up than to defy gravity itself.

Next were the memories, little fuzzy snapshots all jumbled and out of order. He tried to organize them: afternoon football practice—Coach impressed as hell —hanging out at the drive-in with friends—drinks—Cynthia Harris in the backseat of his car—more drinking…hanging out. Why did his head hurt so much? Trying to grab his Louisville Slugger. Why? Daniel Miller standing by his bed…clutching the baseball bat.

That last memory smashed him into conscious reality. His eyes snapped open, the effects of his heavy drinking still weighing considerably on him. He was behind the wheel of his car—in his underwear. Something warm and wet was trickling down his face, dripping off his chin. He reached up tenderly and felt a giant knot on his forehead, from which blood issued. That son of a bitch Daniel was a dead man! He went to start the car. There were no keys in the ignition.

For the first time since coming to, Robbie started to take notice of his surroundings. It was still night and his headlights were on, illuminating a red and white sign about a dozen feet in front of, and to the left of his car. He couldn't quite get his eyes to focus, but he was pretty sure he could make out the words: DANGER, WARNING, and Keep Out! painted in red. The rock quarry.

He'd been here hundreds of times. It was a popular place to park with the kids, right above the big cliff. It was fun to chuck rocks out over the two hundred foot drop and watch them explode on the boulders below. But at the moment, he seemed to be the only one up here, no other cars around. *What time is it anyway? Must be late.*

Maybe he dropped his keys on the ground. He grabbed the door handle and gave it a yank. Nothing. The handle wouldn't engage the mechanism. *What?* His concussed brain tried to muddle through the puzzle. That's when his eyes, as unfocused as they were, caught a movement in the rear view mirror. Daniel Miller was standing behind the car looking back at him, the same bone chilling sneer on his face from before. A very bad feeling washed over Robbie.

He watched in horror as Daniel placed both hands on the trunk of the car and...started to push. The car lurched and began rolling—slowly at first.

"What are you doing?" Robbie screamed. "You bastard! No!" He put his foot to the brake pedal, but it wouldn't budge, something was wedged behind it. He tried to shift the car into gear, but the clutch pedal was blocked as well. The car began to pick up speed. Forget the car, it was time to bail out. He remembered the broken door handle. He grabbed for the window crank. It wasn't there, it had been removed! Reaching across the seat he tried the passenger side. Same thing, broken door handle and no window crank. Trapped!

The car was getting closer to the edge and picking up speed, as there was a slight downhill grade. He frantically jammed the gear shifter against first gear, grinding the gears in vain. He turned around to look back at Daniel. There were black, shadowy shapes all around him, his face a mask of ruthless indifference like a snake. "Okay!" Robbie pleaded, tears welling up in his eyes. He was going to die. "I'm sorry, okay! I'm sorry!" He could see the edge now, a black abyss yawning wide like the jaws of hell, the car hurtling toward it.

He felt the warm sensation of urine, pooling under him as he lost control of his bladder. Crying out, he rammed the gear shifter with every last ounce of desperate strength. The gears growled in protest, but he felt the stick at last grind into its place. Instantly, the tires locked up and the car started skidding for the edge. The car was slowing, but the momentum was still going to carry it over the side.

Bringing his left arm all the way across his body, Robbie smashed his elbow as hard as he could against the driver's side window. Spider web cracks formed in the thick glass as a searing pain shot through his arm. He didn't care. On the second attempt his elbow drove through the glass, sending shards flying. He scrambled to dive out the window, his extremities shaking to the point of uselessness.

Something caught him across the tops of his thighs. He looked down. The seat belt! When they had bought the car, seat belts were an option. His dad had insisted on them, had said that the day might come when they would save his life. His fear-numbed fingers fumbled at the clasp. It was jammed shut. It was loose enough, if he could just scramble his legs through it, like worming out of a pair of pants.

There was a jolt and an awful noise as the front tires dropped out into space, the undercarriage scraping on rocks and dirt. The car came to a sudden stop, teetering on the edge. Robbie held his breath. Where was Daniel? He looked into the rear view mirror. He was shocked to see a gorgeous, blonde woman sitting in the backseat looking back at him, a wickedly beautiful smile on her face.

"You're mine," she said, leaning forward and wrapping her arms possessively around his neck.

Suddenly, the car tipped and started to slide. He was going over, but couldn't break eye contact with the woman in the backseat. Tears streamed down his face as he cried like a baby. The back tires bounced over the edge, the car went vertical, and everything was silent, except for the sound of his own cries.

For a second he was weightless, eyes still locked on the image in the mirror. Then, in an instant, as the car began to descend through space, she transformed. He screamed at the top of his lungs in absolute terror at the maggot-infested corpse that was now behind him, clawing its rotting fingernails into his flesh.

Robbie screamed all the way to the bottom of the quarry.

CHAPTER 9

The phone was ringing. Chet jumped out of the shower, dripping, and threw a towel around his waist. Leaving tiny puddles of water on the hardwood floor, he half jogged down the hallway to the front room of the small house he rented and snatched the phone off the hook. "Hello." No greeting from Caroline the operator this time, just a click as his line was connected.

"Hey, Coop, did I wake ya?" Rick asked on the other end of the line. There was an edge of concern in his voice. It was Sunday afternoon. Sundays were generally slow and the small department usually operated with only one officer. Rick had relieved him earlier that morning from the night shift.

"I was just in the shower, what's going on?"

"I just got a call from Brian Jensen, the maintenance foreman down at the quarry."

"Yeah?"

"He went in to work a little while ago to check up on some equipment for tomorrow. He says there's a smashed up car at the bottom of the quarry. Says it looks like it went over the cliff."

"Suicide?" Chet wondered out loud.

"I'm headed over there right now to check it out. I can call you back when I get there."

"No, that won't be necessary, I'll meet you out there." He hung up without saying goodbye.

It was his day off so he quickly dressed in jeans and a casual button-up shirt instead of going full uniform. He eased the slide of his Colt back and verified there was a round in the chamber before holstering it at his hip. *Never trust your memory.*

Standing in front of the bathroom mirror he ran a comb the best he could through his tangle of damp wavy hair. He stopped, laid the comb down next to the sink, and stared at his reflection. For a moment he didn't recognize the man staring back at him. The other man seemed older, more tired. There was a sadness in his eyes, a slouch to his shoulders. He leaned in closer to the mirror, half expecting the other man to blink, but he just stared back, the memories of another lifetime swimming deep beneath the surface of his brooding eyes.

Then he remembered Kate and the wonderful time they had spent together the day before. He thought about her laugh, the intoxicating scent of her perfume, and the soft sensation of her lips pressed gently against his. He noticed the man in the reflection was smiling now, and the smile was real.

Eagle Point Quarry had suffered during the war, losing almost half of its workforce to either the military or other more war-driven industries, such as steel and rubber manufacturing. During the time that the United States had fought against tyranny and madmen there hadn't been much need for the granite slabs the quarry produced...aside from tombstones.

Now, three years after the surrender of the evil axis, Americans were looking forward with hope and confidence toward the dawn of a new age. The economy and industries were on the rise. Marriages were on the rise too, as couples with great enthusiasm grabbed a hold of the future with both hands and held on tight. Construction was booming for homes and businesses. As a result, Eagle Point was beginning to show signs of life again. The cranes, bulldozers, and other giant earth moving equipment, that had slept dormant for three years, were awakened anew, their diesel engines chugging thick clouds of black exhaust into the air on a daily basis.

This Sunday afternoon the great prehistoric-like machines sat in silent repose as Chet's patrol car navigated the gravel road that encircled the rim of the gaping pit. There was no fence, but *keep out* and *danger* signs were posted along the perimeter in fifty yard intervals. Chet and his deputies were no strangers to the area. The edge of the pit was a popular hang out for the local teenagers on weekends. Just the usual, harmless kid stuff. Parking, drinking, listening to music, and the occasional fist fight. It was a pretty regular part of the job to head out to the quarry and drive off the kids on a Saturday night.

Rick's black and white was pulled off to the side of the road, just up ahead, a white, older Buick parked next to it. Rick and Brian Jensen were both leaning against the hood of Rick's car. They watched as Chet pulled his Chevy up alongside and shut the engine off.

"Afternoon, Brian," Chet said, nodding at the quarry's maintenance foreman as he climbed out of his car.

"Afternoon, Sheriff." Brian spewed a jet of dark-brown tobacco juice through a large gap in his two front teeth. Brian Jensen was in his mid forties, heavy set, broad shouldered, and round in the face. He was shorter than average, but was a man born into his own natural strength, built like a fireplug. The light breeze tussled his thick, curly mop of sandy-blond hair. His stout thumbs were hooked behind the shoulder straps of a pair of worn, faded overalls.

"This where the car went over?" Chet asked.

Rick started walking toward the edge of the pit. "Yeah, there's tire tracks in the dirt that go right over the side."

Chet studied the tracks as he followed behind Rick to the edge, Brian hanging back with the cars. They carefully inched their way to the lip of the cliff and peered over the side. Two hundred feet below they could see the exposed underside of a crumpled car, smashed amongst massive granite boulders.

"Now for the sixty-four dollar question," Rick said, his voice grim. "Is there a body down there?"

"It doesn't look good." Chet walked back a dozen feet, peering down at the tracks in the dirt.

"What makes you say that?" Rick asked, coming over to join him as he squatted down for a closer look.

"Well, see how right here the car basically went into a skid before going over? Looks to me like someone was in the car and slammed on the brakes just before going over the side."

"So whatcha thinking, Coop? Suicide, 'cept he gets cold feet at the last second?

"Maybe. We don't even know if there's a body in that car yet, so let's not get ahead of ourselves."

As they were walking back to the cars Chet stopped. "Wait a second," he mumbled. He paused and squatted near the ground again, studying the marks left behind. "You guys both walked down there before I showed up, right?"

Rick and Brian nodded.

"Let me see your shoes," Chet ordered. "The soles."

Brian's face was quizzical as he looked at Rick. Rick shrugged his shoulders and lifted his foot off the ground and Brian followed suit, one hand on the hood of his car for balance.

Chet nodded. "Okay, good enough, guys."

The two men put their feet back on the ground and turned to Chet for an explanation.

"We may be in luck gentlemen," he explained. "There might not be a body down there. I think someone pushed that car over the side."

"How can you tell that, Sheriff?" Brian asked. The wad of chew in his cheek made the words come out slurred and sloppy.

Chet pointed back to the tire tracks. "There's a set of footprints between the tire tracks. They follow the car almost all the way to the edge, and from the looks of it, they were really digging in. Which tells me they were pushing something heavy."

Rick scratched at his salt and pepper hair. "So, if they pushed their car over the cliff, who slammed on the brakes?"

"I don't know," Chet admitted. "Maybe it slipped into gear just before going over." He stared a moment more at the tracks in the dirt. "Well, I think we've seen all there is to see up here. Let's head down to the bottom and have a look."

Brian spat more chew. "You want me to stay up here, Sheriff?"

"Actually, how about you lead us down there?"

Brian led the way in his Buick with Chet in tow, Rick taking up the rear. The small convoy continued around the perimeter road, the tires of their cars grinding and popping on the rocks and gravel. Reaching the other side of the pit they passed an empty guard shack, the pivoting gate arm left up, pointing like an accusatory finger at the azure sky. Several feet beyond the guard gate they passed the main office, a small two story structure with corrugated metal siding. Waves of warm air shimmered above the dull, rust-streaked panels.

After passing the office, the road hooked sharply to the right and began a steep decent to the bottom of the quarry. It grew wider to accommodate the heavy equipment that frequented it. Looking out of his window, Chet could see the other side of the quarry and the mangled car lying on its top, motionless, like the carcass of some strange animal left to decay in the heat of the afternoon sun.

After a few minutes, the road flattened as it reached the bottom of the quarry and skirted along the edge of the massive pit. They drove by a large crane, a bulldozer, a mammoth-sized dump truck, and a front end loader as they made their way to the other side of the pit. Finally, Brian brought his car to a stop.

The three men exited their cars and gathered next to Chet's. The twisted wreckage of the ill-fated car lay several yards off to their right, half-concealed by boulders as large or larger than the car itself.

"Stay here," Chet ordered Brian. He motioned for Rick to follow him as he started carefully picking his way through the jumbled forest of granite boulders and slabs. The car was unrecognizable, upside-down, disfigured, the cab crushed and wedged completely between rocks and boulders.

Rick squatted near the partially exposed grill, the vertical slats twisted and bent from the crushing force of the impact. "Looks like a Desoto," he said, standing erect again.

Chet made his way around to the side, scrambling over a large boulder to get a better look. Though most of the top portion of the vehicle was concealed, he could see the sun reflected in the car's jet-black paint through numerous fissures and spaces in the rocks. Then, he saw the all-too-familiar, shiny, chrome lug nuts and polished dust covers on the exposed wheels. He felt his heart quicken as he inched closer to the wreck, looking for the final clue that would tell him to whom the car belonged.

Chet placed both hands on a rough, angular rock about the size of a basketball and shifted it to the side, revealing a portion of one of the tell-tale, custom-painted, yellow flames of Robbie Pritchard's brand-new 1948 Desoto. *Dear Lord, don't let him be in there!* he thought.

"Whatcha got up there, Coop?" Rick's voice floated over the rocks that separated the two.

"It's the Pritchard kid's car, no doubt about it."

"Oh no! He ain't in there is he?" Rick's voice was flecked with concern.

"Can't tell, it's too wedged and buried in the rocks. We're gonna to have to hoist it out."

It took a half an hour for Brian to start up the crane and maneuver it into position. He swung the giant boom out over the jumble of boulders and dropped the main hook until it was hovering just above the undercarriage of Robbie's Desoto. It took another fifteen minutes to rig a couple of beefy chains between the crane's hook and the frame of the car. Chet and Rick walked back to a safe distance while Brian sat in the cab of the idling crane, waiting for the sheriff's signal.

Chet nodded and Brian engaged the powerful hoisting mechanism, the engine of the crane revving up as it provided the necessary power. The hook slowly began to ascend, pulling the heavy chains taut. The car resisted, as if it were holding onto some terrible secret it didn't want to reveal. Brian gave more gas and the engine revved faster. The frame of the Desoto began moaning in protest as it submitted to the powerful strength of the crane. Then came the awful, wrenching sound of metal grating and scraping on rough rocks as the boulders gave up their hold on the car and it started rising in the air.

As the mangled hulk slowly rose, the crumpled hood flopped open and hung slack, like the jaw of a corpse, allowing oil and other automotive fluids to cascade over its edge, splashing on the dirt and rocks below. Chet signaled for

Brian to swing the wreck out over bare ground. The boom swung in a slow, deliberate arc, the Desoto leaving a trail of dripping fluids. Chet held up a hand and Brian brought the boom to a halt, the wrecked car swinging on the chains.

Chet motioned again and the foreman reversed the winch, bringing the car closer to the ground. When the car was nearly touching the dirt, Chet made a motion across his throat with his thumb and Brian disengaged the winch, leaving the car groaning on the chains as it gently swayed a foot above the ground.

The lawmen cautiously approached, each peering, trying to see into the dark slits that once were windows, hoping for the best, preparing for the worst. They walked around the car, looking in the windows. "I can't see a dang thing," Rick said. "Too dark in there. Too much debris."

Chet tried to open the driver's side door but it wouldn't budge. "Let's see if we can get this door open." He motioned for Rick to join him. That's when he noticed a buzzing sound coming from inside the car. His heart sank. He had been around enough death to easily recognize the sound of a multitude of flies converging on a corpse.

He shut his eyes tight to ward off the memories, the macabre scenes of dead men sprawled, their limbs grotesquely twisted. And the flies, always there, with dull, red eyes and greasy, black bodies crawling on the faces of the dead, over their open eyes, and in and out of their gaping mouths.

Rick's hand on his shoulder pulled him back from the edge of the swirling chasm. "You alright, Coop?"

A cold sweat had formed on Chet's brow. "I'm okay," he replied, opening his eyes. "I think there might be a body in there though."

Rick nodded in understanding and grasped the door handle. "Well, there's only one way to find out."
They pulled, timing their efforts with each other, yanking on the handle of the warped car door, but it wouldn't budge.

Finally, Rick put one cowboy boot against the side of the car and counted out loud, " One...Two...Three!"

Both men concentrated all their effort into a combined, powerful jerk. There was a dull pop, followed by a sharp squeal, as the door latch gave out and the two men wrenched the door open on its battered hinges.

Instantly, a swarm of flies came boiling out of the door, zigzagging aimlessly, landing on the the two men only to take to flight an instant later, darting back into the car and out again. The men swatted at the flies as they came around the side of the door so they could see into the car.

The Summoning

Even covered in flies, bloated, and smeared in blood, the body of Robbie Pritchard was unmistakable. It lay bent in half on the roof that had crushed him when the car had impacted the ground. Attached to a broken neck, his bruised, swollen head was twisted around at an impossible angle. His face was frozen in a contorted, blood-spattered mask of sheer terror, mouth open, eyes wide, looking right through them.

IT FELT GOOD TO BE OUT IN THE WOODS, breathing the crisp air and listening to the crackle of the fall leaves beneath his feet. Kevin Baxter tried to shake off the memory of Reverend Gannon's droning sermon from that morning, but he could still hear the man's dry voice scraping on his ears like old sandpaper. If that hadn't been bad enough, Ma had insisted that he go to the Sunday school class right after that. Which wasn't too bad after all, he decided. Old Mrs. Whitcomb, the Sunday school teacher, had told the story of David and Goliath, which turned out to be a pretty neat story.

Arriving home from church, he'd snatched up his .22 rifle and headed into the woods for some alone time, hunting squirrels, or anything else that moved. He tried to get Rusty to come along, but his big brother said he wanted to stay home to read comics and flip through his baseball card collection. Kevin felt a wave of sadness wash over him. His older brother was changing. Everyday, it seemed Rusty grew less and less his good buddy and partner in crime. Ma said it was cause Rusty was getting older, having changes in interests, starting to notice girls and what not.

He sighed audibly and tried to take his mind off it. He scanned the low hanging branches of the nearby trees for signs of movement. He noticed an odd tree in front of him shaped almost like a human. There were two broad branches sprouting from its trunk like the arms of a giant. The tree reminded him of Goliath from the Sunday school lesson. He tried to imagine what it must have felt like to be little David, armed with nothing but a slingshot.

He stooped, picked up a rock from the forest floor, and threw it as hard as he could at the imaginary Philistine. The dull thud of the rock impacting the tree echoed around him. He grinned in satisfaction at his marksmanship. Grabbing another rock from the ground he aimed carefully, preparing to deliver another deadly blow, when a movement to his left caught his eye. He froze, just like Dad had taught him so as not to scare off whatever it was. Could be a rabbit, maybe even a small deer! It was watching him, he could feel it. He slipped the rock into the front pocket of his faded, patched jeans and slowly reached for the rifle slung over his shoulder. Carefully, he turned his gaze to see what it was.

A boy, about his age, was standing motionless in the shadow of an elm, about thirty yards away, staring at him. His clothes were dirty, covered with leaves and twigs. His brown hair was a matted tangle that contrasted sharply with his pale face. His dark eyes appeared dead and flat, his cheeks, puffy and swollen.

"Hey," Kevin said.

The other boy just stood there, staring.

"Cat got yer tongue or something?" Kevin took a couple steps toward the boy trying to get a better look at his face. "You lost?"

Without a word, the boy slowly turned and began walking away, his footsteps stumbling and awkward.

"Hey kid!" Kevin shouted following after him. "You deaf or what?" He felt himself growing angry, but he was also aware of an uneasy feeling beginning to rise inside himself. Something definitely was not right about that kid.

"Hey dammit, I'm talking to you!" He felt guilty for cursing on Sunday. He pointed his .22 into the air and fired a round off. The crack of the rifle pierced the air sending a half-dozen nearby birds fluttering away, their wings beating furiously to obtain the safety of the open sky.

The boy froze in place for a moment, then turned to face Kevin. His eyes, though vacant and dead, were wide open and bloodshot, the whites yellowed, the pupils too dark and too large. His mouth moved, as if trying to form words, but nothing came out. He tried again without success and clutched a pale hand to his throat. That's when Kevin noticed the ugly, purple and yellow bruises encompassing the boy's throat and neck. The boy seemed to be growing desperate, glancing around sporadically as he repeatedly mouthed a single word.

Kevin braved a few hesitant steps forward, the dead foliage crunching under his feet like the cracking of tiny bones. "Hey kid, you alright?" he asked with another step forward. Then recognition hit him: the sandy brown hair, the dimpled chin dotted with light freckles, the wide-set eyes. "Levi? Levi Henderson, is that you? Everyone's been worried sick—"

"Get out!" Levi's voice was forced and raspy, as if he were being strangled. "Bad!" he croaked louder.

"What?" Kevin stammered, his heart hammering in his chest, his fingers cold and numb gripping his rifle.

Levi's arm seemed spastic and twitchy as he raised it and pointed in the direction Kevin had come from.

"Wha-what are you talking about?" Kevin barely managed to mutter. His tongue felt thick and clumsy in his mouth. The forest suddenly grew dark and a cold wind began rustling the dead and decaying leaves around them. He shivered against the chill of the wind and the ice water pumping through his veins. Levi continued to point off into the woods, a dark sadness lurking in his eyes.

Instinctively, Kevin staggered a few steps backwards, never taking his eyes off Levi. A tree root caught his foot and he fell, landing on his back. Looking up, he saw that a smoky, black vortex had begun swirling at Levi's feet, like a small tornado. Twigs and dead leaves caught up in the funnel, purled around Levi, increasing in speed and height with each pulsating revolution.

Kevin could hear voices—raspy, whispering voices—coming from the churning cloud. Levi was shaking his head now, tears rolling down his ashen colored cheeks as the swirling mist fully encompassed him, masking him from Kevin's sight. Suddenly, the swirling slowed as the leaves and other forest debris began to collapse inward, toward the center of the mass, until there was only a ball of leaves and twigs left hovering in the air. Levi was gone.

In dumb amazement, Kevin watched the ball of leaves and sticks hover for a second and then explode in a violent rush of air, showering him with debris. At that precise moment he heard Levi's strangled voice choke in his ear. "Get out! Bad! Bad!"

Forgetting his rifle, Kevin jumped off the ground and started beating a path for home as fast as he could run. His fear turned to panic as he crashed with reckless abandon through the undergrowth of the forest. His legs felt like lead as he sprinted. It seemed like every root, vine, and branch was reaching out to snatch and entangle him. He was almost positive he could still hear those raspy, grating voices on the wind, as if they were chasing him. He jerked his head around, risking an awful headlong crash, trying to catch a glimpse of his invisible pursuers.

Was that kid really Levi? And what was wrong with him? A cold, dark feeling washed through him as he concluded that, if he had really seen Levi Henderson, the boy was most certainly dead. Was that Levi's spirit? A ghost? The thought sent a new wave of fear and panic through his body and he surged even faster, flying for the edge of the woods, and for the safety of home.

He hurdled a fallen log as a tangle of cold, leafless branches stretched out in front of him like long, skeletal fingers whipping and clawing at his face. He threw his arms out to protect his eyes and spurred himself to crash blindly through the thick brush. He hit something solid, stopping him dead as a pair of strong hands gripped his shoulders. The scream that exploded from his heaving chest was as involuntary as his own pounding heartbeat. He was a short moment away from death and he clamped his eyes shut waiting for the killing blow, praying it would be quick and painless.

When the death blow didn't come, he opened his eyes to find himself standing in the grasp of the older neighbor boy, Daniel Miller.

"Whoa there! Where's the fire, Kevin?" Daniel's voice was confident, in charge, almost grown-up. He was no longer the shy and unsure-of-himself teenager. Daniel smiled down at him and laughed, "You look like you've seen a ghost."

Kevin took a step back, unable to speak as he labored for air. He studied the older kid's face. The laugh, the smile…something odd about them, not right, like the craftily manufactured grin of a carny at the county fair, luring you in to play one of their fixed games. The smile might be warm and friendly, but not quite able to mask the flinty, reptile eyes of a predator about to strike.

"You okay?" Daniel asked again.
"Uh, huh," Kevin uttered between gasps as he took another step back. "Well, what's the big hurry, kiddo?" Daniel's eyes penetrated into his, a knowing glint reflecting in their hazel depths, the generated smile still pasted in place.

"N-nothin's wrong. I Just remembered I gotta get home or Pa's gonna be real sore with me."

"Oh." The smile faded from Daniel's lips. "I see." He looked around as if trying to see something that wasn't there. "Well, we sure don't want Pa to be angry." He paused, there was an awkward silence as he held Kevin's gaze for a second or two. "Well, you'd better be going then."

"Yeah, I should get going." Keven offered a tentative smile and turned his eyes to the ground, unable to hold the older boy's gaze any longer. He took a step past Daniel, fighting the urge to break into another panic-driven sprint, but was stopped short by an iron grip on his shoulder. He turned with wide eyes, "Yeah?" he asked, his mouth dry.

Daniel ran his thumb tenderly across Kevin's cheek, just below his left eye. His thumb came away smeared in dark-red blood. He turned his thumb to show Kevin. "Better have your ma take a look at that, bud," he said, a sly smirk playing on the corners of his mouth.

Kevin reached up and touched the hot streak that was starting to sting. "Yeah," he stammered breathlessly, "I will. Uh, thanks."

"You're welcome."

DANIEL WATCHED AS YOUNG KEVIN BAXTER DISAPPEARED into the tangle of the undergrowth, the snapping of twigs and branches echoing loudly, even after he had vanished from sight. Obviously, the boy had seen something out there that had scared him half to death. Not long ago, Daniel had sensed some kind of disruption. Something was amiss in the woods.

He had wandered aimlessly for a while waiting, hoping for any kind of sign from her. How he longed to see her again, to behold her tantalizing beauty, to feel her unconditional acceptance, simply to be in her presence. Disappointed, he was returning home when he had happened upon the terrified lad, running like the devil through the forest.

Questions arose: what had Kevin seen? Obviously something. Had this been his sign? Had she led him here for a reason? Perhaps, young Kevin Baxter was to be his next kill.

Shouldn't be a problem, he thought. He brought his blood streaked thumb to his lips and savored the sweet taste of the hunt.

CHAPTER 10

I don't get it, Robbie had everything going for him." Rick was rambling in the passenger seat as Chet drove the car through the tasteful contours of Lexington Street. "Football, girls, money, popularity…"

It was Monday morning and the two men were headed to the Pritchard house to talk to Robbie's parents, a task Chet was not looking forward to.

"It just don't make sense, Chet."

"No, it doesn't," Chet mumbled, lost in his own thoughts.

"I mean, I knew Robbie pretty good. Hell, I've hauled his butt down to the office enough times to feel like I've half raised the kid myself," Rick continued. "He was not suicidal, Coop." Rick shook his head in disbelief as meticulously groomed hedges flashed past his window unnoticed. "Not even depressed, let alone suicidal."

"Well, that's what we're going to try to find out." Chet turned left, off Lexington, onto Maynard.

The Pritchard home was a spacious, two-story, craftsman-style house situated on a large two-acre lot, where Maynard Street came to a dead end. Immaculate, square hedges and a neatly cropped lawn were framed in by an iconic, white-picket fence. A perfect row of young maple trees lined either side of the wide driveway, half of their red and golden leaves lying on the ground, victims of the recent colder nights.

They pulled into the drive and Chet shut off the car. As they climbed out, the front door of the house opened and Orrin Pritchard stepped out wearing a custom-tailored, gray suit. He was tall, walking erect, his demeanor commanding respect as his polished, patent leather shoes echoed on the flawless cement walkway. His carefully parted and waxed hair combined with his thin, neat mustache gave him the appearance of a taller, leaner Clark Gable.

He greeted them, his voice deep and authoritative, "Sheriff Cooper and Deputy Shelton, good morning, gentlemen." He unlatched the gate that allowed access through the picket fence and gestured for the men to enter.

Orrin extended his hand as they came through the gate. The banker was putting up a brave front, but as Chet shook his hand, he could see that his eyes were red, swollen, and too shiny. The man obviously had been suffering immensely since he had received the crushing news, just yesterday.

They followed him in silence as he led them through the front door and into his house. Chet was immediately struck by the beautiful interior of the home as they were led down a hallway. Wood panels, decorative arches, wide floorboards, and small alcoves all flowed together, conspiring with intricate hand carvings and exquisite brick work to give the impression one was walking through an enormous work of art, rather than just a house. Even the paintings and wall hangings seemed to be an integral part of the structure, rather than personalized afterthoughts.

"You have a beautiful home, Mr. Pritchard," Rick said, running his hand along the polished surface of a thick, wooden support beam.

"Thank you," Orrin replied, as he opened a heavy door at the end of the hallway and led them into his study. The design and architecture from the hallway flowed naturally into the study, interrupted only by a thick pad of high grade, forest-green carpet, the zigzagging pattern of a recent vacuuming crisscrossing its plush surface. A large, oak desk, polished to a mirror finish, dominated the center of the room. Behind the desk, two matching bookcases filled with leather-bound volumes stood against the wall. Each bookcase was flanked by an elegant gun cabinet with decorative etchings in the glass doors and small interior lights that illuminated the expensive contents. Chet could almost hear Rick salivating at the sight of the collection of rifles, which were works of art in their own right.

Orrin made his way behind the desk and seated himself in a high-backed, brown leather chair. He gestured to two polished, wooden chairs opposite his. "Won't you gentlemen be seated?"

"Thank you," Chet said, as he and Rick sat down, their duty belts creaking. "Mr. Pritchard," Chet began, "is your wife home?"

"No, she's at her sister's in Greenville. She left yesterday, after we got the word. She couldn't stand to be in the house, had to get away. I'm sure you can appreciate the fact that she is utterly devastated." Orrin interlocked his fingers, rested his elbows on the inlaid leather pad of his desk, and peered with weary eyes over his knuckles at Chet. "What do you need from me, Sheriff?"

The man didn't beat around the bush. "Just a few routine questions."

"Go on."

"Mr. Pritchard, do you have any reason, whatsoever, to believe your son would have taken his own life?" Might as well get it over with and out of the way.

"Absurd!" Mr. Pritchard smacked the palms of his hands hard on the surface of his desk, an intense flame of conviction burning in his brown eyes. "Absolutely not! My son did not kill himself, Sheriff Cooper! He was a happy young man with a great future ahead of him. Besides, he was raised to be tough, grab life by the horns, conquer his obstacles. Suicide would have never entered my son's mind, even in the worst of times, I assure you."

Chet cleared his throat. "When was the last time you saw Robbie?"

"We had breakfast Saturday morning. He left for football practice and to be with his friends, doing whatever they do on a Saturday, and shortly after I headed for the golf course."

"You didn't see him later that night? You, or your wife?"

"That was the last time we both saw him."

"So, he never came home?"

"Oh, he came home at some point, and then left again. His clothes are still laying on his bedroom floor."

Rick spoke up, "He was found with no clothes on, Mr. Pritchard." There just was no way to be tactful. "Why would he come home, take off his clothes, and then leave again...in his underwear?"

The grieving father leaned forward on his elbows. "Gentlemen, may I be frank?"

Chet nodded. "Of course."

"Something is not right here about my son's death. I know you're thinking he committed suicide, or at the very least got stone drunk and had a bad accident."

"Nobody's saying that," Chet interjected.

Mr. Pritchard waved a dismissive hand. "Sheriff, my son was not an idiot, nor was he a suicidal basket case." He rose to his feet, his chair rolling backwards to bang into one of the bookshelves. "There are some bizarre circumstances surrounding the death of my boy." His voice cracked and he paused to regain his composure as his eyes welled with tears. "You come to my home with routine questions, but there isn't anything routine about what's happened to my son."

Rick came to his feet. "That's why we're here, Mr. Pritchard, to try to get to the bottom of this."

"Deputy Shelton's right," Chet said, also rising from his chair. "We aren't saying anything at this point. I'm just trying to get an understanding, and unfortunately, there are certain questions I need to ask. Look, I understand this is very difficult for you. Maybe it would be better if we came back tomorrow."

Orrin placed clenched fists on his desk top and leaned forward, pinning Chet with eyes that seemed to be made of liquid fire. One solitary tear escaped the corner of his eye and streaked unheeded down a chiseled cheek. "Sheriff Cooper, you can ask me all the routine questions you want, but the answers will mean nothing until you ask yourself the biggest question of all." He paused, his eyes boring into Chet's. "Who murdered my son?"

"Murder?" Rick exclaimed, his eyes wide. "In Clear Creek? With all due respect Mr. Pritchard—"

Orrin thumped the desk with his fist. "Sheriff, I want you to order a full autopsy, and I want you to investigate Robbie's death as a homicide."

"Sir," Chet said, "there's hardly any evidence, at this time, to warrant an autopsy, let alone, a murder investigation."

"So that's it, huh? My son, the football star, model student, popular boy, happy kid, commits suicide? Case closed? Well, I've got to say Sheriff, that's some real fine police work!"

Rick took a step forward and stabbed a finger at Orrin. "Now you hold on just a darn second! That ain't no way to—"

"Rick, take a seat," Chet ordered, placing his hand on his deputy's shoulder and pulling him back.

Rick sat down, folded his arms and stared at the floor, a vein popping out of the side of his neck.

"Mr. Pritchard," Chet said, "let me assure you that I'm not even close to calling this a suicide, or anything else for that matter. If I thought it was that open and shut I wouldn't even be here. Now, let's all calm down and see if we can help each other figure this thing out."

Mr. Pritchard slumped wearily into his chair and dug his thumb and forefinger into his red, swollen eyes. "I apologize, gentlemen. I was out of line."

"It's okay," Chet said, "I can't imagine going through what you are right now."

The room went silent as Mr. Pritchard reached into his coat pocket and produced a leather cigarette case embossed with silver studs. The two policemen politely refused his offer of a cigarette and sat patiently while their host placed one between his lips and lit it.

The banker inhaled deeply, the tip of the cigarette glowing a bright orange. He spoke as he exhaled a plume of white smoke, "You do what you've got to do, Sheriff." He took another drag. "But I'm telling you, my boy's death was no suicide, and no accident. The sooner you reach that conclusion for yourself, the better for us all."

Chet crossed the room to stand in front of one of the gun cabinets and admired the gleaming weapons it contained. "Do you hunt much?"

"Mostly big game." Orrin stood and came to stand next to Chet. "Although I do enjoy going after fowl on occasion: ducks, pheasants, partridge, that sort of thing."

"Well, this is quite a nice collection you have here."

"Thank you."

Chet leaned close to the glass. "Nice Winchester."

"You have a good eye for guns, Sheriff." Orrin opened the cabinet and pulled one of the rifles from its felt-lined rack. "Model 1873 carbine, passed down from my grandfather." He handed the antique rifle to Chet. "The gun that won the West."

"Beautiful," Chet said, hefting the rifle with genuine appreciation. He ran his palm tenderly over the wooden stock, the stain darkened from the passage of time.

"Sheriff Cooper," Orrin said, "I know it probably doesn't make sense to you, but I know my Robbie didn't kill himself."

"Actually, I don't believe your son killed himself either." He handed the rifle back. "but, I can't just rule out an accident and launch a murder investigation. Not without any evidence."

Orrin nodded in silence, placing the Winchester back in its rack with great care. "Did your son have enemies? Anyone you would suspect?" Chet asked.

Mr. Pritchard closed the doors to the gun cabinet. Shaking his head he let out a sigh. "I suppose it does all sound kind of crazy, when you come right out and ask it like that."

"It's just your gut trying to tell you something, Mr. Pritchard. If there's one thing I've learned, it's to listen to those gut feelings—even the crazy ones."

"Does that mean you will start a murder investigation?"

"No. Not on an official basis anyway. But, I tell you what: I'll start looking into it quietly, nose around a little bit, talk to some people, ask a few questions, see if I can stir anything up. Until then, we'll call it a tragic accident. Will that be good enough for the time being?"

Orrin took a few thoughtful paces over to one of the bookshelves, rubbing his chin. "Okay, Sheriff, I think I can live with that for now. He absently pulled a gorgeous, red, leather-bound book from the shelf and leafed through the gilded pages. "You'll keep me apprised of anything that turns up, of course."

"Of course," Chet consented. "But, it's vital that this stays between us. Nobody outside this room can know. If it got around that I'm conducting some kind of secret, unofficial murder investigation, then you can imagine the kind of hell that would break loose."

"Agreed." Orrin extended his right hand as if he had just negotiated the terms of a sizable loan from his bank. After shaking hands with Chet, Orrin offered his hand to Rick, who stood and clasped it without a word.

"That's a good man you have there," Orrin said, with a slight smirk. "I do believe he was ready to come right over the top of my desk to defend your honor."

"Yeah," Chet laughed, "I think I'll keep him around for a while longer."

"Is that a fact?" Rick blurted, shaking his head in mock disgust.

The three men shared a brief laugh, and for a moment the prevailing heaviness in the air lightened before returning again, snuffing out the mirth like a heavy gust of wind on a match stick.

"What do you need from me?" Orrin asked, his face appearing more haggard and drawn than even before.

Chet cut to the chase. "Well, Mr. Pritchard—"

"Please Sheriff, call me Orrin."

"Orrin, I'd like it if you could provide us with a short list of his closest friends and associates."

"Not a problem."

"And I'd like to take a look at his bedroom if that's okay with you."

"Follow me, gentlemen."

"Miss Farnsworth?"

Kate looked up from the attendance logs sprawled across her desk to a young boy standing in her office doorway. His blond hair was shaved nearly to the scalp, making it look almost white. He scraped at the floor with the toe of a canvas sneaker, his hands buried in the front pockets of his faded jeans. He had dark circles under his eyes and his skin was too pale. An ugly, red gash in the first stages of healing slanted under his left eye.

"Well, hi there, uh...Kevin, isn't it? Kevin Baxter? I'm sorry, I'm still trying to learn all the names around here," she said, with a smile.

Without raising his eyes, Kevin offered a half-hearted smile that faded as quickly as it had appeared.

"It's recess time. Shouldn't you be out playing with the other kids?"

Kevin stared down at the floor, silent. This was strange behavior coming from the precocious little boy, who just last week, sneaked into the girls' bathroom and dropped a live frog into each one of the toilets.

"Is something the matter, Kevin?" This situation had become somewhat the norm for Kate. She had discovered in recent weeks that as the secretary at Lincoln Elementary she was also the occasional nurse, hall monitor, substitute P.E. teacher, and now and then, counselor. She wasn't sure whether she had volunteered for the extra duties, or if they had been thrust upon her. Whatever the case, a troubled Kevin Baxter had found his way into her office. He looked over his shoulder as if unsure of what to say.

"Is everything okay, dear?" she pried.

He raised his eyes to meet hers and she felt a chill pass through her. There was a fear glimmering in the boy's eyes, a look of terror almost. Involuntarily, she brought a hand to her throat and swallowed.

He spoke in a trembling whisper, "Are there such things as ghosts?"

"SO, HOW DO YOU SUPPOSE TO CONDUCT a secret murder investigation, Coop?" Rick asked as they drove back to the office.

"I really wouldn't call it an investigation, per se," Chet replied. "There were some things Orrin needed to hear to keep him satisfied, so I made it sound a certain way."

"In other words you lied?"

"Let's go with, exaggerated a little."

Rick's silence betrayed his need for further explanation.

"Look, as far as Pritchard's concerned, it's a secret murder investigation."

"But?"

"But, you know as well as I do, that just isn't going to happen. All I can really do is what I said I would; ask around a little. You saw Pritchard back there, his behavior, his state of mind. Besides…"

"Besides, what?" Rick leaned forward to look more directly into Chet's face.

"Never mind," Chet said, keeping his eyes on the road ahead. From the corner of his eye he could see his deputy studying him, his mouth dipped in a frown.

"What?"

"Holy cow! You think there's something to what Pritchard was saying, don't you? You think Robbie could have been murdered!"

Chet sighed. "We might not have any direct evidence of that, but I agree with him; some things just don't add up in all this."

"And in the end, if you don't find anything, do you think Orrin is just going to accept that and move on?"

"I guess he'll just have to accept it."

Rick let out a small sarcastic snort. "Actually Coop, no he won't. Do you need my lecture on small town politics again? Please don't make me bring up Mrs. Reed's flower garden versus Mayor Carson's dog again."

Chet snickered. "What happened to the loyal deputy that was ready to choke the richest citizen in Clear Creek for me a few minutes ago?"

"Didn't the Marine Corps teach you anything about tough love, son?"

"Don't remind me. They gave me all the love I could handle, believe me!"

"And they still had your back?"

"Ten-four," Chet admitted.

"Okay, think of it like that then."

Chet smiled as he turned the car on to Main Street. "Okay, maybe I did step in it back there, but I'm telling you, I've got a feeling."

"A feeling?" Rick shook his head.

"Yes!" Chet said, allowing his annoyance to bubble up. "A feeling."

"You're the boss." Rick leaned back into his seat to stare out of the passenger window. "You know you can count on me, whatever you turn up."

"I know."

They rode in silence until Chet maneuvered the car in front of the office and shut off the engine. As he grabbed the door handle he felt Rick's hand on his shoulder.

"There's something I've been wanting to talk to you about," the deputy said, his face serious.

Chet turned to face him. "Okay."

"I've been wanting to mention some strange reports I've been getting. All day yesterday and even more today."

"They can't be as strange as the last couple of days. What's going on?"

"I don't know, these reports are strange. I mean really out there, Coop."

"Okay, let's have it." Chet was growing impatient.

"Well," Rick paused and looked around as if to make sure there were no eavesdroppers, "the other night, a Willy's Jeep matching the same description as yours was seen driving down Main Street."

"And what's so strange about that?"

"Well, not only does the Jeep match the same description as yours, but according to the reports I've heard, the driver matches your description as well."

"Still waiting for the weird part," Chet said, folding his arms.

"But it couldn't have been you in that Jeep."

"Let me get this straight: the reports say a man, who looks just like me, was seen driving down Main Street in a Jeep that looks just like mine."

Rick bobbed his head up and down.

"Yeah, I guess I just don't see the conspiracy in that. Is it possible that it was actually just me?"

"I just don't see how it could have been you." There was a glimmer of mischievous delight in the man's eyes now.

Chet made a show of checking his wrist watch. "Okay, deputy, out with it."

"It couldn't have been you, because the reports say that there was this pretty young lady riding in the passenger seat, and you were both grinning from ear to ear."

Chet snorted, shaking his head from side to side.

"I know! Crazy huh?" Rick exclaimed, a huge open-mouthed smile on his face. "Sheriff Chet Cooper, out on the town with a girl?"

"Maybe not as crazy as you think."

The older man was laughing. "Just ribbing you, bud. So who is she? My wife's been on my case for two days now to get the scoop." He slapped Chet on the back as they approached the door to the office.

"What, your gossip...I mean, *reports* didn't have that information?"

"Apparently nobody recognized her." Rick held the door to the empty office for Chet.

"Good."

"Aw come on, Coop. Your secret's safe with me," Rick pleaded.

"Oh no it's not!" Chet burst out laughing. "I tell you and it goes straight to Alice, and then to who knows where!"

"Okay, okay," Rick conceded, "you have a point there, but give me a little info."

"Like what?"

"Is it serious?"

Good question. "Look, it was one date."

"You gonna see her again?"

The telephone on Chet's desk began to ring. *Saved by the bell!* "Let me get back to you on that," Chet said, heading for his desk.

"Right, I'm sure you will."

Chet picked up the receiver of the jangling telephone. "Sheriff's Office, Cooper here."

Caroline, the operator, was on the other end. "Morning Sheriff, I've got a Miss Kate Farnsworth who says she needs to talk to you. She won't say about what."

"Please connect us, Caroline."

"My pleasure, Sheriff."

He was pretty sure that he detected a giggle as Caroline connected his line. Couldn't a guy go out on one date, without the whole town going crazy? He waited until he heard the click as his line was connected with Kate's.

He spoke first, "Doesn't the girl usually wait anxiously by her telephone for the *guy* to call *her* after the first date? Or do they do it different in Tennessee?" He smiled at his own cleverness. For once he could be the Smart Alec and she could be on the ropes.

"Shut up, Chet, and listen to me."

The sound of her voice made him realize he had missed her over the last couple of days. "What's going on, Kate? Is everything alright?"

"Everything's fine, but I think you should come over here to the school right away."

"What's going on?"

"It's no big emergency, but I think you'll want to come over. You need to hear what I just heard, in person. Plus, you'll get to see me when you come, and if you're lucky, you might get to take me to lunch."

He was halfway through thinking up a witty response when the line went dead. Shaking his head and smiling, he hung up.

"Kate, huh?" Rick was rocking back in his chair with a huge grin, his fingers interlaced across his midsection. "That wouldn't be that new little secretary down at the elementary school, would it?"

"It was one date!" Chet said, exasperated. It was an exasperation that Rick seemed to be enjoying a little too much. He headed for the door. "I'll be back in a while. Hold down the fort while I'm gone."

"Where ya goin?" Rick asked, still grinning. "What's so urgent all the sudden?"

"She wouldn't say, just that there was something I needed to see for myself." Rick burst into laughter. "Remember you're on duty, Sheriff!"

Chet's face flushed. "Does Alice have any idea she's married to a dirty, old dog?"

Rick was nearly falling out of his chair as Chet walked outside and slammed the door on the echoing laughter.

He took note of what a beautiful fall day it was as he drove to the school. A bright, warm sun radiated from a deep, cobalt sky, without a cloud to be seen anywhere. Just the slightest hint of a chill in the air had caused some to don jackets and sweaters, as they walked the streets of Clear Creek. Others found the temperature to be just right for short sleeves. The oaks and maples lining the sidewalks were still laden by leaves of flaming reds, oranges, and yellows, with not even a wisp of a breeze to stir them.

All seemed right on the surface: people going about their business, shopkeepers tending their shops, housewives out for groceries, delivery trucks making their rounds. An outsider looking in would have never guessed that the body of a teenage boy had been pulled from his car just the day before, or that a few weeks ago, an innocent boy had gone missing, never to be seen again.

As Chet drove through his picturesque little town, an uneasy feeling settled in his gut. A feeling that directly contradicted the benign scenes that flashed by his window. There was something bigger going on here. He could feel it.

He pulled up to Lincoln Elementary and parked out front. His uneasy feelings fled as he looked at the open window to the left of the main entrance. Kate was sitting at her desk with her back to the window, her dark hair catching a beam of sunlight that streamed in. He made his way up the sidewalk and to the front doors, letting himself in. He walked past Principal Grayson's office first; the door was shut, indicating he was out.

He peeked around the edge of the next doorway. He was alarmed by the sudden increase in his own heart rate at the sight of Kate sitting at her desk. She was busy going over some kind of list, her brow creased slightly in concentration as she gnawed on a pencil eraser. She was wearing a plain, yellow dress, but on her, there was nothing plain about it. He rapped with his knuckles on the door frame stepping into view. "Hello, Kate."

She started and yanked the pencil from her mouth. "Good morning, Sheriff Cooper, thanks for coming." She arched her eyebrows and motioned with a subtle movement of her head at the corner of her office.

Chet stepped into the room to have a look. Kevin Baxter was sitting in the corner, kicking his legs back and forth nervously, his shoes brushing the carpet with each pass. His palms were pressed flat on the seat of the chair, to the sides of his legs. He was looking up, his rascally smile acutely missing from his otherwise impish face. He didn't look good at all. Chet was afraid to hear what the kid had done this time.

Kate cleared her throat. "Sheriff, this is Kevin Baxter." She was speaking in that motherly voice. The one that women are able to muster up for any kid, in order to make them feel at ease.

"Kevin and I are well acquainted." Chet folded his arms waiting to hear the worst.

Kate said, "Sheriff, why don't you have a seat? Kevin has something to tell you."

He dragged one of the chairs across from Kate's desk over in front of Kevin and straddled it, draping his arms over the back. "Alright Baxter, let's have it. What do you have to tell me?"

With Kate sitting right there, Chet did his best to put on an air of patience as he listened to Kevin's unbelievable story.

"So, then the ball of leaves exploded and Levi was gone?" Chet repeated the end of the story.

Kevin nodded. "So I figured I'd seen a ghost and took off runnin' for home, sir."

"What happened to your eye there?"

"A branch I guess. I never even felt it happen. Didn't know till Daniel told me about it."

"Daniel Miller?" Chet asked, "Your neighbor?"

"Yes, sir. He was on the edge of the woods, I about ran him right over."

"What was he doing out there?"

"Just walking around, far as I know."

Chet drummed his fingers on the back of the chair rehashing Kevin's story in his head. "Kevin, this isn't one of your pranks is it?" He had to ask given the boy's history, but it was obvious he was really frightened.

"Honest!" Kevin sputtered.

"Okay, Kevin, I want you to calm down. What you saw was probably your imagination playing tricks on you. You know, out there by yourself in the woods, you started thinking about scary stuff, the next thing…"

Kevin was shaking his head from side to side. "I saw him, Sheriff. I saw Levi Henderson and he's dead. An-and he's really upset! Something really bad happened to him." The little kid's voice began to shake as he bit his bottom lip.

In one swift movement Chet was out of the chair and bending down in front of the trembling boy. He placed a comforting hand on his shoulder. "It's okay, bud, there's nothing to be afraid of. Really, there isn't."

He bent down lower to look Kevin directly in the eyes. "Now you're old enough to know that there's no such things as ghosts, Kevin. Or goblins, or any of those things. Now, I'm not saying you didn't see something out there that frightened you, but I know from my own personal experience that when we're afraid and alone, our minds can play all kinds of tricks on us."

"Was it scary for you in the war?" Kevin asked in the blunt and honest way that only a child could.

"Heaven knows I was scared half to death, half the time, son," Chet said, the sincerity of his own voice almost catching himself off guard. He felt the demons stir a moment before he forced them back to sleep. "There's nothing for you to be afraid of. You just keep going about your life as always. Can you do that for me?"

Kevin nodded. "I guess so."

"Maybe except for the pranks and trouble all the time."

The boy blushed.

"Now, I know that Miss Farnsworth here is much prettier to look at than me, but the next time you see something strange you give me a call, will ya?"

Kevin actually cracked a brief smile. "Okay."

"Good." Chet patted Kevin's shoulder and straightened. "Tell ya what: I'll have one of my deputies head over there sometime today and have a little look around, just in case."

"Okay."

Kate came to her feet. "Are you gonna be alright, hon?"

Kevin bobbed his head. "Yeah, I suppose so."

"Good. Now run along to class and remember, anytime you think you need to talk about it, you just let me know, okay?"

"Yes, ma'am," Kevin said, and slid out of his chair to walk past Chet.

He stopped in the doorway. "See ya, Sheriff."

"I'm sure you will," Chet said, disguising his sarcasm with a smile, as Kevin disappeared into the hallway.

Chet turned toward Kate; she was slipping into a white, wool sweater with yellow buttons that matched her dress. "That certainly was interesting," he said.

She pulled a small hand bag from a desk drawer. "I think it's kind of creepy."

"No argument here."

Kate stepped around the desk to stand next to him, and placed her hand in the crook of his elbow. "So, where can a girl get a bite to eat in this town?"

CHAPTER 11

Zoli's, situated just a few blocks down the street from the sheriff's office, was the local butcher shop, owned and operated by Zoltan Horvath. Zoltan had been blessed with the foresight and the financial means to immigrate his family to The States from Hungary, just in time to escape the devastation that swept his country shortly after. It had cost him half of his fortune to get to America, and the other half to convert an old mechanic's garage into a butcher shop. As it turned out, Zoltan was quite the capitalist and had converted a part of the business to a small sandwich shop as well.

A small brass bell jingled when Chet swung the door open for Kate. The inviting aroma of freshly baked bread wafted over them as they walked the short distance to a glass case with a cash register sitting on top of it. Behind the glass, a variety of sliced meats were displayed on metal platters. Little hand written signs were propped in front of each platter, indicating the type of meat and price per pound. To the right and going back, a handful of square tables, draped in white linen tablecloths, were scattered around the small L-shaped room. A few of the tables were occupied by other diners.

Behind the cash register, a door on two-way hinges swung open and Zoltan's wife, Katalin, emerged from a back room, wiping her hands on a white apron. In her mid to late forties, she was slender and shorter than average for a woman, but she exuded an air of strength and resolve, nonetheless. Her dark-brown hair was bundled up beneath a white kerchief, a few rebellious tresses escaping to dangle in front of a set of almond-shaped, hazel eyes. At the sight of Chet, her oval face brightened.

"Good afternoon, Sheriff Cooper!" She exclaimed in a heavy accent.

"Good afternoon, Mrs. Horvath." Chet answered.

"You come for to eat lunch, yes?"

Chet nodded. Katalin's eyes darted over to Kate and then back to Chet, and she brightened all the more. "Yoi, I hear you have girlfriend, Sheriff! Very good, very good."

His cheeks grew warm as they flushed with blood. "Mrs. Horvath, this is my friend, Kate Farnsworth. She's the new secretary down at Lincoln Elementary."

Katalin directed her gaze at Kate. "You are very beautiful girl, Miss Kate, very pretty."

It was Kate's turn to blush. "It is nice to meet you, Mrs. Horvath, and thank you."

"No, you please call me Kati, you too, Sheriff." Katalin said, pulling a pad of paper and a pencil from her apron. "And what for you, today?" she asked.

Chet ordered his usual club sandwich on sourdough bread and highly recommended the combo to Kate, who agreed to go along. "The bread alone is worth the visit," he said.

Katalin promised their sandwiches would be ready shortly, and suggested that they find themselves a table. The other patrons at Zoli's acknowledged the couple with smiles or nods, as Chet led Kate to a table near the back corner. He pulled a chair out for her and then seated himself with his back to the wall—a habit he had formed since his return from the war.

"So, how's your day been so far?" Kate asked, after he had sat down.

"I've had better."

She cocked her head to one side, scrunching her face into a question mark.

"Had to pay a visit to Orrin Pritchard this morning and talk to him about Robbie. It wasn't really the best way to start out the week."

"Oh, I'm sure. He must be devastated. I can't imagine what it must feel like to be a parent and have your child commit suicide like that."

"Well, he's convinced it wasn't suicide."

"Really?" Her eyes widened. "Then what does he say happened?"

"I can't really talk much about it, but he was very adamant that Robbie didn't kill himself. He wants me to look into all other possibilities."

She narrowed her eyes. "Possibilities? Like what?"

He found himself on professional thin ice. "Oh, you know, he thinks maybe it was an accident," he fibbed. "So, I'm going to investigate it a little more before officially ruling it a suicide."

Just then, Katalin appeared at their table to pour them each a steaming cup of freshly brewed coffee. "Sandveeches almost ready," she informed them before whisking off to the next table.

Kate stirred some sugar into her coffee from a small bowl on the table, her spoon clinking lightly against the sides of the porcelain cup. "What do you think? Was it really just an accident? The kid drove off a cliff in his underwear,

Chet." Using both hands, she raised the coffee to her apple-colored lips and sipped gingerly while peering back, her eyes a vivid green.

"I'm keeping an open mind until I've completed a full investigation," he said, also taking a sip of coffee—straight black. "I figure I owe Orrin that much at least."

"Okay, fair enough I suppose."

"Anyway, never mind all that." He moved to change the subject. "What's the latest in your world?"

She shrugged. "I guess nothing too astounding. Mrs. Rockwood, the secretary at the junior high school, is going to be out for a couple of weeks, on account that her daughter just had her first baby. So, you know, she's gonna need some help around the house, taking care of the new addition and all."

"Huh," Chet said, with a smile. "So Martha Rockwood is a mother now, I'll be."

"I take it you know her then?"

"Yeah, we graduated in the same class. We were pretty good friends but I haven't seen her since I left for the Marines. Nice gal."

"I'm sure," Kate said, raising her cup to her lips again.

He watched her gently blow on her coffee, and then cautiously indulge in another sip, her thick eyelashes fluttering slightly as the hot liquid came into contact with her soft, slightly puckered lips. Yeah, she was pretty alright. He fretted for a moment that she might actually be out of his league.

"Anyway," Kate said, placing her cup back on the table and cradling it with her hands, "while Mrs. Rockwood is out, I get to fill in for her."

He caught the sarcasm in the way she said, "*I get to,*" and tried to appear sympathetic, careful not to overplay it. "How does that work? Who fills in for *you* then?"

"Oh, that's the loveliest part!" she exclaimed, brimming with false enthusiasm. "I get to fill in for myself!"

"Really?"

"Yes, sir! I get to start my day out at the elementary school and finish up a whole day's worth of work as quickly as possible so I can be to the junior high by one o'clock, and start playing catch up there until four. And then, it's back to Lincoln, where I get to stay a couple of hours late, making up whatever I missed there all afternoon!"

"Well, at least it's only for a couple of weeks," Chet consoled. "So, starting right away then?"

"Yep. I'm supposed to go over there this afternoon so Mrs. Rockwood can teach me the ropes, and then starting tomorrow, I'm on my own."

Katalin seemed to appear out of nowhere carrying two white plates, each one laden by a heavy club sandwich and a fat dill pickle. She smiled as she placed the plates on the table in front of them. "Please enjoy," she said in her broken English. "You say if you need more anything, okay?"

"It looks delicious," Chet said.

"Thank you, Kati," Kate replied.

Katalin beamed at Kate and then whisked away to her other duties without another word.

Kate scooped up her sandwich in both hands. "Okay, let's see if this is as good as you promised, Sheriff."

"I'll stake my badge on it."

A moment after biting into the sandwich, Kate rolled her eyes to the ceiling, and with her mouth still full of food said, "Wow, you weren't just kidding."

Chet smiled and took that as his queue to start munching into his. They ate in silence for a while, occasionally glancing up to make eye contact and smile.

About halfway through her sandwich, Kate laid it back on the plate. "I'm stuffed," She said, leaning back into her chair. "Whew! That was good though."

"I'm glad you liked it."

"I guess you get to hang onto that tin star a little longer."

They laughed together, then Kate's eyes turned more serious. "So Chet, what do you think of little Kevin Baxter's story?"

He put his sandwich down and rubbed his chin. "I'm really not sure what to think about it; the story is really out there. You know, coming from Kevin Baxter, I'd normally say he's trying to pull some kind of prank."

She jumped in, "I don't think so. You should have seen him when he first came to me. I think he's truly frightened of something."

"Well, sure. His next door neighbor and classmate just ups and disappears one day. It's probably got him on edge. Who knows? Maybe enough on edge that he's seeing things, or imagining them. Add to that, Robbie Pritchard goes over a cliff in his car. Hell, I bet there's a line of kids outside your office right now wanting to talk."

She crossed her legs and folded her arms. "So, you're basically dismissing the whole thing then?" There was an edge to her voice.

He spread his hands defensively. "You did the right thing in calling me, but the kid reported seeing a ghost. I'm not sure what I'm supposed to do with that, except let his parents know about it."

121

She rolled her eyes. "I'm not saying he actually saw a ghost, Chet. But don't you think it's possible he saw something out there? Just because he thinks it was a ghost doesn't mean that there's nothing to his story."

Chet nodded. "Yeah, you have a point I guess."

"Of course I do," she stated, her voice even. "So, are you going to go check it out then?"

"I suppose it wouldn't hurt to send Scotty out there to poke around in the woods a little. He's had a slow day anyway."

"Perfect," she said, and flashed him a smile.

Kate waited, patiently sipping her coffee, while Chet finished his sandwich. The conversation drifted to her family and home. She told him about her dad, his horses and the crazy stuff she did with her brothers when they were kids. He listened intently, studying the changing expressions in her eyes and the glow of her skin as she talked.

"You really love your dad," Chet said.

"I love both my parents, they're good people."

"You must be missing your home and family quite a bit right now."

She began picking absently at the crust of her sandwich. "Well yeah, of course I do. Who wouldn't?"

He leaned forward resting his forearms on the table. "So, do you mind if I ask how you ended up here, in Clear Creek of all places? Cause we're not exactly on the map like New York or San Fransisco."

For a fraction of second, he saw something flash across her face. He couldn't categorize it exactly, a mixture of sadness and panic maybe.

She was quick to recover, putting on an air of indignation by folding her arms and fixing him with a penetrating glare. "Are you complaining? I could start looking for a job in another town if it would make you feel better." She was dodging the question, definitely hiding something.

He decided that letting it go would be the best course of action for now. She obviously had her reasons and wasn't ready to share them. He rocked back in his chair. "No need to go to those kind of extremes!" he laughed. "I think you're an excellent addition to our little town."

"Good! Maybe I'll actually stick around for a while then."

"I hope you do," he said, and he really meant it. He had seen a lot of bad things. Things he would rather forget, but knew he never would. Sometimes when he was alone at night, no matter how hard he tried, he could not force the demons of his mind to stay buried. They would seep out of their graves and, as soft as a dying man's last breath, push their way into his thoughts, dragging his mind into a dark, timeless place, leaving him shaking, cold and alone in the world. Until recently. Since that afternoon at the cabin, the demons felt more subdued than ever, as if Kate's presence in his life had sent them fleeing back, deeper than ever into their dark holes.

An hour flew by quickly, and before long it was time for both of them to get going. Chet dropped a handful of change on the table before helping Kate to her feet.

"Thanks for lunch, it was really good," Kate said, as he escorted her to the front of the shop.

"You're welcome." He held the door open for her. "We'll have to come back here again sometime so you can meet Zoltan. He's a character, I think you'd really get a kick out of him."

He let Kate into the passenger side of his car before climbing in behind the wheel and starting up the engine. Grabbing the radio mic from the hook he depressed the transmit button. "Forks, this is Cooper, do you copy?"

After a few seconds of silence the radio came to life. "Forks here, go ahead."

"Scotty, when you get a chance I'd like you to head out to the Baxters and take a little stroll through the woods behind their place. Kevin thinks he bumped into Levi Henderson out there the other day."

There was a long pause. "Uh, copy that, Sheriff," came Scotty's voice over the speaker, with just a hint of sarcasm.

Chet glanced over at Kate with an *I told you so* look on his face. She simply smiled back and shrugged her shoulders. He hit the transmit button again. "No big deal, Scotty, just poke around out there a little bit and look for anything that just doesn't seem right. I promised Kevin we'd look around for him."

"Ten-four," came the reply.

"Cooper out." Chet put the car in gear and pulled out into the lazy afternoon traffic of Main Street. "Do you want me to take you straight to the junior high then?"

"That would be just fine," she said, smoothing the hem of her dress around her knees.

It wasn't far to drive and within minutes he was pulling the car into the small parking lot in front of Jefferson Junior High School. A marquee in front of the red brick, one-story building read, *The Panthers*. After opening her door, Chet started walking with Kate up the concrete walkway that led to the front doors of the school. A white flagpole jutted out of a small flower bed in front of the doors, an American flag stirred slightly in an almost non-existent breeze.

123

"That's awful sweet of you, Sheriff," Kate said, accentuating her Southern drawl. "But you don't have to walk lil' ole' me all the way to the doors." She batted her eyelashes at him and laughed.

He blushed a little. "Well, ma'am," he replied, trying to mimic her accent, "I'm actually here on a little business of my own."

"Hmmm, not bad. We could almost pass you off as a good ole' boy with just a little practice."

She laughed, and so did he. Her smile was radiant in the afternoon sun and he had to fight the urge to grab a hold of her right there, wrap her in his arms, and press her close.

Once inside the building, they parted ways with a quick squeeze of hands and a simple, *see ya later.* Kate made her way to Mrs. Rockwood's office and Chet headed to Principal Porter's office, across the hall.

The door was open and he could see that Mr. Porter was at his desk shuffling through a stack of papers. He knocked softly on the open door while simultaneously clearing his throat.

Joshua Porter looked up from his task, a heavy pair of black framed glasses perched on the end of his bulbous nose. "Chet Cooper." He didn't seem too surprised. "Come in, young man. Have a seat."

The office was typical: a small rectangular room, a wooden desk at the back, filing cabinets to the right of the desk, and to the left, a large, utilitarian bookcase containing various mismatched volumes. On the wall behind Mr. Porter, framed pictures of his family hung next to a mixture of diplomas and certificates of education. A putting iron lay upright in a corner, a dimpled golf ball resting on the floor next to it.

Chet smiled and gestured to the golf club as he sat down in a chair opposite the desk. "Still at it, Mr. Porter?"

The principal chuckled and wiped a stubby hand over his shiny, bald head. "Unfortunately, yes I am. If anything, my game has worsened over the years, but I don't care anymore. There's just something about getting out there on those greens that keeps me coming back." He smiled as he pushed his glasses back up onto the bridge of his nose.

Joshua Porter was not blessed with the build to be a great golfer: short, thick limbs, and a stout middle, the quintessential fireplug.

"As long as you're enjoying yourself out there," Chet replied, "that's all that counts."

"Exactly!" Mr. Porter stabbed a finger through the air in Chet's direction. "Let's see," he said suddenly, interlacing his fingers and resting his hands on the desk, "the last time you sat in that chair must have been a good fourteen, maybe fifteen, years ago, I'm guessing."

"That'd be about right, sir."

"I seem to recall you were in trouble for punching out Dusty Finch. If I'm not mistaken, you even knocked out his tooth."

"Right again. You really threw the book at me too, if I recall."

Mr. Porter leaned across his desk, his face taking on a conspiratorial expression. "For the record," he whispered, "I was glad you did it. That bully had it coming if you ask me, and more! I hope you know, the punishment was nothing personal."

Chet waved a hand. "It's long forgotten, sir. And I'm sure I deserved it too."

"Well, you turned out all right."

"Thank you, I like to think so."

Mr. Porter's face took on a more serious expression. He removed his glasses and placed them on the desk in front of him. "Well, Sheriff, I take it this is more than a social call."

Chet nodded.

"The Pritchard boy?"

"How well did you know him, Mr. Porter?" Chet inquired.

"I can't say I knew him all that well."

"What kind of kid was he? Was he a good student?"

"Humph." The man shook his head. "He spent plenty of time in that chair your sitting in, if that's what you mean."

"I see. So, he was a troublemaker?"

"Sheriff, over the years I've dealt with a hundred kids just like him." He closed his eyes as if recalling every one of them. "Rich, spoiled, cocky…too big for their britches. They think they've got the world by the tail and Mom and Dad are usually all but checked out."

Chet nodded in silence. Mr. Porter's description was no surprise. "Sir, considering what you knew of Robbie Pritchard, from your dealings with him, would you think of him as one to commit suicide?"

Mr. Porter shook his head, his jowls quivering. "Honestly, not at all. I'm actually quite shocked."

Chet nodded and squared his shoulders. "Did Robbie have any enemies?"

The man's eyes grew wide.

"Routine question," Chet diffused quickly. "I have to ask."

"Kids like Robbie don't have as many friends as they think they do, son. But, they're so wrapped up in their own narcissistic world that they can't see beyond the small, inclusive crowd of sycophants they've surrounded themselves with. For every kid that thinks Robbie walked on water, there's twenty more who are glad he's gone."

Chet nodded. "Nobody stands out in particular?"

A quizzical expression formed on Mr. Porter's face. "I'm not sure what you're getting at here, Sheriff. Are you suggesting that a fellow student may have had something to do with Robbie's death? Because if that's what you're asking me, my answer is: absolutely not!"

Chet rubbed the back of his neck with one hand. "I'm not suggesting anything. By the looks of it, Robbie got drunk and drove his car into the quarry, either on purpose or on accident. You admitted yourself that suicide seems very unlikely. I feel the same way, so I'm just asking some routine questions to try to get a better grip on what happened."

The old principal rubbed his chin with one hand as if weighing Chet's words. "I understand what you're saying, but my answer is the same as before. There's a lot of kids in this school who will not miss Robbie Pritchard, but nobody stands out to me as what I would label an enemy."

"Fair enough," Chet said. "I have a list of some of his closest friends here." He pulled the folded paper from his shirt pocket that Orrin Pritchard had provided him earlier that day. "Would it be alright if I pulled some of these kids from class for a few minutes and asked them some questions?"

Mr. Porter put his glasses back on and blinked deliberately a few times. "I don't see where that would be a problem. You can even use my office if you'd like. I have some errands to run anyway. Mrs. Rockwood across the hall can help you with wrangling up those kids on your list."

"Much appreciated," Chet said. "Would it be okay if I talked to Coach Erickson as well? Maybe he has some insight."

"Certainly." Mr. Porter rose from his chair and walked around the desk. "You know, despite whatever Robbie's negative qualities, he was still just a kid with his whole life ahead of him. It's a horrible tragedy and I hope you find out whatever it is you're looking for."

"So do I," Chet said, coming to his feet.

He followed Mr. Porter across the hall to Mrs. Rockwood's office, who happened to be sitting in a chair next to Kate, showing her the attendance book. At first, the women didn't notice the two men that had appeared in the doorway. Mrs. Rockwood had the stern look of a woman who had spent her entire career dealing with rowdy adolescents. Her graying hair was pulled up into a tight bun and a pair of horn-rimmed glasses magnified her pale-blue eyes. Dressed conservatively, in a gray dress with a white sweater, she looked all business.

Chet was able to catch a candid glimpse of Kate, her brow slightly furrowed as she concentrated on Mrs. Rockwood's instructions. Dark ringlets of her hair played on her smooth cheeks as she gnawed absently on a pencil eraser. When Mr. Porter stepped all the way into the office, she looked up and flashed Chet a quick, discreet smile that made little bolts of electric excitement shoot from his heart and into his extremities.

Mr. Porter left instructions for Mrs. Rockwood and excused himself. Ten minutes later, Chet was seated in Mr. Porter's chair. Across the desk from him was Cynthia Harris: young, pretty and a sobbing wreck.

WHAT A WASTE OF TIME, Scotty thought, as he pulled his patrol car onto the narrow dirt lane that would take him to the woods that bordered the Baxter farm. *Oh well, I get paid by the hour.*

He had just talked to the Baxters a few minutes ago. They were both shocked to hear that their son had reported seeing Levi Henderson in the woods. Kevin hadn't mentioned anything about it to them, but Marley had said that it seemed to explain the boy's strange behavior recently.

Before long, the trees of the forest were looming up ahead, nearly half of their branches gray and barren. Dead, brown leaves fluttered sporadically to the ground, spinning and flipping through the air as if controlled by some unknown force. He shut off his car and got out, his boots crunching on the autumn foliage. It was dead quiet. An ominous feeling squirmed in his breast.

The edge of the forest seemed almost like a wall, as if the trees had clustered together in a conscious effort to keep unwanted visitors out. His right hand instinctively came to rest on the butt of his service pistol, from which he was able to draw a small measure of courage. He shook his head and allowed a short, unconvincing laugh to escape his lips before taking five deliberate steps that carried him into the foreboding forest.

"Just poke around a little," Chet had said. *"Look for anything that doesn't seem right."* At the moment, nothing seemed right. As he entered the woods, there was the eerie sensation he had just stepped through a dark veil and into another world. It was too quiet, too still, and even the colors seemed off somehow. It felt like the trees were closing in, their contorted branches reaching out for him. He pulled up the collar of his jacket to ward off a chill that had

suddenly crept up on him. He scanned the forest in every direction as he made his way in deeper, step by step.

He had been walking for at least fifteen minutes when the hairs on the back of his neck suddenly stood on end. Someone was behind him! His revolver flashed out as he turned. There was nothing there. The pistol quivered slightly in his hand. He stared, expecting something might materialize in front of him at any second. A small chipmunk scurried up a nearby tree, the scratching of its tiny claws on the rough bark unnaturally loud, out of place. He cursed at his jumpiness and slid his gun back into its holster, but left his hand on the grip.

That's enough of this crap! Coop wanted me to check it out, I checked it out. I've got better things to do, he thought, taking several steps back in the direction of his car, eager to be free of the woods.

A twig snapped behind him.

He froze in mid-stride, too afraid to look back. He strained his ears, listening, his fingers becoming slippery with sweat on the grip of his gun. The only sound was the continuous *tap, tap* of the falling leaves as they came to rest on the forest floor around him. He tried to swallow, but his throat had suddenly gone dry.

Slowly, he began to turn around while sliding his gun from the holster. His eyes darted back and forth, from tree to tree, searching for any movement. He thought he detected a brief, shadowy movement behind a scraggy bush.

"Is anybody there?" he called out, his voice cracking.

Silence.

Then he thought he heard a strange sound, alien to his wooded surroundings. The faint whimper of a child?

"Hello?" he called out. It took all the willpower he had to restrain himself from dashing madly back to his car.

In front of him, a small wind began to stir some of the dead leaves on the ground, causing them to tumble and slither like snakes toward him. The small wind became a sudden gust, and a swirling torrent of brown leaves leaped into the air to claw and scratch at him. He threw his forearm up to shield his eyes from the sudden onslaught. Then, just as quickly as it had begun, the wind stopped, leaving Scotty speckled in leaves and dirt, his arm still extended in front of his face.

He wiped his arm across his eyes to clean away some of the dirt. That's when he heard a garbled, choking sound right in front of him. He lowered his forearm and there was Levi Henderson, or some semblance of him, standing a dozen feet in front of him.

The boy was looking right at him, but somehow right through him at the same time. His flat, dark eyes were sunken into the hollows of their sockets with bloodshot vessels sprawled across the sickly, yellow whites, like thin spiderwebs. His skin was as pale as death itself, save for the angry, yellow and purple bruising that covered most of his throat and neck. There were several deep gashes in his skin—curiously not bleeding. Leaves and twigs covered his body and were tangled and matted in his brown hair. The putrid stench of decomposition hung thick in the air. The garbled, choking sound was coming from Levi as he worked his mouth, attempting to say something.

First, Scotty gasped in horror. Then he gagged as the odor of rotting flesh assailed him. By pure instinct, he brought his pistol to bear in a two-handed grip, placing the front site square in the center of Levi's chest and took two unsteady steps backward. His mind was whirring a million miles an hour struggling to comprehend the situation. This wasn't Levi Henderson. This was some kind of monster!

He took another step back, but as he did, Levi took a wavering step forward, his lips still mouthing silent words.

"Stay back!" Scotty yelled, gesturing with his pistol.

Levi took another step, his whole body shaking like he would fall right over at any moment.

"Stay back or I will shoot! I mean it kid!" He stepped back again, but caught his heel on a log. He stumbled, barley regaining his balance.

Levi took two quick and sudden steps, and then two more. He closed half the distance much faster than should have been possible.

Scotty pulled the trigger on his pistol. The Colt .38 bucked in his hands as the shot echoed irreverently off of the surrounding trees and rocks. He heard the wet thud as the slug slammed into Levi's chest. He saw Levi's shirt ripple around the dark hole where the bullet had punched through. The impact would have dropped a grown man like a sack of potatoes, but Levi was just standing there, still working his mouth in silence, seemingly unaware that he had just been shot.

On some level, Scotty wasn't surprised—he had almost expected it—but that didn't bring him any comfort at the moment. He turned and started side-stepping out of there while keeping his eyes and his muzzle trained on the un-dead boy. He was relieved when the boy didn't seem to show any intentions of following. *Turn and run! Turn and run!* A voice deep down was screaming at him.

Suddenly, Levi coughed loudly and a thick glob of black fluid bubbled down his chin to drip onto his chest.

He spoke, "You are going to die." The voice was deep and graveled with a disembodied quality to it.

Scotty felt his bones go soft as his blood turned to ice. There was no malice behind the voice, not like a threat. It seemed Levi was just speaking a matter of fact. *He was going to die.*

Beyond his breaking point, he turned his back on the gruesome specter in front of him and quickened his pace, not even bothering to holster his gun. Almost without realizing it, he broke into a run. The cold fear in his gut was evolving into a blind panic with each step—he was losing it, and fast.

Somewhere in his brain there was a rational voice trying to convince him that he was being childish, even silly for running. As the panic rose from his gut and into his chest, the voice of reason faded and before he knew it, Deputy Forks was in a dead, blind sprint.

Gasping for air he burst out of the woods, the sight of his black and white police car filling him simultaneously with relief and shame. He reached the car and grabbed the door handle, his palm wet and slippery on the cool metal. Before opening the door, he wrenched his head in the direction of the forest. The trees glowered back at him, but there was nothing in pursuit.

He holstered his gun and turned back, catching his own reflection in the window. His face was layered in a sheen of sweat, eyes wide and fearful, his mouth gaping as he sucked in giant gulps of air. The sun glinted off of the polished deputy's badge that was pinned over his thudding heart. In the reflection, the three words engraved on the badge were reversed, but he didn't need to read them to know what they said: *Pietas, Integritas, Animi.* It was Latin for: Loyalty, Integrity, Courage.

He placed both hands on the car door and leaned forward. His heart sank and he forced his gaze from the badge to his own eyes. *You're a coward.* The thought came out of nowhere surprising him, but nonetheless, deep down he knew it was true.

"All your life, acting the tough-guy, putting on a big show, wearing that uniform like you're some big-shot, and then when it all really matters you take off running like a frightened child. The whole town has been looking for Levi and what do you do when you find him? You run away!"

A tear escaped the corner of his eye to mingle with a rivulet of sweat, and run dripping from his chin.

"It's all an act and you know it. Everybody knows it! Nobody respects you, you're the joke of the town. You're not worthy of that uniform or that badge!"

130

That voice of reason, muted in the background of his mind, was wondering what was happening to him, why was he having these thoughts? But when your soul is gutted open in front of you, the truth of who and what you really are cannot be ignored. And it was all true.

Unable to withstand the accusing glare of his badge any longer, he covered it with both hands and turned away. He braced his back against the car door as a sob escaped his dry lips. He slowly sank to the ground clutching his badge, his shoulders convulsing as more sobs spilled out.

"You're worthless."

The tears were flowing freely now, as he looked up into a cold, pale sky. The sun beat down like a spotlight, exposing him, but offering no warmth.

"Why don't you take your gun and do everyone a favor?"

"No...no," he croaked, shaking his head as his right hand drew his pistol back from the security of its holster.

CHAPTER 12

Jack Crandall turned his Oldsmobile into the circular driveway of Jeppesen Funeral Home and Crematory, but didn't park at the main entrance. Instead of following the landscaped contour of the driveway, he continued on a smaller, more discreet path that took him to the rear of the spacious, single-story structure. He was returning from his lunch break and was not looking forward to the job that awaited him in the basement of the old home.

The profession he had chosen wasn't for the squeamish, and by no means did he consider himself such, but every now and then a job came along that gave him his doubts about his chosen career path. But for the most part, he figured he had made a rather shrewd business decision by choosing this particular occupation. After all, no matter how bad or good the economy was, people still tended to die on a regular basis. And dead people needed burying.

He parked his car in front of a door with cracked and peeling mint-green paint. In faded black letters, a sign on the door read: KEEP OUT. He had always been tempted to draw a skull and crossbones under the sign—his second career choice had been art. He snickered to himself. So far in his young career, he had yet to meet a mortician that didn't have a bit of a warped sense of humor. As far as he was concerned, it was requisite for the job.

He inserted his key into the deadbolt to disengage it, but found it already in the unlocked position. He cursed under his breath. Leaving the back door unlocked was a major breach in Old Man Jeppesen's policy. It ranked right up there with taking The Lord's name in vain—especially in the presence of the dead.

He was positive he had locked it before leaving for lunch. He was pretty careful about stuff like that. He couldn't afford to fall into ill favor with his boss, who also happened to be his father-in-law, not to mention from whom he planned to inherit the business someday.

The old door had a tendency to swell in the heat of the afternoon sun so he threw his shoulder against it forcing it open with a pop. A flight of concrete stairs led to the basement from which wafted a potpourri of familiar fragrances only a mortician can identify with. He daydreamed as he descended the stairs. When he took over the funeral home, how would the town accept a name change? Crandall Funeral Home, without the Crematory—he always thought that was kind of a creepy word anyway. Otherwise, it had a nice ring to it, if he did say so himself.

At the bottom of the stairs, a doorway on the right admitted him to a small prep room where he donned a heavy canvas apron, a surgical mask, and thick, black rubber gloves. He opened a cabinet containing jugs of various chemicals, washcloths, and sponges. As he sorted through the cabinet for the supplies he would be needing, he thought of the body waiting for him in the next room.

He had been present when the fire department delivered the body of Robbie Pritchard a few hours ago. What a mess! He certainly had his work cut out for him. Of course he would do his best, but he had a feeling the funeral home would be recommending a closed-casket ceremony to the Pritchard family, based on what he had seen initially.

He loaded his supplies onto a small cart and pushed it toward the washroom, where the corpse lay waiting. He paused at the doorway so he could click on the light, then pushed the cart into the room, preparing mentally for the task at hand.

As he entered he saw that the large, stainless steel basin, where he had left Robbie's disfigured body, was empty. "Huh?" he muttered, looking around the room. He stood a moment in dumbfounded silence before his mind began to conjure up possibilities. Had one of the other workers, or even the old man gotten a jump start on the job while he was at lunch? He found it hard to believe, but peeked his head inside the adjoining embalming room, where cleaned bodies awaited embalming and makeup.

Old Mrs. McMurtrey's body lay alone in the small room, right where he had left her earlier in the morning, but there was no sign of today's newest customer. Maybe the sheriff had ordered an autopsy and the body had been removed.

He checked the ready room, the final stage in makeup and finishing touches before the deceased were brought upstairs and placed in their caskets for viewing. It was empty, and a cold lump began to form in the pit of his stomach. It went against all reason that the body would be upstairs but he hiked the adjoining staircase, all the same. What else was there to do? He was going to have to go to his father-in-law with the news that he may have lost a body. He cringed at the thought.

The Summoning

COACH ERICKSON WAS THE ONLY NAME LEFT on Chet's list of people he wanted to interview. He scribbled a few notes on a pad of paper he had scrounged from Mr. Porter's desk as he waited for the junior varsity football coach to arrive. He had interviewed four of Robbie's closest friends, beginning with his girlfriend, Cynthia Harris.

The interview with Cynthia hadn't gone well. She was still in an obvious state of emotional shock, progressively sobbing harder as Chet's questions sliced into her like razors. She was also very adamant that Robbie had not taken his own life. She had insisted that Robbie loved her too much to do that to her. As far as Robbie's potential enemies? According to Cynthia, he had none. Everybody loved Robbie. He was such a great guy. As uncomfortable as Chet was in the situation, he had tried his best to be sensitive to her grief and when the short interview concluded he strongly urged her to go home for the day, which she did.

He drew a straight line through Cynthia's name on his paper. Definitely not a suspect. Eric, Bobby, and Wes seemed just as shocked as Cynthia, if not quite as distraught. Chet had seen the likes of them many times: typical, latch-on underlings, privileged to coast in the wake of Robbie's success and popularity. Fair-weather friends, only loyal to the point of self-promotion and preservation. Chet had no use for such types, but were they potential murderers? Hardly. So far, he was getting nowhere.

A rap on the door frame pulled him away from his thoughts. Coach Bill Erickson half-stepped into the room. "You wanted to see me, Chet?" His throaty, baritone voice reverberated off the walls.

"Have a seat, Bill." Chet motioned to the pair of wooden chairs opposite the desk.

Bill nodded with a quick bob of his head, took two big strides to a chair and sat down. He was thirty years old, the same age as Chet, and had lived in Clear Creek his entire life. He hadn't changed much and just hearing his voice took Chet back to the high school football games of his younger days.

For a moment, he could see himself on the line of scrimmage, ready to run his pattern. The crowd cheering wildly as his heart pounded out a prayer that he wouldn't drop the pass. And there would be Bill Erickson: six-foot-three, two hundred plus pounds, the quintessential hero quarterback. His commanding voice booming out the count with confidence, his enormous hands spread out like two catcher's mitts, awaiting the snap.

The towering athlete had gone on to play college ball, and had done pretty well from what Chet had heard. But then one day, the Japanese bombed Pearl Harbor. Like so many boys his age he enlisted, and that was the end of football for Bill Erickson.

"How's the arm these days?" Chet asked.

The coach massaged the stump of what remained of his left arm and smiled. "I think it's going to rain tonight. How's the hip?"

Chet smiled. "I think your arm's nuts. My hip says clear skies."

"Next beer's on me if it doesn't rain tonight."

"You're on."

The two men smiled at each other in silence as a feeling of genuine camaraderie passed between them. It was an understanding that could only exist between men who had mutually experienced the hell of combat—even if they had been on opposite sides of the globe.

Chet appraised the man in front of him and decided to forgo anymore smalltalk or BS. It simply wasn't necessary. "Let me get right to it," he said. "I'm trying to wrap my brain around Robbie Pritchard's death."

The coach nodded, his face turning serious.

"You're a straight shooter," Chet continued, "so, I know I can get an unbiased opinion from you."

"Sure thing, what do you need from me?" Bill asked.

Chet stood up and walked around the desk. Leaning against the edge, he folded his arms. "For the moment, I'm working on the assumption that Robbie's death wasn't a suicide." He paused, allowing his words to sink in. "As his football coach, I imagine you probably got to know Robbie pretty well. What can you tell me about him?"

Bill cleared his throat and shook his head back and forth. "He was one tough kid, I'll give him that. Motivated, talented…cocky as hell, but he could back it up too. Did you know Coach Pearce had just snatched him away from me for the varsity team?"

"Yeah, I heard about that. How was he doing on the varsity team?"

"From what I hear, he was more than holding his own. Coach Pearce had to ask him to dial things down a bit in practice. Kids were getting hurt."

"Did he get along with the team? Did the other players like him?"

"For the most part I guess. They respected him at least. He got the job done and was a big factor in the strength of the team. Off the field, I really don't know. He seemed to have friends."

"Yeah," Chet said, recollecting his recent interview with Robbie's so-called friends. "Bill, did you notice any signs or any behavior that would have indicated to you that the kid was suicidal or even depressed?"

"Not at all," the man said, with a shake of his head. "I'll never believe that kid intentionally killed himself. It had to have been an accident. But again, I'm not a professional shrink or anything."

There was a sudden knock on the door and Kate entered the office. Chet couldn't help flashing a smile at her, but the seriousness in her eyes chased it away.

"Sheriff Cooper?" She was all business. "Deputy Shelton is on the phone in the secretary's office. He says it's urgent."

"I'll be right there."

Kate nodded and ducked back out of the office.

Bill came to his feet. "Looks like duty calls, Sheriff." He extended his right hand.

"Thanks Bill, I appreciate your input," Chet said, shaking hands. "Good luck with the team this year."

"Thanks. You should try to make it to a game or two."

"Sure thing."

They entered the hallway together and Chet watched Bill walk away before stepping into Mrs. Rockwood's office. Kate was standing at the desk, clutching the black telephone receiver to her chest with both hands. "Rick sounds worried," she said, as Chet reached for the phone.

He spoke into the phone, "Rick, what's going on?"

"You're not going to believe this, Coop, but I just got a call from Phil Jeppesen, down at the funeral home." He paused, as if unsure of what he was about to say.

"Yeah, and?" Chet snapped.

"Well, apparently Robbie Pritchard's body has gone missing…"

"Missing? What do you mean, *missing*?"

"I mean gone. Phil says his son-in-law came back from lunch a little while ago, went to clean the body, and what not…and it's gone. Says they've looked all over the place and can't find it anywhere."

Anger flared inside Chet at the pure absurdity of it all. "They can't find it anywhere? For hell's sakes, it's not like he misplaced his reading glasses. We're talking about a damn two hundred pound corpse!"

He remembered he was't alone. He looked up at Kate. Her eyes were wide and brimming, her lips parted in a silent question. Mrs. Rockwood was scowling at him.

"Sorry about the language," he apologized, then turned his back to the women and spoke in a loud whisper, "Alright, Rick, see if you can get a hold of Scotty and have him meet me down at Jeppesen's right away. Call Phil back and let him know I'll be there in a few minutes. And not a word about this to anyone for right now."

"Roger that."

He handed the phone back to Kate and saw that both women were still staring at him, obviously not sure what to say.

Finally, Kate asked, "Is everything alright?"

He inhaled and let the air out slowly before speaking, "I really can't talk about it. And I'm going to need you ladies to pretend like you didn't just hear that conversation."

"Of course," Kate said, her emerald eyes glimmering with curiosity.

Mrs. Rockwood pushed her glasses up onto the bridge of her nose and simply nodded.

Satisfied, he turned to leave. "Okay, I'll let you two get back to work then."

"Good luck, Sheriff," Kate said, "with…whatever it is you've gotta do."

"Thanks," Chet said, as he left the office, "I could use all the luck I can get these days."

CHAPTER 13

"T hat's right, now put the gun to your head."
That voice that was his, but somehow not, rasped in his brain. On some level of consciousness Scotty was surprised at how easily he was able to put the cold, hard barrel to his temple and cock the hammer back.

"Pull the trigger. End your miserable existence, you fraud."

He hesitated, his finger poised. Ten pounds of pressure on the trigger was the only thing separating him from now and eternity.

"Do it!"

Hyperventilating through clenched teeth, he squeezed his eyes shut, forcing more hot tears down his cheeks, and began to slowly pull the slack out of the trigger.

"Deputy Forks come in." The sound of Rick Shelton's voice modulating over the police radio in his car, was like a saving slap to the face, awakening him from a nightmare. It really had seemed like he had been in the fog of a dream, a fog that had suddenly fled, taking that awful voice with it. In horror, he realized he was still holding the gun to his head. He threw the pistol into the dirt, repulsed by what he had almost done.

"Shelton to Forks. Do you read?"

He dug the heels of his hands into his swollen eyes, smearing away the tear stains as he struggled to his feet. When he stood up, a wave of nausea slammed him to his hands and knees. He threw up, purging the entire contents of his stomach in one powerful, violent heave. Exhausted, his arms gave out and he rolled onto his back.

He was looking down a long, black tunnel that was quickly closing in. His ears buzzed and his extremities felt numb. Rick's voice crackled over the radio again, but it sounded far away and he couldn't make out what he was saying.

The black tunnel closed and Deputy Forks knew no more.

IT TOOK FIVE MINUTES for Chet to make the drive across town to the funeral home. Phil Jeppesen, owner and founder, was pacing back and forth in front of the main entrance, sucking the last drags from a stubby cigarette.

Phil was in his early sixties, a lifelong resident, and a member of the city council for as long as Chet could remember. The funeral business had been good to Phil. It had earned him a nice home, a couple of cars, college educations for all three of his children, influence in the town, and a great deal of respect. He was shorter than average, slightly on the rotund side, and had a full head of iron-gray hair that he wore combed straight back. He was wearing black suit pants, minus the jacket, with a white shirt and conservative, blue tie. A pair of black suspenders dangled, unslung, from his waistband.

Phil nearly trotted around the police car to the driver's side door as Chet pulled into the circular driveway.

"Sheriff, Sheriff…" he said, his eyes blinking rapidly.

"Phil," Chet greeted, as he stepped out of the car, paying mind not to hit the man with his door.

Phil backed out of the way, running one hand through his hair. "This is just awful." His jowls were trembling and his face was flushed a bright crimson. "Thirty-seven years I've been in business and I never!" He threw his cigarette butt to the ground and stamped on it as if it were a cockroach.

Chet made a small lowering motion with his hands. "Alright, Phil, let's calm down a bit and see if we can figure out what's going on here."

"There's nothing to figure, Sheriff! Somebody stole a body out of my funeral home, plain and simple!" The man's deep-set eyes were little pools of blue fire.

"Robbie Pritchard's body?"

"Yes, the Pritchard boy."

"And you're positive the body is not somewhere in your building?"

"Of course I'm positive! I wouldn't have called you if I wasn't!" He reached into his pants pocket and pulled out a small, brown, leather case. He opened it and took out another cigarette, then offered one to the lawman.

Chet declined with a shake of his head and waited while Phil lit up with a little gold-colored, metal lighter—probably real gold.

"Let's start from the top," Chet said. "Who was the last person to see the body before it…went missing?"

"Before it was stolen?" Phil corrected, then exhaled a cloud of white tobacco smoke.

"We'll see," Chet countered.

The Summoning

Phil led him through the front doors and into the interior of the funeral home. Chet had no love for the place. He was sure that to most people it was nice-looking and tastefully decorated, but to him it was a vault of bad memories. This was where Dad's funeral had been after he had lost his struggle with cancer.

Everything still looked the same as it had that cold winter day, from the plush burgundy carpeting and dark green draperies to the sickeningly sweet fragrance emanating from the various floral arrangements strategically placed throughout the building. As nice as it all seemed on the surface, every now and then, a hint of stringent or some other chemical would permeate the strong floral fragrance, lacing it with the small reminder of the building's primary occupants: the dead.

Phil was in no mood to conduct a tour of the building, for which Chet was grateful. It was bad enough whisking past the viewing room and the small chapel where memories came stabbing like icy daggers into his brain: Mother and his little sister, Connie, in black dresses dabbing at unbridled tears with white handkerchiefs, sitting in chairs next to the casket. He stood next to his mother, the new man of the house at sixteen years of age. In a daze, he shook hands with people he barely recognized or not at all. "At least he's gone to a better place," they would say. Or, "He looks so peaceful. They really did a great job with him." But to Chet he just looked dead.

"The workrooms are downstairs." Phil's voice fractured the dark vision as he rounded a corner and led him down a small hallway and past the bathrooms. The hallway ended with a polished wooden door. A bright red sign was affixed to it and in bold, black letters read: EMPLOYEES ONLY. Phil opened the door to reveal a plain, wooden staircase leading down to the basement.

The familiar chemical odor that had been slightly detectable before was strong now and Chet hesitated a moment before following Phil down. He felt foolish, almost childish, but it *was* a basement full of corpses after all.

At the bottom of the stairs, they walked past a casket—empty, thank heavens —and into an adjoining room. But his luck wasn't meant to last. Jack Crandall, Phil's son-in-law and heir apparent to the business, was bent over another casket —occupied this time—applying some kind of flesh-colored makeup to the ashen face of the recently deceased, Mrs. McMurtrey, with a small, triangular-shaped sponge.

"Sheriff's here," Phil announced as he and his reluctant guest piled into the small room.

Jack looked up from his work. Chet noted the droop in the usually cheerful countenance of the mortician. In his early twenties, Jack was slightly heavy-set —but not unhealthy looking—with broad shoulders, a thick neck, and a square, solid jaw. He had expressive brown eyes, lined prematurely at the corners—from smiling all the time, Chet supposed. He wasn't smiling now as he shot a glance at Phil, avoiding direct eye contact, and nodded a greeting to the sheriff.

Chet felt sorry for Jack. He could only imagine the butt chewing he must have received recently from his perturbed father-in-law. There was a definite tension in the room. Everyone was on edge—except for Mrs. McMurtrey, of course. She actually did look kind of peaceful at the moment. He almost grinned at the irony of it, but it was time to get down to business.

"So you were the last one to see Robbie Pritchard's body?" he queried.

Jack started to nod.

"Of course he was," Phil blurted, "it was his job to prepare the body!"

Chet placed a firm hand on the older man's shoulder and took a step placing himself between the two. He looked Jack in the eyes. "Starting from the beginning tell me what happened."

Under his father-in-law's penetrating glare, Jack recounted the tale. He told how the fire department had delivered the body to the home that morning, how he had left it in the washbasin and gone for his lunch break, and how he had returned an hour later to find the body gone.

"And you say you're sure you locked the back door when you left for lunch?" Chet asked.

"I'm sure I did," Jack said. "It's a habit. I never leave it unlocked, I swear!" He seemed to be talking to Phil more than than he was to Chet.

Phil snorted.

Chet held up a hand. "And the deadbolt was unlocked when you got back?"

"Yes."

"Alright, let's go have a look. I want to see the washbasin and backdoor."

The two men led him through a door and into a medium-sized, square room with what looked like a shallow, stainless steel bathtub mounted on a waist-high pedestal in the center of the room. A hose, with a nozzle attached, hung over the side of the tub.

"This is where I left him," Jack said, pointing to the tub.

Chet walked around the tub, peering at it from all angles.

"It's a washtub," Phil said. "What are you hoping to find?"

"I'm not sure, but I'll let you know when I find it." He continued his inspection without so much as sparing a sideways glance at Phil. "Where's the back door?"

Jack led the way into another room and through yet another door. He flicked on a switch. A single bulb hanging from a bare fixture flickered, casting its dim light on the flight of stairs that led up to the back door.

Chet climbed the stairs, Phil and Jack tramping close behind. He inspected the door and the frame for signs of forced entry: pry marks, splinters of wood, and damage to the deadbolt. He worked the bolt back and forth, as well as the doorknob. He opened the door and checked the hinges. "I can't find any sign that somebody forced their way in."

"It had to have been left unlocked," Phil said.

Jack hung his head and slowly shook it side to side.

"Or," Chet said, "someone used a key. Who all has keys to this door, Phil?"

Phil put his hands on his hips and stared up at the ceiling. "Well, there's myself and Jack, of course." He pursed his lips and furrowed his brow.

"Anyone else?"

"I really don't think so."

Chet turned to Jack. "Do you have your key on you right now?"

Jack fumbled in his pocket for a moment and pulled out a small key ring with a half-dozen brass and silver-colored keys jangling together. "There it is," he said, singling one of the keys out with his thumb and forefinger, allowing the rest to fall and hang from the ring.

Chet turned to Phil. "What about yours?"

Just as Jack had done, the older man pawed around in his pocket and produced his key ring, which contained about twice the amount of keys as Jack's did, as well as a lucky rabbit's foot. He fingered through the keys once, then twice, and then a third time. "I know it's on here," he mumbled, bringing the keys closer to his eyes.

Jack reached for the keyring. "Lemme see."

Phil relinquished the keys. "You've got better eyes than me."

Jack scrutinized each key, sliding them, one by one, along the ring. "It's not here," he said, going through the keys again. "Are you sure it's on this ring?"

"Yes, I'm sure!" Phil exclaimed, snatching the keys out of Jack's hand. "I haven't had that key off this ring since the day I put it on. It's been years!" His search became more frantic, the keys clanging together loudly as his fingers plowed through them. "It really isn't here!"

His angry, red face drained instantly. He looked more like one of his own clients rather than the owner of the funeral home. "B-but who?" he stammered. "Why? Why would someone steal a body?" He looked back and forth between

Chet and his now vindicated son-in-law, neither of whom had an answer for him. "Dear Heavens! What am I going to tell Mr. Pritchard?"

Chet winced. "I'll notify Mr. Pritchard."

"What are you going to tell him?" Phil asked, wringing his hands together.

"What can I tell him besides the truth? His son's body has been taken by someone."

Chet stepped outside into the bright afternoon sun and turned back to the two men standing on the stairs. "I'm going to have a look around the outside of the building and then head back to my office so I can get a proper investigation going. In the meantime, I suggest you get the lock on this door changed right away."

Phil didn't respond. He was holding his key chain in the palm of his hand, staring at it like it was an alien from another planet.

"We will, Sheriff Cooper," Jack said. "Thank you."

Chet spun on his heel to leave. "If you think of anything, and I mean anything, you get a hold of me right away."

Jack nodded. "Yes sir."

"Deputy Forks should be here soon to take an official report." Where was Scotty anyway? He should have been here by now.

Chet pulled the door shut and heard one of the men on the other side instantly engage the deadbolt. He stepped back a dozen steps and took in the whole building, hoping that a clue would reveal itself to him.

Why would somebody want the body? Maybe Robbie really was murdered after all. Maybe the killer got nervous, thought there could be some kind of evidence on the body that would point to him. He'd have to be one audacious bastard to sneak into an occupied building in the middle of the day and snatch a corpse from the basement. A part of him just didn't want to believe it, but here he was.

He took his time walking around the building to his car, but nothing in particular jumped out at him. "Where is that dang kid?" He muttered out loud as he reached his car. He ripped the radio mic from its hook on the dashboard. "Deputy Forks, this is Cooper. Copy?"

Nothing.

"Deputy Forks, come in."

There was a brief squelch break. "Coop, it's Rick, I haven't been able to reach Scotty. He won't answer his radio."

"Roger that. Keep trying him. I need him to come to Jeppesen's and take a report for me. I'm on my way back right now."

"Ten-four. See you in a few."

Five minutes later, Chet opened the door to the office, walked over to his desk, and fell into his chair.

Rick got up from his desk and walked over, a cup of coffee in his hand, and sat down in a vacant chair next to Chet's desk. "That bad huh?"

Chet massaged his temples with his fingers. "Someone stole a key from Phil Jeppesen's key chain and, while Jack Crandall was out to lunch, used it to get into the basement and take Robbie's body."

"For real?" Rick's eyes grew wide.

Chet nodded. "Yup. That's the looks of it anyway."

Rick let out a low whistle. "It don't make sense. Why in the world—"

"Rick, he was murdered," Chet said. "My gut's been trying to tell me all along and this just confirms it. The killer must be afraid there's evidence on the body."

The deputy was shaking his head back and forth. "Coop, murder in Clear Creek? There's got to be an explanation."

"We've got footprints at the quarry that indicate the car was pushed." Chet counted off on his fingers. "Skid marks that point at someone trying to stop at the last second. A half-dozen acquaintances who all swear that Robbie was not suicidal, and now a missing…make that, *stolen* corpse."

Rick nodded slightly, looking down at his feet, allowing the reality to sink in.

"And my guess is," Chet continued, "if we keep digging, we'll find more."

Both men contemplated things in silence for a minute, before Rick asked, "Does Orrin Pritchard know?"

"Not yet," Chet said. "It's the next thing on my list."

"So, you gonna make it official then? Open up a murder investigation?"

"I'd say there's plenty of evidence to warrant it, don't you?"

Rick sipped from his coffee and tapped his index finger on the side of the cup. "As circumstantial as it is…yeah, I'd say you've got enough to validate an investigation. But, I'm thinkin' it might not be the best move."

"Alright, I'm listening." Chet stood up and walked over to the coffee percolator to pour himself a cup.

Rick turned sideways in his chair. "Well, if we actually got us a killer on our hands then he sure does have a set of brass balls, stealing a body in broad daylight and all. Someone that cocky's bound to screw up somewhere. But you launch a murder investigation, all official, with articles in the paper and everything…might scare him. Send him underground, if you know what I mean."

He weighed his deputy's words carefully in his mind. He trusted the older man and put a lot of stock in his advice.

"You're probably right, but I don't think we'd be able to keep this under our hats. Especially once Orrin hears that Robbie's body was stolen. He's not going to keep quiet about it. It just can't be covered up. It's too big."

For a moment, he could see Robbie's mutilated body in his mind, spilling out of the crushed car, flies crawling on his blood-smeared face. "And underground or aboveground, or wherever, we're going to find him. He will face justice if it takes me the rest of my career."

Rick nodded, a knowing smile curving his mouth. "That's a big ten-four, Sheriff."

"How long since you tried for Scotty on the radio?" Chet asked.

"Just before you came in," Rick said. "I'll try him again." He started to stand.

"I got it," Chet said, crossing the room to the base radio unit that sat on Rick's desk. Then the phone on his own desk began to ring.

"And I guess I got this," Rick said with a grin. He answered the phone. "Sheriff's office, Deputy Shelton here."

Chet clicked the transmit button on the base radio. "Forks this is Cooper do you copy?"

There was no answer, just the occasional pop or squeal of static.

"Deputy Forks this is Sheriff Cooper, do you copy me, Scotty?" Chet slapped the desk with his palm. "Where the hell is he? He knows better than this!"

Rick hung up the phone, his eyes grave with concern.

"Now what?" Chet barked. *This day just keeps getting better!*

"That was the hospital," Rick said. "Ambulance just brought Scotty in. They say he's unconscious and barely breathing."

CHAPTER 14

Robbie's half-naked body hit the ground with a solid thud, the swollen, misshapen head colliding hard on one of the exposed roots of the ancient, fire-damaged tree. Daniel bent over and rested his hands on his knees, chugging giant lungfuls of air, while tendrils of sweat coursed down his face. He looked at the stiff arms and legs of the heavy corpse, a dreadful feeling roiling up inside him. He had murdered again.

At least this time his victim had deserved it! Still, a part of him was horrified at what he had done. He wanted to cry out, plead for God to forgive him, let him go back and wipe the slate clean, somehow. It was too late for that. God would never forgive him now.

"What god?"

It was her! He was getting better at separating his own thoughts and distinguishing them from her voice.

"The god who abandoned you? The god who refused to hear your prayers? The god that didn't mind that you were an outcast? You really think you need His forgiveness?"

Her presence was stronger now. She had transcended beyond just a whisper of a thought in his mind. He could smell her lilac aroma ever so faintly. His heart fluttered with excitement. The feeling of dread dissipated. She was what mattered…to please her, to serve her.

"I want to see you again," he imparted with his mind. *"Please."*

Silence.

He straightened and surveyed his surroundings hoping to see her, only to be disappointed. The forest in this area seemed devoid of life. The trees were dark skeletons, their dead leaves covering the forest floor in a depressing medley of flat browns, dull reds, and pale yellows.

His disappointment began to kindle into anger. He had just bent over backwards for her. Stealing Robbie Pritchard's body from the funeral home and lugging it through the forest had been no easy task. The cunning and outright brute strength required to pull it off was nothing short of extraordinary. Sneaking into the the old funeral director's home last night and stealing his key right off the key ring had taken him all night!

Then, there was playing sick this morning so his mother would let him stay home. He had waited a couple hours and then told her he was feeling better. She let him take the old pickup into town so he could finish the rest of his classes for the day. But, instead of going to the school he waited for the mortician to go to lunch.

Parked down a side street, he had watched and waited in his family's truck. When the mortician had left, he drove the truck right up to the back door of the funeral home. He used the stolen key to unlock the door, removed the body, and threw it under an old canvas tarp in the bed of the pickup.

There was the risky drive out to the edge of the forest with a murder victim in the back of his pickup, and then the even riskier hike out to this tree with the body slung over his shoulders. Surely, after all he had done, the least she could do was show herself, even if only for a minute or two. Had he not earned that much?

Trying not to let the frustration build, he scooped up an armload of leaves and dead twigs, scattering them over the body. It was highly unlikely anyone would ever come here but it was better to be safe than sorry.

He looked at the now unoccupied spot at the base of the tree, where he had originally hidden little Levi Henderson's body. He was still trying to get used to the idea of catching the occasional glimpse of the kid limping and shuffling through the woods. Sometimes the hair on the back of his neck would stand on end and he would turn around to see the dead boy standing at a distance, glaring at him. A shiver trickled along his spine—a small part of the old Daniel still left in him, he supposed.

He knew there was no need to fear. Levi was under her power now. But when he looked into those glassy eyes it seemed there was still a vestige of him remaining, somehow trapped between the worlds of the living and the dead. He could feel the hate and the anger radiating from him. Not that he could blame him.

Daniel wasn't sure what purpose it all served. It really wasn't for him to question her will and her purposes. He was content to serve her for now. With each kill his power had increased, and she had promised it would continue to do so. But where did it all end? He had no idea. He hadn't put much thought into it. On some level he may have fantasized about being with her in the end somehow. But the present was going to have to suffice for the time being.

He threw another pile of debris onto Robbie's body. Black dirt cascaded down the face into the half-opened eyes, mouth, and nostrils. He looked into those puffy, lifeless eyes for a moment.

"So, are you going to get up and start walking around too?"

The corpse didn't answer, but seemed to be looking back at him. He took that as a yes.

It was time to get going, he still needed to make an appearance at school. He wondered how things were going there. What were people saying about Robbie's death? Wait until they hear the body is missing! He couldn't help chuckling to himself as he turned to go. *Idiots.*

And there she was, standing—more like floating—several paces from him, even more beautiful than before. She was clothed in the same milky-white, satin robe that clung to her enticing curves, in just the right places, in just the right ways. He choked on his breath in awe, and fell to his knees before her. She was a goddess, of that he was sure.

She smiled and he felt all of his previous anger and frustration melt away. She closed the distance between them, her walk alone a seduction, accentuating her feminine figure. And though she was walking, Daniel definitely took note that her naked feet didn't seem to touch the ground or disturb the leaves.

The familiar and tantalizing scent of the lilac blossoms came rushing like an assault on his senses. He closed his eyes, tilted his face to the sky, and inhaled deeply of the intoxicating fragrance. He could still detect the faint odor of decay riding in the current of the aroma, but he paid it no mind.

With each one of her steps, the air around him grew colder, and he now exhaled vaporous clouds with each breath. She reached out with a long, graceful hand and placed it on the side of his cheek. He felt no physical sensation from her touch except for a slight tingle, almost like a very fast yet subtle vibration on his skin.

"You have done well," she said, her full lips never moving, but her low, soothing voice crystal clear inside his head. *"I am pleased with you, Daniel, but there is much I still require of you. I need your help."* Her crystalline, blue eyes were pleading. *"Will you still help me, Daniel?"*

"Yes." His voice was trembling as his body shivered from the cold. "Yes, I will continue to help you." What could he say to please her all the more? "I am yours to command."

That must have pleased her, because she smiled so radiantly, he thought he would melt like an ice cube left in the blazing afternoon sun. *"I never doubted you,"* she said, her lips motionless. She bent down and kissed him on the forehead.

There was that tingling sensation again. His heart was ready to burst from his chest as he watched her stand erect.

"I will make it all very worth your while, trust me." She took a step backwards.

"No!" he exclaimed, extending a supplicating hand toward her. "Please don't go yet. Stay just a little longer."

"I don't yet have the strength. That is why I need you, Daniel." She started to flicker in and out of reality, and her form became wavy like a reflection in a rippling pool of water. *"Remember I am always with you."*

"Wait!" Daniel cried. "What is your name? What should I call you?"

But it was too late. She glimmered a final time and Daniel found himself alone once again. The feeling was devastating. Ashamed of the wet tears now spilling out of his eyes, he looked over his shoulder at Robbie Pritchard's body.

Robbie was looking back at him, a mocking sneer on his face. "What a sissy mama's boy!" he said, as dark blobs of blood spilled from his mouth to run down his chin.

"You shut your mouth, or I'll kill you again!" Daniel yelled back.

The corpse lay cold and still, the eyes vacant, the mouth gaping, no sneer, no blood on the chin, just as he had left it.

He wiped the tears from his eyes and face. *What is even real anymore?*

"I am real," she echoed in his head. *"And I am always here, with you."*

He smiled, he could feel her there.

As he hiked back to the truck, a million thoughts were bouncing around inside his head: What was this all about? Who was she? Who were any of them for that matter? Where was all this heading? Why did they need him to kill? What he wondered about the most: who was next? And when?

CHAPTER 15

The Clayton County Regional Hospital was an older, two-story, no-nonsense structure consisting of two wings that joined to create an L shape. The nexus on each floor served as a nurse's station, the two wings shooting off at right angles to each other.

Dr. Clarence McConnell was waiting at the nurse's station when Chet and Rick burst in through the main entrance. "Sheriff, Deputy Shelton," he said, acknowledging them.

He was young, maybe just a few years older than Chet. He was of average height, a little thin, and had short, blond hair neatly parted down the left side of his head. He was dressed in standard doctor's garb: a white lab coat over a sky-blue, button-up shirt, a black necktie that hung to the waistband of his light-khaki trousers, and a stethoscope slung around his neck. Chet didn't know him well, but knew he had been a medic with the 101st Airborne. The young doc was plenty qualified as far as he was concerned.

Chet closed the distance to the doctor in what seemed like two giant strides, Rick nearly having to jog behind just to keep up. "Dr. McConnell, how's Scotty? What happened to him?" Chet asked, the words tumbling out on top of each other.

"We're not exactly sure what happened yet," Dr. McConnell said. "Marley Baxter found him on the edge of his farm, near the woods. He said he was lying there, right next to his car unconscious, flat on his back. He tried to revive him at first and when he didn't respond, Marley put him in his truck and drove him here as fast as he could."

Rick stepped forward. "Is he okay now, is he awake?"

Dr. McConnell looked around for a moment, and then turned and walked away, gesturing with his head for them to follow him down the corridor. He stopped and spoke in a hushed tone, "There are some things you should know about this situation."

"Okay," Chet said, "we're all ears. What's going on?"

"According to Marley, your deputy's service revolver was laying on the ground next to him. Not in the holster."

Rick folded his arms. "It could have fallen out of the holster if he collapsed."

"The hammer was cocked back." Dr. McConnell's voice was flat, his eyes flickering back and forth between the two cops.

Chet put his hands on his hips and exhaled a sigh. "Doctor, is he going to be alright?"

"That's the other thing. When they brought him in, they said he was barely breathing. When I began to examine him, I realized that he was just breathing very slowly, very deep. Almost like he was in a trance." He licked his lips and glanced around again. "I thought he was in a deep coma or under the influence of a very powerful drug of some kind. I tried to revive him. You know: patting him on the cheeks, calling his name, shining my light into his eyes…that kind of thing."

"Yeah, and?" Chet said, anxious for the doctor to get to the point.

"Well, this is where it gets even more bizarre." Dr. McConnell lowered his voice a bit more. "Deputy Forks was in the Navy, correct?"

Chet and Rick nodded together.

"My understanding was he never shipped out though, right? The war was over before he could leave stateside?"

"That's correct," Chet said. "To his everlasting shame, from the way he talks. I'm always trying to tell him he was fortunate, but he doesn't seem convinced. Where exactly are you headed with all this, Doc?"

"I'm getting to that. Sheriff, do you know what shell shock is? I'm assuming you're familiar with it."

"Yeah, I know what it is. I had to deal with it once in a while overseas. Sometimes, after heavy fighting, some of my guys weren't themselves exactly. It was different with each case. Some guys would get all jittery and nervous, while others would be just the opposite: stopped giving a crap about anything."

"Exactly, but there are even more extreme cases than that. I dealt a lot with those cases as a medic."

Chet knew what the doctor was talking about. He had seen it once on Tarawa. A Marine from another platoon who had completely lost it. He had to be held down by several of his buddies as he thrashed and screamed at the top of his lungs, *"We're all gonna die! We're all gonna die!"*

War was a strange kind of hell. Some men coped in different ways with it, while some didn't cope at all. He thought of the demons twisted deep into the fabric of his own mind, constantly clawing to get out. No matter how faintly, they were always there, tapping, scratching. So, was that his way of coping? Bury and forget? Maybe, so far so good. It had gotten him by this long, but how long could he keep the demons at bay?

"After several minutes of trying, I was able to get Deputy Forks to wake up," Dr. McConnell said. "When he did wake, he had to be restrained. He was completely out of his head, combative, in a state of panic. He displayed the exact behavior I've learned to associate with extreme combat stress."

"What in Heaven's name?" Rick scratched his head. He was looking at Chet as if Chet had the answer.

Chet didn't have an answer. He stared at his own feet, trying to put the pieces of the puzzle together, but nothing came to mind. "So, what's going on with him at the moment, Doc?" he asked.

"He's asleep for now, I had to sedate him and have the orderlies tie restraints to his wrists."

"Can we see him?"

Dr. McConnell motioned with his hand. "Yes, of course. Follow me."

They followed the doctor past a dozen rooms to the end of the hall. They stopped abruptly before the last door on the right. Dr. McConnell opened the door quietly and the three of them filed into the dimly lit hospital room.

Scotty lay flat on his back on the single bed, unconscious. He was still in his police uniform, the shirt unbuttoned, revealing his chest, slick with sweat as it rose and fell to the rhythm of his breathing. His wrists had been tied with strips of cloth to rails on either side of the bed.

"This is kind of what you'd call our...difficult patient room," the doctor whispered. "We moved him in here after we sedated him. As you can see, it's the only bed in the room. The bed has special rails on the side so we can restrain a combative person and still treat them. And the door can be locked from the outside, if need be."

Chet nodded. "When he was awake and having this episode of...shell shock, did he say anything?"

"Mostly incoherent babbling that didn't make much sense."

"Anything at all? It could be important."

"Well," Dr. McConnell rubbed his chin, the stubble of his whiskers made a scuffing sound, "he kept yelling, 'I won't do it, I won't do it, you can't make me.'"

"Do what?" Rick asked. His mouth gaped open as he waited for an answer.

Dr. McConnell shrugged his shoulders. "Your guess is as good as mine." He walked around the side of the bed and placed two fingers on the underside of Scotty's wrist. He looked at his watch, counting the pulse.

"Did he say anything else?" Chet pried, hoping to find a piece to the puzzle.

"Not really," the doctor said, peeling back one of Scotty's eyelids and shining a flashlight into it. "Oh," he said, snapping his fingers, "a couple of times he shouted out the name Levi."

At the mention of Levi's name, the skin on Chet's neck and shoulders turned to goose flesh as all the hairs stood on end.

Rick's eyes looked like they would bug right out of the sockets. "Did you say Levi?"

"That's right," Dr. McConnell said. "Isn't that the Henderson boy that went missing a couple weeks ago?"

"Yeah," Chet said. "Earlier this morning, I actually sent Scotty out there to have a look around the woods. That's where we think Levi might have wandered off." Chet decided to hold back little Kevin Baxter's report of seeing Levi in those same woods yesterday. "We haven't given up the search officially, we still check on a routine basis. You never know."

"I understand."

"So, Doctor, seein' how our young deputy here has never been in combat, any idea what coulda' brought this on?" Rick asked.

The doctor shrugged and peeled back Scotty's other eye. "I don't know. Maybe some kind of heat stroke, although it really isn't that hot. Could have been a panic attack for some reason. Physically, he checks out pretty good. Temperature, blood pressure, pulse, respirations, all within normal levels. We're just not going to know more until we have the chance to observe him some more and run a few tests."

"Alright, Doc," Chet said. "Fair enough. How long till he wakes up?"

"He should be pretty out of it for at least a couple hours."

Chet mulled over his options. "It won't do us any good sitting around here; we have plenty on our plate right now. We'll come back in two hours then, if that's okay with you."

"No problem here," Dr. McConnell replied.

Chet turned to leave the room, then added as an afterthought, "If you can help it, try keeping him conscious this time. Maybe we can get some answers out of him."

"I'll do my best, to the point of keeping him from seriously injuring himself, of course."

"Of course," Chet agreed, and walked out of the room. "See ya in a couple hours."

The doctor nodded once and continued with his examination as the heavy door clicked shut.

The two lawmen strode quickly down the hall in silence. Chet thought he could almost hear the gears in his deputy's brain spinning in a frenzy. He was sure that if he looked, he would see smoke coming out of the man's ears.

As they passed the nurse's station and turned for the exit, a middle-aged nurse working the desk called out, "Sheriff?" She came around the desk. In her hands she carried Scotty's duty belt, neatly wrapped around itself. The curved grip of Scotty's revolver jutted out of the bundle, an ominous reminder that it had been found lying out of its holster. The nurse held the belt and pistol at arm's length as if the pistol grip was the head of a venomous snake, coiled and ready to strike.

"We felt it best to confiscate this from him," she said. "Dr. McConnell put the gun back in the holster." She extended the belt to Chet. "He said to make sure to give it to you before you leave."

"Thanks," Chet said, accepting the duty belt with both hands and handing it to Rick.

As they made their way to Chet's car, Rick spoke up. "What do you make out of all that, Coop? To me, it almost sounds like Scotty got the tar scared right out of him, or something."

"Who knows?" Chet said. "I guess we're just going to have to wait till the kid wakes up and see if he can tell us what happened."

"I know, I know. But it's strange. I mean, I can see him getting all sick and collapsing with some kind of heat stroke, panic attack or whatever. But, why did he pull his gun? That's what's got me wondering. That, and that strange stuff that he was saying, Levi's name and what not. And for that matter—I"

"Deputy Shelton," Chet interrupted.

"Huh?"

"You're rambling." Chet opened his car door and motioned for Rick to get in. "Come on, I've gotta get back and make a phone call that I'm not too crazy about having to make."

"Yeah right." Rick climbed into the passenger side.

Chet started up the engine and put the car in gear. "In a couple of hours we can ask Scotty himself what the devil happened to him, okay?"

"Sure thing, Coop. Whatever you say, you're the sheriff."

Chet shot him a sideways glance as he pulled out into the street.

"So," Rick said, "since you don't wanna talk about Scotty, how'd things go earlier with you and that pretty, little Miss Kate?"

Chet tightened his grip on the wheel while Rick flashed a toothy grin.

KATE WAS DOING HER BEST TO LISTEN to Mrs. Rockwood's instructions as the veteran secretary droned on and on about Principal Porter's weekly itinerary and meeting schedule. The problem was, she couldn't shake thoughts of Chet out of her mind enough to make room for Principal Porter's schedule. What was going on? She was dying to know. It sounded like a dead body was missing from the funeral home! Chet had sure seemed worked up over it when he left.

Would it be right to ask him about it later? As if he would tell her anything anyway. Maybe tonight she would ask Mable for use of her kitchen. She might bake some cookies and take them down to Chet's office. There's nothing quite like a bit of warm food in a man's belly to get him to open up. A little something a girl learns growing up in a family of all brothers.

What kind of a cookie man was Sheriff Cooper? Chocolate chip? Oatmeal and raisins? It was a crucial decision. Chocolate chip was probably the safer bet. She hadn't met a man yet who didn't like chocolate chip cookies. Of course there were always brownies, or a pie, or even a cake.

"Do you understand everything about Mr. Porter's schedule then?" Mrs. Rockwood asked, peering at Kate through her round glasses.

"Um, I think so," Kate lied, realizing she hadn't heard a word in probably the last five minutes.

"Excellent. Why don't you work the desk here for a while. I'm going to step out for a few minutes. Do you think you can handle that?"

"I'm sure I'll be just fine."

The older woman rose from her chair. "Good."

Kate beamed her best smile as Mrs. Rockwood left the room. Kate rolled her eyes. *You're a school secretary lady, It's not like you sit here splitting atoms all day long.* She decided that she'd had enough for one day. As soon as Mrs. Rockwood returned from her errand, it was going to be time to get back to her real job at the elementary school.

Someone in the doorway cleared their throat.

She looked up to see a boy, obviously a student, entering the office and approaching her desk. He was of average height and build for a young teenage

155

boy. He had a handsome face, but his skin was too pale, especially for the end of summer. His eyes were sunken in with dark circles under them, the irises nearly black. His dark-brown hair seemed unwashed and was combed straight forward, the bangs even with his eyebrows. He wore jeans and a plain button-up shirt. The shirt seemed dirty and stained with sweat.

She noted that his gait contained the confidence of a grown man, not that of a boy as he neared. And his smile didn't seem to match his face, it was too bright, too charming, like it had been pasted on.

"Well, I don't recognize you," he said, his tone friendly, even flirtatious. "Are you new here?"

"Yes, I am." Kate wanted to squirm under his penetrating stare, like an ant trapped in the focused point of light of a magnifying glass. "I'm just filling in for Mrs. Rockwood for a couple of weeks. Her daughter had a baby."

"Wow, that's fantastic," he said. "How great for her, huh?" The response seemed automatic, out of touch. His eyes continued to bore into her, the way a cat stares at its prey just before the pounce. But, the smile never changed. "So, what's your name?"

"I'm Miss Farnsworth, and you are?"

"Daniel Miller." He leaned on her desk with both hands, invading her space. "So, not married?"

She rolled her chair back a few inches. This kid had confidence. "What can I do for you, Mr. Miller?"

Daniel took his hands off the desk. His pasted on smile morphed into a slight frown. It seemed more natural on him than the smile. He reached into his back pants pocket and pulled out a piece of stationery paper that was folded into a square. "I was sick this morning, but I'm feeling better now. I need to check in for the rest of my classes." He extended the paper to Kate. "My mom sent a note."

Kate reached and took a hold of the folded note, but Daniel didn't let go right away, creating an impromptu game of Tug of War. She fixed him with a stare and arched her eyebrows.

"Thank you," she said.

The cocky, hollow smile returned to the boy's face as he relinquished the note. The sooner this creepy kid was out of the office the better. She unfolded the note and quickly scanned the neat handwriting asking that Daniel be excused for illness.

"I'm glad to see you're feeling better, Daniel," she said. "I'll give this note to Mrs. Rockwood when she gets back. You can head to class."

"Thank you, Miss Farnsworth," he said, starting for the door. "It was nice to meet you."

"Likewise," Kate lied.

After Daniel walked out of the office, Kate continued to stare at the open doorway. Something was not right about that boy. She couldn't place her finger on what it was, exactly. She tapped at her lips with a pencil. There was a sadness. Yes, that was it. There was a very deep sadness about him. He was doing his best to mask it with his smile and bravado, but it was there. In fact, he was almost physically dripping with it. She could feel the heaviness of it still lingering in the room, even in his absence.

There was something besides the sadness, something else that went beyond that. She pondered for a moment longer and then sighed, shaking her head. She had too much going on to worry about it.

Where was she? *Oh yeah, cookies.* Chet was probably a chocolate chip guy she guessed, chasing away the unsettling thoughts of the strange boy named Daniel Miller.

THE HALLS WERE EMPTY, but Daniel hardly noticed as he shuffled his way to Mr. Phelps's world history class—apparently late. His mind was still swimming from his other-worldly communion in the woods. The beautiful woman, the goddess, mistress, whatever she was, had physically touched him today. Twice!

He had been sure from the beginning that she was only a spirit, that she didn't possess a physical body. But he found he was still disappointed to have it confirmed. All that mattered to him was to be with her somehow, when this— whatever this was— was finished. But, how was he to be with her if she was only a spirit of some kind? He turned a corner in the hallway that led to Mr. Phelps's classroom. He could hear the eccentric history teacher from clear down the hall, lecturing passionately about something.

The questions continued to flow into Daniel's mind. If she didn't have a body, what kind of spirit was she? Was she someone who had lived once? A ghost? Then what was she doing here? Hadn't he been taught his whole life that when you die, God judges you and you are sent to either Heaven or Hell? So, maybe she was something entirely different. Be that as it may, it didn't solve the problem of how he was going to be with her. Levi Henderson had been dead for two weeks now, and yet he seemed to have no problem walking around in the woods. That had to have something to do with it.

As he reached the door to the classroom the image of Miss Farnsworth, the pretty little substitute secretary, suddenly popped into his head. It caused him to pause, his fingers resting lightly on the doorknob. She was a very nice looking girl and young—not too old for him. She could use a lesson or two on manners though. She would behave differently if she had any idea who he was. Maybe in time she would get the chance to know.

A sensation stirred in his belly, like he had swallowed a live fish and it was flopping around down there. Suddenly, he could see himself with Miss Farnsworth, alone together in some field, sitting on a blanket, perhaps under a big tree. She, the perfect combination of beauty and submissiveness—maybe even a little afraid of him. No, not afraid, just properly respectful. His belly stirred and flopped again. He imagined kissing her hard on the mouth, taking her to the ground, his body pressing down on hers. She resisting a little at first, until his hands…

He shook his head, snapping himself from the lustful daydream. He reminded himself that his thoughts were no longer his own. No doubt his mistress was aware of his recent wayward thoughts. Would she be angry with him now? He felt ashamed as he turned the doorknob and entered the classroom.

Mr. Phelps glanced at him as he shut the door, but didn't miss a beat in his lecture. Daniel walked to his assigned desk and sat down. He expected to receive some kind of harassment from the other kids over being late. Undoubtedly one of Robbie Pritchard's cronies was about to jump at the chance to get in a good dig. But surprisingly, everybody remained silent. That's right, Robbie was dead! The little minions didn't know what to do or how to act without their fearless leader.

He slowly swiveled his head back and forth, observing his fellow students. Shock and disbelief were etched on many faces. The ones who didn't appear affected were probably former victims, just as glad to be rid of Robbie as he was. He laid his arms across his desk and half buried his face in them to conceal his grin. If only the little worms knew who sat amongst them and what he was capable of doing!

It was hard not to laugh as he looked around again. *Any one of you little maggots could be next. You're all just pathetic little bugs that I could decide to squash in an instant!* He laughed inside himself and he could feel his mistress laughing with him. Maybe she wasn't angry with him. He was a man of flesh and blood after all. He allowed himself a brief indulgent thought about the pretty secretary, but kept his mind tuned into his mistress, trying to probe her thoughts and feelings. His heart skipped a beat as he realized she didn't seem upset at all. In fact, she almost seemed to approve.

For the duration of the class his mind was like a rubber ball, bouncing and careening from subject to subject, Mr. Phelps's lecture going entirely unheeded. One minute he would be thinking about the next kill, and in an instant, he would be daydreaming about the secretary. During one of these daydreams, which were becoming increasingly erotic, Miss Farnsworth's face shimmered and was suddenly replaced by the beautiful face of his mistress. Okay, maybe he had taken his daydreams too far and she was letting him know.

The bell rang, yanking him from his roller coaster thoughts. Daniel rose from his desk in unison with the other kids, but delayed long enough to let everyone get ahead of him—he had become uncomfortable having anyone walk or stand behind him lately.

As he crossed in front of Mr. Phelps, sitting at his desk, the teacher said, "Daniel, do you have a few minutes?"

"Uh sure," Daniel replied. *Great! Now what?*

Mr. Phelps was actually a great teacher. Truth be told, the old Daniel had really liked him. Of course, now he didn't seem to like anybody. Mr. Phelps was just another slug to him now. He was in his late forties, maybe early fifties with thinning red hair that he would habitually run his fingers through. He wore black-framed glasses that he seemed to be constantly removing and polishing. He possessed a booming voice that often thundered into other classrooms when he got on a topic which excited him. Daniel was sure that when Phelps had covered Abraham Lincoln, the school's foundation had been damaged beyond repair.

"I'll get right to it, son," the teacher said, interlacing his fingers across his stomach. "I'm starting to worry about your grade in this class. I've noticed over the last several weeks that your work has been in decline. And it isn't just my class, Daniel. I checked with some of your other teachers and they have the same story to tell. In a matter of weeks, you have slipped dramatically from one of my best students to the bottom tier. You're not turning in assignments and the ones you do turn in are sloppy and, many times incomplete. You do manage to do well on the tests, I'll give you that, but that's not going to cut it. Now, is something wrong? I mean at home?"

Daniel knew he was in trouble. The last thing he needed now was anybody focusing special attention on him. He had been a fool to let his grades lapse. Mr.

Phelps wasn't going to be satisfied with a simple, *No*. He was going to have to give the man a portion of truth. "Honestly, sir, I have been having problems."

Mr. Phelps leaned forward in his chair and removed his glasses. "What's going on, Daniel? I just want to help."

"I've been having these nightmares that started about a month ago. I can't sleep at night because of them." Daniel tried to make his voice sound as pathetic as possible.

It was working. Mr. Phelps's eyes were now dark-brown pools of sympathy. "I see," the teacher said.

"You don't need to worry, sir. I had an appointment with Dr. Steinmetz not long ago. He got me some medicine that has been helping." It was a lie. He hadn't needed the pills since the day he murdered Levi. He continued, "I'm really sorry about my grades. I accept full responsibility, and I promise that I will do better from now on."

Mr. Phelps was polishing his glasses with the tip of his plain, black neck tie. "Now why didn't you say something before? We could have worked something out so that your grades didn't suffer so much."

"Guess I just didn't realize I was slipping so badly." Not so much a lie. He had been so preoccupied with his new identity, his new life, that school had been the farthest thing from his mind. He would have to be more careful about that.

Mr. Phelps ran a hand through his auburn hair. "I want to help you, Daniel. Mind you, I don't believe in charity for students that are goof-ups and all around wastrels, but you are neither of those. You're a good student that's hit a bump in the road is all, so I'm going to offer you the chance to earn some extra credit points."

"Yes, sir," Daniel replied, trying to sound enthusiastic. Where in Hell's Half Acre was he going to find the time to earn extra credit points? If this guy didn't back off, there was going to be some extra activity all right!

Mr. Phelps smiled, and leaned back in his chair. "I think I've got just the thing for you."

CHAPTER 16

Reverend Lucas Gannon's black, leather shoes echoed on the sidewalk that led to the main entrance of Clayton County Regional Hospital. A half an hour ago, his mid-afternoon nap had been interrupted by a frantic phone call from Lucy Forks, one of the more regular attendees to his Methodist congregation. She had blubbered out a barely coherent explanation that her son, Scotty, had been admitted to the hospital with some kind of illness, or possibly an accident on the job. Could he please come quickly and pray with them?

His modest three-bedroom bungalow was only two blocks from the hospital, so as usual, he chose to walk the short distance. It had been forty years since he had assumed the spiritual mantle from his father and the responsibilities of caring for the congregation had become his to bear. For forty years now, literally following in his father's footsteps, he had walked this route to the hospital, his King James Bible grasped firmly in hand, ready to pray with and for the members of his flock who needed him.

How many had he lost over the last four decades, including his wife? It was impossible to keep track of them all. It was usually the old, as it should be, but sometimes it was the young who were taken in the prime of their lives. Why the young? People always asked him. Why would God want to take so and so in the prime of his or her life? An entire lifetime spent studying the scriptures, trying to understand God's will, and the answer to that question still eluded him. He would usually respond that God had his purposes, purposes which mankind could not comprehend. Sure it was true—a good answer, right out of the manual —but it still felt like a copout whenever he said the words.

Over time, he had come to the personal conclusion that the only way to completely understand death was to go through it for yourself—not a doctrine he preached from the pulpit, by any means. Now, quickly approaching sixty-eight years of age, he figured the mysteries would be opened up to him soon enough.

He chuckled to himself as he dismissed the heavy thought. He was still young by Gannon family standards.

He paused when he reached the hospital entrance and donned the customary black suit coat that had been draped over his arm. Straightening his slightly bent frame, he assessed his reflection in the glass doors and tightened the knot of his necktie before entering. Without hesitation, he strode directly to the nurse's station where Janice Ward, the head nurse, was busy filling out charts.

"Afternoon, Janice," he said.

"Oh!" Janice looked up from her paperwork. "Good afternoon, Reverend. I'm sorry I didn't see you come in."

He held up his hand. "That's alright. Could you please tell me which room Scotty Forks is in?"

"He's in room seventeen, Reverend."

"Thank you, Janice." Having no need for directions, he headed for the wing on the left.

As he walked down the hallway he tried to mentally ward off the pungent scent of disinfectant mingling with the sickly sweet tang of body odor, a smell he'd never grown accustomed to, even after forty years. He knew of the secure room which had been reserved for patients who were battling mental disorders, or the occasional criminal who needed medical attention, and he wondered why Scotty would be kept in such a room.

He knocked lightly on the door and waited, both hands clasping his Bible in front of his waist. The door swung inward, revealing the dimly lit room. To his left, Scotty lay on his back in a hospital bed, his wrists tied to the rails.

The young man, his pale face glistening in a sheen of sweat, was slowly turning his head from side to side. His eyes were scrunched shut, like he was trying to squeeze out what little light was in the room, and he was mumbling, "No...no." It was barely a whisper.

Lucy Forks, Scotty's mother, was seated at her son's side, dabbing at his forehead with a damp cloth, tear tracks staining her thin cheeks. His father, John, stepped toward Lucas from the foot of the bed and extended his hand, his dark-brown eyes flecked with worry.

"Thank you for coming, Reverend," John said, as they shook hands.

Lucas stepped deeper into the room. "What happened, John?"

"Marley Baxter found him layin' in the dirt, out on the edge of his farm. He was unconscious. He woke up when they got him here, but Dr. McConnell says he went all crazy, yellin' and shoutin' a bunch of nonsense. They had to knock him out just to keep from hurting anyone, or himself. Doc says he's starting to wake up. Shouldn't be long."

"Did the doctor say what is wrong with him? What happened?"

Lucy spoke, her voice choking, "He doesn't know. He said it's some kind of anxiety attack maybe, but he's not sure." She stood and worked the cloth in her hands. "Can you pray for him, Reverend?"

"We all can." He stepped to the foot of the bed and placed his Bible on the mattress. John and Lucy stood to either side of him, and the three joined hands.

They bowed their heads and Lucas began to pray. "Dear Lord—"

The prayer was suddenly shattered when Scotty shot upright in the bed, the rails clanging as his wrists jerked against the restraints. His eyes were wide open, but the irises were rolled up into his head so that only the whites were visible. The veins on his neck popped and writhed under his skin, like thick worms trapped beneath the surface. He swiveled his head from side to side, as if looking around the room, but with unseeing eyes, while gnashing at the air with his teeth.

Lucy cupped both of her hands over her mouth stifling a scream, and the three jumped back, shocked and horrified.

"Amen!" Scotty shouted, his head weaving back and forth like a snake. Then he roared an angry, defiant laugh, bits of spittle flying from his teeth.

"Scotty!" Lucas exclaimed.

Scotty stopped swaying and fixed the jaundiced whites of his eyes on the Reverend. His upper lip curled above his teeth and formed a snarl. "Hello, Lucas," he hissed, tilting his head, "do you remember us?"

Lucas felt a cold, dark chill course through him, like someone had poured a bucket of ice water over his shoulders. "What are you talking about, Scotty?"

Scotty laughed the same hateful laugh and said, "We remember you, Lucas! The tree...the church..."

"You aren't making any sense! What do you mean?"

Scotty went limp and collapsed back onto the bed. He began to whimper, "Help me...help me, please."

The door burst open and Dr. McConnell rushed into the room followed by a nurse. "We heard yelling, is everything alright in here?"

An icy fist was clutching at the reverend's heart. He turned away numbly as the others in the room gathered around the bed. The dark feeling in his breast was familiar and something was gnawing away at him. The hair on his arms stood on end as he realized that whoever he had just spoken with was not Scotty Forks.

163

He didn't feel good. He needed to go home and lie back down. Amidst the bustle of everyone else devoting all their attention to Scotty, the reverend quietly slipped out of the room, glad to be gone.

CHET DID HIS BEST TO KEEP FROM JOGGING down the hospital hallway, Dr. McConnell struggling to keep up with his long stride. Rick had stayed behind to keep an eye on the office.

"How long has he been awake?" Chet asked.

"About a half hour. He came out of it sooner than I expected," the doctor replied, his white lab coat trailing in his wake. "His parents are with him right now."

They dodged a medicine cart left unattended in the hall.

"Is he talking? Has he said anything about what happened out there?" Chet asked, his eyes fixed on the door to Scotty's room just ahead.

Dr. McConnell gripped Chet by the elbow, reining him to a slow walk. "He is lucid, but emotionally, he is in a very fragile state. When I try to ask him about it, he pretty much shuts down on me."

They stopped just outside Scotty's room and Dr. McConnell placed a hand on the doorknob. "Now, Sheriff, he just might be willing to talk to you, and maybe he won't. I do want to be clear though, my top priority is his health and recovery."

"As is mine. That's why I'm here."

"Good," said Dr. McConnell as he produced a stainless steel syringe from his coat pocket with the deftness of an assassin. "Then we're both on the same page."

Chet did not like needles, and he felt his body recoil inwardly at the sight of the instrument reflecting too brightly in the pale light of the hallway. "What the hell is that for?" he said, resisting the urge to flatten himself against the wall.

"Relax, it's just a little something to settle Scotty down if he gets all rambunctious on us again."

"Oh," Chet said, feeling foolish as the blood returned to his face.

Dr. McConnell chuckled as he turned the doorknob. "It's a good thing the Japs were shooting bullets at you, instead of throwing syringes." He flashed a grin at Chet that betrayed his youth.

"You're hilarious," Chet said. "Just open the door and let's get this over with."

Dr. McConnell swung the door inward and entered with Chet on his heels. Lucy Forks was seated in a chair at her son's bedside, her hands folded in her lap as they held a white handkerchief. John Forks stood leaning against the far wall, his hands in the pockets of his dark slacks; he nodded a greeting in Chet's direction. Scotty seemed to be sleeping, his head turned away from the door, his wrists still bound to the bed rails by strips of white linen.

"How's he doing?" Dr. McConnell asked in a low voice.

"Better, I think," Lucy answered, her eyes watery and red. "He seems to have calmed down some." She tried to smile. "Thank you for coming, Sheriff. You mean a great deal to him."

"He means a great deal to us," Chet said.

At the sound of Chet's voice, Scotty opened his eyes and slowly turned his head. He managed to force a smile, that didn't quite touch his eyes. "Hey, Coop." His voice was weak and hoarse.

Chet stepped closer to the bed. "You really put us through a scare, Scotty. How ya feeling?"

Dr. McConnell began attaching a blood pressure cuff to Scotty's right arm. "Just checking your blood pressure, son," the doctor said.

"I'm feeling pretty tired, maybe a little weak, but I think I'm better now." Scotty watched Dr. McConnell pump air into the cuff on his arm. He tugged his wrists against the restraints. "I'm pretty sure this isn't really necessary, Doc."

Dr. McConnell only smiled as he released the valve on the cuff's air bladder and listened with his stethoscope while the cuff gently hissed. He nodded in silence as he listened to the throbbing of Scotty's pulse come and fade. "Looks good."

Chet stood at the foot of the bed and folded his arms. "Scotty, what happened out there today? Can you tell us?"

Scotty's eyes seemed to instantly well up with tears. He turned his head, unwilling to make eye contact.

Lucy placed a hand on her son's arm. "Scotty, you can talk to us. Everyone in this room loves you and cares about you. Sheriff Cooper and Dr. McConnell need to know what happened to you so they can help."

Scotty stared at the wall on the other side of the room for a silent moment. He sniffed as a lone tear escaped the corner of one eye and ran down his cheek. Then he began to slowly nod his head. "Okay," he relented, turning back to face the others again. "I'll talk, but only to Chet...alone." He glanced down at his bound wrists. "And can you cut these off, Doc? I'm tellin' ya, I'll be fine, I promise."

165

"You seem calm enough now," the doctor said.

"Go ahead and cut em' off," Chet said. "It'll be fine. You can wait outside the door with that bayonet if you'd like."

Dr. McConnell shot Chet a dry smile as he fished a pocket knife from his pants pocket. After cutting the strips of cloth on Scotty's wrists, he folded the knife and motioned to Scotty's parents. "Come on, folks, let's give him a few minutes with the sheriff."

The threesome filed out of the room. Before shutting the door, Dr. McConnell said, "I'll be right outside if you need anything." He patted his coat pocket where the syringe lay concealed, and winked.

"I'll let ya know," Chet said.

The door clicked shut, leaving the room in a heavy, awkward silence. Scotty was holding his recently liberated hands in front of his face, inspecting them, rotating them back and forth, and methodically flexing his fingers.

"Yep, they're yours alright," Chet said, breaking the silence. "Had them since you were born." It was meant to be funny, but any lightheartedness that may have been intended was engulfed immediately by the pervasive darkness in the room.

Scotty didn't miss a beat. "You sure about that, Coop? Cause I ain't so sure."

"What are you talking about?"

A weak chuckle escaped Scotty's lips, like he was laughing at his own inside joke. He let his arms collapse, his hands falling into motionless heaps on the bed as he shook his head back and forth. Chet walked around to the side of the bed and sat on the small wooden chair, the same one that Scotty's mother had been occupying.

"Alright, Deputy Forks, what happened to you out there? Now out with it."

Scotty sighed, his lower lip began to tremble and his voice cracked as he spoke. "This is going to cost me my job, Coop."

"ACCORDING TO SCOTTY, THAT'S WHEN HE SNAPPED out of it and threw his gun down. I guess he blacked out after that."

Back at the office, Chet finished telling Scotty's bizarre story to Rick, his one remaining deputy. Glancing out of a window, he noticed the waning afternoon sun was already casting long, dark shadows that stretched across the street and crawled up the sides of buildings and parked cars. The days were growing shorter as the nights were finally beginning to cool. Hunting season was right around the corner, a whole new set of headaches for the department.

"Anyway," he summed up, "that's the last thing he remembers."

Rick rounded his lips and let out a low whistle. "Sounds like the poor kid's completely lost his marbles." He took his feet off of his desk and leaned forward in his chair, placing his elbows on his knees. "What do you make out of all of it?"

"I don't know," Chet replied, staring into his coffee mug, as if the answer somehow lay in its steaming, black contents. "One thing's for sure, it's gonna be a while before he's back on the job."

"Obviously. But, you gotta find it a bit strange that we now have two witnesses sayin' they seen Levi Henderson out there in those woods—one of em's a sheriff's deputy, by the way."

"A suicidal deputy, apparently. And both of our so-called witnesses claim Levi's walking around dead." Chet blew on his coffee and took a cautious sip. "How am I supposed to react to that?"

"Don't know. I guess just chalk it up to coincidence?"

"For now, but maybe you can take a drive out there tomorrow and have a look around."

"Maybe *we* can take a drive out there, you mean."

Chet put his coffee down on his desk. "Are you kidding me, deputy?"

Rick's face was stone serious. "No, I certainly am not kidding…Sheriff."

"Unbelievable!" Chet said, his face cracking into a wide grin. "I never took you for a superstitious man, all scared of goblins and ghosts!"

"Hey!" Rick spread his hands and shrugged his shoulders. "Let's not forget what happened to the last deputy that went out there to have a look around."

"Alright, alright, fair enough. I'll worry about Levi Henderson's ghost after I deal with this whole Robbie Pritchard thing. That's our priority for now."

"Agreed," Rick said.

Chet was just reaching for his coffee when the front door flew open and Orrin Pritchard barged into the office, clutching a baseball bat. "Sheriff Cooper, I've got something to show you!" he steamed. His white shirt was rumpled and untucked, his hair sprawling in a dozen different directions, the opposite of the comely, well-groomed man they had visited earlier that day.

Chet remember now, he'd forgotten to inform Orrin that his son's body was missing from the funeral home. He felt his stomach twist into a knot. This was not going to go over well.

Rick came to his feet in one fluid motion. At the same time, he hooked his right thumb into his duty belt, just inches from the butt of his revolver. The subtle movement was not lost on Chet.

"Evening, Mr. Pritchard," Chet said, as he eyed the bat with a certain amount of trepidation. Maybe Orrin had heard about the theft of Robbie's body, had gone totally insane, and was here to beat someone's brains out.

Orrin ignored Chet's greeting and marched straight away to his desk, holding the bat out in front of him. Chet stood up, eyes still focused on the bat, his own hand slipping for his right hip. He saw Rick take a few steps forward and position himself tactically behind Orrin.

"What can I do for you, Mr. Pritchard?" Chet asked, taking one step back while trying hard not to be obvious about it.

"You can go ahead and open that murder investigation up for Robbie," Orrin said. His voice quivered with hot emotion, along with the strain to keep his breathing under control. "I have all the evidence you need right here!" He slammed the bat onto Chet's desk, scattering several papers into sudden flight. Orrin's eyes were intense and unblinking, searing into Chet's.

Chet glanced down at the bat, then back up to meet Orrin's burning gaze. "I'm sorry, but you're going to have to enlighten me. What's so special about the bat?"

Orrin rolled the bat a quarter of a turn so that the Louisville Slugger logo was face up. "Look closely, Sheriff, just under the logo."

Chet took a step forward and bent down to have a closer look. A dark, red spot, about half the size of a dime caught his eye. Blood, no doubt about it.

Orrin read Chet's mind. "It's Robbie's bat, he always kept it by his bed. A while ago, I was in his room cleaning up when I knocked the bat onto the floor by accident. When I went to put it back in its spot, I noticed the stain. Sheriff, I guarantee that's blood...I guarantee that's Robbie's blood."

Chet rubbed at the rough stubble on his chin as he considered the implications and possibilities.

By this time, Rick had made his way to Orrin's side and was examining the stain for himself. "I have to agree, looks like blood."

Orrin folded his arms across his chest, his hawk-like eyes never breaking their gaze. "So, what are you going to do now?"

Chet eased himself down into his chair and let out a long sigh before speaking. "Mr. Pritchard, have a seat, there's something I need to tell you."

"What more do you need? It's as plain as the nose on my face! Robbie was murdered!"

"Sit down. Please."

Orrin sank down into the chair across from Chet's desk but did not relax. He gripped the arms until his knuckles grew white, as he squirmed in place like a man with a severe bowel problem. "What's this all about?"

"I have some really upsetting news for you," Chet said.

THE COOKIES WERE STILL HOT AND GOOEY when Kate piled them onto two separate plates in Mable's kitchen. She cracked open the window above the sink and set the plates on the ledge, allowing the crisp evening air to cool the steaming treats, the tiny pools of chocolate slowly gelling back to their solid form.

As the cookies cooled, she bustled about cleaning up the mess. She was on her hands and knees wiping up a bit of flour that had spilled onto the wood floor, when Mable Johnson entered through the swinging door.

The older woman made a show of inhaling the sweet fragrance, her head tilted toward the ceiling, her hands clasped in front of her ample bosom. "Well, my dear, I sure hope that Sheriff Cooper isn't going to get all of those cookies, cause they sure smell delicious!"

Kate smiled and brushed a stray lock of curls out of her eyes. "No, he'll get that plate there." She pointed to the plate on the left. "The rest are for you and your husband, or whoever else would like one. I don't want to send the wrong message by giving him an entire batch."

Mable laughed. "Certainly not! You bake a man an entire batch of cookies, it goes straight to his head."

"Exactly." Kate stood up from the floor. She wrung the dish rag into the sink. "One plate is just enough to let him know I'm interested, but that he's still got a lot of work to do."

"Right you are! And it's just enough to leave him wanting more."

"That's what I'm hoping for, but Chet's a hard man to read. He's complicated, not like the boys I knew back home. I mean, he can be really warm and friendly, and then, just when it seems like he's about to really open up and let you in..." She dropped the dish rag into the sink. "It's like he's a thousand miles away sometimes."

"You're probably more right about that than you know," Mable said.

Kate furrowed her brow. "What do you mean?"

169

Mable walked over to the small table in the corner of the kitchen and sat down in one of the chairs. "How much has he told you about what happened to him over there?"

"He hasn't said a word about it," Kate confessed, pulling a chair out from under the table for herself. "I know he was wounded, but when I asked him about it, he just made a joke and changed the subject."

Mable nodded. "That's his way. He'll never brag about it, or even admit it, but make no mistake, that boy is a hero." Her eyes glistened in the soft glow of the kitchen lights. "I'm not too up on all the gory details. I don't much care for all the stories that our boys brought back with them. Not the ones about all the killing and such, anyway. I get too upset by it all."

"Well, that makes two of us," Kate said. "My brothers all volunteered, but fortunately, none of them got into anything too serious or dangerous. They don't have any horror stories to tell."

"What a blessing for your family."

Kate's curiosity was burning. Maybe if she knew more about what Chet had gone through, she would be able to help him get past it, or at least be able to deal with it. "What can you tell me about it, Mrs. Johnson?"

"Like I said, I don't have a lot of the details and I don't know all of what happened, but one time, he saved the lives of a whole bunch of his men."

Kate placed her elbows on the table and leaned closer.

Mable continued, "According to the story I heard, they were on one of those islands, clearing the Japs out of all the caves and tunnels they'd dug, when Chet and his boys walked into some kind of trap. There was heavy shooting coming from every direction, pinning our boys down so they couldn't get out. Even taking cover and crawling on their bellies, they were still getting killed. It was just a matter of time before they would all be dead."

Kate tried to picture some far off jungle, the awful scene of human carnage, and poor Chet in the middle of it all. She felt a small lump form in her throat.

"Well, Chet was the sergeant and he knew it was up to him to get those men out of there. So what does he do? He stands up, pulls a pin on a grenade and runs straight at a machine gun nest. By all rights he should have been killed, but by the grace of God, he avoids getting hit. When he gets close, he throws the grenade and dives to the ground." Mable mimed the action of throwing the grenade. Then she slammed her palm hard on the table. "Boom! The grenade goes off, taking out every Jap in that nest."

"I had no idea," Kate said.

Mable reached across the table and patted Kate on the hand. "He wasn't finished there, dear. He used the machine gun in that nest and turned it back on the other Japs that were shooting at his men. After seeing what he had done for them, the other men took courage and fought back. With Chet leading them, they rushed the remaining Japs, and killed or captured them all. If it weren't for him charging that nest like that, they'd all be dead."

Kate shook her head in amazement. She had heard stories like that before. She knew things like that had happened during the war, but it was different to actually personally know the man, the big hero. It made the whole thing much more real. Maybe even a little dangerous.

A part of her saw Chet in a new light, a new light that allowed her to see beyond the rugged, handsome looks and good-natured easiness that she had originally been attracted to. From the get go, she had seen something lurking in his sky-blue eyes, like an unwelcome guest. Most men hid their vulnerabilities, and Chet was no different, but he couldn't hide from her. As much as he kept it inside, his eyes always betrayed a hint of his pain, like a clean window with one lone, black fly crawling on its sparkling surface.

So, what kind of issues was he carrying with him and how deeply did they run? Could a man with his demons be capable of carrying on a normal life, let alone a relationship? How far was she willing to stick her neck out?

Mable grabbed Kate by the hand. "That man has been through a lot. More than you and I could ever imagine. He's seen a lot of killing, and even done some himself. That kind of experience does something to a man, it changes a core part of him. No woman's gonna step into the life of Chet Cooper and make everything all right again—Heaven knows plenty of girls in this town have tried."

Kate felt defensive. "I don't suppose to make everything all right in his life. I expect that after what he's been through, nothing will ever be all right again. Anyway, I'm just interested in being his friend right now. I just hope he feels the same about me. Maybe someday it will grow into something else, but for now, I think we're both fine with being friends and taking things nice and slow. I'm in no hurry."

Mable smiled, more to herself than to Kate. "Did I hear correctly, that he took you up to his cabin the other day for your date?"

"He did," Kate acknowledged. "Not that that's anybody else's business," she added, flashing an indignant pout for good measure.

Mable chuckled as she rose to her feet and began ambling for the kitchen door. Before exiting, she turned back to Kate. "Hon, that's farther than any girl's made it with the man so far!" She burst into laughter and pushed through the door, leaving it to swing back and forth on its two-way hinges. "Friends!" she exclaimed, sarcastically between chortles.

"You were probably riding on the back bumper of the Jeep the whole trip, knowin' you," Kate muttered under her breath, rolling her eyes.

She sat in silent thought, staring blankly at the flowery design on the tablecloth in front of her. She remembered the unforgettable afternoon at Chet's cabin. The two of them sitting there on the hill, watching the sun set over the valley—a page ripped right out of a fairytale book. She knew one thing for sure: sitting there, cuddled up next to the man and listening to the steady rhythm of his heartbeat, she had felt nothing but safety and contentment. To be honest, she didn't recall noticing the haunting glint in his eyes that day. A good sign or just a coincidence?

With a sigh and a shake of her head she stood up and took the cookies from the window ledge. She set one plate in the center of the kitchen table and draped a clean dish towel over the other. She made her way to the front entrance and selected her red flannel jacket from the cluster hanging from the coat rack. After shrugging into her jacket, she opened the door and stepped out.

She loved the fall, and the cool evening air would have felt refreshing after baking in a hot kitchen, but her mind was grinding on the unpleasant thoughts of war, killing, and Chet, a man plagued with memories he would never be rid of. Walking down the path, the chilled air seemed heavy as it gathered around her, the shadows of the growing darkness too black.

"He better like chocolate chip," she said.

CHAPTER 17

It was like waking from a long, dreamless sleep, where time had no place or meaning. It was as if his brain was wrapped in a thick fog that refused to dissipate. It had been a long, long time since he had felt the sensation of movement, the ground beneath his feet. Never mind the fact that the appendages moving him around weren't actually his. As if on cue, his sluggish feet got hung up on a tree root and he fell to the ground. Feeling nothing, he struggled back up.

It was taking a painfully long time to learn to control this new body, a boy's body with its short legs, short arms, and low center of gravity—not exactly what he had been accustomed to before. But this vessel was now his, though it had not been easy to wrestle complete control from its previous owner.

At first, the boy had refused to depart, had refused to recognize that he was no longer a part of the living world. Like a little parasite he had clung to the former shell of his mortal existence, often invading and taking over, just long enough to interfere with the plan.

Although his ability to comprehend the passage of time remained distorted, he was sure it had been a while now, since he had vied against the boy for the space which he now occupied. Surely, he had at last achieved liberation. Liberation from the accursed tree which had served as a prison to his soul these many years. Finally, he was free again.

"Not free." The thought bubbled up from some dark, murky place to explode on the surface of his consciousness. He remembered: a moment of desperation, a noose around his neck, a pact made in haste, the crush of his windpipe, the black tunnel opening into Hell's abyss, falling into the burning flames of hopeless regret and self-loathing. And then she was there, plucking him from the inferno at the last moment.

She had really saved him after all, just as she had promised! He was elated, but it was to be short-lived, and he instantly found himself in another kind of hell: his eternal soul, along with his followers, incarcerated in the suffocating blackness of the hanging tree. It was only then he realized she had set him up, had been luring him into her trap all along. The incantation he had recited at the time of his death, had sealed his fate along with the others who had followed him and trusted his leadership.

But the real hell began when she had started to feed, supping on their paralyzed souls, a ruthless arachnid dining with leisure on the helpless insects trapped in the morass of her sticky strands. And feed she did, until his soul had been shriveled into a dried out husk, barley a vestige of its former state.

For years, he had clung to the remnants of himself that made him an individual: his memories, passions, loves, lusts, hates, even fears. One by one, she drained them away, feasting on each part of him as if it were a rare delicacy.

She had deceived him from the very beginning and he had been the fool that went along, doing her bidding, lusting after her, murdering for her, and finally, betraying his own followers to her. Now, as the dead boy's legs staggered on her errand, carrying him through the lifeless forest, he knew on some level that his usefulness was almost worn out.

She had not fed for some time now, she was hunting again, spinning a new web from which she hoped to feast for many more years to come. And then, it would be to the abyss with him, back to the unquenchable flames.

He emerged, suddenly, from the tangle of the trees into a wide clearing of long grass, the dry blades whispering as his pant legs brushed past them. Through dim eyes that could only see in varying shades of black and gray, he saw a dilapidated, old church in the center of the clearing, its blackened bell tower jutting up in stark contrast to the bright, afternoon sky. He had a connection to this place. He struggled to pry from the muck of his broken mind what that connection might be as his legs stumbled forward mindlessly.

She wanted him there, at the church, her overpowering will pulling him like a dog is pulled on a leash. For what purpose, he knew not.

THE SUSPENSION ON THE OLD PICKUP squawked in protest. Reverend Lucas Gannon struggled to keep the cracked, rubber tires from slipping into the deep ruts of the dirt road that carved a jagging path through the countryside, skirting fields and etching through small groves. The late afternoon sun imbued everything in a sheen of hazy, autumn gold. A raw wind drove clusters of dry leaves and bits of chaff to swirl across the road like small schools of brown and yellow fish.

The old Salem road was seldom used, save for the occasional hunter wishing to access the span of woods that sprawled up the slopes of the foothills to the east. Sure there were deer in the area, but the road—if one could call it a road—was really going out of the way, when much easier hunting was to be had closer to town.

Five minutes had lapsed since he had passed the last stubbly wheat field where most hunters usually abandoned the road, figuring they had come far enough. Since then, the path had become progressively worse as it increased in elevation and the trees became thicker.

Lucas worried about the rusting, faded blue Chevy as it clambered onward. For too long it had sat uselessly in his backyard, neglected under a rotting canvas tarp, he being more inclined to walk wherever he needed to. It took some coaxing, and a little old-fashioned know how, but the tired engine had some life in her after all, and an hour later, here he was.

A voice inside wouldn't stop asking what he was doing out here. A part of him knew the answer and recoiled at what he was doing. Fragments of lost memories from his childhood began to flit through his mind, as if they were the shards of a broken mirror, each one reflecting a glimpse of a lost memory. Lost or suppressed? After all, it was *he* who had shattered the mirror. Had shattered it long ago, and swept the pieces away into some dark corner of his mind to be forgotten.

As he continued to ease the truck through and around the worsening ruts, his mind, like a naughty child making a mess, dragged the broken fragments from their proper place, spread them out in plain view, and started reassembling the puzzle.

He was eight years old the last time he had traveled this road. Back then it had been no more than a narrow footpath. He remembered, from all those bygone years, that it had been late into the night, or the early hours, just before dawn. He had been on the back of a horse, clinging to his father's waist, burying his face into the back of the man's coat, allowing the thick wool to absorb his tears, hoping his sobs would be muffled.

They were coming back from a place. A bad place. Through the dim mists of a faded memory, a certain sinister image—once forgotten—began to coalesce in the forefront of his consciousness. The old church house, decrepit and abandoned. The memory of it—even now, sixty-one years later—sent a chill up his neck where it collided with the base of his skull. The pieces were coming together more quickly now, the big picture coming into focus, one jagged fragment at a time.

As from the grave, he heard his father's voice, reaching across time and space. *"They were bad people, Lucas. You know that, don't you? We had to do what had to be done. There's no shame in doing The Lord's work."*

The tires slammed hard over a tree root and the entire Chevy shuddered as if it would break apart into a million pieces. He shook his head at his own carelessness and exhaled as he realized he had been holding his breath. He tried to focus back on the road, but the naughty child in his head continued dragging more puzzle pieces out, adding them to the growing picture that was beginning to take up all the free space in his mind.

"Someday the flock will be yours, Lucas, and you will find that if you truly love them, you will be willing to do what it takes to protect them."

Father and son hadn't been alone on the trail. There were others who had come with them. Several prominent people from town, including members of the church, had taken part on that dark night. The dull clip clop of several horses' hooves on the packed earth had been the only sound in the darkness, except for Father's whispers, which were few and far between.

The steering gear groaned as the reverend cranked the wheel sharply to the left, trying to stay on the road as it angled sharply around an enormous tree. He eyed the rough bark and thick branches warily, as they floated by his window. The sight of the arboreal giant flung another shard of memory skidding across his brain.

Nooses—how many, he didn't recall exactly—swaying in the soft breeze, moving together in unison, like the young lovers at the town dances on Friday nights during a slow song. The coils forming the knot were identical and neat, as if to bring a sense of order to the chaotic task at hand.

The thing that had stood out the most to young Lucas Gannon was the loop in the rope, the part that was slipped over the head of the victim…so deadly and yet so simple. It was a hole, a dark portal to another world, a passage to the very pit of Hell. He had spent all eight years of his young life listening to Father preach about Hell and damnation. In his mind, once the noose was slipped over someone's head, they were occupying two worlds at once. All that was needed was for the knot to cinch tight and transport the condemned the rest of the way.

"They're burning in Hell now. They won't be able to hurt anyone ever again," Father had promised.

Burning in Hell. He had never doubted it—at least, not until the incident a few days ago. As far as he knew, a soul burning in the pit would not have had the power to possess Scotty Forks.

Lucas had watched them all die with his own eyes, Father had made sure of that. Was it possible that they had escaped God's judgment somehow? Surely not! Then what had taken place back in Scotty's hospital room?

He turned his attention back to the road. The leafless trees yielded to an open field of brown grass and the road eased up a gentle slope. The Chevy ambled up the incline and the reverend scanned the sky ahead. The wind whipped at the clouds like tattered bedsheets flailing on a clothesline. Then it appeared, almost imperceptibly, a black point on the horizon. It seemed to grow right out of the hill as he neared, the tip angling out to the sides, to form a rectangular shape that ended in a point.

A shudder ran through him as he recognized the steeple of the Salem church rising out of the ground like an old weather-beaten tombstone, abandoned on some forgotten prairie from a time long past.

Salem had been a small village in the foothills at one time, but there was nobody alive that could remember back to when people had actually last lived there. How old it was or why it had eventually been abandoned, no one could say. The old church, made from chiseled blocks of granite, was the only remaining evidence of the settlement's existence.

There were a few old folk tales and local legends about what had happened to the people of Salem: an outbreak of smallpox had destroyed the population, a massive feud had killed most of them off, a hard winter, there was even a story of a curse. Lucas subscribed to the theory that a massive fire had burned down the village one night—hence the lack of other structures—and the people just never bothered to rebuild. The village was probably already in some state of decline at the time anyway.

Whatever the real reason, people tended to avoid the area altogether. Sometimes, a few teenagers would venture up on a dare, but even the bravest never stayed around long. There was a malodorous quality to it, not in the sense that one could physically smell, but rather felt it. Some described the feeling as an invisible, heavy cloud, oppressing, stifling. Others guffawed and called such descriptions nonsense. It was just an old, forgotten building. Nothing less, nothing more. He thought it was ironic that most of the skeptics were people who had never even been up here.

Now, from the top of the slope, the Salem church was in full view and he brought the truck to a stop. As buildings went, the church was nothing impressive, except maybe its ability to withstand the ravages of time and weather. Rough, angular blocks of granite, blackened over time and varying in size, formed a rectangular structure, the front end topped by a squat, solid steeple. A large square hole had been formed in the top of the tower to accommodate a church bell, which had long since been removed. A sagging pile of rotten wood shingles was all that remained of the roof. Certain sections of the roof had caved in completely, exposing the heavy rafters beneath, like giant, sun-bleached ribs, perhaps from the decaying carcass of some giant, mythological creature.

His eyes naturally followed the vertical line of the steeple downward, tracing the angle of the roof to the corner of the building, and all the way to the ground. He focused his attention on a piece of ground adjacent to the building. It was that bit of land that had brought him here. The cemetery.

He shut off the engine and immediately regretted it. He just hoped that it would start back up again. He slid out of the truck and turned up the collar of his leather jacket, to ward against the chill from the wind, but another kind of chill was seeping into his bones, a chill that no jacket could defend against. Jamming his hands into the front pockets, he felt a small relief as his right hand came into contact with his Bible.

"There's no shame in doing the Lord's work," he repeated his father's words out loud, but they seemed to echo hollow as he started walking.

There was little to indicate that the ground he was standing on was a cemetery. Only a few wooden grave markers remained, leaning precariously, choked by tufted clumps of brown weeds. Other markers lay buried in the grass, the hand carved inscriptions filled with packed dirt, making them all but unreadable.

He paced back and forth, turning in circles, looking for any disturbances in the earth. He had to verify for himself, had to know that *they* were still there. He needed to know that under his feet, down in the cold, dark clay, *he* was rotten and mouldering into dust.

"What are you doing out here?" he scoffed aloud to himself. "What did you expect you'd find? Open graves? Undead walking around?" He snorted at his own foolishness, shaking his head.

Suddenly, he stiffened as a large puzzle piece in his head clicked into place, and awful memories came rushing with the impact of an icy waterfall crashing on his head. He remembered the old man's name was Cyrus. He could still envision the lanky scarecrow body, eyes the color of dull, tarnished metal always reflecting the maniacal glint of religious fervor.

Cyrus was insane. Even at eight years old, young Lucas Gannon could tell just by looking him in the eyes. On that night, sixty-one years ago, those lunatic eyes were darting back and forth, the whites glowing luminous in the lantern light. The noose was shoved roughly over his bony head, causing his wispy, gray hair to flail chaotically as if in silent testimony to the man's madness.

Uncaring, frenzied hands tightened the noose and Cyrus went stiff, as the reality of his situation became more pronounced. That's when he locked those metallic eyes on Lucas. Even now, the memory of that gaze caused his knees to grow weak with fear. The old man started to mumble strange, unintelligible words, perhaps some other language.

There were no last words offered, no official ceremony or fancy trap door like in the movies. Without any kind of evident order, four men—his father amongst them— seized the other end of the rope, and heaved together. The rope made a sawing sound on the thick branch it was slung over. Cyrus may as well have been a sack of potatoes as he suddenly appeared to float into the air. The kicking and choking seemed to last forever, his lips purple and puffy as they continued to utter the strange words, his glassy eyes nailing Lucas in place.

He was barely aware of sinking to his knees in the old graveyard, barely aware of the tears now trickling from the corners of his eyes as the dark memory overwhelmed him. He became cognizant of his own voice uttering in the wind, "Just die! Why won't he just die, already?"

An imperceptible amount of time elapsed as he knelt, surrendering to the memories, allowing them to flow freely from the dark corners and spaces of his mind where they had remained locked away for all those years. Questions started to gnaw at him like the faint itching of a scab, begging to be picked at. The sense of the questions grew until they had formed large enough in his mind, pushing aside the memories long enough for his attention.

He was positive it had not been Scotty back in the hospital. Someone or something had taken over Scotty's body and delivered a message. The feeling that he felt when Scotty had laughed at him was the same feeling he had felt watching Cyrus hang. But why? Why, after sixty-one years, were these things starting to stir? Maybe nothing was stirring, maybe he was losing his mind. Something had caused him to come way out here. But for what? Answers?

"Oh, come on!" He slammed a fist into the ground. "Would you listen to yourself? Get it together!" He noted how his voice seemed out of place, awkward, like a bratty kid talking out loud in the middle of one of his sermons. "You've become a ridiculous old man," he said, as he stood up. "People die, they are judged by God and are sent to their reward. The end." What happened with Scotty was just a bizarre occurrence, nothing more.

He was turning to walk back to the truck when a loud, hollow thud echoed from inside the church. It sounded like a large board had fallen and clattered to the floor. He froze in mid-stride at the sudden clamor, his senses coming alive. The wind must have blown down a rotting timber from the roof. His hand searched in his pocket for his Bible.

The wind seemed to hum in anticipation as he strained to hear more. Then a faint scraping sound. Was that the scuffling of feet from inside the church? How could it be? Gripping his Bible, he scanned the cemetery for signs of recently disturbed earth, despite the better part of him knowing it was a superstitious and foolish thing to do. And yet, there was the sound again, dry and rasping, like an old newspaper being scraped across a rough plank of wood.

Almost against his will, he took several steps toward the building, his legs filled with liquid lead. Now the building in front of him seemed more oppressive than ever. The granite blocks that formed the old church looked as if they each weighed tons, the entire structure so heavy that it threatened to sink into the earth at any moment. He could almost see the ground concaving around the building, like an old mattress with a heavy bowling ball placed at its center.

Drawing nearer, he kept his eyes trained on one of the window frames, the glass long since shattered and gone. It gazed back at him like the hollow eye socket of a skull. Inside, a collage of black and gray shadows hung like thick curtains, pierced only by a random shaft of sunlight that had managed to breach the collapsed and rotting roof timbers. He fixated on that shaft of light, a literal ray of hope shining in the darkness. Even as shivers of fear and apprehension coursed over his body, the biblical parallel was not lost on him. *And the light shineth in darkness; and the darkness comprehended it not* – John 1:5, one of his favorite versus.

Taking courage, he removed his Bible from his coat pocket and gripped it firmly with both hands. He closed the distance between himself and the window. Some of the shadows became solid shapes: piles of rubble and trash, timbers from the collapsing roof, and broken, overturned pews.

The shuffling sound was coming from somewhere too far into the dark chapel for him to see. He would have to insert his head through the window opening if he wanted to see more clearly. He decided against that course of action.

"Is anybody there?" he said, doing his best to maintain a calm voice.

The shuffling noise ceased immediately. The only sound was the low moaning of the wind as it caressed the vacant opening.

"Hello?"

Silence.

He hurried to the next window on his left to gain a better view of the area where the sound had originated. As he moved away, the rhythmic, unmistakable sound of someone running, exploded across the floor, followed by the crash of a door being flung open. His heart was hammering in his chest as he thrust his head through the window. The front door of the church was now open, swinging on battered, rusty hinges that screeched in the wind. Whoever…whatever it was, was now outside. Outside with him.

Any courage he had been able to hold onto, melted away in an instant. He nailed his eyes to the corner of the building, expecting something or someone to appear from the other side at any second. He risked a glance at his Chevy. It seemed so far away. How long would it take him to run to the safety of the steel cab? Ten, maybe fifteen seconds? An eternity. He suddenly felt keenly aware of his age: the steady deterioration of muscle and bone over the years, the aching in his joints, the constant shortness of breath. He was an old man, older than he had ever been willing to admit.

A tall, thin shadow appeared at the corner of the building: two arms, two legs, head, torso. A human shape. The lanky form immediately brought to Lucas's mind the image of Cyrus, standing beneath the massive tree with a noose around his neck. The wind rippling the dead grass, served to accentuate the stillness of the lone figure.

He held the Bible out in front of him as if it were a shield, gripping it firmly with both hands. The sight of his worn, leather book brought him a degree of strength. He drew on it, remembering the courage of little David who had stood against Goliath, the giant Philistine, trusting that The Lord would deliver him.

Despite his best efforts, his voice trembled slightly as he called out. "Who's there? What do you want?"

There was a sudden lull in the wind and the whispering grass went static, matching the stillness of the dark apparition projecting across its wispy blades.

"I know you are there, and I know you can hear me," Lucas continued. "No sense in hiding. Now come out and show yourself."

The shadow on the grass slowly began to shift, and time seemed to slow down as a filth-covered boy materialized from around the corner of the church. His face and hair were caked in dried mud. Bits of leaves and broken twigs were embedded in the crusty surface. His eyes were like empty pits, non-reflecting, devouring. His frayed and tattered clothes flapped gently as the wind began to pick back up, carrying upon it the stench of decaying flesh.

Lucas thought that it was the most pathetic child he had ever seen in his life, save for one glaring contradiction. He appeared to be grinning. Not the happy kind of smile Lucas was used to seeing on a boy, full of mirth and mischief. The puffy, swollen lips were barely parted in the cold, unfeeling rictus of a bird's beak. Gaping, red fissures formed a series of fleshy crenelations that lent to the illusion of a second row of blood- stained teeth.

A wave of apprehension passed through Lucas and he took a step backwards, the Bible in his hands trembling. His heart was going to explode right up through his chest and into his throat. He wanted nothing more than to take off on a sprint for the truck, but his legs and knees felt like jelly. He probably wouldn't make it more than a few steps.

The grinning gash of a mouth moved, a dark, thick liquid spilling out to drip down the boy's chin. Then he spoke, "Lucas."

Two voices speaking in accord—a woman and a man—accompanied by a sloppy, gurgling sound, blending to create a twisted chorus, haunting, with malicious undertones. The woman, he didn't recognize, but there was no mistaking the voice of Cyrus, the crazy, old man they had hanged. Cyrus, who had been buried later that night in this very cemetery sixty-one years ago, was talking to him…from the decomposing body of a dead boy.

"Stay back, abomination of Hell," Lucas said, through clenched teeth, his Bible extended out in front of him.

Gurgling laughter spewed out, malignant and venomous as Cyrus took a slow, heavy step forward. "Is that the way to greet an old friend?" the two voices chimed together. "You know, I always liked you, Lucas. I hated your self-righteous, murdering father, but I always liked you."

Lucas took another step backwards and sideways, a subconscious move toward the truck. "My father was a man of God."

The hollow, black eyes seemed to flash for a moment. "We know what your father was, what he did!" Another step forward. "Even now, he burns for his sins."

"No!" Lucas cried out in defiance. "My father was a good man. He did what was necessary!"

"Poor little Lucas. Made to watch. Made to take part. Such a burden to carry all these long years. But we can lift that burden, we can stop the pain." Cyrus extended his yellow-gray hand. "Come to us, Lucas. Come and know the truth. Come and know the true peace."

Lucas shook his head and took another step back, feeling a sudden sense of imminent danger.

Cyrus pressed on. "Aren't you the faithful one? But, that's what I really liked about you. You had real faith, a true believer. Now that is a rare and powerful thing. Not like your fear-mongering, traitorous father. No, I had my eye on you back then. So much potential." He shook his head. "All for naught."

Lucas side-stepped for the truck once again, making no pretense to stay and continue the conversation.

Cyrus glanced sideways and seemed to notice the truck for the first time. A knowing grin spread across his face, causing the mask of dried mud to crack and flake. "I suppose it was too much to hope that you would see the light and join us." He took a step that obviously was intended to cut off Lucas's angle to the truck.

They stood staring at each other, like gunfighters in a western film at high noon, waiting for the other to make the first move. Cyrus grinned the cold, dead grin of a snake as he waited to strike, his black, merciless eyes almost begging the prey to run.

For the first time in his life Lucas felt his faith abandoning him. Would God really save him now? Would God interfere and perform a miracle to save him from this living nightmare? What was so special about Lucas Gannon that God should see fit to save him?

His Bible seemed as heavy as a sack of rocks, forcing his weary arms to droop. The book no longer seemed to be an object of power that could protect him. It was just a book after all, wasn't it? He was a foolish, old man to believe that a collection of stories pressed between two flaps of leather could save him from the hellish thing glowering at him now. No, this was it. He was going to die right here, right now, at the hands of some kind of Satanic aversion.

The fiend took three quick steps toward him, but froze when a pair of grouse exploded from a clump of tall weeds near his feet, their wings beating as they desperately sought the safety of the sky.

Lucas envied the birds as they gained altitude and let the wind carry them away. If only he could join them and be gone from this God-forsaken place. The grouse became imperceptible dots in the leaden sky, when a sudden thought drove into his brain like a railroad spike. *The shotgun!*

Back when he had driven the Chevy more, he had often kept a loaded, double-barreled, twelve gauge shotgun under the seat for hunting birds. More than once he had pulled the truck to the side of a country road and blasted a pheasant or grouse.

Was the gun still there? He had forgotten about it a long time ago. Was it loaded? If so, would it even fire after all this time? A new hope surged through him and he felt a tingle of energy pulse in his legs as they seemed to regain their strength. Maybe, just maybe he could reach the truck and get to the gun.

As Cyrus took another step, Lucas played the only card he had. He threw his Bible directly at the demon creature's face. Without even waiting to see if his aim was true, Lucas sped off on a sprint for the truck and, hopefully, the shotgun resting under the seat.

There was the sound of pages fluttering through the air as he ran, then a thump, followed by an angry snarl as the Bible hit its target. Then footsteps coming, impossibly fast. He refused to turn around and look. He knew that the sight of the demon boy running at him would most likely sap the strength right out of his body.

The truck was just a dozen yards away, he was making better time than he had thought he would. He allowed himself to hope as he willed his legs to pump faster.

Just when it seemed he was home free, something struck him in the back with inhuman force, blasting the air from his heaving lungs. For a moment, he was caught in a space absent of time, as he sailed through the air, numb of any sense of sound, motion, or feeling. Then, he crashed to the earth and, like a rubber band being pulled and released, time and space snapped back to the present, and he found himself tumbling violently through the dirt and grass.

He felt a sharp pain in his side and heard a muffled snap from deep within his body as he slammed into something hard. He felt himself slipping away into the oblivion of unconsciousness, until a hard, racking cough forced him to remain in the world of the living, for at least a little longer. With each coughing spasm the pain in his side stabbed like a twisting knife. His eyes tried to focus, but everything was blurry, and the ground was swaying like the waves of the sea.

He rubbed his eyes and gradually everything started to come back into focus. The cough remained persistent, however, and the sharp pain was only worsening. He made a quick inventory of the situation as he battled to get to his feet. He was able to feel with his hands behind him and determine that he had slammed into the front tire of the truck. The shotgun was almost within his grasp!

His eyes darted quickly, scanning, searching for Cyrus, but the abhorrent thing was nowhere to be seen. Had Cyrus left for some reason without finishing him off? He propped himself up against the tire and endured another side-searing coughing fit. Maybe God had come through after all. Maybe that thing had been struck down by His wrath and was lying dead in the grass. Dead for real.

He struggled to one knee, wincing as every joint seemed to grind and every muscle cramped in protest. Ignoring his body's objections, he placed a hand on the fender of the truck and hauled himself painfully to his feet.

Using the hood and fender of the truck as a support, he pulled himself along to the door. Somehow, between coughing attacks, he managed to open the door. "Please be here," he prayed out loud, "Dear Heaven, please let it be here!"

"Amen."

The ethereal sound of the twain voices turned his blood to ice water and his hope faded. He looked up from where the voice had come, and to his horror, Cyrus was there, squatting on the cab of the truck, like a demonic gargoyle grinning fiendishly back at him. He was holding a large crucifix in his boyish hand. No, it was a piece of broken window pane, jagged and splintered at one end.

Before Lucas had a chance to recover from the shock of seeing him perched there, Cyrus raised the makeshift crucifix and, almost casually, trance-like, plunged the sharp end deep into the reverend's shoulder, near his neck.

Lucas gasped in pain and horror as he fell backwards, the stick jutting out of him at an angle. As he hit the ground, he heard the rumpling and popping of metal. Cyrus was climbing down from the cab of the truck to finish him off, no doubt. Curling his wounded arm in front of him, Lucas rolled onto his stomach and began to belly crawl for the cab of the truck. The pain was unbearable, and he was again on the verge of passing out as he clawed with his one good arm, his feet digging into the cold, gray dirt.

It was the small sneaker of a boy that stepped on his back, but the strength of something else that pushed his chest and face into the ground. Refusing to give up, so close to the shotgun, he continued to claw and scrape across the ground, inch by inch. Another violent coughing fit seized him, coating his lips in frothy blood.

"Lucas, Lucas," the voices said in a tone of mock sympathy.

He continued to scrape along, ignoring them.

"It's over Lucas. It's time to face your fate; you belong to her now."

He reached the open door of the truck and slowly, painfully, pulled himself up to his knees. "Her? I don't know what you're talking about." he said, through clamped, bloody teeth as he slid his hand along the floor and under the seat.

"Your father never explained it all to you? He never told you about *her*?" The conjoined voices laughed in incredulous mirth. "All these years of guilt and self-torment, and you never even knew why?" More gurgling, sinister laughter.

Lucas probed with numb fingers under the seat. It had to be there. It just had to! He slid his hand further under the seat. Salvation was at his fingertips, as they brushed the familiar walnut stock of the shotgun. As his hand closed around the stock, Cyrus stepped forward, grabbed the stick protruding from him, and yanked it free.

Lucas howled as an unimaginable, white-hot pain seared through his body, sending a wave of nausea and weakness coursing through him. He gripped the gun, but feared he no longer had the strength to wield the cumbersome weapon.

"Well," Cyrus said, "it doesn't surprise me that your old man would keep the truth from you. I have to say, I almost feel sorry for you. Oh well, it doesn't matter now, does it? You will know all about her very shortly."

Lucas knew at any second the accursed stick would be thrust deep into his back. He concentrated on gathering all of his strength, like the winner of a poker game pulls his winnings close into himself, embracing them with his arms. He tightened his grip on the gun and braced his mind for the explosion of pain that was sure to follow his next movement.

"I would say good bye, Lucas," the voices said, "but we'll be seeing you very soon."

This was it, now or never! Defying the agonizing pain, Lucas yanked the side-by-side from under the seat and spun around. Nearly passing out from the pain, he leveled the barrels at Cyrus's chest and, with a shaking thumb, cocked both the hammers back. *Please let it be loaded!*

A look of shock and then amusement flashed across the dull black eyes. "You fool, you can't kill me. I'm already dead."

Lucas applied pressure on the first trigger. "Then I'll send you back to Hell!" He pulled the trigger, but there was only a dull *click* as the firing pin struck a dead primer.

The raven's grin split Cyrus's face as he raised the bloody stick for the killing strike. "I don't think so. Not just yet. Be sure to give my regards to Daddy."

Lucas pulled the second trigger just as Cyrus began the deadly strike at his heart. The twelve gauge exploded with a thundering roar, blasting its deadly payload of buckshot directly into Cyrus's chest.

The recoil was too much for Lucas and the shotgun bucked itself free of his weakening hands. Through the cloud of smoke he couldn't believe his eyes; Cyrus was not dead! He stood in the same spot, his arm still raised for the killing blow, his hand wrapped around the stick.

The wound left by the shotgun was devastating, especially on the small chest of a boy, and Lucas could see it gaping through the tattered holes of Cyrus's gunpowder-stained shirt. The dead boy's face was a blank mask of dried mud, now spattered in red splotches the color of over-ripe cherries. The smile evaporated and the eyes looked more dead—if that was even possible.

Just as Lucas was about to resign himself to death, his heart leaped in his chest as Cyrus suddenly let go of the stick. A faint look of shock appeared in the obsidian eyes as he brought his hand to his chest and dabbed at the wound. Taking his hand away—covered in dark, thick blood—he stared at it for a brief moment before collapsing sideways to vanish in the blowing grass.

Lucas stared at the spot where Cyrus had gone down, mesmerized, expecting him to get back up at any second. Another round of coughing snapped him out of the spell. His mouth was filled with the taste of iron and salt, and he spat a thick stream of bloody spittle to the ground. Each breath was becoming more difficult than the last. Coughing up blood, the pain in his side…he must have broken a rib and, most likely, punctured a lung. If he didn't get help soon, he would drown on his own blood as it slowly seeped into his lung.

Newly motivated by this new threat of death, he began the arduous struggle to get off the ground and into the Chevy. Every few seconds, he jerked his head over his shoulder at the spot where Cyrus had fallen. As he rose to his feet, the higher vantage point gave him a glimpse of the body: the body of a boy lying in the grass, a chunky hole the size of a softball in his small torso.

He stared long enough to make sure the body wasn't moving, then turned to make his way around to the driver's side of the truck.

"You can't kill me, Lucas. I told you, I'm already dead." The dual voices rose up out from the ground to echo through him like a thunderclap.

Not bothering to look back, Lucas scratched and clawed his way across the hood of the truck, refusing to stop even when another coughing spasm pulled up more blood and mucus from his injured lung to spill onto the faded, blue paint of the driver's-side door.

"Lucas!" the voices hissed through the wind.

Still refusing to look back, he wrenched the door open and fell headlong onto the seat in practically one motion. Somehow, with a will all their own, his legs folded up under him and onto the floor of the pickup. Grasping the steering wheel with both hands, he pulled himself into a sitting position behind it and grabbed the ignition keys. That's when he saw Cyrus getting to his feet, albeit very slowly, very unsteady.

Fear gripped his heart with icy fingers and he turned the ignition in a panic. The truck lurched and died. *The clutch! Push in the clutch!* He found his leg barely had the strength to push the clutch pedal to the floor. By this time, Cyrus had staggered a few feet and was making his way around the front of the truck, seemingly growing stronger with each step.

Lucas turned the ignition again and the engine made a whirring sound as it turned over, but didn't start. He pumped the gas pedal a few times and tried again. The engine hiccuped briefly as if it would start, only to go back to the whirring sound.

Cyrus was around to the driver's side and making his way to the door, one hand making the slithering sound of a snake as it scraped along the truck's fender. The rictus smile was plastered back on his face. As he got closer to the driver's window. All Lucas could see was the top of his head.

"Lucas!"

He figured he had one more shot at starting the pickup. At risk of flooding the engine, he slammed the gas pedal all the way to the floor and cranked on the ignition. "Start, damn you!" he shouted. "Start!"

The engine alternated between whirring and small hiccups as Lucas cranked, not letting up. Suddenly, the truck backfired, emitting a loud *bang* that reminded him of the shotgun blast. The engine came to life with a roar. He kept the pedal to the floor, filling the carburetor with gas. It took him a second or two, fumbling with the gear shift, to find first gear. Nice and easy now, don't kill it.

Slowly, he disengaged the clutch, being careful not to stall the engine, and the truck began to roll forward. An involuntary laugh of triumph, combined with disbelief, erupted from him as he angled the truck onto the road and gunned it for the trees. He checked his mirror, expecting to see Cyrus, a vanishing dot, left behind in the field of blowing grass and weeds. But he wasn't where he should have been. Then…where was he?

His window burst into a thousand shards, as a bloody hand punched through the frame, grabbing a handful of Lucas's coat in an unbreakable grip. A ghoulish face appeared in the window opening, the smile gone, replaced by a look of pure malice and evil. The running board! He was standing on the running board!

Lucas tried to shake his unwanted passenger by veering the truck recklessly from side to side. That's when Cyrus began to pull; his strength was incredible! Lucas may as well have been hooked up to a winch or a crane, as his body was pulled upward and out of the window opening.

The beginning of the forest was just ahead, if he could just make it into the trees! But, as his body was lifted from the seat of the truck, his foot was lifted from the gas pedal and the truck began to slow down. He pointed the toe of his shoe and gassed the pedal one last time, as his head and shoulders were pulled out of the window and he found himself face to face with the living-dead creature.

Cyrus curled his bloody, cracked lips like a rabid dog, exposing the white, new teeth of a young boy. "Nice try," he said, teeth chomping on each word.

Lucas could see the first of the trees approaching as the truck rocketed toward them. His fingertips groped uselessly with the wheel. In seconds they would rocket past the first big tree…or plow directly into it.

The monster opened his mouth wide, wider than humanly possible, distending his jaw like a snake about to devour its prey. The stench was beyond anything Lucas had ever experienced. It was the foul reek of encapsulated decay and unadulterated rot.

Then, to the reverend's horror, The fiend clamped its festering mouth on his exposed throat and bit down. Lucas screamed as the canine teeth punctured into his vulnerable flesh, and the flat incisors began to saw back and forth. Warm blood began to flow. Given the supernatural strength recently displayed by the creature, Lucas figured his throat would be torn out at any second.

He was barely aware of the sound of his own choked screams as he saw that one, massive tree loom into his field of vision. It took every ounce of his courage and every ounce of his fear, combined with all the strength left in him, as he let out a herculean roar of final defiance in the face of death itself. He caught Cyrus by enough surprise that he was able to move just a few inches back into the cab of the pickup. But it was enough for him to purchase a grip on the wheel with his right hand and nudge it to the left.

Metal squealed and buckled, the left fender ripping away, as the truck made contact with the large tree. There was the splattering *thud* of the solid trunk colliding with Cyrus, scraping him from the side of the truck in an explosion of metal, limbs and bark. The truck was out of control as it careened off the tree, tilting dangerously onto two wheels for an instant, hurtling for the forest.

Lucas fought to bring the truck back under control and onto the road. He knew, instinctively, that he needed to slow down, but the brake pedal was the farthest thing from his mind; there was no way he was giving that thing another chance to catch up with him. He cranked the wheel hard to the left and hammered his foot down on the gas. The rear tires spewed dark earth behind them, digging deep gouges into the ground. The battered truck seemed to explode as it hit the ruts of the road.

The steering wheel had a mind of its own and it was all Lucas could do to keep a grip on it, but he somehow managed to steer the truck back onto the road. *Too fast, too fast! Slow down!* His inner voice was trying to reason with him, but he was too far gone in the grips of panic and fear to heed it. Instead, he gave more gas, until the road and the trees became a steady blur. The truck rattled and bounced so violently that he was sure it would simply disintegrate into molecules at any moment.

He recognized that his breathing was becoming more shallow, more labored, and he was feeling extremely light-headed. He wasn't coughing as much anymore and he knew that wasn't a good sign. His lungs were making a rattling noise when he exhaled. The death rattle they called it, a sound he had come to know all too well over the years, bringing comfort to the bedsides of the dying. It was usually the tell-tale sign that the end was very near. Forgetting Cyrus, a new fear dug its icy finger tips into his heart. He needed medical attention, and he needed it fast!

But, he was fading too quickly; his vision was dimming, he could feel a numbness in his extremities, and the loud rumble of the truck's engine was now just a muted droning. Gradually, his foot relaxed off the gas pedal. Then, one at a time, his hands fell from the steering wheel. He barely noticed the jolt as the truck left the road to crash through the small trees and underbrush.

He still killed me after all, he thought, and there was the sensation of an impact followed by an explosion of white stars in his head, and then everything faded to black nothingness.

CHAPTER 18

The sun dipped below the horizon, relinquishing its rule to the hungry grasp of twilight, transforming the land into an indistinguishable pattern of interlocking gray and black shadows. A light fog was moving in, sifting among the trees and buildings, warping them into ghostly shapes from another world. The streetlights appeared as fuzzy, yellow smudges floating in the distance.

The dirt path that wound through the park was unlit and isolated, but Kate couldn't have felt any safer as she walked with Chet, her hands resting gently in the crook of his elbow. Her little after school visits to the sheriff's office had become more and more frequent of late. It had started with the cookies, a random act of kindness, she preferred to think of it. Over the past couple of weeks it had evolved into almost a daily ritual. Cookies, coffee, sandwiches, soup, a pie. It turned out that Chet was quite a fan of chocolate chip cookies after all. Rick Shelton was quickly becoming quite a fan too!

After her first visit, Chet had insisted on driving her home, but at some point he began suggesting that they walk. She wasn't sure why, but he hadn't driven her home since. Not that she minded, she liked walking with him. She enjoyed the conversations as well as the moments of quiet—nothing but the sound of the leaves crunching under their feet. It was during these walks that he seemed to relax a little, letting down his guard. She felt like she was able to pick away at the wall he had thrown up around himself and every so often, catch a glimpse through the cracks into his soul.

"How's Scotty doing?" she asked as they entered a large grove of neatly trimmed trees.

"About the same," Chet replied. "He's out of the hospital at least, living with his folks now. Me and Rick went by to see him yesterday."

"Rick and I," she corrected.

"Right."

"How did that go?"

"Fine, I guess, considering everything that's happened. He's not going to be coming back to work for a while though. If he even comes back at all."

Kate shook her head. "That bad, huh?"

"He wakes up every morning convinced he's going to die that day. I don't know what to make of it," Chet said, shrugging his shoulders. "Something really shook him up out there. Dr. McConnell has absolutely no explanation for it. Physically, there's not a thing wrong with him. It's like he just snapped or something."

"Does he still claim he saw Levi in the woods?"

"Not supposed to even bring it up—Doctor's orders. It could send him spiraling right back into the hospital."

"Gee," Kate said. "So, what about you and Rick? How are you guys going to handle working with a man short? It's not like you have a lot of extra deputies hanging around."

"As much as I hate to admit it, I might have to face the real possibility of hiring another deputy to replace him."

"Have you got any candidates?"

"I was thinking you might be interested," he said.

She slapped him on the shoulder. "Oh, knock it off!"

"What?" he feigned an injured look. "I really need the help you know."

"Well, I won't argue with you there."

They walked in silence as the darkness of the evening set in and the fog thickened around them like a shroud. After a few minutes, the grove of trees gave way to a spacious area with a large, round stage dominating its center. A white banner spanning two poles hung over the stage. *Clear Creek Fall Social*, was painted on it in fancy red letters. The big fall social was next Saturday; the whole town was buzzing about it. There was going to be music, dancing, oodles of food, a melodrama, gunnysack races, and even a boxing tournament! The event was supposed to last all day and into the evening.

Kate bumped Chet with her hip, causing him to side step off the path. "So, are you going to the big party next Saturday?"

"I'll be here, if that's what you mean...me and Rick."

"Rick and I."

He stopped and looked down at her. "Rick and I," he said, rolling his eyes.

She smiled, patting him on the cheek. "We just might make a proper gentleman out of you yet, Chet Cooper."

He smiled and started walking again. "Am I really that bad?"

"Awful."

192

"Got any advice, besides the need to improve on my grammar?"

"Well, a gentleman wouldn't leave a lady waiting and twisting in the wind for starters."

This brought Chet to another stop. He folded his arms and leaned against the side of the stage. "Whatever are you talking about?"

"Oh, for cryin' out loud, do I really have to spell it out for you?" She gestured with both hands to the banner that was now almost right above their heads.

"Oh," he said, rubbing the back of his neck with one hand. "You want to go to the social together?"

"Thank you for asking, kind sir," she replied, placing emphasis on her Southern drawl, "but, I'll have to think about it. You're not the only man in town you know, and a lady has to keep her options open." She hooked his arm with her hand and started to pull him back down the path.

"Oh for hell's sakes," he grumbled, shaking his head.

"Cussing and swearing scores you no points at all," she said, sticking her nose snobbishly into the air. "And you're gonna need all the points you can get."

Chet continued shaking his head.

They moved beyond the stage and back into the seclusion of the trees that grew in clusters along the edge of the park. Before long, a sidewalk appeared from out of the fog, barely illuminated by the subdued glow of a nearby streetlight. They took the sidewalk, the fog absorbing the sound of their footsteps.

Chet said, "It's not that I don't want you to come with me to the social, I'll just be on duty is all."

Kate snorted. "Nice try." She felt his arm stiffen slightly and she smiled. He was still fun to tease. She gave his arm a squeeze and laid her head against his shoulder and felt him relax. Even after all he had been through, he was still just a boy in so many ways.

"Chet," she said.

"Yeah?"

"Mable told me about it…what happened. I mean to you overseas in the war and all." She felt his bicep go stiff again as his walk slowed.

"Well, it's no big secret. You were bound to hear about it eventually." His voice was wooden, far away.

It wasn't exactly the result she had been hoping for. In her mind she could see the wall sprouting back up all around him, shutting her out. "You don't want to talk about it, and believe me, I understand more than you—"

"Good, then let's talk about something else."

"Fine," she said, "but I just wanted to let you know that if you ever do want to talk about it…or anything really, you can talk to me. I'll listen, middle of the night, whenever. Okay?"

"Thank you, Kate, but I'm fine, really," said the human wall.

She gave his arm another squeeze to reassure him and laid her head against his shoulder, but it didn't have the same effect this time and the ensuing silence was awkward, almost unbearable. She tried a couple of times to bring him back around, asked about the Pritchard case: was he any closer to finding a suspect? Did he have any theories on what had happened to Robbie's body? When that didn't seem to work, she tried a few jokes and some harmless flirting.

He responded to her questions, but his answers were methodical and uninvolved. He even chuckled politely at her jokes and flirting, but it was obvious that his mind was lost elsewhere, probably half a world away on some war-torn island in the Pacific. The Great Wall of Chet was deflecting and repelling all of her attempts to get through.

It seemed to take a long time to finally reach The Cozy Corner and the chill of the night, combined with the fog, had settled right into her bones, but the chill in her heart was the true source of her shivering.

He walked her up the porch steps and they shared a brief hug, but his arms were about as warm as tree branches as they embraced her. She thanked him for walking her home and kissed his cheek; it was like kissing a stone.

They exchanged the usual pleasantries and he even smiled, but his eyes were hard, like glass marbles with that distant, haunted look to them. Then he turned and walked away, his shoulders slumping with the weight of the world, the fog swallowing him whole.

A lump caught in Kate's throat and her eyes began to brim with tears as she realized what she was about to do.

"Chet!" she called after him into the fog.

"Yeah?"

She used the tips of her fingers to wipe away the small trickle that was beginning to flow from the corners of her eyes.

"Chet, could you come back up here, please?"

THERE WAS A DIFFERENT TONE IN HER VOICE as it echoed through the gathering fog, serious yet tremulous, fearful, even vulnerable, and it hit him like a slap to the face. He woke, as if from a dream, a nightmare. He had allowed himself to go into that dark place in his mind, where the demon memories whispered their horrors and pierced him with their accusing glares. And suddenly, Kate's voice was there, pulling him from that god-awful muck.

He turned around and walked quickly back to the porch, the demon voices pushed aside by a feeling of growing concern. She was there, still standing where he had left her, arms wrapped around her chest in an effort to ward off the cold.

"Hurry up, Chet, I'm freezing to death," she said, doing a little dance.

He reached the steps. "You need to start dressing warmer, girl," he said, appraising her outfit: thin, pink sweater, bluejeans that ended mid-calf, and light, leather flats, no socks.

"Yeah, apparently."

"Did you need something? Is everything alright?"

She let out a heavy sigh. "Yes, there's something I need to tell you."

"Okay, I'm listening."

"First, come inside with me before I turn into an ice cube."

He followed her inside. The house was warm and filled with the enticing aroma of baking bread and some kind of meat cooking, maybe roast beef or ham. The Cozy Corner was a good name for the place alright. Mable, her husband, Henry, and Henry's brother, Elmer, were all sitting in the front room. Elmer, as usual, was reading a newspaper while Henry wiped down a rifle with an oily rag. Mable was chattering away to both men.

Mable rose from her chair. "Chet, what a pleasant surprise! Come to join us for supper?" Before he could answer, she fixed a stern gaze on Kate. "Kate, you should have let me know you were bringing a guest for supper! My lands, girl! It's just your luck I made enough tonight, but you might not be so lucky next time. I've got to know a little in advance, not that the sheriff isn't welcome any old time, of course he is."

"I'm not here for supper," Chet said, squeezing into Mable's rant. "Maybe some other time."

"Oh?" Mable said, the frantic smile draining from her plump face.

"Mrs. Johnson," Kate said, "is there someplace where Chet and I could talk in private? I don't mean to impose, but it's kind of cold outside."

The two women stared into one another's eyes for a moment and an understanding seemed to pass between them. Mable nodded rapidly, her double chin quivering. She flew into action, barking commands, prodding Henry and Elmer out of their chairs and herding them from the room like dumb cattle.

195

"Nice to see ya, Sheriff," Henry said, as he was hustled by.

"You too, Henry. Nice rifle, by the way."

"The deer better watch out this year!" These last words echoed as Mable shooed the men down the hallway and into the kitchen.

Chet turned to Kate, who was standing in the middle of the room, wringing her hands, feet fidgeting on the carpet, watery eyes darting about the room. Something was definitely wrong. He had never seen her like this before. Usually, she was so full of confidence and sass. Alarm bells started going off in his head.

"Kate, what in the world is the matter?" he said, stepping toward her, wanting to enfold her in his arms.

She crossed the room to where a love seat sat against a large picture window, and sat down patting the cushion next to her. "Come sit with me, Chet." A lone tear suddenly trickled from the corner of her left eye, and she quickly wiped it away with her hand.

He rushed to her side, producing a handkerchief from his shirt pocket and offered it to her.

"Thank you," she said, accepting the handkerchief. She dabbed at her eyes and smiled. "I guess you're more of a gentlemen than I originally gave you credit for."

"Maybe you give me too much credit," he said. "My mother was a handkerchief fanatic. Always made sure I had one in my pocket whenever I left the house.

"A good man always knows Mama was right."

"Alright, so what's going on here? Are you okay?" he asked.

With the handkerchief crumpled up in one hand she reached over and grasped both of his hands in hers. He could feel the cool wetness of her tears on the cloth. "Daddy told me I was to never speak of this, but I guess I'll just come right out with it," she said. Her hands were trembling.

He gave her hands a reassuring squeeze. "You can tell me."

She took a deep breath and let it out. "Chet, do you remember when you took me to Zoli's for lunch a few weeks ago, and you asked me how I ended up in Clear Creek?"

He nodded. "Yeah, I remember."

"Clear Creek isn't exactly New York or San Fransisco, is how you put it, if I remember correctly.

"Right. I was curious how a young woman such as yourself, ends up leaving a family behind in Tennessee, that she obviously loves and misses very much, to come work at an elementary school here."

She nodded her head. "I know, I know. It doesn't make sense." She paused, looking down at her shoes.

"You can tell me."

"I didn't come here by choice," she began, "I was sent here. Basically, sent away, I guess you could say. I had a boyfriend named Albert. Albert Cromwell. He was the son of my dad's law partner. We were the same age and actually kind of grew up together. When we got older, into our teens, a romance developed. I thought we would get married—so did everyone. We were the fairytale couple of the town, even prom king and queen.

She fidgeted for a moment with the handkerchief. Chet moved his hands so that he was cradling hers and gently pressed her hand to stop the fidgeting.

"Sorry," she said. "Anyway, you have to understand that Albert was extremely popular in our town. He was the star of the basketball team, tall, handsome, charming, came from money…just about anything a girl would want in a guy, right?"

"Sounds like a champ," Chet said, and realized he hadn't done a very good job of hiding his sarcasm.

Kate nodded. "Every girl was jealous of my position. After we graduated high school, he went off to college—law school. We planned to get married, either after he graduated or had finished a few years.

"The only problem was, after dating him through high school, I began to realize I didn't love him. Heck, I didn't even really like him anymore. He was snobby, arrogant, and demeaning to me. I was nothing more than an object to him and college only seemed to have made him worse.

"I tried to carry on, be the dutiful girlfriend, but in reality, all I had done was drag out the inevitable. Finally, one night—he was home for Thanksgiving—he proposed to me, wanted to make it official. I just couldn't go through with it. I realized that the rest of my life was on the line, so I turned him down and broke off the whole thing.

"At first, he was crushed and begged me to take him back. He made all kinds of promises to treat me better. Told me he loved me, but my mind was set on it. I told him we could always be friends, but I thought it had been a mistake for us to have ever allowed our friendship to turn into a romantic relationship.

"It would be an understatement to say he didn't take it well. In fact, he was furious. In his eyes, I had insulted his honor and humiliated him.

197

"One day, not long after, I went out riding alone...I needed to—" At this point she choked on a sob, her eyes welling with tears.

He scooted closer to her and placed an arm around her shoulders. She looked up at him, meeting his gaze, her eyes shimmering and pleading.

"You don't have to tell me," Chet said. "It's okay."

"No!" she said. "Don't you see? I do have to tell you!"

He nodded. "Okay."

After regaining her composure she continued, "So, I went riding a few days later in the hills, where I usually liked to go. I was confused. Everyone was telling me I had made a terrible mistake. I felt like the whole town was mad at me for breaking up with him. I just needed to get away and be alone for a while to clear my head, you know?"

Chet nodded, being no stranger to the feeling.

"Well anyway, I would usually ride out to a particular pond in the woods and let my horse drink before heading back. I slid off Storm's back and led her to the water." Kate paused, her voice choking back a sob.

He felt the tips of his ears burning, not sure if he wanted to hear what she was about to say. The tension in the room was thick, like a heavy cloud hanging over them.

She swallowed hard, gripped his hands tighter, and continued, "I don't know if he followed me or if he was already there waiting for me. I guess it doesn't matter." Her voice was just a choked whisper now.

"Who was there?" Chet asked, fearful of the answer.

"Albert. He just appeared out of nowhere, said he wanted to talk about us. He was angry and drunk. I was scared, so I told him we could talk about it later when he had sobered up. He wouldn't listen and kept insisting that he loved me and we needed to talk.

"He was standing between Storm and I, and he kept side-stepping in front of me as I tried to get past him. I just wanted to get on my horse and get out of there. I finally lost my temper and pushed him." Her tears were flowing at this point, and she was making no more attempts to hold back the flood.

Chet put an arm around her shoulders, they were trembling.

"He fell and I made a move for my horse, but I wasn't quick enough, Chet. I just wasn't quick enough. He grabbed me by the hair and threw me to the ground. The next thing I know...he's on top of me, hitting me and calling me horrible names. He...he started ripping away at my clothes. I fought him. I fought as hard as I could, clawing at his face, kicking, screaming, but it only made him angrier and stronger. He was so strong."

Chet felt his blood boil and had to resist the urge to slam his fist into something, but on some instinctual level, he knew that now was not the time for that. An angry display was the last thing she needed from him right now. What she did need, he wasn't exactly sure, but one thing he knew for certain, he would be there for her. He wasn't even entirely sure what that meant, but he knew it meant something deep, something profound.

Unable to resist any longer, he put both his arms around her, holding her close. She buried her face into his chest and sobbed in silence, while he gently stroked her hair. After a few moments, the sobbing ebbed to a sniffle and she raised her liquid emerald eyes to meet his.

"I'm so sorry for dropping this bomb on you," she said. "Daddy said to never speak of it, but I just couldn't keep on any longer the way we have without telling you. You have a right to know about it. I might not be exactly what you had hoped for. Damaged goods, I guess you could say."

Chet shook his head. "No. I would never say that, and I never want to hear you say it again." He took her face in both of his hands and wiped at her tears with his thumbs, smearing streaks of mascara across her cheeks. "Are we clear on that?"

Kate nodded and a little smile escaped onto her lips. "Yes," she said, "We're clear."

"Good. Okay, so what happened next? How does all this get you halfway across the country?"

"Okay," she said, peeling his hands away from her face to cradle them in her lap. "He was gone as suddenly as he had appeared. I was…I was scared, angry, hurting, ashamed, in shock…I didn't know what to think or feel. I was numb. I went straight home and told my parents what had happened.

"Daddy was furious. He swore to find Albert and kill him, but Mom convinced him to call the police. They came out and took one look at my face and clothes, and began a manhunt for Albert instantly."

"Were they able to find him?" Chet asked. "Was he arrested?"

"They found him later that night in his family's barn. He was dead. He had shot himself."

Secretly, Chet was glad to hear that news. *Good riddance!*

"The next thing I know, the whole town is pretty much blaming Albert's suicide on me."

"What?" he exclaimed. "That's ridiculous! Why?"

"Everyone said I broke his heart. They said if I hadn't left him, he'd still be alive. There were lots of ugly rumors that started to spread about me. I finally decided to go public with what he had done to me, but that only seemed to enrage everyone all the more. I was 'spitting on his grave,' they said."

"Unbelievable."

"I had nobody. My friends had all turned on me, the entire town hated my guts. My family was suffering by me just being there. That's when my dad decided it would be best for me and the family if I went away—at least for a while. So Daddy pulled some strings and got me into a business school in Nashville where I could do a quick crash-course and qualify to do secretary work. He and Principal Grayson are old college buddies, so Daddy got a hold of him and, the next thing I know, here I am. You're the first person I've ever told about it."

They sat in silence for a long time. Chet replayed Kate's story in his mind over and over, wishing he could travel back in time and be there at the pond on that horrible day.

"So," Kate broke the silence, "what are you thinking about?"

"Actually, I was thinking I wish I could go back in time, and be there at the pond waiting for him."

Kate smiled. "That's sweet, but that's not going to happen. What's done is done, as they say. Only thing to do now is put it behind and move on."

"Yeah, move on," Chet said.

Somewhere in the house a phone began to ring. Mable's muffled voice could be heard as she answered it.

"Thanks for listening, Chet. I can't believe how much that helped," Kate said.

"Anytime."

"Promise me something?"

"What's that?"

"Don't shut me out. Let me help you too."

"What do you mean?"

Kate snuggled up to him and laid her cheek on his shoulder. "You know what I'm talking about. You don't have to tonight or anything. Just promise me that when you're ready, you'll let me in, let me help you like you helped me tonight. Maybe you've been good at hiding it from everyone else, but you can't hide it from me. I'm no stranger to bad memories and nightmares."

She definitely had his number alright. He sighed. "Okay."

"So, promise?"

"I promise."

She chuckled and said, "That's probably why we both get along so well."

"Why's that?"

"Because we're both equally screwed up!"

"You're terrible," Chet said.

And they both started to chuckle. Quickly, the chuckle evolved into full blown fits of therapeutic laughter that chased away the gloom and tension that had pervaded the room earlier.

Mable suddenly appeared from the hallway. "Well, it looks like you kids are having a good time," she beamed. "What's so dang funny?"

Chet stood up. "It's nothing, Mable, I was just getting ready to leave."

"Actually," the matronly woman said, "I just got off the phone with Rick, he called from your office. He said something has come up and he's on his way here right now to pick you up."

"Did he say what it was about?" Chet asked.

"No, just said to let you know he'd be here in a few."

"Okay. Thanks, Mable."

"Next time you should stay for dinner," Mable said.

"Next time," he promised.

She bustled out of the room but not before turning back to give them both an inquisitive look. He headed for the front door, Kate trailing close behind. They reached the door and without saying anything, he turned and pulled her into an embrace. Chet inhaled the sweet fragrance of her hair, ignoring the little strands that reached out to tickle his nose.

There was a flash of headlights through the window and two quick honks from a car horn. "That'd be for me," he said, "I gotta go."

"Be careful," Kate said. She raised up on her tiptoes and pressed her lips firmly to his. Chet felt a hunger run through him, but just like that, she pulled away with an impish smile.

"Was that a kiss?" he asked, certain that it was.

"Chet, if you have to ask, then it probably wasn't. I told you before, if I kiss you, you'll know."

"Right. I forgot. See you tomorrow?"

"Get out of here, Sheriff, before Rick loses his patience. Now goodnight."

"Goodnight, Kate."

He opened the door and half jogged to Rick's patrol car, parked in the driveway. He slid into the passenger seat. "What's going on, Rick?" he asked. "Did Robbie's body turn up?"

"Nope," Rick answered as he threw the car's transmission into reverse and started to back out of the driveway.

"You found Robbie's killer?"

"Nope."

"Levi Henderson turned up?"

Rick shifted into first gear, then paused deliberately to look at Chet before launching the car down the street. "Reverend Gannon's been killed."

CHAPTER 19

As Rick pulled the car up to the entrance of the hospital Chet let out a sigh. "You know, Rick, I think I've had about enough of this place for a while."

Rick humphed. "Tell me about it. Give it another twenty years, then come talk to me."

"I'll be sure to make a note of it," Chet said, popping his door open and climbing out. "Dr. Steinmetz didn't give you any information over the phone?"

The deputy came around the front of the car. "Nope, he just said that Lucas Gannon had been killed and that we…make that *you* should get down here right away. That's when I called Mable to track you down." He sidled up next to Chet. "I didn't interrupt anything too important back there did I?" he asked, giving Chet a poke in the ribs with his elbow.

"Let's go find Dr. Steinmetz," Chet said.

They entered the main doors to find the doctor waiting for them at the front desk, dressed in his trademark jeans and cowboy boots. An off-white, button-up shirt and red tie were partially concealed by a black, v-neck sweater vest. He was absently stroking the whiskers of his bushy, gray and black mustache that extended past the corners of his mouth to bristle at his chin.

Chet had known Harold Steinmetz his entire life. In fact, the older doctor had delivered Chet as a baby and had been the Cooper family doctor ever since. He had been dubbed The Cowboy Doctor by his patients due to his penchant for wearing jeans and boots, not to mention the fact that he still competed as a calf roper in local rodeos.

He had been a gentle, guiding influence for Chet and his younger sister, Connie, when their father had passed away from cancer during their teen years. He was an absolute godsend when Mom had died while Chet was away, practically taking Connie under his wing as his own daughter. For that, Chet was eternally grateful to the man.

Shorty after becoming sheriff, Chet had enlisted the old cowboy to come aboard part-time as county coroner and had learned to entirely trust the man's expertise and opinion on matters of the deceased, such as time of death and cause of death. If a corpse arrived at the hospital, Dr. Steinmetz was usually called in for his opinion.

The doctor's dark-brown eyes studied the men from behind a pair of small, wire-rimmed glasses as they approached, his usual smile replaced by a grim frown. Chet didn't like the look in the doctor's eyes. Something told him he might be in for a long night.

"We've gotta quit meeting like this," Chet said, extending his hand.

Dr. Steinmetz pumped his hand, and then Rick's. "Trust me, Chet, I don't like it anymore than you do. You could always get somebody else to do your dirty work you know. I wouldn't complain."

"I'm sure you wouldn't, but I think I'm going to need you to stick it out for just a bit longer, Doc."

The old cowboy nodded with a smile and gestured for them to accompany him down the hall. "Shall we?"

"After you," Chet said, falling in step beside the doctor, Rick taking up the rear.

It was dinner time at the hospital and as they walked down the corridor, nurses and orderlies were bustling about like ants, pushing carts of food from room to room. More than once the trio had to dodge a metal food cart as it was whisked past them, squeaking wheels protesting all the way.

They reached a four-way intersection and the doctor led them to the right. That meant they were heading for the morgue at the end of the hall. This hallway was deserted and the three men slowed their pace, none being in a hurry to go into a morgue.

Rick said, "Doc, you wanna fill us in here? I'm guessing that Reverend Gannon didn't die of a heart attack."

"Well," the doctor began, "he was actually found in his truck, a couple of hours ago, by some hunters out on the old Salem Road. Apparently, his truck had left the road and was found smashed into a tree."

"With him dead inside, I take it," Chet said.

"Not quite dead yet. He was still alive at the time he was found, but he was gone by the time they were able to get him here."

They reached the morgue. Dr. Steinmetz pushed on the crash bar of the heavy wooden door and walked into the room, Chet and Rick following behind.

The morgue wasn't a very large room. It was big enough that it held two rows of five gurneys, four of which were occupied, each covered by a white sheet. The floor was concrete, painted a mint-green with a circular drain in its center. White and matching mint-green tiles alternated to form geometrical patterns on the walls. There was that certain stringent, chemical smell present that Chet noticed at the funeral home, except no flowers were present here to mask it. Instinctively, he crinkled his nose and tried to breath through his mouth.

Rick walked around the gurneys. "So, one of these stiffs is Reverend Gannon?"

"A little respect, deputy," Chet scolded.

"Sorry, Coop."

Chet turned to Dr. Steinmetz. "So, what's the deal here? He had a heart attack or a stroke, lost control of his truck, and crashed it into a tree?"

The doctor walked over to the farthest body on the left. Out of the four, it was the only one that had dark-red spots where obvious wounds of some kind had bled through the sheet. "He crashed his truck all right, but he didn't have a heart attack or a stroke, and the crash isn't what killed him."

"Then what did?" Chet asked.

"That's why I called you," Dr. Steinmetz said, grabbing the sheet by a corner. "You tell me." In a quick, fluid motion, like someone ripping off a bandage, he uncovered the upper half of Lucas Gannon's body.

"What the hell?" Rick muttered.

Chet moved in for a closer look. Despite the fact that the corpse had probably been cleaned up before being placed in the morgue, it was still a mess. There were bruises and lacerations almost everywhere, many of the cuts still leaking small dribs of blood.

Rick's mouth hung open as he stepped closer. "What was he doin' when he hit the tree, a hundred miles an hour?"

Chet had seen the results of a fatal crash before. Car accidents were something he had to deal with on a regular basis and, unfortunately, sometimes people didn't survive. He broke his gaze away from the body and looked at Dr. Steinmetz. "Well, if your objective in bringing me down here was to kill my appetite, then congratulations. But something tells me that's not why I'm here."

Dr. Steinmetz shook his head. "No, that's not why I brought you here. Let me just get right to it." He grabbed Reverend Gannon by the hair and tilted back his head, fully exposing the fleshy throat. There was an oval shaped wound over the left jugular, red and angry with a sickly, yellow bruise extending outward. There were parts of the wound where the skin had been pierced, leaving deep punctures where pools of blood lay coagulating.

"I've examined this wound pretty thoroughly for the last hour," Dr. Steinmetz said. "Do you recognize what this is, Chet? What caused this wound?"

Chet folded his arms. "Can't say that I do."

"That's a damn bite mark," Rick blurted, "a *human* bite mark!"

Dr. Steinmetz pointed his finger at Rick and made a clicking sound with his tongue. "Give the man a prize."

Rick folded his arms and puffed out his chest, his face beaming with pride.

"There's more," the doctor said, moving to the head of the gurney, motioning for Chet and Rick to accompany him. "There's another strange wound here," he said, pointing to a hole between the neck and shoulder. "A very deep puncture wound. Something stabbed him and then was ripped roughly out again."

Chet's mind was whirring as he tried to process what Dr. Steinmetz was getting at.

"And, for the icing on the cake," Dr. Steinmetz picked up the right hand of the corpse, "I found what I believe to be gunpowder residue on his hands. The Reverend has recently fired a gun, from what I can tell."

Chet chewed on his lower lip as he pondered the implications: a human bite wound on the throat, a stab wound in the shoulder, and gunpowder residue on the hands. As much as he hated it, wanted to deny it, his mind finally took the leap. "He was attacked."

"I believe so," the doctor said, clasping his hands behind his back.

Chet squeezed his eyes against the fatigue that was creeping up on him. "Have you been able to determine the cause of death yet?"

"Can't say for sure, but at this point I think he had his ribs broken and one or both lungs were punctured. That stab wound in his shoulder could have contributed as well. I'll know more once I start poking around inside."

"When will you be able to get started?"

"I can get on it right away." Dr. Steinmetz walked over to a cupboard and opened it. Inside were various cutting and sawing instruments. He looked over his shoulder at Chet. "You're welcome to stay and watch. It shouldn't take too long."

Chet had seen enough of what people looked like on the inside without needing to see anymore. "I think we'll check back with you later."

Dr. Steinmetz smiled. "If you say so, Sheriff."

"Who found him and brought him in?" Chet asked. "We should probably go talk to him."

The older man dropped a handful of instruments onto a metal cart and started pushing it across the floor. "It was Roy Hatcher and his oldest son, Trent."

"Did you talk to them?"

"No, they had already gone when I got here. I expect you can find them at home."

Chet motioned with his head to Rick that it was time to leave. "Alright, Doc, we'll let you get to work. I'll give you a call later tonight, or first thing in the morning to see what you found out."

The doctor was just donning a blue apron that he had pulled from another cupboard. "Sounds like a plan. But I gotta tell ya, I think you might have a murder on your hands here."

"That's just what I need right now."

The Hatcher residence was located in a row of twenty homes, lining one side of Fisher Road on the eastern outskirts of town. The row of homes was the last real neighborhood on this side of Clear Creek. Beyond them the community abruptly surrendered to the expansive pastures, fields, and farmland of the countryside.

"It's gotta be the same person who killed Robbie," Chet said, as Rick turned the car onto Fisher Road. "You have to ask, what are the chances that we would have two totally unconnected murders here in Clear Creek?"

"I suppose that makes sense," Rick agreed, "but I just can't see how they could possibly connect. If it is the same person, they sure didn't follow the same pattern."

"Go on."

"Well, with Robbie the killer did his best to make it look like an accident or at least a suicide, but with Reverend Gannon there's no attempt to cover up what happened…he bit him on the neck for cryin' out loud."

"That is pretty weird," Chet said. "I feel like I'm suddenly starring in the latest Dracula picture."

Rick slowed the car and pulled into the driveway of the Hatcher residence. "What makes you think *you're* the star? I *am* the better looking one out of the two of us after all."

Chet sighed as he got out of the car. "You know what, if you want to be the star of this particular nightmare, be my guest."

Rick laughed and slapped Chet on the back as they walked up the drive and mounted the steps of the front porch. "Don't worry, Coop. If we just keep picking away at the threads something will unravel. We'll get to the bottom of all this."

He wished he could share in his deputy's confidence as he rapped with his knuckles on the aluminum screen door. From somewhere inside the house a dog exploded in a canine fit of barking and snarling. The two men looked at each other nervously.

"Sounds like someone ain't had his dinner yet," Rick said.

Chet looked at his deputy and could see that the barking had the man just a bit on edge. "Maybe he's had dinner but just wants a little deputy for dessert."

A muffled voice could be heard as someone behind the door scolded the dog. Soon the barking stopped and Roy Hatcher opened the door.

Roy was middle-aged, somewhere in his fifties, with short-cropped hair the color of wet sand that had been sprinkled with salt. A lifetime of physical labor in the steel mill had actually been good to him, bestowing him with hardened muscles that stacked neatly on his trim, six-foot frame. He wore green wool hunting pants tucked into high leather boots, and a white undershirt that left the arms exposed from his rounded shoulders down.

Sitting in the hallway behind Roy, a fat, stumpy Basset Hound warned the intruders with a low growl.

"That's enough, Butch!" Roy said with a sharp clap of his hands.

Butch the Basset Hound let out a whimper and waddled off, leaving his master to fend for himself, but not before turning and letting out one last growl as if to say, *I'll be in the next room, so don't try anything funny!*

Chet smiled and said, "Evening Roy."

Roy nodded, stepped aside, and motioned for them to enter. "I figured I might be getting a visit from you tonight." He led them to a small room adjacent to the front entry way. The room contained a small couch with matching walnut end tables, a wooden rocking chair, and an old piano squatting in the corner. "Can I get you men a beer?"

"No thanks, Roy," Chet said, "this shouldn't take too long if you've got a minute."

"Sure thing." Roy nonchalantly dragged the rocking chair across the room so that it faced the couch. Settling himself into the chair, he gestured at the couch. "Have a seat, make yourselves comfortable."

The two cops crammed themselves onto the small couch, their shoulders rubbing together. Rick pulled a small notepad and a stubby pencil from his shirt pocket and waited.

Chet leaned forward, placing his elbows on his knees. "I just want you to go over what happened today with Reverend Gannon. Just start from the beginning. Any small details could be important, so try to concentrate on that, okay?"

"There's not much to tell really," Roy began. "Me and Trent decided to go see if we could bag a deer or two this morning."

"Trent's your oldest?" Rick asked.

"And my only," Roy answered. "Sixteen years old. He's in the kitchen doing his school work. You want me to fetch him here?"

"I don't think that's necessary," Chet said.

Rick jotted down a few notes in his notepad.

"Anyway," Roy continued, "we decided we'd take the old Salem Road up past the Danbury farm. I hadn't been up that far in quite some time, but I'd heard there might be some deer up that way. Well, we hadn't gotten too far up into the tree line—maybe ten minutes or so—when I see this old Chevy up ahead. It looked like it had just failed to make a turn in the road and had crashed off into the woods. It was resting against a big old tree. There was still steam coming out from under the hood; it hadn't been very long.

"We jumped outta our truck and ran over to have a look. Sure enough, there's Reverend Gannon lying on the front seat with blood all over him. I thought for sure he was dead at first, then I heard him wheeze and cough."

"Was he conscious?" Chet asked.

"No, he was out like a light. I shook him and yelled his name, but I couldn't get him to respond. He was bleeding real bad from his mouth; I knew I had to get him to the hospital quick. So me and my boy carried him to our truck and drove as fast as we could back to town. But he didn't make it...course you already know that."

Rick looked up from his notepad. "So that's it then?"

"Pretty much, I suppose."

"You didn't see anybody else around? Nothing else strange or out of the ordinary at the scene?"

Roy leaned back into the rocker. "Well, if you ask me the whole damn thing is pretty out of the ordinary."

"How's that?" Chet asked.

The steel worker shrugged his rounded shoulders. "For starters, it's strange that he was even up there. The only reason to be up on that road is to hunt, but

Reverend Gannon was not dressed for hunting, and I didn't see a rifle anywhere. And his truck was pointing downhill, so he had been coming back from up the hill when he had the accident. What was he doing way up there, especially all by himself?"

Chet nodded. "Anything else?"

Roy folded his muscular arms across his chest. "I ain't no expert, but if you ask me, he looked way too bloodied up. It's not like he wrapped the truck around that tree, but he sure looked like he had."

"So you're saying the injuries seemed inconsistent with the accident." Chet stated, more than asked.

Roy nodded.

"Dr. Steinmetz said he died while you were driving him into town."

"That's right. He was coughing up a lot of blood the whole way. I kept talking to him, trying to tell him to hang on, that we were almost there, but he went quiet just as we hit town. When we got to the hospital, they told us he was already dead."

Rick looked up from his notepad and scratched behind his ear with the pencil. "You say you were talking to him?"

Nice Catch, Chet thought. He had missed it completely. Not for the first time, he was grateful to have the older, more experienced man at his side.

"Are you saying he *was* conscious then?" Rick pressed.

Roy bobbed his head up and down. "Yeah, he came to for a while—at least partly.

"Did he say anything?" Chet tried to subdue the sound of urgency in his voice.

Roy spread his hands out in front of him. "I don't think he was right in the head, Sheriff. He was terrified of something. My boy had to hold him down, he was thrashing around so bad, and he wasn't making a lick of sense."

"Did he say what had happened to him?"

"Not that I recall." Roy leaned back into the chair and looked up as if he could see his memories being projected onto the ceiling. "He just sounded crazy to me. He said the demon was back, said it like he was trying to warn me. There was something about his father." Roy scratched at his chin. "He shouted out the name Cyrus a couple of times."

Chet looked at Rick who was scribbling away in his notepad. "The name Cyrus ring a bell to you Rick?"

"I don't think so."

Chet turned back to Roy. "Anything else you can think of?"

"There's one more thing," Roy said. "When he was thrashing around, he was actually trying to see out of the windows. We kept telling him he needed to lay still—he was bleeding all over the place—but he had this horrified look on his face and just kept asking us, 'Where's the boy, where's the boy?' We asked him, what boy?" Roy paused and rubbed the back of his neck with one hand. He seemed hesitant continue.

"And what was his answer?" Chet prodded.

Roy scrunched his eyebrows together. "'The dead boy that killed me.'"

CHAPTER 20

W ell, Daniel, I have to say this is very excellent work," Mr. Phelps said, leaning in for a closer look at the diorama on his desk. His thinning red hair was messed up from a day of running his hands through it and his shirt had come loose from his waistband in various places. His face belonged to a wax figure in a museum, the day's buildup of oil and grease glossing his pale skin in a dull sheen.

School had let out a few minutes ago. Waiting for the hallways to clear sufficiently, Daniel had retrieved his extra credit assignment from his locker and had just presented it to his so-called history teacher. The assignment had been to create a diorama depicting an event from world history that interested him, the topic was to be of his choosing. The temptation to show the assassination of Abraham Lincoln, Mr. Phelps's hero, had been strong, but in the end he had opted for a more subtle form of rebellion.

"Outstanding attention to detail," Mr. Phelps said. "I didn't know you were an artist."

"Thanks," Daniel replied, with a shrug. It was no big deal. He knew the simple-minded teacher would be impressed with it. He did have to admit, it was probably the best diorama project that had ever come across the old windbag's desk. It was museum quality work, from the life-like miniature palm trees to the tiny soldiers positioned amongst them.

Mr. Phelps removed his glasses and squinted. "What is that on the top of the little hill there?" he asked, using his tie to clean the greasy smudges from his glasses.

Daniel would have liked to shove that grease-stained tie down the man's throat and let him choke on it. It took an effort to maintain a calm voice as he explained. "That's a machine gun nest. See how it has these American Marines pinned down in this low area? They've walked into an ambush. There's two more machine gun nests." Daniel indicated with his finger. "Here and here. The Marines are surrounded on three sides by interlocking fields of fire. It's a perfect trap. There's no way out." Daniel pointed out a half dozen tiny Marines, their small, lead-cast bodies disfigured and painted with scarlet wounds. "As you can see, they won't last long."

Mr. Phelps cleared his throat. "I see." He was visibly uncomfortable by the scenario—not unexpected. He stood up and replaced his glasses. "As I said, Daniel, this is very good work and will see you a long way toward some extra credit points."

"I thought you'd like it, sir."

"Just one thing."

Here it comes.

"I'm curious. What inspired you to create this particular scene? Why depict Americans losing? Why not show the same scene, but with the Americans ambushing the Japanese? Doesn't it just kind of seem a bit on the unpatriotic side?"

It was official now. Daniel had suspected it, but it was now confirmed that Mr. Phelps *was* an idiot, just like everybody else. "That's the trouble with the truth, sir." The word *sir* clung with bitterness to his tongue so that he had to spit it out. "The truth isn't patriotic or unpatriotic. It doesn't take sides. It is what it is."

Mr. Phelps straightened like he had been slapped in the face. He took a moment, as if thinking of how to respond. "I'm not disputing that, not at all. I just simply asked you a question, and I believe it's a valid one. You could have just as easily made a diorama depicting the Americans winning. Why wouldn't you?"

Daniel felt his patience with the doddering old fool slipping away. "Maybe I did," he said, through partially gritted teeth.

Mr. Phelps gesticulated with his blocky, clumsy hands. "I hardly see how this depicts the Americans in any kind of winning situation. Why not—"

"Tuesday, November 22, 1943," Daniel interrupted, unable to contain himself any longer. "The Battle of Tarawa, First Battalion, Sixth Marines," he extended his hand slowly over the diorama, like some god about to manipulate his creation. "A large squad of Marines, led by Sergeant Chester Cooper, is caught in a deadly ambush with little or no chance of survival."

Mr. Phelps began to slowly nod his head.

Daniel placed a finger on the head of one of the small figures and continued. "Sergeant Cooper, realizing that his entire squad is on the verge of being wiped out, charges a machine gun emplacement. Defying all the odds, and perhaps even God himself, the sergeant gets close enough to the nest without getting killed and destroys it with a grenade. He then saves the rest of his men by turning the machine gun against the other Japanese emplacements and rallies the rest of the squad to fight through the ambush…onto victory."

Mr. Phelps cut in, speaking slowly, like an imbecile trying to tell a joke to which he's forgotten the punch line. "America goes on to take Tarawa, then Saipan, and eventually all of the Pacific islands." He chuckled. "I've underestimated you, son. In your own way you *did* depict an American victory. Not bad. And you even found a way to include our local sheriff."

"Yes, sir."

Mr. Phelps smiled a warm, sincere smile and asked, "How's the nightmare situation these days, Daniel?"

"A lot better. I just must have been going through some kind of phase or something. Actually, working on that diorama really seemed to help."

Daniel was laying it on kind of thick now, but Mr. Phelps simply beamed back at him. "Well, I'm glad to hear it!" He lifted the diorama in his hands and looked again at the details up close. "I'm going to figure out a good place where I can display this if you don't mind. It would be a crime not to."

"That'd be fine with me, sir," Daniel said. "Can I be excused now? I need to get home to my chores and homework."

"Yes, yes," Mr. Phelps said, continuing to admire the miniature battlefield. "We'll see you tomorrow, Daniel."

Walking the empty hallways, Daniel tried to push the insufferable Mr. Phelps out of his mind by attempting to tune in to *Her* thoughts. She hadn't required anything from him in a while and he was getting anxious. Was she not pleased with him? Was she cutting him off? The thought filled him with dread. He tried to calm down and reminded himself that he had done all that she had asked. There was no reason for her to be displeased. She had a plan, and he was a part of that plan. That much he knew, and for that he was grateful.

Reverend Gannon was dead. She had allowed him to be a part of that, hadn't she? Maybe he hadn't physically been there, but he was as much a part of it as Cyrus or Levi, lending his power and his life force to the deed.

In his mind's eye, he had watched the whole thing unfold through the eyes of the dead boy. He had even felt the impact as the buckshot from Reverend Gannon's shotgun had ripped through Levi's body. It was then that he had felt his own life force combining with the others to give renewed strength to the thrall, so that it could finish the job. He had still not recovered fully from the draining effects. Perhaps that was why he was having trouble communing with his mistress.

As he was nearing the main entrance to the school, lost in his thoughts, Miss Farnsworth, that new secretary, suddenly emerged from the office and into the hall directly in front of him. Instinctively, he flattened himself against the wall and froze like a cat, just before it pounces on its prey.

Like the majority of people she was oblivious to her surroundings and didn't see him, just yards behind her, as she locked the door to the office. He was a statue against the wall watching her as she walked away.

He caressed her with a heavy gaze, every line and curve. With blatant abandon, he admired the well-defined muscles in her shapely calves as they flexed with each step, the sensuous undulation of her nicely rounded hips rising and falling beneath the snug drape of a yellow dress, and the thick, dark, curls of her hair, teasing and beckoning as they bobbed and played about her shoulders.

He was close enough to catch a fleeting hint of her perfume in his nostrils and he felt a hunger growing deep inside him, ravenous and insatiable. The live fish in his gut began to flop around once again.

Unmoving, he waited as she disappeared around a corner. He listened and heard the sound of one of the doors to the main entrance open and then close with a loud snick. He forced himself to wait just a minute more and then made his own way to the main entrance…quietly, slowly.

Once he closed the door behind him, she was easy to locate with her high heels echoing on the pavement nearby. He watched for another minute, allowing her to get a little farther down the street. When he was sure that she was a safe distance ahead, he put his head down and began to follow her.

CHAPTER 21

Kate's hand lingered for a moment on her pink sweater hanging in the entryway of the Cozy Corner. She had changed into jeans and white, canvas tennis shoes, but still, it was such a nice warm day that even the thought of lugging a sweater along with the sandwich-laden picnic basket seemed a hassle. But, if there was anything she had learned over the last couple of weeks in Clear Creek, it was that the warmest of days could turn into very chilly evenings. On her last walk with Chet, she had nearly turned into an icicle by the time he had walked her home.

Her last walk with Chet. She hadn't seen him or talked to him since spilling her guts to him, a few nights ago. He sure hadn't stopped by or called since that night, but to be fair, he was up to his brilliant-blue eyeballs right now with everything that was going on.

She looked down at the picnic basket. Maybe this was a mistake. Maybe he hadn't called or come by because he needed more time to process. After all, she had pretty much dropped an A-bomb on him the other night. Or was she damaged goods now in his eyes? That's what they had called her back home.

No, she would not allow herself to believe that about him! She knew him better than that. There had been so much tenderness and compassion in his eyes when she had opened up to him. She couldn't have hoped for a better reaction. Or was she totally wrong? Had she mistaken pity for compassion? Because there was a difference. A big difference!

A hot, long repressed anger seeped up from somewhere deep in her core. She didn't want his pity! She didn't want anyone's pity! All the pity in the world couldn't take back that awful day. She just wanted to get on with her life without that one ugly event from her past factoring into every decision she made.

She abandoned the pink sweater on the hanger and jerked open the front door. Come hell or high water, she was bringing Chet a dang sandwich today, and he was going to love it!

As she shut the door behind her, a slight movement to the right caught her eye. She snapped her head in that direction. One of the juniper shrubs growing on the corner of the house was swaying, as if being stirred by a light breeze. Only there was no breeze. She watched as the shrub grew still, her heart anything but. Someone had been there watching her!

"Who's there!" she called out, doing her best to sound tough and unafraid. There was no answer—not that she expected one. She took a deep breath to steady and calm her nerves. It was probably just some stupid kids messing around, or even a stray dog.

She shook her head. How long was it going to take? How long until she didn't jump out of her skin every time someone said hello from behind? How long until she didn't see Albert, drunken and ravenous in every shadow and dark corner? How long until she could stop reminding herself on a daily basis that Albert was dead?

"You've just got to get over it, girl, and move on," she whispered, clenching her jaw. She concentrated and forced an image of Chet into the center of her thoughts. The picture of the young sheriff, handsome, strong, and solid, splashed into that dark place in her mind, dispelling the blackness, sending it retreating away, replacing it with light and warmth. She smiled and allowed herself to bask in that moment of peace.

She recalled the picnic basket in the crook of her arm and the yummy food inside. She felt a twinge of excitement as she imagined Chet taking hungry bites while listening patiently to how her day went. And Rick would be there, telling jokes and flashing his toothy grin, while wondering if she had brought him any, but too afraid to ask. And when she gave him some, he would try to control himself so as not to spoil his appetite for dinner at home.

She thrust her chin forward, pulled her shoulders back and stepped smartly down the porch stairs, making her way to the street. Let that stupid bush shake itself right out of the ground, for all she cared.

She reached the corner of Washington and Park without even turning around once to look behind her and, since there was no traffic, she jay-walked to the opposite corner, intending to cut through the park. She snickered to herself. Chet would probably have a heart attack if he saw her do that.

She chose the dirt path that meandered through the center of the park, plunging in an out of small copses of manicured trees and flower beds. She recognized several kids from school playing in the park as they darted across her path like playful birds. As she rounded a particular bend in the path, a small gang of rowdy boys nearly ran her down, yelling at the top of their lungs as they barreled down the path on a mad dash to some youthful adventure or mischief.

"Sorry 'bout that, Miss Farnsworth!" a voice echoed back to her as the mob vanished around the bend.

She felt her spirits lifting. It felt good to be known. She was starting to feel like she was part of a community again. She smiled. *That's alright, boys.*

She reached the recently erected pavilion at the center of the park with the big banner hanging over it. Two men dressed in overalls, caps, and leather work boots were working on fastening a tall metal pole to the center of the stage. They both looked up at her as she approached.

"Afternoon, ma'am," one of them greeted, nodding his bearish head. He was short, a little on the chubby side, but stout at the same time. A hint of a smile barely protruded from the bristling, black whiskers of his thick goatee.

"Afternoon," Kate said. She looked again at the pole the men were holding upright. "What's that pole thing supposed to be?"

"It's a mast," the other man said, focusing his attention from Kate back to the *mast*. He was taller and thinner than his partner, with no facial hair, younger, and perhaps not as friendly.

"Oh, a mast?" Kate said. "So where's the flood?" She giggled.

The thinner man gave her a narrow, slightly annoyed look while his partner laughed out loud.

"Ya hear that, Lloyd?" the bigger man said, giving his irritated partner a nudge to the ribs with his elbow. "She thinks you're building an ark! Maybe we should start calling you, Noah! Ha!"

A wry smile suddenly formed on Lloyd's mouth. "Well, if I'm Noah, then who are you supposed to be, Artie, the hippo?"

Like a wave, Artie's beard rolled over his smiling lips, submerging them beneath a coarse, hairy surface. An instant later, the lips resurfaced in the form of an indignant scowl. "Hey!" he said.

Kate slapped her free hand over her mouth to stifle a laugh, but not before a lone, petulant, little squeak had burst from her.

Lloyd seemed pleased with his own clever comeback, and was now jutting his elbow into Artie's ribs. Artie looked down at Kate, a look of hurt on his round face.

"I'm sorry," she managed to choke out between giggles.

The beard bristled and morphed, and out popped the grin once more. "Ah, it's no biggie. I guess I kinda had it coming." Artie squinted his eyes, giving

Kate a once over. "You from around here, lady? I'm sure I don't know your face, and pardon me for sayin' so, but a pretty face like that ain't easy to forget."

"Thank you," Kate said trying not to blush.

Then Lloyd, who was attaching some kind of guy-wire to the pole, burst in. "Of course she's not from around here, Artie. Didn't you hear her accent?" He peeked his head from behind the pole to look at Kate. "Mississippi?"

Kate shook her head and shot him an icy glare.

Lloyd cleared his throat. "Okay, Georgia then?"

"Oh, Pu-lease!" Kate moaned, rolling her eyes.

Lloyd was biting his lip, looking up at the tree tops as if he could see a giant map of the country projected against them. He snapped his fingers. "I got it! Alaba—"

"Don't you dare even say it, mister!" Kate cut him off, pointing an accusatory finger at him.

Lloyd cowered behind the metal pole like a scolded child.

Kate flickered an assuring smile at him. He wasn't really in any trouble with her. "If you really must know, I'm from Tennessee. I'm new here, I just got hired as the new secretary at Lincoln Elementary. My name is Kate Farnsworth." Then she added a big Southern, "How do ya do?" Just for good measure.

"Ah," Artie said, his face lighting up. "I know who you are now. Aren't you Sheriff Cooper's new girlfriend?"

Girlfriend? She hadn't thought of it that way. Is that what she was? Is that what everyone else was saying? Was that what Chet was saying? She hadn't even kissed him yet! Well, not a real kiss, a seal-the-deal kind of kiss anyway.

"Um, well," she stammered, "Yes, we are friends, but—"

Artie cut her off by holding up his hand and shaking his head. "But nothin', sweetheart, you don't have to explain. That romance stuff gets complicated sometimes."

"Yes, it does."

He continued as if he hadn't heard her. Maybe he hadn't. "Specially right now, what with dating a sheriff and all when there's a killer on the loose."

Killer? She knew Chet was looking into some possibilities, but she hadn't heard anyone just flat come out and say it that way, like it was public knowledge.

"You seem like a sweet gal to me," Artie was saying. "Personally, I despite what others are sayin' and I don't blame the sheriff. He's a man of flesh and blood after all, and he's got the right to a personal life too. Right?"

The budding of a certain dread began to edge its way around her heart, like an inky, black tendril slithering around in her chest, probing, poking, trying to snuff out the light and warmth she had been basking in. "What are others saying?" she heard herself ask.

There was an awkward silence as Artie stopped talking mid-sentence. He looked at Lloyd and back to Kate, his face a giant question mark. "Yeah, you know...the article in this morning's paper? You ain't read it?"

Kate slowly shook her head, a million fears running through her mind. "No, I haven't," she said, suddenly feeling numb.

Lloyd snatched his cap off his head and slapped Artie across the back of the neck with it. "Nice one, Artie!"

A look of pain and regret filled Artie's face. "Awe jeez, sweetheart, I'm sorry for runnin' my mouth! I didn't know."

Kate did her best to flash him a brave smile. "It's okay, you didn't do anything wrong. I'll be just fine, but I really aught to get going now. It was a pleasure meeting you both." She picked up the path where she had left off and decided to double time it to Chet's office and find out what in the world this was all about.

She hadn't gone five steps when she heard Lloyd's voice call out behind her. "It's for lights, Miss Farnsworth."

She spun around. "Excuse me?"

"The mast," he said. "You asked what it was for. It's to string lights for the dance on Saturday. We'll string them from the top of the mast out to the trees. It'll be really pretty!"

"I'm sure it will be, Lloyd," she said, before turning back around and walking away. She heard the two men arguing with each other as she dove into a grove of pine trees and vanished from the clearing.

By the time she reached the sheriff's office she had worked herself into a complete tizzy. She could have forced the front door open with sheer mind power alone if she had wanted to, but still had the wherewithal to do a quick hair and makeup check using the mirror of a parked police car.

After taking a moment to gather herself, she pushed open the heavy wooden door to Chet's office and marched in, determined to get to the bottom of whatever was going on.

To her dismay, the office was void of any sign of life except for the ancient, battered fan oscillating back and forth on the corner of Chet's desk. She shook her head at the sight of the choked clutter. It was a miracle the man could find anything! Going to the desk, she rescued a pile of folders that was threatening to avalanche over the side and straightened it into a neat stack. She placed the picnic basket on the floor since there wasn't even a single piece of real estate on Chet's desk to put it.

The two lawmen must have received a call and had to leave. They did have a job to do after all. They probably wouldn't be gone very long. She could wait for them, maybe straighten up a little bit until they got back. She appraised the rat's nest of papers, folders, and broken pencils sprawling out before her. Where to even begin? And he was a Marine? His old drill instructors would probably have a thing or two to say about this.

She sat down in Chet's chair and started stacking papers in separate piles based on their contents. She rummaged through the drawers—all haphazard jumbles of various office supplies—and found a handful of empty file folders under a box of shotgun shells. "Goodness gracious," she muttered, extracting the file folders from the tangle.

She took a stubby pencil that should have been thrown away about two inches ago, and labeled one of the folders, *traffic*. Another one, *domestic*, and yet another, *theft*.

She began sorting the papers and reports into categories, stuffing them into the folders, and creating new folders with new categories when necessary. It was good busy work, and it wasn't long before she was completely submersed in categorizing and filing, forgetting, for the moment, about her troubles and worries.

She was so absorbed in her work that she let out an embarrassing little scream when the door suddenly popped open and Rick Shelton walked into the office. Rick, in turn, jumped about half way out of his skin like a startled cat.

His hand dropped to his sidearm as he spun to face her. "Holy crap, Kate!" he exclaimed as relief flooded his face. "You about gave me a darned stroke!"

Kate smiled and put her hands up in the air. "Don't shoot."

He took his hand off the butt of his pistol and grinned. "As long as you promise to be good, I'll hold my fire."

Kate made the motion of crossing her heart with her index finger. "Promise."

"Alright then," he said, relaxing his posture, his grin growing wider somehow. He looked at her, then at the desk, and back to her again. "Wait a minute, just what are you doing, missy?"

She put her hands on her hips. "Something that really needed to be done, obviously. Although, why I took it upon myself to do it, I really don't know." She pursed her lips and blew an unruly lock of hair out of her eyes. "It's looking a lot better, if I do say so myself, deputy. What do you think? Will Chet be overcome with joy and appreciation when he sees?"

"If he manages to notice, I'm sure he'll dance a jig on the spot."

Kate planted her fists on her hips. "What do you mean, *if* he manages to notice? How could he not notice?"

Rick laughed. "I'm sure he'll notice."

"Well, he better."

"He does have a lot going on right now, but I'm sure he'll notice when he can't find anything on his desk anymore." Rick chuckled.

"Very funny," she said, doing her best to shoot daggers from her eyes.

Rick started scanning the room, looking at all the desks and table tops. "So, you just stopped by to clean up Chet's desk then?" he asked.

Kate had a strong suspicion that he was looking for her trademark picnic basket which, at the moment, was hidden behind her chair. She could almost see the near panic rising in his eyes as he failed to locate the basket. It was her turn to do some leg pulling.

"Yep," she said, "I was just walking around town and thought I'd pop in, see what you boys were up to this afternoon." She pretended to go back to her filing.

"Oh," Rick said, his shoulders visibly slumping.

He looked so pathetic she couldn't stand it. She rose from her chair, the legs scraping on the wood floor. "You are so ridiculous, Deputy Shelton!" she said, producing the basket suddenly from behind her. "Is this what you were looking for?"

Rick's eyes lit up like a kid on Christmas. "Well now," he said, walking over to her. He was rubbing the palms of his hands together and licking his lips. For real! Actually rubbing his palms, and licking his lips!

"What a pleasant surprise," he said through a wolfish grin as he came to stand beside her.

Kate gave the toe of his cowboy boot a playful stomp. "Surprise, my foot!"

"Ow!" he said, his eyes nailed to the lid of the basket.

She lifted one of the lids and let it rest against the handle. "You know, I think I'm beginning to spoil you two." She reached into the basket and pulled out a ham and cheese sandwich wrapped in tinfoil. "It's getting to the point where you expect it now."

She held the sandwich a moment, not quite offering it to him yet. His eyes had the concentration of a dog with a piece of meat dangling in front of its nose. She couldn't help but laugh. "Oh my gosh, here ya go!" she said, tossing the sandwich into the air.

Greedy fingers snatched the sandwich out of the air with surprising agility.

Kate arched an eyebrow, truly impressed. "Nice catch."

Rick brought the foil-wrapped goodness to his nose. "In a former life, I played some minor league baseball...shortstop. Guess I still got it." He took a good sniff. "Ham and cheese?"

"Apparently, you were also a bloodhound in a former life."

He laughed. "You're probably right, Katie my dear." He unwrapped the sandwich and nearly inhaled half of it in one bite. With his mouth on the verge of bursting at the seems, he smiled.

"Glad you approve," she said.

He only nodded and chewed.

Kate looked back down at the desk. She'd made a lot of progress, but still had a bit to do before the task was completed to her satisfaction. One problem: she had just run out of file folders. "Hey Rick, you wouldn't happen to have any file folders in your desk, would you?"

Rick nodded toward his desk. "I think so. Go ahead and help yourself, I'm gonna get a little coffee brewing." He walked over to the percolator sitting on a table in the corner.

She walked the dozen or so steps to the center of the office where Rick's desk butted up against Scotty's. A hand-written book in neat, flowing script, lying open on Rick's desk caught her attention. It looked old. The pages were yellowed and rough on the edges. The leather binding was cracked and faded. The penmanship was exquisite, obviously from a time when penmanship was taken a lot more seriously, almost a form of art in and of itself.

Mesmerized, she gently picked the book up, cradling it in her arms like a fragile infant. "Rick, what is this book?" she asked, carefully leafing through the pages. "A journal of some sort?"

"Huh?" Rick said, looking over his shoulder. "Oh, that's Reverend Gannon's journal. We took it out of his house today."

"Reverend Gannon's journal? What was he, two hundred years old?"

Rick laughed. "I'm talking about Reverend Gannon, *Senior*."

"That makes a lot more sense. What are you guys doing with it?"

"Chet wanted me to look through it and see if I could find anything that might help us figure out who killed the poor Reverend."

"Talk about scraping the bottom of the barrel. Any luck?"

He finished getting the coffee brewing and came back over to her. "I've leafed through it, but haven't been able to come up with anything. And really, with Scotty out of commission for now, neither of us really has the time to be reading through some old preacher's diary." He sat down on the corner of his desk and began studying his sandwich, turning it over in his hands as if plotting where to attack next.

"I could read it," Kate said. "I've got plenty of time. That is, if you're done with it."

The man shrugged his shoulders. "Knock yourself out, kid. We could use all the help we can get at this point. Chet won't care. And like you said, the diary's a long shot anyway." He chomped into the sandwich again.

"So, where *is* your boss?" Kate asked, after she felt like he'd chewed long enough to allow him to answer.

Rick swallowed. "Mayor called, wanted to see him right away." He clamped down again on the sandwich, tearing off another healthy portion.

"Do you know how long he'll be gone?"

He shook his head as he maneuvered most of the food in his mouth into one bulging cheek. He looked like a squirrel, when they jam their cheeks with pine nuts. "I'm not sure, but Mayor Carson sounded pretty ticked off when I answered the phone. I think Chet's over there getting his a— I mean, his *butt* chewed. Could be a while."

"Getting chewed out by the mayor? What for?"

Rick was about to take another bite, but then stopped, a pained look crossing his face. "Well…" He hesitated.

Kate folded her arms across her chest and fixed Rick with a stern gaze. "What is it, Rick?"

"I'm not sure, but it's probably to do with that article in today's paper." He looked into Kate's eyes, sympathy playing on his face. "You haven't read the paper today, have you?"

She shook her head. "Haven't had a chance, but it sounds like I should read it."

Rick nodded and without a word walked over and grabbed a copy of *The Clear Creek Register* out of the wastebasket, next to Chet's desk. He held it out for her as she crossed the room and took it from him, curiosity and apprehension seeping from every pore of her body.

She placed the reverend's journal on Chet's desk, sat down in the chair, and spread the paper out on a section of recently cleared away surface.

"Front page," Rick said, and walked away to sit at his own desk leaving her alone to read.

Kate read the bold headline of the front page story:

KILLER AT LARGE! SHERIFF DISTRACTED?

Clayton County sheriff, "Chet" Cooper, announced today, that his department is operating under the assumption that the death of Reverend Lucas Gannon on October Fifteenth was a homicide. Sheriff Cooper spoke briefly during a telephone interview, but declined to comment on the details surrounding the alleged murder. "We believe that Mr. Gannon was attacked and murdered. We are conducting a thorough investigation and cannot, at this time, comment on the specifics," said Cooper.

When asked if there was a connection between the murder of Mr. Gannon and the theft of Robert Pritchard's body from the Jeppesen Funeral Home, a few weeks ago, the sheriff declined to comment, but did admit that there are no suspects thus far, in either crime.

A string of recent events has plagued the popular sheriff for over a month now, beginning with the disappearance of Levi Henderson, followed by the mysterious death of Robert Pritchard, the bizarre theft of the body, and now the homicide of local Reverend, Lucas Gannon.

"People are talking and starting to worry. People just don't feel safe right now," said Ross Parker, owner of Parker's Food Mart. "People are starting to wonder what the cops are doing about this."

"Right now, we're doing everything we possibly can to resolve these recent occurrences," Sheriff Cooper stated. But many in Clear Creek are starting to have their doubts, in light of the sheriff's recent social activities...

Kate's heart jumped into her throat making it difficult to breathe while her stomach began to burn as if she had swallowed acid. She didn't want to read anymore, but she plowed ahead.

Some have questioned whether or not Sheriff Cooper is too distracted with his own social life. As most people in Clear Creek are keenly aware, the young sheriff has recently taken up dating a Ms. Katherine Farnsworth. Ms. Farnsworth has been seen frequenting the office of Sheriff Cooper in the afternoons. The two have been seen together around town on numerous occasions, even together in the sheriff's official police vehicle.

"My taxes are paying for Sheriff Cooper to solve these crimes and keep this county safe, not to be cruising around with some dame," said one Clear Creek citizen who requested to remain anonymous...

The Summoning

Kate's vision blurred and a tear suddenly fell from her eye and spattered on the newspaper to form an inky, wet blot in the center of the unfinished article. She couldn't believe it. It was happening all over again! She would be the talk of the town once more and then eventually be exiled to start life again amongst strangers. The tears came in great gushes, beyond her ability to control.

In a sudden seizure of rage she crumpled up the paper with both hands, digging her fingers into the ball of paper until it hurt. She hurled the crushed paper back into the wastebasket, nearly tipping the metal can over. She buried her face in her trembling hands. "It's not fair," she uttered. It was her dad's least favorite phrase in the world, and she felt ashamed. But it wasn't fair! After everything she'd been through back home and everything she'd done to build a new life! Not to mention her budding, yet fragile, relationship with the only man on the planet that might understand her...and now this?

Her shoulders convulsed involuntarily as a big sob, generated from her most inner depths, lurched through her body. She could feel another sob down there, somewhere, forming and building, preparing to erupt.

Then there was an arm around her: strong, protective, almost fatherly, full of compassion, gently squeezing. A handkerchief was pressed tenderly into her palms as the arm turned her sideways, pulling her into an embrace.

"There, there, darlin', it's alright." Rick was kneeling on one knee to the side of her chair, still chewing on a bite of sandwich.

She surrendered and buried her head into his shoulder. "Oh Rick, Chet must be absolutely humiliated by this!" she managed to choke between sobs. "He probably totally hates me right now! The whole town probably does!"

"Now you know that's not true, Kate," he said, patting her on the back like he was burping a baby. It must have looked ridiculous, but it felt good.

She pulled away from his shoulder to wipe her eyes and nose. She saw that she had left a big wet stain on his khaki deputy's shirt, and tried to dab at it with the handkerchief. "You must not have read the same article then. Even the mayor's yelling at him right this second. All because of me!"

"That's not true."

"I'm going to have to leave, Rick. I can't stay here, not now, not after this. I won't go through that again, and I won't put Chet through it."

"That's enough of that talk now, missy!" Rick placed his hands on her shoulders and held her at arms length. "Do you have any idea what that would do to Chet?"

"Chet would survive just fine, Rick. In fact, he'd probably be better off without me in the end." The question was, would *she* survive?

Rick's salt and pepper mustache bristled for a moment and he rose to his feet. "Katherine Farnsworth, if you were my daughter I'd put you over my knee this second and give your butt a good whippin'! Hell, I just might do it anyhow, daughter or not!"

Kate's cheeks flushed with shame. Shame and indignation. "That's something I'd certainly like to see you try, deputy!" She laid her Southern accent on thick. She sounded like a hillbilly straight out of the Ozarks, a regular Hatfield or McCoy. The only thing missing from her performance would have been to spit a stream of tobacco juice on his boots.

Rick put his hands on his hips, looked up at the ceiling, and let out a big sigh. "Chet would kill me if he ever found out."

"I imagine he would, but he'd be too late by the time I was finished."

Rick smiled as he parked his rear on the corner of Chet's desk and looked down into her eyes. "Look, I don't know your whole story, about how you ended up here in Clear Creek. Chet hasn't been too clear on the details."

"That's good to know, since he wasn't supposed to talk about it."

"Right. Anyway, I just want to say, that you need to give us a chance."

"What do you mean?"

"This isn't Emmet, Tennessee, so before you get all in a huff and make the rash decision to leave, I'm just sayin', give it a chance. Give this town a chance to prove that we're different."

"I'd like to, Rick. Believe me, I really would. But how am I supposed to think that this town is going to be any different after reading that?" She gestured to the wastebasket.

"Ok," Rick said, "fair point, but do you know who wrote that crap?"

She shook her head.

"Conrad Fairchild, who just so happens to be the brother of Andrew Fairchild."

"And?"

"Andrew Fairchild was the other guy who ran for sheriff and lost to Chet a couple years ago. The Fairchild family is still very upset over Chet's victory. Ticked off might be the better way of puttin' it. It was a bit of a nasty campaign on their part, claiming Chet was unqualified and was simply coasting on the laurels of his war experience."

Rick walked over to where the coffee had just finished percolating and poured two steaming mugs full. He carried the mugs back over to Kate and offered her one.

"Thanks," she said. She wasn't sure what to think. She wasn't sure what to feel. It was like someone had thrown her heart and brain together into a big blender, mixing the two until they became some abstract concoction of anxiety and illogic.

He perched himself back on the corner of the desk and took a tentative sip of his coffee. "Careful, it's pretty hot," he said. "Anyway, old Conrad jumps at every chance he can to take a stab at Chet. This isn't the first time and it won't be the last. Besides, nobody pays him any mind. Everyone knows it's just sour grapes."

Kate cradled the coffee mug in her hands, feeling the warmth seep into her palms. She watched as the steam curled and wafted upwards. Strangely, it brought a touch of comfort. "The mayor sure seems to be paying a mind to him," she said.

Rick took another sip, but kept his eyes fixed on her over the rim of his cup. "Give it a chance," he said, lowering his mug. "Is that really too much to ask?"

She rose to her feet, set the mug down on the desk, and snatched up the picnic basket. "I've gotta get going. When Chet gets back, just tell him I stopped by." She produced another foil-wrapped sandwich from the basket and put it on the desk. "This is for Chet." She fixed Rick with a stern look. "*Chet.*"

He grinned. "Let me drive you." He dug into his front pocket and pulled out his car keys.

"No, absolutely not!"

"Kate, it's no big deal, really."

"Yeah, and if Conrad sees? Can you imagine what he'd write about then?"

Rick nodded and dropped the keys with a *clink* back into his pocket.

She came around the desk and made her way for the door.

"So what are you going to do, Kate?" Rick asked.

"I don't know, I really don't. But promise me you won't speak of any of this to Chet. If I do decide to leave, he should hear it from me first. So that means you don't say a word to Alice either! Promise?"

"I Promise."

"Thanks, Rick. Thanks for everything." She turned and grabbed the doorknob to leave.

"Wait a second," he said, quick stepping to her side. "Didn't you forget something?" He was holding the old diary in his hand. "You promised you'd look through this."

"If I didn't know better, Deputy Shelton, I'd say you're trying to trick me into staying."

"Wouldn't dream of stooping to trickery," he said, smiling like a fox who'd just been handed the keys to the hen house.

"See ya around," she said, taking the diary.

"Promise?"

She forced a smile, opened the door, and stepped out into the crisp, autumn air. A lump was still catching in her throat. Her world, once again, had been turned on its head.

CHAPTER 22

Chet nearly drove up onto the curb before he brought his patrol car to a lurching stop and leaped out, slamming the door behind him. The car was still rocking on its suspension when he jerked the glass door open and burst into the front office of *The Clear Creek Register.*

He was all too aware that he shouldn't be here, not in his current emotional state anyway. He had tried to shake it off and return to business as usual. He had even made it halfway back to his office after his meeting with Mayor Carson, before flipping a u-turn and speeding directly to the newspaper building where Conrad Fairchild worked.

Chet had actually never been inside the building—a den of snakes as far as he was concerned. There was nothing surprising about the office. A tall counter ran the length of the small room, almost like in a bar, with a door behind it that led to the rest of the building. On the far left, the counter was interrupted by a small gate so that one could gain access to the other side. An unoccupied secretary's desk sat in the corner.

The walls of the reception area had been made into a shrine, glorifying the paper's greatest accomplishments. Plaques, awards, and various honors hung in places of prominence along with framed headlines of some of the bigger stories the paper had covered over the years. One in particular caught his eye:

WAR HERO ELECTED SHERIFF

The heavy odor of ink and chemicals dominated the air, making Chet feel a bit light-headed as he approached the counter, or maybe that was just his own blood boiling. The office was empty at the moment, so he assaulted the little silver bell resting on the counter, hammering it with his palm in rapid succession.

He stopped pounding on the bell when a man's voice called out, "I'm coming! I'm coming! Hold your horses!"

The door behind the counter burst open abruptly, and Terry Cook, the press operator, barged into the room. Terry was young with a stout build, square jaw, heavy brow, short, blond hair, and deep-set, blue eyes, that glowed with irritation.

"Sheriff Cooper?" The hard lines in Terry's face softened into questioning curves and arches. "Is something the matter?"

Chet didn't waste any time. "Is Conrad in the building, Terry?"

A glint of understanding flashed across Terry's eyes. "Um, I think so. At least he should be," he said, wiping his eternally ink-stained hands on his canvas apron.

"I need you to go tell him that I'm here to see him."

Terry hesitated for a moment and then opened his mouth to talk.

"Right now, Terry."

The stout man shrugged his shoulders and showed his palms as if in surrender. "Okay Sheriff, you're the boss. I'll go tell him." He turned and went back through the door, shaking his head and muttering something to himself.

He returned a few minutes later. "He's really busy right now, trying to meet the deadline for tomorrow's print."

Chet started walking for the little gate at the end of the counter. "Well, this will only take a minute."

As he pushed through the gate and headed for the door that led to the rest of the building, Terry moved to block his path. "Sorry, Sheriff Cooper, but that's employees only back there."

Chet locked a withering gaze on the young man. "Terry, you're a good guy, but if you don't get out of my way, so help me."

"You're obviously upset right now, and I don't blame you, but you've got to calm down."

On some level in Chet's mind, Terry's words rang true, made sense, were good advice worth heeding. Hell, Terry sounded just like him right now! But that common sense part of his brain was currently being drowned out, overwhelmed by the memory of Conrad's stinging and unfair article.

It wasn't as if he couldn't handle his share of criticism. Conrad had lashed out at him before and he had always been able to let it go, even laugh it off. This time, it wasn't just about his own pride or dignity. Conrad had directly gone after Kate and dragged her through the mud, in front of the entire town! There was a line and the little weasel had crossed it.

"Step aside, Terry."

Terry visibly wilted and backed away. "Just take a minute to think about what you're doing, Sheriff."

The pressman's words barely registered as he shoved his way through the door. He found himself in a short hallway with a plain concrete floor that had been painted a light cream color. On the walls, more framed headlines and articles from the past hung in egotistical, self-congratulatory tribute.

At the end of the hallway, thick strips of clear plastic, suspended from the ceiling, formed a sort of giant curtain. On the other side of the curtain would be the printing area, full of big rollers, belts, dies, inks, and printing plates: the machinery that could transfer a man's thoughts and opinions into actual tangible form to be distributed to the masses, for good or for bad.

He was pretty sure he wouldn't find Conrad in there with all the chemicals, inks, and heavy machinery. That was Terry's world. Conrad's world would be in a tidy little office, hiding behind a desk as he typed out his vitriol day in and day out.

Before the end of the hallway, there was a door on the right. He figured it had to lead to an office area of some kind. He reached the door in a matter of a few large strides and opened it, revealing another small corridor lined with doors on either side.

No painted concrete here. Instead, a nice pad of light-brown carpet sprawled out before him. The walls, painted beige, were decorated with large photographs of dramatic and contrasting landscapes—Ansel Adams if he wasn't mistaken. Three doors lined each side of the hallway, all six sporting engraved, brass nameplates. The broad, green leaves of a decorative geranium plant arched out gracefully next to a gleaming, white porcelain water fountain at the end of the hall. *This* was Conrad's world.

Chet found Conrad Fairchild's name engraved on a brass nameplate at the very end of the hall. He gripped the doorknob and, from within, he could hear the rapid, sharp, staccato of typewriter keys impacting paper. *Last chance to just walk away.* The thought was merely fleeting, the image of Kate's tear-streaked face taking center stage in his mind. Resisting the urge to kick the door right down, he took a deep breath, turned the knob, and stepped into Conrad's lair.

SLUMPING IN THE CHAIR AT HIS DESK, Rick tried to fight off the wave of sadness that was washing over him since Kate's departure. He was still chewing on the final remnants of the sandwich she had made him, but it seemed to have lost its flavor as he contemplated the idea of her actually leaving. Would she really do it? Probably. She didn't seem like the kind of girl to bluff. Poor Chet. How would he take it if she really did leave?

And what was his place in this mess? Kate had sworn him to secrecy, and he had agreed to it at the time, but now he regretted it. Keeping something like that from Chet sure didn't feel right, but come to think of it, neither did breaking his promise to Kate.

"Dammit," he cursed under his breath and chucked the last bite of his sandwich into the wastebasket near his desk. Looking around the empty office he began to feel his frustration rising. Things were starting to get out of control around here: Scotty going off the deep end, Reverend Gannon attacked and murdered, Robbie Pritchard probably murdered too, his body actually stolen from the funeral home! Not to mention little Levi Henderson was still missing. For all anyone knew, Levi had been murdered as well. And now, this stupid article appears in the paper. As if Chet needed to be dealing with that crap on top of everything else!

He looked at his watch. Speaking of the young sheriff, he should have been back by now. Even a good tongue lashing from Mayor Carson shouldn't be taking this long. Standing up, he opened the top drawer of his desk where he kept his duty belt and hauled it out. He buckled it on as he made his way for the door. He'd just take a drive down Main Street and see if Chet's cruiser was still parked at the city building, and then be right back. The phone could take care of itself till then.

He pushed the door open. As if on cue, the phone on Chet's desk began jangling loudly, almost desperately, as if begging him to stay. He sighed and stomped over to the phone, the door slamming shut behind him.

He snatched the receiver up and resisted the temptation to hurl it across the room. "Sheriff's office, Shelton here," he spoke into the microphone.

"Afternoon, Rick," Caroline's tinny voice echoed into his ear. "I've got Terry Cook on the line, from *The Clear Creek Register*. He says it's urgent."

"Well, put him through, Caroline." The impatient tone in his own voice surprised him, so he quickly added a humble, "Please."

What in the world was *The Register* calling about? What nerve to call here after that smear they'd run today on Chet and Kate! They were probably calling him to try to get some kind of statement out him, so they could twist it and turn it against his boss. But, why was Terry Cook, the pressman, calling instead of that no-good snake in the grass, Conrad Fairchild? Most likely, Conrad had put Terry up to it, lacking the guts to make the call himself.

233

He heard the faint click on the phone as his line was connected with the line at the so-called *newspaper.* "What is it, Terry?" he snapped, and this time he didn't care how he sounded.

"Deputy Shelton?" Terry's voice was reserved, almost timid.

"This is Deputy Shelton alright, what do you want, Terry?"

"Uh well," Terry stammered.

Rick didn't have time for this. "No comment." It was a very useful phrase that he had become very acquainted with over his twenty-five years on the job.

"Huh?" Terry said, after a brief pause.

"No comment!" Rick bellowed into the phone. "And you can tell Conrad that if he wants to talk to me, he can come down here to my office and talk to me face to face like a man, or not at all!"

"Deputy Shelton, I don't know what you're talking about," Terry said, the volume of his voice rising with each word, "but I think you better get down here right now!"

Rick's gut stirred as his senses picked up on the urgent and worried tone of Terry's voice. Okay, so maybe he had been wrong about the reason for the call. The realization that he'd just made an ass of himself was just a mere inkling beginning to take real shape in his mind, as he probed for more information. "What's going on down there, Terry? Is everything alright?"

"Uh, no. Everything is not alright. Your boss just showed up here and pushed his way past me into the building, looking for Mr. Fairchild, and he looked like he was ready to punch somebody's lights out."

Rick slammed his fist onto the desktop. He should have seen this coming! "Listen, Terry," he spoke rapidly into the phone, "I want you to go find Sheriff Cooper and do your best to stall him till I get there. Understand?"

"Yeah, right!" Terry shot back. "He already threatened me once, and I think he meant business. You better just hurry down here, cause I ain't going near the guy."

"I'm on my way." Rick slammed down the receiver and was in his car an instant later.

CONRAD FAIRCHILD WAS SO INTO whatever drivel he was typing up for the next deadline that he didn't even bother to look up from his typewriter when

Chet entered his office. The only acknowledgment he gave at all to someone else's sudden presence, was to briefly hold his left index finger in the air.

It was a medium-sized office with enough room for Conrad's large desk, a matching pair of crammed bookshelves, a couple of filing cabinets, and a small, leather couch against the wall opposite the desk. A shaft of light from the waning sun slanted in through an open window at Conrad's back, forming an obtuse, golden rectangle on plush, white carpet.

The wood-paneled walls of Conrad's office were exactly what Chet would have expected: occupied by framed diplomas and awards testifying of his journalistic prowess and accomplishments, hanging in geometrically pleasing patterns.

Chet grunted in disgust. The only reason Conrad enjoyed his current position as lead reporter for *The Register* was because his uncle happened to own the paper. Sure, he had a fancy college education and little papers hanging on his walls that said he was great at what he did, but in reality, he really wasn't that good. His investigative skills were shabby at best. But, thanks to an uncle who generously turned a blind eye to his journalistic malfeasance, and the fact the paper served a rural population that didn't place much demand for excellence in reporting, Conrad Fairchild was allowed to pump out his blatant bias and downright lies, day in and day out.

The fact he'd clobbered Conrad's older brother, Andrew, in the election for sheriff had not helped Chet's case with *The Clear Creek Register* and its lead reporter. After the election, Conrad had declared war on the new and inexperienced sheriff. The typewriter was his weapon of choice, the nasty lies that spewed out of it, the ammunition.

Chet folded his arms and watched Conrad, in a white shirt and plain black tie, pounding away at the round, little keys of his typewriter. Over-sized, gaudy cufflinks at his wrists danced to the steady rhythm of his feverish typing.

He was shorter than average, on the thin side, and had never been very athletic. Strawberry-blond hair—fine and wispy—swirled about on the crown of his head, which seemed a tad too large in comparison with his narrow shoulders. His pale-blue eyes transmitted a certain intelligence, but a wide mouth and big teeth, combined with an almost non-existent chin and steeply sloping forehead, seemed to convey more of a cunning, devious look, like a mischievous elf in a fairytale. Like what was his name? Rumpelstiltskin, was it? Yeah, that was it.

Chet cleared his throat audibly. Time to get this show on the road.

Conrad removed a pencil he had been clenching in his coffee-stained, rodent teeth and in a nasally, high-pitched voice said, "Just *one* more second Terry, I'm having a streak of genius here."

"Now that, I highly doubt," Chet said, stepping all the way into the room to stand directly in front of Conrad's desk.

The clacking cadence of the typewriter ceased as Conrad looked up, his eyes large and watery, probably from allergies. "Cooper?" He rarely deferred to Chet's official title. "What are you doing? We're closed! You can't just come barging into my office like this!"

"Excuse me if I forgot to call and schedule an appointment," Chet growled, coming forward and placing his knuckles on the desk, "but this just couldn't wait."

Conrad's face began to flush and turn all pinkish and splotchy, making his eyes look even more pale in contrast, if that was possible. He leaned back in his chair to give the appearance of a man at ease. It was almost comical with his reddening face and quivering cheeks betraying his ruse. He attempted a smile, but it ended up in more of snarl as he spoke, "You can come in here and try to intimidate me all you want, Cooper, but I'm not afraid of you. There's such a thing in this country called freedom of the press. Perhaps you've heard of it?"

A burst of adrenaline surged through Chet's body as his blood came to the boiling point. He couldn't believe the gall of this pathetic, little excuse for a man! He fought to keep his voice level and measured. "You think that being a member of the press gives you the *freedom* to destroy people's lives? Do you really think you have the right to spread lies and half-truths about people just to further some personal agenda? Is that what freedom means to you?"

Conrad exploded out of his chair, his face beat red. "Now you hold on just one minute, Captain America!" He made a stabbing motion with his index finger at Chet. "I know you're the big hero in this town, but if you think you can just come barging into my office, accuse me of spreading lies, and then presume to lecture me on freedom, you are sorely mistaken! Just because somebody handed you a gun and then sent you off to war does not make you an expert on freedom!"

Chet was losing the battle for control. The demons stirred as images of the blood and carnage of the past began to flash through his mind. If this went on much longer someone was going to get hurt. He vaguely became aware of a dull ache in his forearms and realized he was clenching his fists tight enough to crush walnuts. He came around the front of the desk, a reckless move given how hot his fuse was burning. Conrad backed up a step, placing his chair between him and the enraged lawman.

"You're right, Conrad," Chet said, "I didn't come here to lecture or debate you on freedom, or anything else."

"Then just what did you come here for?" Conrad asked, glancing at Chet's balled up fists. "You gonna hit me, Cooper, is that it? Huh?"

"As much as you deserve a split lip right now, I really should."

"You go right on ahead then!" Conrad spat back. "You go ahead and we'll see what happens next!"

Chet used his foot to roll Conrad's chair out of the way. His pulse pounded in his ears. "You print whatever you want about me, Conrad, but you leave Miss Farnsworth out of it. Do you hear me? She's a decent person, a citizen of this community. She doesn't deserve this…especially from a coward like you."

Conrad laughed a forced, sarcastic cackle. "Boy, you really are Captain America, aren't you? Well, I got news for you, superhero: as a citizen of this community, Miss Farnsworth's inappropriate activities are subject to scrutiny by the press, even if she happens to be dating the sheriff." He folded his arms smugly across his chest. "Did I mention freedom of the press already? Oh that's right, I did."

"You listen to me, Conrad—"

"No, you listen to me!" The little rat interrupted. "I've got a deadline to make and I've already wasted too much time as it is with you. The fact is, that new dame of yours is just going to have to grow thicker skin if she's planning on being seen with the likes of you." He grabbed his chair, rolled it back into place, and sat back down at his desk. Without looking back at Chet he said, "Now, since you don't seem to be here on official police business and you didn't make an appointment, I suggest you get the hell out of my office."

That was it! In one explosive movement, Chet grabbed Conrad's shirt in both hands, hoisted him right out of the chair, and slammed his back into the wall with enough force to send a wooden plaque clattering onto the desktop.

With bulging eyes and curling lips, Conrad hissed through his gritted, yellow, rat teeth while the young sheriff pinned him to the wall.

"As I was saying!" Chet's eyes were hot drill bits boring into the smaller man's face. "You leave Kate alone!" He gave the little man a good shake. "Do I make myself clear?"

"Let go of me this instant!" Conrad shrieked with rage.

"Do I make myself clear?"

Suddenly, Chet could feel the presence of someone behind him in the doorway. He turned to see Rick stepping into the office, followed by Terry.

"Coop, what are you doing?" Rick exclaimed, a look of incredulity plastered across his face.

"Deputy Shelton, get this maniac off me!" Conrad squealed.

Rick spread his hands out in front of him. "Coop!" he pleaded.

Chet turned back to Conrad. "You leave Kate alone. I mean it!" He felt Rick's hands grasping at his shoulders, gently pulling him back. He released his grip on Conrad's shirt, leaving behind two wrinkled balls in the starched fabric.

Rick continued to pull him backwards, toward the door. "Let's get out of here, this clown ain't worth it."

He felt himself coming back from the brink of a blind rage as they reached the doorway. What had come over him just now? Before exiting, he looked back at Conrad. The little man had not moved, his back still against the wall, his knees slightly buckled, eyes darting like a caged animal. They pushed past an open-mouthed Terry and made their way toward the front of the building.

As they turned the first corner, Conrad's whining voice echoed down the hall. "You'll be hearing from my lawyer!"

Chet let out a deep sigh and shook his head.

"If you don't hear from ours first!" Rick shot back.

They entered the front reception area. Rick said, "What happened back there, Coop? You decided to hold a spontaneous press conference, or something?"

Chet yanked on the handle to the front door of the newspaper building, flinging it into the rubber doorstop bolted to the floor. "I don't know what got into me, Rick. I figured I'd have a sit down with Conrad, maybe get a few things straight between us." He laughed bitterly. "Believe it or not, I thought we could talk out our differences…maybe even mend a few fences, if not entirely bury the hatchet."

"You know where you went wrong, don't ya?"

"Enlighten me."

Rick walked over to Chet's cruiser and opened the door for him. "Let me pass on a little advice that my daddy gave me a long time ago."

"Okay."

"Before you sit down and have a real man to man with someone, there's one important thing that you have to keep in mind."

Chet slumped behind the wheel of his car and waited for it.

The older deputy bent down to be level with him. "You can't have a man to man talk with a pile of horse shit." His infectious grin spread out across his face and he slapped Chet on the back.

Chet smiled, he even almost laughed. "Your daddy told you that?"

Rick just kept smiling as he straightened. "See ya back at the office." He pushed the door shut and walked over to his own car.

As Chet pulled out into the busy, late afternoon traffic and headed back to the office, a wave of shame slowly washed over him. Of all the stupid, bone-headed things to do! It certainly wasn't becoming of a sheriff to behave the way he just had. What was he supposed to do, just let Conrad Fairchild go after Kate like that? No! He smacked the steering wheel with the palm of his hand.

Still, he shouldn't have let the article get to him like that. The meeting with Mayor Carson didn't help. As an elected sheriff, the mayor wasn't his boss technically, but he was forced to work closely with the mayor and city council, as Clear Creek didn't have their own city police force. Not yet, anyway.

Mayor Carson had been furious after reading the article and had made intimations about how maybe it was time for a Clear Creek PD, since Chet and his whopping department of three—two for the moment—didn't seem up to the task lately. Chet had left the meeting in a huff, walking out on Mayor Carson mid-sentence.

The Fairchild article had done a lot of damage. To suggest that he was gallivanting around town, strictly pursuing a social life, while a mass killer was stalking the citizenry was, of course, ridiculous, but it was a deadly seed to plant in the minds of the people. Not to mention the jab at Kate. It was yet to be discovered what kind of damage this had done to her on an emotional level.

Speaking of Kate, she was probably back at the office right now, waiting for him and Rick. He felt his heart gladden at the thought. He imagined her: gorgeous, sitting at his desk, probably with her little picnic basket of sandwiches or cookies. Maybe both. Had she seen the article in today's paper? How would she handle it? That remained to be seen. One thing for sure, until things settled down with whatever was going on around here, they were probably going to need to be more careful about how they presented their relationship in public. He would talk to her on their walk tonight. For now, he needed to hurry back to the office. If Kate was there with a basket of goodies, Rick was not to be trusted!

Chet picked the foil-wrapped sandwich off of his desk and looked around the office in slight bewilderment. "Where's she at?" he asked.

Rick was at his desk, seemingly preoccupied with some kind of paperwork and didn't answer.

That's when Chet noticed the new and improved condition of his desk. The surface was completely clear, except for a neat stack of manila folders, labeled and organized, sitting next to the phone. The insane clutter from before was gone. He picked up the folder on the top of the pile, the tab read, *Traffic* in neat, feminine penmanship. Flipping it open he could see parking, speeding, and traffic tickets, along with accident reports stacked painstakingly in chronological order.

"Kate did this?" he asked. "So, where did she go?"

Rick looked up from some report he was going over. "What was that, Coop?"

Chet held out the sandwich and shook it in the air. "Where is Kate?" he repeated, with more than a little exasperation in his voice. "She's obviously been here, where did she go?"

"Oh, oh yeah," Rick scratched his head like he had just been asked to explain Einstein's Theory of Relativity. "She uh, she uh, said she had to go. Said to tell you 'howdy' and hopes you like your sandwich. It's ham and cheese, by the way. Pretty good too."

"Did she say where she was going?"

"Um no, not really."

An awkward silence hung in the air. Rick was acting strange, not really himself. Something wasn't quite right here. Chet kept looking at him, letting him know that he wasn't satisfied with that answer.

Rick shot him a forced smile. "Did ya see what she did with your desk and all?" An obvious attempt at misdirection. "Sure looks better now, don't it?"

"Cut the crap, deputy," Chet said, walking over to Rick's desk. "I've seen this act before."

"Act? What ya talking about, Coop?" Rick swallowed hard and forced another weak smile.

"I had a hundred different Marines in The Corps try to get away with a hundred different things on my watch. I learned how to recognize someone covering their tracks pretty quick."

Rick's false smile drooped into a frown. He looked like a kid with his hand caught in the cookie jar.

Chet sat on the edge of the older man's desk. "You're a good man, Rick. And you know what makes you a good man?"

Rick shrugged his shoulders.

"You're a really crappy liar."

Rick shook his head slowly back and forth in surrender.

"That's a compliment, by the way," Chet continued. "Now, are you going to tell me what's going on with Kate?"

"She made me promise to keep my mouth shut, but I guess you woulda found out one way or the other, eventually." He looked up with pleading eyes. "Just don't tell her I said anything, okay? If she finds out, she's likely to kill me!"

Chet folded his arms. "Out with it."

The man sighed in resignation. "When I got back from a call, she was here with food and all, and was cleaning up your desk. She was in a good mood and everything, but then, just by chance, she ended up reading Conrad's article."

Chet cursed under his breath.

"She got pretty upset," Rick continued. "She started crying. Said something about, 'it's happening all over again.' I didn't get that part. Then, she said she was thinking it might be better for her to leave, start over in a new town. She was afraid that she was damaging your career and your reputation."

Chet felt like he'd just been kicked in the gut by a mule.

"I told her that Conrad was nothing but a bitter, old cow turd, and not to pay him any mind, and to stay and give things a chance."

Chet stood up and started pacing, still holding the sandwich. "What did she say to that?"

Ricked shrugged his shoulders. "She just said she had to go. She slapped that sandwich on your desk, swore me to secrecy, and then she left."

He walked over to his desk and fell into the chair. Anger and frustration began welling up from deep inside of him, rolling in great waves. Damn that Conrad Fairchild! He should have smashed him in the face when he had the chance! His world seemed to be suddenly collapsing all around him.

Was Kate serious about leaving? Would she actually do it? How could she? How could she just toss aside everything like that? Was it possible that he had been mistaken about what was going on between them? Had he been a fool all along to think there was actually something there?

No! He shook his head, refusing to entertain the thought for another second. If she was running, it was because she was scared. The thought made his heart ache for her. At the moment, there was nothing he wouldn't trade to be able to take her into his arms and embrace her, chasing out the fear and the doubt once and for all. The thought of her leaving was simply unacceptable.

Then, for the first time, he acknowledged to himself that he truly needed her. He couldn't imagine life without her. In almost dumbfounded disbelief, he suddenly arrived at one simple conclusion. He was in love with her.

CHAPTER 23

Kate quickened her step. Walking faster kept the tears at bay, as if she could outrun her own thoughts. When she slowed down, her thoughts seemed to catch up to her and then she was apt to dwell on certain things. Those certain things were apt to make her cry. She didn't want to cry. Well, actually she did want to cry, but it was going to have to wait until she got home. Then she'd probably fling herself across the bed and bawl her eyes out like a teenage kid.

She stopped at an intersection and waited for traffic to pass. Chet was probably back at his office by now wondering what in the heck had become of her. She didn't leave Rick much ammunition if Chet got too inquisitive. Not that it mattered; if he was curious enough, he might show up on the front porch of The Cozy Corner and demand an answer directly from her.

What would she say then? *Sorry to inconvenience you, but I'm thinking of running away to start anew somewhere else...thanks for the good times?* She envisioned Chet's handsome and chiseled features crumbling away to a mask of confusion and pain as she tore his heart out of his chest and punted it down the street like a football.

Luckily, the traffic cleared just in time. She crossed the street, resuming her brisk pace with the image of the emotionally shattered sheriff quickly giving way to other thoughts. "Settle down," she whispered out loud to herself, "it's not like you're leaving on the next bus or anything." Ahead, she could see the park, about a block in the distance. She picked up her pace even more, as if making it to the park would somehow solve all of her problems, like a kid playing tag in the schoolyard, running for base, where they would be safe from their pursuers.

But she wasn't a kid anymore. Pigtails and hopscotch were a thing of the past. She knew, all too well, there was no such thing as running to base where you were safe. And that's why she had to leave. She had foolishly allowed herself to think she could escape what had happened back home in Emmet, had allowed herself to let down her guard and believe that the worst was behind her.

Today had proven she had been wrong. Once again, she was about to find herself the talk of the town, her name like a bad taste on the lips of anyone who spoke of her.

She would have to move to a bigger city, a place where she could literally blend in, disappear, and just become one more nameless face in the crowd. She stood a better chance of moving on with her life in a place like that. And Chet would be fine. In fact, his life would probably be a lot simpler if she was just out of the picture anyway.

Her lips began to swell as two teardrops tumbled down either of her cheeks. She quickly wiped them away. That was quite enough! Now she was starting to wallow in self-pity. She had been raised better than that!

Before she knew it, she was in the park. She didn't take her usual route that would lead her through the groves of trimmed trees, skirting past manicured flowerbeds, and on her way home. Suddenly, the idea of sitting in her rented room and crying on her rented bed didn't seem like such an appealing option anymore, so she just started to wander, moving from tree to tree, her feet crunching on a kaleidoscopic carpet of recently fallen leaves.

What she needed was a good distraction for a little while. Something to take her mind off things. She knew finding something else to concentrate on for a time would help her to think more clearly and sort out the myriad of thoughts that were currently plaguing her.

She could go back to the junior high or elementary school and play a little catch up on her work—she still had a few letters she was supposed to transcribe and type up—but she was sure she'd actually prefer going home and bawling on her bed over that.

She remembered the old journal that Rick had given her! It was in the picnic basket. She did promise to have a look at it, not that she thought there would be anything in a hundred year old journal pointing to Reverend Gannon's killer. That was okay, she had an affinity for old stuff and antiques anyway. Delving into the personal writings of a reverend that had died decades ago just might provide the distraction she was looking for.

It didn't take her long to locate a vacant park bench near a semicircular stand of pine trees, safeguarding a small, granite slab that served as a memorial to the early settlers and founders of the area. It seemed fitting, so she placed her picnic basket on the polished, wooden bench and sat down next to it.

She carefully withdrew the diary from the basket and placed it reverently on her lap. She used both hands to turn back the worn, leather cover, crossed her legs, and began to read.

The Summoning

FROM HIS VANTAGE POINT, he had a perfect view of the beautiful Miss Farnsworth, sitting on a park bench reading. She went by Kate, but her real name was Katherine. He liked Katherine better. It was elegant, much more fitting. Her casual attire of jeans and white canvas sneakers did not diminish that elegance, even slightly in his eyes as they peered at her through the prickly branches of the pine trees.

A beast deep inside him stirred as he observed her beauty: a delicate neck arcing gracefully, lazy ringlets of ebony hair catching the gilded rays of the autumn sun as they frolicked and played about the smooth contours of her face and shoulders, tender lips, the hue of red roses in full blossom, moving slightly in concentration as she read.

She was pretty and he was attracted to her. Who wouldn't be? That's why he had decided to follow her today. That's what he'd thought anyway. Now he was suspicious that he may have been nudged, or helped along to make that decision. He could sense the will of his goddess mistress. She seemed just as interested in Miss Farnsworth as he was. He was starting to get the feeling that this pretty newcomer was going to have a role to play before all was said and done.

Her budding friendship with the local sheriff could prove to be a problem if that was the case. Sheriff Cooper was obviously one to steer clear of, but he was just another local yokel, dealt with easily enough if things came down to that.

He looked around to see if there was anybody nearby, but the immediate surroundings seemed to be deserted. It was getting late and kids were beginning to migrate back to their homes, suppers and homework awaiting them. The chances of anybody happening by were slim to none.

He circled around the stand of trees, back to the walking path that meandered past the memorial and the park bench that *Katherine* was occupying. He made sure he stayed well out of her sight before he entered the path. Then he started walking casually back in her direction. That way, it would just seem like a chance encounter. Completely innocent.

KATE WAS SO ENGROSSED IN THE JOURNAL that she wasn't aware of anyone's approach until the dipping sun suddenly cast a long shadow across the old, weathered pages.

Startled, she gasped and jerked her gaze upwards to lock eyes with a teenage boy standing just a few feet away. At first, he only looked familiar, but then he smiled at her, a passionless, almost soulless smile, completely detached of any expression that would normally be observable in the eyes.

In a quick instant, she recalled her brief encounter with young Daniel Miller, not long ago in the school office. She remembered the awkward, threatened way he had made her feel that day, coming on to her so boldly, completely irrespective of boundaries and proper social protocol. She recalled thinking that something just didn't seem right about the boy. The worst part, the part she remembered the most, were his eyes.

There was a darkness in his eyes, but not in the way that people differentiate between light, shadow, and color. His eyes were obviously brown, a very pretty shade of brown to be honest, like a creamy, milk chocolate sort of color. But they were still darker than dark. And now, here, alone with him in this isolated place, she realized it wasn't just his eyes. It was his entire countenance; it was dark in a sense that you could only know if you were in his actual presence. *If darkness had a smell, this kid would reek of it,* she thought.

Only one other time in her life had she felt the same kind of oppressiveness from another human being's presence. That cold afternoon when she had been raped by her boyfriend, Albert.

Even now, as she looked up into Daniel Miller's eyes, she could feel the smothering crush of Albert's weight, smell the reek of alcohol on his breath, and hear her own desperate screams distantly echoing as if they hadn't been her screams at all.

Daniel's voice pulled her from the nightmare playing in her head to the present which, unfortunately, didn't seem to be much of an improvement. "Looks like I'm not the only one who decided to enjoy this fine afternoon," he said with all the smoothness and congenial charm of a door-to-door tonic salesman.

"It is a lovely afternoon," she replied, determined to be normal and polite, regardless of how the boy made her squirm inside. "I would have figured you would be home by this time, Mr. Miller."

The young man laughed. "Please, call me Daniel. School *is* out for the day, you know. There's really no need for such formalities here. Don't you agree, Katherine?"

She forced a smile. "Yes, school is out, Mr. Miller. But I believe that the proper terms of mutual respect always apply between teacher and pupil, regardless."

The Summoning

His otherwise impassive eyes flashed with annoyance briefly, but the charming smile did not waiver in the slightest. "As you wish, Miss Farnsworth," he said, stepping nearer. "But technically, you realize that you really aren't a teacher and, technically, you don't even work at my school."

He was testing her somehow, like a boxer in the ring, circling his opponent, throwing small jabs, searching for a weakness. On an instinctive level, she knew she couldn't let this person find any weakness in her.

She cleared her throat, hoping that her voice would exude confidence and strength. "Be that as it may, a true gentleman—which I have no doubt you are—should have no issue with addressing a lady properly." She smiled, trying to appear pleasant, but not overly-friendly. The last thing this kid needed was encouragement! She was a snake charmer with a venomous serpent before her, swaying, attuned to her every movement in a precise dance, where the slightest misstep could mean death.

He seemed to ponder it for a moment, and then nodded his head. "Spoken like a true lady, Miss Farnsworth. I am sorry if I offended you, that wasn't my intention."

"No need for apologies."

Then it happened so quickly she almost couldn't be sure. For just a moment, she saw the hard glint in his eyes yield to a certain softness, a softness that seemed to convey a profound sadness. In that very brief space of time, he was just a kid. A kid in some kind of pain, crying out desperately for help, or maybe attention, or maybe for somebody out there to just give a damn.

It was there, and then it was gone.

He stepped closer, officially invading her space, but was either oblivious to his incursion, or just simply didn't care. She suspected the latter.

"What are you reading?" he asked, bending slightly at the waist and squinting his eyes. "Looks interesting."

Kate put a hand over the exposed pages of the journal, as if the boy's gaze would damage the fragile, time-worn paper. "Oh, it's nothing really, just a dusty old book." She closed the journal and placed both hands atop the cracked, leather cover. "Nothing you would be interested in, I'm sure."

She looked up at him and offered a polite smile, but his focus was on the journal, his eyes aflame with a strange, intense curiosity.

His words came out slow, mechanical, "Actually, you might be surprised what I'd be interested in." He tilted his head to the side, the way a curious dog might when hearing a strange sound it doesn't recognize. "Did you know that history is my favorite subject?"

"I did not know that."

His eyes never left the book. "Sometimes, the oldest books are the best ones, and pardon me for saying, but if you're reading it, it must be interesting. I can't see someone like yourself settling for a boring book." His eyes darted away from the journal to fix with hers. "Right? You wouldn't settle for a boring book would you?"

"Of course not," she said, getting to her feet. This was getting too uncomfortable. Time to extract herself from the situation. "It was nice running into you, Mr. Miller, but I should be getting along now. The sun will be down soon." Turning, she bent over, opened the picnic basket, and gently placed the journal inside.

When she straightened, she was startled to discover he had somehow maneuvered to stand directly in front of her, closer than ever. This had gone beyond ignorance of the social norms, or even a little rudeness, to flat out inappropriate behavior. He was so close she could smell the scent of his breath, mingled with the natural musk of his body, a heady concoction of testosterone and lust.

It was Albert all over again. She felt her knees turning to useless liquid as the blood drained from her head. She wanted to run, but doubted she would make it more than two or three strides before collapsing. She took a deep breath, and then swallowed hard against the sensation of fainting.

He smiled, arrogant, defiant. "What's the book, Kate?"

"What?" she asked, taking a tentative step back.

He stepped with her, maintaining the intimate space between them. "The book, Kate. What's the name of the book you're reading?" He reached up and twirled a lock of her hair in his fingertips. "I'm interested."

With his touch, a wave of disgust and fear swept through her, but it was the flood of anger that came rushing from deep within that prevailed. "That is none of your damn business," she said, in a cool voice. It wasn't the panicked, shaking voice of a victimized, frightened woman. It was the voice of an angry woman who would not be victimized again.

She stepped back, just out of his reach, her hair falling from his grasp. Daniel's cocky smile vanished and his face became inscrutable, emotionless. He moved to take another step, perhaps pushing his luck or simply testing her will.

She thrust her right arm forward, striking him on the chest with the flat of her hand, leaving it there as a barrier. She could feel the heat of his skin through his shirt, it seemed abnormally hot. His heart was pounding through his ribcage, thrumming against her palm. The smirk returned, but more sinister than before.

The rage that had given her strength, began to disintegrate under the continuous, crashing waves of fear and doubt.

He leaned into her hand with his body weight, his grin seemed to intensify. She quickly realized, that he was becoming aroused by the fact that she was touching him! She jerked her hand back. He closed the distance once again. This time she stood her ground, unwavering. She refused to run. Not this time!

"What's the book?" he asked again.

"You are wildly out-of-line, Mr. Miller," she said, craning her neck so that she could maintain eye contact. She would not give into fear. "I suggest you turn around and walk away this instant, before you do something you regret."

He stood still and seemed to be contemplating his next move. A moment of indecision that she took advantage of.

She surprised him by being the one to step closer. Their bodies brushed against each other as she held her thumb and forefinger an inch from his nose. "Young man, you are this close to spending the night in Sheriff Cooper's jail. Now, I urge you in the strongest terms possible to turn around and go home."

The sneer was gone, again replaced by the mask of indifference. Except for the eyes, which seemed to always be brimming with a certain level of hatred. He stepped backwards, raising his hands in a show of acquiescence. "I'm sorry," he said. "You're obviously upset about something. I think you totally misunder—"

"Go," she said. "Just go."

Snorting, he shook his head, as if she were some kind of lunatic. Shrugging his shoulders he moved past her and onto the path, from where he had come. He stopped and held her gaze for a moment. "See ya around, Miss Farnsworth," he said, his voice dripping in sarcastic sweetness.

Kate watched, never taking her eyes off him until he had vanished down the path into the gathering twilight of the cool, fall evening. Finally alone, she allowed her iron will to crumble away and the tide of emotions that had been battering against it came all at once. A flood of fear, doubt, and memories crashed against her, forcing her to the ground. Great sobs racked her body. They came on and on, unchecked.

She had no idea how long she had lain there, curled up in the fetal position next to the bench. It was full on dark now. The cold, humid air, like frozen, stiff fingers raked her skin, seeking to penetrate into her bones. The tears were long gone, the crying done. A dull ache in the back of her throat was the only remaining testament to her previous emotional collapse.

She allowed her thoughts to run with abandon, coming and going as they may, no holding them back, no quelling of emotions. Completely cried out and emotionally drained, she drifted in her own consciousness like a ship without a sail or rudder, until the sound of feet crunching on leaves behind her hit like a cement truck.

She bolted up and whirled about onto her knees, dried leaves scattering around her. It had to be Daniel! He had come back! This time he wouldn't leave until he got what he wanted.

A distant light was behind him as he approached so that she could only see his darkened outline.

"You'll have to kill me," she said, low and threatening. "That's the only way you'll get what you want. You'll have to kill me first, you hear?"

The silhouette stopped walking when she spoke. She tried to steel herself for what was about to happen, reaching deep down, searching for the strength to fight, even if it meant to the death.

"Kate, is that you?" the figure said.

Relief flowed through her body when she recognized the voice.

"Deputy Forks!" she exclaimed, as she struggled to get to her feet.

The figure ran forward, the thin, youthful features of Deputy Scotty Forks coming into view. He reached her side and hoisted her up by her arm. She held onto him until she felt steady enough to stand on her own.

"Kate, what in the world are you doing? Are you alright?" Scotty said, using his hands to brush leaves off of her shoulders and out of her hair.

It was Scotty alright, but not the old, cocky, swaggering Scotty she had first met when she had moved to town. Now standing in front of her was the sad, broken Scotty, the mentally unstable, *suicidal* Scotty.

He had lost a lot of weight since that day he had been found, collapsed and unconscious next to his police car, his pistol next to him on the ground. The doctor had diagnosed him with having something similar to severe shell shock, like some soldiers get after being in really heavy combat. The strange part was, he had never seen combat.

"You're ice cold," he said, slipping out of the light green cardigan he was wearing and draping it over her shoulders.

Normally, she would have put on her tough girl act and refused it, but she gratefully accepted the warmth that the wool fabric offered. "I guess you can be a gentleman when you want to be, deputy."

He smiled an unconvincing smile, his eyes and cheeks dark and hollow in the shadow of the distant street lamp. "It's just Scotty for now, Kate. I'm afraid my deputy days are over."

"That remains to be seen. Anyway, you look like you're doing much better," she lied.

"Thanks. Now, what are you doing out here by yourself in the dark, Kate?"

"Nothing."

"Nothing?" He fixed her with a suspicious glare. "Really?"

"I could ask you the same thing?"

"I was going for a walk," he said. "And you were what, taking a nap?"

She looked down at the ground. "I'd rather not talk about it. Please."

He reached out and used the knuckle of his forefinger to raise her chin so that her eyes met his. He looked into her eyes and she felt like he was looking right into her soul. There was a sudden twinkle of understanding in his eyes—understanding and fear. He swallowed nervously and swiveled his head in every direction, as if expecting to see someone or something in every shadow and behind every tree.

"You've been touched by it," he said.

A chill ran down Kate's spine. "What are you talking about?"

He licked dry lips. "Have you heard the voices? The whispers?"

"No! What? Scotty, I don't understand. What are you talking about?" The poor guy was obviously still sick.

He stared into her eyes again, like he was looking for something. Finally, he shook his head. "I'm sorry, didn't mean to scare you." He looked up. "You shouldn't be out here alone like this. You going to the office to see Chet?"

"No. Just came from there, I'm headed for home now."

"Why didn't Chet walk you home?"

She didn't answer.

"You'd rather not say."

Kate looked around at the surrounding darkness and shivered involuntarily. "Could you walk me home?" she asked, feeling a little foolish.

Without saying a word, he offered his arm.

HIS PRIDE WAS STILL STINGING as he watched the couple walk within just a few feet of him. He had concealed himself earlier in a flower bed, overgrown with wilted and dying day lilies, along a particularly dark and secluded section of the path. They were close enough he could have reached out and grabbed her ankle, if he wanted to. He smiled to himself. Wouldn't that be a show to see!

He eyed the picnic basket swinging in the crook of her arm. Inside was that book! There was something important about it. He felt it the moment he laid eyes on it. There had been quite the stir about it in his head. The book was dangerous to him somehow. Dangerous to his mistress and everything they had worked for up to this point. He was going to have to find a way to get it away from Kate.

He wasn't too worried about it at the moment. Things might not have gone as well as he had hoped for tonight with her, but there would be another opportunity, and she would eventually warm up to him. She was just shy. Maybe a little scared because of the age difference. Of course, that didn't excuse the way she had acted tonight.

He was upset with her. Her behavior had been totally unacceptable. But all lovers had their quarrels, didn't they? He'd read somewhere that the most important thing in a relationship was forgiveness. Or was it trust? The forgiveness part he was sure he could do, but she wasn't helping at all on the trust end of things. The way she was hanging onto that low-life of a loser cop, wearing his sweater around like the cheerleader whores at school, flaunting their boyfriends' letterman jackets…. It was disgusting and filled him with rage.

She was probably doing it on purpose, knew he'd be watching, was getting back at him by making him jealous. Girls did that all the time: liked to make guys jealous on purpose. Some girls liked it when two guys fought over them. He never had her pegged for the type to play those games. "Be careful what you wish for," he whispered, as he watched them fade into the darkness beyond.

CHAPTER 24

Rick's voice echoed across the office, jolting Chet out of his stupor, "You been awfully quiet over there. Everything alright?"

Chet was sitting at his desk, resting his weight on his forearms and working his hands together. His sandwich lay to the side, unwrapped but untouched. He looked up at his deputy and friend. Solid Rick: good-natured, wise, reliable, well-liked. He was looking back at him, the smile on the corners of his mouth belied by the glimmer of concern in his brown eyes.

Chet cleared his throat and shook his head. "I wouldn't exactly say that everything's alright, Rick."

The deputy got to his feet and hooked his thumbs into his duty belt. "Okay, stupid question. How about I rephrase?" He walked the few steps to stand in front of Chet's desk and folded his arms across his chest. "Are *you* alright?"

Well, that was getting right down to it. He didn't know how to answer. Sure, he was alright as far as being able to function, going through the motions of doing his job and continuing to blunder along through the normal aspects of daily life. But was he really alright? The woman he loved was in pain, pain she didn't deserve, pain caused by her association with him. And there didn't seem to be anything he could do to help her. To make things worse, he apparently was going to be denied the chance to help her. She was leaving.

Rick planted his rump on the corner of the desk. "You know, she ain't gone yet, Coop. Question is, what's to keep her here?" The question hung in the air. "Does she know how you really feel about her? Cause I think if she did, there'd be nothing that could make her leave."

Chet looked up at his friend. "So now you're a shrink?"

His deputy snickered. "I might not have the degree, but I've got the qualifications."

"Yeah?"

"Yeah! It's called twenty-three years married to the same woman, and raising three boys!" Rick laughed.

Chet rubbed the palms of his hands across the surface of his desk, as if he were smoothing out invisible wrinkles. "So what are you saying, I should head on over to her place right now, tell her I'm in love with her, and beg her to stay?"

"Well, that might be the direct, Marine Corps, storm-the-beach method of doing it. There's also the smoother, gentler, Rick Shelton way, which I happen to highly recommend."

"Do ya, now?"

Rick's face turned serious as he held up his left ring finger and wiggled it back and forth. The gold wedding band glimmered. "Twenty-three years, buddy! Twenty-three years!"

"Right. So what's the smoother, gentler Rick Shelton way?"

THE CHILL OF THE EVENING had managed to find its way through her flesh and all the way to her bones, as Kate made her way with Scotty down the front walk of The Cozy Corner. Their footsteps echoed hollow on the wooden stairs of the front porch, interrupting the silence that had prevailed during the rest of their walk together.

At the front door, she retrieved her hand from the crook of his arm and, with some reluctance, slipped out of the cardigan he had given her to wear earlier. "Thank you, Scotty," she said, handing the cardigan back to him. "It was very kind of you to walk me home."

"It was no trouble," he replied with a shrug. "I was only going for a walk anyway. I just hope you're alright."

"I'm fine now, thanks. Are you going to be okay to walk home? Would you like to come in and warm up for a while?"

Scotty slipped back into his cardigan. "I'll be fine, it's not really that cold."

"Are you kidding? I think it's freezing!"

He chuckled, it seemed a bit forced, but it was nice to see him coming around. Maybe he really was going to be alright after all.

"You think it's funny that I'm nearly a human Popsicle?" she teased.

"No…" He looked down at the ground with an almost child-like smile. "I just can't wait to see you in a couple of months, if you think it's freezing now."

Kate placed a hand to her throat. "Oh, don't even say that!"

"You're probably gonna want to invest in a good coat before too long," he said. "Check at Flossy's, they've probably got some set out by now. They'll even order one for you from Sears-Roebuck, so you don't have to pay the extra on the postage."

"Thanks, I'll go have a look sometime this week." *If I'm still here.*

A shiver of cold rippled through her body, and she suddenly found the idea of a warm bath very appealing. "Well, it was good to see you, and thanks again, Scotty. You were a lifesaver tonight."

"It was really no problem," he said, turning. "I'll see ya around."

"Okay, see ya."

He took two steps, then stopped and turned back, his movements halting, unsure. The stark glare of the porch light accentuated the pale, sallow quality of his skin, the gaunt sharpness of his facial bones, and the deep hollows of his cheeks. He was a shadow, a specter cloaked in a mere semblance of his former self.

"Kate," he said, his voice low and deadly serious, lacking any note of the congeniality from moments before. "You need to be careful."

"I'm always careful, Scotty." She forced herself to chuckle, trying to hold on to the more lighthearted mood that was rapidly evaporating.

Scotty looked down at his feet for a moment, and then lifted his head back up, his eyes penetrating. "When I first saw you tonight, laying on the ground, I thought I saw it—felt it, actually—but I wasn't sure..." He seemed to lose his train of thought, his gaze moving through her, seeing something beyond, that wasn't there.

"Felt what?" she asked.

He seemed to recover as if from a stupor. "I know I sound nuts, but just hear me out. There's something going on in this town...something evil. It took a hold of me out there in the woods at the Baxter place; still has a hold of me, and whatever it is, you have been touched by it too...in some way."

He was right, it did sound nuts. But all the same, his words sunk in, deep and low, down in that God-given sanctuary in the soul where the truth resides in all creatures, unshakable and undeniable. She shivered once more and lied to herself that it was just the cold air getting to her again. "I don't even know what to say to that, Scotty. I—"

"You don't have to say anything. Look, like I said, I know how it sounds. If I were you, I'd think I was crazy too."

"I don't think you're crazy."

"Call it what you want, Kate: sick, crazy, screw loose. Maybe I really am crazy for all I know. But believe me on this one thing if you never believe another word I say." His hands were shaking now, and she could see the striations of his jaw muscles contracting beneath his cadaverous skin. "There is an evil presence at work here in this town and, for whatever reason, you have attracted its attention. I can feel it!" His eyes were burning into hers, his pupils were little points of intense flame.

She opened the front door, sneaking one foot inside. A wave of warm air flowed through the open gap, beckoning. "Okay, Scotty, I really need to go now. And so should you before it gets any later."

His eyes were glistening as if he were on the verge of crying. "Just be careful Kate—"

"I will, thanks." She stepped the rest of the way inside.

"Pay attention to your surroundings for anything that doesn't seem right—"

She started closing the door. "I will, I promise. Thank you, good night."

He looked around for a moment, hesitating like a lost child who didn't know what to do. At last, he turned, put his hands in the front pockets of his pants, and shambled down the porch steps to vanish into the night.

Kate leaned her weight into the door until she heard the bolt click into place. Scotty's words echoed in her mind as she made her way past the unoccupied front room and up the staircase. *There is an evil presence at work here in this town.... You have been touched by it too.* She could still see the intensity that had burned in his eyes.

Suddenly, Mable's voice boomed from the bottom of the staircase jarring her from her thoughts, "Katie dear, you're home! Why so late? And where's Chet? Didn't he want to come in?" She paused her interrogation to squint through her beady blue eyes. "My goodness, girl, you look awful!" Her pudgy hand flew to her bosom, her eyes widening. "Have you been crying?" It was an accusation more than a question. "Come down from there and let's have a talk. I'll warm up a bowl of potato soup for you."

The last thing Kate wanted to do, at that moment, was go into a time-consuming explanation to her new, self-appointed guardian about the day's events. "I'm sorry, Mable, I really don't mean to be rude, but it has been an exhausting day, to say the least." She paused a moment to fight back another wave of tears. How her body was managing to manufacture more tears after tonight was beyond her. "All I want right now, is a warm bath and bed."

Mable's lips compressed to form a white line of concern, her eyes studious and searching. "Fair enough, dear," she said. Her mouth widened into a matronly smile. "Heaven knows I've had my share of those kinds of days, you're entitled to yours I suppose."

"Thank you," Kate sighed, turning and taking another step.

"We'll talk tomorrow," Mable announced, with all the authority of a boarding school mistress.

Kate felt herself stiffen slightly at the announcement. "Sure, tomorrow," she answered without turning. *Warm bath and bed, warm bath and bed...*

"Goodnight then, dear."

"Goodnight."

Opening the door to her room, she stopped and surveyed it for a moment, like a guest seeing it for the first time. Her bedroom was pretty much just that: a room with a bed in it.

The single bed, covered by a patchwork quilt of colorful material, was pushed into the far corner to make the most of the tiny space. The brass bed frame was tarnished, but still managed to reflect some of the dim light emanating from the single, shaded lamp perched on the small nightstand next to the bed. The hardwood floor, like the bed, was dulled by age and use, the surface scratched and marred by the countless guests and occupants who had rented the room over the years.

A circular rug, handwoven from rags matching the quilt, covered a small patch of the scuffed wooden floor by the bed, serving as a barrier between cold floors and bare feet on chilly mornings.

Across from the foot of the bed, pressed against the wall, stood a polished wardrobe with brass handles that housed her clothing, shoes, and most of her belongings. At the edge of the wardrobe, the ceiling sloped sharply downwards to flow into a cozy dormer with a white-paned window. A pair of crisp, off-white curtains hung, bunched up, off to the sides. A narrow writing table had been fitted into the alcove with a plain wooden chair tucked under its surface. A short row of her favorite books and novels lined the edge of the table, under the window sill.

Laying the picnic basket on the floor next to the writing table, she opened the lid, fished out the late reverend's old journal, and placed it gently on the desk. Maybe after her bath she would read some more before going to bed. Maybe. What would be the point to that if she was going to leave this place anyway?

She walked over to the window. The darkness of the night seemed to be almost watching her through the panes. With a shudder she yanked the curtains shut, leaving the blackness to itself. She sighed and crossed the room to the wardrobe, extracting a fluffy lavender bathrobe and matching towel—gifts from her parents when she had left home. She tossed the robe and towel onto the bed and began to undress, the thought of lowering herself into the soothing, encompassing depths of a steaming bath sounding better and better by the second.

Although she had shut and locked the bedroom door, she still faced it while undressing. Ever since enduring her attack from Albert on that fateful day, she did not like to leave her back exposed to any door, locked or otherwise.

One by one, she stripped off articles of clothing and hung them over the foot of the bed frame. Retrieving the robe, she draped it over her shoulders, welcoming the warm caress of the plush material against her chilled skin.

As she was fumbling with getting the sash tied in place around her waist, a faint sound from behind caused her to freeze in place. It was nearly inaudible, almost a sigh, like the hushed sound of a snake's coils slithering across the ground. As impossible as it seemed, she could also feel someone behind her, watching.

She clutched at the robe near her throat with her hands, pulling it tight. It had to just be nerves from her crazy night playing tricks on her. She was just tired, frazzled. There was nobody standing behind her!

Another noise. It was like a dry, scraping flap, a wispy flutter. She felt her eyes welling with tears of horror as she turned around to face the window.

The white, ghoulish face of some tormented man was staring at her through the paned glass, the mouth twisted in silent anguish, the black eyes burning with unspeakable, endless remorse and self-loathing. There was a dark red hole in the side of his right temple about the diameter of a .45 caliber bullet; globules of blood issued out of it, dull and viscous. The left side of his head was an eruption of brain and skull fragments matting in his sandy blond hair—a bullet's exit wound. There was no mistaking the disfigured and tortured countenance. It was Albert!

A bone-splintering scream erupted from the very depths of her soul as she simultaneously jumped backwards, her body crashing against the door. Her knees completely failed her, buckling from the surge of terror shooting through her, and she crumpled into a ball.

After collapsing, she shoved the knuckles of her hand into her mouth to prevent another scream from escaping as she riveted the window with tearful eyes. The spectral image was gone, as if it had never been there at all. Only the ethereal black of the night was visible now, yawning endless beyond the glass.

With some difficulty she rose to her feet on wet noodle legs and tried to collect her wits. The sound of heavy running mixed with concerned, frantic voices echoed throughout the old boarding house. Mable, her husband Henry, and probably every guest in the house would be crashing into her room at any moment. There would be no sense in trying to stop them, so she unlocked the door in advance of their arrival.

She kept her gaze on the window as she took a step closer, trying to pierce the darkness outside for any sign of the face that had been there moments before. Then a certain realization hit. Her skin rippled like goose flesh and her heart pounded so hard it felt as if she were going to faint.

She knew for a fact that she had shut the curtains before undressing. And yet, here she stood, looking out into the night through a considerable gap in those very curtains.

Albert had been here! Albert was dead! And yet, someone had opened her curtains! As the full weight of the realization sunk in, she felt the blood drain from her head. Her hands and feet began to tingle as the room spun before her eyes.

The door flew open and banged hard into the wall. Mable burst in followed by a wild-eyed Henry.

"Good gracious Almighty, girl! What happened? Are you okay?" Mable exclaimed, her eyes covering the room in one glance.

Everything slowed down and she felt herself falling. "A-a man in the window," she heard herself say. Then the floor was floating up to meet her. And then, nothingness.

She became aware of a sound like rushing water in her ears, or was it the soft buzzing of bees? The buzzing faded, replaced by human voices, the words indiscernible. A soft light at the edges of her vision slowly encroaching inward, followed by a flood of memories: Daniel Miller practically assaulting her in the park, Scotty walking her home, Scotty coming unglued, warning her. There had been something else. Something nightmarish that had caused her to faint.

Her vision and her mind began to clear as she came around. She was lying down, someone was shaking her, patting her on the cheek. She could make out a face looking down at her. The final memory exploded suddenly into her fragmented mind. That ghastly face watching her undress in the window!

She screamed and clawed at that face, desperate to escape. One of her fingernails gained purchase into warm flesh, gouging a line that was sure to draw blood. Her wrists were seized and her arms restrained by hands with the strength of steel. The grip was strong but not painful, and the restraint was firm, but gentle.

At last she came to, her faculties returning as her heart finally managed to pump an adequate supply of oxygen to her addled brain. Relief flooded over her as she recognized Chet, his ruggedly handsome face creased with worry while he looked down at her, his eyes the color of azure gems.

She stopped struggling and then gasped when she saw an ugly, red scratch streaking down the left side of his face, a light trickle of blood just beginning to seep. "I am so sorry, Chet! I didn't know…I thought you—"

"It's okay, Kate," he said, his voice tender, but riddled with concern and urgency. Mable appeared in her field of view and pressed a moist towel to the bleeding gouge on the man's cheek.

"Thank you, Mrs. Johnson," he said, wincing and grabbing the towel. His eyes, flickering with intensity, never left Kate's as he spoke, "What happened, Kate?"

Kate shook her head, trying to clear the lingering fog of unconsciousness. She tried to sit up and noticed that she was still in her room, lying on the bed, the concerned sheriff sitting on the edge of the mattress, next to her.

To her own horror, she also realized that she was still dressed only in her bathrobe! A flare of indignation sparked inside of her. For Chet to see her like this—half of the skin on her body was probably bared for all to see!

She raised herself onto her elbows. "Chet, what are you even doing here?" she scolded.

He placed large, warm hands on her shoulders and began pressing her back down. "Take it easy for a minute," he said.

At first she resisted, upset by the man's violation of her modesty. But his eyes, brimming with innocent concern and tenderness, disarmed her quickly and she lay back down, using her hands to close the robe across her chest, covering what little she could.

"Mable phoned the office a few minutes ago. She said you screamed and then passed out, and then something about a man in the window."

All thoughts of indignation and immodesty fled from her mind at the mention of the man in the window. She swallowed hard and nodded.

Chet's face took on a quizzical expression. He looked at the window in the corner of the room and back to her. "You're sure? What was he doing?"

"I heard something behind me, so I turned around—"

"He was here in the room?" Chet interjected, his eyes suddenly blazing.

"Well, no. I mean, not when I turned around he wasn't. When I turned around he was outside, staring at me." She decided to keep the *Albert with his head blown off* part to herself for the time being.

"So, your window was open? Somehow he climbed in and then back out?"

Feeling exasperated and now confused by her own story, she let out a deep sigh. She sat up, propping her back against the bed frame and allowed Chet to place the pillow behind her shoulders.

Henry appeared in the doorway with a glass of water and pushed his way past his wife to Kate's bedside. "Here ya go, missy," he said, offering the glass.

As Kate took a long swallow of the cool water, Rick entered, filling the room to capacity. "Had a look around, Coop, no sign of anybody in the yard. No footprints or nothing. Whoever it was has probably high-tailed it outta here by now."

"Thanks, Rick," came Chet's reply.

"You want me to call Dr. Steinmetz?" the deputy asked, leaning his weight on the door frame.

"No!" Kate blurted. "No thank you. I'm fine, I don't need a doctor."

"You're sure?" Chet asked.

She nodded and took another sip of water. "I'm fine really, just a bit shaken up." She took in all the faces looking at her. "And maybe a bit embarrassed," she added.

Chet seemed to take the cue. "Okay everybody, let's give Miss Farnsworth some breathing room and a little privacy." He motioned with one hand for everyone to clear the room.

Mable and Henry nodded as they shuffled their way past Rick and out the door. Kate could be sure they wouldn't stray too far from earshot. Rick offered a friendly wink as he pulled the door closed, leaving her alone in the room with Chet.

The sheriff waited a moment and then spoke softly, "I want you to start over from the beginning and just tell me what happened. Can you do that?"

She nodded and swung her feet past him so she could put them on the floor and sit upright. Cradling the glass in both hands, she stared into the clear water to organize her thoughts.

She rose slowly and stood a moment, making sure of her balance, Chet's hand on her back providing support. When she felt confident enough to walk, she padded across the floor to stand in front of the writing table.

"I was getting ready to take a bath," she began. She turned and faced the door. "I was undressing right here." She blushed, suddenly realizing that her underwear was still draped over the bed frame. Trying her best to be nonchalant about it, she snatched the towel from the foot of the bed and draped it over the exposed unmentionables.

The movement didn't seem to be lost on Chet as he cleared his throat and averted his eyes. To his credit, he remained totally professional. "You said you heard something behind you?"

"I heard a noise behind me, so I turned around. That's when I saw him... looking at me." Her eyes welling up, she pointed at the window. "He was right there, just staring! He had so much sadness in his eyes." She began to shiver.

He rose from the bed, came over to stand next to her, and put a reassuring arm around her shoulders. "There's just one thing that's bothering me about all this." He walked over to the window and parted the curtains all the way. He pushed on the window frame, testing the latch. He turned and faced her. "Kate, this window is on the second story of the house. There's no tree branches, no lattice work, no adjoining gable, no ledge, or anything for someone to use to look through your window."

It hit her like a ton of bricks. She hadn't even questioned it herself until now. He was right. How could anyone have been outside her window? But Albert had been there! She had seen him as clear as she could see her own hand in front of her face. Had it all just been a figment of her imagination? Some hallucination brought on by her past, mixed with the emotional stress from earlier in the park? It was certainly possible.

Chet was watching her silently, leaning against the writing table, chewing on his bottom lip. His voice was barely louder than a whisper, "Sometimes, I see things or hear things that aren't really there too. I think it kinda comes with the territory."

Obviously, he didn't believe her. He hadn't even bothered to ask for a description, a fact she was actually grateful for. How would she have answered that? *I think I saw my dead ex in my window?* Insane. She wasn't so sure about it now herself. *Except!*

"The curtains, Chet!" she said, stomping her foot on the floor with a thud, and folding her arms. "I know I closed them before undressing, and when I turned around they were open! Open just enough for him to see in here!" A realization dawned on her. "That must have been the sound I heard that made me turn around...it was the curtains sliding open."

"Kate," his voice was firm, "listen to yourself. You aren't making any sense. The curtains didn't move by themselves, you must have forgotten to close them."

He was right again, of course. She was losing her marbles.

"Look, I think you had the right idea," he said, stepping forward to grip her shoulders in his hands. "A nice warm soak in the tub and a good night's sleep will do you wonders. In the morning, it'll be a new day and this will all just seem like a bad dream."

"You're probably right," she admitted.

He smiled. "Smart girl." He took his hand and gently brushed a stray lock of her hair back behind her ear. His fingers trailed lightly down the side of her neck, tracing the contours of her collar bone, and back to her shoulder.

A different kind of shiver coursed through her body, an exhilarating pulse of warmth and longing that frightened and excited her at the same time. Something inside her came back to life as if resurrected. It was a part of herself she had assumed to be dead, a part of her that Albert had stolen from her forever. She fought to control the trembling of her limbs and joints.

He brought his hand up to her ear again and repeated, tracing his fingertips along the rim of her ear, following the line down to her neck.

She reached up and grabbed his hand in hers, pulling it away. "Okay, you really need to stop that," she said.

He turned his hand around so that he was holding hers. "I don't want you to leave."

So Rick had spilled the beans. It sure hadn't taken him very long!

Chet continued, "You don't have to worry about Conrad at the newspaper. I took care of him, so just stay. I can protect you…let me protect you."

Kate stared into his eyes, holding his gaze in silence for a long moment, a moment she wished could last all night. Then she wrapped her arms around him and pulled him close to her, burying her head against his chest. "Okay, Chet, I'll stay," she said. "We might as well ride this all the way to the end and see where we end up."

"I promise, you won't regret staying," he said, as he turned to leave. "I'll call and check on you in the morning. Let me know immediately if anything else happens, no matter what time it is.

She smiled and nodded. "Sure."

Chet had been right: a warm bath was exactly what she needed, and so she allowed her body to drift listlessly in the soothing water. The liquid heat sapped the tension away from her weary mind and body to rise and dissipate in the clouds of steam wafting up from the clawfoot bathtub.

So, she was staying now. Whether it was the right thing to do or not, she didn't know. She was rolling the dice on Chet and this town with nothing less than her heart—and probably her sanity—on the line.

In a way, taking the guess work out of her situation was a relief. She had set her course. All that remained was to see where it led her. But she couldn't deny that there were definitely some storm clouds on the horizon. She could feel that she was sailing straight into a hurricane and the thought filled her heart with terror. *What kind of idiot sails right into a storm on purpose?*

She sighed. Well, she was committed now. The phrase reminded her of her father. Sometimes, he would go out on a limb and breed one of his mares with a certain stallion that seemed against convention, hoping to achieve certain results from the foal. Others would sometimes second-guess his methods, but once the mare was pregnant, all he would say was, *"Well, we're committed now."*

"Except I'm not a horse," she uttered out loud to herself, before plunging her head under the surface of the water.

She wasn't sure how long she spent in the tub, soaking and washing, and soaking again. Long enough to turn her toes and fingers into little raisins. Finally the water grew lukewarm, almost chilly, and she pulled the plug. The drain sucked ravenously at the soapy water as she got out and grabbed her towel.

After drying off, she quietly padded down the hallway, swaddled in her bathrobe, the towel wrapped around her head like a giant purple turban. She turned the doorknob to her room and poked her head around the door before setting foot inside. To her relief, the curtains to the window remained closed, so she slipped into the room, smiling at herself, feeling just a bit foolish.

Rummaging through the wardrobe, she found her nightgown she'd brought for cold nights: plain-white with no frills, made of heavy, warm cotton that nearly reached her ankles. Tossing the nightgown over the bed frame, she unwound the towel from her head and used it to dry her damp hair.

That's when she saw it. She gasped and swore under her breath. It was as plain as day. Why hadn't she noticed it before? She had been so overwhelmed with Albert's apparition in the window—not that anyone could blame her—that it had escaped her attention. Until now.

Her heart began to pound heavily as she was suddenly able to recall and pinpoint the source of the second sound she had heard earlier; the dry, scraping flutter. It had been the sound of the pages of a book being rifled through, one by one.

It was all she could do to keep from hyperventilating as she stared in perplexed fear at it. It may as well have been a coiled up rattlesnake on her desk.

Reverend Gannon's journal was laying there. Open.

CHAPTER 25

Scotty tightened his shoulders against the chill of the night, lost in his thoughts as he made his way for home. It was getting late and the streets had become uncomfortably vacant. The park had grown especially dark and foreboding since the sun had gone down.

He did his best to navigate his way around the darker shadows, staying along the lit paths and walkways, as sparse and scattered as they were. A yellow, waxing moon was slowly rising, partly concealed by a thickening shroud of dark, tattered clouds. A faint rumble echoed across the evening sky, possibly indicating the approach of a storm. A slight breeze had picked up, driving the fresh scent of rain before it.

He shook his head as he recalled his recent conversation with Kate Farnsworth on her front porch. He had never meant to scare her. He was only trying to warn her—somebody had to! She had been touched by the evil now in someway…like he had. The memory of his confrontation with the boy Levi, dead and yet somehow alive, forced him to swallow hard against the sour, acidic swelling in his esophagus.

Now that voice: since that day, a malicious presence that seemed to always be with him. It was vile, threatening and mocking. Sometimes, it took all of his faculties to shut it out and keep it at bay. And sometimes, he just wasn't strong enough to fight it. The evil would enter like a disease, consuming and devouring until he could muster the strength to push it out. It was a never-ending battle and he was growing weaker while the evil seemed to gain in strength. He knew it was only a matter of time before he was wholly consumed by it.

Kate had to be warned. Whatever it was that was attacking him was somehow focusing its attention on her as well. Earlier, when he had come across her lying on the ground in the park, he had felt the malignant, vulgar residue of its presence still lingering in the air. But from the look in her eyes, she thought he was a total lunatic. Maybe he should go to Chet with his concerns. He sighed in frustration. Chet pretty much figured him for insane too. He just hoped Kate had taken him seriously.

His heart jumped as he realized that with all his deep thinking and contemplating, he had allowed himself to inadvertently wander into a particularly dark and isolated section of the park. It was a path of habit, a route that, up until a few weeks ago, he would have walked without a second thought. But under the current circumstances, it could be a fatal error and he cursed at himself for his carelessness.

He immediately angled off of the path, onto to the leaves and grass, and made a bee-line for the nearest streetlight in the distance.

"MAY I BE EXCUSED?" Daniel pushed his chair away from the dining table.

His mother flicked a glance to his dinner plate and creased her forehead. "You hardly touched your dinner, Danny, are you not feeling well?"

She had started calling him *Danny* again, resurrecting the old nickname of his childhood. He wasn't exactly sure what she was trying to do, but it was ridiculous and it annoyed him immensely. It was probably some kind of attempt to subconsciously regress into the past to what might have been happier days for her as a mother, but days of misery for him: a time of weakness, doubt, and self-loathing.

"Don't worry, Mom, I'm fine," he said, and shoveled a heaping spoonful of mashed potatoes into his mouth to put her mind at ease.

His father might as well have been on another planet, a spread out newspaper effectively shielding him from any contact with his family.

The mouthful of potatoes apparently did not have the desired effect on his mother as the lines in her forehead deepened. "Danny, you just got home. Now don't get me wrong…"

And here she goes.

"I'm really happy that you're keeping busy and have some new friends and interests, but we've hardly seen you lately. You don't come home till after dark, usually wolf down your dinner, and then shut yourself up there in your room the rest of the night."

He jammed another heaping spoon of potatoes into his mouth and chewed slowly as if it were a pile of gravel. It had been easy using Mother's hopefulness and trusting nature against her, telling her lies that she wanted to hear and knowing that, because she wanted to believe, she would believe.

He figured she would be so happy at the prospect of him making new friends and doing wholesome activities with them after school, that she would turn a blind eye to his late nights and his self-enforced solitary confinement in his room. Up until now, it had worked. She had even become pretty liberal about letting him drive the old Ford to school so that he could stay in town with his new friends and come home later.

"Why were you so late tonight anyway? You usually aren't this late."

He really didn't have time for this. Tonight was the night, and if he didn't get away from this woman with her stupid concerns and irritating, prying questions, he was going to miss everything! He played his ace card and said, "I was at that new kid, Clark's, house." Another lie.

"Clark Benton, right? The one that just moved here from Nebraska?"

"Yeah, that's the one. We have a debate competition coming up and we were studying for it."

His father grunted from behind his newspaper. His son on the debate team apparently not meeting his approval. Daniel couldn't care less. He stared at the old man's dirty fingernails and heard the air whistle through his nose as he breathed behind his newspaper wall. *Disgusting.* When the time came, killing the old man would be a pleasure.

Mother sighed. "Still, Danny, it's awful late for you to be out."

"I know, Mom," he said, pausing for effect as he prepared to deliver the line that would buy him some more time and lenience with the insufferable woman. "It's just that…" He tried to force himself to blush and smile. "It's just that Clark has a sister—a twin—and her and I kind of got to talking."

Mother's eyes widened as a slight smile began to play at the corners of her mouth. "Really?" She was taking the bait. Time to set the hook and reel her in. *Just tell the woman what she wants to hear. Too easy.*

"Her name is Wendy," a good, chaste sounding name he figured, "She's pretty Mom, and I…" He stirred his fork in his food.

"Annnnd?"

He looked up at his mother, hope pooling in her plain, brown eyes. "And I think she might kind of like me."

"Oh, Danny," she gushed, "That is wonderful!"

"Anyway," he cut her off before things got out of hand. "Because of Wendy, I probably didn't get as much studying and homework finished as I should have." He scooted his chair back from the table a little more to add emphasis.

He glanced over at his father and noticed the man was peering at him over the top of his paper, his eyes narrowed in suspicion. His mother was easy enough to lie to, Dad was a different story. So far the man had remained silent, willing to go with the flow, and that was good enough.

"Okay," Mother said. "Go on up, but at least take your plate and eat some more. No point in starving." She was absolutely beaming.

"Thank you," he said, lifting his plate as he stood. He could feel her gaze boring into his shoulder blades as he walked from the dining room. She would be crushed when she finally realized all of it had been a lie. He figured the day would come when he would have to kill her. The thought of it almost made him feel sorry for her.

He closed and locked his bedroom door, shutting out the world of the mundane while embracing the quiet solitude of his sanctuary. No need to flick on a lamp, he was perfectly at home encompassed by darkness and shadow.

He let the cold dinner plate land with a thump on his bed and walked over to the edge of the large, tan rug in the center of his room. He squatted and began rolling up the rug, revealing an intricate pattern of symbols and geometric shapes of a ritualistic nature, meticulously scribed in white chalk on the wooden floor boards.

He set the rolled up rug off to the side and stood for a moment, admiring his handiwork with reverence before stepping into its center. He closed his eyes and breathed deeply as he concentrated on centering himself. After a while, he could feel his mind and body drifting together as they came into a state of equilibrium and calmness.

Stepping out of his circle, he walked over to his nightstand and pulled a large hunting knife from the drawer. He stepped to the edge of the circle, placed the blade against the fleshy part of his left palm, and drew it slowly across. He winced as the blade bit into his flesh and the wound began to throb as dark blood gushed forth.

Mesmerized, he watched the reddish black fluid seep from the gash until a small pool had formed in the middle of his palm. He dipped the knife blade into the reservoir of coagulating blood, and began using it to smear the thick liquid over the entire surface of his palm. When he was finished, he laid the knife on the floor and pressed his bloody hand into the center of the pictograph, leaving a perfect, red hand print.

Slowly, he rose and took a step to stand in the center of the circle. Closing his eyes, he concentrated and waited. Soon, the air began to tingle with energy, like the electric spark in the atmosphere just prior to a lightning strike. The tingle began to intensify as it gathered and focused in on him. The time had come and he started saying the words that she had taught him—an incantation she had called it. Each time he repeated the incantation he felt a new surge of power and strength enter into his body; the sensation was intoxicating.

And then, suddenly, he was no longer alone. He could hear *them* chanting along with him, the voices from the tree. He recognized each one of them, but instead of inside his head, they were all around him. The chanting gradually began to rise in intensity and speed, the syllables forming an undulating beat, until the chanting had become almost feverish. When he opened his eyes he was startled—but not surprised—to see he was not alone in the room.

He counted thirteen people, men and women, holding hands in a circle around him while intoning some dark being of ancient and terrible power. They were dressed in the rough, homespun clothing of a time gone by and, based on their translucent, flickering appearance, he judged them to be spirits of the dead. But he wasn't scared. Why should he be frightened of ghosts? He had a body of flesh and blood, and that made him more powerful than they by far.

Directly in front of him was the tall, gaunt spirit he had seen before, haunting his dreams by night and lurking at the edges of his vision in the day. Daniel could sense he was somehow the leader of this group of people. He could feel that the lanky figure commanded a certain level of respect and deference from the rest of them. The man's eyes were hot, black coals of hate. Leader of the group, yes, but he was in some kind of servitude to yet another. Daniel smiled. *Her.*

He realized the strength he was receiving came from this circle of spirits. He was consuming their energy. In essence, he was feeding off of their souls and he delighted as he gorged himself with power. He closed his eyes again and let it all in, drinking deeply.

There was a strange pulsating sensation that resonated with the tingle and they seemed to come into tune with one another, along with the chanting. They harmonized like some alien form of music and he felt himself become as light as the air. Then there was the sensation of moving through a wall. When he opened his eyes he was floating, looking down at his own body as it stood in the circle, rigid like a statue, and just as vacant of life.

In thrilled amazement, he held his hands up in front of his face. They appeared solid to him, but his skin glimmered with a silvery sort of energy, his life force, he surmised. He looked around at the people chanting in the circle, they no longer appeared transparent or flickering, but solid. Silvery streams of energy flowed out from each of them, and into him.

Suddenly, the chanting ceased and then she was there, standing by the window. His beautiful mistress! As always, she was garbed in her satin robe that seemed to be able to consciously manipulate its own form to caress the curves and lines of her figure in every complimentary way. And as always, her bare feet seemed to hover just slightly above the floor. Her seductive lips smiled, warm and inviting as she beckoned to him with a curled finger. Through no doing of his own, he floated across the room as if she were drawing him toward her with her eyes.

That's when he saw the boy, Levi Henderson—his spirit anyway—standing by her side. She held the boy's hand, possessively, like a mother would cling to her child's hand on a crowded street. As he floated across the room to her, Levi pierced him with eyes of sadness and hate. Daniel sensed that the boy now belonged to her in some way…like a captive. As he neared, he could see something behind her, low and hunched at her feet. He recognized the bully, Robbie Pritchard, on his knees, head hanging, spirit crushed. He never even glanced up as Daniel approached.

He noted that the spirit of the preacher wasn't there. Maybe because he hadn't made that kill himself. Maybe only the people he happened to kill himself and take to the tree ended up as her prize.

As he floated across the room, he had to admit on some level, that he felt a little bad for Levi; the boy had never done anything to him. But seeing Robbie in his current situation gave him a deep sense of gratification. *Not the king anymore,* he thought. *How the mighty have fallen.*

He wondered for a moment if a similar fate also awaited him once all was said and done. But he only needed one long gaze into her impossibly blue eyes to dismiss the thought entirely. She and he were going to be together in the end. They were both growing stronger with each day, with each kill, and soon his mistress would have the power and strength to transcend into this world, the world of the living—not as a mere mortal, but as a goddess! And he would be there, by her side. First, a physical vessel would be required, one worthy of her magnificence and beauty with a soul strong enough to sustain her for a long time.

He smiled because he knew this vessel had already been chosen. Miss Katherine Farnsworth had no idea of the high honor that awaited her in the near future! It was ironic that she had been so fearful of him earlier that afternoon in the park. She couldn't know, couldn't comprehend that he was merely watching over her, protecting her. Someday she would understand…someday soon.

His out-of-the-body self came to rest directly in front of her. Still smiling, and holding him captive with her eyes, she reached out with a slender hand and stroked the side of his face. In his current physical state he could actually feel her caress, like a prickling of electricity, and he leaned into her touch.

Her voice had a melodious quality as she spoke, "The young policeman has become a danger to us. He spoke with her today, tried to warn her, and now she grows wary. This cannot be allowed."

"I understand," Daniel replied, a small thrill building inside him as he began to realize where this was going.

"Wilt thou help me? Will thou not do that which I bid thee?"

"I will, just tell me what you need me to do."

She smiled and kissed him on the forehead. "The man must die. You must take his life."

"And take him to the holy place?" Daniel asked.

She seemed to contemplate that for a moment, then shook her head. "No, I do not require it."

She reached down and stroked Robbie Pritchard's head with perfectly manicured fingernails. Robbie flinched in fear and began to tremble and sob. She smiled again. "I have that which is sufficient for my needs." Then she turned her head to look out the window and pointed into the night. "I have delivered thy prey into thine hands. Go now to thy task, and fail me not!"

In an instant he was flung by some force right through the wall, and he found himself flying at an impossible rate of speed over the countryside. There had been no sensation of acceleration, yet ten miles of fields, forests, and farm land raced past in only a matter of seconds. The deceleration was equally as instantaneous as he flew over streetlights and then trees.

Again, came the feeling of moving through a wall and, suddenly, his limbs felt awkward and heavy, almost clumsy, but extremely strong and powerful. He took a moment to get his bearings and take inventory of where he was or, perhaps more importantly, who he was. The voice of his mistress echoed in his head. *"Fail me not!"*

THE LIT PORTION OF THE PATH was not far now and Scotty quickened his pace. In the light he would be safe. Under normal circumstances he would never have been out in the dark like this, alone.

Walking Kate home had really thrown a wrench in the gears of his routine. Always a sucker for a pretty face, even in his current screwed up state of mind.

But hell, what guy wasn't? The dame even had Chet all wrapped around her pretty little finger, so who could blame him if he happened to like the girl too?

Reaching the lit path didn't make him feel as safe as he had thought it would; it was still late and the park was as deserted as a graveyard. The silence was unsettling: no other footsteps save his own, no distant voices or dogs barking, only the wind as it scattered the occasional leaf and caressed the bare branches of nearby trees.

He was in a no man's land at the moment, but he knew that beyond the confines of the park lay the town with its sidewalks, lights, and streets with cars. He just needed to make it through that grove of pine trees up ahead and he would be in the clear. Five more minutes and he'd be home.

As he entered the grove of pines he instantly sensed that something wasn't right. In fact, something was very wrong. It was the exact same sensation he had felt back in the woods behind the Baxter place, when he had seen Levi's dead corpse walking around. It was the unshakable feeling of being watched. No, it was beyond that...more like being hunted.

Suddenly, on instinct he froze, like a squirrel caught exposed on the trunk of a tree. He had always enjoyed shooting and hunting, and had probably shot dozens of the chattering creatures over his lifetime. Usually, when a squirrel sensed danger it froze, holding perfectly still against the bark of a tree. It was a tactic that relied on camouflage and a little luck, hoping to evade detection from a nearby predator or threat.

The problem was it didn't work very well for the squirrel if it had already been spotted. It actually just made it all the easier to line up your sights and take a well-aimed shot at the oblivious critter. How many of his bagged squirrels over the years would have escaped if they had just scurried off for their lives?

Freezing in place: it really was a stupid reflex.

A putrid, gag-inducing stench assailed his senses first, immediately followed by a heavy blow across his shoulder blades that sent him sprawling to the ground like a rag doll. Nearly unconscious, with his vision fading in and out, he tried desperately to recover, but his arms and legs were slow to respond. That awful odor of rot and decay slammed into him again as his attacker closed the distance.

The powerful stench worked on his muddled brain like smelling salts, and he managed to roll onto his back, his right hand instinctively groping at his belt, searching in desperation for the service revolver that he knew wasn't there. Milky-white light from the rising half moon permeated through the dense pine boughs and reflected off of grayish, waxen skin that hung too loose from the heavily muscled frame of an unclothed man.

His assailant stumbled toward him on heavy, thick legs, his ape-like arms swinging in a silent manifestation of raw strength. As the attacker neared, Scotty could see his naked body was covered in wounds, deep gashes and punctures, as if he had been dragged through a giant pile of railroad spikes—curiously, all bloodless. He felt a sick hopelessness fill his body as he realized that nobody could have survived wounds like that. The image of the dead, yet living Levi Henderson, materialized in his panicked mind and, even in his current state of shock, it wasn't too difficult for him to see the similarities between Levi and this abomination.

The thing bent over, grabbed him by the shoulders with hands of iron, and began lifting him off the ground, seemingly without any effort. There was a glistening, wet sheen on its blanched skin, as it oozed, rotting and decomposing. Its movements were accompanied by a wet, sickening sound like spaghetti noodles being stirred in a bowl. Scotty retched. It was all he could do to not throw up as he was brought to eye level with the creature.

The flat, broad face was almost decayed to the bone, the eyes sunken in and black, the lips shriveled into a permanent snarl, but up this close it was instantly recognizable: Robbie Pritchard.

The thing spoke, but obviously with some kind of supernatural help, as neither the desiccated lips or withered, black tongue moved. "Times up, Deputy Forks."

There was no doubt in Scotty's mind that he was about to die, just as the dead Levi had said he would. But in that moment of stark realization, he felt the fear drain away and a small ember of courage take light in his breast. A part of him was actually relieved to have this all finally over with. He was tired of living in fear, his manhood taken from him along with his sanity.

Survival was out of the question, this thing was too strong to fight. So, if he was going to go out, then why not on his terms? At least he would go out like half a man, not the sniveling, paranoid worm he had been reduced to over the last few weeks. He would die proudly.

Scott William Forks, Clear Creek County Sheriff's deputy, clenched his fists at his sides, looked right into those foul, soulless eyes, and flashed his best wise guy smirk. "We've been looking all over for you Robbie, where ya been? Jeez, you look like you was set on fire and put out with a baseball bat!"

The undead Robbie just continued to hold him there, seemingly a bit taken back by such a display of nonchalant bravado in the face of death—literally in the face of death.

"By the way," Scotty said, scrunching up his nose, "You ever hear of a toothbrush kid? Your breath could wake the dead."

The iron grip tightened on his shoulders and he winced in pain.

"Do you really think you can laugh and joke your way out of this?" came the hollow reply.

The grip tightened even more, causing Scotty to grunt. "Yeah, that's it," he panted, "that's the spot."

The creature drilled him with its black gaze. Scotty got the definite impression that he was talking to some spoiled brat kid, a kid about to throw a temper tantrum.

"You should have stayed away from the girl," the corpse said, a tinge of jealously detectable even in that disembodied voice.

"You aren't Robbie Pritchard," Scotty said, sweat beginning to pour down his face as the crushing grip on his shoulders continued to send jolts of pain through his nervous system. "Who are you really, huh? I think you're just some loser kid that figured out a witch's spell. Made a deal with the devil, did ya?"

The grip on his shoulders lessened slightly. Bingo! In spite of the pain, Scotty laughed. "That's it, isn't it? Well, I got news for you kid: it ain't gonna turn out for you like you think!"

"It has so far," the monster said. It lifted him higher into the air, fully extending its arms, like a playful father would lift a child up high. "Before you die, know this: the girl, Sheriff Cooper, all your friends…are going to die."

Scotty started to kick and thrash with all the strength he could muster. This was it! "You leave them alone!" he shouted.

"Goodbye, Deputy Forks."

Scotty stopped his useless struggling to look the thing in the eye one last time. "You'll burn in Hell," he said.

"We'll see about that."

The next thing Scotty knew, he was flying through the air, tossed as if he were nothing. He felt the impact of his body colliding with a large tree trunk, the shattering of his own bones filled his ears. The reanimated corpse was walking toward him as he crumpled to the ground, his body broken beyond repair. Warm blood filled his throat and he didn't even have the strength to cough. He realized he wasn't even breathing at all as darkness closed in upon him.

The Summoning

As the light of the living world fled from his eyes, his final thoughts were of Kate Farnsworth. As he had suspected, this creature, or whoever was controlling it, did indeed have a deep interest in her; she was in extreme danger. He had done the right thing to warn her tonight. He could only hope that she had taken him seriously.

After all, it had cost him his life.

CHAPTER 26

Despite the fact that it was raining, a substantial crowd had gathered and was milling about the large grove of pine trees that dominated the south end of the city park. Men dressed in rain-drenched overcoats and fedoras, along with women wrapped in shawls and clutching umbrellas, watched with grim expressions as Chet and Rick briskly made their way across the damp leaves.

Artie and Lloyd, the two city workers tasked with getting the park ready for the festival on Saturday, had called the sheriff's office just a few minutes prior, to report they'd found a body in the park. Chet had expected to meet the two men who had called it in, but was not prepared for the gawking crowd that had formed.

Sometimes he forgot how quickly word could spread in a small town. Word had spread fast enough, that Rick was still chewing on the piece of toast he'd been eating for breakfast when the call came in. *A dead body turns up in the city park and the man still has the compulsion to cram food into his face. Unbelievable!*

As they neared, the crowd parted for the two lawmen, a couple of voices calling out, "Make way for the cops!"

Chet pushed his way through the onlookers, Rick close behind him. Artie and Lloyd stood like gatekeepers where the path vanished into the trees.

Chet stopped in front of the two city workers, the drizzling rain pattering steadily on his khaki uniform. "Have you kept everyone out of there like I told you to on the phone?"

The men exchanged a look, and then Lloyd bobbed his head. "Yeah, pretty much."

"Pretty much?" Rick spouted from behind Chet. "What is that supposed to mean?"

Just then, a brilliant flash of light burst from out of the trees, followed by a muffled pop. The tell-tale signature of a camera going off, a camera that happened to be equipped with a large press bulb.

"I told you guys to keep everyone out of there until I got here!" Chet unleashed on Lloyd and Artie as he pushed past the two men.

"Dang, Sheriff, we're sorry," Artie mewled, "Mr. Fairchild said he was a member of the press and that we had to let him by."

"Mr. Fairchild is about to become a member of my jail!" Chet retorted as he left the two workers behind him and entered the grove. Apparently, slamming Conrad Fairchild against his office wall hadn't done much to shake him up; the man was just as impudent as ever.

The cold drizzle was noticeably less under the heavy canopy of pine boughs, but it was also dark, the overcast sky doing little to add much light to the situation. He paused a moment to allow his eyes to adjust to the gloom. The odor of death and decay hung thick in the air, sending his mind wheeling back to a time when that particular stench had been common place for him. The demons began to stir. Behind him, he heard Rick curse under his breath.

He forced the demons into silence and focused his attention to the center of the grove. About twenty-five yards in front of him, almost smack dab in the center of the grove, lay the naked, rotting corpse of a man. The body was almost shapeless, a pile of human flesh, contorted and heaped about without substantial form.

Standing over the corpse with a handkerchief pressed over his nose and mouth was Conrad Fairchild of *The Clear Creek Register*, a big newspaper camera hanging around his neck from a leather strap.

"I want you and your camera out of here, right now," Chet ordered, doing his best to keep his voice level and professional.

Conrad straightened in surprise, then looked at his wrist watch and nodded in feigned admiration. "Wow Cooper, great response time! I figured you for another five minutes at least."

"I'm sure you did," Chet said, beginning to slowly walk toward the body. "Now get out of here before I arrest you."

"For what? Doing my job, reporting the news?"

Chet had covered half the distance, his hands clenched at his sides. "For tampering with a possible crime scene and obstruction, that's what. You're making this too easy, Conrad. Now get out."

The reporter sneered and started walking in Chet's direction. "Fine, be it far from me to question the law of the land."

276

The two men glared at each other as Conrad approached, things obviously far from over between the two.

"Slam any citizens against a wall lately?" Conrad asked, his voice dripping with venom as they walked by each other.

There was a thudding sound behind Chet, followed by a grunt of pain. He whirled around to see that Rick had Conrad in an arm lock, and had just wrangled the large camera off the reporter's neck.

"Hey!" the little man protested, as Rick shoved him away. "You can't take my camera!"

"Shut up you idiot, I'm not taking your camera," Rick said, and started to fumble with the retaining clasps on the back of the device. After a couple of seconds, the back of the camera popped open, exposing the light-sensitive roll of film inside.

Conrad's rat face was as red as a beet. "Come on! Freedom of the press, guys! You ever hear of *The Constitution!*"

"Know all about it," Rick said, grabbing the film with one hand and ripping it from the camera, one end trailing like a black streamer. "You ever hear of common decency, Conrad?" Rick shoved the camera back into the man's shaking hands, causing him to take a step backwards.

"You're just going to let your deputy get away with this obvious abuse?" Conrad stammered at Chet, bits of spittle flinging from his pointy teeth.

Chet folded his arms and didn't say anything.

"That's fine!" Conrad fired back, making his way down the path. "You can tear the film out of my camera, but you can't open up my head and tear out what I saw." He swept one hand across the air in front of himself. "Tomorrow's headline: Murdered Body of Robert Pritchard Found. Sheriff at a Loss." He turned his back on the two and stormed for the edge of the grove.

"Hey!" Rick shouted after him.

Conrad spun around. "Now what?"

Rick crumpled up the film into a ball and threw it at the ground near the newspaper man's feet. "Pick that up," Rick said, "or I'll cite you for littering."

Snarling like a coyote with rabies, Conrad stooped and snatched the film up with a claw-like hand. Without another word he was gone, most likely racing to his office to type up the greatest work of his career.

"That man is rotten to his core," Rick said, staring after the retreating reporter.

Chet barely heard his deputy as he approached the corpse. Conrad had said it was the body of Robbie Pritchard. Could it really be? The size of the frame and the muscularity were certainly consistent with the Pritchard kid. As he worked his way to the other side of the body so that he could get a look at the face, he was taken back by the amount of injury and damage that had been inflicted to it.

Every kind of conceivable wound covered the moldering corpse: lacerations, contusions, cuts, scrapes, punctures, gashes.

Rick spoke behind him, "Sweet mother of all that's holy, Coop. What has this guy been through?"

Chet bent down and pried a stick out of the mud and squatted near the head of the corpse. He shook the mud off of the stick and then used it to lift the swollen, rotting head out of the muck. He took a deep breath and exhaled forcibly, trying to ignore the gnawing mental fatigue and stress that seemed intent on spiraling him into a nervous breakdown.

Dropping the stick, he stood up and faced his deputy. "Conrad was right. It's the Pritchard kid, sure enough."

Rick shook his head and put his hands on his hips. "Well, he sure didn't look like this when we pulled him from his car. I mean he didn't look pretty then either, but look at him now…kid looks like he got into a fight with a wood chipper!"

"This was all done to him postmortem," Chet said, "by whoever stole the body."

"And probably by whoever killed him," Rick finished the thought.

"Probably," Chet agreed. "And now they've left the body right here in the middle of the city park for us to find."

"I don't get it, Coop, why? Why take that risk? We weren't any closer to finding this body than the day it went missing."

"I don't know, Rick. I just don't know. I'm still trying to wrap my brain around this. Someone might be sending a message, or maybe it's a taunt."

"Taunt?"

"You know, catch me if you can sort of thing."

Rick ran his fingers through his short-cropped salt and pepper hair. "Coop, we got ourselves a problem. I mean, between the Henderson kid up and disappearing, Robbie Pritchard most likely being murdered, Reverend Gannon getting killed, and now this, not to mention Kate's creepy window peeper last night…"

Chet rubbed at his temples with his fingers. "What are you getting at, Rick?"

The older deputy folded his arms. "Okay, I'll just say it. We have some kind of psycho killer on our hands."

"What?"

"I'm starting to think it's all connected, Coop."

"Maybe," Chet said. "But that's a pretty good stretch at this point don't you think? There's nothing similar about how Robbie and Reverend Gannon died, and Levi is still missing, not murdered."

"As far as we know."

"Yes, as far as we know. And until we do know, I'm not going to jump to conclusions and scare the hell out of the whole town by announcing we may have a mass killer on the loose."

Rick put his hands up in the air. "I don't wanna fight with ya, and if we were in New York City or someplace like that, I wouldn't be saying this. But this is Clear Creek we're talking about here! Up until a month ago, the biggest crime around here was Melvin down at the filling station cheating at checkers." Rick walked around to the other side of Robbie's dead body and gestured with his hand at it. "And who does this? Who? Someone totally screwed in the head, that's who."

With his hands on his hips, Chet stared at the ground, letting his deputy's reasoning register in his brain. The only sound was the periodic splatting of large drips of rain that managed to find their way through the thick branches of the surrounding pines.

"I'm not saying you're wrong," Chet said, lifting his eyes to meet Rick's gaze. His next words caught in his throat at the sight of his deputy. Rick's face and head were covered in blood. Tiny, reddish rivulets trickled down his face and onto the collar of his shirt. It was a bizarre sight. Even though the man looked like he had just been cleaved in the head with a hatchet, there he stood, calmly blinking as if nothing had happened at all!

"Rick!" Chet exclaimed.

Rick's eyes grew wide as he looked around in alarm. "What is it, Coop?"

Chet stepped over Robbie's body. "Rick, you're bleeding like a stuck pig!"

The man looked down at his chest, searching wildly for the unfelt wound that had his young boss on the verge of hysteria.

"No, it's your head!" Chet was next to him now, parting the deputy's short hair, looking for the gash.

Rick reached up and patted a hand on his head and drew it away, red and dripping. "What the? I didn't feel nothin' hit me."

Just then, as Chet was still searching for the cut, he saw a big, red drop from above, impact on Rick's scalp, mingling with the rain water to run freely down the side of his head.

"Did you find it?" Rick asked, probing now with his hands across his head.

Another droplet of blood fell from the sky and hit with a splat. Chet craned his neck to look up into the boughs of the trees that loomed overhead. About twenty feet up, he could make out the soles of a pair of shoes in the gloom. A second later, he could see legs attached to the shoes, then hands and arms, then a torso.

"It's not your blood, Rick," Chet said, a sick feeling rising up from his gut. He pointed skywards.

Mouth agape, Rick sidestepped out of the path of another glob of blood as it fell to vanish into the mud and leaves on the ground. "Tell me that ain't another dead body hanging up there."

"Sure looks as if," Chet said, unable to tear his eyes away from the macabre scene.

"Can you see who it is?"

"It's too dark up there, too many branches in the way."

Rick stepped over to the trunk of a nearby tree and grabbing a hold of the lowest branch, hoisted himself up with the agility of a gymnast.

"Not a good idea, deputy," Chet warned. "I don't wanna be adding you to the list of casualties today."

"I got it," Rick replied, scrambling up a few more feet, his cowboy boots slipping precariously on wet bark.

Chet watched in silence as Rick clambered his way higher.

"Looks to be a male victim," Rick called down. "He's hanging from a rope around his neck. He's facing away from me, but I think I can get him turned here. Just a sec."

Chet could hardly stand the suspense as he watched his deputy and friend struggle to hang on to a branch with one hand while attempting to turn the hanging corpse with the other.

"Almost got it," Rick's voice floated down, followed by a long moment of excruciating silence. "Oh no," came the voice again. "No, no, no, no!"

"What is it?" Chet called up, hardly able to contain his anxiety.

"It's bad." Rick's voice was trembling. "It's very, very bad."

"Can you tell who it is?" Chet wasn't so sure he even wanted to know.

Rick let go of the body and stabilized himself with both hands, the body slowly rotating back to its original position. Rick's eyes were little pinpoints of light looking down at him from the shadows of the pine branches.

"It's Scotty…he's dead."

KATE SAT ON HER BED, her legs folded in front of her like chicken wings, the old reverend's journal resting in her lap. It was nearing midmorning, but she was still in the same heavy nightgown she'd slept in all night. The bed hadn't been made and her hair was gathered up into what was supposed to be a ponytail, but had turned out to be more of a snarled mess.

Earlier that morning, Mable had come into her room with a steaming bowl of oatmeal and a slice of toast. She informed her that Principal Grayson had just phoned, absolutely forbidding her to go into work today. She was to spend the day resting from her harrowing night.

She tried to protest, but Mable wouldn't have any of it and had apparently assigned herself as Kate's own personal jailer. Chet's fingerprints were all over her sudden incarceration and she thought of ruthless ways to punish the man as she ate her oatmeal.

Not wanting the day to go to complete waste, she decided to give Reverend Gannon's journal a real go over. After the night's events, she couldn't ignore that there was some significance to the old book. Someone, or *something* had opened that book to a certain place and now here she sat staring at that same page.

All the other entries that she had read were nothing out of the ordinary, just brief descriptions of each day's events, interlaced with a spiritual thought or a muse, but this particular entry stood out. It was different. It had no date written at the top of the page like the other entries in the journal, and it didn't make any sense:

Nothing is as it seems
for reality has become the dream
Seek the truth and it shall be found
where the sins of the righteous man are bound

That was it. Just a weird poem, or riddle of some kind all by itself in the middle of the page. There was no explanation. The rest of the journal just continued on the next page, right where it had left off.

It had to mean something, but after spending the last hour staring at it, she still had no clue. It was like being on the right path, but having no idea where that path led. She flipped through the journal looking for other poems or riddles, but there weren't any other entries that seemed out of the ordinary at first glance. Maybe she would have to read the entire journal for the answer.

The Summoning

She sighed and threw herself back onto her pillow and straightened out her legs, her knees stiff from sitting cross-legged for too long. She stared at the ceiling, repeating the riddle over and over to herself, hoping that her brain would miraculously latch on to some hint or clue buried in the rhyme. The morning rain drummed on the rooftop and against her bedroom window, providing a natural cadence for the poem as it cycled in her mind.

Her thoughts gradually wandered away from the maddening riddle to the memory of Chet's gentle caress the night before. She could see his blue eyes again, filled with the innocence and vulnerability of a child as he had asked—begged—her to stay. She could feel again the soft, warm touch of his fingers on her neck, hear the sweet, protective tenderness of his voice. The way it had all made her feel! More alive than she had felt in a long time.

Her heart increased its pace as she remembered her promise to stay, and her palms began to tingle and sweat as she pondered the implications. She cursed herself. A pair of gorgeous blue eyes comes along and common sense goes right out the window! Oh, there were other features of his to blame besides the eyes: a tall, muscular build, olive skin, chiseled jaw, wavy hair the color of chestnuts, an earnest smile that could…

"I've gotta get out of this room," she blurted, as she bolted out of the bed. Within minutes she was dressed in a pair of comfortable, faded jeans, canvas sneakers, and a gray, baggy sweatshirt. After quickly applying just the bare essentials of makeup: blush, eyeliner, and a light coat of lipstick, she spent a few extra minutes taming her curls into at least a semblance of a ponytail. She tucked the rest of her hair under her baseball cap, scooped up her breakfast dishes, and went downstairs.

"You are supposed to be resting in your room, young lady," Mable scolded, when Kate brought her breakfast bowl and spoon into the kitchen.

The matronly landlady was standing at the kitchen table in a flour-covered apron, beating the living snot out of a giant blob of bread dough. Her jowled cheeks were flushed and she was perspiring from the effort. Her copper hair was restrained in its usual, tight bun on top of her round head.

"Remind me never to do whatever he did," Kate joked, nodding to the lump of dough before placing her bowl and spoon in the sink.

Mable allowed a chuckle to escape before pressing her hands into the soft mixture to knead it. "Well, it seems your spirits are up."

Kate hopped up to sit on the counter top, her feet dangling. "I'm feeling alright, if that's what you mean."

"I'm glad to hear it, but you should rest. You had quite a night last night."

Kate watched as Mable kneaded and pounded for a minute, then asked, "Mable, what can you tell me about Reverend Gannon? The elder I mean, not the one that just died."

Mable paused for a moment to flash an inquisitive look in her direction. "What on earth for?"

Kate shrugged her shoulders. "Curious."

"Lucas was a good, decent man of God. What happened to him is a tragedy that this town will not get over very easily." Mable delivered a loud spank on the bread dough. "His father died when I was very young, I barely even remember him. The word, *stern*, comes to mind, but I imagine he was probably every bit a man of God as his son turned out to be."

"That's it?"

"Well, missy, what do you want to know, his life story?

"Yeah…kind of, I guess."

The older woman eyeballed Kate with suspicion as she picked bits of dough from between her plump fingers. "Well, I suppose you could go talk to old Nathan. He might be able to give you the story."

"Nathan?"

Mable stumped over to a cupboard and removed a stack of bread pans and started separating them on the table. "Yeah, Nathan Hobbes. He's the librarian down at the city library. He's also the unofficial town historian, if he can't fill you in on the details, I doubt anyone can."

"Thanks, Mable!" Kate lighted off the counter and sprang for the swinging kitchen door.

"Whoa, girl!" her self-appointed substitute mother bellowed. "You're not going out like that are you?" Her pale-blue eyes squinted in disapproval. "No offense, but a young lady can't just go strolling around town looking like a… like a bat boy for mercy's sakes!"

Kate laughed.

"I mean it, girl. What will people think?"

Kate stepped over to the stout woman and embraced her warmly. "I love you, Mable, but as of last night, I stopped giving a rat's furry, little fanny what people think."

Mable's eyes widened and her jaw slackened in shock as Kate patted her on the cheek and walked away. "I'll be at the library."

The Summoning

Kate shook the rain drops from her umbrella before folding it up and dropping it into a container near the library entrance, noting that only one other umbrella occupied the metal can.

The so-called city library had turned out to be just a couple of spare rooms set aside in the basement of the tiny city building.

She was standing in the first low-ceilinged room that took less than a second to glance over, the four walls lined with books stacked row by row in wooden shelves. A little wooden desk was to her left, unoccupied at the moment. Nondescript, brown carpet covered the floor and the musty odor of old books hung in the air.

At the back of the room, a doorway appeared to open up into yet another book-filled chamber. She could hear the unmistakable thumping sounds of someone shelving books coming from the other room. It had to be the old librarian, Nathan Hobbes.

She took casual notice of the book titles as she passed by them on her way to the adjoining room. Some of the poor books looked like they hadn't been moved in a coon's age, while others were in such disrepair, they belonged in a trash bin as far as she was concerned.

The second room was pretty much identical to the first room, just a tad bigger, and instead of a librarian's desk, there was a scarred and battered wooden table with four chairs in the center of the room. A radiator, painted white to match the walls, knocked and hissed out its warmth in a corner. A rectangular window near the ceiling ushered in the gray light of the gloomy day while holding at bay the steady barrage of rain drops that pelted its rippled surface.

An old man, looking to be well into his eighties, was in the far corner of the austere room, bent over with an armload of books. He slowly straightened as best he could when she entered, his frame stooped from age.

The man was thin and of average height, though he stood hunched. He may have even been a tall man once, in his younger years. She guessed that his oblong, bald head, currently covered in freckles and liver spots, had probably showcased much more hair at one time as well. He wore light brown slacks and a matching sweater vest from which protruded the folded collar and long sleeves of his white shirt.

He seemed surprised by her appearance. He used one bony finger to push a pair of thick, black-framed glasses off the end of his thin nose, to study her for a moment with magnified, brown, blinking eyes. Kate wasn't sure if he was so surprised because he didn't know who she was, or if he was just that shocked to have a customer. Probably a little bit of both.

"Good morning," she greeted, taking a step closer and smiling.

"Good morning," he replied, with a watery voice, still peering through thick lenses at her. "Is there something I can help you with Miss uh…"

"It's Farnsworth, but please just call me Kate."

"Farnsworth, Farnsworth…" He scratched at his chin and looked at the floor, his brow wrinkled in intense thought and concentration. If he recognized her name from the recent newspaper article that mentioned her, he certainly didn't show it.

"I'm not from around here," she said, before the old codger burst a brain vessel. "And you would be Mr. Hobbes, the librarian, I presume."

The old man shuffled to the center of the room. "Everyone round here just calls me Nate," he relaxed his hold on the stack of books in his arms and they slid onto the surface of the table, remaining neatly stacked, as if under his command, "no reason for you not to do the same, Kate, my dear."

"Okay, Nate," she said stepping closer to join him at the table, "I can do that."

He scratched at short gray whiskers on his chin and then smiled, revealing straight, white rows of teeth that didn't match his otherwise aged and weathered countenance. "Nate and Kate," he said, nodding in approval. "Kinda has a nice little ring to it, don't ya think?" He shuffled a little closer, smiling like a hyena, his white teeth flashing.

Holy cow, was he making advances?

"Um, yeah I guess so," she half laughed, watching incredulous as Nate advanced closer.

Before she knew it, her left hand was ensnared in his leathery grasp and being swiftly drawn to his purplish, puckered lips.

"Oh, Nate, really that's quite unnecessary. Seriously…"

The kiss was a little too wet, a little too cold, and lingering, but Mother had raised her to be a lady—at least how to act like one when it was required—and so she bore it with all the grace she could muster.

"Thank you," she said. "You're too kind…thanks again…. Okay." She withdrew her hand from his reluctant grasp and hungry lips.

"Might I ask where you're from?" he asked, his brown eyes floating up and down her body. Thank goodness for baggy sweatshirts and jeans!

"Emmett, Tennessee, up near Nashville," she said, hoping to get past the current awkwardness of the moment.

"It must be a beautiful place."

"It is very lovely."

Nate crinkled his brow. "So, what brings you here?"

He was obviously referring to Clear Creek, but this was her chance to head old Don Juan off at the pass. "Well, I came because I was hoping you could tell me a little about the late Reverend Gannon. Senior, not Junior."

"Oh?" There was a demand for an explanation cloaked in the simple response.

Of course, she couldn't just barge into the library and expect some old man to willingly answer whatever questions she put to him, especially as an outsider. Fortunately, she had come prepared with a little, white lie. Who was she kidding? More like a bald faced lie. Lying had not been part of the curriculum of her good Southern upbringing, but a skill she had acquired nonetheless—as a matter of survival, being the only girl in a household of brothers!

"Well," she said, sidling up next to him. "I've been doing research into my genealogy. You know, family tree stuff."

Old Nate bobbed his head.

"I think there might be a distant family connection. I'm just trying to find out more about him. I was going to talk to his son, Lucas…"

"That isn't going to happen anytime soon," Nate said. "You heard what happened to him didn't ya? Murdered."

"Just awful. I understand he was very much respected and loved."

Nate shook his head. "Murder, hard to believe something like that could happen here in our little town."

"I'm sure."

Nate fixed his milky eyes on her. "So, you came here from Tennessee?"

She nodded.

"To get more information on a long-gone, possibly-distant relative?"

She nodded again, but had the distinct feeling of someone picking at the loose threads of what was suddenly starting to look like a poorly conceived lie.

"A man who's son just so happens to be the victim of a recent murder?"

She didn't even have the resolve to keep nodding. It did sound ridiculous, repeated back to her like that. She felt the uncomfortable heat of blood flushing to her cheeks. "I—I'm sorry, Mr. Hobbes. I didn't mean to offend you." She spun away, intending to beat it out of there. "I'm sorry I wasted your time, have a good day."

She barely made it two steps.

"Whoa now, hold your horses, young lady."

She stopped and turned. There were those gleaming choppers, like a brand-new white picket fence, lighting up the room.

He took a cautious step toward her in a manner reminiscent of how her dad would approach a horse with harness in hand—slowly, so as not to frighten the animal off. "You still want to know about Reverend Gannon?" He didn't wait for a response. "I'll help you, but on one condition."

She shuddered to think what that might be while nodding her head in silence.

"I want the truth. All of it. And I'll do what I can to help you."

"All of it?"

He nodded, a smile touching his lips.

"Okay," she said, "but you probably won't believe it."

He pulled a chair out from under the table and began lowering himself into it —a seemingly painstaking process. As his bones settled, he motioned for her to do the same. "I've been around a long time, Kate. You might be surprised at what I'm willing to believe at this point down the road."

With a sigh of surrender, Kate let her purse flop onto the tabletop and seated herself across from Nate. He leaned forward, elbows on his knees, eyes blinking in anticipation.

"The reason I'm here," she began, "is because I'm helping Sheriff Cooper look into the murder of Lucas Gannon..."

Over the next ten minutes, she laid it all out in the open for the decrepit librarian with the teeth of a Hollywood star—and apparently the libido. She started with the day she met Chet and helped him look for the boy, Levi Henderson, and how they had hit it off pretty much right away. She went over the death of Robbie Pritchard, the theft of his body, and then Scotty Forks collapsing and claiming to have seen Levi, except walking around dead somehow. Scotty Forks trying to warn her of some kind of *evil* that had come after him, and was now targeting her.

Nate raised a thin hand to stop her. "What did he mean by that? Was he saying a killer was after him and you too?"

Kate sucked in air and blew out. "Maybe, but he made it sound like something else, something more...spiritual, like supernatural."

"Demonic?"

An involuntary shiver radiated down her spine. "Yes, more along those lines, I think."

Nate leaned back in his chair, the wood creaking. Or was it his old bones? "And what does all this have to do with the late Abel Gannon, Lucas's father?"

Kate steadied herself. "Okay, this is where it gets weird."

He raised his silver, shaggy eyebrows and motioned with his hand for her to continue.

She unbuckled her purse, slid the journal out, and placed it on the table. "This is Abel's journal. It was found by Deputy Shelton in Lucas's house, after he was killed. I think Deputy Shelton was just feeling sorry for me and wanted to give me something to do, so he asked me to go through it and see if I could find any clue or information that might point to an enemy of the family, or whatever."

"And you've found something?"

She nodded. "You're going to think I'm nuts, Nate, but last night I had what you might call...an episode." She opened the journal up to the page with the riddle and spun it around on the table for him to read it. "I have reason to believe that this page is extremely significant to what is going on around here."

He pursed his lips as he read out loud, "Nothing is as it seems, for reality has become the dream. Seek the truth and it shall be found, where the sins of the righteous man are bound." He laid the book back on the table. "What makes you think this is so important?"

"Last night, someone showed me this page. Someone I know to be dead."

And that was all of it. She studied his face, searching for any sign that could possibly indicate whether he believed her or not.

Nate tapped his finger against his chin, his jaw working on some imaginary morsel. After a moment he spoke, "Let me just be clear. From what I gather, you are saying that basically, we have a killer on the loose here in Clear Creek?"

She nodded.

"And you have come to believe that the answer to who this killer is lies somehow in Abel Gannon's journal, and not only that, but specifically this little riddle that you were um...*shown?* By someone beyond the grave, to be exact."

Kate shook her head half disbelieving her own story. "I know, I know. Call the paddy wagon, right?"

"No, no, not at all!" He reached out a bony hand and patted her on the knee. "I find the whole thing quite fascinating actually."

"So you'll help me?"

"I'm not sure how I could be of any help, but I'm willing to do what I can."

Taking his hand off her leg would be a great start. She stood up and began to pace. "Okay, for starters, how about that riddle? Does it mean anything to you? Can you make heads or tails of it?"

He skimmed over the passage again. "I have no idea what it means, but the placement is very strange. It's just sitting there all by itself in the middle of a blank page, no explanation. Almost cryptic in a sense."

Kate grabbed a random book from the shelves, and slid her thumb along the edges of the pages, just to give her hands something to do. "Did you know Abel before he died?"

The old man interlaced his fingers across his midsection. "Oh yes, I attended his congregation as a matter of fact. I was in my late teens when he passed away."

"What was he like?"

"He was serious, I never saw him smile or laugh, and every sermon seemed to be fire and damnation. He could preach hot hell in the freezing snow, they used to say."

"Yeah," Kate said, still feathering the pages of the book with her thumb, "I know the type: hellfire, damnation, and brimstone."

Nate smiled. "But, he wasn't always like that. At one time, he was very much the opposite. Most people agreed it was his wife's passing that changed him, but some insisted that he started changing before his wife died."

"And what do you think?"

Nate's eyes took on a vacant expression as he seemed to transport himself back in time. "I think he started to change when those religious lunatics moved into town."

"Religious lunatics?" She shelved the book she had been playing with and hurried to sit back down in her chair. "Like what, Masons? Polygamists?"

Nate laughed. "No, not quite. I can't remember what they called themselves exactly...The Children of something or another. They were into worshiping some kind of ancient fertility goddess, or some kind of nonsense like that. Their leader was named Cyrus, if I recall, a real fanatic."

"Wow," Kate said. She could only begin to imagine what sort of ceremonies and practices could be associated with that religion. "So what do you mean, they moved in? Are you saying they just showed up one day?"

"Well yeah, pretty much. A group of them bought a big old place on the outside of town and they all lived there, like a commune, growing all their own food and what not. There was probably around fifteen of them or so. They pretty much kept to themselves out there. Once in a while, you'd see two or three of them come into town to buy some supplies, but that was about it."

"I can imagine that the good reverend didn't take too kindly to having a cult move into his town."

"You could say that. In fact, nobody took too kindly to it, including the sheriff and the mayor. Especially after a few townsfolk up and disappeared without a trace."

Kate thought of Levi's disappearance as a sliver of fear stabbed into her heart. Could something like that be going on now? "So, what happened? Was this cult responsible for the missing people?"

The old man shifted around in his chair, searching for a more comfortable position. "Most folks blamed them, sure. But there never was any proof. The sheriff even searched the property, but came up empty-handed. The people wanted them gone, but their hands were tied by the law—freedom of religion, you know."

"Interesting," Kate said, trying to imagine it all in her head. "And the missing people…were they ever found?"

Nate slowly shook his head. "They were never seen again. There was speculation going around that they had been murdered by the cult—human sacrifices."

It wasn't cold in the room, but Kate felt the need to wrap her arms around herself to prevent a shiver from running through her. "What happened? Was the town ever able to get rid of these people?"

Nate's face grew serious as he held her in his milky gaze. "One night, there was a fire that leveled the house to the ground. Everything burned. Nothing was left by morning, except a pile of smoldering ash."

Kate's hand crept to her throat. "How horrible. Did any of them make it out?"

The ancient librarian didn't answer, as if considering how to put his next words.

"They *all* died?" She found it hard to believe that fifteen adults could all perish in a house fire without a single survivor.

"That's just it," Nate said, "nobody knows exactly what happened to them. There was absolutely no evidence of any human remains in what was left of the fire. Rumors spread through town as quickly as those flames had spread through that house.

"Most people figured they were guilty of kidnapping and murder, and had decided to cover their tracks by burning down the house and skipping town."

"Makes sense I guess," Kate said.

"Yes, I suppose it does, but there were some who believed a group of vigilantes might've taken matters into their own hands and done away with the cult themselves." He arched grizzled eyebrows at her. "All I know is, none of them were ever seen around here, again."

Kate let her eyes rest on the old reverend's journal laying on the table. "That's when Abel Gannon's demeanor began to change?"

Old Nate nodded.

"Do you think Abel had something to do with the fire and the disappearance of the cult?"

"That's a dangerous question, young lady, perhaps best left unanswered."

For a long moment, no words passed between them as she tried to sort the crazy story out in her mind. It was definitely an interesting story to be sure, but was she any closer to figuring out the riddle in the journal?

Rick had told her to read the journal and see if she could find any clues that might point to an enemy of the Gannon family. If Abel had played a part in murdering fifteen people…

The main door to the library swung open in the other room. A gust of cool, moist air rushed through the small space. Footsteps thumped across the floor and a familiar voice, high and nasally, called out, "Kate?"

A short man, small of frame with narrow shoulders and a pinched face appeared in the doorway. It was Porter Thomas, the chain smoking Marine that had helped out with the search for Levi the night they had stumbled across that machine gun nest. He was the poor guy that had suggested she stay behind, that the woods were no place for a woman. She had about bit his head off.

"Miss Kate," he said, laying eyes on her.

She rose from her chair. "What is it, Porter? How'd you know I was here?"

"Stopped by the boardin' house, talked to Mrs. Johnson. She said you had come here."

Kate cocked her head sideways. "What's going on?"

"Sheriff Cooper sent me to get ya. I'm to take you down to the sheriff's office."

Grabbing the old journal and her purse, she took a tentative step toward him. "What for, and why would he send you?"

Porter shuffled his feet on the carpet as he answered, "Chet just deputized me a while ago—on a temporary basis. Something…something has happened. I'll explain on the way."

Her mind began racing as a feeling of dread crept up into her breast. She could sense it in Porter's voice and see it in his eyes; something very terrible had happened. What could it be? There was only one way to find out, so on numb feet she followed Porter as he lead the way to the front door.

The wiry man waited, holding the door for her as she pulled her umbrella from the container and stepped into the drizzling grayness.

"You're welcome back anytime, Kate," the old librarian called from behind, curiosity etched across his wrinkled face.

She managed to force a wooden smile before Porter closed the door and led her by the arm to a rusty, old, Dodge pickup, parked and idling along the curb. He opened the passenger door. She had barely scrambled in when he slammed it shut, the door clanging like a metal garbage can being thrown against a brick wall. He hustled around the front of the truck and jumped into the driver's seat. He put it in gear and gave it some gas, the truck backfiring loudly as they pulled away.

The interior of the truck was pretty much what she expected: dirty and smelly. Cigarette butts and ashes spilled out of the ashtray which could no longer contain its contents. A mix of food wrappers, receipts, old spark plugs, and empty bullet casings cluttered the dash and floorboards. She crinkled her nose at the overpowering odor. It reeked like someone had thrown a dead, wet dog into a fire and then thrown it under her seat.

"Sorry 'bout the mess," Porter said, leaning close to the windshield. The wipers whipping back and forth were doing a better job of smearing gunk across the surface than wiping away the rain.

"It's fine," she lied. "Now what's this all about? Is Chet okay? Rick?"

Porter glanced sideways at her for a second before returning his eyes to the road. "They found the Pritchard kid's body this morning…in the park. Looked like it had just been dumped there by somebody overnight."

There was more to the story than that, she could tell. He was holding something back, something awful.

"That's kind of a good thing, isn't it?" she said, praying that her instincts were wrong.

Porter exhaled heavily and licked at dry lips. "There was actually two bodies. The other one was Scotty Forks…murdered."

CHAPTER 27

I s Kate here yet?" Chet blurted as he stormed into the office, the door banging shut behind him. "I saw Porter's truck out there."

Rick looked up from a pile of paperwork, his shirt still stained in Scotty's blood. Porter stood in the corner by the coffee, cradling a steaming cup in his hands. Rick motioned with his head at Chet's desk, his face a mask of pain and concern. Chet turned in time to see Kate running around the edge of his desk. She flung her arms around his neck and buried her face in his chest.

After a moment she looked up to meet his gaze, her eyes glistening with unshed tears. Her voice cracked slightly when she spoke, "Is it true? Scotty's dead? *Murdered?*"

He used his finger to tilt the brim of her baseball cap back so he could see her eyes better. "I'm afraid so. I just got back from the morgue with Dr. Steinmetz."

Rick came over, his cowboy boots clumping on the wood floorboards. "What did Dr. Steinmetz say?"

The couple released their embrace to face the longtime deputy. Chet took a moment to organize his thoughts while simultaneously trying to push the horrific images of Scotty's battered corpse, laying on a stainless steel gurney, out of his mind. He knew it was useless. Those images were burned into his brain now and filed away with all the other memories of death and decay, guaranteed to emerge later, on some dark and sleepless night when he was all alone in the world.

He looked at Kate, her green eyes brimming, yet she was remaining strong— strong for him. He drew from that strength, drinking from her well of light and goodness, and felt his courage return. "For starters, he wasn't killed by hanging, his body was hung up like that after he was dead."

"So, how'd he die?" Rick asked.

Chet put his hands on his hips and looked down at the ground. "The doc hasn't done a complete autopsy, but said it looked like he died from a severe blow to the upper body, like he'd taken a bad fall, or been hit by a car. His entire ribcage was pretty much shattered by the blow. Broken ribs probably punctured his lungs and heart."

Rick exhaled, shaking his head. "And then he gets strung up in a tree. But why? Why Scotty?"

Chet walked over to collapse into his chair. "I don't know, bad luck I'm thinking. He probably accidentally stumbled upon our killer in the middle of dropping Robbie's body off in that grove of trees. The killer simply eliminated a witness."

"With what, a wrecking ball? How did he inflict those kinds of injuries, Coop?"

Chet felt a burning frustration smoldering down deep inside him, a white-hot anger clawing for release. Since Levi Henderson's disappearance it had been one baffling occurrence after another. People in his town, people he had sworn to protect, were dead and he had no answers, not even one clue to what or who was responsible!

"Coop?" came Rick's voice, asking for an explanation to yet another inexplicable mystery.

"I don't know, Rick, maybe he dropped a damned piano on him!"

Rick absorbed the verbal blow without so much as a wince. "It's okay. We'll know more once Dr. Steinmetz gets finished with the autopsy."

A wave of guilt slammed through Chet. The last person that deserved to be yelled at was his trusted friend and deputy. "I'm sorry I lost it, Rick. I'm just so frustrated with all of this. I didn't mean to take it out on you."

Rick waved a hand like he was swatting at a fly. "Don't sweat it." He scratched his head for a second. "Um, do Scotty's folks know?"

Porter mumbled from the corner, "Whole town's gotta know by now." It was an irrefutable fact.

"One of us should probably go over," Rick said. "You want me to go and check up on 'em?"

Chet nodded. "Yeah, that's probably a good idea. Thanks."

"You bet," Rick said, heading for the door. He grabbed the door handle and then paused to look back. "Don't worry, we'll get this all sorted out and catch the son of a bitch. It's just a matter of time before he makes a mistake."

Chet nodded in agreement, even though at the moment he was having serious doubts. "Oh, Rick?" he said, before the man could leave.

"Yeah?"

"Might wanna change your shirt before you go over there."

Rick looked down at the bloodstains on his shirt and his face drained of all its color. "Oh crap! Yeah, I'll swing by my place and change first."

As the door closed, Kate made her way over to Chet's desk, dragging a nearby chair with her. She sat down next to him, her movements stiff, her face wooden and pale. Something was wrong.

"Anything else you need me to do, Sarge?" Porter piped up from the corner.

"No," Chet answered. "You can go ahead on your daily business. If something comes up, I'll get a hold of you. Thanks for finding Kate for me."

Porter took a final sip from his coffee cup before setting it on the counter next to the percolator. "I'm off then," he said and gave a sloppy salute as he strode past on his way to the door.

Normally, Chet would have chastised the former Marine and reminded him that this was not the Corps. Instead, he turned to Kate before the door had even shut. "Are you okay? You look like you've seen a ghost."

Her eyes suddenly took on an incredulous glint. "Really, Chet? After last night, that's your choice of words?"

He sighed. "Yeah, bad choice of words. Sorry, I'm not exactly at my best right now."

Her face softened. "That's okay, neither am I."

"So anyway," he said, grabbing a notepad and pencil from a desk drawer, "are you okay to talk?"

"I suppose."

I had Porter round you up and bring you here because you may be the last person that saw Scotty alive."

She swallowed a little too hard and nodded. "I probably was. How did you know?"

"Last night, before I left, Mable told me that Scotty had walked you home." He managed a snicker. "She was afraid that he was pulling a fast one, trying to steal you away. She was uh...giving me a heads up."

She reached into his shirt pocket and snatched away the folded hankie that he always kept on him. She dabbed at her eyes with it, apparently losing the battle with her tears. "He was nothing more than a complete gentleman doing his duty, as he saw it."

"So he did walk you home last night? About what time would you say it was when he left you?"

"Well, it would have been pretty close to the time that you were called. I went straight up after he left, to take a bath, and that's when I saw...the ghost, the peeping tom, or whatever you want to call it."

"Right. So, how did he seem to you?"

"Well, you know how he'd been acting ever since his…episode, all paranoid and kind of crazy?"

Chet nodded.

"He was pretty much like that, but worse in a way. I mean he was really scared. To be honest, he sort of started scaring me. I almost had to kick him off the porch." She dabbed again at her eyes. "I felt bad for him. I should have insisted that he call a ride. Instead, I let him walk off all alone, out there in the dark."

Chet wondered what in the world Scotty was doing walking Kate home in the first place, but was afraid that if he asked, it would maybe come across as accusatory, so he let it go. "Okay, so he was more scared and paranoid than normal. What kind of stuff was he saying?"

"That there was evil at work in this town, a darkness, and that I had been touched by it somehow. He warned me to be careful. He said this so-called evil was focusing its attention on me."

The hairs on Chet's arms stood up. He sure didn't like the sound of that! "What was he talking about, Kate? Did he say what this evil was?"

She shook her head, "No, he just said that something took a hold of him that day in those woods, that it still had a hold on him, and now I had been touched by it."

An ominous feeling seemed to press in from all sides. Kate shivered and hunched her shoulders. "Do you think he was right, Chet? Am I in danger?"

He scooted his chair closer to hers and draped an arm around her shoulders. "I don't know what's going on, but I swear I'm going to get to the bottom of all this. Don't you worry about all this talk of evil. Scotty had lots of problems. All this talk of you being in danger, there's no reason to believe it."

Leaning into him, she placed her hand on his chest and started to fidget with one of the buttons on his shirt. "If I could stay like this, I know I wouldn't have to worry."

He used his arm to crush her delicate frame even closer into him, relishing her warmth and her scent. But a little stray thought was running through his mind, bouncing around back and forth in a panic, unwilling to settle down no matter how good the moment with Kate was feeling. Could she really be in danger? What did Scotty know? He was murdered after all, maybe he really did know something. Not to mention the man in the window!

He cleared his throat. "Just to be on the safe side, have you noticed anyone following you, or acting strangely around you, or anything weird?"

She raised her head to look up at him, a hesitant, almost guilty look in her eyes. She exhaled as she shook her head. "I wasn't going to say anything cause it's probably nothing, and I think I took care of it."

Alarm bells went clanging in his head and that panicky little thought was now running around screaming, *"I told you so! I told you so!"*

She got to her feet and began pacing back and forth, rubbing the palms of her hands together. "There's a boy at the junior high, an eighth grader. He's been really forward, very brazen, making advances, trying to flirt, I guess."

Chet tried his best to smile hoping it would help assuage her worries, and perhaps chase away a bit of the heavy, pervading gloom. "Well, I certainly can't blame him for trying."

She responded with a quick sideways glance and a half-hearted, fleeting smile. "Yeah, except this kid scares me, Chet. He's not normal. He's very intelligent and talks a good game, but there's a hostility there, I can feel it. Social protocols seem to mean nothing to him: he crowds too close, he's suggestive, arrogant, totally inappropriate. It doesn't seem to be of any concern to him that he's just a kid."

"What's this kid's name?"

"Daniel Miller. Do you know him?"

Chet hoisted himself out of his chair, the shrapnel wound in his back making him wince. "I know who he his. Usually a quiet kid, kind of an outcast really. Not quiet enough it seems. Sounds like he could use a good talking to."

"That's just it though," Kate exclaimed as she sat back down and pressed her hands between her knees. "What if I'm blowing it all out of proportion because of what I went through with Albert?"

The young sheriff's temper flared at the thought of that kid making unwanted advances on the girl he loved, scaring her. "So what if you are? He's being disrespectful and making you uncomfortable. I'll have a talk with him and his parents."

She reached out and grabbed his hand. "No," she said. "I don't think it's necessary."

"Why the heck not?"

"Because, I already took care of it at the park last night, just before I ran into Scotty."

"You saw him last night? What happened? What was he doing at the park? He should have been home at that hour."

"I don't know, he just kind of appeared out of nowhere while I was reading. He came onto me, stronger than ever, and I told him that he needed to leave or I was going to report him to the police. He stopped what he was doing and left. He complied, and hopefully that's the end of it. Can't we just let it go for now?"

Chet sucked in a deep breath and let it out. "I don't know, Kate. I don't like it one bit."

She smiled as she stood and took his face in her hands. "Are you sure you're not just jealous?" She used a finger to lightly trace the wound she had left on his cheek from the night before.

He let out a snort. "Okay, we'll leave it alone for now, but I want to know the very instant he tries anything again. Deal?"

She raised herself up on tiptoes, kissed the scratch on his cheek, and whispered into his ear, "Deal."

THE ENTIRE SCHOOL WAS BUZZING like a hornets' nest that had been jabbed with a stick over the news. Two bodies had been discovered that morning in the park, Robbie Pritchard and Deputy Forks. Daniel pretended not to hear any of it, while secretly soaking in every word.

The rumors and speculation ricocheted through the halls and classrooms, careening from mouth to mouth with a life of their own: Robbie's body was so badly mutilated that it wasn't even recognizable—the deputy had been found hanging in a tree—there was a mass murderer on the loose—no, Deputy Forks was the killer and now he had committed suicide over the guilt—no, it was actually a deranged inmate that had escaped the asylum, and was on a murdering rampage.

Daniel moved through the halls like a shadow, unnoticed as always. Unnoticed and unloved. He yearned to shout his crimes out loud, and then see the dumbfounded looks on their stupid faces when they finally saw him for the first time. Saw him for who he really was: a killer, a predator, a transgressor filled with power, one who would take that which was most precious from them without hesitation.

That sure was some trick, he thought as he took his seat in algebra class, remembering the night before. He was still trying to wrap his head around it; the fact that he had left his body! Not just that, but that he had been able to take possession of Robbie's dead corpse and control it! It had been the perfect crime. No evidence would be found to link him to the cop's murder.

It was unfortunate that Robbie's body was too far gone now with rot and decomposition to be of anymore use. That was the downside. He guessed that

Levi's body was lying out there in the woods somewhere, beyond its usefulness as well. He supposed that soon another body would be needed, another kill.

He was growing in power. He flexed his fingers and watched the muscles of his forearms ripple in response. Yes, his physical strength was increasing, but he could feel a power inside himself that transcended physical strength. He could feel it, but didn't understand it. He knew that he had tapped into that power last night when he had made that incredible jump into Robbie's body. He had drawn from a source deep inside of himself and he sensed that with each kill, that source increased greatly.

She was growing in power too, somehow drawing from his kills as well. Before, it had been a major effort for her to appear to him and speak into his mind. Now, her presence was almost continual and each time she appeared to him her form was more and more substantial. She was nearly ready to make her entrance into the physical world. Once she took a vessel of flesh and blood for herself, she would be all-powerful, truly a goddess. And he would be there, by her side, enveloped by her love and beauty.

Pretty Katherine Farnsworth had been chosen as the vessel that would provide—an honor for her—but not to be slaughtered like some dumb animal, not like the others. No, his mistress would not inhabit a stinking, rotting, corpse. Kate would still be alive, still be in there somewhere. She was just going to have to learn how to share is all.

His hands grew clammy and he licked his lips, imagining how it would be, as images from his darkest fantasies flashed through his mind. There would be no more stupid mind games, no pulling away, no idle threats to call the sheriff. Kate would just be along for the ride. Powerless. Would she be aware? Conscious of everything going on, just unable to do anything about it?

Forbidden images flickered across the stage of his imagination. His body pressed against hers, flesh against flesh, gazing into those stunning green eyes, the eyes of his goddess mistress. But they were Kate's eyes as well and she was in there, experiencing it all. If he looked hard enough, would he see the fear? Would he sense a slight tremble in her fingertips as they caressed his skin?

He could always hope. Couldn't he?

CHAPTER 28

S cotty Forks, Lucas Gannon, Robbie Pritchard, Levi Henderson. Were they all connected somehow, or were they just randomly selected victims? Chet stopped pacing and allowed himself to crumple onto the old, broken-down couch that served as the only piece of furniture in the tiny living room of his rental.

It was in the afternoon, but having worked the graveyard shift the night before, and then having slept through the morning and part of the afternoon, his day was just getting started. The stress of recent days was apparently taking its toll. After prying himself out of bed, he had remained in the shower, standing under the faucet in a daze of weariness until the hot water had turned to lukewarm, and then to downright freezing. He had shaved with cold water—not a new experience for a Marine—and was now dressed only in his khaki pants and a white undershirt. The thought of putting on his whole uniform seemed an insurmountable task at the moment.

He pressed a cold beer—not the worst breakfast he'd ever had—to his forehead and stared at the four names scrawled on a large pad of paper he'd hung on the opposite wall. When he had written those names, he had envisioned that, eventually, he'd be able to draw connections, add names, possibly even come up with a motive or even a suspect. But so far, the four names remained alone in stark, glaring contrast, defying him to solve the riddle they represented.

He had stared at those names for two days and, so far, couldn't make one single connection between them, or come up with a motive of why anyone would kill them. As far as he could tell, someone was killing at random and killing for the pleasure of it. And with the latest stunt, leaving two bodies for him to find in the park, the killer was growing more and more confident, throwing it right in his face, challenging him.

He was at a loss with no clues, no leads, and no answers. To make matters worse, Conrad Fairchild had made good on his promise and had released a scathing article in the paper, calling on Chet to seek outside help from the state police, declaring out right that he wasn't up to the task. Even going so far as to suggest a recall vote on his election.

The worst part of it was, as infuriating as it had been to read the blistering article, a large part of him wondered if Conrad was right. Maybe he wasn't cut out for this crap after all. And if *he* was thinking it himself, how many people out there were reading the paper today, nodding their heads in silent agreement?

The faces of the victims' families flitted through his mind. So far, he had let all of them down. He'd failed to protect their loved ones and now seemed utterly incapable of at least giving them the justice they deserved. Especially painful was the thought of having to attend Scotty's funeral in a couple of days. He and Rick had both been asked by the family to say a few words. The thought of standing up there, in front of the people he had failed, speaking at their dead loved one's funeral, was an agonizing proposition to say the least.

Maybe it would just be better for everyone if he resigned and left town for good. He wondered if Kate would go with him. How would she feel about following a disgraced sheriff to some random town to eek out a living doing whatever? What about his sister, Connie? Could he just leave her, his only family? She would never forgive him.

He cursed under his breath as he went to take a sip of beer and realized he'd forgotten to remove the cap. As he got to his feet to fetch a bottle opener from the kitchen, a knock came at the front door, immediately followed by Rick's voice, slightly muffled, "Coop, it's me."

"Come in," Chet called back, continuing into the adjoining kitchen on his quest to liberate the bottle cap from his beer. The sound of the front door opening and closing barely reached his ears as he yanked open his silverware drawer and started pawing through the utensils.

He located the bottle opener and turned around to face his deputy who had just entered the closet-like space that was supposed to be a kitchen.

"Morning, boss," Rick said, leaning a shoulder against the wall, his eyes dropping to the brown bottle in Chet's hand.

He ignored the trace of disapproval in the man's eyes and pried the top off the bottle, allowing the bent cap to fall plinking onto the cracked, yellow linoleum floor.

"Beer for breakfast?" Rick asked.

Chet tipped the bottle to his lips and took a swallow without breaking eye contact. "Yep, liquid breakfast. No hassle, easy cleanup." He took another swallow, secretly wishing he had something a bit stronger than beer around.

Rick held out a hand. "Horse pucky, that ain't no breakfast and you know it. Now give it here."

"Get your own, there's more in the fridge."

The older man fixed him with the well-practiced, stern gaze of a seasoned father. "You hand me that beer, or I call for reinforcements."

"What reinforcements? You mean Porter?" Chet laughed. "All I have to do is toss him a beer too, and he'll be about as useful as a screen door on a submarine." He tipped the bottle back again and wiped his mouth with the back of his hand.

"No, I didn't mean Porter, I was talking about getting Kate over here."

Chet felt the wind spill out of his sails, and the aftertaste of the beer was suddenly even more bitter than usual.

Rick grinned, exposing his big teeth. "Yeah, I thought that might get your attention. You know, I bet I could have her over here in ten minutes or less, don't you? Heck, maybe five minutes when she hears that her big hero is drinking beer now for his breakfast." He thrust his hand out again for the bottle, his eyes twinkling with victory.

Chet shook his head. "You're a dirty fighter, you know that, deputy?" He handed Rick the bottle and walked past him, back into the living room. He lowered himself down onto his knees and then leaned forward and placed his palms on the floor. "I'm guessing you didn't come by here to tell me that you caught our killer while I was asleep."

"Wish I could tell ya that, Coop. I was just in the neighborhood, thought I'd stop by is all."

Chet raised his knees off the floor, tightened his abdominal muscles, and made his whole body a perfectly rigid plank. "Why don't you give me the rundown of the day so far," he said, as he began a series of methodical pushups, executing the movements with perfect form and fluidity—not too fast, not too slow. His muscles began to engorge with blood and burn as they stretched and contracted.

Rick plopped onto the couch nearby. "As far as police stuff goes, it's been quiet. The festivities started up not too long ago, down at the park. Looks like just about the whole town is down there right now."

Chet was slowing now, the muscles in his arms and chest starting to fatigue. Was it Saturday already? Dang, he had let the big fall social totally slip his mind! "So you've been down there then?" The words escaped in labored grunts as he strove for just a few more pushups. "Everyone's behaving themselves so far?"

"So far, yeah. But just in case, I gave Porter one of my deputy shirts to wear. He's at the park now, showing a presence and keeping an eye on things."

"Good," Chet said standing up and letting the blood pump through his arms and chest while he caught his breath.

Rick came to his feet as well. "You planning on taking Kate to the big dance later?"

"She really wanted to go, so I kind of had to compromise with her. I told her that I would take her, but that technically, I was on duty—we're always on duty—so I'd be in uniform and everything, gun and all."

"She knows you can't dance right?"

"I can dance just fine."

"I can't wait to see you jitterbug with that big old sidearm flopping around on your hip."

Chet smiled and held up a finger. "That big old sidearm will be a perfect excuse for me *not* to Jitterbug."

"You know, you're pretty smart for guy who drinks beer for breakfast."

"And you've got a pretty smart mouth for a guy who happens to be talking to his boss."

Rick let out one of his big guffaws, his face split wide by a huge grin, and then clapped Chet on the shoulder. He pulled his hand back feigning pain. "Ouch! Careful, man of steel here!"

"That's enough," Chet said, heading for the narrow hallway that led back to his bathroom and bedroom, "I'm going to finish getting ready."

As he rifled through the clothes in his bedroom closet, he could hear Rick making some sort of ruckus in the kitchen, probably pouring all his beer down the sink. He smiled. Good old Rick Shelton. What would he ever do without the man? Loyal to a fault, dependable, and always positive, almost to the point of being annoying.

He found a clean shirt and pulled it off the hanger. The budget was tight. Very tight. Small counties like his didn't have money to throw around, but he would have to figure out a way to give the man a pay raise. Somehow.

He finished getting ready, taking a little more time than usual to comb through his wavy hair and even splash a little cologne on his neck. As he was buckling on his duty belt, he detected a faint, yet delicious aroma drifting its way into his room. Pancakes?

"For crying out loud Rick, you didn't have to go and do this," he said, taking in the scene before him as he entered the kitchen.

Rick was standing over the little gas stove that took up nearly half the space in the kitchen, pouring white, lumpy batter from a glass mixing bowl into a frying pan. The thick mixture sizzled as it made contact with the hot surface of the pan and oozed outward into a circular shape, little bubbles appearing on its surface.

The deputy set the mixing bowl to the side and picked up a spatula. "Let me introduce you to a little something called, breakfast," he said, gesturing with the spatula at the kitchen table, that amounted to little more than a plank of wood just big enough to push two chairs under.

A plate of golden, brown pancakes, fluffy and steaming, had been set in front of one of the chairs, a fork lying to the side. Chet shook his head in disbelief at not only the speed in which the man had been able to pull it all off, but that he had actually been able to locate any ingredients for such good looking pancakes; the grocery shopping had gone a bit neglected lately.

"Sit down and eat, Sheriff," Rick said. "You'll need your energy tonight. Something tells me that Kate isn't gonna take your flimsy excuse to get out of dancing."

Chet sat down in front of the plate. "You don't have to ask me twice," he said, using the fork to tear a bite-sized chunk off of the top pancake. He paused before taking the bite. "Answer me one thing though, Rick. Where'd you get the milk? I know for a fact I don't have any milk in my fridge."

Rick used the spatula to flip the cake in the pan over and cleared his throat. "Well, I guess you could say I improvised and referred myself to my grandpa's old recipe. Now come on, time's a wasting, eat up!"

It was delicious, but not your typical pancake like he was used to eating over at Fatty's Diner out on the highway north of town. There was a familiar bitterness to it, followed by a slightly sweet and pungent aftertaste. As he swallowed the bite down, he looked at Rick, who was staring back at him, an expectant look of mischievousness playing across his face.

"Good?" the deputy-turned-cook asked.

"Beer?" Chet said in disbelief. "You used *beer* to make pancakes?"

Rick's horse-faced grin was answer enough.

"After all the crap you just dished out to me about having beer for breakfast, you don't find it just a little hypocritical that you then, immediately proceeded to make me beer pancakes?"

Rick's shoulders heaved up and down as he laughed at the irony. "It's fine Coop, they're harmless now. Most of the alcohol burns off when you cook 'em." He reached into the pan, pulled out the last pancake, and tossed it back and forth in his hands a few times before taking an enormous bite out of it. "Delicious, if I do say so myself," he somehow managed to say. "Now eat up!"

Eat up he did, thoroughly enjoying the moist, fluffy goodness while Rick cleaned up. With decent food in his belly his mood lightened considerably, and he grew increasingly excited about the idea of spending the evening at the social with Kate. It would be a great chance for her to meet the townsfolk in a lighthearted and friendly atmosphere, and perhaps make some friends. Hopefully after tonight, she would feel a stronger sense of community and belonging. Hopefully.

As they made their way through the living room to leave, Rick paused in front of the giant pad of paper hanging on the wall and studied it for a moment.

"Just looking for some kind of connection," Chet explained, feeling somewhat foolish because the paper was totally void of any ideas. "So far I've drawn a blank."

Rick scratched the side of his face for a long moment, then drew a pencil from his shirt pocket. He traced a line from Scotty's name to Levi's name, then turned to face Chet, his face serious. "Levi goes missing, and not long after, Scotty claims to see him in the woods—dead, but walking around. Levi informs Scotty that he is going to die, and he does."

Chet rolled his eyes.

Rick didn't seem to notice as he drew another line between Reverend Gannon's name and Levi's. "Reverend Gannon is attacked and killed. Before he dies, he claims it was a little boy who killed him. Another connection to Levi?"

"Are you saying our killer is a dead Levi Henderson? Do you know how ridiculous that sounds?"

"I'm not saying anything, I'm just making connections based on the very little information that we have. If you got something better, I'm all ears."

"Okay, deputy, I'll give you that." Chet said, and then stabbed at Robbie Pritchard's name with his finger. "But what about Robbie? He didn't see any dead little boy, how can he be connected to all this?"

Rick didn't hesitate and drew a line from Robbie's name over to Scotty's. "Well, Robbie and Scotty were both found together, and we can assume left there by the same killer." He placed a hand on Chet's shoulder. "I know it sounds a bit far-fetched, but one thing I've learned over the years in this job: where there's smoke, there's usually fire. Never be too quick to discount something, even if, at the time, it seems ridiculous."

Chet followed the sage deputy outside, into the embrace of a beautiful afternoon. The sun was a shimmering, golden ball, drifting in a cloudless azure sea. It was unseasonably warm, almost like a summer day, except for the slight hint of autumn's crisp chill conveyed by a gentle breeze; a reminder that the grip of winter was not far off.

As he put his car in gear and drove away, he pushed the image of the four names on his wall from his mind. For just this one night, maybe it would be okay to let go a little, enjoy himself, have some fun with Kate. Live for a night.

The entire proposition sounded good to him. He just needed to take care of a few things at the office—one, maybe two hours tops—then pick up Kate, and off to the fall social. He smiled. Maybe he *would* jitterbug after all. He pressed down a tad on the gas and his cares and worries seemed to evaporate behind him as the car accelerated down the road.

CHAPTER 29

Kate stood in front of the full-length mirror that hung on her bedroom wall, her feet together, hands clasped in front, appraising her appearance with a critical eye. With a twisting motion of her hips, the dark-gray, wool skirt swished back and forth around her calves, the pleats mimicking an accordion as they opened and closed with her movements. It was stylish enough, yet would be warm as well.

Satisfied with the skirt, she selected a light-yellow blouse with long sleeves from her limited wardrobe and slipped it on. As she did up the buttons, she couldn't help but to stare at the stupid journal lying open on her desk, that accursed riddle sneering up at her, taunting and teasing.

Her attention for most of the afternoon had been divided between getting ready for the social and pondering over the journal, trying to unlock whatever clues or secrets it was concealing.

As she tucked the blouse into the skirt, she thought about her visit with Nate at the library, and the bizarre history lesson he had given her: a goddess cult, strange disappearances, a mysterious fire…. Vigilantes!

The image of Albert in her window, half of his head blown away, forced its way into her brain, the memory still all too fresh. She had been shown that page and the riddle that was on it. Somewhere in that journal, hiding between the lines of that strange poem, lay a clue or information that, in some way, connected the past with the present. She just needed to figure out what the heck it was. So far, staring at it and repeating the verse over and over to herself had failed to yield any results.

There was a supernatural element to what was going on. She knew it, but was still struggling to get herself to truly accept it. She wanted to talk to Chet about it, somehow make him see it too, but he was probably already on the verge of having her committed to an asylum as it was.

She sighed in a bout of frustration as she bent over and scooped up the shoes she'd decided on for the night: a pair of sturdy, brown, leather oxfords with a slightly raised heel—perfect for a cool night of walking on grass and possible dancing. She pulled a pair of yellow ankle socks from one of the drawers in her wardrobe and sat down at her writing desk to put them on.

It could have been the way she was leaning forward as she glanced at the journal, or the angle at which the afternoon light beaming through the window struck the surface of the page. Perhaps it was a combination of the two, but she noticed something that made her pause midway between slipping on her shoes.

She pressed two fingers and ran them along the open spine of the book, feeling an uneven, slightly jagged resistance against her skin; the tell tale sign of torn out pages. Missing pages! She clapped a hand over her mouth certain she had stumbled across a major development.

Old Able Gannon had torn pages out of his journal and then left behind the cryptic poem:

Nothing is as it seems
for reality has become the dream
Seek the truth and it shall be found
where the sins of the righteous man are bound

It was a message! It had to be! He must have written something in those pages, tore them out, and hid them somewhere. The poem was a riddle that told where to find the missing pages. She leaned forward, resting her elbows on her knees and tapping a finger against her pursed lips; lips that still needed an application of lipstick. As a matter of fact she hadn't done anything with her hair or makeup yet, and Chet was going to be here soon to pick her up.

She finished putting on her socks and tying her shoes. She stood again in front of the mirror, smoothing her skirt with her hands while passing judgment on her chosen outfit. It was cute. Cute enough, anyway.

The riddle was just going to have to wait. She closed the journal and scooted it off to the side, simultaneously attempting to shelve it away in her mind, for the time being. Tonight would be a night to leave her cares behind her. A night for laughing, dancing and good food…maybe even meeting some new friends. But mostly, spending time with Chet.

She smiled, feeling suddenly enthused about the prospect that the evening promised. She grabbed her makeup bag and headed for the bathroom across the hall. The downstairs radio was pumping out that new song, "Love Somebody" by Doris Day. Kate hummed along to the tune while applying a coat of dark-red lipstick.

She puckered her lips in the mirror and made a big smooching sound, followed by a girlish giggle. At the moment, Chet was standing a good chance of finally getting that kiss…if he played his cards right.

Chet brought his patrol rig to a slow stop beneath the sweeping branches of an ancient oak. Considered to be the oldest tree in the city park, it was affectionately known by the townsfolk as Old Abe. He set the brake and stole a quick glance at Kate sitting in the passenger seat. She beamed at him, her eyes glittering in the golden light of the waning sun.

His heart stuttered and his gut did a quick flip flop as he got out of the car. He was that awkward, pimple-faced kid again on his first nerve-racking date! He marveled at how this woman could have that effect on him. In some ways, maybe this *was* kind of a first date; a new beginning for the couple, after having gotten a few things out of the way. He opened her door and offered his hand.

"Why thank you, kind sir," she said, slightly exaggerating that drawl of hers and taking his hand for support.

He secretly admired the beauty of her form and the grace of her movements as she exited the car, one leg at a time, to stand beside him, holding onto his arm with both hands.

He guided her down the footpath that meandered past shrubs, wooden benches, and through small copses of trees, toward the big clearing in the center of the park with the pavilion. As they drew closer, the sounds of people laughing and mingling grew increasingly louder.

"So, how's everything going?" Kate asked, still clinging to his arm as she looked up into his eyes.

"Well, you know," he said, not exactly sure how to honestly answer without destroying the mood of the entire evening.

"Actually, don't answer that," she said. "What I meant to ask was, when does the dancing start? I don't hear any music."

He chuckled to himself. She was quick on her feet, that was for sure. "Usually, once it starts to get dark, they turn on the lights and start the music."

"I can't wait! I used to love dancing, but I haven't been to a dance in a long time. Not since…" She bit her lower lip and stared straight ahead.

He looked down at her. It was as if he could see right through those dark, curled locks and straight into her head. He could see that her demons were currently gnawing and clawing at her, dragging her down with them into an abyss of horrific memories. Time to throw a lifeline.

"Well, I hope you know how to jitterbug then," he said, almost having to grit his teeth just to get the words out.

She seemed to immediately perk right back up, gripping his arm tighter while flashing a pretty smile. "Well, you're in luck tonight, Sheriff Cooper!"

He tried to picture what he might look like doing the jitterbug and immediately concluded that *ridiculous* would be the right word for it. Of course there would be Rick, probably watching with that big idiot grin plastered across his face.

Kate started pulling him down the path, walking faster. "Come on, get moving you lollygagger!"

He laughed and picked up the pace. So what if he looked ridiculous trying to dance the jitterbug, didn't everybody?

A moment later, she was tugging him into the big clearing, a wide smile spreading over her face as she took in the sights of the festivities.

From what he could tell, half of the town was mingling around the dozens of tables lining the edge of the clearing, all laden with everything from food to arts and crafts, most on display for one kind of contest or another. The other half of the town was mobbing a group of concession booths, clamoring to satisfy their cravings for whatever greasy, fat-fried treats tickled their fancy.

Men in dress hats and jackets smoked and talked in small groups, while women stood in their own clicks nearby, laughing and gossiping. A pack of kids chased each other in a game of tag, darting in and out and between the tables and clusters of adults; the little girls splitting the air with squeals of utter abandonment.

On the stage, a group of men in matching white jackets positioned folding chairs and music stands into ranks. Black cases, some oddly shaped, lay about the stage floor.

Kate pointed. "That must be the band getting ready!" Her eyes darted back and forth over the scene. "Oh, a dance floor even?" she exclaimed, pointing to the raised, wooden platform just below the stage. "Y'all know how to throw a party, I'll give you that."

The intoxicating aroma of hot scones mixed with fries, hamburgers, and who knew what else, reached him from those food stands, making his stomach growl. "You want a hamburger or something?" he asked.

"Sounds great, I could use a bite to eat."

He was relieved to see that they were met and acknowledged by mostly friendly and approving faces as they made their way through the throngs of people to the food area. After Conrad's latest newspaper article, he'd half-expected to be dragged up onto that stage to be tarred and feathered. He took new hope that the citizens of Clear Creek had seen the article for the hack job it really was.

Locating the hamburger stand, they took their place at the back of the line. Chet grew envious watching recently served customers walk past them, holding thin cardboard containers stuffed with cheeseburgers and handfuls of sizzling fries. Luckily, the line moved quickly. Before long he had their food and was leading Kate to a group of tables and chairs where they could sit and eat.

"It's good," Kate said after swallowing her first bite and wiping her fingers on a paper napkin. "A little on the greasy side, but pretty dang good."

"The greasier, the better," Chet said around a mouth full of fries.

She smiled. "Well, I was about due for an oil change anyway."

"Hey, at least it's real beef," he said. "There's a lot worse out there, trust me."

She raised an inquisitive eyebrow. "Like what?"

He started to laugh as a forgotten memory pushed its way into his brain.

"What's so funny?" she asked, leaning in closer.

"Oh, I was just remembering this guy in my platoon...Rumsey. We came out together all the way from basic. He was this crazy cowboy from Nebraska, I think. He grew up on a cattle ranch. Funny guy.

"Anyway, we were stationed on some little no name island for a while, in the middle of nowhere, going crazy with boredom, waiting for orders. Well one day, Rumsey starts craving steak. I mean he had it bad! Going on and on about how he could grill the best steak and burgers you ever had. Meat that would melt in your mouth upon contact, that kind of stuff."

Kate laughed. "I'm guessing steak was in short supply on this island?"

"Not a cow in a thousand miles I'd say, but the island was full of these big, enormous rats."

She crinkled her nose. "You didn't! Tell me you didn't eat rats, Chet Cooper!"

He broke down laughing. "Are you kidding? No way!"

"Well, that's a relief! So, what happened?"

Chet popped a fry into his mouth before continuing. "Some of the guys built this little miniature corral and filled it with about a dozen rats. They even *branded* them believe it or not!" He could barely keep his laughter under control to finish the story.

"That's awful," Kate said, fixing him with a stern look.

"They told Rumsey they had a surprise for him and led him to these rats they'd caught. The look on his face was priceless! Just imagine these big rats with USMC branded on their butts running around in a stupid little corral!" He

311

picked up his burger, waiting for his own laughter to die long enough to take a bite.

Kate shook her head with a smile on her lips. "Okay, that is pretty funny, but I still feel sorry for those rats." She put her elbows on the table and cradled her chin in her hands. "So, whatever became of Rumsey?"

"I'm not sure," Chet said. "As far as I know, he's back in Nebraska eating a big, old, juicy T-bone right now. At least I hope he is."

"I'm sure he is." She reached across the table and slipped her fingers into his hand and squeezed.

He looked into her eyes, they still glimmered somehow even with the sun now below the horizon. "I've never told that story to anyone before."

"Why not? It's a funny story."

"I don't know," he said, rubbing the back of her hand with his thumb. "I had almost completely forgotten about it. It's a good memory too."

She furrowed her brow and pursed her lips together for a moment. "I think you've tried so hard to put that part of your past behind you, that you've failed to realize there are good memories mixed with the bad, so you just buried everything…even the good stuff."

He nodded in silent agreement. She was right.

She continued to expound. "It's okay to remember, Chet, and it's okay to talk about it. Those experiences are a part of what makes you who you are. If you completely bury your past, then really, you are burying a part of yourself."

She reached with her other hand and placed it on his cheek. "I'm not interested in just getting to know a piece of Chet Cooper, I want to know the whole man. I want everything that's in there."

For just a moment, as he met her gaze, something seemed to form between them. An emotional gap had just been bridged, forming a stronger bond, drawing them closer together. Somehow, she understood him. Somehow, she got it and could put it into words in such a way.

Suddenly, there was a glow over their heads and the gathered crowd cheered and clapped as the strung lights slowly increased in brilliance, casting the entire area in a soft, white radiance. The band launched into their first song of the night: "In The Mood" by Glenn Miller.

Kate's eyes lit up like a little girl on Christmas morning. She nearly yanked his arm out of the socket as she jumped up from the table. "I love this song, Come on!"

A wave of self-conscious heat radiated up from his collar as he watched other men being dragged by their women up onto the dance floor. "Right now? The very first song?"

"Oh, come on, you big baby! You know how to dance, don't ya?" She pulled him to his feet. "This one's easy, you just bounce around to the beat. It's fun!"

With some reluctance, he allowed himself to be pulled closer to the dance floor. "It's not that I don't know how to dance, it's just been a while. I'm probably a little rusty."

"Well, good thing you just pounded down that big, greasy burger and fries. You should be good and oiled up now."

Resistance was futile, and he went like a lamb to the slaughter.

He had to admit, by the time the first song was done playing he was having a good time. He didn't recognize the next song, but it was a slow waltz. He tried to picture a little square on the floor and concentrated on stepping on the corners to the beat without stepping on her toes.

She looked up at him as she moved flawlessly to the music. "See, isn't this nice?"

He smiled back. "I could get used to it."

He wasn't sure how many songs they danced to as the band made seamless transitions from number to number, perfectly balancing between slow and fast songs.

At some point, it all became an experiential blur, a mashing and blending of the senses: the lights reflecting in Kate's eyes, the heady scent of her perfume in his nostrils, the feel of her delicate hand in his, the rhythmic swaying of her hips against his other hand, the soft, almost sensual tones of her voice, and the enticing way her full lips moved as she spoke. It was like being in some kind of delirious dream, a dream he didn't care to wake from.

After a while, the music ceased and the dream came to an abrupt end as the conductor announced that the band would be taking a fifteen minute break. The dancing couples clapped their appreciation as they slowly vacated the platform.

Chet's back was starting to act up anyway, a dull throb pulsating where he had taken that piece of shrapnel. He reached back with his hand and dug his knuckles deep at the source of the pain.

Kate placed her hand there too, rubbing with her thumb as they walked off the stage and onto the grass. "How's that?" she asked.

"Perfect, as long as you never stop."

"One of these days I'll have to work you over real good."

"Yeah? I kind of like the sound of that."

"I bet you do," she said, slugging him on the shoulder. "So now what, more hamburgers?"

Chet shrugged his shoulders. "Wanna go look at all the stuff on the tables?"

"Why not?"

He offered his elbow.

Instead of taking it she grabbed him by the hand, intertwining her fingers with his. "Lead the way, Sheriff."

It all felt right as they made their way through the crowd, hand in hand, even though he could feel every eye upon them. But for the first time in a long time, he didn't care.

"Aren't you supposed to be on duty, Sheriff Cooper?" The male voice came from behind, accusatory and contentious.

Chet's ears burned with indignation. The nerve of some people! He whipped around, his face flushing with anger. He came face to face with a grinning Rick Shelton, his wife, Alice, at his side.

"Go—sh...dang it, Rick!" A dozen or so profanities of the worst kind immediately had leaped to the tip of his tongue, but as he was in public and in the presence of women, it was all that he could think to say.

Rick bellowed with laughter, even slapping his knee to add to the effect. "Gotcha!" He started laughing again.

"Boy, you sure do crack yourself up, deputy," Chet said.

"Now that you mention it, I am pretty hilarious."

"Well, you came *this* close to a knuckle sandwich. How hilarious would you be then?" Chet said, knowing it was a stupid thing to say, even as he said it. He glanced over at Kate, who was holding her hand to her mouth, unsuccessfully stifling her own giggles. He was having a hard time seeing why this was all so funny.

Alice stepped forward and extended her hand toward Kate. She was slightly on the plump side, but a woman of beauty and elegance with shimmering blonde hair that hung in layers to her shoulders, and large, angular, hazel eyes that bespoke intelligence, kindness, and a good nature. "Well, if these two buffoons aren't going to introduce us, then I guess I will. I'm Alice Shelton, and I'm guessing you must be this Kate Farnsworth that I keep hearing about."

Kate took Alice's hand. "It's nice to finally meet you, Alice."

"The pleasure is all mine, I assure you. I have been dying to meet you ever since Rick started coming home with these stories of an Elizabeth Taylor look-a-like hanging around the office."

Kate visibly blushed. "Oh, I don't know about that."

"Oh, I think so!" Alice stepped back, her eyes scanning Kate from head to toe. "Yes, most definitely. Don't you think so, Chet? Doesn't she look a lot like Elizabeth Taylor?"

Chet scratched his head. "Sorry, Alice, but I don't even know who this Elizabeth Taylor is. Some actress I guess?"

Alice placed a palm to her chest. "Are you kidding me right now, Chet?"

"I'm afraid not, Alice, but if she looks anything as pretty as Kate, then I'm a fan."

By this time Kate was almost as red as a ripe tomato. Chet decided to rescue her from what was obviously becoming a very awkward moment for her. "Where's the boys?" he asked.

Rick waved a dismissive hand. "Around somewhere. Probably back in line at the kissing booth."

"I still say they're too young for such a thing," Alice said.

"Someone's running a kissing booth?" Chet asked, looking around wondering how he had missed something like that.

Rick hooked a thumb over his shoulder back in the direction of the food booths. "The cheerleaders are doing it to raise money." He looked at Alice. "So it's for a good cause and they're only kissing on the cheek, no lips."

"Sounds harmless enough to me," Chet said.

"They could've baked pies," Alice said, folding her arms, "right, Kate? No need to degrade themselves like that."

Kate smiled for a moment as if thinking. "Well, I say if the boys are dumb enough to fork over their hard earned money for a dab of spit on the cheek, then more power to those girls. I hope they rob the boys blind." She laughed.

Alice's eyes popped wide in surprise, then she started laughing too. "I hadn't thought of it that way, but you're right. They're just playing it smart, aren't they?"

Kate wrapped her arms around Chet's neck. "You bet they're playing it smart, don't you agree, Chet?" She pulled him close and kissed him on the cheek.

"Yes," he said. "Smart."

"See?" Kate said, releasing his neck and sliding her hands down his arm to grab back a hold of his hand. "It's just a matter of time before us girls are running this world."

"Yeah, that'll be the day," Rick said, rolling his eyes.

Alice leaned in closer to Kate, a conspiratorial look in her eyes. "Dear, we already do, the men just haven't figure that out yet."

Both women giggled like school girls, leaving the men to shrug their shoulders at each other.

"Well," Alice said, "be that as it may, I don't want our boys spending all their money for dabs of spit on their faces. We better go locate them before it's too late, husband."

"Probably a good idea," Rick said.

Alice took a hold of Rick's arm and began steering him away. "It was nice to meet you, Kate. I want to get to know you better for sure. We'll have you over for dinner one of these days."

"I'll be looking forward to it," Kate said.

"See ya around, Coop," Rick said before turning his back and being lead away.

Chet and Kate resumed their path through the crowd to the tables where the arts and crafts were on display.

"Well, I think you have Alice's approval," Chet said. "Bravo and well done."

"I think we hit it off okay," Kate replied. "She seemed nice, if not a bit opinionated maybe."

"Maybe a bit," he said with a chuckle. "That bit about women running the world: pure genius on your part, right up her alley. Good one."

She stopped walking, put her hands on her hips and fixed him with a stern gaze. "What, you think I was kidding?"

"Well uh, no…not exactly…I mean…" He rubbed the back of his neck with one hand, feeling like he would soon melt under her stare.

She belted out a good laugh. "You know, for a sheriff, you are kind of gullible!"

"Ha! Good one. You know, between you and Rick, I don't even know what's going on around here anymore."

"Come on, you," she said, "I think I see a table over there with some quilts on it. I love quilts."

Quilts weren't really a particular passion of his, but it turned out that he did rather enjoy watching her admire the handiwork of each quilt: the joyous expression in her eyes, the way her lips parted slightly as she ran her hands over the fabric, and the way she would look up at him every now and then, a certain radiance in her smile.

They moved on, working their way down the line of tables, the talents of the locals on full display. Kate took her time looking at a collection of watercolor paintings, painted by members of the local art guild, while Chet found an interest in a table displaying beautifully crafted, handmade, hunting knives.

The band had resumed playing dance music by the time they made it to a table full of art projects that had been done by the local school kids. The art projects, mostly drawings, progressed by age group from the obvious increase in talent and sophistication as one moved along the table. They laughed together at some of the more imaginative scenes, like second-grader David Wimple's depiction of a giant, green dinosaur attacking a futuristic moon base, complete with men in spacesuits firing ray guns at the rampaging monster.

At last, they arrived at the very end of the table where the final art project sat, somewhat isolated from the others. A wooden, rectangular box contained what appeared to be a miniature model of some kind. There were little rises and depressions covered in tiny but very real looking trees and grass; a jungle scene by the looks of it.

"A diorama," Kate said. "It looks really good too, like what you would see in a museum."

Chet bent down to read the small note card that had been stapled to the front of the wooden frame.

The Hero, by Daniel Miller, eighth grade

"What does it say?" Kate asked leaning in close to read it for herself.

Chet straightened. "Looks like your boyfriend is a pretty decent artist." That's when he first noticed the little men scattered throughout the diorama. He looked closer. Not just miniature men, American Marines, cast in lead, weapons in hand, pitched in battle, some lying dead, their wounds painted by a skilled hand in exquisite, crimson detail. There were also Japanese soldiers, yelling, pointing, firing. The Marines were trapped in an ambush, a hopeless situation, Jap machine guns raining down a hellish barrage of flesh shredding rounds.

One by one, certain undeniable details began to jump out at him: the exactness of the terrain, the placement of the men, even the appearance of the trees. It was an exact recreation! His knees grew weak, as bile from the deepest depths rose into his throat. The little diorama seemed to shake back and forth and then grow in size, threatening to pull him right into it. His mind zeroed in on one particular figure, the sergeant in the center of the trapped platoon. It was him. And even though the figure was small, he could see the fear, confusion, and hesitation on the face; fear and hesitation that had resulted in the deaths of his men. The man was no hero as the title of the art piece suggested.

He slammed his eyes shut, but it did nothing to hold back the flood that was now engulfing him. He could hear it: the gunfire, the earth rending explosions, the cries of the terrified, the haunting moans of the dying, and his own heart surging in his ears. He was there again, at that terrible place in his past, as if he had never left.

He leaned on the table with both hands trying not to vomit. A white, stabbing pain blistered through his skull as dark, suppressed memories rushed headlong and unadulterated to wreak havoc on his psyche.

"Chet, are you okay?" Kate's voice echoed across the nightmarish turbulence like the soft, early morning song of a distant meadowlark floating over a war-torn landscape, ignorant of the irony of its own presence. The warm and tender press of her hand on his back was a reassuring connection to the reality that he knew he had momentarily slipped away from.

He broke into a cold sweat as he fought the tide and struggled to find his way back across the gulf, the bile in his throat rising, his head pounding. "I'm going to be sick," he just barely managed to murmur.

The next thing he knew, Kate was pushing him past the table and into the surrounding trees with surprising strength.

"Come on," she said, her hand on the small of his back, guiding him away from the party and deeper into a stand of pine trees.

He placed a hand on the rough bark of a spruce tree and leaned forward, taking deep breaths, pushing back the urge to throw up while the demons of his past ran rampant through his mind, each one evoking some awful memory or another.

She rubbed his back, her voice soothing and calm. "Everything's going to be fine. Just breathe, you have to breath, Chet. Nice, slow, deep breaths. That's it."

The horror began to fade with each breath as he regained control of his thoughts and emotions. Kate's voice was a beacon guiding him through the turmoil and back into the present. He straightened and dug for his handkerchief so he could mop at the droplets of sweat that had formed on his brow.

"I'm sorry you had to see that, Kate," he said, turning to face her, afraid of what he would see in her eyes. "I don't know what happened back there."

She stepped to his side and continued to rub his back with one hand. "You had a flashback or something?"

He exhaled heavily. "Yeah, but this was different. It's never just overtaken me like that before. It was so vivid and so sudden. Everything just came rushing at me all at once, I couldn't hold it back…not like I normally can."

"Do you think it was that diorama that triggered it?"

He had been so occupied dealing with his waking nightmare he had completely forgotten about the diorama that had set off the whole episode in the first place. "That diorama," he said, suddenly recalling the accurate detail of the art project. "Impossible."

"What's impossible?"

"I don't even know how to say it without sounding crazy." He spotted a nearby bench and began walking toward it.

She walked with him, matching his stride. "You won't sound crazy, trust me."

He sat down on the bench and gathered his thoughts while she sat next to him, using her fingers to lightly brush his hair. Her caress was soothing. He wanted to lay his head down in her lap and go to sleep under the protection and safety of her watch.

He leaned forward, his elbows on his knees, and looked down at the ground. "Kate, that diorama back there…it's like an exact depiction of something that happened to me overseas."

"Well, it's understandable that seeing something that looks so similar to what you went through would trigger a flashback. There's nothing crazy about that."

"That's not what I meant." He sat up and looked her in the eyes, hoping that he could get his point across without freaking her out. "It's not *similar*, it *is* an exact representation of a certain event that happened to me. From the placement of the men and the machine gun nests, to the shape of the terrain and the trees. It's like that Daniel kid was able to reach into my mind and snap a photograph, and then recreate it in a three dimensional model. Not only that, but it's not just some random event, it's the one that haunts me the most. It's the one memory I wish I could forget…but can't." He shook his head. "Impossible, I know."

Kate took his hand in both of hers. "Chet, I know you don't like people saying it, but you're like the town hero. Everyone knows what you did. I've heard the story from at least a half dozen people. It's not that inconceivable that Daniel was able to reproduce a pretty close depiction of the whole thing."

"There's one thing that nobody knows about," he said, a wave of shame and guilt flowing through him, "but somehow the Miller kid seems to know."

"What does he know?"

He hesitated. What would she think of him if she really knew the truth?

"Please, Chet, don't shut me out." Her eyes burned with intensity and compassion. "Talk to me. You can trust me with it, I promise."

He rose from the bench and took a step so that he had his back to her; he didn't want to have to look her in the eyes. "Everyone around here calls me a hero, but they couldn't be more wrong."

She came off the bench to stand at his side. "Yes, you are! I've heard the story, how you charged those machine guns with no regard for your own life and saved your entire platoon from being cut down. Pretty heroic stuff if you ask me."

He shook his head. "I'm no hero."

"Are you saying it didn't happen that way?"

He let out a heavy sigh and grabbed her by the hand. "What I'm about to tell you is something I have never talked about…with anybody."

She pulled him back down onto the bench. "Then it's high time." She fixed him in her green, fiery gaze. "Talk," she commanded.

He rubbed the palms of his hands together. "Well, the truth is, when we got ambushed in that ravine, I froze up. I froze with fear and hesitated, and it cost the lives of some of my men. Boys, Kate, just boys straight off the farm." A lump rose up in his throat. "They're dead. They're dead and I'm a hero with a medal."

She began rubbing his back again. "War is a horrible thing, Chet. I can't even pretend to sit here and act like I have a clue of what you went through, but you can't blame yourself for what happened to those boys."

"I know, but I do anyway."

"So what you did that day doesn't account for anything? The fact that you saved the entire platoon?"

He bit his lower lip for a moment, giving his mind a different pain to focus on. "My actions weren't really as brave or courageous as they might sound. After I snapped out of my frozen daze, I saw that some of my boys were dead and more were in the process of being cut to ribbons. I was immediately overwhelmed by guilt and despair at that moment." His eyes were welling up and he feared that he might actually start to cry.

He took a deep breath and exhaled. "Kate, I gave up at that moment on God, life, humanity, hope…everything. I wanted to die. I charged those gun emplacements with every expectation that I was going to be killed. I wanted death, and yet somehow I survived. Through some cruel twist of fate my suicide attempt ended up winning me a medal.

"I survived, and now I live with the guilt. Every time someone buys me a drink, or calls me a hero, it's just a reminder of the men who died under my command. Men who were killed because of choices I made. Men who might be alive today if I had just acted quicker, had listened to my instincts better, had not led them down that ravine."

He looked into her eyes. "So now you know just how messed up I really am. So much for being the big hero right?"

"I don't think you're messed up," she said. "I think what you did was extremely brave. Right now there are men out there who are with their families and loved ones, living their lives because of what you did. Even what's his name, the cowboy from Nebraska with the herd of rats."

"You don't get what I'm saying," he said. "Because of me—"

She jumped to her feet in front of him and put her hands on her hips, leaning forward so that her nose almost touched his. "Well, I guess it was my fault then I got raped?"

"No, of course not! Don't be ridiculous."

She arched her eyebrows, her eyes almost glowing in the darkness like a cat's. "Well, why not, Chet? I mean, I made some bad choices didn't I? I shouldn't have gone out riding by myself that day."

"There's no way you could've known."

"Well, then maybe I just should have been quicker getting into the saddle before he could grab me, or maybe I just didn't fight hard enough." She cocked her head to the side and folded her arms.

He looked down at the ground, breaking away from her intense gaze. "You should never blame yourself for what happened to you."

She placed her hands on the sides of his face and squatted down to his eye level. "You bet I blamed myself. For a long time I did. To tell the truth, sometimes I still do." She grabbed his hand and sat down next to him. "But since coming here, I've become a different person, and I have you to thank for that. You've done more for me than you know." Her eyes were becoming moist and she was blinking a little too much. "Awe, dang it, now my makeup's going to run. See what you've done now?" she said, standing back up as one lone tear tumbled from the corner of her eye.

He sat still, admiring the beauty of this spirited girl that had somehow come into his life, with her ebony curls and full lips the deep shade of red wine. She fanned at her eyes with her hands while that singular tear trickled down her cheek, and at that moment, he *knew* he loved her.

She said, "Anyway, all I'm trying to say is—"

"I know what you're trying to say," he said, rising to his feet and pulling her close. Using his forearms to hold her against him, her palms pressed against his chest, he cradled her head in his hands, gently caressing the rims of her ears with his thumbs.

She snaked her hands up his chest and clasped them together behind his neck. "Oh, so you're a mind reader now?" she asked, looking up at him, her eyes dancing with mischief. "What am I thinking right now then?"

"This," he said, pulling her body even tighter against him and pressing his lips against hers in a soft, lingering kiss. He felt her whole body tremble slightly. A soft moan escaped her as he pulled away.

She slowly ran her tongue over her parted lips as if savoring the kiss. "Good guess," she said, "but you were off a little bit."

"I was off?"

"let me show you what I was *really* thinking." Suddenly, she grabbed him by the face with both hands, and pulled his lips against her hot mouth, kissing him long and hard.

His blood stirred in his veins as his heart pumped double time and little electric jolts went zinging through his extremities. He became aware of all of her: the unique scent of her skin as it blended with her perfume, the warm caress of her breath on his cheek, the scrape of her fingernails across his scalp, the feminine contours of her body, and the steady, rhythmic pounding of her heart as it beat against his chest.

He wasn't exactly sure how long the kiss had lasted, but it sure didn't seem nearly long enough when she pulled away.

"Wow," she said, with a heavy breath while yanking the handkerchief from out of his shirt pocket. "We actually just did that." She started wiping his lips with it, staining the cloth with waxy, red lipstick. She stuffed the handkerchief back in its place, produced a small mirror and lipstick from her purse, and began applying a fresh coat.

"So," Chet said, "was that a kiss then?"

She responded first with a sweet smile, and then a rather hard punch to the shoulder. "You have to ask?"

"Ouch!" He rubbed his throbbing shoulder.

She tossed her lipstick and mirror back into her purse. "Holy cow, you are such a baby!" she teased. She took his hand in hers. "We should be getting back to the party before people start making the wrong assumptions."

"Yeah okay," he replied. "To be continued then?"

She started leading him by the hand, through the trees, back to the party. "We'll see." She shook her head. "I think I've created a monster."

As they walked past the table containing the art projects, Chet stopped, pulling Kate up short to stare at the strange diorama. He took a few steps toward it.

"Are you sure you want to do that?" Kate asked from behind.

"I'm okay. I just want to get a closer look." He hunched over the miniature to scrutinize it better. He felt the soft touch of Kate's hand on his back as she came to stand beside him.

He felt steady, the demons locked securely back in the vaults of the past. He shook his head. "How did Daniel come so close to duplicating it?"

Kate leaned in and pointed at an area on the diorama, her finger hovering over a Japanese machine gun nest. "Chet, doesn't that look familiar?"

Was she trying to be funny? Yeah it looked familiar to him, he was there wasn't he? Instead of answering, he just gave her a sideways look.

"Oh!" she said. "That's not what I meant. Of course it looks familiar to you. I mean, remember the machine gun nest in the woods when we were searching for Levi? You were baffled, wondering who could've built it because whoever did seemed to have some kind of special knowledge or something."

He remembered alright! That night in the woods when they had stumbled across not just the expertly made, but tactically placed machine gun nest just sitting out there.

Kate leaned in for a closer look. "I mean, look at this thing, it looks identical to the one we found. And doesn't Daniel Miller live over there by those same woods?"

The words tumbled out of his mouth slowly as the thoughts formulated in his mind. "Daniel Miller built that machine gun nest."

Kate chimed in. "Remember when little Jimmy Parson said that Levi had been playing with a new friend, an older boy?"

"Do you still have keys to get into the junior high?"

She scrunched her brow. "Yes, they're right here in my purse."

"Good, let's go," he said, heading in the direction of the car.

"What's at the junior high?" she asked, hurrying to keep up.

"I'll explain on the way over."

CHAPTER 30

Kate slid her key into the lock on the front door of the junior high and rotated it, the bolt whispering as it slid away. The heavy hinges creaked as she pulled the thick, metal door open. A draft of warm air gently issued forth, buffeting her curls as she stepped into the dark entryway.

"I'm not sure where the dang light switch is," she said, running her palm along the plaster wall.

Chet knew where it was, he had spent three years of his life in this building after all. "Here, let me get it." He stepped in front of her and flipped the switch, the lights flickering a moment before illuminating their immediate surroundings.

She turned to look at him, a bright smile on her lips. "You act like you know your way around here or something."

"I've spent a little time here."

"Yeah? I bet mostly in the principal's office."

"Hey," he said, following her down the hallway, "I was a pretty good kid, ya know."

She laughed a conspiratorial laugh. "Not according to Mrs. Rockwooooooood,"

she sang in a childish, teasing voice. She reached the office and jimmied her key into the lock. "She warned me that you were quite the troublemaker."

"Oh yeah?" He suddenly felt a sense of horror at the realization that here in his home town, Kate was in a great position to dig up all kinds of dirt about him from just about everyone she ran into.

She opened the door to the secretary's office and turned on the light. "From the sounds of it, you preferred to let your fists do the talking when you were a kid."

"Okay, but for the record, I wasn't a troublemaker," he said, following her around the desk to a set of wooden filing cabinets.

She narrowed her eyes at him as she pulled open a cabinet drawer.

"It was just a couple of bullies that needed help seeing matters in a different way is all."

She patted him on the cheek. "I guess that's one way to put it." She pulled a thick logbook from out of the cabinet drawer and carried it over to the desk. "I hate bullies anyway, so I say good for you. Hopefully, you helped them see things from a whole new perspective...like through a pair of swollen, black eyes."

She flopped the log book down onto the desktop and turned to face him, her hands on her hips. She absently rounded her lips and blew a stray lock of hair out of one eye. She was as beautiful as ever, and he suddenly regretted pulling her away from the party. A few more slow dances would have been nice.

"So, what exactly are we looking for?" she asked, growing serious.

"Levi Henderson went missing on August twenty-fourth. Let's see if Mr. Miller was at school that day."

Kate licked her thumb and started flipping through the pages of the logbook. "That shouldn't be too hard to find out." She stopped on a certain page and began sliding her finger down a list of names, mumbling to herself, "Miller... Miller, there you are!" She slid her finger across a horizontal row of check-marked boxes. She stopped on an empty, unmarked box and looked up at Chet, her eyes growing large. "Absent."

On some level, somewhere deep in his psyche, he felt a piece of the puzzle click into place. But like an incomplete jigsaw puzzle, he still couldn't see the picture and had no idea what he was looking at, only that two pieces had finally been joined. Now, it was a matter of finding the next piece and snapping it into its proper place. "I wonder what you were doing that day, Mr. Miller."

Kate's eyes were even wider. "Chet, you don't think Daniel—"

"I don't think anything right now, Katie dear, but let's pick at this thread a little more, shall we?"

She nodded. "Now what?"

"Robbie Pritchard died the night of September eleventh, when his car went into the quarry. That was a Saturday night, or early Sunday morning, but his body was stolen from the funeral home the following Monday, which would have been the thirteenth, I believe. Let's see if our friend was in school that day."

"Okay," she said, flipping to the next page and scrolling her finger down the list of student names. "By the way, did you just call me, Katie?"

"Maybe. You don't like it?"

"Besides making me sound five years old, I love it." She found the box she was looking for. "The thirteenth, right?"

"Yes." Chet leaned into her from behind, resting his chin on her shoulder so he could get a look at the book. "Was he here, that day?"

"Yes," she said.

The air went out of his sails, the two puzzle pieces suddenly torn asunder.

"Wait," Kate said.

"What?"

"See how instead of a check mark in this box, there's just a line drawn through it diagonally?"

"Yeah?"

"Well, that means he was here, but for only part of the day!"

The puzzle pieces snapped back together, plus one. "Which part of the day was he here?"

She looked up from the logbook. "There's no way to tell." Then suddenly, her mouth dropped open as she furrowed her brow. "Chet, I remember this day. It was the first time I met him. It was actually my first day training with Mrs. Rockwood, right here in this office! He came in late, sometime after lunch, with a note from his mom saying he had been ill. I remember his clothes were kind of dirty, and he just had this odd, icky feeling about him. I couldn't wait for him to leave."

Chet straightened and rubbed at the stubble beginning to sprout on his chin and jaw. "Alright. So, we know that Levi's new, so-called friend was probably Daniel Miller, which is weird in and of itself, him being so much older than Levi. Then, Daniel just so happens to be absent from school on the day Levi goes missing. He also is unaccounted for at about the time Robbie's body was stolen from the funeral home. An interesting couple of coincidences wouldn't you say?"

Kate shut the book and went to return it to the filing cabinet. "Interesting, yes. And believe me, that kid is a creep, but the last time I checked, a coincidence does not amount to proof."

"It may not amount to proof, but it does amount to a lead, and I'll take any lead I can get right now."

She put the attendance book back in the cabinet and faced him, folding her arms and blowing a puff of air again at that one unruly lock of hair. "What's the next move, Sherlock?"

"I think it's time me and Daniel had ourselves a little chat."

"Daniel and I," Kate said.

A STEADY RAPPING AT THE FRONT DOOR downstairs slowly drew him out of a deep slumber. From the angle of the sun driving its accursed light through his bedroom window, Daniel surmised it to be midmorning. Who comes knocking on peoples' doors on a Sunday morning?

He was alone in the house, his parents having gone to church without him after he feigned illness, yet again. How many more times would he be able to get away with that one? Not many more by the look in Father's eyes as he and Mother had left earlier that morning. It didn't matter, he wouldn't need lies and excuses much longer. Soon, his parents would no longer be an obstacle to him. Nobody would be.

The knocking continued. He realized whoever it was—a traveling salesman perhaps—was not going to go away, so he sat up in bed, blinking the sleep from his eyes. He actually felt fully rested, even though he had only slept for a few hours, sleep becoming more and more irrelevant as he gained in strength and power. Not just strength and power, but wisdom and cunning as well. He could feel his mind developing a keen edge right along with the hardening of his muscles and the lengthening of his stamina.

He got to his feet and walked to his bedroom door. He was about to shout to the ignorant bastard beating on the front door that he was coming and to calm down. That's when he heard *Her* in his head and he froze in his tracks. *"Don't answer the door!"*

What? Why? he mentally imparted back at her, but she had gone silent, even withdrawing slightly from him. He crept to his window as the infuriating knocking continued, even growing louder.

A man's voice called out, muffled by the walls of the house, "Hello, anybody home?"

Daniel approached his window from an angle that would give him a view of the driveway, and part of the front porch without exposing him full on. He changed his angle gradually, increasing his field of view by little incremental slices at a time, making sure to keep his head as low as possible, but still be able to see out and down.

A black Chevrolet with a big round light mounted on its roof came into view. He cursed under his breath. It was either Sheriff Cooper or his one, remaining deputy down there, pounding and shouting at the door! Instantly, his skin flushed and his heart began to beat harder and faster.

He adjusted his angle by a few more degrees until he had a view of the front porch. Because of the roof blocking his view, he could only see the cop from the waist down. Why was he here? Daniel was confident that he had left behind no clues anywhere. He tried to calm himself down; there was no way they could have anything on him. He had been too smart, too clever. Besides, if the cop was here to arrest him, he certainly wouldn't have come all alone.

Finally, the incessant hammering stopped. The man's footsteps thumped on the porch as he descended the wooden stairs, heading back to his car, apparently coming to the conclusion that nobody was home. It was about time!

Daniel watched as the lawman emerged into his field of view. He saw the thicker, wider shoulders combined with the unmistakable crop of wavy, light-brown hair that always had a tussled look to it. It was the meddlesome sheriff himself.

The sheriff reached his car, yanking his door open. Daniel exhaled a large sigh of relief and realized he had been holding his breath the whole time. He was sweating too, cold and clammy. As the cop was about to get into his car, he suddenly stopped and looked back at the house, like he was thinking about something.

Daniel froze like a stone. The slightest movement could give him away. He hoped that the sun glaring off the window was enough to keep him concealed. His heart sank as Sheriff Cooper slammed the car door shut and strode with hurried purpose back up to the porch. He had been seen!

He quashed his fear. So what if he had been seen? The stupid cop could knock until his knuckles bled for all he cared. He just wouldn't answer the door is all. He'd figure out some excuse later: he was asleep and didn't hear the knocking, he was scared because he didn't know who it was…something.

He concentrated on slowing his breathing as he waited for the pounding on the door to start up again. But it wasn't the racket of impatient knocking that followed, rather the sound of the doorknob being turned instead, the front door creaking as it was slowly pushed open. His moronic, trusting parents hadn't locked the door!

With the stealth of a cat he glided in his socks over to his nightstand, retrieving the hunting knife from the drawer. He then silently made his way into the hall. Edging along the wall, he came to the top of the stairs and risked a peek around the corner just in time to see the sheriff's back vanish behind the wall that separated the front room from the downstairs hallway.

His heart was hammering a hundred miles and hour as he tried to calculate the sheriff's position in the house by listening to the creak of the floorboards and the dull thud of the man's footsteps. He scraped the blade of his knife across his thumb, testing the edge; it was sharp. He had come too far, was too close now to let anything get in his way. If the imbecile came up the stairs he was a dead man. One lightening quick slash across the throat. It would come out of nowhere, too fast, too brutal. He would be dead before he even realized it.

Daniel tried to calm his breathing and heart rate by reminding himself who he was. He had been chosen, he was special. Some country bumpkin, small-town sheriff was no match for his prowess. He was a hunter, an apex predator in a world of bawling sheep. He was a being of power now, a dealer of death, one who watched from dark places and walked unseen in shadows.

He smiled as his courage began to return. He flexed the muscles in his chest and arms, the blood rushing to fill the taut fibers. He focused his attention on the blade in his solid grip and visualized, step by step, how and where to make the slashing attack that would end Sheriff Cooper's life. He was ready and found himself actually hoping the big hero would choose to come up the stairs. *Come on. Come on up and meet your fate, Sheriff!*

IT WAS JUST TOO QUIET, even for a supposedly empty house, and Chet couldn't shake the feeling he was being watched. As he moved from the dining room and into the kitchen, he slid his right hand to the Colt on his hip, debating with himself on whether or not to draw it. Logic told him that drawing his pistol would be premature, but the hair standing on the back of his neck was in strong disagreement. He compromised by undoing the holster's retaining strap, leaving his hand on the grip.

He had to ask himself what he was even doing here. For starters, he was entering a private residence without a warrant, so there was that. The door *was* unlocked—a convenient little loophole—but still, what had he hoped to accomplish by coming inside? Walking around in a family's empty home was a bit off the original plan of just driving out and having a talk with Daniel Miller. It didn't matter now. He was in, and might as well have a look around. Maybe he would find something after all.

The kitchen was clean and tidy, a dishrag hanging over the sink faucet the only sign anyone had ever even been there or used it. He moved through the kitchen, into a narrow hallway that ran underneath the stairs and reconnected back to the front entryway.

A door on his right turned out to be a closet full of coats hanging on hangers, and dusty work boots lining the floor. A door on his left led down a rickety set of stairs into a darkened basement. Based on the accumulation of cobwebs lining the doorway, the basement had not been visited in some time. That brought him to the stairs that led up to the bedrooms.

The stairway had an open banister on the left that curved around, leaving the hallway to the left exposed to the entryway, like a balcony. The exposed hall to the left was empty, but he would have to go all the way up the stairs to clear the hallway leading to the right.

The first stair creaked like he had stepped on a bullfrog. He froze, sucking in air through his teeth. The second stair was much better, as well as the third, but as he took the fourth stair, a very familiar feeling suddenly oozed its way into his chest. That same feeling had made him pause once in the mouth of a jungle ravine, a platoon of Marines at his back, waiting for his decision of whether to go through the ravine or around. At the time, he had chosen to ignore that urgent feeling, that inner voice of warning…and men had died.

The Colt 1911 made a quiet, scraping sound as he slid it from its leather holster and brought it in front of himself with both hands, into the low ready position. The fact this was the first time he had drawn his weapon as sheriff was not entirely lost on him. He held his breath and tried to access all of his senses for even the slightest hint of something awry.

He sensed something alright, but not anything that could be confirmed by sight, touch, smell, or sound. It was just that innate, inexplicable way a human being can sometimes just sense that they are sharing their space with another person. Maybe on some subconscious level, his brain could tell that the shadows on the walls upstairs weren't exactly right, or maybe he could feel the slight changes in the surrounding air pressure and currents created by the other person's breathing.

The explanation didn't matter much to him at the moment. Someone was up there, and he knew it. "Alright, who's up there?" he called out, his voice loud in his own ears.

He was met with only an eerie silence. Beads of sweat broke out on his forehead as he took another stair, trying as hard as he could to see beyond that hidden corner to the right. He sensed a threat was there, somehow lying in wait for him. He placed a foot on the next stair, but hesitated taking another step. That would place him within range of an attack, if indeed someone with bad intentions was there waiting for him.

The same fear and subsequent hesitation that had caused him to freeze up when his platoon had been ambushed in that ravine, were now creeping through him like little icy tendrils, clawing and intertwining along his extremities, twisting and flowing for his heart. And then, an oppressive darkness assailed him, filling him with self-loathing and doubt. A voice in his head was calling him a coward, a fraud, a hypocrite.

Kate doesn't love you. Kate could never love a broken, cowardly fraud who practically killed his own men with his own hands! It would be better for everyone, especially Kate, if you just ended your own life right here, right now!

The onslaught was crippling. His knees suddenly buckled and he fell into the wall, nearly losing his balance. It was all he could do to train his pistol sights on the space in front of him. What was this, some kind of flashback? No, these weren't vivid memories, this was some kind of outside attack against his mind and soul! He thought of Scotty Forks, how he had described going through something similar in the woods, not far from this place. A voice in his head, convincing him to commit suicide.

At the thought of Scotty, a surge of anger kindled somewhere inside of him, and he was able to use it to push back the darkness to a degree, and regain his balance and composure. Gripping his Colt in both hands, he aimed it at the corner of the wall.

"This is Sheriff Cooper, Clear Creek County. I know there's somebody up there. Now why don't you come on out before someone gets hurt?"

Silence.

"I just want to talk is all. Nobody's in trouble."

"Sheriff? Sheriff Cooper, is that you?" The voice of a teenage boy, fearful and uncertain, echoed from around the blind corner.

Chet took a step backwards to make space. "Yes, it's Sheriff Cooper. Come on out now. Nice and slow."

Young Daniel Miller stepped out from behind the wall to stand at the top of the stairs, his hands held out in front of him, a good-sized knife clutched in his right hand. He was shirtless and wearing an old, faded pair of blue jeans.

Chet was impressed, and somewhat caught off guard, by the boy's lean, muscular physique. Hardened, bunched up muscles flowed and tied into one another across his torso and arms while large, vascular veins writhed just below the surface of his tight skin. How was it that this kid was a picked on outcast? He looked like he could handle any bully that came his way. For that matter, with a build like that, why wasn't he the captain of the football team with the head cheerleader hanging all over him? Robbie Pritchard had nothing on this kid!

Chet kept the Colt's sights aligned at the base of the kid's sternum: center mass. "Put down the knife," he ordered.

Daniel looked at the knife, and seemed almost startled by its presence in his hand. "I'm sorry, Sheriff Cooper," he said, squatting and placing the blade on the floor. "I heard someone in the house. I got scared and grabbed my hunting knife, praying whoever it was wouldn't come up here." He rose back to his full height. "Boy, was I relieved to find out it was you and not some robber, or worse."

He was being polite, cooperative, even submissive—the perfect teenage kid. Maybe too perfect. It was the kid's eyes that gave him away. He could plaster whatever facial expression he wanted on his face, except for the eyes, which remained black, passionless, pits. Kate had been right: there was something off about the boy.

"You wanted to talk or something, Sheriff Cooper?"

The kid made for an imposing specimen. Chet hated to holster his weapon, but did so. "Yes, Daniel, I just wanted to ask you a few questions. It'll just take a few minutes."

"Sure," the boy said, gesturing with his hand for Chet to lead the way downstairs. "We can talk in the front room."

"Where's your folks?" Chet asked, allowing Daniel to pass by him and lead the way into the front parlor.

"They went to church," Daniel answered, leaning a shoulder against the wall. "They'll head out to Fatty's for lunch after."

"Why aren't you with them?"

Daniel shrugged his rounded shoulders and actually seemed to be admiring his reflection in the glass of a painting hanging on the opposite wall. "I wasn't feeling too good this morning."

"Sorry to hear that," Chet said, doing his best to get a read on the kid's demeanor. There was no sense in small talk and he wasn't feeling all too patient at the moment anyway, so he decided to dive right in. "Daniel, how well do you know Levi Henderson?"

"I can't really say all that well. He was a few years younger than me."

Was? Daniel had just referred to Levi in the past tense. "You were neighbors," Chet countered. "Surely you can tell me something about him."

"Sorry, Sheriff, what can I say? It's not like we were friends."

"That's interesting, because one of Levi's friends told us that, just before he disappeared, he had talked about playing with an older boy after school and even building a secret army fort with him."

Daniel's flinty eyes darted back and forth just for an instant. He was not enjoying this conversation and where it seemed to be heading.

"I got to thinking," Chet continued, "who's this older boy that Levi could possibly be playing with and building forts with after school? I mean, it's not like he has a whole lot of options out here, does he?"

Daniel shrugged while pretending to stifle a yawn. This kid was playing it way too cool. "Well, there's the Baxters, maybe you should go talk to them."

"I already did. They don't seem to know who this older boy is either."

"Could've been some kind of imaginary friend. Wouldn't be the first time a lonely kid made one up?"

"So now you're telling me he was lonely?"

Daniel flashed a brief smile, like the acknowledgement a chess player might offer after losing one of his pieces to his opponent. "I only assumed he was lonely, being raised alone by his grandparents over there."

"Lonely…like you?"

"Yeah sure, why not? Like me. I guess I would understand as well as anyone. Being an only child out here in the middle of nowhere can get a little lonely sometimes."

"Would you say lonely enough for two boys to form a friendship, despite an age difference?"

Daniel narrowed his eyes into angry slits. "I'm not sure I like where you are heading with this, Sheriff Cooper. I think I already told you that Levi and I were not friends. He was just a little kid that happened to live over on the next farm." He folded his arms and flexed the substantial muscles in his chest, fibrous striations popping to the surface of his skin momentarily.

"I'm just asking questions," Chet said, not feeling comfortable with the increasingly aggressive stance that the kid was taking. "How about the day Levi went missing?"

"What about it?"

"I did some checking and noticed you were absent from school that day."

"I was sick."

"It would seem, you were also sick on the day Robbie Pritchard's body was stolen from the funeral home."

"So? Is it against the law to get sick now?" The boy's eyes were flashing with intense hate, his pale cheeks beginning to flush.

So much for the cooperative, submissive teenager. He was getting awfully defensive, possibly hiding something. Chet picked at the thread some more. "Well, one thing's for sure: you seem to get sick a lot, especially for one in your kind of physical condition."

"If you don't believe me, feel free to ask my mom, she'll tell you that I haven't been well lately, as if it's anybody else's business anyway." He started walking to the front door. "I don't appreciate you breaking into my home and interrogating me as if I'm a criminal when you have no proof I did anything wrong, Sheriff. Our little discussion is at an end."

He opened the door wide. "Look, I'm sorry about Levi. I know it's a major blow to you personally that he can't be found, so I'm going to cut you some slack. But maybe it's time you came face to face with the reality that he's gone and he's not coming back. Nobody is blaming you."

This kid was lying to high heaven! It was barely within Chet's control not to bash his teeth in with a well-placed elbow as he walked past him to stand in the doorway.

Daniel thrust his hand out to him. "I'm sorry I couldn't be more help. I hope you find Levi, I really do. He was a good kid. Now, can we just let bygones be bygones and forget about all this? Are we square, Sheriff Cooper?"

Chet looked at the offered hand. He would have rather grabbed a handful of maggots. Instead of shaking his hand, he decided to stir the pot just a little more. "Oh, before I leave, there was one more thing."

"Sure."

"Stay the hell away from Miss Farnsworth. If I so much as hear of one more incident of you harassing her, you and I are going to have a very big problem. Are we square on that?"

Daniel's body went rigid as his whole countenance darkened despite his pallid skin. His lips formed a thin, compressed line, while the muscles in his jaw stood out and pulsated. "Yes, sir," he said, the words forced and heavy with concealed rage.

"Good," Chet said. He turned and walked outside. Without looking back, he said, "I hope you get feeling better."

He could feel those dead, psycho eyes drilling into his back as he got into his car. *Those eyes!* He started the engine and put the car in gear. The last time he had been here, he thought he had recognized something familiar about the teenager's eyes, but was unable to make the connection at the time.

Now, as he drove away, it dawned on him what it was he thought he had seen reflecting back at him from the boy's eyes. He saw it every time he looked into a mirror: the haunted gaze of a man who had killed.

DANIEL WATCHED FROM THE FRONT WINDOW as the black Chevy pulled away, the rear tires spitting out plumes of dust that rose into the clear, autumn air, slowly dissipating into thin, brown clouds. Through the glass panes of the window, he listened to the chugging of the Chevy's engine, as the car turned onto Crowley Road and accelerated back toward town.

He slammed his knuckles against the window frame, causing the glass to ripple with tiny pulsations. Apparently Sheriff Cooper wasn't such a bumbling, hillbilly sheriff after all. How much did the big hero know? What other kinds of suspicions did he hold that he hadn't revealed just yet? Did he have any proof? Probably not. He was pretty sure that the sheriff would have arrested him if there was any proof linking him to Levi or Robbie and he would be riding, handcuffed, in the backseat of that car right now.

The fact that the cop was suspicious at all was problem enough. Daniel could sense the tenacity in the man, like a damn bloodhound catching a hold of a scent and refusing to break off from the chase. He had obviously caught a whiff of something and would probably pursue this line of suspicion until it was completely exhausted.

There was something else about the lawman that Daniel sensed. He was a dangerous opponent, not to be underestimated. Sheriff Cooper was in possession of some kind of survival instinct. How had he known that Daniel was laying in wait for him at the top of those stairs? He had come so close to stepping into his own death, only to see the danger at the last second. If today would have been a dual to the death, the hero sheriff would have been the victor.

He was going to have to be dealt with, but not directly. A full on confrontation with Sheriff Cooper was not in his best interest at the moment and could actually prove to be his undoing. He would have to be handled in some other way—marginalized somehow. Taken out of the picture through more subversive means.

Daniel was smart enough to figure something out. He had one thing working on his side and that was knowledge of what was really going on. The sheriff was clueless to the wasps' nest he had just kicked over and that would be Daniel's advantage. He smiled as an idea began to formulate in his head. He was smart enough not to underestimate Sheriff Cooper, but it was obvious the cop was underestimating him.

CHAPTER 31

S o, the kid actually kicked you out of his house?" Rick asked, carrying two mugs of steaming coffee, fresh from the percolator, over to Chet's desk. "Not exactly the act of an innocent man." He placed one of the mugs on the desktop and sat in an adjacent chair, taking a cautious sip from the other.

"He's far from innocent, Rick. I've got the worst kind of feeling about that Miller boy." Chet wrapped his hands around the warm mug, letting the heat seep into his fingers.

It was early yet, and Monday morning had dawned cold and blustery, a frigid wind out of the north shoving its way through town. Desiccated leaves scoured the sidewalks and streets to congregate as swirling clusters in alleyways and against shop fronts. The American flag outside the front door snapped and cracked in the stiff wind like a bull whip as the old building creaked and groaned in a dozen places.

"What do we have on this kid?" Rick asked.

"Unfortunately, not much." Chet took a sip of his coffee. "So far, just theories and circumstantial evidence that links him to Levi and Robbie."

Rick shook his head. "I find it hard to believe he could just overpower a kid like Robbie."

"Rick, you should have seen him. He's got a build like ...some kind of Greek god or something. He's got to be the strongest teenage boy I've ever seen. By a long shot."

"Eats his spinach, huh?"

"By the truckload, from the looks of him."

"So what are we gonna do with no proof, boss?"

Chet leaned back in his chair, cradling the coffee mug in his hands. "This is the only lead we've got, so we're sinking our teeth into it and not letting it go. That kid lied to me and then threw me out of his house. Maybe he isn't our murderer, but he's guilty of something and I intend to find out what.

"I say we ratchet up the pressure. We poke around some more, pay him a couple more visits, watch his every move, or make him think we are. Get him so paranoid he feels like he can't even take a crap without us knowing about it."

"You think he'll crack under the pressure?" Rick asked.

"He's pretty cocky, but has a temper too. I think we can maybe flush him out and get him to snap."

Rick started to nod his head. "Okay, I agree. Operation Thumbscrew: let's do it."

Chet stood up and grabbed his leather bomber's jacket from off the back of his chair and began shrugging into it. "I'll figure out a battle plan on exactly how we pull this off." He zipped up the front of the jacket. "We better get going, Scotty's funeral is about to start."

THROUGH TEAR-BLURRED EYES, KATE WATCHED the collage of flowers on Scotty's casket shudder and sway in the cold, shifting breeze that had assailed the ceremony from the start. Her knees and feet were starting to ache from standing too long in one spot, and she felt a little guilty at her growing impatience for the reverend—a younger man, filling in for the late Lucas Gannon—to hurry and wrap it up already.

She tore her eyes away from the dancing flowers on the casket to take a glance up at Chet, standing next to her. He had just given his remarks, and she had to admit that he had done a good job. Now he stood, his hands tucked into the front pockets of his leather jacket, straight and tall, strong. A Marine, seemingly oblivious to the wind tussling his light-brown, wavy hair.

She slipped her hand into the warmth of his pocket, entwining her fingers with his and giving a reassuring squeeze. When he looked down at her, she whispered, "You did a good job."

"Thanks," he whispered in reply.

She admired his stoicism under the current situation. In fact, it was almost annoying! She had only known Scotty for a couple of months and here she was about to come totally unglued, but Chet almost seemed unaffected by the loss. She knew better than to think that though.

As if on cue, two renegade tears escaped from her eyes to run down both her cheeks. She used her other hand to snake through the front zipper of Chet's jacket to the handkerchief she knew would be folded up in his shirt pocket.

"You came to a funeral without a handkerchief?" he breathed out of the corner of his mouth.

"Thanks to you, I'll be fine," she whispered back.

He started to say something else until she quietly shushed him by putting a finger to her lips, and then pointing to the reverend who was now reading some passage from The Bible, the wind whipping the words away from his mouth, effectively muting anything interesting he might have had to say.

She turned her head back to the young, inexperienced clergyman and made a show of paying proper attention. As she turned her head, she caught a quick glimpse of Chet rolling his eyes.

At length, the replacement reverend finished his sermon and offered up a prayer. Following the *Amen*, the gathered crowd dissipated, flowing around the neat rows of tombstones like a river of dark suits and black dresses, leaving behind a few lingering family members who couldn't bring themselves to walk away.

"New coat?" Chet asked, guiding her by the hand around a white, marble cross.

"Do you like it? I bought it down at Flossy's Drug." She ran a hand down the soft, wool fabric. "Seems like a pretty good coat. I hope it's warm enough, I hear winter can get pretty nasty over in these parts."

"Looks warm enough to me. How about a pair of boots though?"

"You think I'll need boots too?" She had already spent plenty of dough just getting the coat.

Chet grinned revealing a dimple on his cheek. "Trust me, sweetheart, when the snow flies, canvas sneakers and high heels aren't quite going to cut it."

"Great."

"Sheriff?" came the watery voice of an older woman from behind.

The couple turned together. Standing behind them, arm and arm, were Scotty's

parents. Their names were Lucy and John, if she remembered correctly.

Chet took a step toward the grieving couple, closing the distance between them and himself. Kate stayed back, trying to give proper respect and privacy. She lowered her eyes and watched the hem of Lucy's black dress flutter in the stiff breeze.

"We just..." Lucy had to swallow hard before she could continue. "We just wanted to thank you, Chet, for speaking today. It meant a lot to us and it would have meant a lot to Scotty." She choked on the last few words, and had to bring a wad of shriveled, damp tissues to her eyes.

"Scotty really looked up to you, Chet. Being your deputy made him so proud," John said. His voice was gruff, his eyes red and puffy.

Chet took one more step and placed a large hand on each of their shoulders. "I was proud to have him. I could always count on Scotty and I'm going to miss him."

"Thank you," Lucy said.

John just nodded, his mouth set in a stalwart frown.

"If there's anything I can do," Chet said. "Anything Rick and I can help with…"

Lucy looked up, and even standing back a little, Kate could see a fire smoldering in her eyes. Sure, she was a meek, somewhat elderly and devout Christian woman, but she was still a mother. A mother who had just lost her child, and as a woman, Kate could see the lioness in her eyes, the raging mother grizzly that would rip anything apart that threatened her cubs.

"Just catch the bastard who murdered my boy." She didn't yell, and her voice didn't shake or warble. She started to nod her head up and down slightly, as if to agree with herself. "Catch him, Sheriff Cooper."

"I promise," Chet said, his voice a dagger cutting through the wind. "If it's the last thing I do."

Without another word, John put his arm around his wife and steered her away. Kate moved to join Chet at his side, and together they watched the couple walk slowly back to the graveside of their son.

"How did your little chat with Daniel Miller go?" Kate asked.

Chet turned the car from the cemetery entrance onto the road that would take them back into town. "Very interesting." The muscles in his jaw were pulsating.

She reached and started playing with the heater controls on the dash panel. Her feet were freezing. "Interesting, how so?"

He looked over at her, his face becoming pensive. "First of all, I want you to avoid that kid, Kate. He's dangerous."

A ball of ice formed in the pit of her stomach. "You don't have to tell me, but what makes *you* say so?"

"Besides acting guilty as sin, lying to me, and practically throwing me out of his house, I've just got the worst feeling about him." He spared a glance at her from the corner of his eye, and licked at his lips like he wanted to say more, but wasn't sure.

"What kind of feeling is that, Chet?"

The steering wheel made a creaking sound as he tightened his grip on it. "I feel stupid saying it, but it's not that he just acts guilty and suspicious, it's almost like he's…well, like he's evil or something."

She knew feeling all too well. "Like a sad, but at the same time, angry darkness about him?"

"Yes," Chet affirmed, "exactly. A darkness, but not just about him. It's like the darkness is coming right out of him."

She wrapped her arms around herself trying to chase off the chill. "The night Scotty died, he warned me that something…evil was going on in this town. He told me I'd been touched by it and that it was focusing on me. Do you think he was talking about Daniel?"

Chet's knuckles grew white on the steering wheel and his eyes looked as if they could bore holes through the windshield. He inhaled deeply and then let the air out through rounded lips. "Scotty wasn't playing with a full deck, Kate. You know you can't place too much stock in anything he said."

"But what if he was right, Chet? What if he knew something?"

"Like what?"

"Like what if something *is* going on in this town that can't be explained, and he knew about it?"

He placed his hand on her shoulder. "Kate, Scotty claimed he saw Levi Henderson's dead body walking around in the woods, for crying out loud."

She reached up and pulled his hand off her shoulder and threw it back at him. "Yeah? And I saw my ex-boyfriend in my bedroom window with half his head blown away! Guess I ain't playing with a full deck either?"

The look of hurt in his eyes instantly made her feel guilty. He shook his head. "It was Albert in your window? You told me you just saw some man. Why didn't you tell me you saw Albert?"

"I just did, okay?" She grabbed his hand off the steering wheel and plopped it back on her shoulder, then folded her arms and sat back into the seat. From the corner of her eye, she saw him look at her a moment and then smile.

He started twirling her hair with his fingers, causing little shivers of pleasure to scatter across her shoulders and down her back. "Look," he said, "I don't know about evil forces and ghosts, or the undead and all that hocus-pocus. All I know is I have a bad feeling about that Miller boy. I believe he's dangerous, maybe some kind of psycho or something. He might even be evil, but he's still just flesh and blood. If it turns out he's responsible for what's been going on around here, then I'm taking him down."

She reached up to grip his hand in hers and brushed her lips across his knuckles. "I think you're right," she said, "he is dangerous, so please be careful."

He nodded and squeezed her hand. "I will. And don't worry about me, he *is* just a kid."

CHET PULLED HIS CAR AWAY from the curb at Lincoln Elementary after watching long enough to ensure that Kate had made it down the sidewalk and into the building safely. The wind picked up speed, buffeting the Chevy and sending brown and yellow leaves scampering across his path.

He thought about Kate and how she hadn't kissed him as he had dropped her off at the school. Had he been too forward with her the other night and now she was trying to dial things back? Given her past, he had to tread so carefully; maybe she wasn't ready for that level of intimacy yet. But, it had felt so right at the moment, and she had kissed him back—very passionately, truth be told. He was still waiting for his head to come out of the clouds and his feet to touch back down to earth.

As he neared a quiet intersection, a loud clap of thunder boomed and rumbled in the sky above. By the time he had made it through the intersection, his windshield was beginning to collect small droplets of rain.

Maybe she was leaving it up to him now to make that move. Maybe she was sitting in her office right now, wondering what was wrong with him. Why hadn't he kissed her goodbye just now?

There was a stabbing flash of lightning, followed by another clap of thunder. "Here we go," he muttered.

As if the last crack of thunder had ripped open a giant sack of water, the downpour started. Plump, icy raindrops began pummeling his hood and windshield. He flipped on the wipers and watched with a certain satisfaction as the rubber blades swept the windshield clear with each arcing pass.

If only relationships came with wipers that you could just turn on, and simply clear up misunderstandings and confusion. Good communication. That was the key, wasn't it? According to all the experts anyway. Maybe he should just ask her next time if she was comfortable with him kissing her again. He took a moment to imagine that scene in his head, and immediately smacked the steering wheel with his palm in frustration. *Yeah right!*

Really, he was probably just over thinking the whole stupid situation. It's just a kiss for crying out loud, no big deal! He kissed her the other night when the mood seemed to dictate it, and he would do it again when the moment seemed right. It was a simple enough plan, a plan he could stick by for now.

"Battle plans don't work when it comes to women and romance!" Rick almost tipped out of his chair with exaggerated laughter, his face growing red from the strain of the apparent hilarity.

Chet snatched a speeding ticket from the pile of traffic violations stacked on the corner of his desk and scrawled his signature across the bottom. "You know what, Rick, just forget I said anything."

The deputy was wiping away tears from his eyes and was in no mood to just forget anything. "I mean, you can't pin her down or outflank her, Marine. Any plan you come up with is going to go straight to pot as soon as she even starts to suspect you have one."

Chet sighed with exasperation. "That's what I'm trying to tell you, if you would clean the wax out of your ears. The *plan* is to not have a plan, just go with whatever the mood dictates."

"You know what?" Rick asked, suddenly growing serious.

"What?"

"That's a good plan, that's what." The deputy slapped his knee and broke into a fit of self congratulatory laughter.

Chet couldn't hold back a grin as he shook his head and grabbed another traffic violation from the pile. "You're a regular Bob Hope," he said, scratching his signature across the paper. He reached for another and signed it.

As he grabbed the next ticket from the pile, he sensed that he was being watched and looked back up at Rick. The older man was looking at him, sure enough: feet up on his desk, eyes narrowed slightly, the smile of a card shark about to lay down a royal flush splitting his face.

"What?" Chet asked.

"She's the one, pardner."

"What's that supposed to mean?"

"It means, exactly what it means. She's *the one*. I can see it."

"Maybe," Chet conceded, while on the inside hoping with all of his might that Rick was right. "Time will tell."

"Time won't tell shit. I'm telling you right now, that girl is the right one for you."

"Well, let's just hope she sees it that way as well," Chet offered.

"She will, if she doesn't already. As long as you don't go and do something stupid and screw it all up, you two are golden as far as I can tell."

Chet smiled and signed his name to another violation. "I appreciate your vote of confidence, deputy, and I certainly intend to make the best go at it that I can, if that helps you feel better."

"Good to hear," Rick said, putting his feet down, "cause if you do something to break that girl's heart, I'll personally tan your hide. Copy?"

"Loud and clear."

"Alright then," Rick said, getting to his feet to walk over and stand in front of Chet's desk. "Speaking of plans, have you had time to figure one out for our little psycho kid, Mr. Miller?"

Chet folded his arms and leaned back in his chair. "Actually, yeah I have."

Rick planted himself on the corner of Chet's desk. "I'm all ears."

"I drove past the Junior High on my way over and noticed that Daniel's Ford isn't there, so he must have ridden the bus to school today. When school gets out, he's going to see me parked across the street from where the buses load. I'll be sure to make good eye contact with him.

"Then, you'll be waiting out at his house. You've gotta time it just right so that he actually sees you pulling out of his driveway as he's getting off the bus. No waving or smiling, Rick. If you make eye contact with him, you're making eye contact with Adolf Hitler himself."

Rick was nodding his head vigorously. "I like it, boss. I really like it. Then what?"

"I'll wait a couple hours and then head out that way, while it's still light out, and park on the road for a bit, just across from the Miller's driveway. Maybe he'll see me, maybe he won't, but I bet he does. If he doesn't, he'll see me the next morning in the same spot when he leaves for school."

"Better yet, have it be me he sees the next morning," Rick said. "That way it will give the appearance of a bigger effort. And you can be there at the school when he gets off the bus." Rick laughed suddenly. "That kid's gonna be as nervous as a long-tailed cat in a room full of rocking chairs!"

Chet smiled. "He'll do something stupid sooner or later, and my bet's on sooner."

KATE WALKED INTO HER OFFICE, letting the armful of attendance logs avalanche onto her desk in a heap. Her heart certainly wasn't in the job today. It probably had something to do with starting it out with a funeral. That was never a good start.

The weather wasn't doing much to lift her spirits either. She breathed a heavy sigh and watched as the wind pelted her office window with fat raindrops that looked like they were trying very hard to be snowflakes. The semi-frozen spatters collided and melded with one another, to run in little forked veins down the glass.

"I hate the cold," she said and walked over to the window and snapped the blinds shut with a quick jerk on the cord. She sat down, leaned forward, and rubbed her shins briskly with her hands to generate some dang heat.

Maybe when she bought herself a pair of boots, she would get the ones she had seen Eskimos wear in pictures, the kind that went all the way up to the knee with fur poking out of the top. She couldn't help but giggle at the thought of herself tramping around town like that. Mable would practically have a seizure!

"Why that's not appropriate footwear for a young lady," her self-appointed guardian would exclaim. "My goodness, child, you look like you're on a walrus hunt!"

The ringing of her phone made her jump. Images of Eskimo boots and Mable's disapproving glares vanished from her mind as she picked up the receiver. "Lincoln Elementary, Kate Farnsworth speaking."

"What are you doing for lunch, beautiful?" a reedy, old voice asked.

It wasn't so much the voice that she recognized, but more the tone and flirtatiousness that gave the old librarian away. "Good morning, Nate," she said.

"That's not an answer to my question," came the reply. "What are you doing for lunch today?"

She thought of the tuna sandwich and apple sitting in her desk drawer. "No plans, just a quick sandwich from home and then back to work."

"Meet me in an hour at Zoli's, my treat."

Was he joking? He was old enough to be her grandfather! "Look Nate, I think you have the wrong—"

"It's Goulash Day, and don't worry, your boyfriend will never know," he said.

She could see his white teeth flashing in her mind.

"See you in an hour."

"Nate, really—"

"Oh, and bring that journal."

The line went dead, leaving her holding the receiver, her mind racing. Bring the journal?

By the time she reached Zoli's, the wind and rain had capitulated to the sun as it broke through the heavy clouds and began burning off the moisture on the streets with its warming rays. Little wisps of steam were rising and curling about her feet as she pushed her way into the deli, the heavy glass door connecting loudly with the little brass bell hanging above it.

Goulash Day was a popular day to patronize the Hungarian-owned deli by the looks of things; almost every table was occupied and almost every customer seemed to have a bowl of the thick, reddish stew in front of them. The heady aroma of garlic, and who knew what other secret spices, combined with the mouth watering fragrance of freshly baked bread, filled her nostrils, sending her appetite into overdrive.

Scanning the room, she quickly located Nate sitting at a table in the back. The old man silently beckoned her with his unnaturally bright smile and a nod of his spotty, bald head. She made her way through the small maze of tables and chairs while acknowledging a few nods and smiles from faces that she couldn't quite place with names yet.

Nate rose as she approached and offered her his chair, even pushing it in for her as she sat down. The man was smooth, no doubt about it. In his younger years, he probably had the girls lining up. She smiled to herself as Nate was settling his old carcass in the chair across from her. For all she knew, he still did have them lining up!

"I'm glad you could make it," he said.

"Hey, free lunch," she quipped, with a smile. Sure he was old, but she was no dummy. This was the kind of man that needed a constant reminder of his proper place.

"How has your day been?" he asked, his eyes blinking behind thick glasses.

"I've had better," she said, with a sigh.

"It has been a rather melancholy day, hasn't it?" He looked at something over her shoulder and his eyes brightened. "Hopefully, this will cheer you up."

Just then, Katalin Horvath appeared, carrying a metal serving tray containing two large bowls of steaming goulash and half a loaf of bread. "Here you go," she said in her thick accent while placing the tray on the table and unburdening it of its delicious cargo.

"I see you took the liberty to order for me," Kate said.

At that, Katalin laughed. "No! Today is Goulash Day!" She laughed again. "You get goulash. Only goulash." She tucked the tray under one arm and bustled away.

"I told you it was Goulash Day," Nate teased.

Kate picked up a spoon and plunged it into the hot mixture. "Yes, I remember now."

Nate chuckled and began using a knife to cut the bread into thick slices. "Zoltan takes Mondays off, so on Sunday afternoon he cooks up a big batch of this stuff in a giant pot…over an actual fire pit in his backyard." He offered Kate a slice of bread. "You're supposed to sop up the stew with the bread. Anyway, since it's his day off, goulash is all that's on the menu. But trust me, after tasting it, you won't want anything else. And Goulash Day is the only day you can get it."

She tore off a chunk of bread from the thick slice and dunked it into the bowl. "Well, from the looks of things, he has a good following," she said, trying to remain patient while wondering what she was doing here, and why he had asked her to bring the old journal along.

The older man was already chewing, a look of savoring delight twinkling in his washy, brown eyes. He gestured with a hand for her to eat. Despite her curiosity over the journal and this meeting in general, the sights and smells had gotten to her and she was rather ravenous.

She forgot about the journal momentarily, as the thick bread, infused with the spicy sweetness of paprika and the tang of garlic hit her taste buds. She actually said, "Mmm."

Nate grinned. "Didn't I tell you?"

She jammed another hunk of goulash-laden bread into her mouth. She knew it wasn't very ladylike to talk while chewing, but she wasn't too worried about impressing the old wolf sitting across from her. "I think Goulash Day is my new favorite day of the week."

She waited until their bowls were about half empty, and an appropriate amount of time had elapsed, before pulling the journal from her purse and placing it gently on the table. "You told me to bring it."

Nate wiped his hands on a napkin before picking up the weathered, old book. "May I?"

Kate nodded.

The old librarian pushed his thick glasses up onto his nose and flipped through the pages of the journal, stopping at the one containing the odd poem. "There we are."

"Did you figure out what the riddle means?" Kate pressed.

"I wouldn't go that far, but I did have a thought on it this morning. I don't want you to get your hopes up too high though."

"I'm all ears," she said.

He gazed at her over the black rims of his glasses. "And what a lovely set of ears at that, if I may be permitted to say so."

She shot him a tiresome look and folded her arms. "You may be permitted to tell me what you have figured out about that dang book."

He chuckled for a moment, placed a crooked finger on the first stanza of the poem, and read out loud, "Nothing is as it seems." He looked up from the page. "Here, he's obviously trying to tell us that we aren't seeing the truth of something for what it is. He's hiding something or we've been led to believe a lie, perhaps."

Kate recited the next line from memory. "For reality has become the dream."

He nodded. "Now he reinforces the idea, that we aren't seeing the whole picture. And actually, we aren't seeing the picture at all. What we perceive to be reality is in fact, not the whole truth. That's my interpretation of it anyway."

"Sounds good to me," she agreed, and spooned a bit of goulash into her mouth. How could she still be hungry?

He continued with the next line. "Seek the truth and it shall be found. Again, he's inferring that there's more to the story, more to the picture. There's a truth out there to be sought and to be found."

She remembered the story of the cult, and the house fire, and how some back then had believed, that the reverend had been involved in some kind of vigilante act against the cult. "So maybe he was living some kind of lie or a double life? Something he felt guilty about, a past crime perhaps?"

Nate shrugged his shoulders. "The last line is the most interesting one, and actually goes along with the previous line." He read them together as one. "Seek the truth and it shall be found, where the sins of the righteous man are bound."

"So, what do you make of that, Nate?" she asked. "I mean, I've read that stupid poem a hundred times and it just doesn't make sense to me."

"Let's break it down." He held up one bony finger. "One: he's telling us that there is a hidden truth." He held up his second finger. "Two: if we look for it, it can be found."

"Right, it can be found in the same place as the sins of the righteous man," Kate said, beginning to feel like this was all turning out to be a big waste of her time. "But if the man is *righteous*, then why does he have sins? It's a total contradiction."

The old man's face cracked into an amused smile. "But remember, we're in a world where 'all is not as it seems, and reality has become the dream.'"

He was right! She hadn't thought of it that way. "In other words, he's telling us that the righteous man is actually a man of sin, an *unrighteous* man."

347

"Excellent deduction! But, he's also saying that on the outside he still seems righteous…until we seek and find the truth."

A small jitter of excitement rippled through her body. She was finally getting somewhere! "So bottom line, we just have to figure out who the righteous man is, and where his sins are bound."

Nate nodded slowly and smiled, while smearing a big piece of bread around the inside of his soup bowl. "That's the key to the whole thing. Where would one *bind* their sins? What exactly does that mean?"

She smacked the table softly with the palm of her hand. "He speaks of hidden sins, and the truth that must be found. Aren't those the same thing? Isn't he basically saying that if we discover the truth, then we will discover the sins, because they're the same thing?"

He nodded his head in approval. "Perhaps, but we still don't know whose sins he's talking about."

"I think I have a pretty good idea."

"Oh?"

She pointed at the book. "Look at the inside of the spine there. See those ragged edges? Those are torn out pages. I think Abel Gannon wrote something down, as in the hidden truth, as in *his* secret sins. He hid the pages somewhere, and the riddle is trying to tell us where he hid them."

Nate put his elbows on the table and rested his chin on his clasped hands, while furrowing his brow and looking down into his soup bowl.

"Is something wrong?" she asked, detecting a shift in the old man's mood.

He looked up after a moment. "You're smart, as well as pretty," he said. Then he peered over the rims of his glasses at her, a frosty glint penetrating through his murky stare. "Do you realize that you're talking about searching for the hidden confession of Reverend Abel Gannon?" His voice was barely above a whisper. "I wonder if this is truly a path that would be wise to continue on, young lady."

His gaze and tone of voice made the skin on the back of her neck prickle and crawl. "Why?" she asked.

"The Gannons were some of the original founders of this town. It's an old and respected name, Abel being the most revered. Think of the repercussions if you dig up some huge scandal. Especially now, right after his son was just murdered for Heaven's sakes."

She wished she had the luxury to simply drop it and walk away from the whole mess. Who cared about what some old reverend did a hundred years ago? But she had a gut feeling that Chet was up against more than he was bargaining for. There was so much more behind these killings then just a kid gone psycho, and if she didn't get to the bottom of it…well, *those* were the repercussions she didn't want to think about.

She placed her elbows on the table and leaned in closer to Nate, so she wouldn't have to talk as loud. "Nate, one of the last acts of Scotty Forks on this earth was to try to warn me that something evil was happening in this town, and that I was directly involved somehow. Now I believe him; something is going on and Reverend Gannon's hidden sins, or truth, or whatever, is the key to figuring it all out. I can't and I won't just give up on this because it might hurt someone's feelings or sensibilities."

The old fossil took his glasses off and began cleaning them on the corner of the tablecloth. "Very well. You do as you think you must, but don't say I didn't warn you before hand." He placed his glasses back on his hawkish nose and blinked at her through the thick lenses, the previous flirtatiousness and jocular twinkle gone from his eyes.

She reached across the table and picked up the journal. "I suppose this is the part where you tell me that you can't help me anymore with this."

He began to stand up, his eyes darting about. "I wish I could be of more help to you, Miss Farnsworth, but I think I've done all that I can with this." He started to shuffle past her. "I'll pay on my way out. Have a nice day."

She was Miss Farnsworth now? She grabbed him by his bony wrist. "Hold on a second, Nate. You're afraid of something. What's got you so spooked all of a sudden?"

He sighed, glancing around for a moment. "Look, when we started on this, it was just an excuse for a lonely, old man to have a little fun. I really didn't have a clue where it was heading. Now that I see, I don't want any part of it. You are a very sweet and pretty young lady, but you are talking about digging up secrets and sins that may be best left buried."

"But Nate—"

"You're stumbling around in a minefield, Kate, blind and clueless of the possible consequences." He used a gnarled hand to peel her fingers away from his wrist and then brought her hand to his lips and gave it a gentlemanly kiss. "Be careful," he said, and then he walked away.

For a few minutes she contemplated the old man's warning, but kept coming to the same conclusion: Chet needed her on this one—even if he didn't realize it—and she intended to follow through. If only she could somehow crack that riddle!

She did her best to not let frustration creep in and cloud her thinking. Maybe it all had just been fun and games for Nate, but the man had helped her a lot, even if that hadn't been his primary intention. In fact, they had just been able to break the whole thing down into one conclusion: Abel Gannon had hidden a secret confession somewhere, and it was connected to whatever was going on in this town. She just needed to find it. But how?

CHAPTER 32

The shade of night was hungrily swallowing up the remaining light of the day and, although it had been somewhat warm earlier, a slight chill was already seeping through the window pane, caressing Daniel's face, his breath fogging the glass.

He could still make out the shape of Sheriff Cooper's police cruiser parked on the road next to the driveway. It had been there for the last three damn mornings and nights in a row. Not to mention the idiot deputy's afternoon visits and the sheriff's sudden and frequent appearances at the school!

He could feel the sheriff's eyes on him as he stood in the window frame. He hoped that in turn, the sheriff could feel him gazing right back, without fear or remorse, a supreme being filled with power and a thirst for blood and vengeance. He understood the little game that Sheriff Cooper was playing, but if the cop expected him to slip up under the harassment, then he would be sorely disappointed.

There was a problem, however. The meddling cop obviously had decided to focus all of his suspicions in Daniel's direction. It was a bit disturbing that after all his cunning and careful planning, the big hero had somehow figured out whom to suspect.

There was also the problem of the constant surveillance. How was he supposed to get anything accomplished with his two new babysitters constantly on the watch? He could feel the impatience of his beautiful mistress as she grew more and more ready to make her entrance into the world. She needed her vessel and needed it soon. He had to eliminate Sheriff Cooper. Take him out of the equation. Somehow.

It would be nothing for him to sneak out to the police cruiser, yank the door open, and gut the pig with his knife. He took a moment's reverie in that thought, but knew better than to follow through on such an impulse. A missing or murdered sheriff would bring the state police crashing down on the town like a tidal wave. And there was the lawman's unsettling survival awareness, a sixth sense, that would probably warn him of a knife lurking in the dark—as it already had. No. Raw power and brute force weren't the answer for this problem. Subtlety would be required.

A few days prior, when the sheriff had paid him that visit, an inkling of an idea had begun to formulate in his mind on how to deal with the infuriating man. He had shelved the idea, not realizing at the time that the man would become such a danger to him and to the important work he was engaged in.

The muffled rumble of the cruiser's engine being started, reached him through the glass. He watched as the headlights flicked on and the car slowly pulled away, the red tail lights looking back at him like a pair of malevolent, glowing eyes, before they vanished down the darkening road.

He paced the floor of his room for a few minutes, pondering, allowing the idea to germinate and slowly hatch. He flexed his arms and chest, enjoying the sensation of his blood rushing to engorge the muscles, causing them to swell.

He stopped pacing and smiled as the idea suddenly formed completely in his mind. He stomped over to his night stand and snatched up his knife, his stomach doing little flips of excitement. He knew what to do now. He stared back out the window, as if he could somehow still see the police car parked out there. He had almost enjoyed this little game, but after tonight Sheriff Cooper would no longer be a problem. Not for him anyway.

His voice was barely a whisper in the gathering gloom. "Checkmate."

CONRAD FAIRCHILD TURNED THE KEY until he heard the deadbolt snap into place, securing the front door to *The Clear Creek Register*. He glanced at his watch as if the time actually mattered. Perhaps, if he had a wife and kids waiting for him at home.

Home? What was that? In truth, the cozy office inside the building he had just locked up for the night seemed more of a home to him than his actual house. But a man had to have someplace to eat, sleep, and shower, didn't he? With a shrug of indifference, he reaffirmed his grip on the leather briefcase in his hand and made his way to the lone, solitary Buick Roadmaster parked a dozen or so yards away, beneath a flickering street lamp.

He was addicted to his work; journalism and the newspaper were his life, even his true love, or so his ex-wife used to say. She never understood it and he often marveled at how few people truly did understand the power of the pen, or the typewriter in his case. The power of the press was where it was at.

Presidential elections, public opinion, even the tides of war and peace were swayed and influenced by it.

It was an incredible time to be in the news business. Nowadays, what with radio and even television getting in on the act, the press was more powerful than it had ever been in the history of the world. And to think, he was a part of that. Sure, he was just a small-time writer in a two-bit town...or now. But he was positive that, given a little more time and maybe a bit of luck, he would eventually find his way out into the big, wide world. Maybe even the *New York Times!* One never knew. Of course, he was in no big hurry to get out there. Out there, he would be just another small fish in a big ocean. Here, he was a big fish in a small pond, and he didn't mind that one bit.

Reaching his car, he popped the door open and slid behind the wheel, depositing his briefcase on the passenger seat. He allowed himself a moment to enjoy that new car smell which still lingered even after almost a year. He patted the briefcase tenderly, like a proud father might pat his son on the head after a well-played ballgame. His latest creation lay inside the case, an entire day's work, so why shouldn't he feel a bit like a proud father?

His latest and perhaps most devastating salvo, aimed at the so-called sheriff and his bumbling, country bumpkin of a deputy, would be ready for the press by morning. He would tweak and refine it tonight, over a glass of brandy perhaps, while listening to the soothing tunes of Tchaikovsky. No, not Tchaikovsky. He was at war, wasn't he? Wagner would provide the more appropriate score for the work at hand.

Would lighting up a pipe and smoking it be too pretentious, even for him? He really didn't like the taste of pipe tobacco, but loved the way smoking a pipe made his mind operate. Some of his best inspirational work had been conceived while pacing the floors of his house during the late hours of the night, his teeth clamped on a distinguished pipe while wisps of aromatic smoke spiraled in lazy curls from its polished, walnut bowl.

He slid the key into the ignition, turned it, and pressed the gas pedal to the floor, activating the ignition switch. With a satisfying roar, the engine came to life, all three hundred and twenty cubic inches of it. He revved the gas a couple of times, just because he liked the way it sounded. He smiled as he shifted the car into gear.

It was indeed a fantastic time to be alive. By his own admission, he was a man small in stature, robbed by nature of the kind of physical prowess that not so long ago would have been required in order for survival. But not in this new, modern world. In this world, a clever man could be just as powerful behind a typewriter as a man twice his size, if not more so.

He gave the Buick a bit of gas and the car accelerated smoothly into the deserted street. He shifted into a higher gear, the vehicle picking up speed easily as the eight cylinders thrummed under the hood, seemingly begging him for more fuel. He happily obliged them while wondering if smaller men tended to like bigger cars as a rule. He wasn't sure about that, but one thing he did know for certain: he *would* be lighting up that pipe when he got home!

Clear Creek was such a podunk town that it never took too long to get anywhere within city limits. Before his car could barely get warmed up, he was pulling it into the driveway of his cramped, single-story bungalow on the corner of Maple and Clark. It wasn't necessarily the neighborhood of his choice, but not the worst he could have done, especially considering the major financial setback from his recent divorce. No worries, he was just in rebuilding mode. He'd get back on his feet soon enough, and then he'd show everyone.

Jamming his house key into the lock on the front door, he was surprised to find that it was already unlocked. He dropped his keys into the front pocket of his navy-blue suit pants and slowly turned the doorknob. More than likely he had just forgotten to lock the door on his way out that morning, but it still didn't hurt to be somewhat cautious.

The hinges creaked slightly as he nudged the door open, and allowed it to swing under its own momentum, until it contacted the wall with a muffled thump. Without stepping a foot inside, he reached into the darkness and flicked the two switches on the wall, turning the hall and porch lights on simultaneously.

He took a brief moment to watch and listen. The newly illuminated hallway yawned ahead to disappear into the blackness of the living room. The kitchen, half obscured in shadow, was situated to the right, the tired fridge clanking softly from its dark corner. Everything seemed normal and it wasn't as if he was paranoid or anything, so he stepped inside, shut the door behind him, and bolted it for the night.

He moved with accustomed familiarity through the kitchen and dining room, flicking on lights as he went. The worn out linoleum floor cracked under his footsteps, trying desperately to remind him of his current, humble circumstances, the dismal, overshadowing silence joining the chorus to mock his loneliness. He brushed those oppressive thoughts away as best he could. Tonight would be a good night, replete with fine brandy, invigorating music, and even a little pipe smoking as he pounded a few more nails into the coffin of Chet Cooper's undeserved, ill-gotten career.

The dining room table was cluttered with dirty dishes, hamburger wrappers, used coffee cups, notebooks filled with half-written and discarded newspaper stories, and opened, but yet to be paid bills. He used his briefcase like the blade of a bulldozer, pushing the collective refuse across the table and creating a relatively clean space for it to rest on, while he went back into the kitchen to grab a bottle of brandy. He wouldn't have to worry about drinking from a glass —one of the few perks of his newly found bachelorhood.

He returned to the dining room, gripping a half consumed bottle of brandy by the long neck with one hand, while loosening and pulling off his necktie with the other. Popping the latches on his briefcase, he flipped the lid open, fished around for a moment inside the pocket folders, and produced the rough draft that would hopefully be ready to run in the next day's printing.

He passed through the little open archway that connected the dining room to the living room where he maintained a small desk and typewriter for working at home. The phonograph and his record collection were in there as well and, if he remembered correctly, the pipe and the tobacco were in one of the desk drawers.

It was still dark in the living room, but he knew his way to the desk and his eyes had adjusted to the point that he could distinguish shapes and objects well enough. Placing the brandy and the manuscript on the desk, he clicked on the adjustable work lamp that was clamped on the edge of the desktop. The light reflected off the shiny surface of the desk, casting the lamp's own shadow on the ceiling, appearing like some kind of distorted, robotic dinosaur that Dr. Frankenstein might have constructed in his lab during a night of madness.

In contrast to Dr. Frankenstein, who was in the business of injecting life into the deceased, Conrad would be about the business of killing tonight— figuratively speaking of course—in terms of Chet Cooper's career.

He walked around the desk and opened the top left drawer. Inside, the pipe rested on a decorative tin of pipe tobacco, next to a small box of matches. He lifted the paraphernalia from the drawer and placed it on the desk. He was ready to get to work, but something was missing. The music of course! He lifted his eyes to his Zenith phonograph and radio combo on the other side of the room next to his big, green, leather chair. Maybe instead of Wagner he would listen to —

He jumped violently and let out a shrill squeak, like a rat that had just been caught in a trap.

There, sprawled out in his big, green, leather chair, staring at him with reptilian eyes, was a teenage boy.

"Who the hell—"

The boy sprang from the chair, as if hurled by an unseen force. Conrad thought he saw the dull glint of a knife, as the kid closed the distance between them.

STORM'S MUSCLES BUNCHED AND SURGED beneath Kate's saddle. The powerful mare's hooves thundered across the grassy meadow that sprawled before her like an immense, shaggy carpet. Ahead, a familiar tree line cut across a metallic sky like a black, jagged gash.

She felt she knew this place, she was sure of it. Yes, it was supposed to be a place of comfort and peace, but now an uneasy feeling was rising up in her chest.

Weather was non-existent, and for some reason she had no sensation of the wind in her face as the meadow became a blurry sea of gray shadows flowing past her. On the other side of the meadow, the forest loomed and threatened like a violent storm cloud. A blurry memory told her that just inside those trees, a trail carved a five mile track, gently meandering until it led to…

A sudden, icy dread gripped her. *Asher's pond! No!*

She pulled back on Storm's reins, but the mare didn't respond. "Whoa, girl!" she shouted, giving the reins a firm jerk, but if anything, the galloping animal increased her speed. The forest became an infinite, black wall of twisted, deformed shapes, stretching from horizon to horizon, and before she knew it, she had plunged into its inky heart.

The horse ran, nearly flying down the angling path as nearby branches and limbs, dead and gray, clutched at her clothes and hair. The sickly-sweet reek of alcoholic breath mingled with day-old aftershave hung in the air, becoming stronger as Storm conveyed her in some kind of mindless frenzy through the groping forest.

Suddenly, the trail broke through the morass of trees and foliage, emptying into the small clearing where Asher's Pond lay reposing in languid, curving banks adorned by drooping stands of cattails while lily pads draped the silvery surface in random clusters.

A violent scream erupted from Storm. She went into a skidding stop and then exploded into a black, powdery fog, leaving Kate to sail through the air and hit the ground rolling. Oddly, the crash didn't hurt.

Kate rolled straight up to her feet and spun a fast three-sixty. She seemed to be alone, but she knew that was far from the truth. He was here. She could feel him, even smell him nearby, the aftershave and the alcohol giving him away.

She continued to circle, knowing that at any second he could appear from behind like a phantom, as he had before. She backed up to the water's edge, searching the ground around her in desperation for a stick she could use as a weapon, or even a good-sized rock. "Not this time," she said in a harsh whisper, "you'll have to kill me first."

She saw a decent sized stick laying half in the water, the other half near her foot. When she bent down to pick it up, the smooth bark morphed into rough scales, and the stick became a writhing thing, that slithered and vanished beneath the water's mercurial depths. She recoiled in apprehensive disgust, sucking in air through gritted teeth, stifling the instinct to scream.

She balled her hands into fists, the way her brothers had taught her; thumbs curled down, over the tops of the fingers, and as her brothers would say, *put up her dukes,* by bringing her fists up to chin level—ready to fight.

"Where are you, you coward?" she said through ragged breaths, cursing inside at how terrified she actually sounded. She swallowed hard. "I know you're here, Albert, you can't sneak up on me this time!" That sounded better.

A gurgling disturbance rippled the water behind her. She spun, fists at the ready, feet shoulder width apart, left foot forward. A dozen or so yards in front of her, the surface of the water roiled as oozing mud from the bottom bubbled up and spread across the pond like a black, seeping stain. The fetid stench of rotten, decaying vegetation crashed into her, making her gag and spit the putrid taste from her mouth.

Albert's head suddenly appeared in the midst of the turbulence of bubbles and mud, his eyes fixed on her. She watched in riveted horror while he rose out of the water, as if his body were being hoisted by some giant, unseen hook, his arms and legs dangling like the lifeless limbs of a broken doll. Pond water and globules of brackish mud ran dripping from his body until at last his feet hovered several inches above the pond's surface.

He began gliding toward her, floating across the pond like a specter.

The marrow in her knees turned gelatinous, the joints threatening imminent collapse at any second. But she stood her ground. She had spent enough of her life running from him, from what he had done to her. And although she was nearly frozen with terror, a hot coal of rage was fanning itself to life somewhere deep down in her guts.

As he neared, she could see that it was the same Albert that had appeared in her bedroom window the night that Scotty had been murdered. A tortured, almost pleading look was etched on his face, a cavernous hole gaping on the left side of his head.

He stopped his gliding approach a few feet from the bank and seemed to regard her with black eyes for a moment. "Kate," he said, water and muck dribbling from the corners of his mouth, his voice a hollow gargle.

"What do you want? What is this place?" She was a bit surprised by the power of her own voice and the fact that her knees had yet to give out on her.

Albert hung his head as a great sob racked his suspended body and his face contorted into a mask of even more pain and anguish. After a moment of this, he seemed to collect himself and said, "This is the place between places. Here, we wait. Here, we see and know our sins. Here, justice makes its claim."

As he spiraled into another fit of weeping and crying, she realized that she had little or nothing to fear from him. He was nothing now but a broken shell of a man, plagued and tormented, a prisoner here in this strange kind of hell or purgatory. But how did *she* get here?

"Am I dreaming?" she asked. "How did I get here? What do you want?"

The crying ceased and he looked back up, locking his burning, black eyes on her. "The book!"

"You showed me the page with the poem the other night," she said. "Why? What does it mean?"

Suddenly, the pond began to churn and gurgle again. Albert started drifting back to the agitated disturbance where he had surfaced moments before. "The book!" he moaned.

"What does the poem mean? Tell me!"

A hot, dry breeze began to gust, the faint moaning of thousands of damned souls echoing within it. Albert reached the point of the roiling waters where a dozen or so arms flailed up from the depths, hands clutching at his legs and feet. The hands began pulling Albert down, inch by inch. A look of anguish more evident than ever was scrawled across his face.

"Tell me!" Kate screamed, hot tears streaking down her cheeks. "Tell me!"

Albert had all but vanished below the surface of the water, the disembodied hands gobbling him up in a frenzy. He opened his mouth and croaked, "The book, the binding…the binding…the—" And he was gone.

There was the sensation of swimming upwards from a great, dark depth, the pressure growing less with each kick of her legs and pull of her arms. She swam frantically, her heart thudding as she envisioned those grasping hands, reaching out to pull her back down. Back down there with Albert.

Then there was light, and precious consciousness, as she fluttered her eyelids and awoke to find herself curled up on the floor of her bedroom at the foot of her bed.

She got to her feet and looked around the room. Her bed was a disaster; sheets and blankets all snarled up, and her nightgown was moist with sweat. Besides that, everything else seemed normal. She looked at the clock on her nightstand; it was just past midnight.

"The binding," Albert's voice echoed in her mind. *"The binding."*

Her eyes fell immediately on the old journal lying atop her writing desk. "That was no dream," she whispered to herself. Grabbing the book she sat down in the wooden chair, and clicked on the small reading lamp.

She turned the book over in her hands, caressing the worn leather, allowing the tortured image of Albert in all of his spiritual agony to fill her mind. He had said something about the binding. "The binding binds the sins," she muttered. *The torn out pages...they must be hidden in the actual binding itself!*

She pulled open the solitary desk drawer and fished around for her Excalibur letter opener, a gift from her favorite aunt, fashioned to resemble King Arthur's famous sword. Locating it, she laid the journal on the desk and opened up the front cover. She used the tip of Excalibur to separate the leather covering from the thick cardboard that formed the binding.

Once she had a little gap formed, she slipped her fingers between the two materials and mentally braced herself for her next act. She actually felt horrible for what she was about to do, but she could see no other choice.

There was a ripping sound as the old materials began to separate. After a few moments of prying and ripping, the leather covering tore free, taking a thin paper backing with it. The book was stripped and naked, except for some fossilized gobs of amber glue adhering stubbornly to the old card stock that made up the binding itself.

The leather cover didn't seem to be concealing any torn out and hidden pages, so she placed it off to the side. How would one go about hiding torn out pages inside of a book? She thumbed through the pages as she had done countless times, still finding nothing out of the ordinary. It was still just a book.

She bit her bottom lip in frustration. "There's nothing here," she sighed, and let the book drop from her hands. It hit the edge of the desk and fell onto the floor, the pages fluttering in the air for a brief moment. A little stab of guilt stung her as she looked down at the journal, stripped of its beautiful leather cover, sprawling face down at her feet, many of the pages now bent and crumpled.

She leaned forward to pick it up—maybe old Nate the librarian could repair it. That's when something caught her eye. There was a thin object slightly protruding from the end of what remained of the book's spine, from out of that thin gap between the backs of the glued pages and the cardboard that served to bind them to the cover. It must have been dislodged from the fall!

She took the book into her lap to get a better look. The edge of some kind of piece of paper peeked out from the spine at her. "Hello," she whispered, taking a hold of it and carefully sliding it the rest of the way out. It appeared to be a folded envelope, yellowed by age, a dried and cracked blob of wax sealing the flap shut.

Her fingers trembled and her heart seemed to be skipping every other beat as she turned it over in her hands and unfolded it. Her eyes watered, and she swallowed hard when she saw the writing on the front.

It was written in the flowing penmanship of an era gone by. It simply read:

The sins of the righteous man.

CHAPTER 33

Sitting at the kitchen table of The Cozy Corner, Chet stared at the remains of Abel Gannon's journal in front of him, shaking his head. "This is insane," he said, glancing up at Kate, sitting in her bathrobe across from him.

"You don't have to tell me." She sipped coffee from a porcelain mug. "I've been up all night trying to come to terms with it. Sorry about getting you out of bed so early, but I couldn't wait another minute."

He looked at the hands of the small clock that hung on the wall above the stove; it was five-thirty in the morning. An hour ago, she had called him, insisting that he come over right away, that she had something major to show him. Of course, he had rushed over as quickly as possible. She had let him in and led him to the kitchen, being careful not to wake anyone else in the boarding house.

After pouring two cups of coffee, she had laid out her case for him, going over the main aspects: Scotty's warning to her, Albert's appearance in her window, the riddle in the journal, her visit with the old librarian, the story of the goddess worshiping cult, then her bizarre dream, and now this secret confession that was simply beyond all imagination.

She rose and came over to stand at his side, placing a hand on his back. "Look, Chet, I know it's crazy sounding, and I'm not even sure what you are supposed to do with this, but I think the sooner we open our minds to the fact that we might be dealing with something…something maybe supernatural—"

He interrupted, "Kate, this letter," he picked up the old pages emblazoned with tiny, flowing script. "This letter talks about a demon that feeds on peoples' souls! And then something about taking on a human host? Are you saying that I should take any of this seriously?" He rubbed his temples with his fingers. "I mean, from what you've told me so far, it just sounds like the good reverend probably went off his rocker."

She moved behind him and began rubbing his shoulders. "I know it's a lot to wrestle with, and I'm not expecting you to just swallow it hook, line, and sinker. But just be somewhat open-minded about it. You have to admit, some of it makes sense."

He sighed. "Well, you're obviously seeing things in all of this that I don't."

"You mean, things that you won't?" There was an edge to her voice, and his instincts told him that he was on very thin ice at the moment.

"I'm sorry, Kate, I don't mean to be dismissive, it's just so much to swallow right now...I've never been...well, what some might call God-fearing. All this talk of demons and trapped souls, and cults, it's just..."

"Totally unbelievable? Trust me, I know. It's not like I'm some kind of holy roller that speaks in tongues and prays with rattlesnakes, ya know. This is just as mind blowing to me as it is to you. I've just had a little more time to digest it is all. Besides, you barely even let me tell you any of it. Maybe you should hear the whole story before you make your judgment."

He reached up to give her hand a squeeze and then took his first sip of coffee since arriving. "Why don't we try again, and I promise to be open-minded this time."

"Okay," she said, with half a smile. She picked up the old letter and sat in the adjacent chair to his right.

"Just give me the dummy notes," he said.

She cleared her throat. "Okay...well, in a nutshell, he tells us that this cult moved into town calling themselves The Sword of Light. They worshiped some kind of ancient, pagan, fertility goddess—he never mentions which one. Not long after they arrive, a few townspeople here and there turn up missing. Of course, most folks immediately suspected their new neighbors. The sheriff looked into it, but could never find any proof or evidence to pin on them."

Chet shifted in his chair. "Sounds familiar."

She continued, as she glanced over the letter, "Now, Reverend Gannon writes that, at some point, he started having visitations from an angel...a heavenly messenger, 'beautiful beyond words', as he describes it. Apparently, it began with just her voice in his head, but eventually led to full blown visits—mostly in the woods, near an especially old tree, that he writes, 'is particularly enormous.'"

"And it turns out she wasn't so heavenly?" Chet said.

Kate took another sip of coffee. "Getting to that. Now, according to this," she gestured to the crinkled page in her hand, "she was some kind of reincarnation of an ancient evil, basically a demon that requires human sacrifice and then feeds on the souls of the victims who are killed."

"So, where did this…*demon* come from? Did the cult bring her with them somehow?"

"No, it was more like the other way around. The cult came to Clear Creek because she was *already* here. But, there's nothing in here that says where she came from. Abel was sure that she at least dates back to a town called Salem. He guessed that the people of Salem had done something to awaken her, or even conjure her somehow. He writes that, *she* was the cause of the collapse of the entire town."

"The Salem curse," Chet said, rubbing his chin.

"What curse?"

"Salem is an old town site up in the foothills east of here—a ghost town. There's actually nothing really left except the ruined remains of the church. It's always been kind of a place of mystery, nobody knows what happened to the town: why and when it was abandoned, who lived there, what happened.

"Most people assume small pox or a big fire might have been the cause. Some of the more…superstitious people say that the town fell under some kind of curse and that it's haunted up there."

Kate's eyes widened as she reached across the table to grip his hand in hers. "Wasn't that where Lucas Gannon had just come from before he was killed?"

There was a sudden Chill in the room. Chet nodded slowly. "Yeah, he was up near Salem when they found him in his truck."

She swallowed and her eyes grew watery. "See what I mean, Chet? Are you connecting these dots?"

"Yeah okay," he said. "So, we basically have a pagan cult move into town, people start disappearing, and Old Reverend Gannon starts getting visitations in the woods from a messenger from Heaven, who turns out actually to be a demon. Correct?"

She nodded.

"What did these visitations entail? What did she want from Abel?"

Kate let out a heavy sigh. "This is where it gets messy, the kind of stuff that Nathan Hobbes warned me about." She angled her lips and let out a puff of air to blow a lock of hair from her eyes and continued, "Over a period of visits, she actually convinces Abel…to begin killing for her. Reverend Gannon was the reason people were vanishing, not the cult."

"He admits to that in the letter?" Chet couldn't believe what he was hearing.

"Yes, and not only that. He also claims that he was in love with her, willing to do anything for her. She made him promises that they could be together. There was just one problem: she needed a vessel, a body to possess so that she could cross into the realm of the living, and they could be together.

"In the meantime, she needed to feed. She needed to gain strength and power, so she would convince him that certain people were evil. He would kill them and take the bodies into the woods, where she could supposedly feed on their souls. And get this: the bodies would come back from the dead, but under her power, basically undead slaves. He calls them, revenants."

"Levi Henderson," Chet said, his voice barely a whisper.

Kate nodded and licked her lips. "You have three different witnesses claiming to see Levi, *dead,* walking around the woods, Chet. Two of those witnesses are now murder victims."

He rubbed at his eyes with his hands for a moment. He was the one about to lose his marbles. As cockamamie as the whole story seemed on the surface, he couldn't deny the obvious connections, and how well things seemed to fit together.

So, Able Gannon was a nut-job killer, who believed he was in communion with a demon, but that didn't make the demon real. Hell, there were plenty of killers and psychos sitting in prisons all across the country, at this exact moment, who claimed to have heard voices. *The Devil made me do it.* The oldest excuse in the book.

"Alright," he said, "how does this story end? I'm guessing not very happy."

"Good guess," she said, flipping a page over. "Okay, so eventually it gets to the point where he has killed—sacrificed really—enough people that the demon is ready for her vessel, but there's one thing standing in the way: the cult."

"Wait a second, how could they be a problem? They are there to serve the demon aren't they? You said they came to town just because of her."

"Not to *serve* her, to destroy her. The letter is fuzzy about the details here, but apparently these people were some kind of anti-demon crusaders. Their main purpose was to hunt down and destroy creatures like this.

"The real kicker is later, Abel found out that this woman, evil goddess, whatever, had also started working on Cyrus, the cult leader, the same way she had been working on him. She was playing both men against each other to her advantage. Smart, eh?"

Somewhere in Chet's brain something began to throb. "Cyrus?"

She nodded. "Yes, the cult leader. Why?"

"Before Lucas Gannon died, he was supposedly mumbling a bunch of incoherent nonsense. According to Roy Hatcher, Lucas mentioned the name Cyrus in his babbling."

Kate swallowed hard, and fixed a wide-eyed gaze on him, that seemed to be saying, *"See?!"*

He tried to ignore the tingle creeping along his spine. He nodded with a frown in concurrence, and motioned with his hand for her to continue with the story.

She took a brief moment to regain her composure, and then quietly cleared her throat. "Basically, to protect his demonic girlfriend, Abel starts using his sermons to stir the town up against The Sword of Light, accusing them, ironically, of being devil worshipers, and of kidnapping and murder.

"Eventually, he was able to convince the sheriff, mayor, and a number of his parishioners, to join him in dealing with the cultists once and for all. So, one night this…mob, led by Abel Gannon, went out to the farm where the cultists were staying and pulled them from their beds. They dragged them deep into the forest—to the big, old tree, to be exact—tied nooses around their necks, and hung them all."

Chet shook his head. "Those poor people…all murdered. How many, does it say?"

She pulled her eyes from the paper to greet his gaze. "Thirteen."

He let out a snort. "That figures. And the bodies?"

"They hauled the bodies up to the old Salem church, not far from this tree, and buried them in the church cemetery."

"The perfect hiding place."

"Afterwards, they went back to the farmhouse and set it on fire, making it look like an accident. The sheriff did his part and convinced everyone that the cultists were either all killed in the fire or had fled town and burned the house to cover up any evidence that they were responsible for the disappearances."

"So now, with the demon killers out of the way…"

"Abel Gannon was free to perform the ritual that would bring this thing into the world of the living."

"But, they needed a host, right? A vessel?" Kate nodded. "Abel chose his wife, Constance."

Chet let out a low whistle. "Boy, this guy just keeps getting better and better."

"He doesn't go into detail of the ritual or anything, but before long, he did take his wife out to the old church in Salem, to make it all happen. Told her they were going on a picnic."

Chet leaned back in his chair and folded his arms. "Well, the town of Clear Creek is still here and standing, and there doesn't seem to be this evil cloud hanging over the city or anything, so something must have gone wrong."

Kate nodded and took a sip of her coffee. "You could say that. He writes that he did perform the ritual, but in the middle of the process he had a change of mind, a sudden awakening to the reality of what he was doing to his wife and the mother of his son."

Chet sighed in disgust. "A little too late for that. Why do you suppose the change of heart now?"

"I don't know. Maybe it was all the religious training and praying he had done his whole life. Maybe that had an effect on him…something this demon didn't anticipate. Either way, he tried to halt the ceremony and save his wife from being possessed, and becoming this so-called *vessel*. But it was too late. Too much of the transformation had already taken place, leaving the demon sort of trapped, halfway…one foot in each world, so to speak.

"The worst part was how it left his wife, writhing in pain and horror, as her spirit and the demon struggled with each other for control. Reverend Gannon describes a scene out of a nightmare: rocks and debris flying through the air, branches and twigs snapping off of trees, an unnatural, growling wind, his wife's body levitating and contorting as she howled."

Kate looked up at him and shuddered uncontrollably. "I hate this stuff, Chet, I'm not as rock solid as you are. This kind of thing gives me goosebumps on my goosebumps."

"Right," Chet said, reaching to give her her shoulder a reassuring rub. "Not exactly a big fan of it myself, but you can't stop there. What happens next?"

She wiped at watery eyes. "For the first time, Abel saw this creature for what she truly was: not a heavenly being or messenger, but a 'denizen of Hell's lowest pit'. He also knew that there would be no saving Constance's life. This demon would eventually win the battle, take over, become more powerful than ever, and enter a cycle of massive destruction, all the while feeding off of his wife's trapped soul."

Kate took a deep breath, obviously steeling herself for the next part. Chet grabbed a hold of her hand, and had to admit, he was hanging on every word now.

"Abel quickly reasoned that he could not allow the demon to enter the world of the living, and that to save his wife he would have to kill her. So he cut her throat." A tear leaked out from the corner of Kate's eye. She didn't seem to notice and continued, "He just let her bleed out."

"And the demon?" Chet asked.

"Without a vessel, and without Abel to feed her anymore, she lost her power. She became trapped inside the tree, along with the souls of the people Abel had murdered for her, including the thirteen cultists."

"Trapped in the tree?"

"It's some kind of protection for her, a sanctuary. It's a place in this world she is able to inhabit. Abel wrote that he wanted so very badly to go into the forest and cut the tree down or burn it, but he didn't dare get that near to her. He spent the rest of his life hearing her voice in his head, trying to convince him to come back to her."

Chet stood up from the table and began to pace, trying to get the whole nutty story straight in his head. "Is that how it ends? He just eventually dies, probably half out of his mind with guilt, while this possessed tree whispered to him?"

Kate got to her feet as well, her slippers making a scuffing sound on the floor as she came to him. She put her arms around his waist and laid her head on his chest. Her voice was soft, almost trembling. "That's just it. From what I gather, she's still in this tree. She's been there these past decades, waiting for the right person to come along, reaching out and searching for another…I don't know what to call it."

"A feeder," Chet said. "She can't operate on her own. She needs someone to *feed* her, until she's strong enough to take physical form."

She pulled her head away from his chest and pierced him with soul-searching eyes. "Chet, I think she has found him. I think it's Daniel Miller."

He stepped away from her to continue with his pacing, his hands on his hips as he mulled over everything. He was aware of Kate watching him, chewing on a hangnail, waiting for him to say something. And say what? What did she expect him to do? Haunted trees, demons, trapped souls, apparitions…

"What are you thinking about?" she asked.

He stopped pacing and leaned back on the kitchen counter, crossing his ankles and folding his arms. "It is *a lot* to take in, Kate. I'm sorry, but I think I'm going to need a while to digest all of this. You understand, don't you?"

She nodded. "I understand, Chet, but if all this is true"—she gestured at the confession on the table—"I don't think you have a while."

"You have to understand, I'm already pursuing Daniel as hard as the law legally allows. Unless I can dig up some kind of hard evidence that directly links him to a crime, I have no choice but to wait for him to make a mistake. I have to deal with physical evidence and the facts. Whether this thing that feeds on souls is real or not."

She crossed the floor over to him and placed her hand on his. "I realize that, Chet, I really do. Believe me. But maybe it's important for you to realize what you're possibly up against. I'm afraid that when all is said and done, this will all boil down to more than just making an arrest on a teenage kid."

He ran a hand through her curled locks. "Okay, maybe I am up against an ancient, evil, demon lady. I'll keep that in mind when I'm slamming Daniel Miller's face onto the hood of my car and arresting him for murder." He tried his best to flash a cavalier smile. "Does that make you feel better?"

She rolled her eyes. "Not hardly. I need you to take this more seriously, Chet." Her eyes were pleading. "Remember how she played Abel and Cyrus against each other at the same time?"

Her eyes grew wide. He thought he almost saw a little light bulb click on above her head. "Chet, she could try that with you and Daniel! You need to be prepared for that possibility!"

He put his hands on her arms. Slid them up over her shoulders and neck, to cradle her head, his fingers penetrating and entwining in her hair. He felt her shiver as he pulled her into him. "No need to worry about that. There's only one indescribably beautiful, goddess-like creature haunting my dreams these days, and she's standing right here."

She smiled, and put her hands around his back, interlocking her fingers. "You are too smooth."

He pulled her closer and tilted his head down. As he closed his eyes, he felt her raising on her tiptoes, felt her breath against his lips. And then they were kissing. And for a brief moment, nothing mattered to him, but her. Nothing else existed, but her. No demon-possessed, murdering teenagers, no secret confessions of dead preachers, no dead walking the woods—

"Good gracious!" Mable's voice dismantled the moment with all the finesse of a toddler kicking over a tower of wooden blocks. A normal person would have maybe blushed for a moment, excused herself, and then retreated from the room. Mable was no normal person.

Her ruddy cheeks, the size of small apples, flushed as she buried her fists into the plump padding of her hips. "What in the name of Sam Hill are you kids doing in here?" she asked, as if it weren't obvious.

Kate didn't even turn around—not right away—and rolled her eyes at the ceiling as she released her hold on his torso.

He tried to muster up the most innocent, disarming smile he could. "Good morning, Mable," he said, allowing his hands to drop to his sides as Kate stepped away from him, finally turning to face her self-appointed governess.

"I'd say it looks like a good morning alright." Mable's eyes flicked back and forth between them. "Thought I'd get an early start on breakfast this morning, but looks like you two already got a jump on things in here."

Chet laughed, he couldn't help it. The whole situation seemed ridiculous to him: two grown adults, blushing in shame after getting caught in an innocent kiss by this fiery, red-headed, matron of a woman who somehow perceived herself as their chaperon.

Kate must have felt the same way, because she began to giggle too, a weightless, musical sound to his ears. She took a step forward. "I'm sorry, Mable—"

Chet interrupted, "I tried to stop her but she just kept coming on to me. She had me trapped up against the counter…there was no where to run. You gotta believe me."

Kate spun and punched him hard on the arm, her emerald eyes blazing, her teeth clenched in an incredulous grin. This made Chet laugh harder, despite the throbbing pulses of pain now radiating down his arm. He made a mental note to avoid angering girls who had grown up with lots of brothers in the future.

Despite the display of puritanical abhorrence at what had been taking place in her kitchen, Mable, being the consummate match maker at heart, finally cracked. "You may as well hold back the tide as try to hold back true love, I suppose." She stomped across the floor and flung open the refrigerator door.

"I suppose," Kate said, flashing Chet a conspiratorial smile.

Mable produced a large package wrapped in white butcher's paper from the icebox. The word *bacon* was written on the top in heavy, black pencil. With one hand she aimed the package at the couple like it was a sword. "You two just mind yourselves now." She stabbed at the air with the bundle, accentuating each syllable, "This once, I'll look the other way, but I can't have people thinking I'm running some kind of brothel here, now can I."

"No, ma'am," Chet said with as much seriousness as he could muster.

The copper-haired woman nodded, the tight bun on the top of her head pitching back and forth like a little fireball zagging through space. "Good," she said and walked past the couple to fetch a frying pan from a cupboard. She plunked it down on the stove. "You'll stay for breakfast."

This was a proclamation, not a question. But he was starving, so he didn't argue.

Meanwhile, Kate had discreetly folded up the old parchment from Reverend Gannon's journal and placed it in the pocket of her bathrobe. Chet nodded his approval, putting his finger to his lips. The reverend's insane story should remain between the two of them…for now, anyway.

Mable struck a match and lit the burner on the stove, the blue flames guttering for a moment and then growing steady. She turned, her eyes appraising, her lips a thin line. "Young lady," she said, "you need to go get dressed."

CHAPTER 34

I don't know about you, Rick," Chet said, getting up from his desk, "but I've about had it screwing around with this Miller kid." It was getting close to lunchtime and Mable's bacon and eggs from earlier that morning were starting to wear off, leaving his stomach to grumble in protest.

Rick, sitting at his desk, feet up, nodded his agreement. "Yeah, he don't seem to be showing any signs of cracking does he? In fact, I think he's almost getting a kick out of the whole thing if you ask me."

"How's that?"

"This morning, that little bugger walked right past my car, looked me dead in the eyes, and then smiled and winked at me! I hate to say it, but he just thinks this is some kind of big game."

Chet thought about everything Kate had told him earlier. If that preacher's confession had any validity to it, then yeah, this all probably was some kind of big game to him. Could any of that really be true? At the time, in the quiet dim of Mable's kitchen, he had to admit, he almost felt convinced. Kate was right. It sure did explain a lot and made it easier to connect some of the dots.

He had even come close to telling Rick all about it. But now, under the glaring light of day, the whole idea of supernatural forces at play was just too much. He was fairly certain Daniel Miller was guilty of something—the disappearance of Levi Henderson at least. Beyond that, he wasn't sure about much. All he had to go on was his gut, a hunch. Evidence…he just needed evidence!

"It's a game to him because he knows we don't have any proof." Chet smacked a fist into his palm. "If only I had something on him, I'd drive down to that school right now and drag him out of class in handcuffs!"

"Do it anyway," Rick said, taking his feet off his desk.

"I wish I could."

Rick interlaced his fingers over his stomach. "Ya know, Coop, I saw this picture once—can't remember the name of it, or who was even in it. It really wasn't very good. Anyway, it was about this big homicide detective in New York City, who was in kind of a similar situation as us. This detective had nothing on this guy, but he knew the guy was guilty of murder. So he got the guy to slip up by letting on that he was really close to obtaining some evidence— even though he wasn't. Anyway, in the picture it worked. The bad guy was caught returning to the scene of the crime looking to hide his tracks.

"You might not be able arrest him, but you can bring him in for questioning. You know, pull him outta class in front of the other kids…make a big scene. That might rattle his cage a bit. Then, work him over back here. We could tell him we're close to having what we need to arrest him."

Chet mulled it over and decided it wasn't a bad idea. It wouldn't be the first time the older, more experienced deputy had come up with a good one. He lifted his leather coat from off the back of the chair. "We could tell him we found fingerprints on Robbie Pritchard's car, see if he'd be willing to let us fingerprint him to make a comparison."

Rick got to his feet. "I'm not promising it'll work, but it'll sure as heck ratchet things up a bit for him. A lot more than just staring at him from our patrol rigs anyway."

Chet shrugged into his bomber's jacket. "Alright then, grab your coat and let's go get Mr. Miller."

"Ten-four!" Rick said, trotting to the door and snatching his denim jacket off the coat rack. He slipped into it, opened the door, and held it for his younger boss.

As Chet was rounding his desk the phone rang, stopping him in his tracks. Rick sighed and allowed the door to close.

"Sheriff Cooper," Chet said into the receiver.

Caroline's voice crackled over the speaker, "Morning Sheriff. I just got a call from Terry Cook. He wants you to meet him over at *The Register* as soon as you can make it."

"Did he say why?"

"No, he wouldn't tell me," she sounded offended, "he just said it was urgent."

"Was that it?"

"Like I said: he wouldn't say."

Chet thanked Caroline and hung up the phone.

"What was that all about?" Rick asked.

Chet sighed. He really wanted to get down to the school and implement his latest plan on Daniel. "There's something going on at *The Register*. Terry Cook just called Caroline and wants me down there as soon as possible. He didn't say why."

Rick snorted. "Sounds like some kind of mischief from Conrad Fairchild if you ask me. He probably wants you down there so he can ambush you with his lawyer or something. And that'd be just like him too, having Terry call you... doing his dirty work." He put his hands on his hips and shook his head. "I wouldn't even go if I was you."

"I have to go, Rick. I can't just ignore it."

"Hey, how about if I go see what Terry needs and you go to the school?"

Chet considered it.

The deputy took a step forward and spread his hands apart. "Coop, it's not like the building's on fire. I can handle whatever's going on over there. You can go scoop up the psycho kid and we'll both meet back here. Give 'em the old one, two...Pow!" He made an uppercutting motion with his fist, doing a decent imitation of Jack Dempsey's form.

Chet leaned against his desk, giving it some thought.

"Ah, come on," Rick said, grinning wide. "Think of the satisfaction of tossing a big old monkey wrench into the gears of whatever Conrad's got going on over there!" He smiled wide, exposing his horse teeth.

"Well, when you put it that way..."

"I do put it that way. Now come on...I'll take care of Conrad and you go get that cocky, little shit."

RICK ACTUALLY COULDN'T WAIT to get over to the newspaper building. He looked forward to seeing the look on Conrad's face when it was himself getting out of the car instead of Coop. He put a touch more throttle to his vehicle than he probably should have, considering that he was slightly breaking the very speed limit he was paid to enforce. The irony made him smile, not that he enjoyed the feeling of being a hypocrite, but he was enjoying the prospect of stuffing the rat's little scheme right back down his throat.

He rolled to a stop at an intersection where the light had changed to red— running the light would probably be going too far. He took a moment to recall his high school days, some twenty-five or so odd years ago. Even back then, he had hated Conrad Fairchild's stinking guts. Always whining and sniveling about this or that, blaming everyone else for his own mistakes, acting like the world owed him something.

The guy sure hadn't changed much since then. He shook his head. Conrad couldn't have fallen into a worse career given his vindictive, him-against-the-world personality. The light changed to green and Rick barreled through.

He wondered what kind of crap Conrad was up to now. He thought of Chet and all the pressure he had been under lately with these killings. He thought of Kate and how she had seemed to show up in Chet's life at the perfect time, like an angel sent on some kind of secret mission, to buoy up the young man. Chet would be a basket case by now dealing with the pressure if not for Kate being in the mix, he was sure of it.

To be honest, when the rookie sheriff had taken over, Rick had been nervous. Sure, the kid had some good things going for him—war hero for one thing—but he was still very wet behind the ears when it came to the job of running a sheriff's department, even one as small as Clear Creek County's.

It hadn't taken long for Rick to notice the signs of a man, haunted and beleaguered by his recent past: periods of depression, sudden mood swings, moments where he seemed mentally checked out, to name the most obvious. The kid had been pretty good at keeping it all hidden and tucked away from everyone else, but when men work long hours together and sometimes life and death are on the line, it's nearly impossible to conceal that kind of thing from each other. Over a short period of time, the young hero had become the little brother Rick had never had.

It went both ways. Chet was at a point where he could tell within minutes of the start of the day if Rick and Alice had been in a fight the night before. Just as Rick could sometimes, with one glance at his young boss's eyes, tell that the man was seeing things that weren't really there, hearing things that had already happened.

But ever since Kate's arrival on the scene, Rick had observed a remarkable change in Chet. Sure, the ghosts were still obviously there to some degree, but maybe not so much anymore. The ghosts had diminished. Or maybe it was that the ghosts were still there, but he wasn't bothered by them so much as before. Whatever was going on, it was because of Kate, no doubt about that.

He pulled alongside the curb in front of *The Clear Creek Register.* A feeling of protective anger surged up in him as he got out of his car and yanked the front door open.

Terry was standing behind the counter, a worried look on his smooth, ink-smudged face. "Deputy Shelton," he said, coming around the counter, the little wooden gate banging against the wall.

Rick glanced around the room. No sign of Conrad or a slick lawyer anywhere. "Where's your boss, Terry?" He walked over to the counter and peered over as if Conrad might be hiding behind it.

"That's why I called," Terry said, wiping meaty hands on the front of his stained printer's apron. "I'm afraid that something might be wrong with Mr. Fairchild."

Rick resisted the opportunity to whole-heartedly agree that, yes indeed, something was *really* wrong with Mr. Fairchild. Instead he folded his arms and asked, "What makes you think that something is wrong with him?"

"Well, he didn't come to work this morning, which is totally not like him at all. Sometimes, I think he practically lives here."

"I assume you tried to call him at home."

"Yeah, but he wouldn't answer, so I went over there to check in on him. I tried knocking on his door, ringing the bell…"

"Maybe he decided to skip town for a bit."

"If he did, he left his car…it's in the driveway." Terry shook his head in a show of frustration. "He had this big…article he wanted to print today that he was all excited about. He was going to take it home and work on it so we could run it in today's issue. I've been holding up the run now for over an hour. Trust me, something's wrong. There's no way he would have missed the run this morning."

Rick wanted to spit at the mention of a new article from Conrad. "What kind of article would that be, another hit piece on Sheriff Cooper? Or better yet, on an innocent school secretary that's just trying to get along as best she can in a new town, far away from home?"

Terry sighed, shook his head, and put his hands on his hips. "Look, I know that your boss and mine aren't really seeing eye to eye these days—"

"Ya think?"

"But that doesn't mean you and I have to be at war. Like you, I'm just trying to do my job. You know what, Rick? I don't even read the paper. I just run it through the press, try to get home as soon as possible, and sneak in a little fishing when I can."

Rick felt bad, he always did like Terry. It wasn't like he was to blame for Conrad's shenanigans. He looked down at his feet. "You're right, Terry, me and you got nothing to be hostile toward each other about."

Terry offered a smile and a nod.

Rick put his hands on his hips. "I guess someone ought to go over to Conrad's place and check on him."

"That's why I called. I figured if anyone is allowed to kick his door in, it'd be the cops."

Rick nodded and couldn't help a grin. "A chance to kick Conrad's door in? Now you're talking."

CHET POKED HIS HEAD into Principal Porter's office, catching the stout, little man in the act of putting a golf ball across the smooth, brown carpet. Chet watched as the dimpled ball collided with the edge of an empty coffee mug lying on its side, and bounced away, hitting the wall.

"Son of a…" The old principal restrained himself from finishing his chosen phrase, as he used his putting iron to collect another ball from a small pile off to the side. Chet watched another failed attempt. This time, he thought the mug had been in serious danger of being broken. The bald head turned a strange mixture of pink and purple, and the old educator showed less restraint this time in his choice of words to express his displeasure.

The poor guy just had no finesse, and Chet found it hilarious that of all the hobbies for Joshua Porter to decide to pursue, he had picked golf. It was like watching someone trying to wind up a pocket watch with a pipe wrench.

"It's a putt, Mr. Porter," he said, stepping into the office, "not a home run."

Mr. Porter looked up, his eyes blinking in surprise behind black framed glasses. He let out a low chuckle and walked over to his desk, placing the putting iron in the corner by his bookcase. "Sometimes, I let this silly game get the best of me," he said, plopping down into his high-backed leather chair.

"It only gets the best of you when you quit trying." Chet offered encouragement, even though he really thought that maybe giving up on the game might be in Mr. Porter's best interest.

Mr. Porter removed his glasses and began wiping them with a handkerchief from his pocket. "Now that's good advice to live by. I like it." He perched the glasses back on his nose. "So Chet—Sheriff—what brings you down to my neck of the woods?"

Chet strode into the office and took a seat in the chair across from his old principal's desk. In his day, it had been known as the *hot seat* by the students unfortunate enough to find themselves in it, squirming under Principal Porter's penetrating glare. He leaned forward, his elbows resting on his knees. "I told you the last time I was here that I was suspicious that Robbie Pritchard's death was not a suicide."

376

Mr. Porter nodded, his jowls shaking. "After recent events, it turns out you were probably right about that."

Chet rubbed his palms together, they were sweating. The *hot seat* still had its effect, apparently. "There's a student here, Mr. Porter, that I believe has at least knowledge about, if not something to do with Robbie's murder."

The older man's eyes grew wide, his mouth clamping tight, compressing his fleshy lips. He didn't say anything, just looked shocked.

Chet continued, "Not just the death of Robbie Pritchard, but Lucas Gannon too. And Scotty Forks. Even the disappearance of Levi Henderson."

Mr. Porter looked like he had been slugged in the stomach. He took a deep breath and let it out, some of the color returning to his cheeks. "If this is the case, then why have you not arrested the suspect? I'm assuming you must have some kind of evidence?"

It was Chet's turn to take a deep breath and let it out. "That's my problem. All I really have is circumstantial, nothing solid. That, and a strong hunch. I can't legally place him under arrest just yet."

"But you're sure this student is your man?"

"I don't know for sure, but like I said, I have a strong hunch."

"May I ask who this student is?"

Chet straightened in his chair. "None of this leaves this room."

"Understood." Mr. Porter's eyes were drilling holes into him, the thick lenses of his glasses magnifying the heat of his stare.

Chet whispered, "Daniel Miller."

Mr. Porter's face was indiscernible for a few seconds, and then he began to slowly nod. "Now that you mention it, if I had to accuse any of my students of being a murderer, Mr. Miller would be my choice. He's really undergone quite a change over the last several weeks. Some would say for the better, but I don't know about that."

"Why's that? What kind of change?"

The principal leaned his solid bulk back into his chair and looked up at the ceiling. "Well, Daniel Miller has always been one of those kids who just can't fit in, no matter how hard he tries. I've always felt sorry for him. He's extremely intelligent and has a passion for learning, especially history. But for some reason, he's always been a kid kept at arms length by the others, an outcast, so to speak.

"He has a sensitive side to him; he can write, composes fairly good poetry, and he's always done well in school art contests." Mr. Porter shook his head. "I think the pain of being an outsider cuts deeper in him than it would some other kid. A few times he's tried to break free…tried to climb out of the hole that the others have put him in. He tried out for football; it must have required a level of courage that most people can't identify with. But he didn't make the team; the other boys made sure of that."

"You say, he's *changed* over the last several weeks though?" Chet said, actually feeling a little sorry for Daniel himself.

Mr. Porter interlaced his fingers and placed his hands on the desk. "Yes, he has. It's hard to explain really. He used to shuffle through the halls between classes like a shadow, trying not to be seen, doing his best to stay invisible. Probably just trying to stay off of Robbie's radar.

"But lately…. Well, the best way I could describe it is, he's gone from shuffling through the halls to strutting. Nobody wants a thing to do with him still, but the weird thing is, he doesn't seem to want anything to do with them either. It's like he's stopped trying and has decided to embrace the solitude and exile.

It's like he has this new-found, kind of aloof confidence, and you can see in his eyes: he thinks he's superior to everyone here…including his teachers. The strangest part, is the way the other kids have gone from teasing and mocking him to avoiding and fearing him. You can see it in the halls."

Chet would have bet dollars to donuts he already knew the answer to his next question, but he asked it anyway. "When did you first start noticing this change in Daniel?"

Mr. Porter twisted his mouth and scratched at his chin. "Let's see…"

"About the time of Robbie Pritchard's death?" Chet asked.

Mr. Porter leveled his gaze at him and nodded. Chet could almost hear the gears and wheels in his head clicking and turning as the man put two and two together.

Mr. Porter removed his glasses and tossed them clattering onto his desk. He rubbed at his eyes with a thumb and forefinger. "You don't have evidence enough to arrest him, so what are you doing here, Sheriff? What does this have to do with me?"

Chet stood up—he couldn't sit for one more second—and started pacing around the office. "Over the last few days we've been trying to flush him out by keeping obvious tabs on him. You know, just seeing if we can get him to choke under a little pressure, maybe make some kind of mistake that will give us an opening. But like you said, he's smart. He's got us figured out. I need to take a new tack. So in a few minutes, I'm going to go drag him out of whatever class he's in and take him down to my office."

Mr. Porter rose to his feet. "I thought you said you didn't have enough evidence to arrest him."

"It won't be an arrest. I'm just taking him in for questioning."

"So why don't you just take him in after school, why come in here in the middle of the day and disrupt the whole school? Do you have any idea the ruckus you're going to leave in your wake?"

Chet put his hands on the principal's desk and leaned forward to make sure he had the man's full attention. "Look, the kid is cocky and has a temper, I've seen it first hand. I think that's going to be his weak spot. Right now, he thinks I'm playing around. Well, after today's humiliation, he's going to realize this isn't a game and I mean business."

Mr. Porter was shaking his head in total disagreement. "I don't like it. You said yourself, you're not one hundred percent he's guilty. What if he is innocent? What if your hunch is wrong? You'll be doing irreparable damage to the poor boy."

It was a good point, but he had his mind made up. He folded his arms across his chest. "With all due respect, Mr. Porter, I don't need your permission on this. I came in here merely as a courtesy, hoping for your cooperation."

Mr. Porter slumped back into his chair with a heavy sigh. His face suddenly looked older, tired. "No, I suppose you don't need my permission, but for the record, I'm not on board with the idea."

"Fair enough," Chet said. "Now which room is Mr. Miller in right now?"

"Are you sure about this?" Mr. Porter asked, his hand resting on the handset of his phone.

Chet nodded. "Which room?"

Before the man could pick it up, the handset buzzed, causing him to jump. He recovered after the second buzz. "Yes, Mrs. Rockwood." He looked up at Chet. "The sheriff? Yes he's here in my office right now. Yes, certainly…yes, just put him through to my line. Thank you, Mrs. Rockwood." He shrugged a shoulder and extended the handset to Chet. "Deputy Shelton is on the line asking for you."

He accepted the handset and put it to his ear. "Everything okay, Rick?"

There was a slight pause and then Rick's voice, metallic and scratchy in his ear. "Coop, you need to drop everything and haul ass over to Conrad's house asap."

Even over the poor connection Chet could detect the agitation in Rick's voice. A jagged lump of ice formed in his stomach. "What's going on, Rick?"

"Conrad Fairchild is dead."

CHAPTER 35

C het turned his cruiser onto Clark Street. A few blocks down was Conrad Fairchild's house, on the corner of Clark and Maple. As he neared, he could see Rick's cruiser pulled parallel with the street. He also recognized Dr. Steinmetz's car parked right behind Rick's. An ambulance was pulled into the driveway behind Conrad's big Buick. Two medics stood leaning against it, smoking cigarettes and talking. He recognized one of them as Phil McCray. The other one looked familiar, but he didn't know him.

"Have you got the body in there?" Chet said, as he approached the ambulance.

"Nah," Phil said, "He's still in the house. Deputy Shelton and Dr. Steinmetz are in there with him."

"Have you been in there and seen him yet?"

Phil shook his head. "Nope, not yet. They won't let anyone else in. Apparently, there's not a whole lot for us to do in there. We're just the meat wagon at this point, I guess."

Chet moved past them, heading for the front door of the house, which was hanging halfway open on one hinge. Chunks of splintered wood—the remnants of the door jam—were scattered about.

He stepped through the threshold onto the decrepit linoleum floor and pushed the door fully open. The one remaining hinge creaked its protest.

"That you, Coop?" Rick's voice echoed from the front room.

"Yeah," he answered, taking a few more steps down the hall.

"In here."

As he neared the end of the hallway a familiar, sickening odor hit him, stopping him in his tracks. It was the coppery, metallic scent of blood. He grimaced and wasn't so sure he wanted to continue. He knew that for blood to actually give off an odor, there had to be a lot of it.

The demons started to claw. He did his best to shrug them away. Steadying himself, he walked into the front room. He had been right about one thing: there was blood…a lot of it. The walls were practically slathered in big arcing patterns of congealing, dark-red splatter.

Of all the carnage he had seen overseas, he had never seen anything like it. Conrad's body, the torso at least, was lying on the top of the desk, like the victim of a human sacrifice left on the altar; the head, the arms, and the legs had all been hacked off, leaving stumps of bone jutting out, white and jagged. The abdomen had been opened up. All of the sticky insides were pulled out, left to hang over the sides of the desk, still attached.

He fought the urge to wretch from the combined sight and the unique stench that accompanies a human body that's been turned inside out. He pulled his handkerchief from his pocket and jammed it over his nose and mouth, resisting the urge to toss what was left of Mable's eggs and bacon all over the floor.

Forcing his eyes to look away from the dismembered corpse, he noticed Rick and the doctor were both standing there beside it, looking at him. Dr. Steinmetz also had a handkerchief shoved into his face. Rick was trying to stifle the odor with the sleeve of his shirt.

"Where's the rest of him," Chet managed to say.

Rick gestured with his head. "Dining room table."

Without a word, he walked past the desk toward the dining room, being careful not to step in the areas of carpet that were saturated in blood. He was barely aware of Rick and the doctor following behind.

What was left of Conrad Fairchild was laid out on the table, the severed limbs were where they would be anatomically, if still attached to the torso. At the far end of the table, was the head, jammed neck first onto a large candlestick, like a head on a pike. The jaw was distended, the mouth wide open, and the cheeks bulging, like a squirrel storing nuts for the winter. There were no eyes, just black, bloody sockets.

"What's in his mouth?" Chet asked stepping around the clutter on the floor to get a closer look.

"Not sure," Rick said, his voice muffled by his shirtsleeve. "It looks like balls of newspaper…we thought it best to wait for you."

"One way to find out," Chet said, cringing inside as he extended his hand toward the macabre display.

Dr. Steinmetz stepped forward. "Allow me, Chet," he said, brandishing what looked like a pair of stainless-steel, long-nosed pliers in his hand.

He had no problem with that, and stepped back.

The doctor inserted the instrument into the mouth and clamped down on one of the crinkled, paper balls. It was packed in tight and he had to give a bit of a tug to free it from the cluster of other wadded up, paper balls that had been jammed into Conrad's mouth. This caused the candlestick to wobble and the decapitated head fell over with a whump onto the table. Two more balls were jarred loose by the impact and rolled out, one after the other.

"Good hell," Chet said.

The doc shot him a sheepish look. "Sorry." He took the wadded up newspaper from the clamps and began to open it with his hands. He set it down on the table and ironed it out with his palm. It was a page from *The Clear Creek Register.* An article written by Conrad himself, the headline all too familiar:

KILLER AT LARGE! SHERIFF DISTRACTED?

Chet reached for one of the other loose wads of paper and spread it out on the table. Another Conrad story from the paper, heavily criticizing his department.

Rick held up a third. "Another one about you, Coop," he said. "Written by Conrad, questioning your experience."

It took five more minutes to extract the rest of the crinkled, paper wads from the mouth of Conrad's decapitated head and smooth them out.

After holding up the last of them so everyone could see it, Dr. Steinmetz placed it on the stack of the others and fixed his eyes on Chet. "It would seem, every criticizing article that Mr. Fairchild ever wrote about you and your department is here, Sheriff."

"But why?" Chet said, his head swimming in an overwhelming mire of confusion. "Who would do this?"

"Someone who obviously hated Conrad," Rick offered. "A lot."

"This is more than hate," Chet said, "The dismembering, the blood and gore, the placement of the limbs, the whole ritualistic nature…it's a message."

Rick took his arm away from his nose and mouth. "Yeah, but for who? And what's with the news articles? If anyone had a reason to be upset with Conrad enough to kill him, it would be you, Coop. After all, it's been you and Kate he's been after so hard lately."

There was something about Rick's last sentence that had a kind of ominous ring to it. On some level, Chet knew there was significance to it that he should recognize, but his thought process was too rummy to be able to discern it.

Dr. Steinmetz put his hands on his hips and shook his head. "I think we have a big problem here."

Chet felt himself almost coming undone. "A problem? You mean besides the fact we're having a discussion in a man's dining room, where his head is jammed on a candlestick?"

The doctor let the little eruption pass. He folded his arms. "Chet, if you were asked, who in Clear Creek was Mr. Fairchild's biggest enemy, the one person in this town with enough motive to murder him…objectively, who would you say that person would be?"

Chet swept a hand over the grizzly scene before them. "I don't know anyone in Clear Creek who would do something like this, regardless of what Conrad had written about."

"It's you, Coop." Rick's voice was quiet, but cut through the din in his brain like the first thunderclap of an approaching storm.

A dull ache began to throb near the base of his skull. He clapped his hands behind his neck and applied pressure to the pain, as if it were a bleeding wound. He had to stop the flow…had to stop the demons of the past from spreading any further into his brain. "What are you saying exactly, Doc, that I'm the prime suspect?"

Dr. Steinmetz picked up the stack of newspaper articles. "I'm saying, that somebody sure wants you to look like the prime suspect." He dropped the papers back onto the table.

Rick stepped forward to stand next to Chet. "Well, anybody with a brain can see this is just a setup. And not even a very good one at that!"

"Well, yes of course, but…" The doctor motioned them toward the kitchen. "Let's talk about this outside where we can actually breathe," he said.

They followed him through the kitchen and outside, regrouping on the chipped and cracked cement steps that led to the front door. Chet inhaled deeply of the crisp, morning air. Being rid of the sights and smells of the carnage inside had an immediate, mind-clearing effect.

Rick nudged a loose brick by the door with his foot. "Okay, Doc, you say we have a big problem, but I say it's an obvious setup that doesn't hold even a drop of water. So what's the big problem?"

Dr. Steinmetz had one hand in the pocket of his trench coat, fiddling with his keys. "You're not going to like this, Chet." He took a deep breath, exhaled and watched the steam from his mouth dissipate. "I think you're going to have to step down…temporarily, until this all gets cleared up."

"No offense, Dr. Steinmetz," Chet said, "but that's the craziest thing I've ever heard you say. There is no way I'm stepping down." He hooked a thumb over his shoulder. "Not while there's a psycho killer, who's responsible for *that,* running loose in my town!"

"I understand how you feel, son, believe me I do, but you need to realize something here." The doctor ran a hand through his thick mustache. "Everything in that house is going to have to go into a report…everything, including those newspaper articles."

Rick kicked the loose brick hard enough to dislodge it from the wall. "Those papers don't prove shit! You know it, I know it! It's ridiculous! If Coop really was guilty, why would he do something so stupid as cut the body all up, and then incriminate himself by stuffing—"

"There's something else," the doctor cut in. "Something that complicates the issue even more."

"Like what?" Chet asked, not really wanting to hear the answer, but knowing it was unavoidable.

"You understand what doctor-patient confidentiality is, right?"
Chet nodded. "Doctors can't go blabbing about their patients to other people."

"And the only reason I can tell you now, is because the patient I'm about to tell you about—" He glanced back at the house. "—is dead. Not long ago, Conrad came to me complaining of back pain, neck pain, and headaches. He wanted me to examine him and check him out." He paused to pierce Chet with a concerned gaze. "The day after I examined him, I was visited in my office by Calvin Finch, Attorney at Law, and asked to sign a legal affidavit based on my examination."

"You're kidding," Chet mumbled.

Dr. Steinmetz breathed a heavy sigh. "Apparently, you had some kind of recent altercation with Conrad? Slammed him against the wall of his office by the neck?"

Chet cursed under his breath. If the fresh air had been doing him any good a minute ago, it was losing its potency. He felt the throb in his head returning with each beat of his heart.

"I'll take that as a yes," the doctor said. "What you need to understand, is that Conrad had just filed a major lawsuit against you, the department, and the county. I was going to have to testify against you when it came to court. I wanted to warn you, but I was legally bound to silence. It is…or I guess *was* just a matter of time before you were served."

Chet battled against the sudden urge to put his fist into the side of the house, even if it meant destroying all the bones in his hand on the brick surface.

"Do you see what I'm getting at here?" Dr. Steinmetz asked. "As outrageous as it sounds, you are the prime suspect in this."

Rick began shaking his head, muttering and cursing under his breath.

Chet couldn't believe what the man was saying. "Well, I didn't know about any lawsuit for starters—"

"Do you think anybody is really going to believe that?"

"There's no hard evidence!" Chet said, his voice cracking. "It's all circumstantial!" He took a deep breath and tried to calm down. "Doc, I'm being set up here, it's obvious."

"Well, obviously," Dr. Steinmetz said, "but you can't continue to function as a sheriff and investigate a murder in which you are a suspect. You must recuse yourself until an investigation can be completed."

As much as he hated to admit it, the doctor was right. "I don't believe this."

Doctor Steinmetz placed a comforting hand on Chet's shoulder. "Look, I doubt it will be for very long. These crimes can't continue to go on without the killer making a mistake somewhere. Chances are, there's evidence right here in this crime scene that points to the killer's identity."

"And in the meantime…who takes over for me? Rick all by himself?"

"Hey," Rick butted in, "if I wanted to be sheriff, I woulda ran for the office a long time ago. Thanks, but no thanks."

The doctor continued as if he hadn't heard, "Rick is more than qualified to fill in for you while you are gone, and as county coroner, I have the authority to help out with the investigation. You've already deputized Porter Thomas as a reserve deputy. You might want to make him temporarily full time, and possibly deputize one more person— either as a reserve or full time. That can be left up to Rick, depending on how comfortable he feels with all of this."

Chet nodded. It was a good plan…well thought out. Harold Steinmetz was a wise, sensible man. There was no arguing with his rationale, but he found himself unable to actually face the reality of letting go on this one. The image of Daniel Miller's face, his arrogant, dead, black eyes smiling in victory, flashed into his mind. He spun on his heel to head back into Conrad's house.

The doctor clapped a hand on his shoulder, causing him to turn slightly. "Whoa," he said, like he was reigning in one of his horses. "Where do you think you're going, son?"

Chet tried to shrug the hand off casually, but felt the doctor's fingers tighten up on his coat. "Like you said, there might be evidence in there. Maybe if I do a real thorough search—"

"You can't go back in there, you'll compromise the investigation."

"I haven't stepped down yet, Doc. Hell, I don't even know if I will."

His leather coat squeaked as the fingers tightened on it. Steinmetz let out a heavy sigh. Chet turned back toward him, doing his best to remain calm, keeping his voice as neutral and smooth as possible. "The last time I checked, I was still the sheriff around here. Now, please take your hand off of my jacket, so I can go do my job—what I was elected by the people of Clear Creek County to do."

The older man drilled him with an intense yet sympathetic gaze, like a reluctant father who was about to deliver a good spanking to one of his children —not because he wanted to, but because he *had* to. It was a *this is going to hurt me a lot more than it hurts you* kind of look. "Don't make me do this, Chet."

Chet turned to fully face him. "Do what?" he said, through clamped teeth.

Dr. Steinmetz released his hold on Chet's jacket. A look of sadness tinged with a bit of fear swept across his face. He took a step back. Chet was angry and frustrated, but he hadn't meant to take it out on the good doctor, a lifelong friend. Feelings of guilt and remorse bubbled up. But dammit, how was he supposed to just let go? Walk away? How was he supposed to just let Daniel win?

That reluctant parent look came back into the doctor's eyes. "Chet, as county coroner, I have the authority to relieve you of your position, if I see a cause to do so."

"What? That's ridiculous! I appointed you to the position in the first place, how can that be? I'm an elected official, it's not like you can just *fire* me." He shot a desperate look at his deputy.

Rick seemed to be struggling to make eye contact with him. "It's true, Coop. In extreme cases, the county coroner has the authority."

Chet turned back to the doctor. "So if I understand you correctly: what you're saying is, either I step down voluntarily—"

Dr. Steinmetz interrupted, "I'm saying, that it would be the wise thing to do in this situation, Chet. Step down, *voluntarily.*"

Or be relieved of his duty. Chet had no problem reading between the lines. The doctor was doing his best to avoid that situation. He turned back to Rick. "What do you think?"

The lawman folded his arms, shook his head, and grimaced. "I hate to say it Coop, but Dr. Steinmetz has a point here." He nodded toward the house. "Whoever did this was smart. I mean with all the blood and guts, and the hacking off of limbs and what not. When word of this breaks, it's going to be a sensation. It's going to sweep across the county and beyond, placing you right direct in the spotlight." He sighed. "As your friend this is hard to say, but you need to be ready for it." He paused a moment to wipe a hand across his face. "Some people are going to wonder if you really didn't kill Conrad and then butcher him up like that."

"That's ridiculous," Chet argued, "anyone that knows me, knows that I would never do something like this."

"When people hear the facts: The ongoing feud with Conrad, your altercation with him, the lawsuit, the grizzly crime scene, complete with newspaper articles jammed down Conrad's mouth…" He seemed to stop short, unwilling to go on.

"What is it, Rick? You were going to say something else."

The deputy gave Dr. Steinmetz a sideways glance, as if asking the doctor to bail him out of a tough spot.

Chet took a step closer to Rick and put both hands on his shoulders. "Like you said, Rick: you're my friend. You can tell me. What else were you going to say?"

The deputy took a deep breath and exhaled. "Some people are going to think you snapped." He winced as he said the words. "They're going to think that… the war made you…. Dammit Coop, I don't even know how to put it across without sounding like a big jackass!"

"They're going to think that what I went through overseas made me unstable and that I eventually snapped and butchered Conrad."

"I'm just sayin' that *some* people are probably going to say that." He looked down at the ground and kicked at the brick he had knocked loose earlier.

A numbness began to creep up through him and he felt a strange detachment, a cold distance separating himself from everything he cared about. It was like watching a badly written movie, one where you could care less how it ends or what happens to the main character, except that *he* was the main character. "Alright," he said, unpinning the metal badge from his shirt and extending it to Rick. "Looks like you're the man in charge now…Sheriff."

Rick looked down at Chet's extended palm, the silver badge glinting dully under the noon sun, and shook his head. "That's not necessary, and don't call me, *sheriff.* I'm just fillin' in while you're gone…like you was going on a vacation or something." He snapped his fingers. "As a matter of fact, that's exactly what you should do! Just disappear for a while. You and Kate can take a road trip up north and—"

"How would that look, Rick?" Chet said. He let his badge slide into the front pocket of his pants. "The prime suspect in a murder, skipping town?"

Rick scratched at his scalp. "Yeah, I suppose you're right about that."

Chet stepped off the cement stairs onto the grass. "I'll drop my patrol car off at the station and walk home." He started walking.

"Coop," Rick said, his voice full of pity and concern.

"Don't worry, I'll be okay," he said, without turning or slowing. Then, as an afterthought, he added, "Just let me know as soon as you nail that son of a bitch."

Chet slammed himself into his patrol rig and smacked the steering wheel with the palm of his hand. It felt good, so he smacked it two more times while spewing profanities he hadn't uttered since his days of motivating young Marines under his command.

He cranked the engine to life and let it warm up as he watched Rick and the doctor vanish through the doorway, back into the blood-soaked house. It would no doubt be a long day for Deputy Shelton: photos needed to be made, a complete sweep of the property, gathering of evidence, interviewing neighbors, notifying family, removal of the body—what was left of it—and dealing with the press.

The press: they would come clamoring for him as well; not just from Clear Creek, but from towns all over the state. An army of bloodsucking leeches, camped out on his front lawn, squirming and pressing against each other, vying for the big scoop.

The thought made him sick. He rammed the car into gear and gunned the gas. The tires chirped briefly on the asphalt as the Chevy lurched into the street, leaving a ghostly, white plume of exhaust in its wake.

As he drove through town, random people waved, smiled or nodded at him. The people were about their daily business, unaware that just a few blocks away a member of their society, one of the flock, lay butchered and dismembered in his own home. A wolf had come preying in the night and had killed. Those who were expected to watch over the flock and protect it from such slaughter had failed. Each wave or smile directed at him filled Chet's heart with shame and self-loathing.

The wolf was still out there, still hunting…waiting. Waiting for the right time until he would strike again and pull down another victim. And what could Chet do now to stop it? Nothing. Nothing but trust in others to do the job, to play the roll of the sheepdog.

He parked the car in its usual place and went inside to drop off the keys. The office was quiet, cold, almost unwelcoming, like he had just stepped through a portal into an alien dimension. He dropped his keyring on Rick's desk and it clanged with the finality of a judge's gavel. *May God have mercy on your soul...*

Shaking the thought, he gave his desk a quick once over, making sure he wasn't leaving anything behind that he would need or want. He had purchased all the equipment on his duty belt with his own money, so he considered those items as his. Finding himself at the door, he breathed a heavy sigh and pushed it open.

As he walked down the street, he was forced to endure several more smiles and other various greetings. Word wasn't out yet; people still thought he was their trusted sheriff. So far, he hadn't detected the type of apprehension, suspicion, or hidden whispers that a murder suspect might expect. That would be changing soon. This was most likely the last peaceful stroll he would take through his hometown for a long time...if not forever.

Depression seeped through him like a slow moving poison, penetrating as it sought out all of the hollow and empty spaces, until it had filled him in like a thick, heavy grout. Thoughts of permanently resigning crossed his mind more than once. He could just work a regular nine to five at the quarry or the mill. Work hard all day, come home to a reclining chair and a couple cold beers every night, holidays and weekends off, no hacked up dead bodies to deal with, no psycho killers to catch...a normal life, like everyone else.

A normal life seemed nice as he first rolled it around in his brain, but for some reason, the longer he thought about it, the more depressed he became. He loved being sheriff. He loved working with and for the people, the fresh, day to day challenges—you never knew what was going to happen in a day's work—to see justice applied and mercy bestowed, to hold the trust and confidence of the people, to serve and to protect. Now it was all gone. Just like that. With the flick of a killer's knife it had all been carved away from him.

He'd left the office with the intention of going home. In fact, he had every intention of spending the rest of the day decimating his supply of beer. Instead, he now found himself standing on the sidewalk outside of the elementary school. He didn't remember even making the conscious decision to come here. It was like his feet had made the choice for him, acting under their own volition while he had been preoccupied with wallowing in self-pity.

Kate's office window was open and the blinds pulled up. It occurred to him that the afternoon *had* warmed up considerably, but he had not felt it, even wrapped up in his thick bomber's jacket. For him, the sun overhead held no warmth. It seemed pale, dull, and sick. The light breeze in the air carried with it the gnawing of winter's chill.

The Summoning

He could hear the distant *tap, tap, tapping* of her typewriter issuing out of the open window. In his mind's eye he could picture her slender, graceful fingers stroking the keys with practiced and fluent efficiency. Periodically, the typing would cease and her head, shrouded in dark ringlets and curls, would suddenly appear in the window frame as she leaned forward to inspect her handiwork. Then her head would vanish back out of sight and the staccato sounds would resume, *tap, tap, tap.*

He just stood and watched. What was he doing here? Why had he come here instead of going home? The answer came to him like a slap in the face. He needed her. He was wounded, hurting, and he needed the kind of comfort you don't get out of a bottle. The kind of comfort he knew only she could provide him.

He took a dozen or so steps down the sidewalk that led to the front door of the school. He stopped. What was he thinking, that he could just barge into Kate's office, broken and hurting, expecting her to make it all better? As much as he felt he needed her right now, the thought of her seeing him like this was too much.

She deserved better. She had been through much worse than he had, but lately it seemed like it was her that was providing all the emotional strength in their relationship.

She'd come to Clear Creek in an attempt to escape the horror of what had happened to her in her hometown. But instead of escape, she had found herself strapped with a whole new burden. Him.

It occurred to him that it had been extremely selfish of him to pursue a romance with the poor girl. The pain she must be in! And yet, the focus always seemed to be on him. Not that he had meant for it to be that way. Certainly not! They were both survivors of terrible things, the haunting memories of which were constantly threatening to pull them down into a dark pit of misery. So they clung to one another because they could understand the other's pain.

It was that mutual familiarity with pain and suffering that brought a level of intimacy to their relationship. An intimacy he'd never experienced before with any other person. But there had to be more than that to a relationship. A relationship had to be built on much more than just a shared understanding of one another's suffering. They had to be more to each other than just a buffer against the nightmares and the memories.

He loved her, he was sure he did. Or was it just the way she made him feel that he was in love with? Was he just using her, like a bottle of booze, to dull the senses and chase away the demons? The thought terrified him. She deserved to be loved, cherished, taken care of…not used like some bottle of pain pills. Maybe he did truly love her, but if he were honest with himself, could he say that he wasn't also using her, draining her like some kind of parasite for his own emotional needs?

The typing stopped and the dark curls appeared again, leaning into the frame of the window. At this distance he could see her face: the smooth cheekbones tinted with a hint of red blush, the perky, upturned nose, and the full lips, coated in a light pink shade of lipstick. She was gnawing on a pencil—a habit that had become an endearing little trait to him, of late. She was a tough and headstrong girl, but right then, as he watched her chewing on that pencil—undoubtedly a habit formed and carried over from childhood—he thought she looked so very fragile, so very delicate.

A swelling gush of love flowed through him and it was all he could do to restrain himself from sprinting to her, gathering her up in his arms, and then maybe the two of them could skip town. Leave and start fresh, somewhere new, never to return.

It was wishful thinking only. He knew better than to run from his problems. You had to stand up to your troubles and your fears or, just like a bully, they would chase you for the rest of your life.

He loved her, but did he love her enough to walk away from her, set her free for her own good? If he truly did love her, then he would do the selfless thing, the right thing for her, not for him.

Her head disappeared again, moving out of the window frame, the rhythmic clattering of the typewriter picking back up.

He stuffed his hands into his coat and turned his back on Kate's open window…her open arms and warm embrace. "Do the right thing," he said quietly to himself, as he walked away. "Do it for her."

CHAPTER 36

Kate smacked the flat of her hand repeatedly on the smooth surface of the wooden door. "Chet Cooper!" she called for probably the umpteenth time. "Chet, you open this door this instant!" She knew he was in there and continued to berate the door.

Three days! It had been three days now since Conrad Fairchild had been found murdered and the whole town turned upside down. Three days Chet had been shut up in his tiny rental home, refusing to come out or even answer his phone. Figuring that he would be devastated by the latest events, she had at first tried to give him his space. She didn't really blame him for not answering his phone—it had probably been ringing off the hook with reporters.

And no wonder. Word had spread quickly about Conrad's hideous murder and the strange macabre nature of the crime scene. Of course, not all of the gruesome details had been released to the public, but word that the sheriff had stepped down from his post had every tongue within a hundred miles wagging. The rumor was that he was somehow implicated in the crime. And so the wild speculations had begun: *Why, if anyone had a motive to kill Conrad Fairchild, it'd be Sheriff Cooper.*

The rumors and the seeming willingness of the townsfolk to throw the man over a cliff without so much as an afterthought made her sick. It dredged up awful memories of her own, how her town had turned on her like a pack of hyenas, bloodthirsty and eager. When she was a little girl, her father had gone on an African hunting safari with a few of his wealthier clients. He had once told her about hyenas.

Cowards by nature, hyenas first circle the wounded prey. Staying just beyond his reach, they gauge their victim's strength while waiting for their numbers to increase until the odds are overwhelmingly in their favor. Then, they dart in and dart out, always attacking from the back, teeth snapping on exposed flesh, weakening their prey with each flash of their teeth until the prey finally succumbs. Then the whole pack rushes in for the final kill, ripping the victim apart in a violent free-for-all.

The predators were only circling Chet at the moment, but very soon the first flesh rending attacks would begin—probably beginning with the newspaper as soon as it felt like the numbers were on their side. She understood his desire to be locked away from it all, but it wasn't fair for him to shut her out like this. Not *her* of all people, not after everything!

"Chet..." Her voice cracked with a sob. She slapped the door one more time. She left her arm there and leaned up against it, putting her weight on the door. "I'm not leaving until you at least talk to me, you hear?"

The muffled sound of shuffling feet reached her ears followed by the snick of the deadbolt being worked. She took one step back, blinking her eyes against the excess moisture that had suddenly accumulated in them.

The door swung inward, revealing Chet's tall frame with the lean muscles and the broad shoulders. Only, the shoulders seemed to sag somewhat, giving his whole countenance a stooped and defeated appearance.

Her eyes went directly to his. They were red, from lack of sleep no doubt, and the skin around them was puffy and scoured raw. A dim caul seemed to preside where, usually, burned a fierce and indomitable intellect. It scared her, and she couldn't help but suck in a small gasp. She hoped it had gone unnoticed.

"I wish you hadn't come over here," he said, his voice a dry croak.

She felt her anger return, overcoming the initial shock of seeing her knight in shining armor slumping in defeat. She tossed her head, flipping a stray lock of hair from her eyes, and thrust out her chin. "Well, Chet Cooper, you really didn't give me much of a choice, now did you? How long were you planning on letting me twist in the wind? Another day...a week?"

He breathed out a heavy sigh, the pungent odor of beer heavy on his breath. "I'm sorry, Kate, it's just that...well, look at me...I'm a wreck. I didn't want you to see me like this."

She was pretty sure she didn't really want to see him like this either. From the looks of the stubble bristling on his face and his greasy, disheveled hair, he hadn't showered or bathed in at least two days...probably three.

She stopped herself short of asking if he was okay. The answer to that was obvious. "Are you drunk?" she asked instead.

"I don't think so," he answered. "Not very anyway."

"Were you sleeping?"

"Sort of, I guess. Not really what I would call sleep though."

His eyes were blue orbs of ice giving credence to her sense of a cold detachment coming from him. The cursed wall that she had been chipping away at now for weeks, ripping out great blocky chunks of it in order to gain precious access to this man, had been reconstructed and fortified. Even higher and thicker than before.

"You wanna come in?" he asked, stepping aside.

The house was dark and full of intertwining shadows of gloom. The thought of him just in there, by himself, hurting, drinking.... Albert had been drunk too, that day at the pond. "I don't think that's a good idea," she said, taking a step back.

"I would never hurt you," he said. "You have to know, Kate. I would never —"

"But you *are* hurting me," she interjected. "It's killing me to see you like this, Chet!" Two large tears straggled out from the corner of each of her eyes. She let them run down her cheeks unheeded.

A wave of anguish passed over his face. "Kate, I—"

"You are supposed to be my strength, don't you understand? My rock." More tears. "But a little trouble comes your way, and you just fold up and collapse like a cheap lawn chair? That isn't you, Chet, I know it! Where's the man that led men into battle? Where's Sheriff Cooper? Where's the man I fell in love with?"

His eyes had gone from balls of ice to shimmering pools of pain. His lips were moving but no words were coming out of them. Finally, he said, "I don't think I'm the man that you need me to be, Kate. I've been able to pull off the act pretty good up till now I guess, but the truth is, I'm broken and I don't know if there's any fixing me."

A cold, jagged stone formed in the center of her heart and was migrating up into her throat; it was getting difficult to breathe. "I'm not exactly all put together perfectly either, in case you haven't noticed. That's why we work, why we're so good together."

"You deserve so much more than me." He was looking down at the floor. "You would be better off—"

"Shut up!" she hissed, crossing her arms beneath her breasts. "Just shut up! If you think I'm going to stand here for one more minute and listen to a...a man who's drunk and needs a bath, try to break up with me as he wallows in his own self-pity, you've got another thing coming, buster!"

"I'm serious, Kate," he said, "I'm no good for you. And I'm not drunk."

"I could have left, Chet...I wanted to leave, but I stayed. Do you want to know why?"

He didn't say anything, just lowered his eyes more—if that was even possible.

"I stayed for you…I stayed for us, because I believed in us. I thought that between the two of us, we could turn our weaknesses into strengths. I'm a better person for having known you and I would hope that you would say the same about me." More tears came to streak down her cheeks.

He was shaking his head slowly back and forth.

She reached a hand and cupped his chin with it, forcing his eyes to meet her gaze. "Are you going to stand here and say that I was wrong, that it was all a big mistake? Because if that's how you feel…" She swallowed back a huge lump in her throat that was trying to climb right up into her mouth. "Because if that's how you feel, then I'm on the next train out of here. Tomorrow morning."

A glimmer of shock and pain flickered in his glassy eyes. "I don't even know what to say," he said, his voice a scratchy whisper. "You're the best thing that's ever happened to me, Kate…by a good long shot. But I don't think I'm right for you. I'm afraid that you would never be as happy with me as you might be with someone else…someone with more to offer."

She narrowed her eyes. "You know, I just can't do this with you, Chet. I'm not going to stand here and beg you. You either love me enough to hang onto me, or you don't. It's no more complicated than that." She used her coat sleeve to wipe away the tears running down her face, swallowed back the big lump, and fought to gain control over the water works.

"So, I'm going to make things real easy for you. Tomorrow morning, the first train out of Clear Creek departs at seven-thirty, and I intend to be on it. Then, I'll be out of your life for good and we can both move on, in whatever way we can."

He opened his mouth to reply.

She cut him off. "Don't say another word, not right now…not like this. You have the rest of today and tonight to sober up and think good and hard about what you want—and hopefully take a shower and shave. Then, if you don't want me to get on that train, you have until tomorrow morning."

She turned and stepped smartly off his stoop, took two more steps, and then turned back to face him. She employed every ounce of her faculties and will power to hold back the sobs, chokes, and tears assailing her. "If I don't see you between now and tomorrow morning, then take one last look, Chet Cooper, and know that I *did* love you."

She held his gaze for a brief moment and offered him what could be her last smile. "Goodbye," she said, then turned on her heel and strode away. She could feel his eyes on her back. She hoped that he couldn't see the shaking of her shoulders as she lost the battle with her emotions and the sobbing overtook her at last.

She could only hope and pray that the fool man would come around to his senses. Before it was too late.

HE WATCHED AS THE LIGHT OF HIS LIFE walked away, her black heels echoing sharply on the pavement with the finality of hammer strikes, pounding nails into the coffin of his newfound happiness.

The desire to chase after her was almost beyond his control to resist. He even made it a few steps out the door before common sense brought him to a halt. Everything was crashing down all around him: his career, his beloved town, his self-worth, his relationship with Kate. In one fell swoop, it had all been taken from him and his entire life seemed to have been reduced to no more than a pile of rubble, like the bombed out streets of London he had seen on the newsreels during the war.

But at least in those newsreels, one could always see the people of London in and amongst the destruction gathering their belongings, salvaging what could be saved, cleaning up, helping their neighbors. But not so with him. The destruction of his life had nobody picking up the pieces in order to move on. In his heart, the rubble lay in blackened, smoldering heaps and the task of salvaging any kind of order from the chaos seemed insurmountable.

He shuffled back into his house and closed the door, shutting out the light of the day. He thought he could still hear Kate's footsteps echoing faintly. It was probably just in his head—it probably always would be.

Darkness. An impenetrable, oily darkness swallowed him whole and he collapsed onto the floor, curling up into the fetal position. Kate's footsteps were thunderclaps in his brain, *click, clack, click*.... The image of her standing on his walkway, offering a final half-hearted smile, before turning and leaving, burned in his brain like a brand.

Like the bursting of a great reservoir, everything came rushing all at once. He audibly groaned from the intensity of the pain that came crashing against him as it utterly overpowered and washed away all of his carefully constructed defenses.

Rendered as no more than a sobbing and convulsing wretch, he finally surrendered to the blackness and the demons that seemed to swirl around in it.

There would be no more running, no more hiding. For good or for bad, there would be a reckoning of himself, his life, his choices…everything.

Despair encompassed his soul until he felt he would drown in it, except for one lifeline echoing through the darkness: *click, clack, click, clack.* He reached out to the sound as if he could literally grasp it, embrace it, and it would keep him afloat.

He held on with all of his strength and, when things seemed to be at their darkest, he could hear himself calling out her name.

After an indiscernible length of time, the darkness began to slowly recede and he realized that it would pass. Somehow, he had made it through. Although he had survived, he knew it was just one battle in a war that he would probably have to fight his entire life.

He pulled himself off the floor and fell onto the nearby couch, his head throbbing—the early onset of a slight hangover. He supposed he had been drunk after all. Kate had been right.

Kate. He could still hear her fading footsteps echoing in his mind. He had let her go, let her walk away. And why shouldn't he have? She was better off without him. After today, it was more obvious to him than ever. Pangs of remorse prickled at his heart nonetheless. Was he really doing the right thing?

A slight rap of knuckles on his front door made him flinch. A ray of sudden hopefulness slanted through him. Maybe she had changed her mind and come back! "Yeah," he called out, his voice a hoarse rasp.

"Coop?" The door swung inward, a widening bar of afternoon sunlight following behind, sending the gloomy shadows scurrying down the hall and around the corners.

He blinked and squinted his eyes against the light as Rick Shelton took a few tentative steps into the living room. The man placed his hands on his hips and gave the room an appraising scan before letting his eyes settle on Chet. His eyes reflected a mixture of disappointment and pity with a touch of anger. Chet felt himself growing defensive, perhaps even a bit angry himself.

Finally Rick opened his mouth and said, "What the hell, Coop?"

Chet shrugged his shoulders. What was he supposed to say?

Rick walked over to the telephone hanging on the wall that separated the kitchen from the living room. He picked up the receiver, held it to his ear, and then replaced it back on the hook. "Well, it looks like the your phone ain't broke after all." He paused a moment, leaning one shoulder against the wall and pinning Chet down with his gaze. "So, why ain't ya been answering when I call then?"

Chet leaned forward with his elbows on his knees. "Just needed some time alone, I guess…clear my head, work through things."

Rick folded his arms across his chest. "Is that right? Well, from what I hear, you've managed to about work your way through the best thing that's probably ever happened to you. Or ever will."

"You talked to Kate?"

He nodded, his mouth pulled into a glum frown. "She wanted to know if I could give her a ride to the train station tomorrow morning."

She wasn't bluffing then, not that he ever believed for one second that she was, but he had certainly been holding out the hope.

"So, what's the problem, you just decided you don't like her anymore, or what?"

Chet looked down at his hands hanging limply from his knees. "I love her, Rick. I love her, and that's why I have to let her go."

"That don't make any sense at all."

"I'm no good for her. She deserves to be with someone who can give her everything she needs. I'm not that man. I'm afraid I would only end up being a constant burden to her. Because of my past—"

"What a load of crap!"

Chet looked up at Rick in surprise.

The deputy hooked his thumbs into his duty belt and came to stand over him, like a father scolding a child. "Listen, you were fine, you and Kate, until this Conrad mess popped up. Now I get it. You're shaken up by what's been going on around here lately.

"You're depressed and your self confidence has been rattled big time. It's understandable that a guy would get to feeling down, and even sorry for himself. I can't say I blame you, but you've gotta figure out how to pull yourself out of this—" He looked around the room. "—whatever *this* is, and get back with the program."

Chet nodded slowly, trying to be respectful, trying not to explode in a rage. Rick was probably his best friend, but the guy had no idea what he was going through. If he could experience, for five minutes, the darkness that always lurked just beyond the shadows of his thoughts, and the seemingly constant battle to keep it there, he would know better. It was not a simple matter of just pulling yourself out of it and *getting with the program.*

Rick took a seat on the couch next to him and placed a hand on his shoulder. Then, as if he had been listening to his thoughts, he said, "Chet, I know you've seen things and experienced things that an old country boy like myself can't possibly understand. That goes for most people. Sure, we hear the stories, see the photos, watch the movies, but there's no way most folks will ever fully understand what you go through every day just to maintain." He paused and gave Chet's shoulder a reassuring squeeze. "That's why you can't let her go, Coop. Kate gets it. Somehow, that girl has the ability to understand you. You're never going to find another one like her.

"And she needs you too. I know you think you're doing the right thing for her sake, but trust me. Trust someone who's standing back far enough to see the forest; she needs you more than you know. I don't know what special bond the two of you share, but I'm here to tell ya, it doesn't happen like that every day. Letting her walk away will be the worst decision of your life. For you…and for her."

Rick slipped his hand off of Chet's shoulder, and both men sat in silence; it was a rare moment of seriousness and sobriety from the ever jocular deputy. His friend's words were sinking into him, embedding into the fabric and fibers of his being. *She needs you more than you know….* He hadn't thought of it that way. She was the strong one, the one who would go on and be fine without him— better without him.

But Rick was right: they did share a unique bond. They had hit it off from the very get go, and things had only gotten better between them since. Had he been so focused on how she was making him feel, and how much she was changing things for him, that he had failed to realize that maybe, just maybe he might have been having the same effect on her.

A realization began to slowly dawn on him like the dissipation of heavy storm clouds as the heat of the sun's rays burned through them. His pulse kicked up a notch as that realization formed into an actual, palpable thought: *Don't let her go!* And he would not! The darkness in his heart began to lift away as the thought solidified and he felt his will strengthening around it.

Suddenly, Rick slapped him on the back, smiling his typical, toothy grin. "Besides," he said, "did I happen to mention that she's a hell of a looker?" He followed up with a slap to his knee and a big guffaw.

Chet laughed. It was a real laugh from a real place inside him. It almost surprised him that he had it in him to do so.

"I mean," Rick said, still chuckling, "Only an idiot would let a catch like that get away, and I know you ain't no idiot!"

Chet turned and clapped a hand on his friend's back. "You're right, Rick. You are absolutely right."

Rick grinned. "Of course I am. So, you want me to give you a ride over to her place, so you can get down on your lousy knees and beg for her forgiveness?"

"Uh…no."

"You sure? 'Cause I'd totally be willing to do that for ya. I could even give you some pointers on proper groveling techniques on the way over."

"Oh, I'm sure you could, Rick, I'm sure you could. And I'm guessing you'd be sticking around for the show as well."

Rick shrugged his shoulders in mock innocence. "You gotta admit, it's probably gonna be a heck of a show."

"Well, I hate to disappoint you, but nobody's going to be groveling on their knees."

"Ha!" Rick slapped his knee again and stood up. "You still have a lot to learn about women!" He nodded and his eyes narrowed into knowing slits. "If a woman wants you on your knees…she usually finds a way to get you there."

"Noted," Chet said, with a chuckle and got to his feet. A sudden wave of gratitude hit him, followed by another wave of shame. "Look, Rick, I'm sorry you had to come over here and see me like this, but I'm glad you did. I think you just might have saved my life. Thank you."

"Don't worry about it. Just make sure you don't let that girl slip away now."

"I won't. In fact, I was just thinking, I'll surprise her in the morning by being the one who shows up to take her to the train station."

"You're gonna wait till morning?"

"That'll give me time to…clean myself up, get some sleep—"

"Work on your groveling techniques?"

Chet let out an exasperated sigh.

"Rick laughed out load and started walking for the front door. "I guess I better get going. Lots to do."

Chet followed him. "I know that, technically, you can't talk to me about the case, but can you tell me anything about how the investigation is going? Do you think I'll be back on the job soon?"

Rick stopped and seemed to be pondering what he could or could not say, his brow furrowing into large folds. Finally, he said, "Things are actually moving along pretty quick. Doctor Steinmetz and I have been working things pretty much around the clock between the two of us. Things are looking good on your behalf, Coop. You were framed, and it was a sloppy, last-minute job. We just need to button down a few things—just some formalities and paperwork—and you'll be back with us in a matter of no time. You just have to be a little patient."

"Good to know," Chet said, and then dropped his voice down to a whisper, "Any evidence pointing to Daniel Miller? Anything at all?"

The deputy shook his head. "No, there's nothing, but I'll still bet you dollars to donuts it was him. If anyone had motive to frame you, it would be the killer. And why would he do that, especially so hastily? Because he felt pressured… like he had no choice but to act, and act now."

Chet nodded. "He was the one we were focusing on so hard. This was his retaliation for our pressure on him."

"Exactly right, but what confuses me," Rick scratched at his salt and pepper hair, "is he had to know that this little frame job wouldn't cut it, that you'd be back in a matter of a short time. So, why did he bother?"

"Maybe he's just trying to buy time."

"Time for what?"

A story from Reverend Gannon's confession materialized in Chet's mind. The one about the ceremony, where the reverend had offered up his wife as a vessel to the demon. It was supposedly a grand and final act that would have greatly empowered the demon. It had actually been the cause of the destruction of the town of Salem. Could Daniel be planning something similar? Is that all he needed, just a little more time?

"I don't know," he said, "but you'd best keep your eye on that kid."

"I will," Rick said, stepping outside into the waning light of the day. "Good luck with Kate, all joking aside."

"Thanks."

Chet watched his deputy and friend climb into his patrol rig, start it up, and drive away, throwing up a friendly salute. He returned the salute and went inside. He opened up all of the drapes, allowing the golden sunlight to bathe the small house in warm and promising light.

His mind went to Kate and the newborn hope for the future that might exist for them. He got down on the floor and started cranking out push ups. Time to get cleaned up.

CHAPTER 37

It wasn't the best laid plan and he had been forced to execute it hastily, but it had accomplished what he needed it to; Sheriff Cooper was now out of the picture—at least for a little while. That still left Deputy Shelton in play. The man had done his share of sniffing around, but Daniel wasn't too worried about him. The cop was simply out of time…he would never piece the puzzle together fast enough to stop the events that had already been set into motion.

So, let the old hound sniff and sniff all he wanted. And if by some miracle he did manage to get too close, Daniel would simply deal with him, like he had everyone else who had gotten in the way. He even had further plans for Sheriff Cooper—not now…but later. Later, when an all out victory was ensured and the sheriff's uncanny luck and survival instincts would be a non-factor. This thought made him smile.

In his bedroom, the last slanting rays of the day were glinting off the window as the sun squatted stubbornly on the horizon, refusing to sink any further, taunting him with its accursed brilliance. He had rolled his rug up, revealing the intricate pattern of symbols and pictographs that he had drawn on his hardwood floor weeks before.

He knelt in its center, concentrating and meditating on the moment and the task to come. On the floor, between his knees, his own hand print glared up at him, stamped in his own dried blood. He turned his left hand over and looked at the palm where he had cut it that night, a deep and biting gash. No evidence of the wound remained, not even a faint scar. It was as if it had never happened. The healing had been extremely quick he recalled. He took that as a sign, a good omen to be sure.

The fading light in his room told him that the sun was indeed sinking, as badly as it seemed to be fighting to stay up. The sure and steady rotation of the planet was something that was out of the sun's power to control. So it was, that even that mighty, blazing star, the center and the driving force of the solar system, would eventually succumb, and give way to the darkness.

Closing his eyes, he tried to concentrate and force his mind to relax by practicing some deep and slow breathing. It was somewhat effective, but the reality was, he was nervous. This was it, the culmination of everything he had worked for, sacrificed for…sold his soul for. He now either stood on the cusp of success or was teetering on the brink of failure, and the next several hours would prove which one it was to be.

With a giant mental shove, he pushed the idea of failure far from his mind, choosing instead to focus on the sweetness of success and the rewards that would soon be his: power, strength, respect, even love and adoration. His mistress, finally free to love him, to be with him.

No more loneliness, no more rejection, no more sad and empty days feeling like an exile, banished to wander, fearful and rejected in the outer shadows of a supposed *polite society*. Couldn't they have seen that all he had ever wanted from them was some semblance of acceptance?

He had tried, hadn't he? Tried damn hard to fit into the the tightly woven fabric of their association, bending and weaving himself, conforming, trying his best to follow their unwritten, unspoken rules. But utter rejection and humiliation had been the only reward for his efforts. Rejection: cold, cruel, and uncompromising.

That had all changed the day he heard *Her* voice in his head. At the time, he hadn't known who she was or where the voice had come from, but it had been a voice of friendship, a voice of acceptance and compassion. He realized now that he had probably fallen in love with her at that very moment, had become bound to her.

The nervous feeling began to fade as he pondered these things. His fate was irrevocably bound to her. He had crossed lines, passed over into territory from which one did not simply return. There was no going back. That door had slammed shut the day he had strangled Levi Henderson in the woods.

A burst of rage flared up in his breast. Why would he want to go back? Go back to what? Levi Henderson hadn't been the only one to die that day; the old Daniel Miller had perished at the same time. And good riddance! He would gladly welcome death rather than have to go back to the way things were.

A cool calmness came over him. There was no need to dwell on death and the way things used to be. He had actually been reborn in a sense. The old Daniel was hardly even a memory anymore. He didn't have to hope for success, or even look for it. He would make his own success. He could make it because he was willing to do what was necessary for it. He was willing to go to lengths and places that most people weren't.

That was why *She* had selected him in the first place. She had seen the potential in him, she had been willing to take a chance on him during a time when he had given up on himself, given up on life. She had saved him. He owed her this much at least.

At last, the final rays of the dying sun faded to twilight, leaving his room shrouded in a comfortable darkness. A heavy, sundry aroma of spices, frying meat, and baking bread reached him; dinner would be ready soon. He could hear his mother working in the kitchen, the floorboards creaking in familiar patterns beneath her feet as she moved from cupboard to stove, and back to cupboard.

Beneath the din of his mother working, he could hear the faint crackle of a news program being broadcast over the radio in the living room. In his mind's eye, he could see his father sitting in his easy chair, jeans dirty, stocking feet resting on a footstool, the newspaper spread out in front of him like a barrier, shielding him from the monotony of interaction with his wife and kid.

A wave of disgust passed through him. To think that there was a time that he craved the man's approval, would have done almost anything to gain it! He had tried out for the school football team of all things, just for the old man. He had hoped against hope that he would make the team and at last earn that coveted nod of approval. He didn't make the team, and the nod of approval never came.

A sharp pain in his hands caused him to realize he was clenching his fists so hard that his fingernails were cutting into the flesh of his palms. He forced his hands to relax and unclench. There was no need for anger now. That was the old Daniel who had so desperately needed approval from that bastard, not who he was now, who he had become.

He got to his feet and unrolled the rug back over the big pictograph, then put on a clean shirt so he could go down for dinner. He smiled in the darkness, his hand poised on the doorknob. Before this night was through…before the sun peeked over the opposite horizon, he would finally see the respect in his father's eyes that he so deserved. Respect…and fear.

CHAPTER 38

The harsh, clanging ring of the telephone jolted Rick from an impromptu nap. He hadn't meant to fall asleep, but apparently the fatigue of the last few days had taken its toll. He shot a quick glance at the clock hanging on the wall as the phone clamored. *Almost midnight! Who the heck...*

"Sheriff's office, Shelton here," he spoke into the receiver, doing his best to not sound like a man who had just been asleep.

There was the clicking sound of a line being connected. Janice Locke, the night switchboard operator, was less inclined to make conversation as her daytime counterpart.

"Rick?" It was his wife, Alice. "I just called to check up on you. Are you okay? You said you'd be home around ten, but it's—"

"Awe, dang it, sweetheart, I'm really sorry," he said. "Looks like I accidentally fell asleep right in my chair. Probably would've slept the whole night if you hadn't just called."

"That's because you're exhausted, dear. You've practically been living in the office the last three days."

"You can say that again. Between dealing with reporters, investigating a murder, and trying to get Chet his job back, I've been hopping around like a flea on a hot rock."

"How's that going, by the way?"

"I had a meeting today with Dr. Steinmetz and the prosecuting attorney..."

"Paul Gentry?"

"Yup. He's not going to pursue anything against Chet, we just gotta pretty much wait for a bit of paperwork to get finished up and he'll be back in business. Maybe even as soon as tomorrow."

"Well, that's some good news."

He could hear her breathing into the phone, imagined her sitting at their kitchen table, smooth legs protruding from her white, silky robe, bare feet perched on the rung of the chair, like two little lovebirds, her silvery, blonde hair cascading like a platinum waterfall over one shoulder…. Damn, he missed her!

"You hungry?" she asked.

"Famished."

"How about you get that skinny butt of yours home and I fry you up a ham and grilled cheese sandwich?"

"Now that's a deal I can't refuse," he said.

"And…I may have a little dessert for you after," she said, a flirtatious quality edging into her voice.

"On my way!" He made a kissing sound into the phone and then hung up. He grabbed his jacket from the back of his chair, walked over to the radio, depressed the transmit button, and spoke into the microphone. "Porter, it's Rick, you copy?"

"Yeah, I can hear ya," Porter Thomas replied.

Rick had made Porter a full time deputy on a temporary basis, the same day Conrad's murdered body had been discovered. The man was a night owl by nature, preferring the night shift, which was working out just fine for Rick.

Porter would work until three in the morning. Rick would basically be on call after that, and then work the whole day—and into the night—with Porter starting again at three in the afternoon. It was a slipshod jumble of a schedule, that had left him working too many hours. He needed at least a part-time, third man before he burned himself out. But if all went well, Chet would be back soon.

"What's going on, boss," Porter asked, his voice crackling over the radio's speaker. "I figured you'd be home by now."

"That's where I'm headed right now. Just letting you know I'll be ten-seven till morning."

"Ten-seven, as in out of service, right?"

"That's a ten-four, Porter," he replied. He was beginning to have doubts the man would ever learn the basic ten codes that they used. "It's all yours for a few hours."

"Okay…uh, ten-four then."

Slipping into his jacket, he walked over to the front door and opened it. It was snowing. The white stuff was coming down in fat, heavy flakes that fell straight to the ground, melting on impact. He thought he could actually hear the sound of the snowflakes as they whispered through the air.

The phone began to ring again. It was probably Alice calling back for some reason. He walked over to Chet's desk and snagged the phone off its hook.

"Sheriff's office," he said, listening to the familiar click of the connection being made.

Silence on the other end.

"Sheriff's office," he repeated. "Hello?"

Nothing.

"Alice?"

"I'm sorry, Deputy Shelton," said Janice, the operator, "the connection seems to have been lost. I think the other party hung up."

There was nothing crazy about that. A lot of people dialed the police on a whim, only to change their mind once they heard a voice on the other end of the line. Usually, it was just some kid messing around with the phone. Or sometimes, it would be some poor woman who had just gotten smacked around by her husband. She had every right to call and get her husband's ass thrown into jail, but all too often the abused spouse would just hang up the phone, lying to herself. *He was a good man...he would change if she could just...*

"What did they want?" he asked.

"It was a woman," Janice replied. "She was whispering and just asked for the police, so I rung you up. "I heard a man yell something," she added, "then the line just went dead."

Just as he'd thought. *Poor woman.* He was torn. The right thing to do would be to have Janice look up the identity of the caller and either go out there himself, or at least send Porter. Or he could just go home, eat his grilled cheese —probably frying this very second—and have his *dessert.* If it was really an emergency, and that woman truly wanted the police, then she'd call back. Right?

He sighed, shaking his head, almost angry with himself as he heard the words come out of his mouth, "Janice can you look up the number of the caller and tell me who it was?"

"Just a second." A brief silence as Janice referenced whatever it was she had with her. "Okay," she said, after several seconds, "Miller. Will and Trina. Thirteen-forty-one, West Crowley Road."

The hairs on the back of his neck rose up and hummed like tension wires in a stiff wind. Thoughts of sandwiches and his wife's legs broke apart and fled like the shards of a broken dinner plate scattering across the floor. "Janice, can you ring the Millers back for me?"

"Certainly," she said.

He waited.

A minute, maybe two passed in silence, then Janice was back with him. "The line at the Miller residence is dead."

"You mean they aren't answering?"

"No, the phone won't even ring. Either the receiver has been left off the hook, or the wire has been cut, or something…. The line's dead."

"Alright, thanks."

"Is there anything else?"

"Yes. Could you please call my wife, tell her something came up and I'll be home as soon as I can, but not to wait up for me?"

"I sure can," she said.

"Thanks." he hung up the phone, got back on the radio, and instructed Porter to meet up with him at Fall Creek Bridge, about a quarter mile from the Miller residence. The way his gut was talking to him, there was no way he would go out there by himself, right now, or expect the same of Porter.

He slid his Colt .38 from the holster, checked it to make sure it was loaded, and went to the door. Remembering the snow, he turned up the collar of his wool-lined denim jacket, shut off the lights, and went outside to his patrol car.

The windshield wipers fanned back and forth hypnotically, barely keeping up with the blinding snowflakes that assaulted the glass in furious, split-second attack waves, only to be swept away in an instant. The temperature must have dropped a bit since he left the office; the snow wasn't melting anymore upon contact. The flakes had grown fluffy instead of heavy, accumulating in small drifts and piles already.

He shook his head and held one hand over the warmth of the defroster vent, trying to keep his fingers warm. It wasn't even Thanksgiving yet. He wondered how severe the winter ahead would be if it was already coming at them like this.

The snow was coating everything by the time he had made it out of town and turned onto Crowley Road. The asphalt had grown slicker than snot and the rear end of his Chevy kept trying to come around on him. He needed to slow down or he'd find himself off the road for sure. It reminded him that a huge majority of people—apparently himself included—tended to forget how to drive in the snow, just over the course of a summer. The thought made him inwardly groan at the probable traffic accidents he would be dealing with in the morning, maybe even some tonight. The idiots would be out in droves.

He rounded a bend in the road, making sure to take his foot off the gas as he did so, allowing the inertia of the car to carry itself through the turn, rather than have the back tires fishtail him into a spin. As he came out of the curve, he could see a dim set of red tail lights in the distance. That would be Porter, waiting for him on the bridge.

He rolled up alongside the matching black Chevy—Scotty's former patrol rig. On the passenger seat was his winter hat, one of those fur-lined deals with the ear flaps tied up over the top that you could let down to protect the sides of your face. It had a smaller version of his deputy's shield pinned to the front of it. He fetched it with one hand, jammed it onto his head, and exited his vehicle.

As Rick approached Porter's door, the newly deputized man cranked down his window and vented a plume of tobacco smoke from his nostrils, the lit cigarette held loosely between the first two fingers on his other hand. "So, what's the story here, boss?" he asked, squinting his eyes against the snow sailing in through the open window and smacking him in the face.

"Someone from the Miller place called into the office a little bit ago, but then hung up. It's probably nothing, but I figured we'd better check into it."

Porter nodded. "Yup, probably a good idea." There was an all-business-like tenseness in his face and voice. He had been fully briefed about the whole Daniel Miller situation and didn't need to have the significance of this particular response explained to him.

Rick vigorously rubbed his hands together to create a bit of warmth. "Like I said, it's probably nothing." The words came out as small puffs of steam. "But you've got your sidearm all good to go with ya, right?"

"Yup."

"Good. Okay, let's go then," Rick said and turned back to his idling car.

He led the way, scores of snowflakes darting through the path of his headlights—there an instant, then gone—as his beams stabbed through the white flurry.

The Miller house was completely dark, illuminated only by his headlights as he neared the end of the long, dirt driveway. Not so unusual considering the lateness of the hour. Logic told him that the family was just slumbering in their beds on a cold, snowy night, but as the lights of the two cruisers angled across the house, the window panes just seemed…darker, like an oily blackness was coating them. The house gave

off a sort of *boarded up* vibe, without the boards. Vacant…abandoned.

Everything seemed so quiet, he noted as he got out of his rig. Even with both vehicles chugging in idle, there was a sense of silence that he couldn't quite explain.

Porter's footsteps crunched loudly on the snow behind him. "Seems awful quiet," he said, as if he was a gypsy mind reader.

"Yeah," Rick said, "I know I wouldn't sleep for long with these two Chevy's idling in my driveway at one in the morning."

Porter shrugged his shoulders. "Sound sleepers?"

"Maybe."

Porter squinted against the falling snow. "Course, you'd have to be dead to sleep through that."

It was about the poorest choice of words the man could've come up with and Rick almost laughed. Only a guy like Porter could say something like that and still remain oblivious to the portent of what he had said.

Rick started walking toward the front porch. "Well, I guess we're going to have to wake 'em up," he said, as if he could cancel out Porter's ominous statement by remaining positive.

Without a word, Porter followed.

The screen door wasn't latched and it wailed like a banshee when Rick pulled it open. He stopped and listened, positive that after that ear-rending screech of metal, he would hear footsteps inside—at least a light or two should have flicked on. Nothing. He glanced over his shoulder at Porter, who simply shrugged in return as he slid a cigarette between his lips and produced a match from his coat pocket.

Rick reached out and stole the match from the new deputy, shaking his head in silence. Knocking on someone's door while smoking wasn't professional. Porter nodded his understanding and slipped the cigarette back into a shirt pocket, his jaw muscles tensing somewhat. The man was nervous.

Rick gave the front door three sharp raps with his knuckles, waited several seconds, then knocked again. They waited a full minute before he knocked once more, this time speaking in a loud, firm voice, "Mr. and Mrs. Miller? Clear County Sheriffs."

There's nobody here, go away! The house seemed to be saying in a silent response.

He pounded with his fist this time, the blows echoing like thunder back at him. "Hello!" he shouted. "Police, open up!" The sound of his own raised voice caused an immediate surge of adrenaline to pump through his system that only served to accentuate his already heightened sense of foreboding. *No way anyone had slept through that!*

Still nothing.

"They either ain't home," Porter said, "or they just ain't answering the door."

Rick put his hands on his hips and took a step back. "I sure hate to do this, but we might have to break the door in."

"I thought you had to have a warrant to do that?"

"That's if we were going to go in and search the house. This is more of an emergency.... We're checking on the well-being of the family. Firefighters and paramedics have to do it all the time. This is kind of like that."

"Oh, I get it," Porter said.

"Door looks pretty sturdy though," Rick said, thinking out loud. "I doubt I could kick it in. I have a crowbar in my trunk. I could probably—"

"Is the door even locked?"

Feeling foolish, Rick placed his hand on the doorknob, slowly rotated it, and felt the latch recede from the jam, releasing the heavy, wooden door to swing inward under its own weight. The entryway lay before them, as dark and silent as a cave. "Clear County Sheriffs," he called out, but his words seemed to be swallowed up by the blackness yawning in front of him.

With his right hand snugged up on the grip of his pistol, he took one tentative step inside, and then another. Groping the wall with his left hand, his fingers came into contact with the light switch and he flicked it on, squinting his eyes against the expected flood of light. But nothing happened; he was still encompassed by an almost unnatural darkness.

He worked the switch up and down a few times, but still no light. *That's just great!* A chill crawled across his skin and the hackles on the back of his neck began to stir.

Porter, who had followed him inside—nearly on his heels—cursed softly under his breath and then said, "That ain't a good sign."

"Might just be a bad bulb," Rick said, using his thumb to free the retaining strap on his holster. "Let's move into the living room, see if we can get a lamp or something turned on in there."

It took what seemed a lifetime to fumble their way into the living room, the hard soles of their boots clomping too loudly on the wooden floor. The ludicrous image of a horse walking around in the living room came to mind. There were two lamps standing on opposite ends of the couch, and one smaller lamp sitting on an end stand, next to an overstuffed easy chair. None of the lamps were in any better working order than the entryway light.

"Wait here," Rick whispered, "I've got a lantern in my car, be right back."

"*You* wait here," Porter said, and moved to follow.

There was no arguing that point.

Two minutes later, they returned and began a cursory walk-through of the main level, the beam of Rick's lantern glancing off walls and casting eerie shadows that seemed to slink into corners and slither down hallways.

The Summoning

They rounded a corner into the kitchen. Rick's light skipped across the floor and landed on the telephone—ripped from the wall, smashed and broken into pieces. There was a dull, scraping sound as his gun cleared leather—the first time he had drawn his weapon in twenty-five years as a sheriff's deputy. Behind him, he heard Porter follow suit.

"Well this ain't no shit," the nervous deputy muttered behind him. "Shouldn't we like...you know...call somebody?"

"Yeah, except we *are* the *somebody*." He wished with all of his might that there was somebody else he could call. But who, Dr. Steinmetz? *Sorry ole' boy, but I'm afraid you're it. Come on now, time to earn your pay.*

He swallowed back the fear that was climbing up his throat and scanned the room with his lantern: a turned over chair, shards of broken plates littering the floor, the kitchen table tipped on its side, the floral-patterned tablecloth lying rumpled next to it, the refrigerator door hanging ajar, a woman's shoe sitting alone and upright, as if on display in a department store window...the bloodless, yellowish-gray foot that belonged to the shoe, protruding from under the table cloth.

The sharp intake of air through his teeth made a hissing sound as his light landed on the naked foot. It was colorless and frozen, the toes jutting upward under the glare of the lantern light. A bright red shade of polish decorating the nails stood out in stark contrast to the blanched skin, like big drops of blood congealing on sooty snow.

He brought his pistol sights to bear on the appendage, as if the foot itself was some kind of threat. Not the foot so much, but what it was attached to, whoever or whatever was lying under the tablecloth. The reports of a dead Levi Henderson being seen, *walking around*, were not lost on him at the moment, and he could very well picture the foot beginning to twitch, and the tablecloth shifting and morphing as something underneath began to writhe. Perhaps, it would moan as it began to rise up off the floor, the tablecloth taking on the shape of a head and slumping shoulders...

"I guess that's Mrs. Miller," Porter said, in a detached, mechanical voice.

A small gust of shame passed through Rick as he roused himself from the macabre vision. *How about we deal with the reality of the situation here?* He was standing in a kitchen with a dead body—Trina Miller's, more likely than not —and there was a good chance that the killer—Daniel Miller, more likely than not—was still in the house, hiding around some corner, or in a closet, under a bed.

As they approached, he could begin to make out the vague humanoid form concealed beneath the tablecloth. Handing the lantern to Porter, he reached down and grabbed a fistful of the cloth. He slowly pulled the material toward him, sliding it, gradually revealing the hidden corpse beneath, inch by inch. In a strange sort of way, it made him feel dirty, as if he was violating the decency of the poor, dead woman, the cloth sliding over the curves and contours of her body.

Porter focused the light on the face as soon as it had been exposed.

Trina Miller's head had been bludgeoned in on one side with a heavy, blunt object—Rick thought of the smashed up telephone on the floor—the force of the blow apparently enough to also snap her neck, by the awkward and unnatural angle at which her head seemed to be resting on her shoulder. There wasn't a lot of blood, just a thin, dark trickle issuing from her parted, blue lips. Her vacant eyes stared at nothingness through heavy, half-closed lids, giving her face an ironically serene expression.

The contents of Rick's stomach rose up in his throat, and he thought he just might puke all over the tablecloth—all over that nice flowery pattern. He reminded himself that he had seen much worse than this over his career—hell, in car accidents alone, not to mention what had been done to Conrad Fairchild and Robbie Pritchard! Maybe it was the idea of a child bashing in his own mother's head, that was getting to him. Matricide: did it get any more evil and vile than that?

Like a circus magician flourishing his cape after performing a trick, Rick flung the tablecloth back over the body. He watched it billow and then settle back into place, giving Mrs. Miller back her privacy. Except for that lone, bare foot still sticking out, white and exposed, like the jagged end of a bone poking out from a compound fracture.

He bent down and used a bit of excess cloth and covered it up. He had the melancholy thought that Trina Miller had recently sat down somewhere in this very house and applied the nail polish to her toes—they wouldn't have been gray and cold then—just trying to look pretty, just dolling herself up a bit. Perhaps, she'd hummed a tune to herself during the process, having no idea that her life would soon come to a violent end at the hands of her own son.

He chased those thoughts away and took the lantern back from Porter, who was gaping at the now covered up corpse. They needed to keep moving. There was nothing they could do now for poor Trina. He motioned with his head for Porter to follow him through the opening that would take them into a hallway. The man swallowed and nodded. The guy definitely looked shaken up, but

413

appeared to still be with it enough to continue, and Rick silently thanked God for that.

The narrow hallway made a direct right turn, running beneath the stairs before meeting back up with the front entryway and the living room. A door, about halfway down and to the left, was open, blocking the rest of the hall. Based on the layout of the rest of the home, Rick knew that would be the door leading down to the basement. People didn't usually leave the door to their basement or crawl space hanging wide open.

He looked back at Porter and pointed to the door. As one, the two lawmen approached, the floorboards creaking beneath their feet. Rick used the lantern to give the door a slight nudge, allowing them both enough room to angle past it.

He aimed the lantern's beam down into the darkness, but the pale, yellow light didn't do much to penetrate what almost seemed like a black mist hovering just below the first few stairs. He took two steps down, his cowboy boots thudding on the bare wood. A dangling cobweb whispered against his cheek. He brushed it aside with the barrel of his gun and took two more steps down. There was the eerie sense that the darkness was somehow a living thing, clinging to him, trying to devour him with each step.

He cursed the dark and wished he hadn't failed to put a new battery in his lantern as he flicked the pallid light back and forth in front of him. The light exposed flashing glimpses of rough, wooden floor joists and support beams as he neared the bottom of the stairs.

He figured the fuse box was down here somewhere, probably with a box of new fuses next to it. Maybe they could locate it and get the electricity flowing again. All this bumbling through a murder scene with only the dim light of a dying lantern to guide them was ludicrous, fraying his nerves to their limit. The only comfort he felt, as his feet touched on the cement floor, was the thump of Porter's footsteps right behind him.

He waited for Porter to get off the stairs and then continued straight ahead, looking for the back wall where the fuse box would most likely be located.

And sure enough, there it was, twenty or so feet in front of him, mounted to the wall. He trained his light on it and, despite the weakness of the beam, he could see that the box was open, and that the main switch on the side of the box was in the *off* position. He figured this was somewhat good news, since it meant they would probably have some real light to work with in a moment. *Just a flip of the switch.*

He turned back to Porter, "Let's get some lights on around here," he whispered.

Porter grunted with a nod, little droplets of perspiration beading up on his pasty forehead.

After a few steps, something made him stop in mid-stride; a familiar, coppery odor, like the scent of dirty pennies. It was very reminiscent of the smell that had dominated the scene of Conrad Fairchild's butcher-like murder. It was the smell of pooled blood…stagnant and coagulating. It was all around him, *as if he were standing*…he pointed the lantern down at his feet…*right in the middle of it.*

In the pervading darkness, the blood looked black, like he was standing in a puddle of tar. Except where the lantern's beam hit the gelling surface directly, there was a deep auburn tint that gave away the true nature of the substance.

Porter leaned an elbow on a support beam to his side and wretched. The sound of the vomit splattering on the cement floor was just about enough to send Rick over the edge himself, but he somehow maintained control over that particular bodily function—probably because there was nothing in his stomach in the first place.

"You okay?" Rick asked over his shoulder when he could hear that his partner's system was finished with its little tantrum.

"I am now," came the answer through a couple of coughs, and a sniff. "Where'd all this blood come from?"

Rick angled the lantern so that the light traveled away from his feet, across the dull, bloody surface, toward the wall. He stopped just short of where the floor and the wall joined together. A man in his pajamas was sitting there, his back to the wall; one leg folded up underneath him, the other sticking straight out. His chin was resting low on his chest—almost too low—and his arms hung limp at his sides, the hands and fingers curled up beneath the wrists. His entire front was saturated with blood as if it had gushed down him, cascading like a waterfall to form the sticky morass now slathering the floor.

The bald spot at the crown of the head and the thick, calloused farmer's hands were enough for Rick to identify the man. "Will," he called softly. He didn't expect a response and he didn't get one. He didn't need Dr. Steinmetz's professional opinion to determine the man was dead…very dead.

"The power," Porter said, a tinge of panic circulating along the outer edges of his voice. The whites of his eyes glowed luminously in the dim, residual glow of the lantern light.

"Right," Rick said, and handed the lantern to his partner. He took a few steps toward the corpse and nudged its foot with the toe of his boot; there was no response. He transferred his gun to his left hand, stepped over the stiff, extended leg, and used his right hand to shove the main switch on the fuse box into the *on* position.

There was a brief crackling sound inside the fuse box followed by a humming surge as electricity began to flow. Much to his relief, a couple of naked light bulbs hanging from the ceiling took to life, illuminating the basement. A quick glance around told him that they were alone down there, and he stepped back to have a look at the blood-soaked body sitting on the floor.

Porter, still clutching the lantern, edged a few feet closer, his mouth locked in a grimace of revulsion. Rick squatted onto his haunches in front of the corpse, reached out with his hand, and lifted the head back against the wall; there was a sticky, raw meat sound. He wasn't that surprised to see that Will Miller's throat had been slashed.

The cut was deep—nearly all the way to the bone—and it ran from ear to ear, leaving the severed ends of sinews, vessels, tubes...all that kind of stuff, exposed and open. He eased the head back down onto the chest and stood up.

Porter swallowed, it made a loud clicking sound. "He killed his parents," the man said, sounding like he was in shock—he probably was.

Rick turned to face him. "Looks as if. My guess is he got into some kind of argument with his parents and decided to kill them both. He grabbed a knife, came down here to the fuse box, killed the power, and waited in the dark for dear, old Dad to come down here to try to fix the power. Then, he ambushed him from behind. Cut his throat."

"About cut his whole damn head off," Porter said, popping a cigarette into his pale, trembling lips.

Rick put a hand on Porter's shoulder to reassure and steady him. "Are you okay?" he asked.

Porter hesitated a moment and nodded. "Yeah...I guess so."

"I know this is a lot more than you bargained for when you took the job, Porter, but you're doing just fine." He reached up and pulled the cigarette out of the man's mouth. "But we have to have a look at the rest of the house. That psycho kid might still be here."

"Right," Porter muttered, nodding slightly.

"Now, from things I've read, and other cases like this I've studied, chances are, we'll find the kid dead as well. Usually, in a situation like this, the killer goes and punches his own ticket after he's killed his family...after the reality of what he's done sinks in. A murder suicide they call it." Rick stepped in front of the temporary deputy to lead the way back up the stairs. "Just hang in there with me a few more minutes and, before you know it, you'll be lighting up and enjoying your smoke."

"Okay," Porter said, stepping in behind.

They moved through the main level again, clicking on every single light switch and lamp that they came across. They both paused again where Trina Miller's body lay underneath the table cloth. Rick thought about pulling it off to have a better look at the body, now that the lights had been restored, but changed his mind. Having a better look right now wouldn't change the fact that she was dead. They needed to clear the rest of the house and find Daniel.

He was nowhere to be found. The house was empty. Apparently, the kid had decided against meeting his maker tonight—not that Rick blamed him for that, after what the little bastard had done.

The last room they came to was actually Daniel's bedroom at the end of the upstairs hallway. The big rug had been rolled up, and what it revealed on the bare floor made Rick's guts twist into knots.

"What the hell has this kid gotten himself into?" Porter said, stepping into the room with Rick.

"What the *hell* is right," Rick answered, his voice coming out as only a whisper.

A big circle—maybe five feet in diameter—had been drawn on the floor in white chalk. There was a drawing of a big tree in the middle, with strange symbols lining the trunk and branches. Other symbols, along with crisscrossing lines, made up the inside of the ring, complete with a single hand print stamped in what appeared to be blood in the very center. There were nonsense words too —some with the letters reversed—scrawled along the outer edge of the whole thing.

"It's some kind of devil worship or witchcraft," Porter said, his eyes bulging slightly from their sockets.

"Well," Rick said, walking around the design to get a closer look, "this certainly explains a lot. Question is—now that he's gone and murdered his own parents—what's his next move...what's he up to now?"

"If I was him, I'd be getting out of town."

"That's because you're not a psychotic megalomaniac who happens to worship Satan. No, that's not our Daniel, skipping town and running away. He's got some kind of twisted plan, he's had one all along. Killing his parents was probably a part of it from the very beginning. Except, I don't think he figured on his mother getting a call out before he could kill her, which means she threw a wrench into the works. And now, maybe his hand has been forced before he was ready. He's gotta follow through now…tonight, tomorrow at the latest."

Porter was squinting at the drawing on the floor and rubbing the back of his neck. "Yeah, but what does that mean, 'follow through?' You talking about killing more people?"

Rick slowly nodded. "If recent events are any indication, I'd say he's planning a bloodbath. We've got to find him and stop him."

Porter echoed the very thought that was draping itself over Rick's brain like a tangled net, "Yeah, but how?"

Rick holstered his gun—the kid wasn't anywhere near here—and put his hands on his hips, mulling over his options and the implications of everything that had transpired—everything that was yet to transpire, for that matter. He spun for the door, shouldering past Porter. "Let's go," he said, "we can't do this, just the two of us alone."

Porter stepped in behind. "Where we going?"

"To the neighboring farm, the Baxter place." He hit the stairs, taking two at a time, the banister creaking under his hand. "Gonna use their phone to call Coop."

"I thought Doc Steinmetz had relieved him of his duty," Porter said, struggling to keep up.

Rick reached the front door and turned to face the deputy before opening it. "Actually, if you want to know the real truth, Chet stepped down voluntarily, so that Steinmetz wouldn't have to." He opened the door, snowflakes the size of quarters churned about in the entryway. "After tonight, there's not going to be much Dr. Steinmetz or anyone else is going to be able to say or do to keep him off the job."

"I hope you know what you're doing," Porter said, following him out to the patrol rigs, still chugging faithfully in the driveway. "I wouldn't want to see *you* get into trouble either."

Rick reached his car. "I'm acting sheriff, I'm making the call. If someone wants to fire me when this is all over, they can go right ahead. But right now, all I care about is catching that little son of a bitch before he kills anyone else. And I don't see me and you getting that job done without Chet." He yanked his car door open. "The sooner the better, so let's go."

CHET FELT LIKE HE HAD BEEN ASLEEP forever when his ringing telephone began to pierce through the mud of his subconscious. He wasn't aware of any dreams in particular, but his mind seemed to be trying hard to hold onto a ghostly image of Kate, smiling and beautiful, but evaporating before him like a mist with each incessant ring.

Like the snapping of fingers, his eyes popped open and the lovely vision was gone; he was awake. He grabbed the small wind-up clock off his nightstand as he swung his feet onto the floor. It was just past one-thirty. The telephone in his kitchen blurted out another impatient burst.

He slammed the clock back down on the nightstand, as if that could somehow shut the telephone up. He stomped in his bare feet down the hall, still feeling groggy, maybe even a little hungover, and yanked the phone off its receiver in mid ring.

"Hello," he said.

CHAPTER 39

Throbbing blood surged through every artery and vein, and his skin radiated heat like a furnace, vaporizing falling snowflakes as they came into contact with its fever-hot surface. His hands were shaking uncontrollably in the pockets of his jacket as he walked.

Apparently, the killing of his parents had more of an effect on him than he figured it would. Now his body was reacting to the strange flood of emotions that were washing over him; feelings of ultimate liberation enhanced by the promises of the future, but mixed with an undercurrent of fear, anxiety, and yes…even horror.

He supposed the old Daniel still existed to some extent, slinking and cowering somewhere in the deepest recesses of his being. His days were numbered though. With each kill for his mistress, another piece of the old Daniel died as well, and after tonight, he would be altogether extinguished.

The thought did little to still the shaking of his hands, calm the hammering of his heart, or block the images of what he'd just done from replaying over and over in his head.

Things had pretty much gone just as he had planned, if not as smoothly as he had wished. Ambushing his father in the basement had been all too easy—the old man hadn't even grabbed a flashlight before coming down to check the fuse box. Of course, the first thing he noticed was the main switch had been turned off, and so he turned it back on, but by then Daniel was already behind him.

How the man had managed to get out a scream before Daniel's knife had severed his vocal cords, along with pretty much everything else, was a mystery. After his throat had been cut, his father managed to turn around to face him. In an act born of instinct and desperation, the dying man put his hands to the savage wound. Astonishing gouts of scarlet, frothy blood spurted through his fingers, unconstrained…flowing, gushing.

Of course, with such a devastating and complete severing of the brain's blood supply, the man had only a few fleeting seconds of consciousness before that cold and eternal darkness took him. It was long enough. Daniel locked eyes with him, as the man's legs gave out and he slid down the wall into a sitting position. The old man knew…knew and fully understood what had happened to him. Daniel saw it in his eyes before the light went out of them.

He had intended to enjoy this occasion, to savor it and relish the moment of his liberation, but his mother, upon hearing the sudden scream cut short by Daniel's blade, came down the basement stairs to investigate.

Daniel's back had been turned to the stairs, so he never did get to see the look on her face as she beheld her loving son, bloodied knife in hand, standing triumphantly over the body of her murdered husband. It was probably a good thing he hadn't seen her face, there was no telling what effect it might have had on him right then.

He had only heard a gasping yelp behind him, followed by the staccato *clack, clack* of his mother's shoes, as she ran up the stairs and into the kitchen. He heard her run across the kitchen floor to where the telephone hung on the wall by the back door.

A phone call to the police would have been his ruin, so thinking quickly, he shut the power switch back off, figuring that would kill the phone as well. He was wrong—she was talking to someone—and in the dark he sprinted for the stairs, calling out to his mother, "Wait, Mom, wait!"

As he dashed into the kitchen he heard her shaky whisper, asking for the sheriff's office. Without a moment to lose, he ripped the phone from the wall, snapping the wire at the same time. His mother screamed then, a wretched, howling sound, a hideous conglomeration of every emotion possible in the human experience.

He took some comfort, maybe even a little pride, in the fact he had no desire, took no pleasure in killing his mother. It wasn't as if he was some kind of beast, a pitiless monster, incapable of love or affection. He had even tried to reason with her, explain things to her, get her to see things as he did. He even tried to give her a way out…her death wasn't absolutely necessary.

But she had been beyond reason, past intelligent thinking. Backed against the wall, next to the kitchen table, she just kept screaming and screaming that horrid, piercing wail. When he approached, she flung the table over on its side, trying to hit him with it. Of course, a table lying on its side was of little consequence, and as he neared, the screams became unbearable for even one more second. At that moment, the look on her face suddenly filled him with a black rage.

She was just some dumb, uncomprehending animal, bleating and shrieking against the inevitable, like a sheep or a cow being led to slaughter. He was still holding the telephone in his hands. He looked down at it. He had always thought it looked like a silly face, with the two brass bells for eyes that rang when you got a call, and when you talked, you spoke into its long nose.

Without another thought, he swung the telephone with both hands as hard as he could. There was a terrific sound of wood splintering, the cracking of bone, and the floppy thud of his mother's body hitting the floor. Followed by silence. Dead silence.

But now, as he turned onto Washington Street, the final cries and screams of his mother refused to let go, like large, hooked talons embedded in his brain. He shook his head violently from side to side, his hair, now wet from the falling snow, whipping back and forth. *After tonight,* he told himself, *everything is going to be different!*

There was a slight curve in the street so that The Cozy Corner was not in view yet, but it would be in moments. Kate would be asleep by now in her bedroom on the second story, warm under her covers, feeling safe and sound, unaware of the storm quickly approaching in the night.

Unfortunately, he was heading into this whole thing with only a semblance of a plan, no real details or specifics worked out in advance—not how he had foreseen things going. But with the possibility that his mother had talked to someone on the phone, he had no choice but to move things along a little faster than he had originally planned. He had to operate with the assumption that time was not on his side.

He still had the advantage of surprise, and therefore, a good chance of success. In his history lessons, he had learned that in war, the side that struck first and was able to surprise their enemies, usually came out of the battle as the victor. That would be him tonight. He also had every reason to expect that his dead parents would not stay dead for long. Most likely, they would be playing a role in helping him before the night was through.

He had driven the old Ford into town, utilizing back roads and alternate routes from any that responding police might be using. Five minutes ago, he had parked the truck in front of a dark and empty lot, beneath a broken streetlight, just a couple of blocks away.

The plan for now: get inside the boarding house quietly, incapacitate Miss Farnsworth somehow, and whisk her away to her fate. If all went well, it would be morning before she was missed, and too late for anyone to do anything about it. But what if Kate got off a scream like his dad had, or what if someone else in the house were to wake up and interfere? What if things went badly in the boarding house?

He reached in his jacket and traced his fingertips along the handle of his knife, sensed the reassuring weight of the blade riding in the inside pocket. He would cross that bridge when he came to it. He smiled, but then quickly chased it away. Of course, he hoped it wouldn't come to that, he told himself. *You're not a monster, remember?*

THIS TIME, SHE HAD NO RECOLLECTION of how she had arrived, but here she was again, standing on the banks of Asher's Pond. This time, she knew it was a dream, but also knew, on some level where her conscious and subconscious minds came together, that the ability to wake herself was not in her power.

She looked around, taking in the details of her surroundings. The surface of the pond was a mirror, reflecting a dull, chromium sky. The sun was a cold, indistinguishable blur, that offered no warmth or comfort. The banks of the pond were festooned with reeds and cattails, but noticeably absent were the dragonflies that should have been darting in and out of the foliage. Missing as well: the chirping of birds, the constant droning of insects, and the occasional croak of a bullfrog. For that matter, not even the slightest breeze was there to ripple the water, or wave through the tall grass.

This is a dead place, she thought. The dead…and she remembered Albert. He had come to her the last time she'd dreamed of this place. He had delivered a message and helped her with cracking the secret to the journal. Was that why she was here again? Was Albert going to show up with another helpful message?

As if her thoughts had flipped a switch somewhere, a breeze began, an unnatural stirring of air that didn't seem to be blowing in any given direction. It soughed through the surrounding evergreens, tugging erratically at the branches and treetops. The cattails, grass, and reeds swayed back and forth against each other, like opposing armies locked in a pitched battle.

On the breeze was the scent of an all too familiar aftershave that made her insides shrivel and twist into knots. And then there was the gurgling disturbance out on the surface of the water, with oily, decaying sludge churning in the roil.

"I'm done with all of this!" she shouted at the frothing turmoil. Tears began to fill her eyes.

The top of Albert's head appeared.

Her hands were clenched into tight fists at her sides, the hot wind tussling through her hair with dirty, intimate fingers. "I said, I'm done! I'm leaving Clear Creek and this whole mess behind me!"

Albert's face rose from the surface, his black, crow's eyes focused on her without even blinking as pond water ran into, and out of them.

Her knees were beginning to shake. "Did you hear me? I don't need any messages or advice from you...I'm through with it all!"

Albert continued to rise from the gurgling water, seemingly heedless of anything she had to say on the matter.

She remembered it was just a dream. She tried to will herself awake and swim out of the depths of her subconscious. She was met by a barrier, like having fallen through the ice of a frozen river, the swift current sweeping her downstream as she flailed in vain at the frigid, impenetrable surface.

Albert was suspended above the pond now, and began to float across the water, toward her, a strange look of...was it concern on his face?

She decided to leave. *Why not? It's my dream. Just turn and walk away.* But when she tried to move, she realized her feet were ankle-deep in mud, and some of the grass had snaked and twined its way around her legs, cementing her in place. She was stuck, a captive audience.

Albert was almost upon her. She could smell the rot and decay, heavy and pungent as he approached. *It's only a dream...it's only a dream.* But she knew better.

"Whatever you have to say," she said, through gritted teeth, "I don't want to hear it...I told you—"

"You're out of time, Kate," he said in a gargled voice. "Listen to me." He looked over his shoulder for a moment and then turned his gaze back to her. "To defeat the shadow, you must first descend into the darkness."

"Another riddle? You've got to be joking! What does it mean?"

He shook his head. "I don't know, but you will...*you* will." Again, he glanced over his shoulder.

Something in the trees, on the other side of the pond, shrieked. It was an angry, furious, reverberating sound; human...and yet, not so much. The sound of it curdled the very marrow in Kate's bones. It seemed to pass right through her, sapping every ounce of her courage with it. She collapsed, her knees and hands driving into the soft mud. A thin cry escaped her lips and tears began to flow.

"It's here!" Albert cried, and he started drifting back out over the water. "Remember, Kate, what I said!"

She could only stare down at the mud oozing between her fingers, too terrified to look up and see whatever thing had made that sound. A thing, or *her?*

Albert was already sinking back down into the pond, into whatever private hell of his this was. "It's here now," he said, with a certain solemn finality. "I'm so sorry, Kate." He was almost submerged now, the water bubbling around his chin. "You have to wake up now…it's here."

She was being swept downstream again, under that barrier of ice that kept her from waking out of this hellish nightmare. She could sense the barrier thinning, diminishing, and she pushed against it, trying to break through.

As that boundary between the two worlds in her mind thinned, she became aware of the very real sensation of cold across her entire body. She was shivering. The boundary became as thin as a silk veil.

She opened her eyes. The air in her bedroom was frigid, and even in the dark she could see the white vapor of her breath as she exhaled. She sat up slowly in bed, gathering her blankets around her chest and neck. A shiver tumbled along her backbone. She wasn't sure if it was the chill or the dream that had caused it. Where was this cold coming from? Had the furnace gone out in the middle of the night?

She swung her feet out of the covers and onto the braided rug—even it was cold—and stood up, wrapping her arms around herself for warmth. With great reluctance, she took a gingerly step off of the rug onto the freezing hardwood floor, as if she were about to step onto a bed of broken glass. "I hate the cold!" she whispered to herself as she padded over to the wardrobe where she kept her big fuzzy bathrobe and slippers.

A breeze…an actual *breeze* pulled her up short as it ruffled the hem of her satin nightgown. She sensed it before she saw it; the bedroom window was wide open. Snowflakes the size of bottle caps tumbled freely through the opening, drenching the writing desk and windowsill. In the middle of the desk, surrounded by tiny puddles of melted snow, was the impression left by a muddy shoe.

Her body went stiff with fear as the implication of that muddy footprint hit her with full force. Her breath clotted in her throat and her jaw started to shiver uncontrollably. Albert's incorporeal voice from her dream echoed in her mind, *"You have to wake up now…it's here."*

Her eyes were riveted on the window; it was the ravenous, yawning maw of death, trying to swallow her up whole. At any second, she would be pulled into an invisible vortex and sucked through the gap. The window would slam shut behind her like the teeth of a dog on a piece of raw meat, and she would never be heard of again.

She took a slow, deliberate step backwards, away from the gaping, hungry mouth, as if any sudden movement could cause the jaws to snap out at her. She went to take another step and bumped into something. Somebody!

The scream of a lifetime quickly formed deep in her chest and shot upwards through her like a small volcanic eruption. Her mouth opened to unleash the vocal explosion, but before she could even make a squeak, a heavily muscled arm struck with the speed of a snake from behind, catching her throat in the crook of its elbow, and constricted, completely cutting off her airway. She could feel the attacker's other arm pushing the back of her head forward, into the other arm, making the choke hold all the more devastating.

Instinctively, her hands grabbed at the forearm across her throat in a desperate attempt to wrench it away. It was no use. The arm might as well have been a steel bar. Panic clutched at her as her vision began to blur and a tingling began in her extremities. She knew that in a matter of seconds she would lose consciousness. She had to do something. Now!

She brought her right foot off the floor, pushed her hips forward to generate power, and brought her heel in a sharp backwards kick, into the attacker's shin bone, just below the knee—a little trick her brothers had taught her. She felt the knee give a little, and her attacker grunted with pain, but the python-like hold continued uninterrupted, cutting off the flow of precious oxygen.

Her vision was going black now. She was looking down a long, dark tunnel that was quickly closing. She thought that maybe there was time for one more heel strike to the knee, before the tunnel closed for good. As she tilted her hips forward and brought her leg up to deliver the blow, the attacker hoisted her up in the air, her toes barely brushing the floor. In this position, she wouldn't be able to generate even half the power she had with the first kick.

She kicked anyway, but it had little effect. She struck with her left foot, then again with the right, to no avail. Her vision was gone, and she was falling into blackness, her arms and legs hanging now, numb and useless.

As the last vestiges of her consciousness slipped away, she became minutely aware of the attacker's lips suddenly next to her ear. "Just let go, Kate. It's okay, I'm not going to hurt you…just let go."

The last thought to flutter in her mind was, *Daniel!* Then the darkness took her completely.

"WE SEARCHED THE WHOLE HOUSE before you got here," Rick said, guiding Chet up the stairs of the Miller home. "No sign of the kid."

Thus far, it had been a grisly tour. It had first commenced with a look at the corpse of Trina Miller in the kitchen, followed by the butchered body of her husband, Will Miller, in the basement. The tour was to be culminated in Daniel's bedroom. Rick had said that there was something up there that just had to be seen for himself.

"Have you notified anyone else?" Chet asked, as they reached the top of the stairs.

"No."

"Good, let's hold off for now."

Porter spoke up from behind, "Shouldn't we call somebody: the funeral home, Dr. Steinmetz, someone to deal with…with the bodies, I mean?"

Chet spoke over his shoulder as they made their way down the hallway to Daniel's room, "I don't want to tip off our killer that we're on to him. He'll be more likely to make bolder moves and more mistakes if he thinks he's still in the clear."

" Ah, gotcha."

"Anyway," Rick said, "like I was sayin', we looked through the whole house and I don't think he's anywhere. Unless, maybe hiding out on the farm some place, like in a silo or something."

"Nah, he's gone," Chet said.

Rick paused at Daniel's bedroom door. "What makes you so sure, Coop?"

Chet shrugged his shoulders. "The Ford's gone. He must have taken a drive right after killing his parents."

"Probably two counties away by now," Rick said, shaking his head.

"Your guess is as good as mine, but I have a feeling he's still around."

"Why's that?"

"I don't know. He just doesn't strike me as the type to get out of town…go on the lam. He's up to something…like a big master plan, and this is just the kickoff. It's game time now."

"Well," Rick said, motioning Chet to follow him into the bedroom, "maybe you can make sense of his game plan then."

Chet studied the bizarre drawing on the floor, walking around it, and squatting in places to get a closer look at some of the symbols and nonsense words. His two partners watched in silence.

"Can you make anything out of it," Rick asked, "other than Daniel Miller's crazier than a rat trapped in a tin shit house?"

Chet stood up. "He's into witchcraft, sorcery…devil worship, whatever you want to call it. A cold wave washed through him as he suddenly began to recall all the stuff that Kate had found in old Abel Gannon's secret confession: the demon, the killings, the disappearances, the search for a vessel.

"He's found the vessel," Chet said. His words sounded far away to him, like somebody else had spoken them.

Rick tilted his head. "He found the what?"

CHAPTER 40

O kay, that is officially the craziest thing I've heard in twenty five years as a deputy," Rick said when Chet finished relating the down and dirty version of Reverend Gannon's confession. "Aside from the fact that it sure puts all the puzzle pieces nicely into place."

Chet rested his hands on his hips. "I'm not saying all the demons and hocus-pocus stuff is real, but we have to assume Daniel Miller is operating as if it is."

Rick nodded. "Well, regardless if it's real or not, someone out there is in a world of trouble right now. I mean, if this kid has decided he's found this *vessel,* right?"

"Who knows what he's got planned."

"Well, you're the one who said it's game time, Coop. My guess is that, whatever he's got planned, it's happening tonight…as in right now."

Chet nodded. "Well yeah, I think you're right, Rick. We have to work under that assumption, of course. It's just figuring out where we go from here—"

Rick interrupted, "We've only gotta figure out two things: the who… and the where. Who's the vessel and where would he take them?"

"Unfortunately, that's easier said than done."

"Ain't it always?"

"Okay, so let's think about the who then. Who might Daniel go after as the host for his demon girl?"

Porter, who had been leaning against a wall, quietly smoking the final remnants of a cigarette, cleared his throat. "Well, if it were me that was fixin' to be with a demon girlfriend, trapped in a mortal body, I'd be picking out the prettiest dame I could find…some gal I was already interested in. Did this Miller kid have a *human* girlfriend he might have been dating?"

"Chet!" Rick exclaimed, his eyes growing so wide that he resembled an owl. "Kate! That little psychopath has it big for Kate!"

Chet's blood turned to a cold slush and a wave of panic washed over him, causing him to momentarily freeze up. It was the ambush on Tarawa all over again, Japanese machine guns ripping his platoon to shreds. How could he have been so stupid? He should have sent Kate away the very *second* that he suspected Daniel to be the killer!

Rick grabbed his shoulders and shook him hard. "We have to warn her, Chet! We have to warn Kate now!"

"Alright, alright," he said, squeezing his eyes shut. "Give me a second here." Concentrating on what had to be done, he was able to shove aside the panic and indecisiveness that was trying to cripple him and come up with a hasty plan of action.

"Porter," Chet said, pointing at the man, "you go directly over to the neighbors, the Baxters, and telephone the Cozy Corner. You warn Mable and let her know I'm on my way over there right now. Tell her to make sure her doors are locked and not to open up for anybody until I get there."

Porter nodded and swallowed hard. "Ten-four that," the deputy said. "Then what?"

"Let me know once you've talked to her. Then get back over here and keep an eye on this place. Stay in your car where I can reach you by radio." Chet took two huge strides to the door, then paused. "And be careful, Porter. He could come back."

Porter nodded once, then dashed out of the bedroom.

Rick placed a hand on Chet's shoulder. "You and me both going to Mable's?"

Chet shook his head and started walking, Rick right on his heels. "I'm going to Mable's," he explained, as they hit the stairs together. "Chances are, everything's fine there; it's a house full of people...people with guns for that matter. I don't think he's stupid enough to try to get her out of the house in the middle of the night. If he's smart, he'll wait until she's alone somewhere, like walking to work or something, but I'd rather not take any chances."

They burst through the front door in time to see Porter's vehicle jostling down the driveway. "So, what do you want me to do then, Coop?" Rick asked.

Chet stopped at his patrol car and pulled the door open. "If this insanity really is happening, and he has Kate or anyone else, he'll most likely be heading up to the old Salem church to do the ceremony, or whatever he needs to do."

"You want me to head up to Salem," Rick guessed.

"I'll catch up with you as soon as I've checked on Kate and made sure everything is okay at Mable's."

"I'm on the way," Rick said, jogging to his car.

Chet slammed the radio mic back onto its hanger in frustration. He was already halfway to town and still no word from Porter. *How long does it take to make one damn phone call?* Maybe it was taking so long because nobody was answering. That was a possibility that he didn't like to entertain. He gave the Chevy police cruiser a little more throttle, even though the rear tires had already threatened to spin out on him a couple of times.

He flicked on the mounted top light and blew right through an intersection without even slowing down. The radio crackled for a second and then went quiet again. Rick, who was following behind, must have been about to say something —probably telling him to slow down—but then had thought better of it.

He watched in his rear view mirror as Rick's car slowed at the same intersection and then swung a hard left onto the road that would take him out to the foothills, the car fishtailing in the snow as he accelerated back to speed.

Come on Porter! What in the name of all that is holy is taking so long? The snow was beginning to let up some and he could see up ahead, where the lights of Clear Creek were forming an iridescent halo in the night sky. So much for surprising Kate in the morning; he had planned to be the one to pick her up for her ride to the train station instead of Rick. Hopefully, she would be in the mood to accept his apology now, even if it was in the middle of the night.

Just as he was reaching to grab the radio mic off its hook and try for Porter again, the deputy's voice crackled faintly over the speaker. He sounded far away, like he was speaking into a tin can—probably interference from the storm. "Sheriff, it's Porter, do you copy?"

"You're coming in pretty weak, Porter, but I copy," Chet spoke into the mic. "Were you able to get a hold of Mable?"

"Yes…I mean, ten-four. She says it's all been quiet tonight…"
Chet exhaled an audible sigh of relief.
"….She said her doors and all the windows are locked. She and Henry are on the stairs with a loaded twelve gauge, waiting for you."

Good for them! Chet strongly appreciated a citizen that was willing to defend themselves if need be. He had heard a saying once: Having a gun in your hand was better than having a cop on the phone. As a sheriff, he could personally attest to that sentiment and, at the moment, Henry Johnson and his loaded shotgun, sitting on the very stairs that led to the room where Kate was sleeping, brought him a great degree of comfort!

"I'm on my way back over to the Miller place right now, like you asked," Porter continued.

"Alright, sounds good, Porter. Just stand by there until you hear back from me. Nobody goes in or out of that house."

"And if the kid shows up?"

"Place him under arrest, and If he makes one aggressive move at you…shoot him."

"Copy that."

Rick's voice, also faint and masked with static came over the radio, "You still want me up at Salem, Coop?"

The man obviously was not in love with the idea of going up there, especially all by himself. Chet could sympathize. As lifelong residents of Clear Creek, they had heard all of the ghost stories and superstitions about the old abandoned town site since they were kids. No matter how old or grownup you got, little pieces of those things just seemed to cling to your psyche.

He depressed the transmit button on his mic. "Ten-four, Rick. Just in case our hunch about Kate was wrong and he's got somebody else up there already. Just keep heading up there and I'll catch up. I just want to swing by and check things out at Mable's. Make sure everything is okay there."

"Ten-four," Rick said, the lack of enthusiasm in his voice still detectable through the static.

Five minutes later, Chet pulled his car up to the curb in front of The Cozy Corner boarding home. All of the downstairs lights were on, as well as the porch light. *Now just be careful not to get cut in half by a twelve gauge,* he thought as he exited his vehicle.

Halfway up the walk, he saw the curtains in the front window part slightly, revealing a round, ruddy face peering at him through the glass. The door was flung wide for him as soon as he reached the threshold.

Henry Johnson, in his pajamas and a bathrobe, clutching a double-barreled, side-by-side shotgun, stepped away from the entry. "Come in, Sheriff," he said.

Mable was standing by the banister, wringing her pudgy hands together, her blue eyes burning bright with worry. Her copper hair, liberated from the standard tight bun, hung to her broad shoulders from a loose ponytail. "Chet, what in the devil is going on?" she blurted. "One minute we're sound asleep, and then Porter Thomas calls us and says we need to—"

Chet jumped in, having no time for Mable's habit of running off at the mouth at a hundred miles an hour, and in a hundred different directions,

"I don't have time to explain everything right now beyond what Porter already told you over the telephone. I need to talk to Kate real quick."

"Well, she's sound asleep in her room," Mable said. "I'd have to—"

432

"Wake her," Chet said. "Right now, please."

Mable shook her head, apparently at the impropriety of such a request, and turned to huff her way up the stairs. Chet watched her disappear down the hallway toward Kate's door. The sound of Mable gently knocking and calling Kate's name drifted down to him. He suddenly remembered the last time he had spoken with her.

His palms broke into a hot sweat, and his heart—already thrumming a good bit— kicked up the pace a notch. In a few moments, the girl that had just walked away from him, sobbing and at the end of her patience with his crap, would appear at the top of the stairs. How should he act? What was he going to say? He hadn't had time to think any of that through!

Mable knocked a second time, a little louder. "Miss Kate, are you awake? You uh…you have a visitor. It's Chet. Miss Kate?"

I'm so sorry, Kate, please forgive me, I was an idiot. Please don't go. Stay here and I promise, you won't regret it. I'll do everything in my power—

"Miss Kate…"

Was Rick really serious about getting down on my knees? He had to be joking, you don't get on your knees unless you're giving her a ring…

"Girl could sleep right through a train wreck, I swear," Mable could be heard muttering to herself, along with the sound of a door knob being worked.

Henry grinned at Chet as if they had just been made privy to some kind of intimate knowledge. And maybe they actually had. He wouldn't know any different.

Suddenly, Mable belted out a scream that rent the air like a thunder clap. Chet's heart came to a dead stop.

AS SHE SLOWLY STARTED COMING TO, Kate first realized that she had been hog-tied, her hands and feet bound together behind her back with what felt like strips of cloth.

As she tried to open her eyes, she found that she had been blindfolded as well. Something had been jammed and tied into place in her mouth. She could smell and taste the laundry detergent in the fibers, and recognized it: a pair of her own socks—at least they were clean.

As the fog of subconsciousness began to lift from her brain, she incrementally became aware of more and more things. She was laying on her side and being jostled about, the growl of an engine droning in her ears, along with the sound of wind and roadway rushing past. She was in a car, or maybe a pickup.

She was cold and wet, her satin nightgown clinging to her body, and her damp hair sticking to her face. At least a blanket was draped over her, providing some warmth. Where was she? Why was she tied up like this? Who…

Daniel Miller! And she suddenly remembered it all: the open window, the muddy boot print on her desk, the choke hold, her fighting, her kicking…her losing. A sickening horror filled her as full realization hit her. She tested the strength of her bonds. They were secure, and she was helpless.

Suddenly, his hand was there, rough fingers tracing the contours of her face and twining themselves in her hair. "Rise and shine, Kate," he said. She could envision the arrogant grin on his face as he said it. "Have a good nap?"

The sound of his voice combined with his wretched touch launched her into a frenzy of disgust, panic, and anger. She mustered every ounce of her strength, pulling against the strips of cloth that bound her, thrashing and contorting her body with all of her might, but the knots held fast and the strips began to bite into her wrists and ankles. She let loose with a scream—the one that had been choked off earlier—but it was sufficiently muffled by the gag in her mouth.

"My goodness," he said, brushing a fingertip lightly along her bottom lip. "There's really no need for behavior like that. It won't do you any good anyway. The knots are all very tight, you're going to have to be cut free with a knife. So, you might as well just relax and accept your fate—a great honor, actually."

She hated herself for crying. She cursed herself from the depths of her soul, but couldn't hold it back. The gag muffled her sobs and the blindfold soaked up her tears.

"There, there," he said, like he was talking to a baby. "It's okay, really. You don't have anything to be afraid of. I'm not the monster you seem to think I am. I'm not going to hurt you. In fact, I love you, Kate. I have since the first time I saw you." His hand slipped from her face, found its way beneath the blanket, snaked along the back of her neck and under her nightgown, where it began to caress her bare back. "How does that feel, better?"

She clenched her teeth on the gag, fighting back the urge to scream again. She had to get a hold of herself, gather her emotions and put them in check. It was her only hope of getting out of this alive. His clammy hand migrated further down her back, sliding under her arm and onto the side of her hip. She physically shuddered as his fingertips brushed across the waistband of her panties.

"How about that?" he said, his voice thick with lust. "Does that feel good?"

She choked back the tears. There would be a time and a place to cry—later, if she survived this—but right now, she needed to focus on a way out of the situation. She tried to say something, but of course the gag prevented it from coming out as anything intelligible. But it did have the desired effect; his hand ceased it's disgusting probing and stroking.

"What was that," he said, "did you just say something?"

She mumbled again.

"If you want to talk, I can take the gag off, as long as you promise to behave yourself. Do you promise?"

She nodded.

He slid his hand from off her back and began using it to untie the gag, the other hand obviously occupied on the steering wheel of the truck. "Don't break your promise now," he said, as the gag loosened. "If you do, then I'll have no choice but to hurt you, and I really don't want to have to hurt you, Kate. Okay?"

She simply nodded again. The gag came off. He plucked the rolled up socks out of her mouth. She worked her jaw against the stiffness that had already begun to set in. She took a few deep breaths now that she could breathe better.

"Now, you were saying?"

The psycho didn't waste much time. He seemed anxious to talk, maybe she could use that against him somehow. Under the circumstances, talk seemed to be her only weapon anyway. "Please untie me, Daniel," she said, trying her best to sound calm. "All of this really isn't necessary. I promise to behave."

He laughed and patted her lightly on the cheek. "Nice try, my dear, but I think everything will go much more smoothly if you remain just like this...for a bit longer anyway."

In her anxiousness, she had overreached, asked for the whole kit and caboodle. *One thing at a time, step by step...like boiling a frog,* she thought. "Well then, can't you at least, please take off this blindfold?"

Silence. He was considering it.

"I mean, I don't see how it can hurt anything for me to be able to see the floor of your pickup do you? And am I not behaving?"

There was a tug on the blindfold and it came off. "I figured you as high maintenance," he said, with a little laugh.

She blinked her eyes and tried her best to look around and get a better handle on her situation. She was facing the back of the seat, her head next to Daniel's right leg. A lot of good getting the blindfold off had done. Her knees were touching the passenger door; she could feel the cold metal of the handle rubbing against her skin every time the truck rumbled over a bump.

She had no idea how long she had been unconscious, but it was dark in the cab of the truck so she knew it was still nighttime. The constant flip-flap of the windshield wipers told her it must still be snowing heavily.

"Aren't you going to ask me what's going on, Kate? Why you're here… where we're going?" he asked.

She didn't need to ask, really. After what she had read in Abel Gannon's journal, it wasn't all that difficult to figure out. She cursed herself. How could she have been so blind as to not have seen this coming? She had been so worried about Chet underestimating what he was up against, and diving headfirst into a supernatural buzz saw, that she had missed all the obvious signs. Even after Scotty had warned her, she had missed it. It was obvious now; she had been chosen as this so-called, vessel, the living body that the demon would take to enter into the world of man. And apparently, tonight was the night.

"I guess I figured you wouldn't tell me if I asked anyway," she responded. *Get him talking, find a weakness to exploit.*

"I'm sorry, I didn't want it to have to be like this," he said. "I really did try my best, but you couldn't see me…you *wouldn't* see me through your silly, school-girl crush on Sheriff Cooper." He took his eyes off the road for a moment to look down at her, and once again started playing with her hair. "So, you see… this is really your fault that I had to do it this way."

A flash of anger flared up in her and, if she could have, she would have turned her head, bit off one of his filthy fingers, and spit it back in his face. "You're a kid! What did you expect, Daniel?" Probably not the smartest thing to say.

His fingers tightened on a fistful of her hair until she winced from the pain. "I expect!" He pulled even tighter. "A little common, damn courtesy! Is that too much to ask for, Kate?"

"Ow, you're hurting me, Daniel! Please stop! I'm sorry, okay?" she mewled. That had been foolish. She couldn't afford to anger him again. She was going to have to be smarter than that, play his game until she found an opening… somehow.

He let go of her hair and grabbed the wheel. "I think maybe you were better off with a pair of socks in your mouth," he muttered.

"I'm sorry, I didn't mean to make you angry." She injected as much submissiveness into her voice as she could. "But you and I…I just figured because of my position at the school and our age difference, that it wouldn't be appropriate. You know? I could get into a lot of trouble and lose my job."

For a few minutes, he just drove in silence, not saying a word. It could have been a bad sign, but so far he hadn't stuffed her mouth with socks again, so that was a plus. "Where are you taking me?" she finally ventured.

He chuckled, then came the revolting, clammy hand again, petting her neck and bare shoulder. "Why to your wedding, my love! Tonight's your big night, Kate! *Our* big night, I guess I should say." His hand began to wander again, tracing along the edges of her curves suggestively, but not quite committing.

She recoiled as if it were a big, hairy spider crawling around under her nightgown. It took every bit of her faculties to look up at him and smile. "Hold your horses there, tiger, we're not married yet, ya know."

He winced a bit and removed his hand back to the steering wheel.

"You're right," he said, blushing a little—he was still just a boy when all was said and done. "I've waited this long, I can wait a little longer."

She breathed a sigh of relief. Hopefully, that would be the end of his groping hand for a while. *But now what? Let's see if we can boil a little more of that frog.* She clenched her teeth and let out a little groan of pain.

"What is it?" he asked.

"My legs are starting to cramp up from being bent behind my back for so long. I need to be able to straighten them for a bit."

"Just hold on a little longer." His voice was flecked with indecision. "We'll be there in just a little bit, and then I can untie you."

"You don't have to untie me completely, Daniel. Just cut the cord connecting my ankles and wrists—*one step at a time*—so I can sit up for a bit and stretch my legs." Looking up at him, she could that he was biting his bottom lip, mulling it over in his mind.

"I don't know," he said.

"What could I possibly do with my hands tied behind my back and my feet tied together? Besides, I think I'm getting car sick…I need to be able to sit up and watch the road or I'm going to puke all over. What kind of wedding will it be with a puking bride?"

She saw the dull glint of metal from the corner of her eye as it hovered over and then behind her. There was a ripping sound as the binding was cut in one quick slice. Without slowing or taking his eyes off the road, he put his hand under her head and heaved her up into a sitting position as if she were nothing more than a small child.

He tossed the blade onto the dashboard. "Better?"

"Oh, much better, thank you," she said, straightening her legs, trying to work the stiffness out of her knees. She stared at the knife laying there, not even an arm's reach away. If she could just somehow convince him to cut her hands loose. She would have to think of a reason, but not too quickly, or he would catch onto her little game and probably kill her right on the spot.

She began watching out the window, but of course nothing at all looked familiar to her. All she could determine was, they were driving on a rural, snow-dusted road out in the country somewhere. Over the last several minutes they had begun to climb up and around rolling hills, dotted with copses of leafless trees.

As they drove, she couldn't help but start to wonder if there was any chance at all that she would get out of this. It was the middle of the night as far as she could tell, and she had been abducted right from her bedroom. She wouldn't be missed until late in the morning, when Mable would make the command decision that she had slept in long enough and knock on her door.

By then, she would surely be raped or murdered...probably both. Or maybe even be hostess to a demon entity, which would probably be worse than being raped and murdered. And here came the water works. She didn't sob or choke, but she couldn't stop the tears from peeping out of her eyes to run down her cheeks.

Her situation was hopeless. Daniel wasn't stupid, he wasn't going to be fooled into cutting her hands or even her feet loose. Nobody was going to miss her until later in the morning, and even once she was missing, how would anyone even know where to look for her? Even she didn't know where she was being taken, for crying out loud!

She swallowed back the tears for a moment. "So, where's this wedding?" she asked.

"The chapel, of course," he said, with a sly smile splayed across his hollow features.

She had no idea what he was talking about and knew it would be fruitless to ask. She was sinking into despair, knowing there was no way out, the cloth strips biting into her skin, a constant reminder of just how helpless she really was.

Daniel started to chuckle to himself, shaking his head. "You know, your boyfriend, the sheriff, was actually getting pretty hot on my trail there for a little bit. Had me truly worried there for a few days. He turned out to be smarter than I gave him credit for."

She thought of a few good replies to that comment, but decided that holding back would be the wiser course of action.

"Of course, in the end, I proved to be the smarter one." He laughed some more. "Boy, did I do a number on him, didn't I? The last I heard, he was a total mess: locked away in his house, not seeing anyone—not even *you*, probably drinking himself to death. I guess that taught him."

She kept her eyes straight ahead, but could feel him staring at her, looking for a reaction. He could stare all night, he wasn't going to get one. He finished with a laughing sigh and shook his head, like a kid remembering his favorite Christmas.

She wondered for a moment if it would be possible to lunge for the knife, snatch it up with her teeth, and plunge it into the little bastard's throat. He had done a number on the man alright, preyed on his weaknesses and practically ruined him. Ruined everything she and Chet had built together.

Wait a minute! What with all the recent excitement of being kidnapped by a devil worshiping lunatic, she had forgotten about Chet! All was not lost! She thought about her last conversation with him. She had given him an ultimatum and walked away. Told him she was leaving town on the early morning train, and that if he wanted a future with her, then he had until then to convince her to stay. But by bedtime, she still hadn't heard from him and she had literally cried herself to sleep.

She remembered how he had looked when she walked away. Not good. Really, she hadn't been holding out much hope that he would be able to pull himself out of it. Guilt now sunk its talons into her, wrenching and twisting at her heart. She had been so selfish to walk away from the man at a time when he likely had needed her most, despite the stubborn front he was putting up.

Black clouds of despair began to sink in, enveloping her heart. She fought them off and grasped at what little hope remained, and held it, embraced it with her whole soul. A doubtful little voice in her mind tried to tell her that this wasn't the movies, Chet wasn't going to come riding up on a white horse in shining armor to save her. She silenced the voice of doubt, and pushed it deep into the recesses of her mind. She had to believe that Chet was coming... somehow, she knew he would come. He would...he *would* come.

Suddenly, Daniel steered the truck off of the pavement and onto a rutted dirt track that wound uphill, into thick trees. The truck shuddered and jolted as the tires slipped and sloshed in and out of the deep ruts. She became even more apprehensive as the trees, with their naked, spindly branches enshrouded the vehicle, cutting them off from any traces of civilization.

He turned to her, his eyes gleaming in the dim light of the truck's instrument panel with a kind of frenzied madness, his mouth twisted into a victorious smirk. He cupped a hand to his ear. "Do you hear that, Kate?"

She shook her head.

"Wedding bells!" he shouted, and then laughed raucously. He reached over, put his hand on her thigh, just above the knee, and let it creep a few inches upwards. "We're almost there. I hope you're ready for what's to come."

Something inside of her snapped. This little game was over. She looked him square in the eyes, unflinching, a white-hot fire burning in her chest. She spoke each word slowly and concisely, her voice even and deadly. "Take your filthy, murderous hand off my leg, you pathetic, twisted freak."

His eyes widened, a look of shocked disbelief replacing the cocky smirk on his face. He took his hand away and brought the truck to a halt. She maintained his gaze, refusing to look away as his eyes narrowed to angry slits and his mouth contorted into a vicious snarl. It came so fast she didn't even see the stinging backhand that caught her across the cheek and mouth, snapping her head painfully to the side.

The blow nearly knocked her out, her vision spinning momentarily as a trickle of blood began to run from the corner of her mouth. Before she could regain her senses, he snatched his knife from the dash. With his other hand he yanked her head back by the hair. He set the point of his blade against the soft tissue just below her eye and let it dig a little.

"I should cut your eye out and feed it to you for that," he sputtered through clenched teeth.

The knife point pressed harder, on the verge of puncturing skin.

"I doubt that *she* would be very happy if you brought her a vessel with a missing eye," Kate hissed back, surprised at the lack of fear in her own voice.

He let go of her hair, flung the knife back onto the dash, and began driving again. "So, how much do you know about all this then?" he asked. "Who else knows about it? Sheriff Cooper?"

She kept quiet. She was done talking to him. She would keep her eyes open for an opportunity now—whatever it turned out to be—and take it when she had the chance.

He snorted. "Go on and clam up if you want, you're much prettier with your sassy mouth shut anyway. Besides, it doesn't matter. Your boyfriend is already too late as it is." He chuckled in an attempt to appear unaffected, but it was obvious he was still stinging from her sharp words. "In a very short time from now, you're going to be all mine...and hers, actually. I don't know exactly what's to become of you—your soul, your essence, or spirit I mean—but actually, I hope a part of you stays...trapped inside that pretty little head somewhere, with a full knowledge of everything. That's what I hope for you, Kate."

"You're sick," she muttered, expecting another vicious backhand.

Instead he let loose with a laugh that was a bit too loud and too long. He reached over and twirled a ringlet of her hair around his finger. "You know, you're right about that, and you're about to find out just how sick I can be."

She pulled away from his touch. "I thought you weren't a monster."

The smile dripped away from his face, and his mood seemed to pivot on a dime. He shrugged his shoulders. "I'm not."

She could tell that social hour had now come to an end. He was paying her no more mind as he concentrated on navigating the pickup along the narrowing and ever more winding road.

The snow was letting up and through the window she could see the full moon, a milky smudge shrouded by thinning clouds, looking down on her like a huge cataract eye. She dredged up an image of Chet from the inner-most chamber of her heart and held onto it. Not the broken and hurting man she had talked to yesterday, but the strong, young sheriff who had swaggered into her office and asked her to lunch just a couple of short months ago.

That was the man she needed now so desperately. It was her only chance, she feared, and so she prayed in her heart silently, *please be coming, Chet! Please be coming!*

CHAPTER 41

Porter lit up his second Lucky Strike since his return to the Miller's driveway, his hands still trembling slightly. He took a long drag, held it for just a second, and expelled the smoke from his nostrils. He figured it was going to take at least two more smokes before his nerves got back to normal—maybe even three!

He had backed his Chevy in between two big trees, next to the driveway, in an attempt to camouflage his presence. The spot gave him a good view of the front door of the house, and if anyone happened to drive up, they most likely wouldn't see him until they were right even with his car. Not too shabby of a job, if he did say so himself.

He kept his attention on the house, the windows staring back out at him like soulless, blackened eyes. *Yeah, we see you sitting there, smoking your cigarette. You don't fool us. Hey, you wanna know a secret?*

Oh, he knew the secret alright! Knew more about it then he cared to. *Nope, I'm just fine right here, thank you!* He took another drag, finally feeling some of the mellowing effects of the nicotine as it moved through his system. But still, if he closed his eyes, even if only for just a second or two, there they were: Trina and Will Miller, taking up center stage in his mind. Trina, with her head completely bashed in, and Will sitting in a sticky pool of his own blood.

Another big pull on the cigarette.

He shook his head, even chuckled a little. *Oh, Porter, some of the stupid shit you get yourself into sometimes.* "Hey, Porter," he said, doing his best impersonation of Sheriff Cooper, "How'd you like to make a little extra money? No big deal. You know, standard police stuff: enforcing the speed limit, stopping a bar fight here and there, responding to barking dog complaints…walking through darkened homes with murdered corpses around ever other corner, maybe sitting all alone, watching the house with the bodies still inside, and the killer still out there."

Well, at least his sense of humor seemed to still be intact after everything he'd been through this night. He cranked his window down just enough to flick the cigarette butt out. *Another one bites the dust.* He rolled the window back up and produced cigarette number three from the pack in his jacket pocket. *One more just about ought to do it.*

He stabbed the cigarette between his lips, struck a match, and glanced up at the house just in time to see the front door slowly open.

CHET TOOK THE STAIRS THREE AT A TIME, Henry following behind with the shotgun, but much slower. He didn't remember drawing the Colt from its holster, but he was gripping it with both hands by the time he reached the top. Down the hallway, a dozen yards or so to his right, Mable stood in the open doorway of Kate's room, one hand clamped over her mouth and the other pressed against her chest.

"Step back, Mable!" he shouted, sprinting for the bedroom, fearing the worst.

Mable barely cleared the doorway in time. Chet rushed into the room, pistol up in the firing position.

For the first few seconds, his mind couldn't understand why Mable had screamed; there was nothing here, the room was completely empty. His heart seemed to freeze again, as the word flashed in his mind like a giant billboard sign: EMPTY.

"Wh-where is she?" he asked, lowering the pistol, barely conscious of it in his hands. "Where's Kate?"

Then his eyes started to really take in the room. The first thing he noticed was the window above her writing desk was wide open, and the room was freezing cold. The books on the writing desk had been knocked over—some onto the floor—and the desk itself, was covered in slush and snow.

The blankets and sheets had been stripped from the bed and were lying in a pile in the middle of the floor. Stepping closer to look at the pile of linens, he saw that the bed sheet had been all cut up. The cuts were rough and uneven, as if they had been made in haste, and possibly with a knife, not scissors. A couple of remnants lay to the side as long, irregular strips. A numb fear began to creep through his body as his mind began to piece it all together.

Mable was suddenly at his side, her voice trembling. "What's going on here, Chet? Where's Kate?"

"He took her," he answered, mechanically. "Came in right through the window, tied her up with strips cut out of the sheet, then left with her...the same way he came."

"Through the *window*?" Mable said, in obvious disbelief. "But that would be impossible—not without a ladder. Henry and I would have heard someone clanging around outside with a ladder. Our bedroom window is right next to hers!"

"Not impossible," Chet whispered, "Not when the devil himself is helping you."

"Now what?" Mable asked.

"I'm going to go get her."

PORTER QUICKLY BLEW THE MATCH OUT in his fingers and watched the front door of the house open an inch at a time. He watched until the door swung fully inward and vanished into the blackness of the home's interior. Had they forgotten to latch the door securely? Had the wind—of which there was very little—somehow pushed the door open? Of course, that meant he would have to get out of the car and go shut it—a prospect he did not savor in the least.

Then his eye caught a slight shift in that dark void, a nearly imperceptible movement. A shadow within a shadow. He continued staring, questioning and doubting if he had really seen anything at all. But as he concentrated his gaze he thought he could make out the ubiquitous outline of a person—head, shoulders, torso—just standing there, motionless in the threshold. *Your frazzled mind's got your imagination working overtime is all. Nothin' there.*

One way to find out would be to light the area up with his car's headlights. He grabbed the knob on the dash, but didn't pull it. It was like a huge part of him really didn't want to see what might be in that doorway. It was better not knowing, he reasoned.

Of course, there was the matter of getting out of the car, walking up to the house and shutting the door. He couldn't just sit here and leave it open. There were dead bodies in there for hell's sake. An animal or something could get in there. Then what? Putting both hands on the steering wheel he groaned and slammed the back of his head against the seat headrest. *Okay, one more smoke, then I'll turn on the headlights and go shut the stupid door...and lock it this time!*

Keeping his eyes glued on the doorway, he struck another match and held it to his cupped hands until the tobacco in the end of the cigarette ignited, sending the precious nicotine-infused smoke into his lungs.

He took his time smoking this one, not being in any particular hurry to go about the task he had promised himself he would do once the cig was gone. A couple of times, he thought he saw a shifting in the darkness again, but it was so slight, he couldn't be sure. *What is your problem? Just turn on the stupid headlights and stop this nonsense!*

He reached for the headlight knob, but froze when he saw a naked foot, pale as maggots, appear from the crypt-like darkness and step down, unflinching, into the snow. *The hell?* The foot was followed by another foot—this one clad in a woman's shoe. He could see legs, then knees, the hem of a dress…

He nearly pulled the knob off the dash. The Chevy's lights blared to life, casting the front of the house in a harsh light. There, standing on the porch, defying all logic, was Trina Miller. In the glare of the lights, Porter could easily make out the nasty wound still caving in one side of her head. The strange way her neck seemed to form an obtuse angle to one side, strongly suggested that her neck had, indeed, been snapped.

Earlier, she had seemed as dead as a doornail. He couldn't comprehend how she had survived such horrific injuries. And yet, there she was: alive and even walking around with a broken neck!

The woman took two faltering steps toward him. He cringed and sucked in air through clenched teeth when he saw the way her head bobbed, shoving that angle in her neck outwards a little with each step. *I ain't no doctor, but if she ain't dead now, she will be if she keeps walking around like that!*

He snatched up his radio mic and tried to raise Chet, but got no reply, just a drone of soft static. He tried again and watched with sick fascination as Trina ambled forward a few more steps, then fell down the porch stairs, face into the snow. *If that didn't finish her for good, then she's for sure paralyzed now.*

The half-finished cig dropped from his mouth as he watched her contort herself back to her feet. And he knew it was all wrong…everything: the way she moved—all herky-jerky—the blank expression in her eyes, her pallid complexion, the slack in her mouth and face.

His mouth was as dry as a cotton ball when he tried the radio again. Still no reply, not from Chet, not from Rick…not from anyone! He looked up and saw that she was getting close, one arm extending out for him. Was it a desperate plea for help, or an attempt to grab him? He wasn't waiting around for one more second to find out! He never agreed to this! The dame was on her own.

He rammed the stick into first gear and gassed the engine. In his nervous state he let the clutch out too fast and the tires spun uselessly in the snow. Trina managed to shuffle right up to his window as the tires grabbed some traction and the car began to ooze forward. She struck the window with a fist as he went by, and he was sprayed by chunks of tempered glass as it shattered. He screamed— too shocked to even swear—romped on the gas pedal, and cranked the wheel all the way to the right.

The engine's rpm gauge was redlining because he was still in first gear. The car fishtailed around onto the driveway, spitting streams of dirty snow at the house. Straightening the car out, he risked a glance out of the passenger window and shifted into second gear. Trina was now coming for him at a dead run, her missing shoe causing her body to hitch awkwardly with each stride.

Halfway down the drive, he was getting ready to throw the car into third gear, when an intense, burning pain suddenly flared in his groin. This time, he did have the wherewithal to let out a shrieking, "Shit!" Looking down and half standing, he saw his dropped and forgotten cigarette smoldering away, trapped between the seat and the last place a man wants to see flames!

Raising his butt off the seat, he used one hand to swipe the cig onto the floor. He'd worry about putting it out once he got on the road, and put a little distance between him and Trina Miller—or whatever it was chasing after him.

He looked back up just in time to see a man standing right in his path. No time to swear and no time to scream, he laid on the brakes and cranked the wheel hard to the left. There was a sickening whump, whump, whump, as the car collided with the man, his body flying up and over the right fender, rolling across the hood, smashing into the windshield, then vanishing from Porter's field of view.

The Chevy skidded sideways, its momentum carrying it toward the steep bank of the driveway, a sort of ditch-like feature to help with drainage. If he had been on dry ground, he just might have been able to pull off a save, but the slick, snowy conditions left him no chance at all. He locked his elbows and braced himself as the car slid over the embankment and made one complete roll, coming to rest on its wheels.

During the course of the rollover, Porter had been flung around inside the vehicle like a dried pea in a soup can, the cacophony of breaking glass and twisting, crunching metal filling his ears—he thought he may have even heard the unmistakable snap of a bone or two. Everything hurt, and he felt close to losing consciousness, which at the moment, would have seemed like a blessing.

But he didn't lose consciousness, and was becoming painfully all too cognizant of his situation. Somehow, he had ended up in the back seat, lying on his side. An icy, dull throb below his right knee was letting him know that the bone there was most likely broken—a hot, stabbing agony when he tried to move it, gave him no reason to doubt. Warm blood trickled sluggishly in several rivulets down the side of his face, surely the result of several lacerations on his head.

The car's engine, having died in the crash, was ticking quietly, while a vent of steam hissed softly from a hole in the radiator. Other than those two sounds everything around him was quiet. It gave him the moment he needed to gather his thoughts, pull his wits together. It was the sound of footsteps crunching on the snow in the near distance that jarred his memory—a staggered, hitching walk, like someone with one shoe on and one shoe off.

A second set of footsteps came to his ears, these ones much closer. He remembered the man he'd hit with the car. He must have come out of it okay… maybe it had only been a glancing blow?

"Help!" he cried out, his voice pinging back at him from the surrounding metal. "Help, I'm in here! You have to hurry!"

The footsteps were getting closer. *Good, he heard me!*

"You have to hurry! That lady out there, there's something wrong with her…I think she's dangerous!" he warned his would-be-rescuer. "Hurry!"

There was no change in pace. Was the guy slow in the head or something? *Give him a break, he just got plowed over by a car.* He was right outside the window now, Porter could hear the man's feet shuffling in the snow, probably trying to figure out how to get the car door open.

The man's face appeared in the window above Porter's feet. The diffused light of the full moon splashed across his pale features, revealing a maniacal grin, and to Porter's absolute horror, a deep gash across his throat, gaping and cherry red, like the gills of a fish.

Earlier, there had been no doubt about Will Miller being dead, his throat slit down in the basement, and yet here he was, pulling and wrenching on the car door, trying to get it open. Porter started to scream for all he was worth, the sound billowing out of him unbidden.

He moved to sit up—ignoring the grinding pain in his leg—and pushed his back against the other side of the car, as far away from Will as he could get. Reaching down to his hip, he felt the cold grip of the pistol he'd been issued when Chet had deputized him. He drew the gun, but his hands were shaking so

447

badly he had serious doubts on whether he would actually be able to hit anything, even at this close range.

Just then, as Porter cocked the hammer back on the .38 revolver, Will managed to dislodge the door, the warped metal squealing loudly as he twisted it open. *Bam!* The gun jumped violently in his hand and there was a brief, fiery flash. Will Miller staggered back, a small, dark hole now appearing in his chest near the collarbone. He snarled, and came again, reaching inside the car with his hands, groping at Porter's ankles and pant legs.

Porter kicked with his one good leg and continued shrieking as loud as he could, hoping that by some miracle, someone would hear him. He cocked back the hammer of the gun for a second shot, just as Will managed to capture his ankle. He squeezed down on it with a vice-like pressure. Porter howled in pain, his voice growing hoarse as he fired again, from nearly pointblank range. The round hit Will in the chest, on the left side, right in the heart.

For a moment, the thing—this was no man—appeared to have been stunned, but never loosed his hold on Porter's ankle, and after a second or two, began pulling him out of the car. Porter cocked and fired again, this time aiming for the head. He missed, the bullet flying just to the left, to sail off somewhere into the night sky. He cocked back the hammer once more. *Steady! Make it count!*

There was an awful screech of metal behind him as the other door was ripped completely away from the car. Cold hands, like crab's claws clamped around his neck and began to squeeze with incredible force. He didn't need to look to know that it was Trina behind him, about to choke the life out of him.

He brought the pistol over the top of his head and blindly fired. The hands fell away from his neck, followed by a hideous, vehement wailing. He turned and saw he had put a hole right in the center of her face. The blonde hair on the back of her head was mushroomed out and stained red from the exit wound the bullet had left behind.

She came at him, growling like some kind of animal, flailing her hands and gnashing her teeth at him. At that moment, he knew he was a dead man. Whatever these things were, they were beyond his ability to kill.

Her strength was incredible; his bones cracked and broke from each vicious blow, his skin opened up like wet paper from each slash of her fingernails. Will was still pulling him out of the car by his legs, Trina crawling on the backseat after him, her attack relentless. He tried to cock back the pistol's hammer for another shot, but the gun slipped from his trembling fingers. It was probably no use anyway, but he might have liked that last bullet for himself, he thought as he was pulled from the car, landing hard on the ground.

His state of consciousness seemed to pulse back and forth with each painful beat of his heart: darkness, then light…darkness again, and then he was back. The cold ocean of darkness beckoned him and he felt himself letting go…giving into the pull that would take him away from this nightmare, and into that void of nothingness.

Trina got out of the car. The crush of her feet in the snow was loud in his ears. He looked up through a throbbing black tunnel. Standing over him, she raised her ashen foot high above his face, held it for a second, and then…she put it back down into the snow.

Together, the dead couple turned their heads as if they both could hear something. Suddenly, to Porter's amazement, they both took off on a dead sprint. The crunch of their feet tearing up the new-fallen snow faded away at an unnatural speed. Just like that, Porter found himself alone in the dark, unconsciousness still threatening to overtake him.

But somehow, he was still alive! Blackness began to sweep through his brain. Where were Trina and Will off to in such a hurry? *I wonder where my cigarettes are,* he wondered just before he passed out.

CHAPTER 42

Rick shook his head and cursed out loud as his patrol rig slammed with a tooth-jarring crash back into the deep ruts of the old Salem Road. In his mind's eye, he could envision nuts and bolts, crucial to the operation of the vehicle, shaking loose with each bump and shudder. Of course, it wasn't really the health of the car that mattered at this point. Just moments ago, he had received word from Chet about Kate's likely abduction at the hands of the Miller kid.

Rick was driving the car now like a battering ram, completely indifferent to the obvious damage he was doing to it. *Just get me to the top, baby, that's all... just get me to the top!* He had just radioed back to Chet that, indeed, *someone* had been on this road, and recently, judging from the fresh tracks and the spots where tires had thrown up big chunks of spattering mud across the white snow.

Chet was on his way, but so far, any attempts to raise Porter on the radio by himself or the sheriff had failed. The snowstorm was still causing interference, he supposed. This rescue operation was going to be up to just he and Chet, from the looks of things.

The road gradually became steeper and narrower as he progressed, the ruts deepening as the tires slipped more and more. The car bottomed out a few times in some difficult spots, forcing him to back up and make a run at it. He winced each time at the sound of the undercarriage scraping over the road—if it really could even be called a road anymore.

Just as he was starting to doubt he could go much further, the Chevy slid sideways and down, lurching to a sudden stop, the tires sliding uselessly in the mud and snow. He put the car in reverse and tried to back up, but with no luck at all. He tried rocking the car by rapidly switching between first gear and reverse, but it wouldn't budge.

He spit out a serious curse word—the one you didn't let your wife hear you say—and kicked the door open. His cowboy boots slid in the snow as he made his way around the car to evaluate just how stuck he was. It didn't look good...

not good at all. Somehow, the car had fallen into some deep, but separate sets of ruts, torquing the frame and very effectively wedging itself with opposing forces into place. He kicked the fender in frustration. Out came that word again.

He climbed back into the car. "Coop, it's Rick," he said into the radio mic, "do you copy?"

"Go ahead," Chet's voice echoed across the static.

"You on your way?"

"Ten-four, just on the outskirts of town right now. Are you already up at the old town site?"

"That's a negative, my car is stuck…real bad. There ain't no way I'm getting it out."

Silence.

Rick could imagine the look of fear and pain in Chet's eyes, as the man was probably frantically trying to come up with a plan. "Just get up here," Rick said. "Try to get around my car if you can. I'm proceeding on foot, maybe you can pick me up."

"I'll see you soon," came Chet's reply, his voice cold and distant.

Rick tossed the radio mic back into the car, letting it dangle from its cord. Then he shut the ignition off and carried the keys with him to the rear of the car. He opened the trunk and grabbed his Winchester twelve-gauge, pump shotgun. He always kept it in the trunk of the car for when he might run across a pheasant or grouse while on patrol in the countryside. He never imagined in his wildest dreams he'd be needing it for anything otherwise.

Slamming the trunk of the car shut, he slung the shotgun over one shoulder and started hiking up the road at a fast trot, praying that Chet would have better luck getting up here than he had, and knowing that time was probably quickly running out for Kate.

BY THE TIME THE FORD EMERGED from the trees, at the top of a gentle slope, Kate's heart was beating so hard she felt like it might break a rib. What was this insane kid going to do to her? Was he just nuts, or was all this talk of a demon for real?

Not far up ahead, she saw the outline of an old church silhouetted against the opaque, winter sky—*the wedding chapel*—and she figured her questions would be answered soon enough.

The Summoning

Daniel navigated the truck along the edge of an ancient cemetery, the time-worn, neglected building looming prominently in the windshield. It was a very sturdy-looking structure, made from big, chiseled granite blocks, with a squat, stone belfry in the front. The bell no longer occupied the hollow space at the top.

Some of the roof remained intact, although it was sagging severely in most places. Most of the heavy timbers that made up the rafters were exposed as the majority of the roof had collapsed over the years.

Daniel brought the truck to a stop in front of the main door and killed the engine. For a moment, he said nothing. Just sat there, biting on his bottom lip and wiping the palms of his hands on his jeans. He looked nervous, even frightened.

"Look, Daniel," Kate said, "whatever it is you're thinking of doing here, you don't have to. It's not too late for you to turn back from this."

He turned his eyes to her, a reflection of fear and pain mirrored in them for an instant. "You know, for once, I just wanted to be someone...someone with a few friends—maybe even a girlfriend—belong to a school club, play on the football or basketball team." He shook his head and sighed heavily. He seemed almost on the verge of tears. "But you see, Kate, there are these unwritten rules in society, rules that are designed to keep certain people...certain *undesirables* on the outside, never to be admitted into the precious inner circles."

"Daniel, believe me, just about every kid feels like that at some point in their lives. It's all part of growing up."

"Maybe for some kids," he said, his voice taking on a hard edge. "Kids who are content to be herded around like sheep, but I refuse to be a whipping boy to the likes of Robbie Pritchard, or anyone else. I've been mocked and laughed at for the last time."

"So, somehow you've decided that killing random, innocent people is the answer?"

He narrowed his eyes. "I'm going to let that one go, just because you have no idea what you're talking about."

Stall for time, keep him talking. "I probably know more than you think," she said.

He gripped the steering wheel, his knuckles turning white, the wheel squeaking in his hands. "That book you were reading in the park that day; I knew it was dangerous the second I saw it in your hands."

She was startled. How could he have known that there was anything special about that book? So much for her attempts at rationalizing away any existence of the supernatural in all of this. The demon was real...she knew it. She had known it since that night when Scotty had been murdered just after warning her. "Daniel, whatever it is that you have yourself mixed up in, it's not too late…you don't have to go through with…with whatever you are planning here."

"That's where you're wrong," he replied, his voice flat and emotionless. "She's my mistress, I'm bound to her now…bound by blood sacrifice. The only path for me now is the path that she has laid before me. For me and for you."

Little fingers of terror pawed and clutched at her heart and a wave of desperation cascaded down through her. "It's not a *she,* Daniel…it's an *it!* Haven't you figured that out yet with that genius brain of yours? It's a demon that showed itself to be *exactly* what you wanted it to be!"

He started shaking his head. "No…no, you're wrong, Kate, you are wrong…"

"You know I'm right! You think you're in love with it, when in reality you have only allowed yourself to become a slave!"

"That's enough, Kate!"

"A subservient slave, murdering innocent people to serve the blood lust of some hellish demon that, in the end, will devour you!" Tears were streaking down her cheeks now. "She…*it* doesn't love you, Daniel."

"I told you to shut up!" he screamed.

She softened her voice. "Daniel, untie me now, and—"

He grabbed her rolled-up, pink socks off his dashboard. "That's enough out of you," he said, holding the socks up to her face. "Open," he commanded.

"Daniel—"

He grabbed her by the hair, wrenching her head back, and shrieked like a complete lunatic, "Do as I saaaaaay!"

She cried out in pain, and as she did, he stuffed the socks back into her mouth, and then quickly tied a strip of cloth across her mouth to hold them in place. Kate screamed in frustration and rage, thrashing against her restraints. With an amused look on his face, Daniel just sat there, watching, until weariness overtook her and she finally stopped, her chest heaving as she sucked in air through her nose.

"Are you finished?" he said.

She stared down at her feet in response, catching her breath, refusing to look at him.

"Good girl." He watched her for a few more moments, and then opened up his door to get out. "Well, let's get this show on the road, shall we?"

She watched him walk around the nose of the truck, smirking at her through the window. At that moment, she felt an intense hate building up inside of her, pushing out the fear. The tears had ceased to flow by the time he opened her door. The cold embraced her instantly, a light breeze rippling the hem of her satin nightgown. She began to shiver.

He reached in and adjusted the blanket so that it was around her shoulders and upper body as much as possible. "Sorry about the cold," he said, "but I didn't really have time to pack you a bag." He chuckled. He put his hands on the sides of her face, forcing her to look him in the eyes, and made a show of wiping her tears with his thumbs. "So, here's what happens next: I'm going to carry you now. This can take place in two different ways: with you conscious, or unconscious. Do you remember that little choke hold I used on you?"

She maintained her silence.

"Well, if you start squirming around again, you'll leave me no choice. I will put you to sleep again, understand?" He made her nod her head. "Good. Let's go." He reached into the car, slipping an arm behind her back and another one beneath her knees, and lifted her out with ample ease.

She was amazed at his strength. It was as if she weighed nothing to him. She could feel the hardened muscles in his arms, pressing into her body, as he began to walk. He never staggered or stumbled, even a little, as he carried her up the stairs of the old church building and through the front door.

The inside was darker than night. All she could see were the dim and shadowy shapes of what she assumed were the remnants of the collapsed portions of the roof. Some of the shapes were highlighted with a thin layer of white from the fresh snow that had found its way inside. He carried her through the middle of the building—what would have been the aisle—stepping with familiar ease over the fallen timbers and mounds of plaster and brick that lay in his path.

At the back of the building, which actually would have been the front of the chapel, was a raised dais. Two sets of stairs flanked the dais on either side, permitting access to the platform where the preacher's podium would have been. She realized that Daniel wasn't even breathing hard as he carried her up the short set of stairs on the right.

He moved across the platform to the very back, where a thick, canvas tarp, about the size and shape of a door, hung from the stone wall. A slit had been cut in the center of the tarp. It was through this opening that Daniel carried her into pitch black darkness.

She could tell from the closeness of the air, they were in some kind of smaller room, perhaps an office that the clergy had used when the building was a functioning church. The roof on this part of the building apparently had not suffered as much as in other spots, because Kate could not detect any holes or big cracks. There was also less of a draft in here, even if the air still held the bite of winter's chill.

"Again, I'm sorry about the cold," he said, sounding every bit sincere. "Just bear with me for a little bit." He carried her a few more steps, near the wall, opposite the curtain they had just passed through. He then bent down and sat her on some kind of wooden bench, perhaps an old pew that he had scavenged.

He moved off and in the darkness she could only hear him scuffling around the small chamber. The icy, stone floor chewed on the soles of her feet as she sat there with little options but to wait, listen, and try her best to remain calm—the latter, proving to be an impossibility.

There was the unmistakable sound of a match being struck and suddenly, the room was dimly illuminated in an orange, flickering glow. It was a windowless, semicircular room, about twenty feet across, and twenty feet deep with stone walls and a stone floor. In the center of the room, stood a big wooden table, about three feet high, and large enough for a full grown man to lie upon. Back in the building's heyday, she figured this table most likely held objects of value: relics, figurines, perhaps a large crucifix. Now, it lay vacant, except for four large candles, one on each corner, that Daniel proceeded to light. The only other object in the room was the old pew she was sitting on.

After lighting the four big candles, he approached. She was shivering, and if it wasn't for the gag in her mouth, her teeth would be clacking as well. "Hang in there, just a little bit longer, sweetheart," he said, bending over and dragging a large gunnysack from under the pew. He opened it and dumped the contents, spilling several dozen split pieces of wood clattering onto the floor. He started stacking them against the wall, to her right.

As she watched him work, she noticed there was a small square alcove in the wall where he was piling the wood into the shape of a log cabin. She realized it was a fireplace, and actually found herself willing him with her mind to hurry up. Within a few minutes, he had a decent blaze going, the heat from the licking flames radiating out to warm her chilled, exposed skin.

He looked up at her. "It warms up in here really nicely," he said, actually beaming like a child. Rising to his feet, he looked around the room, his hands on his hips. "I know it's not the Taj Mahal, but we'll be okay here for a while. Nobody will think to come up here to look for us, especially in the winter. There's plenty of wood to burn, and I've stashed enough food up here to last a long time. Long enough for us…*Her* to continue to build strength and power."

He came over and sat down next to her. "I know you probably hate me right now, Kate, but in time, you'll come to realize that this was meant to be. You might even learn to love me back." He sat back and put an arm around her. "Of course, it won't really be you, I guess. I mean, I totally think you are still going to be along for the ride, so to speak, but it will actually be *Her* doing the driving."

"Mmmm, mmmm," she mumbled behind the gag.

"You want to say something?"

She nodded her head.

"Okay, but if you get all sassy again, I'll shut you up, and that will be it, until *She* comes."

Kate continued to nod her head. *Keep him talking!* He untied the cloth strip and removed the gag, tossing it on the bench next to him.

She swallowed back the fear and loathing she felt for him and consciously focused on softening her eyes and face. "Daniel, can't it just be you and I, the two of us? I mean, you're right, this is a perfect place for just the two of us to be happy together. We don't need this other woman, mistress, or whatever you say she is."

"Right, Kate. You hate me now. I can't just leave you tied up forever, and you'd run away the first chance you got."

"I don't hate you, Daniel, I'm just terrified right now. Look at me: I was choked into unconsciousness, tied up, kidnapped from my room, driven up to some abandoned, old church in the middle of Timbuktu, and told that some other being is going to be taking possession of my body. Don't I have the right to be a little scared?"

He shook his head slowly back and forth. "I'm sorry, but you just don't understand the situation here. As I already explained to you, the path has been laid before us. I have no choice but to see this thing through."

She knew this was her last window of opportunity to talk to him and try to sway him from this *path* as he called it; the window was quickly slamming shut. "You are a free man to do what you want, Daniel. You don't have to do anything you don't want to."

He stood up and kissed her on the head. "Everything's going to be okay, I promise. You have nothing to be afraid of." He scooped her up into his arms and started carrying her over to the table. "It'll all be over soon, and you can start the process of accepting your new existence."

"Daniel, no! Where are you taking me? What are you doing?"

"It's almost time now," he said, stopping in front of the table. "And I can hardly wait." He buried his face into her neck, just below her ear, and inhaled deeply.

Turning her head away in repulsion, she saw the table and noticed something about it for the first time. Dangling from each corner, was a short chain that had been bolted into the wood. Attached to the ends of the chains were metal cuffs—the perfect size for a pair of wrists and ankles.

Kate screamed.

COWBOY BOOTS WERE NOT DESIGNED for trudging through the snow, and Rick was cursing the ones on his feet as he hiked up the road, doing more slipping than actual walking. His body was working hard and he was starting to feel too warm beneath his wool-lined, denim jacket. Under normal circumstances, he would have consciously slowed his pace to avoid perspiring, which would dampen his clothes, and possibly lead to hypothermia.

But slowing his pace was not an option tonight. That psycho kid probably had Kate up at the old Salem church at this very moment; every second was crucial. Every second was crucial, and yet, here he was mucking his way on foot through the snow—most likely an hour or more away. At this thought, his heart sank and he knew Kate's chances were not good—even if he broke into a sprint the rest of the way.

Don't give up just yet, mister, Chet's still on his way, he thought. But Chet was driving the exact same make and model that he had just been forced to abandon. What chance did the young sheriff have of making it much farther than he had? Not a very good one, he reckoned, reaching out and grabbing the small trunk of a young sapling to keep himself from falling on his face.

He leaned his shotgun against the sapling, and placed his hands on his knees, gulping for breath. As the thudding of his heart began to diminish in his ears, he thought he heard the undulating growl of a vehicle, back down the road, working its way up the arduous path. With each second, the sound grew louder. He felt his spirits and hopes rise dramatically, as he was able to determine that the vehicle had most likely managed to make it around his stuck car and was still coming!

It had to be Chet, so he grabbed up his shotgun and started half trotting, half skiing his way down the road, toward the approaching vehicle. As he got closer to the sound, it became very evident that he was not hearing the deep, throaty,

V8 rumble of Chet's Chevy. This engine sounded much smaller and was definitely running fewer horses. He could hear the perky torque as the smaller motor revved through its power band, getting the job done.

He stepped off the road into the cover of the flanking trees, racking a round into the shotgun. If this wasn't Chet coming up the road, then who was it? It was better not to take chances, so he watched and listened as the vehicle neared. If it turned out to be Daniel, he had every intention of blowing the kid's head off as he drove by.

No more than a couple of minutes passed before he saw the initial beam of the headlights stabbing through the trees, violently jerking in all directions as the road tossed the vehicle about. A minute later, the actual headlights came into view as the vehicle rounded a bend in the road about two hundred yards below him. He stuffed the butt of the gun into the hollow of his shoulder, bringing the muzzle to a forty-five degree angle in front of him, and waited.

Suddenly, as the vehicle halved the distance to one hundred yards, the iconic, seven-slot grill, and narrow headlights of a Willys Jeep became evident. Quickly, Rick thumbed the shotgun's safety on and started slipping his way toward the oncoming Jeep, waiving his hand. As he closed the distance, he could see Chet in the driver's seat, pouring it on, pushing the little Jeep to its limits.

Chet began to slow up, as he neared, but Rick yelled over the whine of the engine, "Don't let up, Coop, or you'll get stuck for sure! I'll jump for it!"

Chet still slowed up some, but maintained enough forward momentum to prevent the snow and mud from sucking him down. Rick tossed the shotgun onto the backseat, and then started running next to the Jeep with one hand stretching out for something to grab onto, like a hobo hopping a train. Just as one of his boots slipped out from under him, he was able to get a hold of the windshield frame. He pulled himself into the passenger seat and shouted, "Go, go!"

Chet barely acknowledged him and put his foot to the accelerator, the muscles of his jaw standing out.

Rick patted the Jeep's dashboard, like patting a dog on the head. "Good thinking, Coop. Anywhere that Daniel goes in his old Ford, this little baby will be able to follow."

Chet grunted in agreement.

"Did you ever get a hold of Porter?" Rick asked.

The younger man looked at him and shook his head. "Stupid storm must be playing havoc on our radios. Looks like it's just you and me." He had to down shift to make it over a steep little knoll in the road. "I just pray we aren't too late."

Rick placed a hand on his boss's shoulder. "Those tracks look pretty fresh, if you ask me. I'd say we're right on his tail."

"Let's hope so."

"Coop, she's going to be okay," Rick said. "He's just one deranged kid on the run and he couldn't a picked a worse place to run to. Once he's at the top, there's gonna be nowhere else for him to go. We'll have him trapped."

The Jeep was launched briefly into the air by a large bump in the road, Chet wrestling with the wheel to keep the small, squirrelly vehicle under control. Rick had to use his hands to hold his own butt to the seat to keep from being bucked right out.

Chet shook his head as he urged the Jeep on. "Don't underestimate this kid, Rick. I've got a very bad feeling that it's not going to go quite so easy." He risked a quick, sideways glance at him, his eyes a glacial blue. "We need to be prepared for anything, Rick…and I mean, *anything*."

CHAPTER 43

The small fire had warmed up the area, just as Daniel had promised it would, but she was shivering uncontrollably anyway. *Trembling* was probably the better word for it. You shiver when you are cold, but when you are really scared or frightened, you tremble.

The metal shackles encasing her wrists and ankles were cold though, and she supposed those would never heat up, regardless of how warm the fire made everything else. She hated the trembling. It was like her own body betraying her to the enemy, broadcasting in the clearest means possible, just how terrified she really was.

But fear and terror were the only things left to her now, as she lay helplessly shackled, hand and foot, in the middle of nowhere. A human sacrifice on the altar of a murdering lunatic.

She had fought him when he cut her loose from the cloth strips in order to put her in the metal cuffs. She had fought with everything she had in her: kicking, punching, screaming, biting, raking with her nails, throwing knees and elbows, all she had. She had been nothing more than a kitten to him. His strength was…preternatural. He absorbed the worst of her blows—even a brutal kick to the face—as if they were nothing, while forcing her into the shackles.

The kick to his face had torn his lip open and a trickle of blood flowed from the corner of his mouth. Once she was secured and unable to move, he dabbed at the blood with his finger. Smiling, he extended his bloody fingertip to her face and drew on her forehead, uttering something unintelligible. As he did so, an inexplicable, hot gust of wind filled the room briefly. On the wind was the trace scent of lilacs, mixed with the subtle stench of decay.

Grinning, Daniel lifted his nose to the air and inhaled, then looking at Kate he said, "She's here."

That was when Kate had started trembling.

After replacing the four candles that she had knocked over, he stepped away, beyond the edge of her vision, while she struggled desperately to regain her courage and her wits.

"You look so beautiful," he said, his voice all around her at once. "I could just stand here and look upon you forever."

She stared up at the conical ceiling of the room, watching the shadows created by the four guttering candles and the flickering fire dance and dart about. She was all too aware of the sheer, satin nightgown barely draping her body and could practically feel his lustful eyes groping her. And there it was, that tiny, yet angry little coal of indignation coming to life deep inside her. "M-maybe you should t-take a picture," she stammered.

He stepped out of the shadows, knife in hand, the candle light glittering in his eyes. "Maybe I'll improve the scenery just a little." He slipped the blade of the knife beneath one of her gown's shoulder straps and angled the blade against the delicate material.

She lifted her head to look him directly in the eyes, and said, "So, now the monster comes out…after all."

Frozen, he held her gaze, his nostrils flaring, his lips compressed together forming a thin, white line. After a long moment, her heart sank as a wicked smile slowly seeped across his face.

"So be it," he said, his voice thick and deep. "I'm a monster."

She felt her nightgown lift from her skin ever so slightly, as he applied pressure to the shoulder strap with the blade. She closed her eyes, two tears egressing in thin streaks down either side of her face, to vanish into her hair. *Be strong, girl! You can get through this, just be strong!*

He was taking his time, obviously to draw out the suspense and increase her personal agony. She opened her eyes. Her body was still shaking, but pure rage and hatred had replaced fear and terror as the main cause. "What are you waiting for? If you're going to do it, then just do it already!"

He bent low, and whispered into her ear, "If you say so."

A loud slam from somewhere in the main part of the church pulled him up straight, and he quickly withdrew the knife. His face blanched as he stared at the curtain. Kate recognized the sound of footsteps echoing through the building, heading in this direction. A new thrill of hope and salvation surged through her whole being. It had to be Chet! Who else could it possibly be? Somehow, he had missed her before dawn and now he was here!

Daniel, obviously arriving at the same conclusion, spun and placed the edge of his blade across her exposed throat. He hissed, his voice low and guttural,

"One sound, and I shut you up forever." He applied just enough pressure so that she felt the blade's cold bite on her soft skin.

She hardly dared to breathe, knowing that one slip from her...or from her captor would mean instant death. She could barely hear beyond her own blood thrumming in her ears, but the footsteps were definitely growing louder, *clomp, shuffle, clomp, clomp....* If that was Chet, he sure wasn't being very stealthy about it—especially for a former Marine! In fact, the sounds conjured up the image of an intoxicated person stumbling through the church. The only thing missing was the occasional hiccup.

"They're coming this way," Daniel whispered, as if it weren't obvious. He slipped into a dark shadow, off to the side of the slit in the center of the curtain, and all but vanished in it. "I'm just two steps away from you, Kate. I can still end you in less than a second."

There was no way she was just going to lay there, in subdued silence, and watch this kid ambush and butcher Chet as he came through the curtain. She would warn him, but would have to time it just right, at the last second, but still give him enough time to defend the attack. Barely breathing, she fixed her concentration on the ragged slit in the old tarp that served as the makeshift doorway into the chamber, and waited for Chet to appear.

The shuffling and stomping grew louder and louder until it paused, just behind the curtain. She couldn't see Daniel, but rather could feel him tensing up, coiling himself like a rattlesnake about to strike. The curtain began to billow and sway as somebody pawed at it from the other side, searching and groping for an opening.

This was it, she prepared herself. *Your left!* That's what she had decided to yell out the instant Chet's head poked through the opening.

But instead of Chet, a woman suddenly lurched into the little chamber on the stiff, inarticulate limbs of a marionette puppet. Kate recognized the creature for what it was, as the intermittent firelight illuminated its features: yellow-gray skin, crooked neck jutting out at the wrong angle, bloodied, misshapen head, and an obvious bullet hole in the center of its face. A plain house dress hung in ragged tatters, the exposed skin covered in dozens of lacerations, cuts, and scratches.

Kate screamed in unconstrained horror and utter disbelief. The thing turned and looked at her with expressionless, dead eyes, and at that moment, Kate new beyond a doubt, that all of it was real. The Salem curse was real. The demon woman that needed her as a vessel...real. Murder victims, reanimated after death...

The woman—the *dead* woman—took two hitching steps to stand beside Kate at the altar. Kate pulled weakly against her restraints, all of her strength having gone out of her along with the last scream. She grew lightheaded, knew she was breathing too fast and too hard. Her world began spinning.

A deep, grinning blackness enfolded her in its depths, pulling her down into its tranquil bosom. As the oblivion of unconsciousness smothered her final thoughts, she heard Daniel's voice from the corner of the room. "Hello, Mother."

CHET PULLED HIS JEEP OVER to the side of the road, halfway up the final rise that would lead them to the old Salem town site. He shut the ignition off, the silence almost immediately overwhelming in the absence of the motorized growling of the engine and the squawking of the suspension. Time was not on their side and his initial instinct had been to plow full force, right up to the old church and charge in with guns blazing.

It had been Rick that convinced him of the foolishness of such a maneuver. Daniel would hear the Jeep's engine as soon as it crested over the hill, he had argued. The kid would likely panic, and there was no telling what drastic actions he would take then. Conceding to his deputy's cooler and more experienced head, he had finally agreed with the man's strategy.

Without wasting a second, both men slid from the open cab—Rick grabbing his shotgun from the backseat—and began working their way up the last hill. The snowstorm had passed, leaving behind a thin veil of clouds surging sluggishly across the sky. Slightly obscured, the full moon was a bright smudge high in the zenith of its course, casting the entire landscape below in contrasting, silver-white highlights and pitch-black shadows.

The two lawmen hiked without a word. Fifteen minutes later, they found themselves at the top of the hill where they paused momentarily to catch their breath and survey the scene. The abandoned Salem church was a silent, stone hulk, squatting stoutly before them just a hundred yards or so away; there was no sound or movement.

"It's awful quiet up here," Rick whispered. "You're sure this is where he woulda taken her, Coop?"

The possibility he might have been wrong, sent bolts of panic arcing across his chest like little electric shocks. "This has to be it," he said, "this is where Abel Gannon took his wife. It's right in his journal."

"Look!" Rick thrust a finger toward the front of the church. "His pickup. He's here all right!"

Chet peered ahead, and sure enough, there was the Ford, parked just in front of the door of the church, half concealed by the black shadow being cast down by the steeple. He drew his Colt from the holster on his hip and pulled back the slide just far enough to verify a round in the chamber. "Truck first, then the church," he said, and started moving in the direction of the vehicle.

The two men moved parallel to each other, making sure to keep about a five foot distance between them—the farther they were apart, the tougher it would be for a shooter to hit them with rapid, successive shots. They were nearly trotting as they approached the Ford, both men feeling the expediency of the situation increasing, both now willing to sacrifice some stealth for speed.

Chet reached the passenger window and brought his gun up to the glass as he peered inside. Rick circumnavigated the rear of the truck, his shotgun tucked into his shoulder as he cleared the bed. The truck was empty. They met back up at the front of the pickup. Chet put his palm on the hood; it was warm.

"inside?" Rick's voice was barely a whisper, his eyes fixed on the dark hole that was the open front door of the church.

Chet nodded and led the way up the stairs. Upon entry, the church appeared to be empty and dead inside, except for a few broken and rotten pews strewn amongst scattered piles of debris and rubble. Tight, constricting desperation pawed and clutched at him. Empty! The church was empty! *Nobody here! I'm too late!*

Suddenly, Rick nudged him with his elbow and pointed into the blackness at the back of the church. "Do you see it?"

Chet strained his eyes into the darkness, and sure enough, he saw it too. A thin, orange light, flickering intermittently in the deepest part of the gloom. A fire was burning.

Side by side, the two men worked their way forward as silently as they could, navigating around rotten roof timbers and various detritus that was littering the floor. As they drew closer, the orange light became brighter and Chet thought he could see shadowy movements in the light.

He had been here before and knew the place well enough to remember that there was a room at the back of the church. He had always figured it was an office or private chamber for the reverend. As they made it to the stage, where the podium would have stood, he could see that a tarp had been draped over the entrance as a makeshift door. The tarp didn't quite touch the floor, and it was through that small gap that they had been able to see the escaping firelight.

464

He eased himself up onto the stage and winced as a floorboard moaned under his weight. After a moment, Rick joined him, gripping his shotgun with white-knuckled fingers. Chet brought his pistol up to chest level and nodded once to his deputy before continuing forward.

They slowly closed the distance until he could actually hear the crackling of the fire coming from behind the tarp. Other than the popping of the fire, it was dead quiet. This gave him much cause for alarm. That, along with the fact he hadn't noticed anymore ghostly movements in the firelight since that creak of the floorboard moments ago.

They were within five feet of the curtain now. Chet used the back of his hand to wipe the sweat out of his eyes. *Please be in there Kate! You have to be in there!* He took his eyes off the curtain long enough to give his deputy a glance. Rick nodded—he was ready to go—and fixed his gaze on the curtain, waiting for Chet to make a move.

As Chet took a step forward, the curtain suddenly exploded outwards, revealing the interior of the room for a brief instant. In that half of a second, his brain was able to register two things: Kate was in that room, and a woman was running now, full speed right at Rick, an unearthly wail bursting from her lungs.

The roar of Rick's shotgun was deafening as it discharged a load of buckshot into the shrieking woman's chest at near pointblank range. Like the flashbulb of a camera, the shotgun's muzzle flash illuminated the woman's face, freezing it in time for a microsecond; Chet recognized the insane and all-too-dead face of Trina Miller.

The impact of the buckshot made her stagger backwards, but she quickly regained her balance and charged again at Rick, who was in the middle of pumping another round into the shotgun's chamber. Not quick enough. Trina fell upon him with a ferocious attack, slashing at him viciously with her fingernails and gnashing her teeth like a feral animal. Rick was stumbling backwards, using the shotgun like a shield to fend off the assault, a deep gash on his cheek, already weeping blood.

Despite his state of utter disbelief, Chet instinctively trained the sights of his .45 on the woman's back, hoping for a clear shot, praying he wouldn't hit Rick, but the woman's movements were too erratic and he didn't dare take it. The struggle went to the ground as Rick fell over on his back, Trina landing on top of him.

"Get her off! Get her off!" Rick screamed, as he rammed the shotgun with both hands into the thing's face, with little to no effect.

Chet took two deliberate steps forward and placed the muzzle of his pistol directly against Trina's skull. It was then, he saw the hole—an obvious exit wound—gaping from the back of her head, tiny skull fragments and brain tissue matting in her blonde hair. The wound had not been there before, and he quickly connected the dots; Porter must have shot her in the head. And then what?

He started squeezing the trigger on his Colt, but based on what he was seeing, he had serious doubts that two holes in the head would be any different than one. Suddenly, he was hit by something that sent him flying. He landed in a painful sprawl on the rough wooden floor. Stunned, he rolled onto his back just in time to see Will Miller pouncing through the air at him, the gash in his throat forming a bloody grin.

THE LOUD BOOM OF A NEARBY GUN blast catapulted her back to consciousness, to the here and now, followed by the sounds of a struggle on the other side of the curtain. A man was screaming; it sounded like Rick, but she couldn't be sure.

She was still lying on the table, but no longer shackled by the iron cuffs. Her hands were at her sides now, but something was definitely wrong. The room seemed to be spinning now, and when she tried to move, her limbs felt like they were made of cement—heavy and barely responsive.

Daniel Miller was at her side. He seemed to be in some kind of frenzy, chanting strange words as he drew the blade of his knife across the palms of his hands. She remembered being filled with hate and horror, but for some reason those emotions seemed beyond her now, and she merely gazed on, watching her abductor with a strange detachment, as if she was merely a spectator watching a film or a bizarre play.

I must have been drugged with something, she guessed. *Or I'm in some kind of hypnotic trance?* It was hard for her to even care, let alone guess much about it. She just wanted to go back to sleep, but another gunshot rang out from beyond the room, quickly followed by another. This seemed to be cause for great alarm for Daniel, and he became even more frantic with his chants and cutting.

Suddenly, she saw that she was surrounded by a group of people—men and women both. She had no idea where they had come from, but they were also chanting along with Daniel. The air seemed to crackle all around her, as if they were drawing the energy from all of the surrounding atoms.

The air next to her—the opposite side from where Daniel was standing—began to shimmer like a mirage above a country road on a hot summer day. A gust of warm wind passed over her body, rippling her nightgown and tussling her hair. The fire increased in intensity and the candles began to glow, their flames sprouting upwards. The air ceased to shimmer and there stood a woman of utmost grace and beauty, looking down at Kate with a warm and benevolent smile.

The woman leaned forward, placed her hands on the sides of Kate's face, and looked her in the eyes. Immediately, Kate was falling into those liquid, blue pools, being swallowed up to drown in their bottomless depths. It was beautiful, warm…soothing.

She was barely aware now of the chanting going on around her, barely recognized another gunshot, as a thousand tiny fingers began pushing on her from every direction, poking and probing the outer edges of her very soul, trying to find a way in. She resisted these subtle attempts to gain access, it being as natural to her as breathing, but she could also feel that resolve weakening as she sank deeper and deeper into those glorious eyes.

She was losing the fight, could feel this other woman's presence pushing her out, exiling her to some other place in her own mind; a dark and secret corner from where she knew there would be no escape. Beyond caring anymore to fight it, she began to ease up and felt herself slipping away.

CHAPTER 44

Just before the dead thing landed on him, Chet was able to lift one leg and jam his foot into its stomach. Driving with his leg, he used the forward momentum of his assailant to send the foul thing flying overhead. The creature, now inhabiting the murdered corpse of Will Miller, sailed over the edge of the stage and crashed into a heap of old roof tiles.

Chet struggled to his knees and watched in horrified fascination as the creature quickly collected itself with disjointed, scrabbling movements, like some kind of giant, grotesque beetle. After righting itself, it charged at him on all fours like a rabid dog. The Colt rocked in his hands as he fired a single, well-aimed shot that struck the undead attacker in the middle of the forehead. The .45 caliber round practically obliterated Will's entire skull. His limbs collapsed beneath him, but he continued to convulse and writhe on the ground, his fingers leaving bloody tracks in the floor as he clawed and raked at it.

Chet lined his sights up and fired another round that decimated what was left of the creature's head. The body finally went limp…back to being dead. Whatever these things were, apparently they still required at least a semblance of a nervous system to maintain their control over a body.

Quickly, he jumped to his feet and rushed over to where Rick was still on his back, fending off Trina's savage attack. His heart lurched when he saw that the man had lost his hold on the shotgun, now lying uselessly a few feet away.

His best friend's face was covered in blood. His gritted teeth were a row of white islands in a sea of red as he flailed his arms, desperately trying to deflect the barrage of blows raining down on him. "Coop!" he cried, his voice weak and muffled.

As Chet approached, Trina turned to face him, her eyes rolling wildly. "You're too late, cop," she hissed, and licked at her lips provocatively.

"The girl is mine!"

Without a second thought, he destroyed her face with two quick rounds. The nearly headless body slumped sideways onto the floor, one bare leg still draped over Rick's heaving abdomen.

"How bad is it, Rick?" he said, kneeling beside his deputy. "Are you seriously hurt? Can you walk?" He flung the dead woman's leg off the man's stomach.

"Not good, Coop," Rick said, between grunts of pain. "She did a pretty good number on me."

"Hang on, buddy," Chet said, slipping out of his leather jacket and draping it over Rick like a blanket.

Rick reached out with a feeble hand and gripped Chet by the collar. "Kate! Go save her, kid! Don't worry about me, I'm right behind ya."

Chet pulled Rick's revolver from the holster and placed it in the deputy's hand. "They hate head shots," he said. He picked the shotgun up off the floor. "I'll be right back, this should only take a minute. You just hang in there, ya hear?"

"Go," Rick said, coughing up a gout of blood. "Go get your girl, and send that kid straight to hell, where he belongs."

"That's the plan."

Holstering the .45, Chet put the butt of the shotgun to his shoulder, and approached the curtained doorway. Reaching out with one hand, he ripped the curtain down, letting it fall to the floor. Despite having just killed two people who were already dead, he wasn't prepared for the sight that lay before him.

The small room was awash in a kind of sickly, pinkish glow. A ring of people, their hands linked, surrounding an old, battered, wooden table in the center of the room were chanting, their voices low and monotone. Their faces were gaunt and creased with suffering—they were here against their will. They were flickering, like an old light bulb that was fixing to give out. Trickles of cold, fear-driven sweat began to run down his forehead as he realized these people were actually the disembodied spirits of people long dead.

His heart just about stopped in mid beat when he saw Kate, floating in the air! Actually levitating, just above the heads of the surrounding circle of people, and slowly rising higher. She looked like she was asleep, lying on her back, her white night gown hanging from her suspended body like a translucent, silken veil. She looked as beautiful as he had ever seen her, but then, like the chanting, incorporeal spirits beneath her, she flickered.

Kate was gone. Floating in her place was another woman. The woman lolled her head to the side and looked directly at him with gorgeous, burning blue eyes of pure hatred. She was exquisitely beautiful—too beautiful. Like the unrealistic creation of some pimple-faced, pubescent kid's ultimate fantasy come to life. She looked like a twisted conglomeration of all the best parts taken from a selection of pinup girls. The result was a plastic woman, void of any defining characteristics or endearing features; just a thing…a sex object, and most definitely the demon woman from Gannon's journal.

Another flicker and Kate returned, then another brought the demon back again, only to flicker out and be replaced with the image of Kate once more. He had seen enough, it was time to crash this little party. He took a determined step into the room, making a beeline for Kate.

"Chet, lookout!" It was Kate's voice, but it was inside his head, like he had thought it to himself. He barely caught a sliver of movement from the corner of his left eye, and it was just in the nick of time. Something glinted in the firelight as it swept through the air toward his face.

He brought the shotgun up in front of himself defensively. Something metallic sparked as it glanced off the barrel in a high-pitched clang. Another slashing attack forced him to stumble backwards in an attempt to create some separation. In that brief moment, he could see Daniel Miller emerging from a dark shadow, pressing the attack, unwilling to lose the advantage of surprise.

The boy was whipping his hunting knife in wide, violent arcs, managing to stay inside Chet's gun, too close for him to use it. He was backed up against the wall when he saw an opening, and snapped the gun straight out, catching Daniel on the bridge of his nose. The kid's head whipped backwards from the blow, his nose broken, a thick stream of blood running freely from each nostril. It hardly seemed to slow him down at all.

Reaching out with one hand, Daniel snatched the shotgun from Chet's grip, as if he were just a child, and hurled it across the room, smashing it to pieces against the far wall. The psycho had Chet cornered. He grinned. The blood from his broken nose flowed over his teeth, giving him the appearance of a ravenous wolf that had just made an especially bloody kill.

"Chet!" Kate screamed in his mind, *"He's going to stab you…"*

And precisely at that moment, Daniel lunged forward, his blade angling upwards into Chet's guts. Chet got both hands on Daniel's wrist and sidestepped. There was a ripping sound as the knife sliced through his shirt. He felt a hot sting as the blade bit into his side, drawing a quick flow of blood; fortunately, just a cut.

The boy was overextended now and off balance. Maintaining his grip on the kid's wrist with his right hand, he brought his left elbow down into the tender, meaty portion of the forearm, just below the elbow, with every ounce of power he could muster.

Daniel howled as his knife went clattering to the floor. Releasing the wrist, Chet flicked out his left fist in two quick, successive jabs that snapped Daniel's head back. He followed up with a jaw-shattering right hook to the side of the head that sent droplets of the kid's blood flinging through the air as a thick, red mist. Stunned, Daniel staggered for a moment, but somehow managed to stay on his feet.

Chet's right hand flew to the grip of his Colt, but before he could draw the pistol, Daniel roared like an enraged beast and charged into him, headlong. The collision was like being hit by a freight train, the air exploding from his lungs as his back crashed against the wall. His knees buckled and he gasped painfully to get his air back. Daniel brought a fist crashing down on his face, the blow sending him to his hands and knees.

The superhuman kid lifted him up with an iron grip by his shirt and slammed him hard against the wall, pinning him there. "You should have left well enough alone, Sheriff. You know what I have to do now."

"Daniel," Chet managed to say before he was seized by a short coughing fit, "you are under arrest for the murders of Levi Henderson, Robbie Pritchard, Lucas Gannon, Conrad Fairchild, and your own parents." He looked at Kate, still levitating in the air like some magician's lovely assistant at one of those magic shows. "And kidnapping," he said, trying to get a grip on his pistol with fumbling, numb fingers that refused to cooperate.

"Cute," Daniel said, sneering. Then he smashed Chet across the face with a hard right that sent him wheeling to the floor.

Blackness was all around him, and he could hear Kate's voice in his head, screaming, *"Wake up, Chet! Wake up, now!"*

Lying flat on his back, he forced his eyes open just in time to see that Daniel had retrieved his blade and was kneeling next to him, the knife poised over his head. Daniel brought the knife down in a plunging attack aimed right for Chet's heart. He caught the boy's wrist with both hands, and redirected the momentum of his downward motion to the side. The knife missed his heart, but sliced a jagging cut over his ribcage before plunking into the stone floor.

Chet saw the flicker of surprise in Daniel's black eyes just before he kicked his leg up, booting the kid hard in the face; once, twice, and again for good measure. Then, he wrenched Daniel's arm until he heard the loud snap of his shoulder popping out of the socket. Again, the knife clattered to the floor as Daniel wailed with rage and pain.

Chet didn't release the arm. Instead, he wrenched it even farther until he could hear ligaments and tendons snapping and popping.

Daniel was crying, bent over in pain, and throwing a howling tantrum, like a spoiled child. "She's mine! She's mine! You can't have her...no!"

Maintaining his grip on the limp and useless arm, Chet got to his feet and looked up at Kate. She was still levitating there, flickering back and forth between herself and the image of the demon. Only, now the demon seemed to be the stronger, more tangible image of the two women. Kate was fading, and she would soon be gone.

He cranked on Daniel's wrist, eliciting a cry of agony. "Stop this," he shouted. "Send that bitch back to hell, or wherever she came from, or I swear I'll rip your damn arm off!"

The psycho just started to laugh. It was a disturbing, hollow, grating sound. "You're too late, Sheriff Cooper, there's no stopping it now. Kate's already gone, and any minute now, my mistress will make her entrance into the..."

"Chet!" Kate's voice came again into his head, but sounded so faint now, like she was shouting to him from across a wide and distant gulf. *"Daniel is the key...the source of the demon's power. You have to...you have to kill him to stop her!"*

Without giving it a second thought, Chet pulled his Colt from the holster and pointed it right at Daniel's head. "This little shindig is over, kiddo," he said, cocking the hammer back. "But I get the feeling your party is just getting started."

"Oh, I wouldn't if I were you," Daniel said. "If you kill me, Kate dies right along with me."

Chet hesitated. Was he telling the truth?

"I know she's been talking to you, Sheriff. I can hear her too. And she's right: if you kill me, then you stop all of this. Kate just failed to mention one little, annoying detail: she dies too." He laughed. "You know, Abel Gannon ran into the same dilemma with his wife. He ended up cutting her throat to put her out of her misery. Do you think you can handle that, Sheriff Cooper? Are you willing to cut Kate's throat to save her soul?"

"He's lying, Chet!" Kate said, her voice echoing distantly. *"Able could have saved his wife by killing himself. He was the power source, but he was too cowardly to do the right thing, so he cut his wife's throat to save himself!"*

"She doesn't know what she's talking about," Daniel spat. "Are you really willing to risk her life...her soul, on wild speculations?" He started to straighten himself up, seemingly oblivious to the further grinding and snapping coming from his deformed shoulder joint as it rotated to an impossible position. "If you're positive, then do it. Shoot me, Sheriff Cooper.... Come on."

"Do it, Chet! Do it for me. I'd rather be dead then trapped in a body with a demon at the wheel. You...we...can't allow this thing to come into the world. Please, you owe me that much."

"I love you, Kate," Chet said, as he began to take the slack out of the trigger.

"I love you too."

Chet looked into Daniel's coal-black eyes, they were wide with fear and panic.

"Don't you do it!" Daniel said.

At that moment, the entire room seemed to shake as the air was rent by a shrill, ear-splitting scream. Chet looked away from Daniel to Kate, where the shriek had come from. Suspended in the air, with her head thrown back and her body jerking and contorting, she was howling. The sounds coming out of her were completely inhuman. Kate opened her eyes and looked at him. He was horrified to see her green eyes smoldering with the hate of the demon, a sinister smile of victory playing across her full lips.

He had failed. Kate was gone.

"Kate!" Chet cried, feeling the strength almost go out of him entirely. He let go of Daniel's wrecked arm and the kid crumpled in pain to the floor. He took two hesitant steps toward the levitating woman, the woman that looked like Kate, but was now something else all together. She was still drilling through him with eyes that bespoke an unfathomable loathing. She was slowly descending through the air now, as the circle of beings seemed to be winding down their chant, and blinking out one by one.

He just watched in stunned disbelief. Kate was gone, consumed by some otherworldly abomination that he couldn't even begin to believe in, let alone understand. She came to rest on the table and began to slowly stretch and flex her limbs in a languid seductive fashion. In moments, the demon would have complete control over the faculties of its new tabernacle. And then become this unstoppable, evil force that had been described in the Gannon journal.

"I'd rather be dead..." Kate's final words played through his mind. *"...you owe me that much."*

Suddenly, in one fluid motion she swung her legs over the side of the table, and sat up, her feet dangling like a child's. It was now or never. Hot tears blurred his vision and rolled down his cheeks as he aimed his .45 at Kate's face—Kate's perfectly beautiful face—and squeezed the trigger.

CHAPTER 45

The report of the gun blared off the walls of the small room, but his shot had gone wide, missing the mark by mere inches. A searing pain in the upper portion of his back had caused him to flinch just as the gun had gone off. He spun around. As he did so, there was a hot, wet, ripping sensation in his back. His hand went numb, releasing its hold on the pistol. Daniel was standing in front of him, his right hand dangling from the useless arm at his side. His left hand was clutching the knife, stained and dripping with fresh blood.

He had no idea how serious the stab wound to his back was—the pain told him it was bad—but for the moment, his heart was still beating and his lungs were still working. That was good enough for the Marine.

Daniel took a step sideways, brandishing the blade in front of him, making small darting movements with it at his face. Chet had to gain control of that knife, and from the feel of the warm flow pouring out of the wound in his back, he needed to be quick about it. *Get inside his attack, gotta get inside,* he thought, trying to recall his military training.

He circled left, toward Daniel's crippled right arm—the kid's weak side. This forced Daniel to have to reach across his own body to make attacks. It was a sound strategy, one employed by boxers and prizefighters to great effect. But boxers and prizefighters didn't usually go up against demons and kids with superhuman strength.

Daniel made a sudden slash at Chet's face. The sheriff faded back, out of reach of the knife, and answered with a solid left jab to the boy's already broken nose.

"Chet, it's not too late." Kate's voice was a remote echo that barely registered in his mind this time. *"Im still fighting the demon off, but I can't hold on much longer. You have to kill him!"* There was still a chance to save her!

With a renewed hope surging through him, he threw all caution to the wind and let his fists fly. The punches were catching the kid; some were just glancing blows, but others were landing hard. Daniel began to wither under the assault, slashing out in wild, uncontrolled attacks with his knife. Chet's forearms were bleeding from a dozen cuts where the blade had stung him, but it was the deep wound in his back that had him concerned the most. His shirt was now sticking to his back like he had run through a lawn sprinkler.

The kid was taking a beating that most likely would have killed a normal person by now. He wondered how much longer Daniel could hold out, and how much longer he could keep taking the fight to him.

"Just run, Daniel!" It was Kate's real, physical voice behind him—the demon was talking. "Don't let him kill you or all will be lost. Just run away, stay alive. I will deal with the sheriff."

Daniel offered Chet one quick, smug grin that said, *I win...you lose,* and took off on a run around one end of the table. Chet lunged after him, and might have caught the boy, but as his fingers brushed the back of Daniel's shirt, the demon leaped off the table and delivered a bone-shattering kick into Chet's abdomen. The blow sent him reeling backwards to crash onto the floor in a heap of senseless, writhing pain.

His vision was a clouded, pulsing blur as he watched her walk toward him. He saw his gun laying on the floor, within arm's reach. He stretched out toward it but she had seen it too, and sent it skidding across the floor with a casual flick of her foot.

She knelt beside him, smiling petulantly, and began to brush her fingers through his hair. "Poor Sheriff Cooper...you tried so hard, came so close to saving your beloved." She grabbed his face in both hands, the flesh of her palms was hot, like she was burning with a fever. "You couldn't save your Marines, and you can't save her. She's in here with me right now, Sheriff...still clinging on to what little bit of herself she can. She's a strong one, I'll give her that much. It was one reason why she was chosen." She bent her head toward his face. "Shall we give her one last memory of happiness before I devour her?"

He tried to sit up, tried to force his pain-racked body to fight, but she pushed him easily back to the floor with the palm of her hand. She kissed him, full and hard on the mouth. The kiss was almost violent, devoid of any kind of love, affection, or even lust, a base act of hate and mockery. When she pulled away, he choked for air, his lungs battling to recover from the shock of the brutal kick.

She stood up and seemed to regard him for a moment with merciless, reptilian eyes. Nonchalantly she placed her foot across his throat and leaned her weight on it. His airway was immediately crushed shut. He quickly grabbed at her ankle with both hands, trying to twist and throw her off balance. But much to his shock and dismay, he couldn't budge her.

Choking, he arched his back and tried lifting her leg straight up, a task that he knew he had ample strength and ability to do—Kate was not a large person—but she may as well have been a two ton block of cement standing across his throat. His already oxygen-deprived brain began to fade as he kicked, writhed, and tried to twist out from under the crushing force. Blackness was closing in. *I failed you, Kate...I'm sorry.* He hoped that somehow she could hear him.

"She hears you," the demon said, applying yet a little more pressure to his neck. "She's watching you die at this very moment. She can even feel it, Sheriff: the soft yield of your throat against the sole of her foot as she crushes down, the weakening of your pulse as your life force slips away. She's screaming your name, Chet. Screaming and screaming and—"

"Well, I guess we'll have to do something about that then, won't we," said a voice on the other side of the room.

The foot was suddenly lifted off of him. He rolled onto his side, inhaling giant gulps of precious air, ignoring the pain it caused in his ribcage and back. As his vision cleared, he saw one of the most wonderful sights he could have imagined. Daniel was backing away from the door, into the corner of the room, his hands in the air, a look of surprise and horror splayed across his battered face.

Holding the boy at gunpoint was Rick, covered in his own blood, his clothes ripped and tattered, his body bent slightly at the waist, one arm cradling his ribs. He looked at Chet, lying on the ground at Kate's feet, gasping and struggling for air. "You two having a lover's quarrel over there or something?"

Chet thought of Kate. The demon had said she was still hanging on. Maybe there was still time...just maybe! "Kill him, Rick!" Chet shouted, his voice coming out as a hoarse rasp. "Shoot him in the head!"

Rick gave him a look of shock. "I think I've got this under control, Coop. No need to kill the kid in cold—"

"Do it, Rick! That's an order!"

An ungodly shriek suddenly erupted from the demoness, as she sailed through the air, right over the table, in a single flying leap toward Rick, her hands and feet extended out in front of her like a pouncing cat.

Time slowed as Chet yelled, "Shoooot!"

Like a snapshot in time, he could see every detail of the scene: The orange firelight rippling off the creamy folds of Kate's nightgown as she flew through the air, Rick's eyes, wide with surprise at the sudden leaping attack, Daniel's sudden move for Rick's gun…Rick, picking up on the kid's movement at the last second…

The bright spout of flame from the revolver's muzzle as it discharged, combined with the sharp report, brought the passage of time back into alignment with the present. Daniel's head fell backwards, a dime-sized hole appearing in the center of his forehead. His legs buckled and he fell to his knees, his arms hanging at his sides. He froze like that for a brief moment, then toppled over onto his back.

Daniel Miller was dead.

The very moment the gun went off, killing Daniel, Kate crashed into Rick with a cry that pierced the air like a shock wave. The bloodied and broken deputy collapsed under the impact to the floor and lay motionless. Next to him Kate was writhing and screaming as if she were being consumed by flames: arching her back, thrashing her arms and legs, digging her heels against the stone floor.

Chet labored to his feet and stumbled toward her, calling her name, his voice sounding distant in his own ears beneath the ungodly shrieking coming from her. He fell on his knees at her side and tried to hold her down, fearing she was going to hurt herself. As he pinned her shoulders to the floor, she opened her fiery, green eyes and gnashed her teeth at him.

"She's mine!" said the demon. "Mine!" She thrust her fingers like claws at his face, but suddenly jerked her hands back, and slapped the floor at her sides instead.

For a moment, he was confused, then he realized that it was Kate that had held back the demon's attack. She was in there fighting back, wrestling with this thing for her freedom!

"Let her go!" he yelled. "Daniel's dead, you have no power now! Do you hear me, you are through!"

"No!" the demon howled.

He placed his hands on the sides of her face, and spoke gently, "I know you're in there, Kate. I know you can hear me. You've gotta fight, sweetheart… you've gotta give it all you've got. Take control, Kate…take control."

"Chet?" It was just a whisper, weak and thready, but there was no mistaking Kate's unique inflection.

"That's right, Kate. I'm right here, darling, I'm right here!"

Suddenly, she began panting heavily, her chest rising and falling in rapid, heaving movements. Her skin started to glisten in the flickering firelight as beads of sweat rolled down her body.

"You've lost," he said. "Slither back into whatever hell pit you crawled out of, and let Kate go. It's over for you."

The demon smiled, her eyes piercing him with hatred. She laughed a guttural, ugly laugh. "You fool, it's never *over* for me. Like death, I am timeless. I'll return someday and feast again."

"Enough," Chet said. "Now let her go."

She laughed again. "Not before I break every bone in this beautiful body." She shrieked a horrible sound, like the wail of a thousand tortured souls, and started thrashing violently against the stone floor.

"No!" Chet yelled, diving on top of her, trying to pin her down. He used his arms to secure her head against his shoulder to keep her from slamming it against the floor, but he could feel the rest of her body convulsing and contorting wildly beneath him. "Stop it!" he shouted. "Leave her alone!"

She let out a cry of pain. He squeezed himself against her tighter, but she was too strong. He couldn't protect her. He braced himself for the imminent sound of her bones beginning to break under the strain. "Hang on, Kate," he said. "Hang on."

Suddenly, a hand was placed on his shoulder. "I got her legs and feet, Coop!"

Chet looked over his shoulder to see Rick, grimacing in pain, as he prostrated himself over Kate's kicking legs and then bear hugged her knees to his chest. She continued to thrash with her legs, buffeting Rick back and forth across the floor. He held on while Chet pinned her under the whole weight of his body, completely immobilizing her.

The flailing ceased and Kate went rigid, as if every muscle in her body had seized up. She cried out. It was a cry of one final, exhausted effort, like a pregnant woman delivering her baby with one last push; giving everything she had left in her, to the point of near death. Then, her body went as limp as a fresh corpse.

The fire burning in the fireplace and the candles on the table roared brighter, as if someone had poured gasoline onto the flames. A flat form, blacker than the darkest shadow, appeared like an inky puddle beneath Kate's slack body and oozed across the floor toward the fireplace. Chet watched as it seeped away, a low, gargled growl emanating out from it.

In front of the fireplace, the black puddle began to ripple up through the air, taking on a three-dimensional shape, forming around curves and contours until the demon was standing there in the form of the beautiful, blonde woman.

She stared at Chet for a moment, a look of disgust on her face, before turning her gaze to the body of Daniel Miller in the corner. She held out a hand to the body and beckoned with a long, red-tipped finger. A silvery, transparent visage of Daniel suddenly appeared next to his crumpled body. He was looking around, as if confused. An expression of horror crossed his face when he looked down to see his own lifeless body on the floor, a bullet hole clean through the head.

He looked up from his body back to the beautiful woman, as if for an explanation, but she was gone. Instead, where once stood the woman, some kind of black, spectral thing floated there. It had a humanoid, but asexual appearance, with stretched, thin arms that ended in long, hook-like claws.

Daniel began to drift toward this being. He opened his mouth in a terrified scream, but he made no sound, like an actor in an old silent movie. He looked to Chet, his eyes pleading. *"Help me!"* he mouthed, over and over again. Then, *"I'm sorry!"*

There was nothing Chet could do for the boy, but watch as the spindly, clawed hands of the dark being reached out and grabbed him, pulling him into its bosom with ravenous greed. Then, as the candles and fire returned to normal, the demon, still clutching a screaming Daniel, shimmered and vanished in a ripple of air.

"What the hell did we just see?" Rick asked, crawling to join Chet at Kate's side.

"I don't know and I don't care, so long as I never see it again," Chet said, giving Kate an assessing look, his heart thudding with worry.

She was breathing, he noted right away with relief. Her white nightgown was stained in big blotches and smears of blood—all belonging to he and Rick he quickly surmised. Both men checked for broken bones by prodding and squeezing her arms and legs, but found all to be intact.

"Let's see if we can wake her up," Rick said, taking one of her hands into his and patting it vigorously. "Wake up, Kate. It's all over, wake up now."

Chet gently shook her shoulders. "Come back to me, Kate," he whispered. "Please!"

She started to move her head back and forth, moaning softly.

"She's coming around," Rick said, darting a hopeful glance at Chet. "That's it, girl…come on now!"

Like a newborn butterfly flexing its wings for the first time, her eyelids began to flutter slowly and deliberately. Her emerald eyes drifted listlessly for a moment before scanning Chet's face, then Rick's, and back to Chet, full recognition manifesting in their depths.

She reached a trembling, dainty hand to the side of his face. "Chet, you came…you came for me. I was afraid that you—"

He scooped her up, and pulled her in close to him, kissing her tenderly on the forehead.

She started to sob, burying her face into his shoulder. "It-it was so horrible, Chet. I can't even...it took over, I had no control...I was standing on your throat, watching you die. I could feel you dying and it...was laughing at me." Her shoulders convulsed with another string of sobs.

"But you beat it back, and I didn't die," he said, rocking her like a baby in his arms, stroking her hair. "It's over. You're safe now. You're going to be okay."

"Which is more than I can say for you, Coop," Rick said, from behind. "Did you know you have a hole in your back?"

"Yeah, I kind of figured. You don't look so good yourself, deputy."

Kate's crying stopped suddenly, like someone had turned off a cry switch somewhere inside her. "We need to get you two to the hospital!" she said, pulling herself from Chet's embrace and getting shakily to her feet.

"Kate, what do you think you're doing?" Chet said, suddenly feeling very lightheaded. "You shouldn't be walking arou—"

"Shut up, Chet." She walked over to the old pew on the other side of the table and grabbed a blanket. Picking Daniel's knife from off the floor, she used it to cut a large square piece from it. "Rick, are you okay to drive, or do I need to?"

"I think I can manage it."

"Good, let's get going then. Chet, can you walk?" She draped the blanket over her shoulders like a robe.

Chet started to get up. "I'm fine, just a little weak, I think." A wave of dizziness washed over him and he fell back to one knee.

She was at his side in an instant. "You've lost a lot of blood. I'm sorry, but this is probably going to hurt." She pressed the square piece of material over the wound on his back, applying firm pressure. "That should help, but I think we need to hurry."

Together, Kate and Rick helped him up, and the trio began slowly making their way out of the building leaning on each other for support like the legs of a tripod.

The floor was rocking back and forth under his feet as if he were aboard a ship being tossed about on a stormy sea. They walked past the sprawling bodies of Mr. and Mrs. Miller. Kate gasped.

"It's a long story," Rick said, his voice sounding muffled, like he was speaking under water. "For another time, let's just get out of here for now."

Darkness was pressing in on him from every side and his own breath seemed to be clogging his throat, his temples throbbing with every beat of his heart. His legs were growing heavier with each step and he began to wonder how it was that he was even on his feet at all.

Kate and Rick were talking…about something, their words now just a distant humming in his ears, echoing softly inside his skull.

Rick's voice penetrated through the fog for a moment, "Be careful not to step on an old, rusty nail or a piece of broken glass, sweetheart. I should give you my boots—"

"No time," Kate said. "Don't worry, I'll be fine. I spent half my life running barefoot through the Tennessee woods, mind you." She went on talking, saying something about chasing her brothers—climbing trees—hunting squirrels—riding bareback—

Her words trailed off as darkness took him and he fell into the black chasm of unconsciousness.

Kate's voice chased after him, as he plummeted away, "Chet…Chet!"

CHAPTER 46

"Chet...Chet, honey, can you hear me?" said a voice that was sweet, lovely and filled with compassion.

He opened his eyes. He wasn't sure how long he had been asleep. Like a newborn baby, fresh from the womb, he had no comprehension of the passage of time. His last memory was of Rick, Kate, and himself, stumbling through the old Salem church. Then he had passed out; it could have been a year ago, it could have been five minutes.

It only took a second to realize he was in a hospital bed. A dull ache throbbed in his wrist. He lifted his hand in front of his eyes and saw where an intravenous needle had been inserted and taped into place.

"Chet?" said that sweet voice again. Only this time, as the clouds of obtuse oblivion drifted away, the voice was fully recognizable.

He slowly turned his head toward the voice, blinking the fog from his eyes. Kate was standing at his bedside. To him she was an angel in a sweatshirt and jeans. Her face filled his vision as she leaned toward him, dark ringlets of hair swaying forward.

"How are you feeling?" she asked, gripping him gently by the hand.

He performed a cursory mental check of himself and didn't notice anything hurting too much. "Okay, I think. What happened? I remember walking through the church...you and Rick were helping me walk...then I...I guess I passed out?"

She tilted her head to the side, her face growing serious. "You nearly died, Chet."

"Really? I didn't feel like I was hurt that bad."

"When Daniel stabbed you, he nicked an artery. That's why you were bleeding so much. Dr. Steinmetz said that if the knife had gone just a few more millimeters, you would have bled to death before we could have gotten you back to town. It's still a miracle you didn't."

"How long have I been out?"

"About a day. We got you to the hospital early this morning. Doctors Steinmetz and McConnell performed emergency surgery on you until dawn. You've been asleep ever since. It's late in the afternoon now, around four-thirty maybe. Your sister was here for a while. She had to leave, but said she'd be back to look in on you."

He squeezed her hand a little harder. "And how are you doing?" he asked. His throat felt like it was coated with sand.

She sighed and licked at her lips. "Physically, I'm fine, but I don't know if I can come to terms with what happened up there, Chet." Her eyes became moist.

He closed his eyes and awful images from the night before flashed through his mind like smudged slides in a projector. "I'm with you there," he said. "How's Rick doing by the way? I thought he looked worse than me at the end there."

"I'll live." Rick stepped out from the other side of the bed into the golden bar of sunlight that was beaming through the small window near the bed. "Just some good contusions and scratches…a few broken ribs. Doc patched me up pretty good, but I'm gonna have to take it easy for a while."

Chet was relieved to see that the man did look a lot better than the last time he had seen him, wheezing and covered in blood. Besides a black eye, some red scratches, and a good-sized bandage on one cheek, he seemed to be okay.

The door swung open and Dr. Steinmetz entered the room followed by Rick's wife. The cowboy doctor smiled as he approached. "Hello there, sleepy head. Alice said you were starting to come around. You sure gave us a pretty exciting morning, son."

"So I hear," Chet said. "Thanks for working your magic on me, Doc. I hear it was a close shave."

Dr. Steinmetz nodded gravely. "It was, I won't lie. But you should really be thanking this young lady standing next to you. She saved your life. If it wasn't for her quick thinking, you wouldn't have even made it to my operating table."

Chet looked up at Kate. "Is there something you haven't told me?"

Kate shrugged. "I was doing what I could, that's all."

Dr. Steinmetz put a fatherly hand on Kate's shoulder. "When you arrived last night, you weren't even breathing. She was doing it for you…giving you mouth to mouth. I'm convinced that's why you're even alive right now."

Dr. Steinmetz spent the next fifteen minutes examining Chet: shining a light in his eyes, checking his blood pressure, listening to his heart and breathing, checking his dressings and stitches.

"When can I get out of here?" Chet asked when the doctor was finished.

"I'd like to get you up and walking around as early as tomorrow," the doctor said. "Let's wait and see how that goes. Then we can go from there. Fair enough?"

Chet nodded.

Dr. Steinmetz moved for the door. "Alright people, he's going to be fine. We should all go now so the man can get some rest." He pointed at Rick. "And the same goes for you, mister. You may not be hospitalized, but you need to rest those ribs."

Alice put an arm around Rick's waist. "Don't you worry about that, I'm taking him home right now and putting him straight into bed."

"How 'bout one of them grilled cheese sandwiches you promised me last night," Rick said. "I'm about half-starved."

"If that's what you want," Alice said, guiding her husband to where the doctor was holding the door open.

Rick looked over his shoulder at Chet. "I'll come by and see how you're doing tomorrow, Coop." He turned back to his wife. "Seems like you was promising *dessert* too," he said with a grin.

For some reason, Alice's cheeks blushed as red as apples. That made Rick laugh, which then cause him to put a hand over his ribs and groan. Alice, still blushing, bustled him away and out the door. The sounds of Rick chuckling lightly while Alice scolded him in hushed tones, echoed as the two made their way down the corridor.

Kate cocked an inquisitive eyebrow at Chet. "What was that all about?"

"I have a feeling we don't want to know."

"Okay, missy," Dr. Steinmetz said, "let's let him have some rest." He motioned at the door like an usher in a theater.

"Can I please just stay a little while longer?" Kate begged. "I promise to let him rest."

Chet watched as she batted her eyelashes innocently, her head tilted slightly to the side. He smiled inwardly; she knew exactly what she was doing and it seemed to be working.

Doctor Steinmetz nodded with a smile. "Okay, I suppose there's no harm in you staying for a while, but promise me you'll let him rest. Deal?"

"Deal."

The doctor exited the room, closing the door behind him.

Kate stood a moment, silently listening to the doctor's footsteps fade away. "Don't get too comfortable," she said, sitting on the edge of the mattress, her face all business, her eyes boring into his. "I need to ask you something, and I need you to be one hundred percent honest with me."

"Okay."

"So, putting all this Daniel Miller and his demon crap aside, things between us had taken a turn for the worse, I think you could say."

"You were leaving town…yeah, I guess you could say things weren't so hot as of last night."

"Right, so here's what I need to know…right now." She closed her eyes and exhaled. "Before you heard that I was kidnapped, were you going to let me leave?" She opened her eyes, green fire burned in them.

"Were you really *going* to leave?" He felt like it was a fair response.

"Not if you did something to stop me," she said, her eyes flicking back and forth across his face as if she were reading it like a book.

He smiled. He wanted to tell her how beautiful she looked right now.

"I'm not messing around, Chet Cooper," she said, arching her eyebrows. "Now, were you going to let me leave?"

"Not in a million years," he finally said.

A look of sincere relief spread over her face and her eyes began to glisten. "Then where were you? I waited all evening at Mable's for you to come and you never did!"

"I'm so sorry," he said, "but I was in no condition to come over. I wanted to clean myself up, sleep off the…the alcohol and surprise you in the morning."

She slowly nodded her head. "Okay…okay." She took his hand in hers and they sat that way for a long time, saying nothing.

He thought that he should be feeling content, but something was just *missing* from the moment. A strange feeling of awkward nervousness pervaded; she wasn't content, she needed something more right then. Instincts told him what she needed, probably because he knew it was the same thing he needed.

"Kate," he broke the silence.

She was looking out the window, watching the sun slowly descend through a gray, winter sky. "Yeah?"

"It's taken me a little while to figure it out, maybe longer than it should have, but with everything that's been going on and all…I mean I've had a lot on my plate you know, and I've been grappling with myself, almost as much as with all that's been going on…"

She furrowed her brow. "What are you getting at, Chet? Are you trying to break up with me or something? Because I'll tell you one thing—"

"No!" he said, laughing as he reached up to place his hands on her shoulders. "No, absolutely not."

She placed a hand on his forehead. "You don't *seem* feverish, but you sure are acting like it all of a sudden. Maybe I should go get a nurse."

"Kate," he said, "what I'm trying to say is…I love you! Okay? I love you. I've known it for a long time now, but just wasn't sure how to tell you. So, now you know."

He would never forget the look on her face at that moment. She stared down at him, as if seeing him for the first time, her eyelids blinking heavily. "I love you too."

"So, I'm kind of new to this step in a relationship," he said. "What comes next?"

"I don't know, I'm new to this too. I suppose we just do what comes natural."

"Like what?"

"Oh, things like this." She placed her hands on either side of his shoulders, straddling him with her arms. She closed her eyes and leaned down, barely parting her lips, her front teeth gleaming white behind them. "Say something if this starts to hurt," she whispered.

"Not a chance."

He closed his eyes just as she pressed her soft, warm lips to his mouth. He reached up and cradled her face with his hands, heedless of the IV tube dangling from one wrist. She kissed him with an almost ravenous passion, her hands slowly raking through his hair. Despite the fact that he was lying in a hospital bed, having nearly died earlier that day, he found himself lost, floundering in a deep and unquenchable desire for this girl; a desire that can only be born of unconditional love, cultivated by mutual respect, and a willingness to sacrifice.

She pulled away and smiled. "In case you're wondering, Chet Cooper …that was a real kiss."

"It's finally good to know," he said.

The next day, just after a breakfast of eggs that had the flavor and consistency of water and a piece of soggy toast, Doctor Steinmetz popped into the room. "How we doing this morning, Sheriff?"

"Better," Chet replied.

Steinmetz nodded with a smile. "I'm actually surprised to find you all by yourself this morning. I figured that little gal of yours was going to spend the night for sure. She wasn't about to let you out of her sight."

Chet didn't say anything, just smiled.

The doctor planted a scrutinizing stare on him for a moment, then smiled back. "She did stay all night then," he stated. "Well, I hope she kept her promise and let you get some rest."

"You don't have to worry about that, she's been pretty much my little enforcer all night. Wouldn't even let me lift my own fork for breakfast this morning, insisted on feeding me like a one year old."

"Did she make little airplane sounds for ya?"

Chet rolled his eyes. "Thankfully, no."

The doctor came to stand at his bedside. "Where's your little nursemaid now?"

"I convinced her that she could go home, get something to eat, take a bath. I had to promise not to die while she was gone."

Steinmetz eased into his standard examination routine: poking, prodding, listening, checking. "I sure do like that little gal, Chet. She's a real peach, that one."

"You don't have to tell me."

"So, you see it for yourself? That's good. Then I won't say another word about it." He pulled a tongue depressor from his shirt pocket. "Open your mouth and say…"

"Ahhh."

After the man removed the giant stick from his mouth, Chet asked, "When are you going to let me out of here, Doc?"

Steinmetz had him get out of bed and walk around the little room for a few minutes. After Chet sat down on the edge of the mattress, the doctor nodded and made some notes on the clipboard that was hanging on the foot of the bed. "You're a quick healer, young man," he said. "You're all set to go if that's what you want."

"Want!" Chet said.

Doctor Steinmetz walked over to the door. "Very well, I'll get a hold of Rick and tell him to come and get you. I'll have him swing by your place on the way and pick you up a change of clothes. You're not going to want the outfit you came in here with, trust me. And I want you to promise me that you will take it easy for a while. By that, I mean nothing more vigorous than checkers for at least a week. Do I have your word on that?"

Chet nodded. "Yes, sir." An hour later, Rick and Kate arrived together in Chet's patrol car—the only one out of the small fleet still in service—with a change of clothes. Kate promised not to peek while he got dressed, but he made her go out into the hallway regardless. A man had to have some dignity after all.

They sat in a bit of an uncomfortable silence during the drive home. The three of them had been through something extraordinary together. It was something that they would only ever be able to talk about amongst themselves—maybe not even then. Nobody would ever understand what had happened up there, in the old Salem church house. They had seen through the veil that separated the world of the living from that of the dead.

The sun was out in full force, a shimmering, golden orb cast against a hard, blue sky. Hardly any evidence remained of the previous snow storm, except for a few slushy deposits slouching in the shadows here and there. Autumn was not ready to give up its place just yet, and winter was yielding its claim for the time being. The citizens of Clear Creek were out and about, bustling to and fro on the streets and sidewalks as if all could sense that golden days, such as this, were breathing their last.

Chet felt like it was wrong to not talk about it, that they shouldn't just sweep it under the rug like it had never happened. And yet, what did one say? How did one even begin to discuss those events? Maybe sweeping it under the rug was the right thing to do after all. *Sweep it under there with the rest of the garbage. There's always room for a little more down there.*

Kate broke the silence, leaning forward from the backseat, her voice subdued. "She'll find another *feeder*," she said. "It's just a matter of time before she does. Then this will all happen again. Then again, and again, and again. She'll continue the cycle of destruction, feasting on souls and luxuriating in blood and horror. She'll never be satisfied...never. We have to stop her."

"How do we stop her?" Rick muttered. "We don't even know what *she* is. I'm still trying to come to grips that any of this even actually happened."

"We all are," Chet said. "We'll probably be wrestling with this for the rest of our lives."

Rick flicked on his turn signal and turned the car onto Washington Street. "So, what do we do then? I suppose we could just treat every disappearance and murder for now on as the possibility that the demon has returned. In the meantime, maybe we should consult some religious leaders, let them in on what's happened."

Chet shook his head. "No, the truth of what happened here stays between us. We can't let something like that get out. The whole town would either go into some kind of panic, or lock us all up in a loony bin and toss away the key."

"The tree," Kate said, thinking aloud and putting a hand on Chet's shoulder.

"What tree?" Chet asked.

"According to Abel Gannon's journal, the old tree is like some kind of power source for her…a refuge even, where she builds her strength. That's where Abel first started meeting her. What if…what if we cut it down and burned it? Abel wanted to do it himself, but never worked up the courage before he died."

"Makes all the sense in the world," Chet said, "except, how do we find one single tree out of an entire forest? Abel never left directions or a map on how to find it and we can't ask Daniel where it is."

"Remember when she was taking over my body, how she was bragging about being able to feel what I could feel, hear my thoughts, know my feelings?"

Chet put a hand to his throat as he recalled his windpipe nearly being crushed under Kate's foot while the demon reveled in how much pain and horror his girlfriend was enduring at that moment. "I'd rather forget."

"Well, unfortunately for her, it's a two-way street."

Rick craned his neck to look back at her. "What are you saying, darling?"

"What I'm saying is, for that brief period of time, the demon and I were sort of…well, connected I guess would be the best way to put it. She knew my thoughts, but I knew hers as well. In fact, I think we're still connected in a way, even though she's gone."

A chill prickled down Chet's spine like a stream of ice water. "Still connected? But I thought—"

"No, it's not like that, Chet. She has no control over me…she's not even here, but we can still sense each other in some way. It's hard to explain, and maybe the feeling will decrease with time, I don't know. But what I'm trying to say is, I think I can find the tree, guys."

"How?" Chet asked.

She shrugged her shoulders. "I could track her. Basically, it would be like following a scent, like a psychic bloodhound, sort of. Before Daniel took me from my room, I was having a dream—more like a vision, I think. Albert was there and told me, 'To defeat the shadow, you must first descend into the darkness.' I think this is what he meant; I had to be taken by her to the extent that I could learn how to destroy her."

Rick pulled the car up to the curb in front of the Cozy Corner boarding house and killed the engine. "So what, we just pick a day and follow your nose—for lack of a better term—to the tree and cut it down…burn it, whatever?

Kate nodded, her curls bouncing with enthusiasm for the plan.

"Sounds pretty risky to me," Chet said. "What if we end up in another life and death struggle with this thing, with your soul on the line, Kate? I have to admit, I feel like we'd be delivering the mouse to the cat."

Kate shook her head vigorously. "I don't think so, guys. I can sense her right now. She's weak and terrified. And with Daniel gone, she's vulnerable and hoping with all her might that we decide not to act on this. Think of it more like delivering the cat to the mouse."

Chet and Rick looked at each other, unsure.

Kate sat back against the seat, folding her arms and crossing her legs. "You two don't have to come," she said, "but I refuse to just move on with my life knowing that there might have been something I could have done to put an end to all of this. Too many lives have been destroyed by this thing already. Bottom line, boys: if I have anything to do with it, that monster's days are numbered."

Chet didn't like it one bit, but knew she was right. If there was even a chance they could end this demon's reign, they had to try. He sighed. "I guess there's not much arguing that," he said.

Rick was just shaking his head back and forth.

Kate leaned forward in the seat, grabbed Rick's face and planted a loud kiss on his cheek. "Cheer up, deputy," she said. "I'll pack sandwiches!"

CHAPTER 47

On Kate's stern insistence, Chet stayed the following week in a spare room at The Cozy Corner, where she and Mable could keep a close eye on him and nurse him back to health. This so-called *nursing back to health* turned out to be an outright violation of his civil and human rights, the likes of which he hadn't experienced since Marine Corps boot camp.

In fact, if not for the endless evenings curled up with Kate on the living room sofa, and the kisses that seemed to be exponentially increasing in frequency and passion, he just might have put his foot down and told them that enough was enough. But the women must have been doing something right, what with the forced naps during the day, the early bedtimes at night, and the constant forced ingestion of herbal tea because after just a week, he was feeling almost one hundred percent again.

Throughout the week, Kate kept referring to their plan to hunt down the demon's sanctuary and destroy it, as the *picnic* they were going on as soon as he was well enough to do so. Mable thought a picnic was a splendid idea and would do Chet a lot of good to get out into the woods, especially while the weather continued in its current warm streak.

Sunday morning dawned crisp and bright, the dewdrops on the lawn sparkling in the slanting sunlight like the ill-gotten gems of a pirate's hoard. After a filling breakfast of scrambled eggs, pancakes, and black coffee, Kate announced that Chet would be well enough for a picnic that afternoon. She went about immediately making the preparations.

As it turned out, Kate had been right about her ability to *sniff out* the old rotting tree that served as the demon's sanctuary. Now, standing before it, Chet had no doubt as to the corrupt nature of the arboreal giant looming before them in the small clearing.

Trees, in general, are things of beauty that have the wondrous ability to display both the randomness and the order of nature simultaneously. But where most all trees seem to be growing by a set of natural rules that dictate the flow of roots and the spread of branches, this particular behemoth, in the heart of the forest, was a stark and ugly contradiction of the natural order of things.

The thick branches, instead of tapering smoothly, bulged oddly in random places, as if a fibrous network of tumorous growths sprawled just beneath the surface of the rough, blackened bark. Instead of spreading skyward, the branches seemed to grasp and clutch at the air in sporadic patterns that evoked a twisting and writhing chaos. It was as if an alien presence had taken hold of the tree and contorted it into everything that stood against beauty, order, and goodness.

"This is it," Kate said, raising a finger to the tree. "She's in there, along with the souls that she holds captive." She walked beneath a large, low-hanging branch that jutted out horizontally from the trunk. It was charred by fire damage and the end was jagged where it had been snapped off. She gazed up at it. "They hung those people from this branch. They are all still here. I can feel them."

Rick took off a backpack he had been carrying, opened the top flap, and tipped it upside down. Several cans of lighter fluid tumbled to the ground at his feet. "Let's get on with this," he said, his voice flat.

They piled up dried brush, twigs, and other flammable fuel at the base of the tree until it looked like an ancient, pagan funeral pyre. Then, they emptied every single can of lighter fluid, drenching the brush pile, and squirting the fluid as high up the tree trunk as they could.

When every can of lighter fluid was empty, the three of them stepped back. The smell of the gas was nauseating. Chet could actually see the air shimmering from the vapors, giving the tree the appearance of shuddering in fear from what was about to happen. He reached into his pants pocket and pulled out a battered Zippo lighter. He snapped it open and flicked the striker with his thumb; the wick caught flame on the first try. He extended the lighter to Kate. "Why don't you do us the honor."

"My pleasure," she said, taking a hold of it, being careful not to burn her hand. She took two defiant steps toward the tree, her chin thrust forward, the reflection of the lighter's flame burning dangerously in her eyes. She looked back at the two men behind her. "She's begging now…trying to make a deal."

Chet shook his head. "I don't think so."

Kate nodded, brought her arm back like a baseball pitcher, and threw the lighter at the fuel-soaked brush pile. "No deal," she said as the lighter disappeared into the tangled snag.

Instantly, the heap erupted into flames with a low roar. It was followed shortly by a hiss and crackle as the flames began to penetrate and consume more than just the lighter fluid. Orange and red tongues of cleansing destruction leaped quickly up the tree trunk to lap hungrily at the lower hanging branches.

Rick started to nod in approval. "The fire looks real good so far, I think it's going to do the trick just fine."

Kate stepped back to Chet's side, her eyes riveted on the flames as they spread from branch to branch. She reached down and intertwined her fingers in his. They watched silently as the tree became a searing ball of fire. They had to squint their eyes against the intense waves of heat that were radiating out from the conflagration.

Suddenly, a loud, cracking sound exploded above the din of the roaring fire as the one low branch fell to the ground in a shower of sparks. Kate gasped and swooned against Chet, putting a hand to her forehead.

"What's wrong!" Chet exclaimed, encircling her in his arms.

She furrowed her brow and squinted her eyes as if in pain or extreme concentration. "She's desperate now…she knows this is the end for her. She's making one last try to…to take me…before the tree dies. Don't worry, she's not nearly strong enough to do it, and she knows it."

More branches cracked and fell to the ground while others bowed to the flames in defeat. The threesome watched, determined to see the job through to the end. There was another loud, cracking sound, almost like a clap of thunder, and the entire tree suddenly split at the crotch. One side fell away, crashing to the forest floor, smoldering, shapeless, and dead.

What remained of the tree seemed to shudder just then, and Chet thought he heard the sound of a deep-throated sigh escape from the dark schism where the tree had been divided.

Kate turned into him, away from the scene. "They're free," she said, tears running down her face. "They're free."

He embraced her as she buried her head into his chest.

The tree shuddered again, and then began to…squeal. It was a shrill, writhing sound: ultimate misery, anguish, loss, and pure hate, congealing and twisting together, rending the air, building and growing louder.

She clutched at him and cried out as the awful sound crescendoed. Then, it began to fade, decreasing in sound and intensity like the rush of a passing car on a quiet stretch of road, until…silence.

"She's gone," Kate stated, looking over her shoulder at the smoldering remains of the giant tree.

"She's dead?" Rick asked,

Kate shook her head. "I don't know if she really was ever alive, Rick. I just know she really is gone."

"Are you alright?" Chet asked, cupping her face in his hands.

She looked up into his eyes and nodded. "I'm okay now. In fact, I feel absolutely fantastic." She laughed, the silvery tone of her voice in clear and beautiful contrast to the charred and smoking ruins before them.

He kissed her and then held her in his arms, never wanting to let go of her. They held each other in a silent embrace. Time had no meaning.

Rick, who Chet had all but forgotten about at this point, suddenly let out a gasp and pointed. "For the love of all that's holy, would you have a look at that!"

Kate spun around as Chet's eyes followed Rick's pointing finger to the remains of the tree, a smoking cinder, still retaining its twisted and grotesque form. A little boy now stood next to the blackened stump.

Chet didn't even need a second to recognize the boy; he had spent weeks searching these very woods for him. The cherubic face with the brown hair and freckles of Levi Henderson would be indelibly imprinted on his brain for the rest of his life.

Levi simply stood there, returning their stares, almost as if making sure he had their undivided attention. He looked every bit as alive and well as anyone of them, and for just a moment, Chet considered the possibility that the boy was actually alive, and had now just happened to turn up. Maybe it was the fire that had drawn him out from some secret, hidden spot in the woods.

He immediately cast the notion aside. The boy was too clean—he literally seemed to glow—to have been living alone in the woods all this time. Levi smiled, his eyes twinkling with an otherworldly light that seemed to come from within him, rather than from reflected light.

"Thank you."

It was the voice of a boy, but heard in his head, not by his ears. The voice was sweet and melodic, like the carefree trill of a robin on a warm spring day. It echoed through the corridors of his mind and seemed to usher an exuberant feeling of peace and love along with it.

Kate was nearly overcome with emotion, bringing a hand to her chest and openly weeping tears of joy. Tears brimmed in Chet's eyes also as he placed a loving and protecting arm around her shoulders. Rick's mouth was agape; he was still pointing at the vision before them.

The boy nodded once, turned around, and began to walk away from them. Gradually, he began to vanish before their eyes, his body becoming more ethereal and translucent with each step. And then, as indiscernible as a storm's final raindrop, he was gone.

The three stood watching, as if they could still see him, each one lost in their own thoughts, trying to make some sense of it all, knowing that they never really would be able to.

Kate took Chet by the hand, giving it a squeeze. "We did it," she said. "It's over."

He kissed her gently on the top of the head. "I like to think that some things are just beginning."

She smiled, stood up on her tiptoes, and kissed him. The moment his lips made contact with hers, he knew everything was going to be alright—*they* were going to be alright. He interlocked his fingers behind her waist, resting his hands on the feminine crest of her hips, and pulled her into him, their bodies meshing and conforming with one another like interlocking pieces of a puzzle; each an incomplete mystery without the other. She pulled away from the kiss, but not before biting his bottom lip in a playful manner that sent his heart pulsing like a war drum.

"You are playing with fire, missy," he said.

She smiled mischievously and pulled his ear to her lips. The warm sigh of her breath on his neck and ear sent tremulous shivers bolting along his nervous system.

"If you can't stand the heat, Sheriff…" She nipped at his earlobe briefly.

"Well, that settles one thing," Rick said, putting his hands on his hips, apparently indifferent to the couple's romantic moment.

"Yeah?" Chet replied, barely interested.

"I'm going to start going to church more, I think."

Kate burst out laughing.

"No, I mean it," Rick said, sounding offended. "We should all probably start thinking about that stuff more, don't ya think?"

Kate continued to giggle as she hooked a hand into each man's elbow and pulled them to either side of her. She started dragging her double escort with her. "Let's get out of here. I've got sandwiches back at the car," she said.

Without so much as a glance behind, the three vanished down a trail and into the woods, leaving the remains of the tree behind them, burning and smoldering to ash.

EPILOGUE

The Jeep lurched and swayed on its suspension, clawing along the primitive track that etched a winding path up the side of the mountain. It was late spring and the wildflowers were in full bloom, cascading down the grassy slopes in a magnificent profusion of blues, pinks, reds, and yellows. Birds zipped from tree to tree, like little colorful, chirping arrows. It was mid-afternoon, and even though they were steadily climbing in elevation, the sun was warm and shone down comfortably.

Chet took his eyes off the trail to steal yet another longing glance at Kate in the passenger seat. Her hair and makeup were still exquisite from earlier that day. She had been so pleased with how her hair had turned out that she'd left in the white veil, fearing that removing it would ruin her hairdo.

The veil didn't exactly go with her pale-yellow summer dress and black flats, but he didn't mind. It only added an exotic element to her look, like a sultan's daughter from some ancient, forgotten realm, buried long ago by the sands of time.

He was waxing all poetic now, and he chuckled inwardly at himself, but he really could appreciate how the beauty of a woman might drive a man to put pen to paper. Maybe he would write her a love poem someday: *Roses are red, violets are blue....* He smiled and shook his head. Poetry was probably better left to the poets.

She stuck her leg outside of the Jeep, the smooth skin beginning to attain a light bronze color from the sun's rays. She stretched it toward the fender, rolling her ankle in circles. "How much looonger?" she asked, imitating the impatience of a little kid. She caught him staring and put a hand to her hair. "What, do I still have stupid rice in my hair or something? I thought I got it all out."

"No rice...you're just beautiful, that's all."

"Well, there's more where that came from, but you best keep your eyes on the road if you would like to live long enough to find out."

"Yes, ma'am," he said, forcing his eyes back onto the road.

She turned in her seat to face him and began to brush the hair over his ear with her fingertips. "So, are you sure that Clear Creek can survive a whole week without her mighty sheriff?"

"I'm sure Rick has it all under control. Plus, it gives him an opportunity to bond a little more with Porter. Those two could use a little bonding time."

She laughed, then leaned over and kissed him on the cheek. "That's good to hear, because I plan on keeping you all to myself just this once, Chet Cooper."

The way she said it, made his palms suddenly start sweating on the steering wheel.

Half an hour later, the road rounded a sharp bend and dumped them into the small clearing that harbored the little cabin where they had spent their first date. He helped her down from the Jeep. "Well, here we are," he said. "I hope you don't get sick of me after a week."

"Not a chance!" she exclaimed. "There'll be plenty to do up here. We've got board games, a deck of cards, a couple of books to read, plenty of food. We can go on hikes, do some fishing. And, if we get tired of all that, there's"—she twirled a lock of her hair playfully with her fingers—"always other stuff."

She walked around to the back of the Jeep, rummaged in a cardboard box that was filled with various supplies, and produced a deck of cards. She shuffled the cards in her hands. "I figured we could start things off with several games of gin rummy."

He came over to her, took the cards, and let them spill back into the box.

"Hey!" she protested.

In one swift movement, he swept her off her feet, cradling her in his arms, and started walking toward the cabin door. "I vote *other stuff* first," he said.

She shot him a knowing look, turned the doorknob for him, and then put her arms around his neck, as he carried her into the rustic, mountain dwelling. She gasped as he set her gently back on her feet. "Chet, when did you have time to pull this off?" she asked.

"It wasn't me," he said, looking around in mild shock. Red and pink balloons with matching ribbons hung from the open beams that spanned the width of the room. On the table, a small card was propped up against a vase of fresh-cut flowers.

Kate picked up the card, unfolded it, and read aloud. "We wish you all the happiness possible in your new life together. Love your friends, Rick and Alice Shelton. PS: Get busy making memories!"

"Sorry, we gotta get home to the kids, my foot," Chet said, referring to Rick and Alice skipping out on the wedding luncheon early—not before Rick had been back to the food table three or four times.

"So sweet of them to do this," Kate said. She took in the room with her eyes again and looked down at the floor. "Oh my," she said, blushing slightly.

He followed her gaze to the floor. A trail of rose petals wound its way to the little ladder that led up to the loft where the bed was. They both looked up from the suggestive, floral path and met each other's gaze. The world grew absolutely silent as they stared at each other for a few moments.

"Wow," she said, "things just suddenly became...I don't know...*real.*" She took two steps toward him. "I mean, after everything...after all we've been through together, and all the circumstances that brought us closer, not to mention the forces that tried to pull us apart. After all that, here we are: husband and wife...Mr. and Mrs. Chet Cooper. Doesn't that kind of blow you away?"

He simply nodded. "It was meant to be, I have no doubt about that."

"Had to be," she said, smiling.

He took a second glance at that blood-red trail of rose petals that refused to be ignored, and then turned for the open door of the cabin. "Better get the Jeep all unpacked, I guess."

"Chet?"

He stopped on the threshold. "Yeah?"

"Don't turn around until I tell you to."

"Okay."

He focused on a chipmunk that was scurrying around at the base of a large pine tree at the edge of the clearing. He thought he heard the sound of a zipper. What was she up to? After an eternity, he heard her padding quietly across the floor. Then she was behind him. She put her hands on his shoulders and turned him around to face her.

Looking past her, his eyes immediately caught sight of her dress puddled on the floor where she'd let it drop off her body. Her shoes sat side by side, encircled by the rumples of yellow, where she had simply stepped out of them.

"I think the Jeep can wait, don't you?" she said while undoing the top button of his shirt.

He had been so caught off guard by this sudden development—he had figured some wine first, maybe a little small talk—that he found he was speechless, and could only manage an awkward stammer.

She giggled as she unfastened two more of his buttons. "Why, Sheriff Cooper, you aren't nervous, are you?" She said, accentuating that Southern accent he found so irresistible.

"No," he managed to say, a bit on the defensive. "Should I be?"

She laughed, her eyes shining with life. "Probably." She pulled him by the shirt into the cabin, while kissing him passionately on the mouth.

She put her foot on the door and kicked it shut.

Thank you, for reading **The Summoning.** If you enjoyed it, please consider taking a moment to rate and review it on **amazon.com**. Your positive input is very important in helping others discover this book and its author.

Do you want more of Brady's work? Be sure to check out **The Fifth Corner,** a highly rated series of action, adventure, mystery, and romance. Available on Amazon in paperback or Kindle. Download the first book **HERE.**

When a teenage girl vanishes mysteriously in the Idaho Rockies, professional adventurer, Jake Preston, is tapped by her wealthy father to find the girl and bring her home. What starts out as a typical missing person's case quickly becomes much more when Jake discovers an otherworldly object that possesses supernatural capabilities. Soon, Jake discovers the earth has a fifth corner, a secret, ancient world, protected by dangerous people, who will do anything to remain in the shadows.

To sign up for Brady's **FREE newsletter** please head over to **www.bradylongmore.com** where you will be kept up to date on Brady's latest projects, upcoming releases, and in general, what's going on in his life. Signed copies of his books are also available on the website. From there you can also connect with Brady on Facebook and Twitter, where he is quite active.

Author's note about PTSD

As I embarked on this project, I never envisioned PTSD (Post Traumatic Stress Disorder) would become a theme in the novel. As a writer it's hard to predict where exactly I'm always heading with a story. I hope that those who suffer from PTSD or have close friends and family who suffer from it will realize it was never my intention to treat this serious condition lightly or flippantly. As a matter of fact, I hold those who have served our country in the highest regard. That includes law enforcement and all first responders who stand at the ready to encounter dangers on our behalf at a moment's notice.

I think I may have subconsciously worked this theme into my writing when a friend and coworker, a veteran of the war in Afghanistan, took his own life. Perhaps, on some level, I needed to work this horrible event out for myself by writing about it.

The truth of the matter is, the characters in this novel are fictitious, but PTSD is very real and those who suffer from it are in need of our love and support. At the risk of sounding too preachy, I'd like to encourage people to do some research into PTSD and possibly look for a charity where they would feel comfortable donating some time and money. Let's not abandon those who have given so much for the freedoms and liberties that we enjoy.

God bless America and the men and women who defend her.

Thank you
-Brady Longmore

ACKNOWLEDGEMENTS

This book would have never been possible without the inspiration, support, and input from several individuals. First off, let me thank my lovely wife, Kimberly. Without her constant and steady support, this book would have inevitably ended up as yet another unorganized jumble of ideas, scribbled into a notebook and buried at the bottom of a desk drawer. She was crucial in helping me find just the right voice for Kate Farnsworth and really bringing that character to life. In her way, Kimberly is my own *Kate*.

Both of my brothers have been invaluable in the creation of this novel, from designing the cover, helping with the layout and format, providing feedback on the story, and providing editing services. May we clasp forearms for a long time to come.

I would be remiss if I didn't single out my parents and give credit where credit is due. I was raised on a healthy diet of ghosts and goblins, literally being taught there were real monsters living in our crawlspace. To prove the point, my dad would often do battle with said monsters. My mom would stand by the door and listen with me to the sounds of banging and cursing coming from the other side. Dad would emerge from the crawlspace, his shirt torn and dirty and his glasses askew from the epic fight. Thank you, Mom and Dad, for the gift of imagination. May the one-eyed ghost never cease to haunt your abode.

Much thanks to my beta readers and other friends and family—sisters included—who provided feedback and moral support. Thanks to those who allowed me to pick their brains and who endured some of my endless babbling as I tried to work through plot holes and other issues.

Finally, let me thank you, the reader, for taking a chance on an independent author. Your support means a lot to me. I know money doesn't come easy to many people these days. I consider it a great honor that you chose to spend a little bit of yours to read my book. I sincerely hope that it lived up to your expectations, that it was worth your time and your money, and that you are looking forward to the next book!

-Brady Longmore

About The Author

Brady Longmore grew up in Idaho Falls, Idaho, where his parents convinced him at a young age that the monsters in the crawl space were real. Although this may have resulted in many sleepless nights, it also ignited in him a love of mystery and a fascination with the supernatural.

Whether he was winning writing contests in school or terrifying his fellow Boy Scouts with campfire tales of deranged killers on the loose or vengeful spirits haunting the woods, it became evident that Brady was born to be a storyteller.

Brady attended Idaho State University for a short time where he studied history. He has worked in many professions including: TV news photographer, graphic artist for a publishing house, and law enforcement officer. But his true passion lies in sharing the fruits of his overactive imagination through the written word.

Brady currently lives with his wife, Kimberly, and their four children in Idaho Falls, Idaho.